Philip Friedman is a practising attorney living in New York City. His previous novels include *Rage*, which was also a film starring George C. Scott and Martin Sheen; *Termination Order*, which the *New York Times Book Review* called 'one of the best spy stories of the year'; *Reasonable Doubt* and *Inadmissible Evidence* – both of which became worldwide bestsellers. His novel of the conspiracy surrounding the assassination of John Kennedy, *Act of Love, Act of War*, was republished in 1994 under the title *Wall of Silence*.

# Grand Jury

## Philip Friedman

HEADLINE
FEATURE

First published in hardback in Great Britain in 1996
by HEADLINE BOOK PUBLISHING

First published in paperback in 1996
by HEADLINE BOOK PUBLISHING

A HEADLINE FEATURE paperback

10 9 8 7 6 5 4 3 2

ISBN 0 7472 5097 9

Typeset by
Letterpart Limited, Reigate, Surrey

Printed and bound in Great Britain by
Cox & Wyman Ltd, Reading, Berks

HEADLINE BOOK PUBLISHING
A division of Hodder Headline PLC
338 Euston Road
London NW1 3BH

For Bob —
mentor, role model and friend — who over the years has changed my life for the better again and again.

Each book I write is a new lesson in the generosity not just of people I already know and value, but also of some I have never met before.

Once again, Dan Castleman gave unstintingly of his time and expertise, despite his increasingly weighty responsibilities in the real world of law enforcement.

Also remarkably helpful were Linda Imes, Margaret Chan, Chan Wing Kee and that most stalwart of stalwarts, Mary Corrarino.

Kenneth Vianale and Ken Ng and Melinda Parsons each got me started down a path I would otherwise never have trod, as did Katharine Muir. And my progress was fostered in many ways by Dan Kleinman and David Erickson, and by Betsy Elias, Judy Mintz and Margit Anderegg.

To them all, and to everyone else who helped (many of whom are mentioned in the concluding Author's Note), my deep and abiding gratitude.

Just as it is presumption to sacrifice to ancestors not one's own, so it is cowardice to know what is right and not do it.

*Master Kung*

They wait in the darkened apartment-house corridor, a half-dozen men wearing blue NYPD windbreakers over their bulletproof vests, guns out and ready, breathing kitchen smells none of them grew up with, listening to the singsong of the indecipherable language from the floors below.

'Police!' one yells, pounding on the door. 'Open up!'

No response.

'Police!' he yells again. Nothing.

The battering ram splinters the door, buckles it inward. The first two rush into a narrow entrance hall darker than the corridor, pistol and shotgun trained on the rectangle of dim light at the hall's end. As they move warily toward the open door and whatever lies beyond, another pair come in behind them.

Their view through the doorway is blocked by a screen of angled panels, ancient black wood adorned with a vista of jagged mountains and twisted trees. Along the edges of the panels crawls a carved wooden serpent with the head of a dragon.

They bring in the battering ram and bowl it along the floor ahead of them. It slams the panels flat.

In its wake, Detective Mick Pullone scoots through the doorway, crouching, shouting, 'Police! Freeze!' eyes and shotgun sweeping the room, seeing no detail but scanning for movement, a sign of anything living, human, a threat.

He ducks his head back out into the entrance hall. 'Okay,' he says and his partner joins him, followed again by the second pair. Behind them, the cops who wielded the battering ram secure the entrance and cover the others' backs as they move on into the apartment.

*Pullone, in the lead running down the hallway toward the bed-rooms, sees motion. 'Freeze! Police! On the floor! Now!'*

*The man is rooted to the spot, his body quivering. His hands are empty.*

*The detective leaps forward, gun up and to the side so his shoulder crashes into the man before he can react. The impact propels the much shorter, lighter man sideways and down, stumbling over his own feet. Immediately, Pullone is straddling him, automatic pistol parting the hairs on the back of the man's neck, pushing hard as the man presses his face against the floor, desperate to escape the cold metal of the gun muzzle digging into the base of his skull.*

# I

## *THE GRAND JURY*

# 1

David Clark shifted in his movie-theater-style seat in the grand jury room, trying to unstick his sweaty trousers from the underside of his thighs without being obvious about it. Not that he thought anyone would notice it even if he stood up and peeled them off altogether: the others were all preoccupied with their own discomfort. Twenty-three strangers waiting for yet another assistant district attorney to come in and present yet another case, in a room with only one window that opened and air conditioning they had been promised would be working again soon. Not the ideal conditions for being alert and observant.

When the notice arrived saying he'd been picked for the grand jury pool, David's first impulse had been to do some research, the way he did with anything new. In New York State, he'd learned, a prosecutor needed a grand jury indictment in order to charge anybody with a felony. It was in the state constitution: 'No person shall be held to answer for a capital or otherwise infamous crime . . . unless on indictment of a grand jury.' And not only were grand juries essential, they were secret. Trials were public, but not grand juries.

The actual summons to serve had come three months after David went downtown to be fingerprinted so they could be sure he wasn't a criminal. By then he was impatient to begin and concerned that he might be disqualified. But grand jurors, it turned out, faced nothing like the exhaustive selection process that trial jurors were famously put through. All that mattered, getting on a New York County grand jury, was that your fingerprint check turned up clean, you were physically able to serve and you understood English reasonably well.

David had assumed he was going to hear every kind of criminal case there was, including at least a few that would be really interesting. Almost two weeks of mornings had revealed that being a grand juror was a lot more fascinating in theory than in practice. Considering that it was the first step in society's attempt to bring criminals to justice while protecting people from being falsely accused, grand jury duty involved a lot of sitting around.

Most of the others fought the empty periods with books or newspapers; a few had put together a recurring card game. David brought professional journals and found he had trouble concentrating on them. For relief, he closed his eyes and visualized the glories of West Virginia whitewater and the trip he was planning for early autumn. And tried not to think too much about the woman in the seat next to him, her pale skin and dark hair, her fine bones and long, graceful body.

Eight permanently anchored seats and one narrow aisle down the same long, curving row, Susan Linwood was still regretting that she hadn't fought the summons to serve. When she'd gotten her notification, her immediate reaction had been to reach for the phone. She'd had jury duty postponed in the past, following advice from a lawyer friend of her husband's, and after that nobody had bothered her for years; she'd begun to feel immune.

But she hadn't made the call. At work, there was only one major client to worry about and no reason not to be out for the month of mornings or afternoons grand jury service would demand. Holding the fort alone would be good experience for Annette, her associate, and an opportunity for her to show she had what it took for Susan to think about offering her a partnership.

And maybe, Susan had thought, it wasn't too much to hope that grand jury duty could provide some relief from her growing sense that she was living her life by rote. At the very least it would be educational. It might even recharge her creatively, give her a whole new mental vocabulary to work with. Only too late did she realize how badly it would eat into this last precious month before her daughter left for college and adulthood and independence.

The door to the grand jury room opened and a man came in, as tall as

6

any prosecutor they'd seen – at least six-two, David Clark guessed, maybe six-four – broad shoulders and chest made his height hard to gauge. He carried his size and bulk with the nonchalant ease of an athlete.

He started by introducing himself, as all the prosecutors did. 'I'm Assistant District Attorney Daniel Mahoney. The case I'm going to present is *The People of the State of New York against Martin Eng and Meiling Cheung Eng*.'

He slowly paced the front of the room – energy, not nerves, David thought. 'This case is going to be a little different from what you're probably used to. I hope you'll bear with me. We can get started today, but we'll have to continue next week, too.'

He stopped pacing and perched a hip on the witness table. 'The first thing I'm going to do that's probably different from what you're used to, is to read you the law at the beginning. That's because this case is likely to be more complicated than the others you've had, and I want you to have some idea of what it's all about when you hear the evidence.' His tone was conversational, and he was looking at the individual grand jurors as he spoke.

'I'll do my best to keep things simple for you. If you have questions raise your hand and tell me and if they're about the law I'll see if I can answer them myself; if they're about the facts I'll ask the witness for you.'

He told them that Martin Eng and his wife were being accused of first degree possession of a controlled substance – heroin – and of conspiring to sell it, a crime whose definition was indeed more complicated than most they had heard before. There were plenty of questions about it.

Since there was no witness in the room and they were just talking about the meaning of the law, Mahoney said, he would let the jurors ask their questions aloud instead of trying them out on him in private first, as they usually did. That way, he said, everyone would learn, without his having to repeat the questions aloud himself.

David was glad to hear the questions in the true voices of the grand jurors themselves, for once. The good news was that though regular trial jurors had to sit and listen in silence, grand jurors got to put questions to the witnesses. But David had been frustrated from the beginning by the New York County practice of asking questions only through the A.D.A. – he wanted to know what questions the others had and what reason a prosecutor gave for modifying or rejecting them, as they often did.

When the grand jurors had run out of questions for Mahoney he looked around at them all and smiled. 'Okay, if you're all set I'm going to bring in my first witness.' He left the room briefly and returned with a man in a gray suit, tall and blocky but not as big as Mahoney himself.

The foreman swore the witness in and Mahoney, like all the other prosecutors, went up the shallow stairs to ask his questions from behind the second row of grand jurors at the end near the door, almost directly behind David. Asking questions from behind the grand jurors led the witnesses to make their replies loud enough to be heard by everyone. And, David had observed the first day, it turned the prosecutor into a kind of disembodied voice of authority for all the grand jurors except the foreman and alternate foreman and secretary, whose single, shared desk at the top of the room was next to where the prosecutors stood or sat or – by the sound of it – paced.

'State your name, please,' Mahoney began, 'and your rank and assignment.'

'Michael A. Pullone, Detective Second Grade, NYPD, and I'm currently on special duty with the New York County District Attorney's office.'

'Can you tell us what that duty is?'

'We have a small group of detectives on special assignment for the D.A.'s office. Our job is to identify and arrest major narcotics traffickers and the people who handle their money for them. And to seize the narcotics and whatever else.'

'Detective, were you on duty the night of July tenth this year?'

'Yes, I was. I was working the four-to-twelve. That's four in the afternoon to midnight.'

'And were you in plainclothes or uniform?'

'Plainclothes.'

'And did you have any particular assignment that night?'

The detective took a notebook from his jacket pocket and got permission from Mahoney to consult it. 'I was conducting a search

8

pursuant to a search warrant on a premises at 419-B Eleanor Street, in downtown Manhattan, apartment twelve.'

'Can you describe that search for the members of the jury?' Mahoney asked him.

'Yes. There were five detectives, and we had some officers from the ESU – that's the NYPD Emergency Services Unit. We approached the premises and identified ourselves.'

'Were you admitted?'

'No.'

'What did you do then?'

'Pursuant to our warrant, we made forced entry.'

'What did you find?'

'The premises was a three-bedroom apartment with a front entrance hall leading to a living room and dining room and a kitchen off that, plus another hallway leading to a master bedroom with a bath, two smaller bedrooms, and a second bathroom. It appeared to have been constructed by connecting apartments in adjoining buildings. It was the residence of a man and a woman, identified to us as Martin and Meiling Eng. We found them, and a search of the premises also revealed a quantity of white powder, some notebooks, and a quantity of cash.'

'Where did you find the white powder?'

'It was recovered from a hidden drawer under what appeared to be an altar or a shrine of some kind: a statue in a black wooden box with no front and a painting on the inside, with candles around it, standing on a dresser in the master bedroom.'

'And was the white powder packaged in any particular way?'

'In a plastic wrapper with a brand on it in red – a circle with some Chinese characters and the words *Double UoGlobe*.' He spelled it for the stenographer. 'And in the middle of the circle there's a couple of lions on each side of a globe of the Earth.'

'Was the package full?'

'No, it appeared to be about half-empty.'

'And where did you find the cash?'

'In several packets behind the drawers of the dresser that had the shrine on it, and in a safe concealed in an end table in the same room.'

'Did you count the cash at the time?'

9

'No, we did not. We placed it in evidence bags which we sealed.'

'Did there come a time when you learned how much cash was there?'

'Yes.'

'How much was that?'

'Something over four hundred and twenty-five thousand dollars.'

'Let me be sure I got that right,' Mahoney's voice said behind David. 'More than four hundred thousand dollars.'

'That's right.'

'And what sort of bills were they?'

'Mostly fifties and twenties. Some hundreds.'

'New or used?'

'Used.'

'And did you find anything else?'

'Yes, we found the keys to three safe deposit boxes.'

'And did you subsequently investigate those safe deposit boxes?'

'Yes, we opened them all.'

'And what did you find?'

'Cash – another six hundred and fifty thousand dollars – plus what appeared to be financial certificates of some kind, bearer bonds I believe they're called, each with a face value of fifty thousand dollars.'

'How many of those?'

'Six.'

'Was that all?'

'There was also a quantity of gold jewelry.'

'What sort of bills were in the safe deposit boxes?'

'Hundreds, mostly. Used.'

'That's more than a million dollars cash altogether and three hundred thousand dollars in bonds, not counting the gold.'

'That's right.'

Mahoney paused for a moment. Letting it sink in, Susan Linwood thought. And it *was* something to contemplate – close to half a million dollars around the house and almost a million more in safe deposit boxes.

'And what, to your knowledge, happened to the white powder?' Mahoney resumed.

'I vouchered it and submitted it to the police chemistry laboratory for testing.'

'And was there anything else that you submitted to the police chemistry laboratory?'

'Yes, we submitted a sample of the money as well.'

Mahoney took him through the vouchering process by which the collected evidence was identified and placed in serially numbered evidence bags before it was transmitted back and forth from the lab where it was tested. Then the prosecutor moved on to a new subject.

'You told us that you found Martin and Meiling Eng on the premises, is that right?'

'Yes.'

'And that you identified yourself as the police?'

'Yes.'

'And requested that they admit you?'

'Yes.'

'And how did you gain entrance to the apartment?'

'We had to break the door down.'

'When you entered, did you observe the defendants?'

'Not at first.'

'But you did, eventually.'

'Yes.'

'And what did you observe them doing?'

'They were fleeing.'

'Where?'

'They appeared to be heading for a rear door in the kitchen.'

'And what happened?'

'We kept them from reaching it. But we had people out there, too, in case they got past us.'

'How did they behave at that time?'

'They weren't what you'd call cooperative.'

'Can you be more specific?'

'Well, yeah. It wouldn't be too much to say they resisted us.'

There was a pause as if Mahoney was deciding what to say next. 'And did they cooperate with you in your search?'

'No, they did not.'

'And at what point did you place them under arrest?'

'After we found the . . . ah, the white powder.'

'Thank you, detective.'

Mahoney walked down from behind the rows of chairs and came to stand in front of them.

'Questions?' He seemed relaxed and pleasant.

A couple of hands went up. Mahoney walked up the center aisle to stand next to grand juror Number Sixteen, three seats from Susan in the second row. A leathery, brown-skinned man with grizzled silver hair, he had announced to the others on their first day that his name was Norman Thompson and he didn't want to be known by any seat number. Mahoney bent to listen to his question, said a few words in response, then straightened up.

'Ladies and gentlemen, on the subject of what the white powder is, we'll be hearing another witness right away.'

The other hand went down and Number Four's went up. In the absence of her fellow grand jurors' names – or any other information about them – Susan had been mentally labeling them based on their appearance and behavior. The showily muscular Number Four had quickly become 'macho man.' He always voted to indict; his rare questions seemed to come from an interest in the police.

Mahoney went over and listened to him, then relayed the question. 'Detective, a grand juror would like to know how you got the safe open.'

'We confiscated it and had it opened for us by members of the police department Safe and Loft Squad.'

No one else had a question. Mahoney dismissed the detective and told the grand jurors he'd have another witness for them right after the break.

# 2

Susan headed straight for the two pay phones in the corridor outside the grand jury rooms, but as usual she was late. Sitting in seat Number Nineteen – where she'd ended up by default, having been in the ladies room when the grand jurors first took their seats – she was so far from the door that at least three or four of the others were always at the phones before she got there. She was fifth this time, which put three ahead of her in line and one already using the single phone that still worked.

As she waited, wondering for how much longer she could keep indulging her aversion to cell phones, Mrs Liu passed by, pausing as if she was about to say something but apparently deciding not to. Susan thought she looked troubled.

The small, rotund Chinese woman had come over shyly to introduce herself to Susan during the mid-morning break of their first day and said something softly that Susan did not understand. The words were Chinese, but in what dialect Susan was not sure. Toishanese, probably – a South China dialect spoken in a few counties west of the Pearl River, and by a large percentage of the long-time residents of New York's Chinatown.

'I'm sorry, I don't speak Chinese,' Susan had said, imagining the woman classifying her as *jook sing*, a mocking reference to the hollow part of a bamboo stalk applied to Chinese-Americans who lacked the substance of Chinese language and culture.

Actually, she wasn't truly *jook sing*. She could speak a little Cantonese, the remnant of a language she had used as a child in Hong Kong but had been reluctant to speak from the moment she arrived in the United States, just in time for the first grade. More than three decades of making herself American had almost extinguished her native language. She could still say a few things well enough to be understood, but she missed almost all of anything a native speaker said, and she could read virtually nothing.

She'd talked briefly in English with Mrs Liu that first grand jury day. Mrs Liu, who lived in the oldest part of Chinatown, only blocks from the courthouse, had seemed at once saddened and intrigued by how American Susan was. Since then Mrs Liu had smiled hello every morning but she had not tried again to make small talk. Susan had been surprised to find her relief diluted by disappointment.

Now, still waiting for a phone, she glanced again impatiently at her watch. The woman on the phone was immobile, oblivious to the needs of the people waiting for her to finish. A slender, dark-haired woman with flawless pale skin whom Susan had labeled 'the actress' before having heard her speak a word, she'd so far made a habit of staying on the phone for almost the whole break.

Susan broke out of the line to try the second phone, dead the last three days, not really expecting it to have been fixed but needing to be in action. It hadn't taken much to show her how unrealistic she'd been to expect Annette and their eager but not very well-seasoned assistant to manage successive mornings' crises without her. And she had to reach her daughter before she went out for the day. But the second phone's receiver was as mute as it had been the last time she tried it.

'Excuse me,' said a male voice. Susan glanced around. It was Number Eleven, the man who sat near the door at the end of the second row – 'the backpacker' as she thought of him. She had noticed him more than she had some of the others because most of the prosecutors stood right behind him to examine the witnesses, and because he often had questions – intelligent ones, it seemed, when the prosecutors were willing to ask them, which they often weren't. Medium-tall, with medium-brown hair, intensely blue eyes and a neatly trimmed red-brown beard, he had been dressed so far in khakis and open-necked cotton business shirts with rolled sleeves, and high-tech-looking hiking boots. He carried his between-cases reading in a well-worn leather backpack.

'There are other phones,' he said.

Her general impatience brought a sarcastic 'Really?' to her lips, but

14

she stifled it and said, 'Thank you,' hoping she sounded civil: she had collided with him once or twice in her rush to get out the door at the breaks each morning, and he had been reasonably gracious about it. 'But I really don't think there's time for me to start waiting somewhere else.'

He shrugged and turned away.

'Wait,' she said. 'I'm sorry. I'm just . . . Do you know where they are?'

He looked at her a moment, with no expression she could read. 'If you're in a hurry, it'll take too long to explain. It's this way.' He started down the corridor.

After a moment's uncertainty she followed – down a flight of stairs she would have never thought to take, along a hall and around a corner past a security desk to a bank of elevators different from the ones they used to get to the grand jury room.

They emerged on the ground floor of the main court building. The phones were arrayed along a wall not far from the front entrance. There were a lot of them, and only a few were in use.

She talked until her watch told her it was time to go back upstairs. Ordinarily she wouldn't have minded being late, but this was a case she wanted to hear. Removed as her life had always been from the Chinatown immigrant experience, infuriating as it was to think that simply because she was Chinese she might be identified with people accused of importing heroin, she could not help being curious.

Turning from the phones, she realized she wasn't sure which elevators to take, or how to get back to the annex that held the D.A.'s office and the grand jury rooms.

'Over here.'

The backpacker was leaning against the marble wall.

'You didn't have to wait. You'll be late.'

'I got some coffee.' He dropped the container into a wastebasket and turned to walk out of the courthouse.

'Where are you going?'

'The only problem,' he said. 'They don't really like us to come back in through this building.'

They went outside and around the corner and showed their grand jury passes to the policemen guarding the D.A.'s office elevators.

The one they got was packed with prosecutors and detectives. 'I'm sorry if I was rude before,' she said to him when the elevator had started to empty out at the seventh and eighth floors. 'I'm sort of preoccupied. It was good of you to help me.'

'No thanks necessary.' The elevator stopped on nine. 'This is us.'

She paused in the corridor to offer him a handshake. 'I'm Susan Linwood.'

'David Clark. Nice to meet you.'

When they got back to the grand jury room, the others were all in their seats but nothing was happening yet. 'Five minutes,' the warden told them. 'The D.A.'s on his way now.'

It was more like twenty minutes, during which David's trousers again glued themselves to his thighs. He found that he was annoyed with himself for having butted into Susan Linwood's business, and with her for having been so ready to dismiss his honestly-offered assistance. He should have known better. She should have, too. No surprise there, though: it was like the oblivious way she had run into him – more than once – in her hurry to get to the phones, as if the world would automatically get out of her way.

He pulled out one of the trade magazines in his bag. He subscribed to thirty or so of them, he'd never bothered to make a count; most were monthlies but some came every week. The one he'd come up with was from the Armed Forces Communications and Electronics Association. He passed over the news of weapons systems, scanning for developments in computer systems architecture or data security. As usual, most of what he saw was of little or no interest to him.

Twice while he waited for the case to resume he glanced down the curved row of grand jurors at Susan Linwood. He didn't want to stare. He thought a lot of men must stare at her, drawn by her beauty: large, exotic brown eyes; precise nose; soft, full lips; smooth skin of some indescribable glowing hue – like pale honey, or the lightest, most uniform possible suntan.

Beautiful as she was, 'polished' and 'prosperous' were the words she had initially brought to his mind. She seemed to have been packaged in some special factory for upper-middle-class women. Even the fact that she was Asian – Chinese, he guessed – seemed less

16

significant than her membership in that other, more exclusive group.

The sparkle of the substantial diamond on her left hand had caught his eye the first time he saw her. Rich husband. Big, fancy apartment, too, he thought. Kids? Probably, and a career, too, otherwise why the urgent phone calls? He thought she might be around his own age, thirty-four, but he couldn't really judge. All those perfectly done-up women, so unreachable behind their meticulous clothes and makeup, their hundred-dollar hairdos: they all seemed forty years old to him, whatever age they actually were.

Mahoney apologized for being late when he came in: his witness had been unavoidably delayed. The witness proved to be a thin man with sparse dark hair slicked down over his sunburned skull. His tan suit had the rubbery neatness of a synthetic fabric, Susan thought: it would make him sweat badly in this heat.

After establishing the man's credentials as a police chemist and declaring him an expert, Mahoney had him testify that he had been given a quantity of white powder and some U.S. currency to analyze. The evidence bags he described bore voucher numbers Susan thought were the same as the ones on the bags Detective Pullone had filled in the Eng home and in their safe deposit boxes.

'What did you determine the white powder to be?' Mahoney asked him.

'Heroin.'

'And did you test its purity?'

'Yes, I did. It was ninety-six percent pure.'

'Is that purity unusual?'

'Yes, it is.'

'And did you measure the quantity?'

'Yes. There was two hundred and fifty-three grams. That's eight and a quarter ounces.'

'Did you test anything else that was described to you as having been seized in connection with this case?'

'Yes. We were given a quantity of United States currency. Primarily in used fifty and hundred dollar bills.'

'And what did you do with them?'

'We tested a sample of them for trace amounts of narcotics.'

17

'And what were the findings of the tests?'

'We found trace amounts of heroin and cocaine on a statistically significant portion of the bills tested.'

How odd, Susan thought, brought back to alertness despite the heat.

'And did you find both heroin and cocaine on all the bills?' Mahoney asked the chemist.

'No. Some of the bills had no drugs on them at all, some only had cocaine, and some had both cocaine and heroin. A very few had only heroin.'

'Based on those voucher numbers, and with reference to the currency that *did* have heroin on it, can you tell us where those bills came from?'

'Yes. We found heroin principally on bills with the voucher number that matches the one from the residence. We also found heroin on some of the bills from two of the safe deposit boxes.'

'Now, from your knowledge of the results over time of testing currency for trace amounts of controlled substances, can you tell us with a reasonable degree of scientific certainty what percentage of U.S. currency, in general, is likely to show trace amounts of cocaine?'

'No, not really. I can't give you a precise statistical answer to that.'

'Well, from what you know of the scientific literature on the subject, and the results of tests like the ones conducted on this money, with which you are familiar?'

'It depends on the denomination. But in the middle ranges – tens, twenties, fifties – according to the literature, you can almost say that any given bill is more likely to have some traces of cocaine on it than not. We're talking very small traces, here. But detectable.'

'I'm sorry,' Mahoney said. 'I want to be sure I understand that. Are you talking about money that's in general circulation, that you or I might have?'

'Yes, I am.'

'So would you say that the presence of cocaine on currency indicates its recent use in the purchase or sale of the drug?'

'No, not necessarily, not with cocaine.'

'And is the same thing true of heroin?'

'No.'

'Is it common to find traces of heroin on currency?'

18

'Not in the same sense as cocaine, where I could take a bill out of your pocket right now and it would probably have some cocaine on it.'

'How does currency get trace amounts of these powders on it, in your experience as an expert?'

'This is naturally speculation as to any particular bill, of course, but in general, if it's in an environment with the drug, if people are handling both drugs and money, you'll find some of the drug on the money. And of course, people use rolled-up bills as a kind of straw for snorting drugs. That's principally true with cocaine, it's one of the reasons why you find so much currency with cocaine on it. And there are other ways: for instance, if the drugs and money are packed together, or are transported in the same vehicle or container, like a suitcase or attaché case.'

'Would it be likely to find traces of heroin on currency if the heroin and the currency were not in close proximity?'

'No.'

'And in the case of a large quantity of cash, where a significant percentage of the bills show traces of heroin, in your expert opinion what meaning might that have?'

'It would be my opinion that the cash had been used in the purchase or sale of heroin powder.'

The grand jury had plenty of questions for this witness, and one at a time Mahoney asked them, even though – typically, David thought – they were largely repetitions of things that had already been made clear: How did you know where the evidence came from? How do you know you tested the same white powder that was confiscated at the Engs's residence? How do you tell different kinds of drugs apart?

In response to the questions, the chemist recapped the method of using sealed, sequentially numbered evidence bags and providing signed vouchers for each transfer. Mahoney didn't seem bothered by the repetition; David had the impression he was eager to make them see that everything had been handled with precision and little room left for careless error.

Mahoney took time, too, to let the chemist give the jury a short course on the chemical analysis of suspected narcotics. David doubted that most of his fellow jurors understood even the broad-brush picture the chemist painted, but he could feel the growing sense of comfort in the room: it was enough that methods to do those things existed and that the chemist spoke confidently about how they worked.

The case was by far the most interesting they'd had. Until now the grand jury had mostly been offered a succession of chain snatchings and muggings – reported sometimes by frightened or angry victims, sometimes by police decoys who had made themselves targets for an inexhaustible supply of snatch-and-grab robbers on the subways and in the streets. A few burglaries and auto thefts. People throwing rocks through store windows and grabbing what they could. No rapes, no murders. In more than a week they hadn't even had a crime that involved a gun.

For the first time, David was as intrigued as he had hoped to be. Trace amounts of cocaine and heroin on the money – he found that completely unexpected. Maybe heroin on the money in the apartment, just from proximity to the 'white powder,' but in two of the safe deposit boxes . . . And most amazing of all was that finding traces of cocaine on the money was so common that Mahoney had made a point of having the chemist tell them it didn't prove anything. But apparently heroin, unlike cocaine, wasn't everywhere . . . yet. So finding traces of it still meant something.

One question occurred to him about that. Mahoney asked it for him unaltered.

'A grand juror wants to know if you tested the composition of the heroin on the bills, and if so, if it matched the composition of the other heroin you tested.'

'No,' the chemist said, 'we didn't do that kind of test. The actual quantity of powder we recovered from the sample we were given was very small, and we more or less exhausted it in testing to see what we had. Plus, we haven't had much time. It's a miracle we got as much done as we did in the few days we've had so far.'

A good point, David thought. Presumably they'd be able to develop more conclusive evidence in time for the trial itself.

'Looks like the morning's about over,' Mahoney said after the police chemist left the grand jury room. 'You've all been very good to pay such careful attention. As I said when I came in, I'm going to come back next week to present some more evidence. Have you had any other cases so far that were continued this way?'

There was a scattered shaking of heads, and a few people said no.

'Okay, then, what I'd like you to do is pick a word we can use to identify this case, something that will stick in all your minds and that you won't confuse with any other case. That way, when I come back, I can just say that word, and it will help you remember this testimony.'

They picked 'Chinatown.'

The fact that it was Friday made the scramble to leave the courthouse more hectic than usual. Susan waited for it to subside before she left. Her phone calls during the break had put out the immediate fires at work, no one needed her there for another hour or two. And she wasn't meeting Lara until the evening.

In the elevator lobby, Mrs Liu was waiting apart from the others, looking back toward the corridor to the grand jury rooms. She beckoned unobtrusively to Susan and stepped forward.

'Excuse me . . . Can you take the trouble to drink tea with an old woman you do not know?'

'It's an honor to have you ask me.' The formal words covered Susan's surprise. She was not sure what to do. She had the uneasy feeling that this had to be about the case they had just heard. She seemed to remember that regular trial jurors were always being told not to discuss the evidence with each other until it was time to deliberate. But she didn't remember anyone's saying that here. The judge had warned them that grand jury proceedings were secret, but it was a secret she and Mrs Liu already shared. And Mrs Liu looked very eager, for all her properly indirect request.

'It will be my pleasure to join you.'

They stopped at a small basement restaurant down a flight of stairs on Mott Street, only a few blocks from the courthouse. The clientele was mostly wrinkled Chinese men eating alone or in twos, but Mrs Liu seemed to be a regular. They ate dumplings with their tea and Susan waited in polite silence for the older woman to broach the subject that had brought them here. Throughout the light meal, Mrs Liu's brief comments were only about the food and the hot summer weather.

Susan began to think that her assumption about the invitation had been wrong.

Finally, when the waitress had wheeled over the cart of desserts and Mrs Liu had pointed to a plate of sweet sticky rice, she looked across the table at Susan and said, 'The story is not true, the story these men tell.'

Susan had expected . . . she wasn't sure exactly what. Not a bald statement that what they had heard was fabricated.

'I don't understand,' she said carefully.

'Martin Eng is person of respect and trust. His wife, same. Not sell heroin.'

'You know them?' Could that be? Wouldn't she have to tell someone, or disqualify herself somehow?

'Mr Eng, president of community association for people from region called Three Districts, in Guangdong province near Pearl River. Mrs Eng – Cheung Meiling, Chinese name – work for many charity in Chinatown.'

'Now I really don't understand. You're saying . . . these people are prominent in Chinatown?'

'Chinatown people know.' Nodding vigorously.

'Everyone knows them?'

'*Many* people know. Community association not large now. New. More people belong to many old association also for Guangdong people.'

'Aren't those associations . . .' Susan didn't want to say the wrong thing. 'Don't they have connections with . . . gangs?'

Mrs Liu looked down at her plate.

'I don't mean to be offensive,' Susan said. Her own spotty knowledge of the subject was built on childhood references to tongs and tong wars, augmented over the years by news reports of extortion and kidnapping and bloody gunfights in Chinatown restaurants. Boatloads of illegal immigrants. Gambling parlors and forced prostitution. Even the gaudy funeral of a man known as Chinatown's Godfather – the former head of a large benevolent association. 'I'm trying to understand.'

Mrs Liu occupied herself with her sticky-rice dessert.

'Can you be sure it's the same people?' Susan ventured. 'There are so many with the name Eng.'

22

Mrs Liu poured tea for them both. 'I know because Chinatown people say police come to house of same Mr, Mrs Eng.'

'Is it general knowledge, then, that they were arrested?'

'I work at history museum in Chinatown. Also at senior center in same building as museum. Hear many stories. This story – police break into house of Mr, Mrs Eng – I hear many places. Read in Chinatown newspaper. Same people.'

Susan drank her tea. On the one hand she found Mrs Liu's defense of the Engs hard to accept; on the other, she supposed the basic facts might be true. And she had no trouble believing that an event of importance in Chinatown might easily go unnoticed elsewhere.

'Mr, Mrs Eng not selling heroin,' Mrs Liu insisted severely. 'Mr Eng honest businessman, follow old Chinese ways. People say, when young man he was important scholar. In China, number-one student, before Japanese come.'

'Before the Japanese . . . But that was more than fifty years ago.'

'Yes.'

'How old is he?'

Mrs Liu shrugged: don't know, doesn't matter.

But it did matter, Susan thought. Japan invaded China in the late thirties: if what Mrs Liu was saying was true, Martin Eng could easily be well over seventy. Susan had imagined that the heroin dealers in Detective Pullone's story were more like somewhere under forty. Maybe even under thirty, except that the amount of money involved brought to mind Mafia overlords and South American drug kingpins – people with more experience and authority than she expected of kids in their twenties – not that much older than her own son, after all.

Then again, this was narcotics wholesaling, and what did she know about that? Twenty-something might be more than old enough. Weren't there stories about teenage drug dealers? What made less sense to her was the idea of elderly Chinese people actively involved in the day-to-day business of drug dealing. She looked around the room at the men bent over their food, some of them worn and translucent as old porcelain. Hard to imagine any of them as a drug lord.

But maybe it was perfectly reasonable. If some of the community associations and merchants associations had gangs – young, violent

23

gangs – to protect their illegal gambling parlors and collect 'dues' from local businesses and keep the other gangs off their turf, why shouldn't they be involved in the drug trade, too? And if they were, who was to say that the head of the association, especially a small association, might not be directly involved himself.

'The police *did* find heroin in their apartment,' she offered.

'Maybe police brought with them. Police have heroin.'

True, but . . . 'Why would they do that?'

Mrs Liu shook her head. 'Mr, Mrs Eng not sell heroin.'

'I'm sorry. I don't mean to argue with you. I don't know if we should even be doing this, talking about it like this.'

Mrs Liu poured tea for her again. 'I am the one to be sorry. I am wrong to think you take this old woman's word.'

'No, no, it isn't that.' She worried that she'd been insulting, some-how. There was so much Susan had forgotten or never learned about the Chinese forms of politeness. Her mother had tried now and then to give her a sense of her heritage, but she had resisted, intent on becoming as American as she could. By the time she realized she had squandered an opportunity to be closer to her mother, it was too late to undo the mistake: her parents, visiting China for the first time since they'd fled the Communists in 1949, had been killed in a massive earthquake outside Beijing, or so the official communiqué had said. 'It's not that I doubt your word, Mrs Liu. I just . . . I don't see why the police would make such a mistake.'

Lame, Susan thought: that's too lame for words. The police made mistakes; everyone made mistakes. The police could be corrupt, too: there were regular headlines about the District Attorney's office arresting cops – and lying about evidence was only the beginning, especially when it came to illegal drugs.

It was the scale of all this that made her doubt there'd been a mistake, or some kind of police corruption. If these people really were pillars of the community, wouldn't everyone be very careful to have their facts straight before arresting them and poking around in their safe deposit boxes?

Mrs Liu rummaged in her purse and brought out the pamphlet they had been given that explained how grand juries worked, its somewhat fragile white pages protected by a plastic sandwich bag. 'This say if

24

have question, ask. I have many question. Why police go to Mr, Mrs Eng house? Who send them? How know to find heroin there? Excuse me, my English not good. Good to understand what they say, not good to ask question. Important question.'

'Yes, they are important.'

Odd that none of those things had come up. Given the fact of the arrest and the discovery of heroin and all that heroin-tainted money, it made perfect sense that the police had raided the Engs's apartment. But that was hindsight. Mrs Liu was right: it all had to have started somewhere. The police didn't get search warrants to break in doors at random, hoping to find half a million dollars and half a pound of heroin lying around.

'Your English is fine,' Susan said, knowing this was a question not of Mrs Liu's ability but of her self-perception, her desire not to embarrass herself. 'But I can ask those questions if you want me to.'

Mrs Liu smiled. 'You make old lady very happy.'

# 3

David Clark got to the grand jury late Monday morning and spent the first two hours of the session in a fog, waiting for the break and a chance to get some quick breakfast, with the emphasis on a large cup of coffee.

He'd been out the night before with a woman he'd been getting friendly with at the gym. He'd thought of her as easygoing and funny, but outside the gym her main topic of conversation turned out to be money and the things it could buy. Mentioning that he was between real jobs hadn't slowed her down.

By the time he'd gotten back to his apartment he'd been too angry to sleep – angry with her, angry with himself and angry with the way he saw his life right now. Having finally fallen into a restless half-sleep he'd had to force himself to get out of bed in the morning.

At the break, he emerged from the grand jury room into a hallway already full of people – another of the grand juries sitting on the ninth floor was still on its break. David pushed his way through the crowd on his way to the elevators. Susan Linwood was not far behind.

'I don't mean to be a nuisance,' she said, 'but I'd appreciate it if you could point me to where you got that cup of coffee Friday. The line at the vending machine up here is longer than the one at the phones.'

'There's a coffee wagon on the corner,' he told her. 'It's a lot easier than hassling with the courthouse.'

The silver truck was in its usual place, one of its sides hinged upward to reveal an unappetizing array of rolls and pastries wrapped in clear plastic. Susan asked for one of the small bottles of water displayed among the soft drinks; David ordered a large black coffee and a bagel.

'Can I talk to you for a minute?' she asked him. 'About one of our cases.'

He hesitated, taken by surprise. 'Sure.'

'Is there someplace . . .?'

He led her back past the door to the D.A.'s office and around behind the building, where there was a row of diagonally-parked police cars. He put his bag of coffee and bagel on the trunk of an unmarked car.

'This ought to be okay,' he said. 'As long as we don't camp out.'

He stirred sugar into his coffee, waiting to see what this was about. Standing close to her like this, he had a more immediate sense of how stunning she was. Yet there was something cool and studied about the perfection of her beauty; he could not imagine her in workout clothes, sweating on a stairclimber. Or struggling up a rocky mountain trail under the weight of a full pack. Or – unlike the theatrically alluring Number Twelve – in bed.

'It's the case about the drug money,' she said into the silence.

'Chinatown.' Not surprising.

'Those people they're accusing – Mr and Mrs Eng – I've learned something about them.'

She seemed to expect that he'd prompt her to continue. But compelling as she was to look at he wasn't sure he wanted her to continue.

She drank some of her water. He tried his coffee – too hot – and looked past her at the fenced-in park and playground that occupied the blocks behind the courthouse. Elderly people from the adjacent streets of Chinatown sat reading newspapers in the shade of trees big enough to have been there for ever, while little children ran around in happy chaos, oblivious of the older kids trying to play a game of stickball.

'I was hoping I could spark your curiosity about them,' she said. 'I've noticed that you seem to be comfortable asking the prosecutors questions.'

'For all the good it does me. Anyway, there's no trick to it.' He looked at her. 'And you don't strike me as shy.'

She seemed surprised. 'No. I suppose I'm not. But all this . . . it's not what I'm used to.'

'Really? I would have guessed that in your work –' whatever it was – 'you get people to do things for you all the time.'

'You're very direct,' she said.

27

'I work with computers.' This was his usual self-description these days – so vague and only generically true that he sometimes wondered why he didn't do better. 'People aren't my specialty.'

'I suppose being direct is a good trait for working with computers.'

'A necessity. You were saying, about asking the prosecutors questions . . .'

'Yes, I'm sorry. This must seem odd to you. There's a woman in the first row who lives here in Chinatown. Number Six. You may have noticed her.'

'Yes.'

'Well . . . Mrs Liu – that's her name – Mrs Liu told me she knows who these defendants are. She says they're very old, and they're involved in community work in Chinatown and very respected for it.' She paused, waiting. When he didn't speak, she said, 'It raises some questions, don't you think?'

He finished chewing a piece of bagel but this time she did not elaborate.

'Like?' Prompting her, in spite of himself.

She hesitated. 'Like why would elderly people who do community service be in the drug business?'

'Presumably they need the money, or if they don't need it they like it. Isn't that why people are in the drug business, at any age?'

'But . . . *old* people?'

'People all ages like money, last I looked.' Try living without it for a while, he thought.

'But how did the police know to go their apartment? I mean, I know they had a search warrant, but how did they know to get it? How do we know the drugs weren't planted, and the money for that matter?'

'Why would the cops do that?' Not that cops planting drugs on a suspect was an unheard-of idea. But money? And where would cops get that much, for that purpose?

'God only knows why the police do things.' She seemed caught between dismay and annoyance. 'Suppose they needed to boost their arrest record. Or suppose they were under suspicion of dealing drugs, themselves, and they were getting rid of the evidence. Maybe somebody else planted it there. Some enemy of the Engs's, and that's who denounced them to the police.'

This isn't China, he almost said, but he saw in time that it wouldn't be smart. Odd, he thought: what this woman called his directness, he himself often saw as clumsiness. If he sometimes said more or less exactly what was in his mind, it was because he was more caught up in the content of the thought than its social consequences. All too often he ended up offending someone as a result. This time, at least, he had caught himself. 'Anything's possible, I guess.' The words did not do much to disguise his skepticism.

She looked discouraged. 'Well, I suppose we should go back up. I hoped you might be able to help me with the prosecutor, but I'm clearly not convincing you.'

'You know, there *is* one thing that does seem funny,' he said as the thought popped into his mind. 'Didn't the detective say those people resisted arrest?'

'I don't remember exactly, but yes, I think he might have.'

'That's something I'd like to know more about. I mean, if they *are* elderly . . .'

'In their seventies, at least. And Mrs Liu said Mr Eng was a scholar.'

'Then he's probably smart enough to have known he was facing a long jail term. That could make even an old man kind of feisty, wouldn't you say – if he thought he was about to be arrested? Especially if he had a bunch of money and drugs in the house.'

'But – a *scholar*. I mean . . . I don't think of scholars as being, I don't know . . . violent. And I thought you said . . .' She let the sentence trail off.

'I still want to know more about it.'

'Will you ask?'

He nodded.

'I really appreciate it,' she said. 'And what about the other questions?'

'What other questions?'

'About how the police knew to go there.'

'I don't think they usually tell us that, do they?'

That stopped her briefly. 'I haven't really noticed. This is the first time it's seemed important.'

'I think the D.A. usually says, "Did you respond to such-and-such place?" and the cop says yes and the D.A. asks what did he observe, or what occurred. Not, "Why did you go there?" '

'But why *did* they go there? They must have had a reason.'

He shrugged. 'Those are *your* questions.'

'Yes, but . . .' For a moment she seemed at a loss for words. 'I'd rather not ask them myself, if I can help it.'

He didn't get it. He wondered if his confusion was clear on his face.

'You *do* understand,' she said, looking at him as if she could make it true by force of will.

'No, I don't, not really. And you're right, we should be getting back upstairs.' He took a mouthful of his untouched coffee. It was still much too hot to drink that way. He got most of it back into the cup by protective reflex.

'I'm sorry.' His lips and tongue felt scalded. 'That wasn't exactly company manners.' He wiped coffee from his hand with an inadequate napkin.

'They shouldn't serve coffee that hot.'

'I really am sorry.' He could feel his face flushing. 'It took me by surprise.'

'Are you okay?'

'I'll be fine, thanks.' He closed the bag around the soggy napkin and the remains of his half-eaten bagel, and dropped the bag and the offending coffee cup in the trash basket on the corner.

'It's because the Engs are Chinese,' she said as they walked toward the building's entrance. 'They're Chinese, and so am I. I'm afraid the prosecutor will think that's the reason I'm asking the questions and he won't take me seriously.'

'You have the right to ask any question you want.'

'But what if he won't ask it for me? They don't always ask *your* questions.'

'Sure, but first they tell me why – because I'm asking for information the grand jury isn't supposed to have, or I want to know about something that can't be admitted as evidence because of some rule they have. They always have a reason, just the way the judge said they would.'

The way it had worked so far, when an A.D.A. had changed or refused David's questions the reasons had not always satisfied him. But he'd been concerned that pressing too frequently for more

30

convincing explanations – all in whispered secrecy – would make him seem ornery or eccentric to the other grand jurors, unlikely to be listened to if it came to a debate during their deliberations.

It would have been different if they could all hear his conversation with the prosecutor, but the only ones who could hear any of it were the people a seat or two away, and based on his own experience they only got bits and pieces. So if he argued with a prosecutor he would have no one on his side. He supposed that was why the system was set up the way it was, to keep everybody isolated and intimidated. Under control.

Susan Linwood said, 'It's not just the prosecutor – I'm worried about what the others will think, too.' Echoing his own unexpressed thought. 'If it comes to a close vote, I don't want them to think the reason I'm making trouble is because the defendants are Chinese.'

'If it's a close vote, that means a lot of the others aren't convinced by the evidence, either. And they won't think you're making trouble.'

'That's exactly why I'm so concerned about how it looks. I want people to make up their minds on the facts, not on our faces.'

He shook his head. 'I'll say this – I may take the prize for direct, but you win for persistent.' And he was certainly in sympathy with her desire to be taken seriously if it came to a debate. 'All right. I'll ask your questions. But don't blame me if you don't get the answers you want.'

Susan's questions did not get asked that day. She sat impatiently through a sexual assault and a liquor store robbery, hoping each time a new prosecutor opened the door that it would be A.D.A. Mahoney.

The day's last case brought them two prosecutors – a short, blonde young woman named Rachel Meisel and a man called Joseph Estrada who looked to be in his middle thirties, as old as any of the prosecutors the grand jury had seen so far. He had compelling dark eyes and an unforced air of authority. Meisel's supervisor? Susan wondered.

A.D.A. Meisel presented a police officer who informed the grand jury that, calling in his arrest of the defendant for picking a tourist's pocket, he had learned there was a warrant out for him for jumping bail on a similar charge. Meisel offered in evidence an indictment on that charge, a class-E felony. A court clerk established that the defendant

31

had failed to appear in court on April first, the day set in his bail order – or within thirty days of that date, or at any time since.

Throughout the testimony A.D.A. Estrada stood in silence in the back of the room, behind the desk where the grand jury's foreman, alternate forewoman and secretary sat. Susan couldn't see why a crime as seemingly minor as bail jumping required two prosecutors.

When the court clerk finished testifying, Meisel came down to stand in front of the grand jurors and announce that the alleged bail jumper himself was going to testify. This caused a murmur of surprise – and Susan thought it might explain the double-teaming. Meisel wiped her palms on her skirt and looked up to where Estrada was standing.

'Let me explain,' she said in a voice more tentative than the one in which she had questioned her witnesses. 'This kind of testimony is not common, but a defendant has the right to testify to the grand jury in his or her own defense, to try to convince you that he or she should not have to stand trial.' She wiped her hands again.

'There are some things I have to tell you about that. First of all, whenever any witness testifies before the grand jury in this State, that witness receives what is called transactional immunity. Transactional immunity means the witness cannot thereafter be prosecuted for any crime related to any transaction he or she testifies about. Any crime at all – except, of course, perjury committed during the testimony itself.

'This broad grant of immunity is for the purpose of encouraging witnesses to make full and complete disclosure to the grand jury. But it creates a problem when a defendant – or anyone being investigated by a grand jury – wants to testify. Because once a person testifies about anything at all that's part of a specific criminal transaction, then as a direct result of testifying about it that person cannot be prosecuted for that crime.

'This means that in order for a defendant – or a potential defendant – to testify, that person first has to execute a waiver of immunity. Then, since the witness has waived his immunity, he can still be prosecuted, if prosecution proves to be appropriate.

'*However* –' she emphasized the word heavily – 'you are not to draw any conclusions about the defendant's guilt or innocence from the fact that he has executed a waiver of immunity.'

32

Similarly, she told them, they weren't to hold it against the defendant if he brought an attorney into the grand jury with him – a privilege reserved for witnesses who gave up their immunity – or if he exercised his right to consult with his attorney at any time.

'If he does confer with his attorney, you'll hear me mention it for the record. I'm not doing this to call attention to it, but merely for the sake of a complete record.'

After Meisel had answered the grand jury's questions about witness immunity and the effects of waiving it, the grand jury warden escorted the defendant into the room. He was a short, pale man with the gaunt and hunted look, Susan thought, of someone who had never known an easy or comfortable day. He was accompanied by the lawyer Meisel had told them to expect. The defense lawyer, graying and battleworn, seemed annoyed to be there, or perhaps just annoyed in general. He and his client took seats behind the witness table, facing the grand jurors. The warden took a chair by the door.

Meisel started by putting the defendant through a series of questions that established that he was in the grand jury voluntarily and that he was freely giving up the immunity usually conferred on grand jury witnesses. That he was represented by counsel who was present in the room and that he knew that whatever he said would be used in court if he came to trial. Then she asked him if he had a statement he wanted to make. He did.

'I come here to tell you I never did nothing like this in my life. I knew I was supposed to go to court, and I woulda been there if I could. First thing I did, I called my lawyer and I told him, I can't make it, let 'em know, do whatever you have to do. So I figured that part of it was okay. I didn't run out on anybody. I been right here where they could find me any time. Thing was, I was gonna go, but it was my girl-friend . . .' He paused there, looking off a bit blankly as if he was visualizing the scene.

'See, the thing is, she was pregnant but there was a problem with it, I don't know exactly. Tubal pregnancy I think they called it, and what happened was she got sick with it that morning, and all I could do, I had to take her to the hospital. I mean, the baby and all, what else could I do? I had to get her to the hospital, and I figured the rest of it was taken care of, because I called my lawyer and said could he take care of it and he said fine.'

'Have you ever failed to show up in court before?' Meisel asked the defendant, a slight catch of nervousness in her voice.

'Me?' He was incredulous. 'Nah. Never. I said, I never did anything like this before.'

But he had – more than once – and the young prosecutor kept producing court papers to remind him of it, in the face of his repeated evasions and denials. One of his many failures to appear was for theft of services, a misdemeanor: he'd walked out on a restaurant check.

'I thought you meant *felonies*,' he said when Meisel pressed him about it. 'And anyway, that food, I couldn't eat it, it was so bad.'

Some of the grand jurors laughed. It was funny, the way he said it, but Susan didn't see how he could be so unconcerned.

'And did you appear in court on that charge?' the prosecutor asked him.

'I did.'

'Are you sure?' She handed him another of her documents.

He did not look at it. 'I don't care what that says. I went there like I was supposed to and I sat there in court all day. I was going to tell them, I never stole nothin' because nobody ought to pay for that, only nobody called me. I don't know why they didn't write me down, but I know I was there.'

Meisel changed tack. Did he know he was supposed to notify the court if he failed to appear for his April first court appearance on the pickpocketing charge?

'I told my lawyer.'

'Did you notify the court?'

'He said he'd take care of it.'

'Did *you* notify the *court*?'

'I told my *lawyer* to.'

'Were you informed that you yourself had to notify the court?'

'But what difference, if my lawyer—'

'*Personally* notify the court?'

'My girlfriend was sick, I was afraid she was going to lose the baby, what did you want me to *do*?'

'How long was she sick?'

34

'I don't know exactly. For weeks, and I had to stay with her. Four, five weeks, easy.'

The prosecutor asked a series of questions about the girlfriend's identity, the circumstances of their meeting and the length of the relationship. She asked the name of the girlfriend's doctor, which the witness professed not to know, and whether she had any relatives or friends who had visited her while she was sick.

'Some, yeah. Some, like, girlfriends who came to see her.' He did not remember who.

'And during the time you are describing, did you ever leave the house?'

It was the first question he didn't have a quick answer for. 'I don't know,' he said finally. 'Maybe. I must have. Went to the store, you know, stuff like that.'

'And did you appear in court at any time in the thirty days following April first?'

'I thought it was taken care of.'

'Did you appear?'

'I already told you –' the witness was all bewildered innocence – 'I told my lawyer—'

Meisel cut him off. 'Did you *appear*?'

'No, but—'

'Just yes or no.'

'No.'

'Was there a reason why in all that time, and all the time since then, you could not appear in court?'

'I said, because my girlfriend was sick. And I thought it was taken care of.'

Norman Thompson was first up with a question, as usual. David thought it was kind of funny, the way each new prosecutor came in seemingly unaware of who the nuts and nuisances were, when it had been obvious to the members of the grand jury for so long. He wondered if prosecutors developed special antennae for that kind of thing, or if they talked to each other about it before presenting a case.

A.D.A. Meisel listened to Thompson's question but she did not ask

35

it. 'Ladies and gentlemen,' she said, 'the defendant cannot testify about the medical specifics of his girlfriend's condition, except to the extent that he observed them himself.'

As she looked for another questioner, David saw the defense lawyer stir from his inert sourness. He shifted in his seat and cleared his throat, but before he could speak Estrada came down from the back of the room to confer with Meisel.

'Ladies and gentlemen, let me clarify what I just told you,' she said, her cheeks flushed. 'The defendant may report on medical opinions he heard to the extent, and only to the extent, that those opinions affected his own behavior.'

Thompson raised his hand again. Meisel went back and listened.

'All right.' She was clearly annoyed. To the witness she said, 'A grand juror wants to know, was there anything you heard of a medical nature that affected your behavior with regard to your failure to appear in court?'

The defendant jumped on the opportunity. 'Well, yeah, it's like I said, I heard about this, about the tubal pregnancy or whatever, that she could lose the baby any time. So I was real upset, and I was afraid to leave her alone.'

Most of the other questions Meisel relayed to the witness were innocuous – and pointless, David thought – as if people were asking them just because they didn't want to miss the chance to ask questions of a criminal defendant. When the jurors tired of asking questions, Meisel excused the witness and his lawyer led him out. The grand jury warden left with them.

Again, Estrada came down from the upper reaches of the room to join Meisel at the front and they whispered together for a moment.

'There's one more item to cover before I can submit this indictment for your vote,' Meisel said, again looking uncomfortable. 'There's another possible witness, but it's not one the People are calling.'

The defendant was offering his girlfriend as a witness on his behalf. But, Meisel emphasized, although the defendant himself had an absolute right to testify in the grand jury, he had no similar right to bring in any other witness. In a trial, yes – but not here.

'On the other hand,' she told them, 'you yourselves have the right to respond favorably to the defendant's request and ask to hear this witness *if you want to*.' She delivered the last words with evident skepticism.

'We're going to leave the room now so you can discuss whether you want us to call her as a witness,' she said. 'Just ring when you've taken your vote.'

There was a silence after the door closed behind the two prosecutors and the stenographer.

Norman Thompson spoke up. 'I think we ought to hear what this girlfriend has to say.'

'What for?' Once again, David noted, Thompson's first challenge came from the grand juror in seat Number Four – a muscular white man half Thompson's age whose basic attitude seemed to be: nobody gets this far who isn't guilty of something.

'The guy is lying,' he said now. 'Anybody can hear that. And she's gonna lie, too. Why else do you think he wants her in here?'

'We can decide that when we hear her,' Thompson insisted. 'The point is, if we don't listen, we'll never know what she might have said. And she's the only one who can tell us what was wrong with her.'

Grand juror Number Fourteen, one of Thompson's regular supporters when he was awake, greeted this with a hearty, 'You tell 'em!'

'We're here to send dirtbags like this to trial,' Number Four said. 'The regular jury can worry about what was really wrong with her.'

The grand jury's foreman was sitting tight, as usual doing nothing to control the proceedings. 'I'm no better than any of the rest of you,' he had said, their first morning. 'Except maybe when it comes to putting up or fixing telephone lines, and maybe not even that, now I'm retired. They just picked my name out of a hat, is all. I'll do my job here the way they say I have to but I'm not telling anybody else how to do things.' So far he'd been true to his word.

'I never heard anybody lie like that in my life,' Number Four was saying. 'And no girlfriend of some guy who can lie like that is convincing *me* of anything.'

'How else are we going to know what was wrong with her, how bad it was?' Thompson persisted. 'If the man had a reason . . . I mean, you heard what he said. If that was my wife—'

'Girlfriend,' Number Four interjected.

'—girlfriend, I'd sure have been staying by her side till I knew she was out of the woods.'

'It can't have been a tubal pregnancy the way he said,' said the pale woman in seat Twenty, who always wore loose summer dresses with flowers on them. David couldn't remember a time when she'd spoken up like this. 'Tubal pregnancies, there's no saving the baby. It doesn't get that far. There's all this horrible pain, and if you don't get it operated on right away it's going to be fatal.'

'That's why we need to hear from her,' Thompson persisted. 'He just probably got it wrong, like any man.'

'Who cares?' Number Four was full of disdain. 'I say we vote.'

'Well, fuck you, Jack. I say we don't.' Thompson was clearly too caught up in battle to worry about the effect his language might have on the others.

'Wait a minute, gentlemen, please.' A tense voice from behind David and to his right. He turned in his seat to look. It was the alternate forewoman, a short, thick-bodied woman in her fifties with heavy horn-rimmed glasses and a professorial air, standing by her chair at the foreman's desk. 'There's no point getting upset. We can work this out.'

Having said that, she looked around, as if hoping someone else would come up with the next step.

'Look,' Number Four said in a more reasonable tone, 'the thing is, is anybody gonna vote any different on this indictment – up or down – after they hear this bimbo? I mean, I already told you I'm not. And I'll bet my friend Mr Thompson over there ain't about to change his mind, neither. *He's* gonna say let the guy off, *I'm* gonna say no. *Whatever* the girlfriend says. Am I right, or am I right? So that's what it's about. If you think she's going to change your mind vote yes. Or else, vote no and we can all save a lot of time.'

There was a scattering of nods and noises of agreement.

David thought both Thompson and Number Four were arguing the wrong side: if the girlfriend testified, A.D.A. Meisel was sure to make her slip up – all those questions Meisel had asked about her had to be a setup. And that would only make the defendant look more like a liar. But the two grand jurors seemed to care only about their immediate conflict with each other. David saw no point in getting himself in the middle of that.

38

'I got a story to tell before we vote,' Norman Thompson said. Number Four groaned theatrically, but Thompson forged ahead. 'I had a court appearance one time. I went there and I sat there all damn day and nobody called my name. All day. So I went home and then later they tried to get me in trouble because they said I wasn't there. So what I'm saying is, I don't think the man was lying when he said that, that he sat there all day. And another thing. They've got him already on picking pockets – twice – so why do they need bail jumping? I think somebody's got it in for the guy. Somebody's up to something.'

'What the hell does that have to do with his girlfriend?' Number Four was indignant. 'Let's do one thing at a time. We're voting whether to listen to this girlfriend. Let's do that first.'

'That's a good point,' the foreman said mildly, involved at last. 'Any objection? Vote to say if you think this girlfriend person could change your mind. And if not we'll go on without her.'

There was no objection, and the vote was clear: by the show of hands, only two of the grand jurors besides David thought that the girlfriend's testimony might be worth hearing. He was intrigued to see that Susan Linwood had started to put her hand up but had apparently reconsidered.

'Great,' Number Four crowed. 'One more liar we don't need to waste time on.' He was already moving on to victory. 'Let's vote on the indictment.'

'Wait a minute,' Thompson protested. 'Like you said, one thing at a time. She said to let them know about this vote. We've got to do that first.'

The foreman buzzed to let the grand jury warden know they'd reached a decision, and the two prosecutors came back into the room.

'We voted no, not to have that witness,' the foreman told them.

Meisel looked at Estrada, who nodded to her, clearly satisfied by the outcome.

'Okay,' Meisel said. 'I guess that means you're ready to vote on the indictment.'

'I think so,' the foreman said.

She read them the definition of bail jumping in the second degree, and again the prosecutors left the room.

'I'm saying,' Thompson resumed, 'that these people are up to

39

something here. Why trump up some dumb business about he didn't go to court? They've got him in jail now on this pickpocket thing, you want to bet. If they need him in court from now on, he'll be there for sure.'

'I agree,' chimed in Number Fourteen. 'Why don't they just get him on a *real* crime? And another thing. Why does it take two of them in here to make a case against him?'

'You see how they didn't want to let me ask that?' Thompson added. 'And throwing in things like that restaurant bill, where he didn't get any service to be the thief of in the first place.'

'This whole argument is so dumb,' Number Four said in disgust. 'You have to know they're going to get him on every damn thing they can, make the sentence as long as possible. That's what I'd want to do, for sure – get him off the street and keep him off. I say we should vote.'

David wondered why Number Four was so confident. From where David was sitting, it looked as if Thompson's misgivings had real support.

'I don't know if this matters,' said the woman in seat Fifteen, across the aisle from Thompson, 'but I just read where there's a big problem with people not showing up for court dates. That there are – I don't know – fifty, sixty thousand people, serious criminals, just in New York, who are wanted for not showing up in court like this. Some of them don't even go into hiding. They just live at home like normal and nobody has the time to come after them. I don't see why this one man should be different.'

'Because they didn't have to go looking for him,' said Number Four, turning in his seat to address her directly. 'He fell right into their hands.' He looked around at the others. 'It's almost one o'clock. Let's vote.'

'That's fine by me,' Thompson agreed quickly. 'So long as we don't make ourselves into a rubber stamp for these people.'

There were only ten votes to indict, including David's own and Susan Linwood's. Number Four was completely unprepared for the outcome, and he was very vocal about it.

'A vote's a vote,' Norman Thompson insisted. 'There's thirteen people here say *no true bill*, and that's all there is to it.' The foreman – reluctantly, David thought – had to agree.

The color left A.D.A. Meisel's face when she heard the news. She stood staring blankly until Estrada thanked the grand jurors for their time and attention and touched her on the arm to let her know it was time to leave.

An elevatorful of grand jurors escaped together from the courthouse. Making his way through the slow-moving group, David passed Susan Linwood.

'Mr Clark,' she called, matching her stride to his. 'I can't get over how irrational people can be,' she said when they'd outpaced the others, walking down Centre Street. 'That man was so clearly lying – it was almost as if he was mocking us – and yet, once they thought the prosecutors were ganging up on him . . .'

'It was Number Four's fault,' David said. 'He was too eager to shoot Thompson down over the girlfriend, so he won the battle and lost the war. I don't think you'll see anything like that again soon.'

'But you can see how easily it turns into a matter of whim how things come out, nothing to do with logic. If they think my asking questions – my interest in these defendants – is only because I'm Chinese, they won't listen at all. That's why I didn't raise my hand to say I wanted to hear the girlfriend. It wouldn't have accomplished anything, and I don't want to be seen as a troublemaker.'

'I've already agreed to ask your questions. You don't need to convince me.'

'I wanted to be sure you understood.'

'I notice that Mr Thompson doesn't seem to care about saving his ammunition for when it counts, and neither does Number Four.'

'No, and so they both have their allies and their enemies, and very little of what they say is persuasive, don't you think?'

'I suppose.'

'And because of that neither of them is going to swing the balance on a close vote.'

'And you think *we* might have, this time? By making it clear to the people who wanted to indict that without the girlfriend they stood a good chance of losing?'

'Assuming we could have done that. I didn't think it was worth taking sides for.'

41

'But you think these people in the Chinatown case are worth it.'

'I only know I'm disturbed by what Mrs Liu told me, and I want to find out the truth.'

'I'm going to ask your questions for you,' he said again. 'But I have to admit to a certain curiosity . . . *would* you be this interested in these defendants if they weren't Chinese?'

Instead of answering she angled across Foley Square, dodging through gaps in the traffic. He followed her.

'You really *are* direct,' she said when they'd reached the Lafayette Street sidewalk.

'I didn't mean to offend you.'

'I'm not offended. You just took me by surprise. And, frankly, I don't quite see what difference it makes, as long as my questions make sense.'

She stopped at a black sedan parked with the motor running. From where he was standing David could not see the driver.

'This is me,' she said.

'I go over to the West Side.' He said it quickly, to spare them both the awkwardness of her offering him a ride – or not. 'See you tomorrow.'

# 4

In the car on the way uptown to her office, Susan tried not to think about David Clark's question. In a sense it was meaningless: if she wasn't Chinese like the Engs she wouldn't even know about them, not beyond the bare facts the prosecutor had presented so far. It was only because the Engs were Chinese – and prominent in Chinatown, at least a little bit – that Mrs Liu had learned about them in the first place, and only because Susan was Chinese that Mrs Liu had come to her with the information.

But just suppose, she told herself: suppose you learned about it some other way, suppose they were African–American, or Italian–American, or even Korean–American. What then? And she knew that she could not be sure she would have cared as much, or at all.

On the other hand, she thought as the driver pulled smoothly to the curb, maybe that was exactly as it should be. After all, she *was* Chinese, and that did count. Even though she had paid little attention to the fact for much of her life and had all but buried it in a marriage to a pure-bred Wasp from an old-established New England family.

Her assistant, Mona, virtually leapt up from her desk when Susan walked into the office. 'We thought you'd never get here! They're foaming at the mouth at Consolidated again.'

It was not what she wanted to hear. Consolidated Health Products was her biggest account – a sprawling company cobbled together out of a dozen smaller ones, it covered virtually every aspect of the medical-supply business. Consolidated had chosen Susan to create a unified presence for the company so it could emerge from the diverse specialty-products niches occupied by its divisions and become

43

known as a single, broad-based entity. Unfortunately, Consolidated's management was not in complete agreement on the shape their image should take or the timing of its revelation to the world. This resulted in occasional tirades by Shelby Portman, their vice-president of marketing, who sometimes behaved as if Susan should have the answers to Consolidated's internal questions. Until Susan had put her foot down, it had also resulted in last-minute changes in direction that meant days or weeks of work being trashed.

Annette, Susan's associate, working to become her junior partner, was waiting by the door to Susan's office. She followed Susan in, talking as she went.

'It's Portman again. He claims they need a full proposal for the whole new campaign by next Thursday – not just an outline, all the details, too, right down to an itinerary for the tour: which cities, what days. I told him it didn't make sense to try to fix it in stone so early, especially not the tour part of it, at least not until we had some of the introductory releases written and sent out, and made some follow-up calls, but I guess I wasn't convincing enough. So if you don't talk to him right away, I don't know . . . we might be in trouble.'

Susan dropped her purse onto her desk chair and went to sit at the small glass table by the windows, where she did her best thinking. Public relations was a business full of crises, real and imagined – too often provoked by the unrealistic expectations of clients. Annette hadn't been at it long enough to resist pumping problems up beyond what reality merited. This one, though, might actually be worse than she seemed to think.

'Have Mona order some Caesar salad from Artie's and that flat bread they have, and then you can tell me exactly what Portman said, and we can see how bad this really is.'

David Clark thought he had put the encounter with Susan Linwood out of his mind, but the annoyance was there, simmering just out of consciousness, and it kept popping back into his mind. She seemed to have just the kind of attitude that went with her glossy exterior and a lifetime of upper-middle-class comfort and privilege. If she ran true to form, she'd probably be critical of the way he asked her questions – even though it would be Mahoney's version she heard, not his.

He stopped himself, amazed that he was getting so worked up about this. If he was going to ask the questions, he would do it for his own edification, not a smile from a beautiful woman.

He checked his e-mail when he got home. Two of the messages were from friends who were going on his whitewater trip, verifying the schedule and affirming that their checks were on the way. Another was from his headhunter: there were three possible jobs coming up, more details to follow. And there was one from Jon Levi, his old partner. 'I've got one word for you. Interoperability.'

It was the most recent of a long series that varied only in the final word. Jon was always coming up with a new area they could tackle together; the underlying message was always that this would finally be the one that really made them rich. Only this time the word wasn't entirely new, and the whole ritual suddenly seemed sour.

David clicked on REPLY and typed: 'In the future please identify your jokes by appending the appropriate emoticon.' It was as close to an insult as he cared to get; despite everything they'd been through, or possibly because of it, he still liked Jon. For emphasis he appended an emoticon of his own, a razz – :-p – a sideways face, two eyes a nose and a mouth with tongue protruding – clicked on SEND and signed off.

He hunted in the refrigerator for lunch, found a bowl of spaghetti from the previous night's dinner. He took himself some of the spaghetti, and threw together a salad to go with it. It was one of the unexpected benefits of living in this part of New York: an abundance of fresh vegetables available day and night. He didn't make a fetish of eating, but he had come to think that a meal of good, fresh ingredients simply prepared was among life's true pleasures.

There was a worn easy chair by the living-room window that he had made his own in the months since his father died. It was the only place in the apartment where you could see the sky, and for David it was a portal to sanity. He had found the chair with its back to the window and turned it so he could look out between the neighboring buildings at the bright sliver of sky beyond them and the tops of a few trees in the park by the river. Now and then a bird flew by, mostly pigeons, sometimes a crow or a seagull, rarely a smaller bird that he thought might be a sparrow or a robin. Recently he had spied a large bird with a reddish tail, soaring by on wide, unmoving wings: he had wondered if it could be a hawk, but what would a hawk be doing in Manhattan?

He heard a thump by the apartment door, the day's snail mail being dropped on the doormat by the elevator man, a service that survived from the building's more elegant past by virtue of the same rent laws that made this apartment too valuable a bargain to give up. The actual tenant of record was his sister, Alice, who had entered the apartment's line of descent in her ex-husband's family by virtue of her tenancy during the good years of her marriage; she had become the legal tenant when her husband ran off to a more exciting and rewarding life in Los Angeles. Then, after the death of her and David's mother, Alice had brought their father down from upstate to live with her. Not long after, she had set out with her twins for a Shangri La of her own, in Colorado ski country.

At the time, David had been living and working outside Boston, where he and Jon Levi and another budding young genius had been building a small company. For a while it had looked as if they might shortly become the sovereigns of a minor high-tech empire. When that dream had failed, coming to live with his dad and helping him through what they did not yet know would be his final illness had seemed to David the right thing to do. He was glad he had done it.

Growing up, he and his father had never had much to say to each other. Larry Clark had been an honest laborer, a man who worked outdoors with his hands, on his best days a craftsman. He had not been prepared for a son who was fascinated by numbers and electrical circuits, who was happier playing chess than football. Not that David hadn't tried football, hoping to please the silent man who came home sweaty and exhausted at the end of every day, who took a bath and had a beer and read the sports page before dinner, asked the same question about school every evening over coffee, and then parked himself in front of the television until he fell asleep.

Retired and ailing, Larry Clark hadn't been a lot more talkative, but he had developed an uncomprehending respect for his son's professional achievements, despite the abyss into which David's grandest hopes had tumbled. 'Wasn't you,' he said when the subject came up. 'Not your fault. It's like getting run over by a truck driven by a blind man. I seen plenty of good men used up and thrown out by big companies in my day. Nothin' new about that.'

True enough, as far as it went, but there was more to it. There was the question of whether he should have been able to see that the truck might run him down, that the driver was blind. David had never shaken the suspicion that someone else in his place, less fascinated by the road to fame and riches revealed in the headlights, would have gotten out of the way in time.

The important thing, though, was just having the conversation. He couldn't rely on his father to pick him up and dust him off – that was his own job. That, and doing what he could to keep his father comfortable and distracted. They played cards together and David taught him chess. Amazingly, he even reached the point of playing with a real desire to win, though he always grumbled when David brought out the board. 'All right,' he'd say, 'but only because you like it so much.'

Susan Linwood's afternoon went by quickly, consumed by work. After a long, conciliatory conversation with Shelby Portman, she and Annette had worked on the releases for Consolidated's new estrogen delivery system. Susan had been campaigning for months to get the company to make this product launch the occasion for establishing their new corporate identity. It was only at the last possible moment that they had agreed, and twice since then Portman's boss had made serious noises about changing his mind. Each time Susan had had to stop work and sketch out alternative approaches. Now, with the launch due in the fall, there was no more time for second thoughts, not if they were going to have time for the usual delays and screw-ups by the copywriters and graphic designers and printers and everyone else who had to implement the program Susan was developing.

She didn't get home until after nine. She had known not to expect to see her husband for dinner – he had a meeting at the hospital. Work often kept Richard away in the evenings; being a prominent neurosurgeon was not a nine-to-five job, and their oddly strained relationship did not prompt him to hurry home except when their son Charles was in from college.

There was a note from Lara: out with friends, don't wait up. Some bar or club, Susan guessed. Lara wasn't old enough to drink but she more than looked the part when she wanted to. Susan didn't kid herself

– alcohol wasn't the real threat, anyway, and it was even easier for kids to get drugs than it was to get a drink at a club. For starters, no drug dealer was going to card them. Not that carding was a major hindrance, either. Susan had heard enough stories about high-school girls – Lara's friends among them – returning from a night at the clubs sodden with drink to know that enforcement of the legal drinking age was not the clubs' first priority. Still, making them off-limits was the answer to nothing.

Susan thought of herself as an alert and concerned parent, but she tried not to be an overprotective one. She had confidence in her daughter: Lara had always had a level head and a clear sense of what was good for her and what wasn't, even as a little girl.

Fixing herself the dinner her housekeeper had left, Susan tried to run over the plans she and Annette had been working on all afternoon and evening, but she'd had enough of Consolidated Health Products and Shelby Portman. Instead, she found herself thinking about the grand jury. She wondered how much of what Mrs Liu had told her was already known to the prosecutor. All of it, probably: he had to know how old the Engs were, had to know they were prominent in the community, as well. And if that was true, then she was back to the thought she'd had in her conversation with Mrs Liu – if the prosecutor knew those things and was presenting the indictment anyway, didn't that mean they had to be guilty, no matter their age or their community-mindedness? Assuming that Mrs Liu had it right in the first place.

Maybe that was what she should do – check for herself who the Engs really were. In fact, she probably should have done that before she put David Clark through the exercise of asking all those questions for her. He was being a good sport about it, she thought, and it hadn't been fair of her to take offense at his question about what made her care about the Engs. It was a reasonable enough question; after all, she herself had been the one to make a point of her being Chinese.

But now that she had set the process in motion, it would be more embarrassing to try to stop it than just to let it play itself out. Besides, nothing would be lost. David Clark would ask the questions, and she and the rest of the grand jurors would hear the answers. If after that she still wanted to find out more about the Engs, she could do it then.

★ ★ ★

Tuesday morning, like all her other mornings in the grand jury, Susan brought something to read during the down time between cases. This time instead of a novel it was her strategy notebook for Consolidated's estrogen system, even though she had never been much good at using short breaks constructively. Once she was focused on something, even this mostly numbing procession of prosecutors and victims and policemen, she was impatient to get on with it.

Every time the door had opened on Monday she had expected to see the tall, athletic prosecutor who had brought them the Chinatown case. Every time, she had been disappointed, and by day's end she had finally resigned herself to a long wait and convinced herself that nothing that happened here – including *Chinatown* – could possibly have any real significance in her life. It was this idea that had made it seem possible to use the time here to do the work that mattered to her. That and the fact that the air conditioning was working again.

Her resolve turned out to be premature. The first assistant district attorney in the door was the Chinatown prosecutor.

'I'm Assistant District Attorney Daniel Mahoney,' he reminded them. 'I brought you the case you codenamed Chinatown. If you'd like, I can refresh your memory about it a little. Anyone?'

There were no hands.

Mahoney's witness was a tall, suntanned woman with graying hair pulled into a bun and no makeup David could see except lipstick so dark it looked black. The prosecutor introduced her as Dr Mary Coronado; his first questions were about her qualifications as a criminologist for the federal Drug Enforcement Agency. Her specialty was the structure of East Asian narcotics-smuggling organizations. At the end of the series of questions, Mahoney pronounced her an expert.

Coronado had brought in an easel and a large flip-chart – the first page was a map of South-east Asia. She used it to point out the area just north of Thailand where two warring Burmese hill tribes cultivated opium poppies under the orders and protection of large, brutal armies. One, whose main territory ran along the Thai border, was commanded by the half-Chinese son of a general in the army of the

49

Kuomintang – the Chinese Nationalists driven out of China by Mao Zedong's Communists.

The warlord had reigned in the area for a very long time, Coronado explained, protected in part by a mountainous jungle that was virtually inaccessible. There, he had built laboratories that performed the first stages in the processing of heroin, transforming the raw opium harvested from the local poppies into morphine base. The thick paste was carried out of the jungle by the warlord's heavily armed followers and increasingly it was being shipped northward through China with the cooperation, and sometimes now even the participation, of China's P.L.A. – the People's Liberation Army – the very army that had defeated the warlord's father.

In that way, she said, the morphine base made its way to laboratories in Macau and Hong Kong – and, more recently, within South China – for the final stages of refining. The end product, a type of heroin called China White, was setting new standards of purity.

In the old days, she said, injected heroin had been the drug of choice for abusers. Then cocaine had become a formidable competitor, and AIDS had made needle use too frightening for a large part of the potential market. Heroin's popularity had waned.

But China White, in its street-saleable form, was potent enough to be smoked or snorted. The fact that the user didn't have to worry about dirty needles expanded the market considerably. 'We're seeing it displacing cocaine as a recreational drug in some settings,' Coronado told them.

The ultra-pure heroin was trans-shipped from Hong Kong and Macau to New York. In New York it was sold by the unit – each unit being roughly a pound and a half – to retailers who combined it with other white powders, often a sweet-tasting relative of alcohol called mannitol, and put it out on the street to feed the growing demand for a drug that was seen as gentler and more benign than crack or cocaine. Usually, Coronado said, the retailers and their street dealers were not Chinese.

The money taken by the Chinese importers was dealt with in various ways, she told them. Sometimes the cash was simply taken out of the country intact. Mahoney led her through a description of one smuggling organization that had packed the money in gift wrap and filled suitcases with these 'presents,' to be carried as luggage by couriers on their way back to Hong Kong. The ring had been caught only when one of the organization's leaders, on his way home with a particularly rich haul of gift packages, had unthinkingly tried to carry his suitcase onto the plane rather than checking it in for storage in the cargo hold.

Most of the cash proceeds of the narcotics trade traveled out of the U.S. by wire, she said, after having been first deposited in a bank, often a Chinatown branch of a Hong Kong bank. These deposits had to be made carefully, since federal law required the reporting of cash deposits of ten thousand dollars or more. The practice had been to recruit people to make many deposits in amounts just under ten thousand dollars. These local runners, called 'smurfs' in some law-enforcement circles, would go from bank to bank, to avoid attracting too much attention. It was a process that had become more compli-cated and difficult since the passage of federal anti-smurfing laws making it a crime to engage in a pattern of behavior intended to get around the ten-thousand-dollar-reporting law.

In fact, Coronado continued, partly due to the growing difficulty of getting cash into banks and out of the country, a certain amount of drug proceeds was simply hoarded until it could be safely transferred. In some cases it was used for the purchase of negotiable securities or of diamonds or other precious stones – anything that could be trans-ported readily and easily reconverted to cash. Some was even used to make business investments in the United States, though that was also made difficult by the restrictions on transferring large amounts of cash.

'In your experience,' Mahoney asked her, 'might a narcotics-distribution organization have large amounts of cash in safe deposit boxes, or even concealed in the residence of one of its leaders?'

'Well, yes. Holding drug proceeds temporarily in safe deposit boxes is not at all uncommon. Or they'll rent an apartment specifically for the purpose of warehousing money in it. And a separate apartment to hold the drugs. Apartments like that are called stash houses, and they keep them separate so that if a stash house gets burned – revealed to the police and raided – then they only lose either the drugs or the money, not both.

'As for keeping money at home . . . that would be a matter of a given person's tolerance for risk and usually only for a short time.'

'And the amounts of money we're talking about now, amounts that you might find in a safe deposit box waiting to be moved, how much money might that be?'

'I think you'd have a large range there.'

'What about the high end?'

'A million, certainly. Perhaps more. It would depend on the organization and how much activity they'd been having. If you've brought in a lot of product in a short time and you've been having trouble moving the money for some reason, I suppose it could go to several million. That would fill several large boxes, of course, depending on the denomination of the bills.'

'And are you familiar with the various brand names heroin is sold under?'

'Yes.'

'And with the provenance – where it comes from?'

'Yes, in most cases.'

'And do you recognize this?' He showed her the Double UoGlobe label.

'Double UoGlobe? Yes, that's very familiar. It's a brand of heroin that's brought into New York.'

'And where does heroin carrying that brand come from?'

'South-east Asia, via China and Hong Kong. Basically the same route I described.'

'This heroin we've been talking about – China White, as typically found in the Double UoGlobe brand – is that commonly imported or sold in any particular size package?'

'Yes. It comes in as what we call bricks, which are actually a lot like bricks, but smaller, more the size of a paperback book. Sometimes it comes in in other forms of course. But as I said earlier, it's sold in what are called units. Each brick is typically one unit.'

'And how much heroin is in a unit?'

'Seven hundred grams, which is a bit more than a pound and a half.'

'So eight and a fraction ounces is . . .'

'A third of a unit, give or take.'

'And if this heroin is the very pure kind – ninety-six percent plus

52

pure – then, in your professional opinion, with a reasonable degree of certainty, is that the sort of heroin someone might have around for personal use?'

'In my opinion if you used heroin of that purity for personal use, you'd be dead.'

'Then how is that heroin used?'

'As I mentioned earlier, it's cut with other materials, diluted – *stepped on* is how they talk about it – so that it's safe for personal use.'

'That process results in a larger quantity of usable drug?'

'Much larger. Many times larger, depending on whether it's intended to be snorted, smoked or injected.'

'And would the value be increased?'

'Yes.'

'How much might eight ounces of heroin be worth, when it's cut to a level that's sold on the street?'

'The typical wholesale value of that much number four heroin, uncut, is between thirty-five and fifty thousand dollars. The street value would be many, many times higher. The exact amount it brought in would depend on how much they stepped on it, and how the market was when they put it out on the street.'

'You said number four heroin. Can you explain that?'

'There's a grading system. Number four is the purest form of heroin, and the kind in greatest demand.'

'And could you keep that much heroin around indefinitely?'

'Not really,' she said. 'Heroin goes bad after a while, though how long it's good depends on how it's stored.'

'Thank you. Let me see if the grand jurors have any questions.' To the grand jurors, he said, 'We've about run out of the time I reserved for this witness this morning. If you've got a lot of questions now, I can try to bring the witness back.'

Grand juror Number Thirteen, a solid-looking woman of middle age two seats down from David, raised her hand. Mahoney came over and listened to what she had to say.

'Okay,' Mahoney said so everyone could hear. 'This grand juror has asked me if we can get the witness back even if she doesn't have any questions right now but some occur to her later. The answer is yes. And, given the hour, and the fact that you're due for a break about now, I'd like to leave it at that. If you decide you want this witness back, just let the warden know and I'll arrange it.'

He excused the witness. When she was gone he said, 'Thank you for your attention once again, ladies and gentlemen. I apologize for having to present this case to you in so many pieces, but these witnesses are all busy people and I can't always get them here for you when I'd like to and when you've got time that isn't already scheduled by another prosecutor. We'll continue to refer to this case by the code name Chinatown, to help you remember it when I come back, which I hope will be later this morning.'

As the others hurried to leave for the break, David stayed in his seat. He knew Susan Linwood would have something to say to him, and he didn't see any point running from it. She was taking her time gathering up her purse and the shoulder-strap briefcase she had also brought with her, letting the others clear the room before she descended. David stood up, but he did not move toward the door, stepping aside so the other grand jurors could pass. He turned toward her when he sensed her approaching.

'Well . . .' she led off in a tense voice.

He didn't answer.

'I was thinking, if you don't want to ask those questions . . .'

'Mahoney said he'd be back.' He had expected her to be more direct – the way she said he was. But maybe that was why she found his directness worth commenting on.

'But—' Her voice was sharper, but she cut herself off before the second word.

'Look,' he said quietly. 'You said you didn't want to get people down on you because you asked those questions. Well, you know how it is when people start asking questions at one o'clock or at the break just when everybody wants to get out. There's a couple of them that do it pretty regularly: think how you feel about them. I didn't want to put myself in that place.'

After a moment, she said, 'I see what you mean. But it might have been good for them to be thinking about an old couple brutalized by the police, while they're out in the hall chatting.'

'Maybe. But this woman is a narcotics expert. I wouldn't expect her to know much about the Engs, and I didn't see asking Mahoney while she was there.' Stop justifying it, he told himself.

She pulled at the strap of her briefcase, adjusting it on her shoulder. 'I apologize. You're doing me a favor. Do it whatever way you think is best. And, really, if you don't want to . . .'

This time he didn't reassure her.

'You're probably right about not cutting into the break,' she said. 'There'll be time later.'

He watched her leave the room, headed for the phones, he supposed. He wondered fleetingly for how much of her life people had been eager to do things for her, wondered if that was what driving him, too – instead of doing this to satisfy his own curiosity and enjoy the challenge of going up against Mahoney, who seemed by far the smartest prosecutor they'd seen.

And who also, David thought suddenly, gave the impression of having a lot at stake in this case, despite his attempts to seem casual about it.

# 5

On his second visit that morning, Assistant District Attorney Mahoney brought them a skinny man in his thirties wearing a gray-green suit with an olive tie, his brown eyes magnified by thick-lensed glasses in a heavy black frame. Henry Allen was an accountant who worked for the D.A.'s office. As with Mary Coronado, Mahoney started by qualifying him as an expert.

'Do you have experience in recognizing and interpreting the records of narcotics enterprises?' Mahoney asked from his post behind David Clark.

'Yes, I do.'

'How many narcotics enterprises' records have you examined?'

'Over two hundred.'

'Have you had any special training in this field?'

'I took a special training program with the FBI.'

'Have you previously testified in court on the subject of identifying and analyzing narcotics records?'

'Yes.'

'How many times?'

'Hundreds.'

'And on those occasions have you been qualified by the various courts as an expert?'

'Yes.'

'Ladies and gentlemen,' Mahoney said. 'As your legal adviser I now charge you that Henry Allen is an expert in the records of narcotics enterprises.'

That settled, Mahoney asked the accountant to describe the various purposes narcotics records served.

Susan was intrigued to learn that narcotics dealers kept records at all. Henry Allen was not the best witness she had heard, but Mahoney's questions, as they had been from the beginning, were simple and clear.

As the questioning went on, she could see why heroin smugglers might have to keep records of their inventory and its disposition, with amounts received and sold, and coded references to customers and sources of supply. After all, it was a business, and in most cases, as Henry Allen pointed out, the people doing the wholesaling of heroin in New York had higher-ups in Hong Kong they answered to.

'You have to understand,' the accountant said in one of his less robotlike answers, 'many of these people in Hong Kong who deal in narcotics are not full-time criminals. They're businessmen. They could be selling anything. Silk, pearls, jade, any commodity at all. Heroin is more profitable right now. The fact that it's illegal is simply a problem of logistics for them. It means they can't ship their product by an ordinary freight forwarder. But they still have to keep track of what goes out and what comes in. And the same is true down the line.'

Mahoney showed him two ledger books bound in heavy green cloth, the old-fashioned kind with red-leather corners that Susan thought must have been used by every small-to-medium-size business in the days before computers became a universal business tool. The ledgers, Mahoney established, were identified by voucher numbers that connected them to the Engs's apartment.

'Have you had occasion to examine them?' he asked.

'Yes, I have.'

'And have you come to any conclusion about what kind of records they are?'

'I have.'

'And what was your conclusion?'

'I concluded that they are the records of a narcotics enterprise.'

'And can you tell the grand jury why that is?'

Like the DEA witness, Henry Allen had a flip-chart. Allen's chart featured enlarged versions of pages from the ledgers – neat columns of numbers and Chinese characters. The numbers were short, none more than three figures. There were a few sets of compound numbers: one- or two-digit numbers connected to each other by dashes.

'Can you explain this to us?' Mahoney asked him.

'I can try,' Allen said, pressing his lips together in something like a smile. 'I want to warn you first that while these *are* business records of a sort, they are different from the business records you and I are accustomed to. They are not prepared with an eye to an annual audit by independent outside accountants, and they are not prepared with an eye to satisfying the IRS.

'The notations in private ledgers like this are usually made in a kind of shorthand, just enough information for the people who keep them and for the people those people expect to show them to, which is to say their bosses. In addition, because the commodity these people are dealing in is illegal, they cannot simply write so-and-so-many grams of heroin at such-and-such a price. Add to that the fact that the language they're written in is Chinese.'

'Given all that, can you tell the grand jury something about what they say?' Mahoney prompted.

'Yes, yes, of course. I'm laying the groundwork. I think it's best to anticipate questions where I can.'

'Of course,' Mahoney said. 'And can you tell the grand jury how you deal with some of the difficulties you've just described?'

'Yes.' To the jury, he said, 'You may have been told that there are two grades of heroin commonly imported to New York by the Hong Kong organizations, number three and number four. One thing that you can see here is that there are only two different characters in this fourth column here and they repeat quite frequently.'

He flipped the chart to one that showed two Chinese characters greatly enlarged. Susan thought they looked familiar but she could not translate them.

'These two,' Allen said. 'For convenience we've called them A and B, and I've got a chart here where each A-character is replaced by A and each B-character is replaced by B.' He flipped to the next chart. 'You can see the pattern. We've made the A's in red and the B's in blue so it's clearer.'

Susan saw that there were far more A's than B's, and that they appeared in nothing she would have called a pattern, with long strings of A's and only a few B's scattered here and there.

'This corresponds with the fact that there is much more number four

58

heroin imported than number three,' Allen told them. 'Number four is higher in purity, and there's more demand for it right now. So we conclude that A stands for number four and B for number three.'

He flipped to a new chart. 'This concentrates on three specific entries. They're not quite the same as each other, as you can see. Each has an A or a B, and in addition they all have a three-digit number in the second column and another number in the fifth column, and they all start with a Chinese character.

'These entries are consistent with the following system: the Chinese characters in the first column represent a particular courier or shipment. There are twenty-two different characters altogether. The three-digit numbers are amounts of heroin. The hyphenated numbers are dates, month and day only. The numbers in column five are prices. Not the total amount, just the first two or three significant figures.'

'Can you explain that?' Mahoney asked.

'What's that?'

'Significant figures.'

'Oh. Significant figures means the first few digits in any given number. For example, 153,247. Three significant figures would be one, five, three. Two significant figures is just one, five.

'Actually, we all do this in conversation. If someone tells you they bought a car for eighteen, five, you know how much money that is. Now, what they've actually done is give you three significant figures of the amount eighteen thousand five hundred dollars. People do it all the time.'

Susan glanced at David Clark to see how he was enjoying the math. He was checking out the others, a faint smile on his face. He caught her eye and she nodded and smiled back. From what she could see a lot of the others looked confused. The accountant gave a few more examples which Susan doubted would help anyone who did not already understand.

'And were all the notations in the books the same as the ones you've described?'

'No, actually. These entries only appear in the one we call book number two. In book number one the entries are different. We're still in the early stages of analyzing those. They appear to represent payments to couriers, and other expenses. There's also a series of entries that correspond to the Chinese characters found on some of the bundles of money in the safe deposit boxes.'

This time he had blown up photographs hastily mounted on poster board to illustrate his testimony.

'The column of pictures on the left is taken from the slips of paper tucked under the rubber bands that secured the money; on the right are notations from the ledger. If you look closely, you can see that they match.' He pointed out some of the similarities. 'We found many notations earlier in the book which also correspond to these characters.'

Susan could see that the characters did match. This time she even recognized a few of the characters and so anticipated what might be coming next, though not the form in which it arrived.

Mahoney came to the front of the room. 'I'm going to interrupt this witness so you can hear someone else on the subject of these characters.'

He left the room with the witness and returned immediately with a tall, willowy Asian woman – bi-cultural, Susan thought on second look, most likely European and Chinese. Susan tried not to envy her height and her slenderness. She was wearing a linen business suit, her only jewelry a large but simple gold watch with an inch-wide band of heavy gold mesh.

Mahoney's questions qualifying her as an expert revealed that she was a curator of art and culture at the China Society and an adjunct university professor of Chinese languages. He asked her if she had seen the books that contained the characters on the poster. She had.

'Do you recognize the characters?'

'I do.'

'What do they represent?'

'These characters represent different animals which are the signs of Chinese astrology. Horse, Monkey, Sheep, Rat, and so on.'

'Were there other such characters in the books you examined?'

'Yes. And some also appeared accompanied by a second word to modify them. So, for instance, I noted a Big Monkey, and a Gray Monkey, a Brown Rat and an Old Rat.'

'How many of these astrological signs are there?'

'In Chinese astrology there are twelve, the same number as in Western astrology.'

'And what do they represent?'

60

'They represent years of the lunar calendar, in ever-repeating cycles of twelve years.'

'Did you examine the handwriting on these photographs?' Mahoney indicated the poster.

'Yes.'

'And is part of your work to analyze Chinese handwriting?'

'Not in the Western sense of handwriting analysis. But calligraphy is an art in China, and it *is* part of my work to recognize styles of calligraphy and individual calligraphers' work.'

'Did you come to any conclusion about these?'

'Yes. They're certainly in the same style – a refined, typically scholarly hand. If more than one person wrote them then at the very least they had the same kind of education in calligraphy.'

'Is it likely, in your professional opinion, to be the same person?'

'I'd say it's extremely likely.'

A couple of people had questions Mahoney did not ask. He came to the front again and said, 'I'm sure a lot of you are interested in Chinese astrology, but as a general matter the details aren't relevant here. If there are any questions about this witness's expertise or about her opinion on the evidence, I'll be happy to ask them.'

Norman Thompson wanted to know if she had looked at Henry Allen's character A and character B. Mahoney showed her the page on Allen's flip-chart as a memory refresher.

'Yes,' she said. 'I did look at those. This one labeled A is the character for *hot*, and the other one is *cold*.'

Number Fifteen, the woman across the aisle from Norman Thompson, asked if any of the Chinese characters meant 'heroin' or 'drugs.'

'None that I saw,' the witness said. 'But I didn't have the opportunity to read every word.'

There were no more questions. Mahoney thanked her and escorted her out, returning with Henry Allen.

'Have you had occasion to speak about these notations with an expert from the China Society?' Mahoney asked him.

'I have,' the police accountant replied.

'And as a result are you familiar with the meaning of some of the Chinese characters in the ledgers and on the slips of paper found with the money?'

'I am.'

'And what do you understand them to be?'

'Signs of the Chinese zodiac.'

'What significance do you attach to that?'

'It's a way you might use to designate different people. It's as if you were to keep your accounts by your debtors and creditors' astrology signs: so much money due from Mr Pisces, so much payable to Ms Capricorn. That kind of thing, except that these animals stand for years, not months.'

'And is there anything about these records that particularly supports that interpretation?'

'Yes, there is. Some of the animals are in the books in more than one form, like there's a Big Monkey, and a Gray Monkey. You'd do that if you had to distinguish among different people with the same sign. Like a first name and a last name.'

'And what significance do you attach to these names and numbers?'

'As to this particular series of entries, that they're payments made and to be made. The older entries have dates on them – days and months – and in some cases check marks. Assume each astrological animal stands for a specific person. The old entries show payments made to or received from that person. The newer entries would be payments not made yet.'

'Is there anything about the newer entries that you noticed in particular?'

'Yes. As you can see from the photographs here, characters in the ledgers match characters on the slips of paper under the rubber bands on the money. If you add up all the money whose associated slips of paper have the same character on them – all the White Rabbit money, all the Gray Monkey money – and you look on the last page of entries, you see the same number listed for that animal in the ledger. Say there's ten thousand dollars in Large Rat money. In the ledger, you see the signs for Large Rat and the number one hundred – one-zero-zero. And one-zero-zero are the first three significant figures of the number ten thousand.'

He stopped and looked around at the grand jurors, smiling encouragingly, as if to say, see, it's not so hard to understand.

'That's really the key to the whole thing,' he continued. 'That's how we unlocked the basic code of this part of the ledger. Because the numbers in the ledger match the amounts of money, and because they're keyed to each other by these zodiac characters, we can deduce that the other numbers in the ledgers must similarly match amounts of money that came in or went out in the past.'

'And taking all the entries, how much money is recorded as coming in?'

'Without breaking it down, in and out . . . based on this interpretation we see a cash flow of approximately twenty-five million dollars.'

It made Susan catch her breath. Several of the others reacted audibly as well. One person, someone in the front row toward the door, said 'Holy shit,' out loud.

'How was that spread out, in terms of time?'

'That represents what appear to be almost two hundred separate transactions over at least three years. Bearing in mind that we can't be a hundred percent sure we're reading all the entries correctly. We've only had these books a few days.'

'Is there any doubt, in your expert opinion – despite the inevitable uncertainties, and given that they were found on the same premises as a substantial quantity of number four heroin and a large amount of cash – that these books are consistent with the records of an enterprise dealing in the sale of heroin in wholesale quantities?'

'Given that they were found in close proximity to a substantial quantity of heroin and a large amount of cash, it's absolutely my expert opinion based on what I've seen that these books are the records of a heroin enterprise. I'm certainly not going to say at this point that I'm a hundred percent sure. I could be wrong.' But his tone made it clear that he did not think there was much chance of that.

Mahoney thanked him and asked for questions. There were fewer than Susan had expected. Either more people understood it all than she had thought, or they were reluctant to admit they didn't. She was surprised to see David Clark raise his hand. She wondered if he was going to ask one of her questions, though they didn't seem to fit here. Mahoney went over to listen to him.

'A grand juror would like to see your first chart, the one with a sample series of entries,' Mahoney told the witness. When the accountant had flipped the pages back, Mahoney said, 'A grand juror asks, shouldn't there be a proportional relationship between the numbers in column two and the numbers in column five, if one number is the amount bought or sold and the other is the price?'

Henry Allen was visibly startled by the question. 'You have an excellent eye, sir,' he said.

'Just yes or no, please, Mr Allen,' Mahoney told him.

'Yes, of course. The answer is yes, in a way. If I can explain . . .'

'Yes, please do.'

'First of all, just as an example, if you were selling apples at fifty cents each, and you had a price list that showed two apples, the price of those two apples would be a dollar. For four apples, you'd have two dollars and for six you would expect to see three dollars.

'I believe I'm being asked why this ledger doesn't seem to work that way. If you look at the quantities and the prices, there is no exact dollar amount per gram that fits all the entries. Is that in fact what I'm being asked?'

Mahoney turned to David Clark, who nodded. 'Yes,' Mahoney said. 'That's the question.'

'There are several reasons. These prices are not fixed. Some days your apples are fifty cents, sometimes they're seventy-five. Different customers get different prices. The same customer might get a different price on different deals, based on the quantity or the quality of the product. Or the phases of the moon, for all I know. And in this case it also seems possible that some of these quantities may be in ounces rather than grams, which is unusual but not unheard of. I expect to be studying these books for many weeks to gain a better understanding of how they work. But that does not for a minute change my opinion that they are heroin records.'

Mahoney had dismissed the witness and moved to the front of the room to thank the grand jurors when David Clark again raised his hand. Susan saw it but Mahoney didn't seem to.

'Mr Mahoney?' the backpacker said.

'I see we have a question.' Mahoney headed over to listen to him but Clark began to talk immediately.

'I was wondering how old Mr and Mrs Eng are.' The comment was loud enough for everyone to hear. 'Can you tell us?'

'Mr Grand Juror!' Mahoney's angry reaction didn't quite drown out the question. 'The rule here is you ask me your question in private, and if it's a proper question I'll ask it out loud and answer it for you.'

'I don't see why. There's no witness here.'

'Because that's how we do it.'

'You let us ask questions out loud before, when there was no witness in the room.'

'When did I do that?' Mahoney seemed genuinely puzzled.

'When you were giving us the definitions of the different crimes. You said it would go more quickly if everyone could hear the questions so you didn't have to repeat them all yourself. I assumed this would be the same. I mean, I can see why you wouldn't want a witness to hear a question that wasn't proper, but there's no witness now.'

'I don't want *anyone* to hear a question that's not proper. Not the witnesses and not your fellow grand jurors. I believe the judge told you about that when he empaneled you.'

'But if you tell us it's not proper we'll understand that. And in the process maybe we'll all learn more about what's proper or not—'

Susan couldn't believe the man was going on like this. What was the point in antagonizing Mahoney – and the rest of the grand jurors, too?

'—and, if we do, that ought to make life easier for everybody. Don't you think?'

'It might, or it might not.' Mahoney paused a moment, and smiled. 'Unfortunately, making things easy isn't necessarily what the rules are about.' Mahoney's smile included them all: this was a joke they could share.

'The way I remember it,' David Clark kept on, 'the judge said asking questions in private was the practice in New York County. I remember he used that word. The *practice*, he said, not the *law*. And in this county. That must mean they do it differently in other counties. So it can't be all that cut and dried.'

Norman Thompson jumped in. 'I think the man's got a point. Maybe we ought to go and talk to the judge. Isn't that what he said – if there's a disagreement like this we should take it to him?'

Mahoney was shaking his head, still smiling. 'There's no need for that. I think, if you're all that interested in learning about the law, we can stretch the rules – the *practice* – enough to discuss the legal questions out loud when there's no witness in the room, as long as we do it in an orderly way, raising our hands and so on, not just shouting out.

'As for this specific question from grand juror Number Eleven, I'm happy to have you get that information, but asking the question now brings us up against some rules we *can't* stretch – the rules of evidence, which are the *law*, not just the practice. The most basic rule of what I do here is that I'm your legal adviser and I'm also an advocate for the People of the State of New York. In either role I'm prohibited from testifying about facts in any way. The only questions I can answer myself are legal questions – I answer them in my role as your legal adviser. Questions of evidence – and any factual question is automatically a question of evidence – have to be answered by a sworn witness.'

He looked around at them as if to be sure they understood. Before anyone could raise a hand or shout an objection, he went on. 'For this particular question, I can call Detective Pullone back in here to answer it for you, and I will. But before I do that, I do think I should tell you that, strictly speaking, the answer to that question is irrelevant. It has nothing to do with what you're here for.' He held up a hand, palm out. 'It's okay. I said I'd get him in here to answer it, and I will.'

He smiled at all of them. Everyone seemed content.

'Good. I want to thank all of you again for your attention today. And before I go I just want to remind you that we're all here for the same purpose, to see whether or not there's reasonable cause to believe these people may have committed a crime, and if so to give them their day in court.'

Mahoney left the grand jury room feeling sandbagged. Joe Estrada had warned him this grand jury was unpredictable. But he'd said nothing about obstreperous, except for some choice words about grand juror Number Sixteen that had certainly not been misplaced. Not a thing about Number Eleven.

Estrada pleaded not guilty. 'I'd have told you about him if I'd noticed anything.'

Mahoney dropped himself onto Estrada's worn vinyl couch next to an unsteady stack of transcripts. 'Mostly, I have sympathy for these people,' Mahoney said. 'I think they're doing a good thing coming in every morning for a month, sitting there and sweating when the a/c quits, doing their duty. But I'm looking at this Number Eleven, pushing me to let them ask questions out loud, and I'm thinking, *you son of a bitch, this is a game to you.* When it's over you go home to your wife and your job and it's like it never happened. I've got bad guys to indict and a career to worry about, and you're giving me grief just to feel like you're doing something.' He shook his head. 'I figured I could make him look like a jerk, at least enough to keep the rest of them from making him a role model, but I could've come off looking like a bully, and I need these people on my side. And all the while I was debating that with myself I knew Number Sixteen was sitting there just looking for a way to make my life even more miserable. So I played Mr Reasonable, or that's what I was trying to do.' Mahoney made a face. 'Sometimes I think I was better off in Appeals.'

The Appeals Bureau had been a terrific challenge, researching the law and drafting briefs to keep the appellate judges from overturning convictions. After five years of writing persuasive analytic prose that too often failed to convince a Court of Appeals seemingly immune to argument from the prosecution side, Mahoney had begun to get discouraged. Besides, he was missing out on the real fun of being a prosecutor – developing a case and putting it in front of a jury, going head to head against a defense lawyer. Or so he had thought when he had requested his transfer.

'You did the right thing transferring,' Estrada reassured him. 'You just have to get to the place where the aggravation is a stimulant.'

'Yeah, well, maybe . . . only right now the thing is, Meiling and Martin Eng are pushing eighty.'

'No kidding.'

'Not that it doesn't happen, mind you. I asked around, heard some stories. This one old couple – Old Uncle and Old Aunt were the only names anybody had for them – the way the story goes they didn't have the energy to do much more than sit in their rocking chairs, from which cozy situation they did a twenty-unit deal. People are amazing. But it's still the kind of thing that makes you wonder, when your perps turn out to be a couple of octogenarians, damn near. And I can't go telling my grand jury about Old Uncle and Old Aunt to make them feel better.'

'I guess not.'

'And the more I think about it, the less I think it's going to be fun having Mick Pullone back in there so they can ask him whatever comes into their heads.'

'I can't say you're wrong about that. I thought Rachel Meisel did a good job presenting that bail jumping case, and they voted no true bill anyway.'

'The funny thing is, they didn't seem like such a bad bunch at first, not until one guy started shouting questions and the other one jumped on me with both feet. *Let's go talk to the judge.* Thank you very much, sir. I mean, not that it's a big deal, going to the judge, but who wants to get them in the habit of doing it for every little thing?'

'Well,' Estrada said, 'as my father used to tell me every chance he got, adversity is a great teacher. Actually he said something more like getting your chops busted, but you get the idea.'

'You know . . . it's funny,' Mahoney said, 'my coming to you for advice like this. I kinda liked it better the other way, you coming to me.'

The two prosecutors had been friends since they started out together at the D.A.'s office just out of law school. When Mahoney was assigned to the Appeals Bureau he had become Estrada's main source of advice on legal questions and his sounding board for matters of strategy and – eventually – questions of life, too.

Now, though, for all his years at the office Mahoney was a relative neophyte in the courtroom world where Estrada had become an expert, and the tables were turned.

'Seems to me I'm still in your office on a regular basis,' Estrada said.

'Not so often, now that you're a deputy Bureau chief and all.'

'Hey, I got a promotion, I didn't get any smarter. The problem is, you were a whole floor and a couple of corridors closer when you were in Appeals.'

'Closer to you and farther from Kevin Horgan,' Mahoney noted sourly. Horgan was his new boss, head of the reconstituted Organized Crime Narcotics Unit, and they hadn't yet made it through their period of adjustment.

'Catch some lunch?' Mahoney suggested. 'I just realized I'm starving.'

They walked east, between the Chinatown park where the D.A.'s office played its softball games and the towering new federal court building, heading for a hamburger joint that was a law-enforcement hangout.

Mahoney said, 'I took a quick look at my transcript to see what Pullone said when he was in there, and, don't you know, he claimed these nice elderly defendants gave him a hard time. I wish I'd caught him the first time I heard it. I mean, not only are these folks in their late seventies, they're about the size of munchkins. The missus isn't even five feet tall, and the mister isn't that much bigger.'

'That doesn't mean they didn't resist.'

'I don't know. What I do know is I could have been a whole lot more careful. Horgan throws this file at me and goes, "The 180.80 clock is running. Get me an indictment yesterday." And I'm thinking, thanks a lot. My first case since I left Appeals and you give me one I have to indict in six days or the perps are out on the street.

'So I look over the file and I put together this dog-and-pony show, based on next to nothing. And then my good friend Joe Estrada comes along and tells me my grand jury just no-true-billed a blatant, habitual bail jumper, so I beef up the whole show – more witnesses, more visual aids, as close to the whole nine yards as I can manage within the six days that section 180.80 so graciously allows us. I did everything but take a good look at exactly what kind of perps I had.'

'Don't beat yourself up about that,' Estrada said. 'People arrested on a warrant in their own home, major amounts of drugs and money right there . . . you don't need a lot more than that. Though I have to admit I don't see why Horgan and Pullone didn't give you more to work with. You'd think they'd have the case all wrapped up by the time they made the arrest.'

'It's one of these fire drill things. Pullone's informant came in and said he knew about some people who moved money for drug deals and right that minute they had a houseful but they were moving it real soon, so Pullone had to hit them right away. That means no time to develop the case in advance, find out who they're connected to on the

69

heroin end of it, nail them laundering money, none of that.'

'And Horgan went for it?'

'Whipped up some warrants and sent Pullone in there the next day.'

'Not everybody would have, naked like that.'

'Well, you know Kevin.'

'Not really. Just that he's a hard charger.'

'That's for sure. Word is he got to put together this little unit of ours because somebody figured he was the guy to keep the cash register ringing. And so far he's done a damn good job of it, as he's only too happy to tell anyone who'll listen. So he jumped right on this one, looking for a quick indictment on whatever evidence they pulled out when they hit the place. And dumped it on my desk to run through the grand jury. Give the new boy some experience.'

'That's kind of him.'

'Oh, he's real considerate that way. Meantime I've got to get them indicted by tomorrow or else section 180.80 of the criminal procedure law says *get out of jail free*. And the minute that happens the perps can start asking for their money back, and you know how happy Horgan'll be about that.'

The restaurant was packed, but Estrada spotted a couple of federal prosecutors paying their check and moved to grab the table.

'Your problem is you spent too long in Appeals. You got used to detailed analysis and legal precision,' Estrada said as they sat down. 'Welcome to the real world, trial Bureau-style.'

'Yeah, thanks very much.'

Estrada waved for a waiter. 'This man is starving. We'd better get him some food.'

'Not to abandon a fascinating subject,' Estrada said when they'd ordered their burgers, 'but if you happen to be interested in a Mets game tonight, Barry Weiss threw a couple of tickets my way.'

'I've got a date.'

Estrada's eyebrows went up. 'That's new.'

'Get back on the horse, isn't that what they say? I figured six months licking my wounds was long enough.'

'Anybody I know?'

'Not if I can help it.'

★　★　★

'Tell the truth, I'm kind of surprised your perps are in jail at all,' Estrada said when they were waiting for their coffee. 'Old folks like that, and we're holding all their money. What kind of flight risk is that?'

'Yeah, but these days people walk away from money all the time. *Never saw it before, officer. I don't know how it got there.* Plus, it seems these particular old folks had a pair of open airline tickets among their effects. To Hong Kong. So when you talk about flight risk, you're being literal.'

'That'd do it.'

'But I still have trouble with the fact that they're so old. I mean, Old Uncle and Old Aunt aside for a minute, how are these folks going to do in prison? Does it make sense to be slapping them with charges that carry twenty-five to life? This kind of case is the very essence of why we talk about prosecutorial discretion. This is a mandatory sentence we're talking about.'

'On the other hand, you can't just let people get away with crimes because they're golden-agers.'

'You know what gets me?' Mahoney said. 'What the hell did Pullone mean when he said they resisted? I mean, a couple of little old folks, half a dozen cops bust down their door . . .'

'And they're holding half a unit of heroin and half a million dollars, remember, which maybe they weren't so eager to walk away from as you think. Plus the keys to those deposit boxes. That could prompt even an eighty-year-old person to resist.'

'Yeah, well, maybe. Only you'll notice that whatever it was they did by way of resisting, Horgan didn't see fit to put it in the indictment.'

'You could ask him about that.'

'No.' Mahoney didn't have to think about it. 'Horgan is all about results, as far as I can tell – he's not the kind of guy you bother with details. The man I want to talk to is Detective Second Grade Michael A. Pullone. I want to pop it on him, see what he comes up with. If the bastard was padding the story . . . I mean, with all the fuss everywhere you turn about cops lying on the stand, it's the last damn thing I need.'

His friend regarded him from across the table. 'Look, you want advice, here's advice. You said yourself, this is your first real case since you decided you preferred the muck and mire of the courtroom

71

to being the golden boy of the Appeals Bureau. People are watching, and not just Kevin Horgan.'

'Don't remind me,' Mahoney said.

'You've got a solid million and a half in forfeitures riding on this case, you don't want to get carried away imagining things. They found the drugs and money. Even if Pullone pushed a lot harder than he had to, even if he took some old man's pure fright and blew it up into resisting arrest to impress the grand jury – the fact is, these people did have all that money, and they did have all that heroin.'

# 6

When A.D.A. Mahoney came into the grand jury room on Wednesday morning he again reintroduced himself and reminded them that his case was the one codenamed Chinatown.

'Last time I was here there was some question about the defendants in this case. As I promised, I've brought Detective Pullone back so you can ask your questions.'

He went to the door and brought the detective in, then reminded him that he was still under oath.

'Detective Pullone, I'd like to direct your attention to the events you described to us in your earlier testimony.'

'Okay,' Pullone said.

'Did you participate in the arrest of Martin and Meiling Eng?'

'I did.'

'And at that time or thereafter did you have occasion to take their pedigree information?'

'Yes, I did.'

'Did you ask their dates of birth?'

'I did.'

'And what did they tell you?'

'Can I refresh my memory from my notes?'

'Please do.'

Pullone took the notebook from his jacket pocket and leafed through it. To David the whole thing looked rehearsed.

'Okay,' Pullone said. 'Martin Eng, born March 31, 1917. Meiling Eng, born February 22, 1919.'

'Thank you, detective. I think that's all.' Mahoney stepped down to the front of the room where the jurors could see him. 'I hope that answers your questions.'

David raised his hand. Mahoney walked over and stood between David and the door. 'Yes?'

David turned to face him, away from the rest of the grand jurors. 'How tall are they?'

'I beg your pardon?' Mahoney himself towered imposingly.

'Mr and Mrs Eng – how tall?'

The prosecutor looked unhappy. 'I want to be sure you understand that I'm trying to be cooperative here, but I also don't want to encourage you to ask the kinds of questions no other prosecutor is going to have patience for. Height and age are simply irrelevant. They're not an element of the crimes you're considering.'

'Didn't the detective say they resisted arrest? I'd think they're relevant to that.'

Mahoney took a breath. 'I can't comment on what he said or didn't say, but even if he did say that, the question still is – is there a resisting-arrest count in the indictment? And there isn't.'

'Can we find out if he said it?' David wasn't going to let it go that easily.

'We can check the transcript, but I'd rather not waste a lot of everybody's time on this. Let me try to clear it up for you right now.'

He turned to the witness. 'Detective, returning again to the events surrounding the apprehension and arrest of Martin Eng, can you describe those events for the grand jury?'

Pullone leaned forward in his chair, his elbows on the long table. He spoke slowly, pausing between sentences as if feeling his way. 'We announced ourselves. When we were not admitted, we broke the door down. Inside the apartment, I found Martin Eng in the hallway outside his bedroom. He was fleeing in what I assumed to be the direction of a rear exit. I identified myself and ordered him to halt.'

'Did he stop?' Mahoney asked, back at his usual post behind David.

'No.'

'What did you do then?'

'I pursued him.'

'Did you catch up to him?'

'Yes.'

'When you caught up to him, then what?'

'I sort of had him cornered and he didn't seem to have a weapon, so I reached out to handcuff him. He ducked and I tried to grab him. He wasn't much of a runner, but he sure was some kind of slippery. I never actually touched him.'

'What did he do then?'

'He continued his attempt to flee.'

'And you?'

'I pursued him again and this time I succeeded in apprehending him.'

'How did you do that?'

'I sort of tackled him.'

'And what did he do?'

'He tried to squirm away.'

'Was he successful?'

'No, I handcuffed him.'

'Did any of the other law-enforcement personnel who were present witness any of this?'

'Not that I know of.'

'Did he use any force against you when you attempted to arrest him?'

'That first time it looked like he was doing some kind of Chinese martial arts thing.'

'If in your earlier testimony you characterized his behavior as resisting you, would you have been referring to the incident as you just described it?'

'Yes.' Nodding, as if now he saw the point of Mahoney's questions.

'But he's not charged with resisting arrest.'

'Yeah, well, I didn't make a big deal about it in my report. He wasn't trying to hurt me, that I could see, just trying to get away. And he's a little guy – they're both kind of small. I didn't think it made a lot of sense charging him with resisting.'

'How tall are they, do you know that?'

'I'd say, from observation, he's around five three, five four and she's maybe five feet.'

'Thank you.' And, to the grand jurors: 'Any other questions?'

David gave the others time, but no one else raised a hand so he did.

Mahoney leaned over the rail behind him.

'Okay,' the prosecutor said quietly. 'What can I do for you this time?'

'I want to know why they went there in the first place,' David told him. 'You don't just get a bunch of cops together and break a door down unless you're fairly sure what you're going to find. So, how did they know to go there?'

'Well, I can understand that you're curious about that, but as the grand jury's legal adviser I have to tell you that this isn't the right forum for that question. Search and seizure issues are for the *judge* to decide, not for the grand jury.'

'I'm not saying there's anything wrong with it.' David was trying to keep his voice level and reasonable despite a frustrating sense he was letting this slip away from him. 'I'm saying I want to know, to put it all in perspective. I think it's something we'd all like to know.'

'That may be. But I'm afraid you're not here to satisfy your curiosity, and I really do have to draw the line somewhere. All you need to know in order to do your duty is whether there's reason to believe a crime was committed and, if so, whether there's reasonable cause to think the defendants are the people who committed it. How the crime was discovered in the first place just simply doesn't matter.' Mahoney gave it a moment, then asked, 'Do you have anything else?'

David thought about Susan Linwood's idea that somebody might have planted the drugs, but he saw that pursuing it was worse than pointless. How was he going to phrase a question the detective could answer? *Did you plant the heroin yourself?* was not likely to do the job. 'Can you ask him how he knew to look for heroin?'

'No, I can't – same kind of question. Anything else?'

'No,' David said. 'I guess that's it.' Even as he said it he felt cheated. No matter that the questions had been Susan Linwood's to begin with, he still wanted the answers. And the one answer he had gotten – an explanation of Pullone's earlier testimony that the Engs had resisted arrest – was a long way from satisfactory. If David stretched, he could just barely accept the detective's story, though it was hard to believe that a man less than five feet four, almost eighty years old, would have been able to squirm very much after being tackled by a detective the size of Pullone.

76

And then something else occurred to him, a question that seemed important to ask. 'Mr Mahoney,' he said quickly, 'do these people have any kind of legal way they could have gotten the money?'

This time Mahoney asked the question for him.

'Detective, a grand juror wants to know if you found any evidence of what their regular legal sources of income might be?'

Pullone said, 'There was nothing we found of that kind, that I recall, except some record slips from Social Security payments and a few check stubs.'

'What was the amount of the Social Security payments?'

Pullone checked his notebook. 'Nine hundred eighty-four dollars and sixty-nine cents for Martin Eng. Four hundred ninety-two dollars and thirty-four cents for Meiling C. Eng.'

'Anything else?'

'There were a few check stubs from –' he consulted his notebook again – 'the Pearl River Garment Company. Total amount, three thousand two hundred dollars.'

'Did you have occasion to make any inquiry of the Pearl River Garment Company?'

'Yes, I did.'

'Did you learn anything with respect to Martin Eng?'

'Yes, I learned that he's carried on their books for an annual fee of five thousand dollars.'

'Did you learn his title?'

'Yes, he's a director of the company.'

'In your search of the apartment, did you find anything else that indicated income to Martin or Meiling Eng?'

'Yes. There were also some check stubs in the name of Martin Eng from the Guangdong Three Districts Community Association.'

'How much were they?'

'One hundred dollars.'

'And did you note the dates?'

'Yes.'

'And did you notice anything in particular about them?'

'Yes, they were each dated the first of the month.'

'Did you have occasion to inquire further into that organization?'

'Yes.'

77

'And what sort of organization is it?'

'It's what they call a benevolent association.'

'And does Martin Eng hold any position there, based on the records you examined?'

'He's the president.'

'Are there other benevolent associations in Chinatown?' Mahoney asked.

'Yes.'

'Are they known by any other name, as a general matter?'

'People call them tongs.'

*'Tongs?'* Mahoney made the word carry a heavy weight of implication.

'That's right.'

'Thank you.'

Grand juror Number One had a question. While Mahoney discussed it with him, Susan's eyes were on David Clark, in the seat behind Number One. All she could think was, *Why didn't he ask about the heroin?* Instead, he'd asked a question about their jobs that had let Mahoney plant the idea that they might be some kind of gangsters. And if she could have that thought, her fellow grand jurors were sure to, at least the ones who'd heard of tong wars, or of the modern connection between some of the tongs and violent youth gangs.

When she saw that Mahoney wasn't going to ask Number One's question, Susan raised her hand, not caring any more what the others might think. She didn't want to let her other questions go unasked.

Mahoney came around behind her and leaned over the wooden rail. 'What can I do for you?'

She twisted around in her seat so she could see him. 'How do we know the heroin was theirs?'

'I'm sorry? I don't understand.'

'How do we know somebody else didn't leave it there? Just because the police found it there . . .'

Mahoney smiled. 'A good question, but it's not the kind of question I can ask. For any witness I can basically ask what they experienced and what they know of their own knowledge. As for what conclusions you draw from the evidence, that's up to you and your fellow grand

78

jurors. If you want to know something about the detective's investigation, I'll be happy to ask him about it for you.' He gave her time to respond, then started to move away.

'Wait,' she blurted out. 'What about fingerprints? Weren't there fingerprints on the package? Surely you can ask that.'

He looked at her for a moment, then nodded. 'Yes, I can ask that. Detective, a grand juror would like to know if you submitted the package of white powder for forensic analysis.'

He did not answer at once. 'Can I refresh my memory?'

'Go right ahead.'

Again, he flipped through the pages of his notebook. 'I did.'

'And did you receive a report?'

'Yes, I did.'

'What did it indicate, as to fingerprints?'

Pullone consulted his notebook. 'They found no usable fingerprints.'

'Is a failure to find usable fingerprints unusual in a case like this?'

'I wouldn't say unusual, no.'

'Detective, earlier you told us your rank.'

'Yes, I'm a detective, second grade.'

'Second grade. Can you tell the grand jury what that signifies?'

'It's more or less an indication of proficiency.'

'It's not an administrative rank, like sergeant or lieutenant?'

'No, it's if you're good at the job.'

'A step up from detective?'

'Yes.'

'And have you done any other investigations of narcotics distributors?'

'Yes, many.'

'In your experience in those cases, is a lot of emphasis put on fingerprints?'

'It's not the first thing we do. Not like a murder case, where identifying the perpetrator is a major issue, and connecting him with the murder scene or the murder weapon, so as soon as you get to the scene you're taking fingerprints off everything. This kind of case isn't like that.'

'Thank you. Does anyone else have a question for Detective Pullone?'

No one did.

Mahoney had one more witness, a bank officer who brought records showing that several times in the past two years Meiling Eng had visited a safe deposit box rented jointly in her name and her husband's.

When the bank officer was done testifying, Mahoney showed him out, then went to the front of the room.

'You've seen and heard all the evidence I have for you, ladies and gentlemen. Now I'm going to read you the law again, as I promised you I would. I know it's fairly complicated and it's been a while since I talked to you about it, so you should feel free to ask about anything I don't make clear to you.'

Susan's heart was still pounding from her unplanned outburst of questions. She did her best to listen.

By the time Mahoney was done reading them the law on first-degree heroin possession and second-degree conspiracy to engage in the criminal sale of a controlled substance, Susan was calmer, but she was still unsettled. As she watched Mahoney walk out and close the door behind him, she had the feeling that she had left something important undone.

The fact that there were no fingerprints to tie the heroin to Martin and Meiling Eng continued to bother her, despite the detective's attempt to minimize their importance. But it was more than that. She was vaguely aware of the grand jury's secretary reading them the counts they were to vote on, then the scrape of a desk chair behind her and to her left as the foreman stood to call for discussion or a vote.

'Mr Foreman!' It was David Clark's voice. Susan was surprised to see him standing up by his seat.

'Can I say something?'

'All right.' The foreman was being his usual accommodating self. 'Whatever you want.'

'There's something about this that really bothers me. Before we have our discussion, I think we need to get one of the witnesses back.'

'What for?' Number Four interjected, predictably.

'If you'll just give me a minute, I'll try to explain. I only thought of this when Mr Mahoney was reading us the law. I work in a technical field, with computers. My name is David, by the way, just so you don't have to think of me as Number Eleven. What I want to talk about is those records they showed us, the ledger books that are supposed to be records of heroin transactions. One of the things I do, working with computers, is think about ways to make one thing stand for another. And I also have to deal with numbers a lot. And what I can tell you, and I'll be glad to explain this, is that nothing that accountant told us about those ledgers makes much sense.'

There was a chorus of disparaging noises, and from Number Four an annoyed 'give us a break.'

*Slow down*, David told himself: Take your foot out of your mouth and start again.

'No, wait,' he said. 'What I mean is that what he told us is only one possibility. There might be hundreds of equally sensible explanations. For one thing, take what he said about significant figures. That was very misleading. You remember he gave us the example of eighteen, five, and how if a car cost eighteen, five you'd know it was eighteen thousand five hundred. But that's only true if you're talking about cars or boats or something like that. If you're talking about the population of a state, it's millions of people. And when you talk about a number that begins one-eight-five, calling it *eighteen, five* is misleading to begin with. One eighty-five makes as much sense, and just one-eight-five is really more accurate. In money that could be anything from a dollar and eighty-five cents to a big piece of the national debt, in billions of dollars, or trillions. The point is, you need outside evidence to tell you what the quantities might really be.'

'What about the heroin?' protested Number Seven, a dark-skinned woman in her thirties with her long hair in hundreds of perfect, tiny braids. 'I'd say that's outside evidence.'

'All we're supposed to do here is see if there's evidence that matches all the different parts of the crime,' said Number Five, a striking woman with dark brown eyes and a light coffee complexion who dressed with a stylishness that had made David wonder if she was in the fashion business. 'I don't remember what that's called.'

'Elements. The elements of the crime,' Number Four supplied.

'Right, thank you,' Number Five said. 'All we need are the elements of the crime, and this crime is possession of heroin. You can't argue about that. It was right there.'

81

'But there's conspiring to sell heroin to think about, too,' David said. 'All those conditions he just read us, about intent, and the necessity for an overt act, all of that. And Mr Mahoney thought it was important enough in order to make his case to show us those ledgers and explain what was in them, so he must think it's important evidence.'

'Okay, so what's wrong with it?' Number Seven was still making life difficult for him. 'I didn't understand it all, but he's an accountant and it sounded like he knew what he was saying.'

A fragile-looking white-haired man at the end of the first row – grand juror Number Ten – stood up and turned to face the others. 'Excuse me,' he said tentatively, 'I'm an accountant, too. A retired accountant, I should say. Retired, like our foreman.' His voice was thin and unsteady, the words spoken with slow precision. 'One thing you learn in my business is that there are a lot of ways to put down the same information. Any set of numbers can mean many different things. I think you should listen to this young man.'

'Thank you,' David said. 'I appreciate that. It's not just the numbers. I work with codes, as I was telling you. Ways to make one thing stand for another. I don't see how he knows that what's in those books isn't a laundry list, or the receipts from a restaurant. I mean . . . two Chinese characters that he called A and B – isn't that what he said? Okay, but if I remember it right from when I was a kid, if you wanted a combination plate in a Chinese restaurant that's how you ordered it – one from column A and two from column B.'

The scattered laughter that greeted the clumsy joke made Susan's face burn. Could they really think that was funny – that Chinese characters were most likely to be a laundry list or a menu? Only a few of the others glanced over at her or Mrs Liu as if they realized there was something offensive about it.

'The point I'm making,' David Clark was going on, 'is that those two Chinese characters he showed us could represent anything, not just two types of heroin. And the characters on the money could mean anything, too. Rats and Monkeys could just as easily stand for business accounts or for the year the money came in – he said the animals stood for years, and so did the curator from the China Society.

'The truth is, we don't know anything about what these people might have been keeping records of. Even if he's right to say that some of the numbers in the ledgers are dates, we don't know what years are involved. The woman from the China Society said the zodiac is a twelve-year cycle. These are old people. Those are old-fashioned ledgers. How do we even know that the ledgers are from any time in the last twelve years, or twenty-four—'

'What's it to you?' shouted the heavyset, ebony-skinned woman in seat Number Eighteen, next to Susan, dressed, as always, in a bus driver's uniform. 'Like we said that other time, with that bail jumper's girlfriend, nobody is going to vote any different.'

'It's good you brought that up,' David Clark said. 'If you remember what happened then, there were three people who said they might change their minds, and the vote on the indictment was ten to thirteen. So depending on what those three people decided, we could have had an indictment instead of no true bill. And the truth is, you can't really know if you'd change your mind until you hear what the person has to say.'

'Well, why didn't you think of all this when the guy was still in here?'

'I did think of it. I just didn't realize how important it was.'

Number Thirteen rose to say, 'Mr Mahoney distinctly told us we could have someone back if we thought of a question later. I asked him that, and that's what he told us.'

'This is dumb,' said Number Four. 'I said it before, I'll say it again, they don't go to this kind of trouble if the people aren't guilty.'

'Don't be so sure,' boomed grand juror Number Nine. He was brawny and red-faced, with red hair streaked with gray that Susan thought had to be premature: she doubted he was as old as forty. 'They get indictments on innocent people often enough. Think about it. Innocent people get convicted at trial, too. Tell me you never heard about that. Prosecutors like to convict people.'

'Good thing, too,' Number Four countered. 'Get the bastards off the street.'

'Maybe so, if you're not the bastard. If everybody they brought to a grand jury was guilty, or even if they all looked guilty enough to go to trial, then tell me what point there is in having a grand jury. That's what we're here for, to make sure they don't slip one by. What harm is there in making them work a mite harder to convince us?'

This was greeted by a moment's silence. Susan wanted to say something to support it but after her earlier outburst, about the fingerprints, she was more afraid than ever that anything she said would be seen as special pleading.

Grand juror Number One spoke up before Susan could make up her mind. He was the only one who wore a business shirt and a tie to the grand jury despite the summer heat.

'I sell cars,' he said. 'I looked at what that accountant showed us, and I suppose I've got to admit this fellow behind me is right as far as it goes. You can't tell for sure just looking at those charts what it all means. The witness himself said there might be other ways to look at it.

'But there's something else, too, and that's that certain kinds of businesses generate certain kinds of numbers. Where I work, we've got prices in a certain range, we've got model numbers that look a certain way, optional-equipment numbers that look a little different. Even the guys on the floor have code numbers – like who made the sale. Point is, a model number is a model number, not a salesman's ID. And you can tell by looking at it.'

'Maybe so,' David Clark said. 'But even then it could be a model number for a car or an air conditioner or a vacuum cleaner. How would you know which it was? Isn't that right, Number Ten?'

The white-haired accountant stood up again, slowly. 'Yes, it is. Exactly.'

'I tell you how I'd know,' said the auto salesman in seat Number One. 'If I found the damn ledger in a warehouse full of vacuum cleaners, I'd figure it wasn't for air conditioners.'

That brought a laugh. They're just having fun now, Susan thought. This isn't *about* anything anymore, it's just a bull session. Even David Clark seemed more interested in the challenge of debating than in learning about the Engs. She wondered why he had started this at all.

'All right,' he said, 'but this wasn't exactly a warehouse. Granted, the way the woman from the DEA described it, eight ounces adds up to a lot of heroin at the end of the day—'

'It's plenty,' said the car salesman bleakly. 'Believe me.'

'But not for a *warehouse*. All this activity in the ledgers, so they say, and just this one package and no other evidence of buying and selling.'

'Who says there's no other evidence?' demanded the burly man in seat Three, his words colored by a barely noticeable accent – Spanish, Susan thought.

'Don't you think if there was anything else, they would have let us know about it?'

'Maybe not,' Number Three said, but Susan didn't think he sounded convinced. 'Maybe Mahoney has his reasons.'

'All I want to do is get the accountant back in here and find out what he has to say about all this.'

'It's so dumb,' said Number Four, macho man. 'So you get him in here. What's he going to tell you? He already said it's heroin. Suppose now he says sure, it could be something else. He already said that once, too, like Number One there just said. So what does that tell us? Nothing. We know that already. And suppose it *was* something else besides heroin – who's going to tell us what? Not the accountant. Not the cop. So this is dumb. Either you believe what they told us or you don't. Let's vote and get it over with.'

'There is *somebody* who could tell us,' Susan said. Everyone looked at her. 'The Engs could tell us.'

'Oh great,' said Number Four, slapping his head theatrically. 'Here we go again.'

'What about them fingerprints?' grand juror Number Two wanted to know. A young man who wore basketball sneakers and shorts that came down past his knees, he had sat in apparently uninterested silence from the first day, but he was full of energy now. 'I'm hearin' a lot about some accountant, but nobody sayin' word one about there's no fingerprints on no damn heroin.'

'He's got a point,' said Norman Thompson gravely. 'He's got a good point, and so has this lady here. If we think there's a chance those ledgers were about something besides heroin, there's nobody better to tell us what it is than those very people whose books they are. I don't think we need to see the accountant, I think we need to see the defendants.'

'This is crazy,' Number Four said. 'You think for a minute those people are going to tell the truth?'

85

'Like the man said before, we'll see, when we see them,' Thompson said. 'At least we'll hear the best story they can make up, something we can put up against what we've heard.'

'How do we do that? I don't see the District Attorney rushing to bring them in here.'

'They have to,' the alternate forewoman said. 'They have to bring in anybody we want.'

'Who says?' demanded Number Eighteen, the bus driver, next to Susan.

'I think she's right,' Thompson said.

'She *is* right,' Number Four said sourly. 'That's what the judge told us.'

'It's in the book they gave us,' the alternate forewoman said. 'Does anybody have it?'

'Ask Mr Mahoney,' suggested Number Thirteen.

'I have it,' the foreman said. 'Does anyone know where to look?'

'Let me see,' the alternate forewoman said. Susan could hear her leafing through the booklet.

'Here it is. It's section 190.50. "The grand jury may cause to be called as a witness any person believed by it to have relevant information or knowledge." Our Mr and Mrs Eng certainly qualify for that. Then it says that the grand jury "may direct the District Attorney to issue and serve a subpoena on such witness and the District Attorney must comply." There's more, but basically it says we can ask for any witness we want.'

'I want the man who looked for fingerprints,' Number Two said, precipitating a free-for-all.

'What fingerprints?'

'They said there weren't any fingerprints.'

'Said the man who tested for 'em didn't *see* none.'

'Nothing useful.'

'I don't think that's what he said.'

'He said they didn't matter in a case like this.'

'Ladies and gents, can we do one thing at a time?' the foreman implored them.

'Sorry.'

'All right. It's all right. We're just getting carried away. Is it okay

86

with everybody if we start with Mr and Mrs Eng? Do we want to ask them questions?'

'Why not?'

'It's a waste of time, that's why not,' said Number Four. 'They probably don't even speak English.' He glanced over at Susan. 'Sorry, no offense.'

'I think Number Four's right,' announced Number Three in his barely noticeable Spanish accent. 'I say no point wasting our time.'

That angered the big redhead in seat Nine. '*Wasting our time?* I suppose we'd use our time better to hear some more chain snatchings! Not to be rude, but this is the biggest case we've had, and it's the only one with real questions in it. I say make the most of it.'

'Don't we have some obligation to process as many of these cases as we can?' Number Thirteen asked.

'And who told you that, madam? Is it that they're paying us piecework, now?'

'Everybody always says the courts are too crowded and they can't move the cases fast enough.'

'And who do we help, grinding another dozen muggings through the mill?' asked the redhead. 'There are other grand juries sitting now where they can do that. The good judge charged six separate panels of us at once, if I remember it right.'

'We're supposed to be here looking for the truth,' said Number Eight, next to him. 'Like Mr Kelly here said before, we're supposed to keep the prosecutors honest. And like he said just now, this case has some real questions in it. If we don't ask them we're not doing our duty.'

'What you talking about – what questions?' boomed the bus driver. 'These folks had a houseful of heroin and a houseful of money and they ran from the police. Did some martial arts thing on them, too – you heard. There ain't no questions except why we wastin' our breath.'

'Don't you want to hear what the Engs have to say about those ledgers?' This was the grand jury's alternate forewoman again, her clear voice and sharp diction belying her frumpy appearance. 'I certainly do. I tell you what else – I'd like to hear what Mr Eng has to say about that Chinese martial arts trick, and how a man born in 1917

87

could have tried to squirm away when Detective Pullone landed on him.'

'Yeah, like he's going to tell the truth about that, too.' The burly Number Three was broadly sarcastic. 'He's going to scream police brutality, what do you bet? I been there, man, I'm in corrections. I know how it goes.'

'Maybe you're right,' the alternate forewoman conceded. 'Why not listen and see?'

'Because I don't need to sit here for a whole lot of bullshit that's just going to confuse things, that's why.'

'They did have all that heroin,' said Number Fifteen. 'Where else could it have come from, if they aren't in that business?'

'Maybe somebody else put it there,' Susan made herself say, not willing to see this chance evaporate. 'Somebody trying to frame them.'

'Where'd you get *that* from?' the bus driver challenged, in her face.

'I'm not saying that's necessarily what happened. I'm saying everybody keeps talking about that heroin as if it proved something.'

'That's because it *does*.'

'No way it does,' countered Number Two. 'Not without no fingerprints on it.'

'I don't believe this!' Number Four looked to the heavens. 'This is nuts.'

'It wouldn't hurt the rest of us to go along with this,' the grand jury's secretary said. 'If people feel so strongly about it. And it *is* our right to ask for witnesses. There must be a reason for that.'

The car salesman stood up. 'I want to say something here. My nephew died of an overdose of heroin last year. So I don't have to tell you I'm no friend of heroin dealers. I think they all ought to fry. But I want to see these people. I want to see close up what slime like that are like. I want to see them sit there and squirm. Only I have one condition. If we get one, we get both. Let's see how good they are at telling the same lie. I just hope I can keep myself from spitting in their face.'

He sat down. In the silence, David spoke up. 'He's got a good point, you know. It's worth something to get them in here even if you think they're going to lie. I mean, think about the bail jumper's girlfriend.

Aren't some of you sorry we didn't listen to her?'

'You bet we're sorry,' Number Four acknowledged. 'Okay, what the hell, let's get them in here. Like Number Nine was saying, we don't have a whole lot better to do.'

'All right,' the foreman said. 'Are we agreed then, we can vote on this? How many want to ask the prosecutor to have Mr and Mrs Eng come in as witnesses?'

Eight hands went up immediately, including Number Four's. A few at a time, eight more joined them.

'All right, we have sixteen of us want to do this and twelve's a majority so I guess we ought to let them know outside.'

'What about the fingerprints?' Number Two wanted to know.

'Sure,' Number Four said. 'Why not? We're going to be dumb, let's really be dumb. Fingerprints, too.'


'What can I do for you?' Mahoney asked when the secretary buzzed for him to come in.

'We'd like to question another witness,' the foreman said mildly.

'Oh, really? Who?'

'I'm sorry, I made a mistake.' The foreman sounded nervous, David thought. 'Actually it's two witnesses. We'd like to hear from Martin Eng and Meiling Eng.'

'Can you say that again?' Mahoney asked in a tight voice. 'I'm not sure I got it right.'

He's playing for time, David thought: we surprised him.

'Martin and Meiling Eng.' The foreman sounded more uncertain.

Mahoney took a moment. 'Well,' he said. 'I can understand that. A lot of people would like to get some answers from them, myself included. But there's a problem.' He paused for emphasis. 'As I'm sure you've been told, anyone who testifies before a grand jury in this State is, by law, given immunity from prosecution for anything he or she testifies about. That means if these people testify about where they got the money, they can't be prosecuted for anything having to do with their possession of that money. If you want them to explain how there came to be heroin in their house, then once they do that they're immune from prosecution for anything to do with the heroin. We can always prosecute them for perjury, of course, assuming we can prove they lied, but aside from that, they go free.

'That's the law, and the law is that way to make sure that grand jurors get all the information that's available. No witness can say to you – I can't answer that question because it might incriminate me. They can't, because for anything they say in here they just simply cannot be prosecuted, whether what they say is incriminating or not. It's not just the testimony itself that can't be used against them. It's anything to do with the transaction they're testifying about, if they're answering a direct question.

'Just as an example, if I ask a witness, "Mr Jones, what do you do for a living?" and he says, "I'm a hit man," then that's it for any murder Mr Jones might have committed before I asked him the question. He can't be prosecuted for any of them. Not under any circumstances. Not even if we get the evidence completely independently of anything he said. Not even if we already have the evidence and there's a policeman waiting outside the grand jury room to arrest him.

'Now, given that, I know you won't be surprised if I tell you that I don't want Martin and Meiling Eng to be immunized from prosecution. Because *these are the very people I have asked you to vote an indictment against.*' He looked around at them all to be sure they got it.

'You're correct to say that you have the right and authority to instruct me that you want to hear any particular witness. But as your legal adviser, I have the right and authority to choose who can be allowed to get this very broad immunity, and who can't.

'So you must understand that by asking to hear these witnesses, you're at the same time asking me to allow them to gain the immunity that comes from testifying, and I can't do that.'

After a long moment of silence he said, 'I'm sorry life has to be so complicated.'

David was about to say something but the big redhead in seat Nine, the one his neighbor had called Mr Kelly, beat him to it. 'It seems to me you're leaving something out. A couple of cases ago we had a defendant in here to testify. The A.D.A. that time told us defendants have the right to do that as long as they let go of the immunity.'

'That's true,' Mahoney acknowledged. 'They do have the right. But in order to exercise that right, then – as you say – they have to be willing to legally give up their immunity from prosecution. That's *not* something people are generally eager to do.'

'Okay, sure.' Kelly was not appeased. 'I remember the A.D.A. put that defendant through a whole inquisition to make sure he was willing to waive the immunity and take the consequences. But he testified anyway, and if I got it right it didn't make him immune to anything.'

'That's right. It's always possible to waive immunity.'

'How do you know these people wouldn't do it?' asked Number Fifteen, across the aisle from Norman Thompson.

'I can't know, one way or the other.'

'Are you saying you're not even going to bother to ask them?' Thompson wanted to know. 'I mean, the least you can do is tell them we want to hear their side of it.'

Mahoney nodded. 'I'm happy to do that for you. So long as you understand that I have the power to make their appearance depend on waiving immunity. I can inform their lawyer you've expressed interest. But whether they will respond, I can't tell you. The rule is that if a defendant wants to testify in the grand jury they have to let us know well before this. And they haven't.'

'No harm asking,' Kelly said.

'If that's what you all really want.' Mahoney looked around at the grand jurors to underline the skepticism in his voice. 'Why don't you talk it over? I can wait outside.'

'We already voted,' the foreman said with surprising strength. 'We voted by a large margin that we wanted to hear them.'

'Okay.' Mahoney's voice was flat. 'I'll see what I can do. Assuming they'll waive immunity, and the judge agrees to extend certain time limits.' He turned to go.

'Mr Mahoney,' the foreman said.

'Yes?'

'There's something else. We voted that we'd like to hear from the person Detective Pullone sent the package of heroin to, to look for fingerprints.'

Mahoney stared up at him. 'You're sure that's necessary?'

'We're sure.'

# 7

Mahoney made himself walk, not run, along the ninth-floor corridors to the Trial Division offices. He knocked on the blue metal partition outside Joe Estrada's office and poked his head around the doorframe. Estrada, on the phone, motioned him in and held up a finger: I'll be a minute.

It was more like five, as Estrada got deeper into what sounded like a vain attempt to get travel money for some witnesses. He was not in a good mood when he put down the phone.

'Bosses,' he said, with as much disgust as he could pack into the single word. 'You wonder what they think we're doing here.'

'Maybe I'm missing something,' Mahoney said, 'but aren't you a boss, yourself, these days?'

Estrada snatched a nerf ball from the corner of his desk and winged it at Mahoney, who got a hand up in time to bat it away.

'That feels better,' Estrada said. 'I needed to throw something at somebody.'

'An arm like that, you should consider pro ball.'

'Speaking of which, I hope you scored better last night than the Mets did.' He looked closer. 'On second thought, you don't seem like a man making a social call.'

Mahoney told him about the grand jury's request to hear from the defendants.

'No wonder you look queasy.' Estrada himself had grown the look of a man suppressing a grin. 'Show me a man can't get a grand jury to indict when he's got a pound of heroin and a million dollars cash hidden in the dresser, I'll show you a man marked for greatness.'

Mahoney was in no mood for this but he knew better than to show it.

'It wasn't all in the dresser,' he pointed out. 'There was a safe.'

'Right. Dumb of me.'

'I didn't figure this was going to make me a hero around the office,' Mahoney said more seriously. 'The question is what's the best thing I can do to minimize the damage?'

'Nothing much you *can* do except call the other side and make the offer,' Estrada told him. 'You might want to do it in person, though. It's not every day you get to see a defense lawyer fall out of his chair.'

'I was trying to convince myself it might be a plus, in a way.'

'Well, you do get this whole record of sworn grand jury testimony where you can find inconsistencies with what they say if they're dumb enough to testify at the trial, too. That's if they don't just convince the grand jury to set them free.'

'You think they'll go for it, then? Come in and testify?'

'Depends. The fact that it locks them into a story generally keeps defendants away. But that's for *volunteering* to testify. This is different.' Estrada crossed the room to collect his nerf ball. 'Who's the defense lawyer?'

'Jeffrey Rosen?'

'*Jeffrey* Rosen . . . Nope, don't know him. Milt and Louis and Ken. And Nancy, of course –' Estrada's co-counsel on the big murder trial that had earned him his promotion – 'but no Jeffrey.'

'He's an ex-legal-aid guy, mid-size firm. He does a lot of drug distributors. Mostly Asians lately.'

'Did he give grand jury notice at the arraignment?' Estrada answered his own question before Mahoney could. 'He didn't, right? He was so sure his clients were getting indicted he didn't bother to say they might want to testify. I suppose, seeing as there was that pound of heroin—'

'*Half* a pound.'

'—and that million or so in cash, he must have thought there wasn't much doubt about an indictment.'

'He wasn't the only one.'

'Now, though, you're going to call him up and tell him the grand jury wants to hear what his clients have to say. And when he picks himself up off the floor, the first thing he's going to think is – wait a

93

minute, what did I miss? Did I misunderstand this case in some important way?

'Because basically you're telling him that this grand jury that he thought was going to indict his people in a New York minute is all of a sudden clearly having trouble with this case. So he'll be thinking maybe he has a shot at beating this thing before it ever goes to trial. And with his clients probably giving him grief night and day about wanting their million-plus dollars back, he's got a major incentive to take whatever shot he can at killing this at the earliest stage possible.'

'So my next job is to work on my cross-examination,' Mahoney said glumly.

'I would. Not that I ever hope to be in that situation, myself.' Estrada bounced the nerf ball off a filing cabinet, snagged the rebound. 'The good people of this city never cease to amaze me. Just when it looks safe to think of grand juries as the dray horses of the judicial system, pulling their load with blinders firmly in place, along comes a bunch that takes the bit in its teeth.'

He looked at the clock. 'Time to grab some lunch. I've got a meeting at two-thirty about this witness-travel money and I can't face it on an empty stomach. You want anything?'

'I'd better go down to my office and call Jeffrey Rosen. I'm not sure I could eat, anyway.'

Susan endured the chain snatching and the clothing-store burglary that rounded out the morning's session. She was lightheaded with excitement at her victory in getting the Engs invited in as witnesses. Excitement and apprehension: What if they refused to come, or if they were bad witnesses? That would make things worse for them, not better. She told herself it didn't matter. All that mattered was that she had gained them a chance to speak for themselves. If they did well with it, or badly, that was their responsibility.

At the elevators, she saw David Clark talking with the white-haired accountant. Before she could decide to interrupt, Mrs Liu touched her arm, nodding and smiling. She was discreet enough to move on without doing more, but in the meantime David Clark and the accountant had squeezed into the first elevator that arrived. Susan took the next one, with most of the other grand jurors.

As planned, her daughter was waiting for her – sitting on the lone chair in the tiny entrance lobby. Dressed for summer, with her long, sun-bronzed legs very much in evidence, Lara was intently ignoring the obvious scrutiny of the cops behind the security desk. She brightened and bounded to her feet when she saw her mother across the security barrier. Susan pointed to the street and headed out to meet her.

They hugged hello and Susan asked her to wait a minute, while she spoke to someone. David Clark and the accountant were standing just off the curb by a parked car, still talking. She thanked them both for getting things rolling and supporting her idea of hearing the Engs, and they thanked her in turn, for thinking of it.

'It's definitely going to liven things up,' the accountant said. 'And – nothing against David, here, for suggesting it – anything's better than sitting through more testimony by an accountant.'

'Who was that?' Lara asked her.

'My fellow grand jurors. An accountant and, I don't know, a computer person of some sort.'

'Don't you know their names, or anything?'

'The computer person is called David.'

'The tall one?'

Susan nodded.

'Nice.'

'Really? You think so?'

'Absolutely. The beard is cool, I mean sometimes they're gross, but I like his, and you can tell he works out. I think he's hot.'

'Lara!'

She grinned. 'Oh, Mom, you're way too easy to shock.'

Susan grinned back. 'No, you're way too good at it. Anyway, I'm a married lady and he's too old for you.' Susan was no more willing than usual to let herself speculate about how sexually active her daughter might be. She took Lara's arm and hurried her along. 'Let's go, we've got a lot of shopping to do.'

Jeffrey Rosen turned out to be ruddy and balding, with an expensive three-piece suit that only partly camouflaged the cylindrical look of an athlete gone soft. It was a fate Mahoney sometimes worried about; so far, genetics and twice-weekly games of take-no-prisoners full-court basketball had kept it at bay.

'I got your message,' Rosen said on his way into Mahoney's office. 'And I was in the building anyway.'

He sat stiffly on the wooden chair opposite Mahoney's desk. 'I want to be sure I understand. You're telling me that the grand jury has specific questions for my clients.'

'I'm telling you that the grand jury has requested them as witnesses.'

'Well and good, but I don't know how eager they're going to be to endanger their interests simply to provide entertainment for some bored citizens. I need some indication of what this is about.'

'You've already heard everything I have to tell you.'

Mahoney wished he had a better sense of what was going on, himself. It was one thing to be tough with Jeff Rosen to keep him from taking undue advantage of the situation. It was another to lose this indictment because the grand jurors thought he hadn't put enough effort into getting the Engs to testify.

'What you've already told me isn't good enough,' Rosen said. 'The risks are too high.'

'I can't read this grand jury's minds, Mr Rosen, but I'm sure when you talk about risks you're also considering the risks of seeming uncooperative.' Jurors weren't supposed to hold the defendants' silence against them, but people did it all the time.

'That sounds a whole lot like a threat, Mr Mahoney.'

'It's not a threat, it's a statement of fact. This grand jury wants to see your clients, whether it's because they're bored or because they have substantive questions, I couldn't tell you. But if your clients don't come in the grand jury's going to blame somebody – and that somebody might be me, I suppose, but it might also be you, or your clients.'

The trouble was, he couldn't be sure it would go that way. Estrada had hinted at the problem: once a grand jury got a sense of its own power, there was no telling what it would do.

'All right,' Rosen said. 'They might come in ... *might*, mind you ... on the condition that when they come in they can make a statement and then answer questions from the grand jury, and that's all.'

'If they come in, they waive immunity and they answer questions like any other witnesses. This isn't *Let's Make A Deal*.'

'At the very least, in my experience, when a defendant comes in to talk to the grand jury, he gets to make a statement.'

Mahoney let it go by: a statement gave him no trouble. It was another chance for them to hang themselves.

Rosen took the inch and tried for a mile. 'The only way I can think of to sell this is if you'll limit your questioning to the territory my clients cover in their statement.' He hurried on to keep Mahoney from interrupting. 'I understand you don't want them selling your grand jury a bill of goods, but what I'm suggesting ought to prevent that. The problem for me comes if they have to worry about your getting into all kinds of areas that go beyond what they've said. At least we ought to exclude that.'

'Maybe I should remind you,' Mahoney said in a tone of weary patience, 'that when your clients testify they'll have to swear under oath that they've been given no promises as incentive to waiving immunity.'

He turned a page on his desk diary as if he didn't already know what was there. 'We have a calendar date on this case tomorrow morning. I expect we'll be telling the judge you're waiving the 180.80 time limit pending your clients' decision, and pending their testifying, if that's what they want to do. Meanwhile I'll try and block out some grand jury time for them, just in case.'

Rosen took a breath as if to protest, then seemed to think better of it. 'I can't make a commitment on the time limit. I know that the Engs are desperate to get out of jail, so I don't think they'll be eager to give up a provision of the law that would spring them tomorrow. But frankly, I'm just staging a holding action here. The Engs are in the process of retaining new counsel. I haven't been told who, yet, but whoever it is should be in place by court tomorrow. So you'll hear that decision from him. Or her.'

Susan and Lara spent the afternoon buying clothes for Lara's college wardrobe and barely got through half their list. Back home they had to turn sideways to get the shopping bags through the door.

'We'll deal with these later,' Susan said and sank onto the living-room couch, her feet – happily liberated from shoes – up on the coffee table.

When she was ready to stand again, she went into the kitchen for a glass of cold water.

Lara came to join her at the refrigerator, pulled the door open. 'What's for dinner?'

As she often found herself doing these days, Susan marveled at her daughter. Tall and lithe and quick-minded, with inexhaustible energy and an equally inexhaustible appetite. And beautiful – Susan sometimes forgot *how* beautiful. Lara's brother, Charles, wore his mixed heritage less handsomely. He was angular and pasty, with big teeth and weak eyes. Heredity had favored him in less visible ways: he was blessed with an ability to remember and to analyze that had fascinated Susan since he was a small boy. And for all his apparent awkwardness, he played a fierce game of squash and could be transformed into tranquil grace by the concentration he brought to fishing, pursuits that united him with his father – and excluded her.

'Let's go out to dinner,' she said to Lara on a sudden impulse.

'Where?'

'Who knows? This is a whim. Someplace you'd like. Someplace you go with your friends.' She noticed Lara's hesitation. 'Bad idea. Never mind.'

'No, Mom, it's not *that* . . .'

'It's okay, I know I'm a stuffy old lady.'

'Well . . . only sometimes.' Lara grinned. 'Just kidding. Okay. I know where we can go. Only you have to let me pick your clothes.'

The outfit Lara chose for her was a white T-shirt and jeans, with most of her gold jewelry removed – not one Susan would ordinarily have picked for going out to dinner, but that, she supposed, was the point.

The place they went to wasn't one she would have picked, either. Packed with hip-looking kids – no one seemed to be over twenty-five – it looked more like a diner than a restaurant.

'This is certainly different.' Even at Lara's age Susan had not been in the kind of crowd that went to places like this.

'It's got great energy and great people-watching. The food's okay.' Clownishly rubber-featured when she wanted to be, Lara stretched her mouth into an exaggerated queasy face. 'Just barely.'

'Speaking of food, are we likely to get any anytime soon? I thought you were starving.'

'I am.'

A lanky young man in black T-shirt and jeans, a white butcher's apron wrapped around his hips, emerged from the throng.

'Hi, sweetie,' he said to Lara with a peck on the cheek.

'Hi. Mom, this is Alan. This is my mom.'

'Hi, Mom.' To Lara: 'Ravenous, as usual?'

She grinned. 'Sure.'

Susan thought Lara looked embarrassed, let the 'as usual' go by.

Alan reappeared instantly with a bottle of beer and a glass of white wine. A busboy followed him with a huge plate heaped with what looked like fried zucchini strings.

'This ought to keep you until I can get over here to take your order.'

He put the beer in front of Lara and presented the wine to Susan.

'Thank you.' Susan was struggling not to comment on his blasé delivery of beer to her underage daughter. 'How did you know what I wanted?'

For a reply he favored her with what might have been a smile as he swivel-hipped away through the crowd.

'It *is* what you drink, Mother,' Lara reminded her.

'Maybe I wanted to be adventurous tonight.' Her tone was unintentionally harsh.

'Do you want something different?' In response, Lara's voice was tight and strained.

Susan reached over to touch her daughter's hand. 'Just kidding. This is perfect.'

'Is it this, then?' – her beer. 'I thought we decided I was old enough. *Responsible* enough.'

'I guess I still think of it as something you do when you're with me and your father.'

'I *am* with you, silly.'

'So you are.' Susan raised her glass. 'To new experiences.'

Lara touched her beer bottle to the wine glass. 'To *good* new experiences.'

'Right. Good ones only.' Susan tasted the wine. 'This qualifies.'

'Glad you like it.'

'Your . . . friend seems to have good taste.'

Lara was attacking the fried zucchini. 'Yum. Nothing like food when you're hungry.'

'Tell me about him.'

'What – Alan? He's just . . . We all come here a lot, and he's funny. We kid around. He likes me, I guess.' She made a face. 'Not that way. I don't even know if he's straight. We just have fun. A bunch of us went out dancing a couple of times, and some art shows. He's an artist, I think. He's very kind of evasive about it. But it's not . . .'

'I just thought, I'd never heard his name, and that's unusual.'

'I can't tell you *everything*. And he's not important, not that way.' She reached for another handful of zucchini strings.

Susan sipped her wine and enjoyed watching her daughter enjoy the food.

Alan came by to tell them about the specials and they ordered dinner. For a quiet moment, Susan looked around at the crowd.

'Lara . . .' Her daughter looked up. 'Have you ever seen anybody use heroin?'

'Mom!'

'It's just a question.' Not one Susan had planned. 'I'm not accusing you of anything.'

'That's what it sounded like.'

'I was thinking about your friends. Not the ones I know – acquaintances, I suppose. Kids at school, or the people you see when you go out.'

'I don't know why you're talking about heroin, anyway. You already gave me the standard lecture.'

'I've been hearing about it in court.' She put the wine glass down. 'It makes the whole issue seem more immediate somehow. Less abstract, the idea that it's around everywhere. But you know I trust you. You've never given me any reason not to.'

'I bet you worry a lot, though, anyway.'

'What – me worry?' Smiling at her little joke. 'I do my best to avoid it.' She took some zucchini. 'Tasty. But isn't it awfully greasy?'

'You have to be in the mood,' Lara said, taking another handful.

They were eating their main course – grilled vegetables with some kind of pebbly grain for Lara, grilled fish for Susan – when Lara said,

'What is it you're hearing about heroin, in court?'

Susan was caught by surprise. 'About how it's imported. About how pure it is these days so people can inhale it and smoke it instead of sticking a needle into their veins. About how it's popular with a lot of people who used to experiment with cocaine.'

Lara paid attention to her food. 'I do know some people who've done it.'

My God, Susan thought. She said, 'I suppose it's inevitable. Anybody I know?'

'I don't want to get anybody in trouble.'

'I'd say they're in trouble already.'

'See, that's what I mean. People pass judgment.'

'It's hard not to.' Wishing for the millionth time she could be more skillful in how she talked to Lara about things that made her feel parental. 'That's scary stuff.'

'Well, see, but . . . that's just the point. If it's scary, that doesn't mean you go *condemning* people for it. Maybe they're just experimenting. People try stuff all the time. As long as you only do it once.'

'It's a narcotic. It's addictive.'

'You think people don't know that?'

'I guess they do.' *Easy*, Susan warned herself, you're sounding like someone's mother again. That's no way to learn anything, or to convince her you're on her side. 'Only, just *knowing* it isn't always enough.'

Lara patted her lips with her napkin, hiding her face. 'No, not always.' Susan saw sadness in her eyes.

'People get in over their heads sometimes,' Susan said.

'Sometimes. Some people. It's a matter of trust.'

Susan did not contradict her.

After a moment of stillness, Lara went back to her food. She did not speak again until Alan came by to ask how everything was.

When they had their coffee in front of them, Lara said, 'Have you ever talked to Charles about any of this? Heroin, I mean.'

Something about the question, following their earlier conversation, made Susan take notice. 'Any particular reason?'

'No, nothing. I just . . . I wondered if you'd ever talked to him about it.'

Susan shook her head. 'This is the first I've talked specifically about it to anybody. Charles and I had the same talk about drugs I had with you –' only infinitely more awkward and uncomfortable – 'and I suppose your father has talked to him about it separately. Why? Is there anything . . .'

'No. I told you, I was just wondering. You're talking to *me* about it, so I wondered if you ever talked to *him*. Let's just change the subject, okay? I'm sorry I brought it back up.'

'I have some phone calls,' Lara said when they got home. She kissed Susan's cheek and headed for her room. 'See you in the morning.'

Richard was not home yet. Susan took her strategy notebook for the Consolidated campaign into the living room, so she would not miss him when he came in.

Getting the notebook, having it with her, was a kind of talisman against idle speculation. Whatever Lara had meant about Charles – if indeed she had meant anything – it wasn't something Susan could divine simply by guessing. Still, even with the notebook open in front of her, she couldn't keep herself from worrying at the question while she waited. Mercifully, she knew the wait would not be long. Richard was almost always home by eleven, even on his latest nights. He couldn't afford to come home later: his mornings began at five-thirty and he needed his nightly six hours' sleep.

'Hi,' he said on his way in, unwrinkled despite the heat. 'I'm surprised you're still up.'

'I wanted to be sure to see you, for a change.'

'Always a pleasure.' He said it as if he were bantering with her, as if they were both always eager to be together. He came over and kissed her cheek.

'Richard, there's something I need to talk to you about.'

'Oh? What's that?' His usual clinical air.

'It's about Charles.'

That got his attention. 'What about Charles?' A wary edge.

'I went out to dinner with Lara tonight. We went to a place downtown, an art hangout, I think.' She watched her husband's face as she talked. He was listening, but she could see in his eyes his impatience with her style: *Get to the point*, he probably wanted to shout. But she would take this at her own pace. There was no shorthand, chapter-headings-only, executive-summary way to do it.

'You know that I've been going to the grand jury in the mornings.'

'Yes, I remember you were asking Andrew Lake about it at that cocktail party at the beach last weekend, something about what a grand jury's powers were, and what the purpose of it was.'

Memory infallible, as always – when it came to facts. 'We've got a case now that involves some people from Chinatown who are accused of dealing in heroin.'

'Oh. Is that . . . awkward for you?' He had never been one to dwell on the fact that she was Chinese, to make her into some kind of exotic trophy. It was one of his good qualities.

'A little. I'm dealing with it. The important part for now is that I'm learning things I didn't know about heroin.'

'Yes, it's getting to be fashionable, it seems. We're seeing it at the hospital more and more.'

'I was talking to Lara about it—'

'To *Lara*? You don't think she's taking heroin?'

'Lara? No. I suppose I worried for a moment, but no. She says she has friends who've tried it, but she seems to be aware of how danger-ous it is.'

'Then what are we talking about?'

'Well, at the end of dinner, after we'd gone on to other things, she said something odd.'

'Yes?'

'She asked me if I'd talked to Charles about it.'

'And?'

'That's all. Just that. *Have you talked to Charles about this?* But it wasn't just the words, it was the context, too . . . We'd been talking about how kids experimented and how some could handle it and some couldn't. She seemed sad, somehow. And then there was something in the way she asked. It worried me, that's all.'

'Worried that what?'

'I don't know, that he's involved somehow.' Susan could see she had made a mistake to bring it up this way. And yet she didn't know what else she could have done.

'Charles? That's ridiculous. Lara said that?'

'All she said was had I spoken to him. But it just seemed odd.'

'Only in your imagination. Charles and heroin? How can you think such a thing!'

'I didn't say—'

'But you thought it. I don't understand. All these years, and sometimes I still don't . . .' He let it trail off – his expression, at once baffled and exasperated, saying more than the words would have. 'Lara asked if you'd talked to him about it. How can you build that into something we need to have a conference about? She asked a simple, natural question – and because of that you want us to have a serious talk about Charles? It doesn't even occur to you to worry about your precious Lara. But *Charles* . . .' He brushed the idea away with the back of his hand.

'I'm his mother, Richard!' Susan was startled to be so close to losing control. 'You two, you and Charles, you close me out, sometimes I feel it's as if I don't exist. I don't know *anything*! How am I supposed to make a judgment? But I'm still his mother and I still care about him and you can't keep treating me as if . . . as if I'm not worthy of being paid attention to.' Her fury passed as quickly as it had come. She turned away, to hide the tears on her cheeks.

From behind her, Richard put his hand gently on her shoulder. It made her go momentarily even tenser than she already was – or was it a shudder? He kissed her hair.

'You're tired,' he said. 'We're both tired. I'm sorry if I sounded harsh.'

He came around and took her hand. 'We should get ready for bed.'

Numb, she followed him down the corridor to the master bedroom suite. *Ready for bed.* That meant they would brush their teeth and go about their other business. By the time she had her makeup off, he'd be in bed, doing some last-minute reading or lying there with his bedside lamp switched off staring at the ceiling. She would come in from the bathroom and he would say good night and roll over to go to sleep before she had even crossed the room. It had been that way for so many years she had long ago stopped expecting they would even kiss good night.

David slept badly and woke up late, in a black mood. It was not the first time.

He'd had another frustrating afternoon and evening, sitting at his computer playing with the developer's kit for the next generation of the world's most popular operating system, the program that allowed a computer to run. If you wanted to develop an application that could run on the millions of computers that were now in almost every home and office, you had to design it to work with the operating system.

But operating systems were moving targets. There was always a new one coming. With every new generation they got more complex and presumably more powerful and easier to use. But, each time, all the application software that ran with the help of a given operating system – word processors, schedulers, spreadsheets, whatever – had to be upgraded to go with it. Obsolescence had never been so thoroughly built into a family of products.

The software companies said it was to take advantage of the increasing power of new generations of the microprocessors that were the computers' brains. The truth was that the new software was so complex and cumbersome it *required* the powerful new processors or it was useless. Some old programs ran on new machines; no new programs ran on old machines.

David had considerable bitterness on the subject. Five years before, he and Jon Levi and a mutual friend of theirs had left the company where they had been developing computer systems under government contract and took a chance that they could make a dream come true. They'd been lamenting the chaos of incompatible operating systems used by home, office and scientific computers, and they had gradually come to believe they could find a way to allow certain widely used kinds of otherwise incompatible computers to work together more easily. It had taken them two years of twelve-hour days, with many false starts and blind alleys, to come up with a workable method.

What they had not realized when they started was that the step up from a demonstration program to a marketable product was a huge one. First, the program needed a lot more development to make it usable by non-experts. Then it had to be tested and debugged, and documentation had to be written. Good as their program potentially was, they could not sell it effectively without support from a large, established company or a major infusion of capital.

Luck arrived in the form of a project executive at a company bigger than any they had thought of approaching. He had worked with David and Jon's partner years before, and the two men had kept in touch. He'd had a rough idea of what they had been trying to do, and when he was named to head a major operating-system redesign for his company he'd thought of them immediately.

The contract they'd hammered out with the big company's lawyers had been heavily slanted in the big company's favor, but it had still been in many ways a dream opportunity for David and his partners. It meant their work would have the kind of muscle behind it that might get it installed on a major share of the world's microcomputers and scientific workstations. They would get a royalty on every copy sold that could mount well into seven figures each, possibly more. The downside was that their elegant solution of a difficult problem would be reduced to a single feature of the big company's operating system, their own tiny company would be swallowed up, and for five years they would be under exclusive contract, to integrate their program with the new operating system and to work on improvements and extensions of what they had done.

It meant having a shot at fortune, without fame or control or independence. David's partners had jumped at it. He had swallowed his initial misgivings and gone along, quickly swept up in the excitement of being part of what looked like it was going to be an information-technology revolution that almost rivaled the introduction of personal computers.

Two years into the contract, in the wake of a huge stock sell-off that halved its market value, the company they'd made their deal with had begun a massive and rapid downsizing. Lopped off in the bloodbath had been the division that was developing the revolutionary new operating system. Unfortunately for David and his partners, the company had kept all the rights to their work, even though the new management didn't seem to have any intention of ever using it.

There had been buyout money – David thought of it as a consolation prize – but the dream was dead. David had taken a couple of months off to let the wounds heal in the expectation that he would get back to work, find a new area that needed the kind of problem solving and innovation that he now knew he craved. It hadn't worked out that way.

At first he'd allowed himself to be distracted by the demands of his father's illness. He'd had no immediate need to work, there was enough money to keep him going for a while. But life had turned flat and without flavor. When he did try to work, he went in circles. After a few months of that kind of frustration he'd decided to start taking contract jobs just to keep from getting completely stale and to keep from using too much of his buyout money. As time passed he wondered increasingly whether his moment in the sun was already behind him. He did his best to convince himself he could be happy doing nothing more than solving other people's problems.

And then there were the days when he couldn't stand that thought, so he'd sit down with a pad of paper and a notebook computer, or go for long walks, and try to come up with something, anything, that wasn't just a patch he'd been hired to paste onto somebody else's clumsily designed and porous structure. But he was without inspiration, and the lines of thought he made himself follow never led anywhere. Those days he felt the dark hollowness of despair, and those nights he slept very badly.

There weren't any cases at the grand jury that morning interesting enough to lift David out of his mood, but there was a lot of intense talk at the break. The grand jurors stood in tight groups in the corridor debating the previous day's decision to ask A.D.A. Mahoney to bring in the 'Chinatown' defendants as witnesses.

'I don't know what these people think they're doing,' David heard Number Four say in a tone obviously pitched to be overheard. 'It's a total waste of time.'

'Like the man said, we gotta be here anyway,' the corrections officer reminded him.

'Yeah, sure, but what about the A.D.A.? I'll bet *he* has better ways to spend his time.' Number Four was looking straight at David as he spoke.

David turned away. There was no point getting into it now: there'd be plenty of time for arguing later on. He didn't see Susan Linwood in the crowd, assumed she'd gone downstairs to make phone calls as she had every day since he'd shown her the courthouse phones.

He walked over to where Manny Klein, the accountant from seat Ten, was talking to his grand-jury-room neighbors. Number Nine broke off to introduce himself.

'I'm Jimmy Kelly.' The redhead offered a strong, square hand. 'And this is Oswaldo Perez –' the big Dominican from seat Eight – 'and I guess you know Manny Klein. I wanted to say my thanks to you for standing your ground about those Chinese books. I was wondering about them myself.'

'David Clark. I'm glad it worked out the way it did – thanks to the three of you, really.'

'I've got a nephew's a cop,' Kelly said. 'So I'm in no hurry to say the police get things wrong. But my own work is, I own a bar – place called the Shamrock, uptown – and one thing I can say, you spend some time in the restaurant and bar business, you see lots of ways to keep books. People get real sharp making one thing look like it's something else. Manny, here, too, being an accountant, you've seen some of that yourself, I'll wager.'

'Well, you know, they had to teach us *something* in accounting school.' Klein was grinning. 'But seriously, folks, I don't know if we'll ever know for sure if those books are anything but what Mr Mahoney says they are. I expect it'll be interesting to hear what these people have to say.'

'If they come.' In his current mood, David was skeptical of everything.

'Would *you*?' Perez asked them all.

'If I had a good story to tell,' Kelly said, 'I surely would.'

# 8

First thing Friday, Mahoney brought them Martin Eng. The repaired air conditioning was straining as if it were still trying to make up for the days it had left them to swelter. Susan felt clammy and uncomfortable, her body tenser than it should have been after her early-morning hour of tennis with Lara and a hot shower. The only thing she could attribute it to was anxiety about the Engs's testimony today.

Mahoney started with the same disclaimers they had heard from A.D.A. Meisel before the bail jumper testified: the defendant was going to waive immunity, he might bring a lawyer and might consult with his lawyer, and they were not to hold any of that against him.

The man who came into the grand jury room was white-haired and boyishly slight. Arms slender and graceful as the legs of a crane emerged from the wide short sleeves of his crisp, white shirt, giving him a look of fragility he would not have had in a suit. His trousers were dark blue, almost black, cut elegantly of soft cloth that Susan thought might be the lightest of summer-weight wool. His shoes were black cap-toes polished to a high gloss. Rich but not gaudy, Susan thought – the standard she'd adopted for herself when she first encountered it in English Lit. Martin Eng's head was large for the size of his body, the pale skin – much lighter than Susan's own – stretched so taut over the bones it looked free of wrinkles.

Aware that the others were staring as hard as she was, Susan looked around, saw frozen fascination, narrow-eyed suspicion, curiosity tinged with what looked like surprise. And no wonder they were surprised: Martin Eng, who seemed at once self-possessed and out of his element as he slowly crossed the front of the grand jury room – limping slightly, Susan thought – hardly bore the aura of evil incarnate that went with the phrase *major drug dealer*. Number Four, she noticed, was studying the ceiling, making a show of how uninterested he was.

David, examining his fellow grand jurors, thought most of them looked less hostile than he had expected. The real question would be how many were curious enough to listen and open enough to hear – and what Martin Eng had to say. David's own mind was far from made up.

Coming in behind her diminutive client, Martin Eng's lawyer seemed taller than she probably was, though the effect was diluted by the way Mahoney towered over both of them. The defense lawyer's silky, sky-blue suit looked businesslike without being mannish. Her glossy brown hair hung straight to just above her shoulders. Oval, silver-rimmed glasses – David wasn't sure whether they were meant to seem hip or scholarly – called attention to her alert blue eyes.

The grand jury warden followed them in and sat unobtrusively in a chair by the door. It had been the same with the bail jumper: David assumed the warden's presence meant that despite Martin Eng's fresh-from-the-cleaner's outfit he was coming here from jail.

After the defendant had given his name and address, Mahoney handed him a typed document and asked if he had read it that day. He said yes and identified his signature on the second page.

'Mr Eng, do you understand that you are appearing before this grand jury not merely as a witness and that you may be charged with the commission of a crime or crimes?'

'Yes,' he said quietly, looking at his hands, folded on the table in front of him.

'Do you further understand your testimony may be used against you in this and other proceedings?'

'Yes.'

'Do you understand that you have the right to refuse to appear and be sworn before this grand jury and to refuse to give any testimony whatsoever that might tend to incriminate you?'

Martin Eng looked at Mahoney over the heads of the grand jury and seemed to draw a long breath. 'Yes.'

'Do you understand that you have a right to confer with a lawyer before deciding whether you will swear to this waiver and testify before this grand jury?'

'Yes.' Looking at his hands again.

'Have you conferred with your attorney for the purpose of deciding whether you will swear to the waiver of immunity and testify before the grand jury?'

'Yes.' He did not look at the lawyer sitting next to him.

'Do you desire additional time to consult with your attorney?'

'No.'

'Do you now wish to swear to this waiver of immunity and testify before the grand jury?'

For the first time, the defendant looked at the grand jurors. 'Yes.'

'Do you do so voluntarily?'

'Yes.'

'Has anyone forced you or coerced you in any way to sign, swear to, or execute this waiver?'

'No.'

'Has any promise been made to you by anyone in connection with your signing, swearing to or executing this waiver?'

'No.'

'If you wish to waive immunity and testify, please raise your right hand so the foreman can swear you to the waiver.'

Susan remembered the bail jumper's being put through something similar, but she didn't think it had been as specific as this – though that could have been because she hadn't been paying such close attention then. This time it sounded scary to her. Not so much the fact that Martin Eng was giving up his right not to incriminate himself – she'd expected that. It was the part about his not having been forced or coerced into doing it, and not having been promised anything in return. As if no one in his right mind would do this, except under duress. And maybe that was right. Maybe no one would.

'All right, Mr Eng,' Mahoney said when Martin Eng had sworn to tell the truth. 'We've agreed that you'll begin with a short statement. I remind you to be brief and to the point. If I have to, I'll interrupt you to make sure you stay within the bounds of evidence that the grand jury is permitted to hear. Has your lawyer explained all that to you?'

Eng looked at his lawyer, who tilted her head slightly. Eng nodded to Mahoney. 'I understand.'

He took a moment to look around at the grand jurors. Susan wondered how much coaching he'd had.

'First, I say to everyone, I am sorry,' he began. 'I apologize for my English.'

Grand juror Number Four snorted audibly.

'Ladies and gents, please hold the commentary for your deliberations,' Mahoney said immediately. 'Mr Eng, go ahead.'

'Thank you.' Eng seemed unruffled. 'I come here to say I am innocent. The lawyers say I cannot talk about my wife, I can talk about Martin Eng, only. All right. To begin, I say this – Martin Eng has no dealing with heroin. Not now, not ever.'

His voice was deep and rich, surprisingly resonant for a man his size. Instead of trying to project to his audience he spoke as if to someone sitting across the table from him, yet his words had a precision that made them unmistakably clear – even to Susan, near the end of the second row.

'On Thursday, last week, police break into my home, take away my life savings. Police say, take money away because money come from heroin. They say, find heroin in home of Martin Eng. Not so.

'They show me package. They say, "Martin Eng, this heroin we find in your house. Find heroin in shrine in bedroom." Shrine in bedroom gift from China. Never see heroin before this time. Not this heroin. No heroin.'

He paused, looked at his lawyer, looked briefly at the grand jury. 'This money they take away belong to my wife. Also, belong to me. Many years, we save money. In China, save money. Hong Kong, save money. New York, save money. Work very hard in China, whole family, many generations.

'Many years ago, ancestors live in China, in Panyu – city on Pearl River delta near Guangzhou, also called Canton, in south of China. Long ago in Panyu, ancestors own much land, many generations, good for farm. After farm, make factory, manufacture silk cloth. After that, make more factory. Manufacture clothing. Two families have factory business together – Eng family and Cheung family, family of my wife.

Factory business very prosperous, much money, pay much tax to Emperor.

'Then, revolution. Emperor gone. Beginning of republic of Dr Sun Chungsan. Called Chungsan after place of birth, small city also in Pearl River delta, same as Panyu. Eng family and Cheung family help Dr Sun Chungsan before revolution. Give money, talk with friends – ideas of Dr Sun. Send sons of family to help. This Dr Sun same man you call Sun Yatsen, very famous. George Washington of China.'

He stopped a moment to catch his breath and took a sip of water from the glass in front of him. His hand shook slightly holding the glass.

'After revolution, time of much struggle in China,' he resumed. 'Much trouble for Dr Sun, trouble for Canton, for Guangdong province. Many armies, many governments, many strikes by working people. Power change every month. Nationalists, Communists, also strong warlords. But factory business very successful. Good trade with foreigners, make much money. Families get help and protection from many friend of Dr Sun, also many friend of General Chiang Kai-shek, most important Nationalist general. In this time Martin Eng grow to young man. In Canton, many faction in politics, much struggle in schools. People have fear of Japan, but civil war does not stop.

'Then Japanese come to south of China, to Pearl River delta. Take everything, kill many people. Torture and kill grandfather of Martin Eng, kill other ancestors, take factory business. Eng family and Cheung family leave China, go to Hong Kong.'

Susan was fascinated by this unadorned statement of survival in the face of tragedy. Glancing around quickly she had the impression that the others were too. There was something remarkably compelling about Martin Eng.

'Soon, Japanese come to Hong Kong. Much blood. Families run back to China, to small part of Guangdong province under control of warlord allies of Nationalist army. Other Panyu people in that place laugh because we go away before, now come back.' He shook his head, with a faint sad smile. 'No other place to go.

'Then war over, Japanese gone. Go home to Panyu, start business again, from beginning. Very much hard work. New factories, new partners – Hong Kong people. Then more civil war, Nationalist

Kuomintang fight Communists, worse than before.

'Nationalists come, take money from family, place officer in charge of factory, force to make clothes for Kuomintang Army. Put family people in prison. Rest of family run to live in Hong Kong.

'Then Communist People's Liberation Army drive away Nationalists from China. Later, Communists make smiling face to Chinese business people, say "Come home to China, make good business, make your country strong—" '

'Mr Eng,' Mahoney cut in. 'I'm trying very hard to be lenient, but I have to insist that you confine your remarks to the charges against you.'

'Yes, yes.' For the first time, Martin Eng seemed ruffled. 'This, story of *money*. Explain how family get money over many years. Much hard work, much suffering. Then, come to United States, nineteen sixties, carry money, also jewelry from ancestors of my wife.'

His lawyer reached into her briefcase for a large manila envelope. She took out a photograph and handed it to Martin Eng, who held it braced against the table, facing the grand jury. It was a full-length portrait of a beautiful Chinese woman in a cheongsam, the colors of the image all faded into delicate pastels. Over the closely fitted dress with its mandarin collar and skirt modestly slit to the knee, the woman wore an elaborate gold necklace encrusted with what Susan guessed was a fortune in jade and sapphires.

'Picture of wife and jewelry,' Martin Eng said. 'Gold, very pure. Also jade, precious stones. Bring here, sell in nineteen seventies. Price of gold, more than eight hundred United States dollars for one ounce. Make much money.'

He paused again, glanced at his lawyer as if for support, then spoke to the glass of water in front of him. 'Also money from gambling. In Chinatown, all people gamble. Fan Tan, horse race, mahjong. Win much money. Put away for old age. Police take all money. All gone now.'

'Stick to the point, Mr Eng,' Mahoney warned again. 'Ladies and gentlemen, as your legal adviser I have to instruct you to disregard Mr Eng's remarks about the current disposition of his money. That's not relevant. We're concerned here only with the elements of the crimes

Mr Eng is charged with. Because large amounts of money, especially cash, can be evidence of criminal activity, the question of where the money came from is relevant to the charge of conspiracy to sell a controlled substance. All right, go ahead.'

'Yes. Sorry. Write record of gambling in notebooks, in special code. In China, always afraid officials come, read records, make trouble, take money. Learn to write in code so they cannot read.

'Also in notebook, buy and sell coin collection. All coins gone now. Sold. Money for old age. All money for old age. Bank account too dangerous. Hard to get money if trouble. Keep money at home, keep money in vault.'

Susan continued to be impressed by Martin Eng's dignity and the simplicity and directness with which he told his story. But his apparent difficulty with the language seemed increasingly odd, given how mild his accent was and how clearly he enunciated the words he spoke. She wondered if he was exaggerating his foreigner's diction as a way to manipulate the grand jurors. To disguise the fact that he was lying.

Yet nothing he was saying rang false. Growing up, she had heard many stories like it. The bits and pieces she'd gleaned of her own parents' stories were not much different.

'Now, tell about bringing money to United States,' Martin Eng went on. 'In China, always much danger, danger from warlords and Nationalist Army, danger from Communists. Any time, need to get money fast, so no one know. Keep money in bank no good. If trouble, government take money in bank.

'Two years, Martin Eng in prison, cannot leave. Then, Martin Eng free, Chairman Mao Zedong declare Great Proletarian Cultural Revolution. Much danger. Family must leave to save life. Sew gold and jewelry in lining of clothes. Walk many miles to seashore. Walk at night, all night long, many nights. At shore, take small boat to sea. Very dark. Storm. Boat sink, near Macao. Whole family must swim to shore. Clothes very heavy. Whole family almost drown. Two children drown.'

He said that in the same quiet matter-of-fact way he had told the rest of his story, but Susan heard the pain in it.

'Mr Eng,' Mahoney said. 'Do you have anything more to tell the grand jury that is relevant to the charges they are considering?'

'All relevant. All important,' he replied, a rough edge of emotion in his voice. 'You say, where does money come from? Money come from clothes of dead children.'

Into the silence Mahoney said, 'Do you have more that you want to tell us?'

The witness shook his head.

'Is that a no?'

'Yes. No more story.'

'All right, then I have some questions for you now. First of all, do you have any kind of employment at the current time?'

'I am president of Guangdong Three Districts Association.'

'What's that?'

'Community association, help people from Panyu, ancestral home. Also Shuntak people, Namhoi people. Three districts.'

His answer stirred something in Susan's memory: she reached for it but it was just beyond her grasp.

'How much do you earn as president of your community association?' Mahoney was asking.

'Each month, one hundred United States dollars, honorary salary.'

'How long have you held that job?'

'Three years.'

'Before that what did you do?'

'Vice-president of different community association.'

'How much did you earn there?'

'No money.'

'No money?'

'Work free. Honor only.'

'For how long did you work for that association?'

'Twenty years. Different jobs.'

'How did you live during that time?'

The witness shook his head, looking bewildered.

'Let me rephrase that,' Mahoney said. 'During that time did you have any other source of income?'

'Garment factory.'

'What kind of job did you do there?'

'Manage factory.'

'When was that?'

116

'First job, nineteen sixties. Work almost thirty years.'

'How much money did you make doing that?'

'Start out, small factory, cheap prices. Make five thousand dollars first year. Those days, pay rent for home, fifty dollars every month. Then factory grow, add more factories, make more money. Same as China.'

'How many factories?'

'Best years, five factories.'

'You managed five garment factories and worked at a community association?'

'Many years.'

'Do you still do that?'

'Only community association.'

'Do you still get money from the factories?'

'Consultant fee.'

'How much is that?'

'For one year, five thousand dollars.'

'Do you have a title there?'

'Director.'

'What kind of coins were in your collection?'

'Sorry?'

'You said you had a coin collection.'

'Yes.'

'What kind of coins were in it?'

'Chinese coins.'

David couldn't help smiling, though he didn't suppose Martin Eng had intended to be funny. David looked for Susan Linwood's reaction, saw only concentration and concern.

'What kind of Chinese coins?' Mahoney asked the witness.

'Coins from before. Old dynasty. Ming Dynasty, Tang Dynasty. Also money from Republic of Dr Sun Chungsan.'

'How much money did you make when you sold it?'

Eng shook his head, whispered to his lawyer. The lawyer whispered back. Mahoney noted the conference for the record.

'I do not remember,' Eng said aloud.

'Help us out here, Mr Eng,' Mahoney said. 'Give us an estimate. About how much?'

'Sorry. Do not remember.'

'How long were you collecting those coins?'

'From five years old, in China.'

'You had a large coin collection in China?'

'Yes.'

'You brought it here?'

'No.'

'I don't understand. You didn't bring it here, but you sold it here?'

'Sell many coins in China when Japanese invade north of country. Send money to Hong Kong, keep only best coins, very valuable. Bury in secret place. Dig up many years later. Bring to United States. Also, in Hong Kong on way to United States buy more coins, also buy in U.S., make new collection, better than old.'

'You said you kept the best coins from your first collection and brought them here. Is that right?'

'Right.'

'Did you have any favorites in the collection? Some coins you liked more than the others, or that were more valuable?'

Eng hesitated for what seemed to David a long time before he said, 'Coin from time of Emperor Ming Huang, in Tang Dynasty, gift from father for passing important examinations. Very valuable.'

'How much was it worth?'

'I do not remember.'

'But you did sell it?'

'Yes.'

'And you don't remember for how much?'

'I do not remember.'

'Even though it was your favorite?'

The witness, silent, looked confused.

Mahoney tried again: 'The fact that this coin was so special doesn't help you remember anything about how much you got when you sold it?'

'Yes. I do not remember.'

'Do you remember how much you got for your wife's jewelry?'

'Gold, very pure, more than eight hundred U.S. dollars per ounce. Highest price.'

'How much of it did you have?'

118

'I do not remember.'

'How many people came to Hong Kong with you from China?'

'Five people. Wife, four children. Two drown.'

'And you brought all your gold sewn into your clothes?'

'No. Make money in Hong Kong, buy more gold there.'

'Where do you do your gambling here?'

Again, he hesitated. 'Talk to lawyer?'

'Go ahead.'

After a brief whispered conference, Eng said, 'Not gamble now. Before, gambled in Chinatown.'

'Where in Chinatown?'

'Many places. All closed now.'

'When they were open, did they employ guards and lookouts?'

'Need guard to protect from robbery.'

'And from the police.'

'I do not know that.'

'But you do know that gambling is illegal in New York.'

The witness did not answer at once. His lawyer touched his arm, whispered in his ear. As with the other consultations, Mahoney noted it for the record.

'I do not admit anything illegal. I do not run gambling place. Only visit.'

'Ladies and gentlemen,' Mahoney said. 'Let me clarify for you that my question should not be taken to imply that Mr Eng himself was breaking the law by patronizing an illegal gambling establishment. Mr Eng, I'll put the question differently. Did you know that running a gambling establishment was illegal in New York?'

'Yes.'

'How often did you gamble?'

'Every week.'

'How much did you gamble each time you went?'

'One thousand U.S. dollars stake.'

Several of the grand jurors had reactions loud enough for David to hear. No wonder, he thought – that's a lot of money to gamble.

'Did you sometimes lose it all?'

'Sometimes lose. Win two times for every one time I lose.'

'And even though you were not breaking the law yourself, you

119

knew that the people who ran the places where you gambled *were* breaking the law.'

'Yes,' he acknowledged reluctantly.

'And you willingly supported and encouraged them in this illegal activity, to the tune of risking and sometimes losing a thousand dollars in their establishments every week.'

A long hesitation. 'Yes.'

'Who did you sell your gold to?'

It took Eng a puzzled moment to make the transition. 'Don't remember.'

'Do you have any record of the sale?'

'No.'

'Did you give the buyer some kind of bill of sale?'

'No need. They keep gold, I keep money.'

'And the coins? Who did you sell them to?'

'Different people.'

'You must remember who they were.'

'No.'

'None of them?'

'No.'

'There can't be very many collectors of old Chinese coins.'

Eng shook his head. 'I think, many people. Many China people in United States, also Hong Kong, Singapore – many places.'

That made sense, David thought. He didn't know much about Chinese culture but he did know that heritage was important. Considering that, and the number of successful Chinese people all over the world, collecting Chinese coins could well be a crowded field.

'Who did you buy from, when you bought coins?'

Again Eng shook his head. He seemed uncomfortable.

'You need to answer out loud, Mr Eng. The stenographer has no way to indicate that you're shaking your head.'

'Sorry. Buy coins in China, Hong Kong, U.S. Many people sell coins.'

'Do you have any records of buying or selling these coins?'

'Only in notebook.'

'You say your coin collection was valuable?'

'Very valuable.'

'Did you get insurance on it?'

'No.'

'Did you declare the money you made on your income tax forms?'

'What money?'

'The income from the sale of the coins. The income from the gold and jewelry.'

'I am honest man. Pay all taxes.'

'Ladies and gentlemen, as your legal adviser I must tell you that is what we call an unresponsive answer. Please disregard it. Mr Eng, the question is, did you declare the income from the coins on your income tax forms when you received it?'

'Accountant fill out tax forms, tell how much to pay.'

'Does your accountant keep records of what you tell him and the forms he files?'

'This accountant, now?'

'Did you have another one?'

'Yes.'

'When was that?'

'Up to ten years ago.'

'Why did you change?'

'Accountant from before is dead.'

'What was his name?'

'American name, Henry Wong.'

'But you have an accountant now.'

'Yes.'

'What is his name?'

'Anna Kwok.'

'Does she have your old tax records?'

'Only ten years.'

'Before you came here to testify, did you make any attempt to determine if you had records to support your claim that this money was yours?'

'I do not understand.'

'You brought us a picture of your wife wearing some of the jewelry you claim to have sold. Did you look for other proof?'

'Old papers gone. Only keep notebooks. Police take.'

'I believe you said you kept some of your money in the vault. Is that right?'

'Yes.'

'Do you mean bank safe deposit boxes?'

'Yes.'

'When did you rent these safe deposit boxes?'

'I think, about two years.'

'Were they the first safe deposit boxes you rented?'

'No. Had other boxes, many years, in other banks.'

'Which other banks?'

'Banks in Chinatown.'

'Do you have any records? Any canceled checks for the safe deposit box rent, or any receipts?'

Martin Eng looked across the room at Mahoney. 'Do you know how old I am?'

'With all due respect for your age, Mr Eng, I just asked you a question and I'd like you to answer it.'

'Almost eighty years. Too many years for keeping papers. Keep papers . . . soon only paper, no room to live.'

'I take it that's a no.' Mahoney did not sound amused.

'Old records all gone.'

'Well, I have your ledgers – notebooks, as you call them – right here.' Mahoney came forward and handed them to him. 'Can you show us the places where you recorded the sale of the coins or the gold, or your gambling winnings? Anything like that you can show us would be very helpful.' Standing next to the tiny seated defendant, Mahoney looked enormous.

Martin Eng took the two books with no enthusiasm and let them sit on the table in front of him unopened. He looked uncomfortable, David thought, in a way he hadn't before.

'Mr Eng? Can you help us with the notebooks, please?'

He opened the top book and paged through it, pausing intermittently to study a page. He closed the book and moved it aside, paged through the second one. Twice, he stopped and regarded a page with extra care but then moved on without saying anything. Finally he closed the second book and pushed them both away from him.

'I am sorry. It is a long time ago. I am an old man. My memory is

122

bad. I cannot tell exactly what this means, about coins or gold or gambling. I am sorry.'

'Mr Eng, do you want us to believe that you can't remember *anything* about what's written in these books?'

'Some things. Some pages look like gambling, some pages look like coins.'

'Can you point those out for the grand jurors, please?'

He did, haltingly, but he could not – or would not – elaborate on the details, even though Mahoney pressed him.

# 9

At the break Susan stayed in her seat. She did not have to go out into the hall to know that Number Four, macho man, was deriding Martin Eng, mocking his performance. It made her cringe to think about it.

She had listened with growing dismay to his answers. She wanted to believe Martin Eng, had been moved by the story he told. She wished he were making a better showing.

'Mr Eng, do you own the apartment you live in?' Mahoney's first question after the break, like most of the questions he had asked so far, sounded to Susan more like conversation than interrogation.

'Not own. Rent. Eight hundred dollars each month.'

'And how big is it?'

'Living room, three bedrooms, kitchen, dining room, two bathrooms. Also, small room for storage. Small room for servant, with small bathroom.'

'How long have you lived there?'

'Thirty-one years. Rent control.'

'And you've said you have children.'

'Four children. Two dead.'

'How old are the ones who are still alive?'

'Son, forty-four. Daughter, youngest child, forty-two.'

'Do they live with you in that apartment?'

'No.'

'Did they ever live with you?'

'Long ago.'

'How are they employed?'

'Garment business.'

'Are they self-sufficient?'

'Sorry?'

'Do they depend on you for money?'

'No.' The single word and the fiery look that accompanied it were full of indignation. Susan could feel his need to lift the implied slur on his children, but he held it back.

'The police found almost a million and a half dollars in your apartment and in your safe deposit boxes, is that right? U.S. dollars,' Mahoney added.

'Yes.'

'You pay eight hundred dollars a month rent?'

'Yes.'

'Do you plan to move?'

'I do not understand.'

'Are you planning to buy a house somewhere, or a different apartment?'

A crease of troubled concentration appeared between Martin Eng's narrowed eyes. 'I do not understand.'

His lawyer leaned over and whispered to him. He nodded, his face smooth again.

'No,' he said. 'Not plan to buy house.'

'And you are how old?'

'Almost eighty years.'

'How much longer do you expect to live?'

The witness frowned and shook his head. He whispered a question to his lawyer and waited for the answer. The answer did not make him happy. He shook his head again and whispered another question. The lawyer thought about it before she answered. This time, her client seemed satisfied.

'Hope to live long life.'

'How long?'

'Hope to live many years.'

'Suppose I told you that the official life expectancy for a man your age is about eight more years. Would you believe that?'

'My beliefs do not allow that thought.' His stern tone made it a rebuke.

'That's all right, never mind. Let me ask you this, instead – about

125

how much money do you spend to live every year?'

'I do not know.'

'Let's estimate it. You said you pay eight hundred dollars a month rent, that's less than ten thousand a year.'

'Yes.'

'Food. Do you spend a hundred dollars a week on food you eat at home?'

'I do not know.'

'Do you eat in restaurants?'

'Yes.'

'How much do you spend on that?'

'I do not know.'

'Two hundred a week? Three hundred a week?'

'I do not know.'

'Do you get social security payments?'

'Yes.'

'How much are they?'

'Approximately one thousand dollars every month.'

'And does your wife get social security?'

'Yes.'

'Do you know from your own knowledge how much she receives?'

'Approximately five hundred dollars every month.'

'Do you have any large expenses I haven't asked about?'

Susan thought she saw where Mahoney was going, and it didn't seem fair to her. If the money was, as Martin Eng said, all that was left not just of his and his wife's working lives but of their families' fortunes as well, why should they feel obliged to use it for ostentatious living? She knew plenty of people who gave no thought to preserving anything, who lived far too high for their actual circumstances, and who were constantly worried about meeting their monthly obligations. Not everyone would choose that kind of anxiety.

'What kind of large expenses?' Martin Eng asked Mahoney.

'Entertainment, travel, anything like that? Personal expenses like clothing or jewelry? Campaign expenses to keep your job as president of the Three Districts Association?'

'I do not understand what you wish to know.'

'Let me make it clear, Mr Eng. You have current pre-tax income that you've told us about of approximately twenty-five thousand dollars a year, including your wife's social security payments. You have no large expenses that you've told us about, and your children don't depend on you for money. You claim you're keeping all the money the police found in your apartment and in your safe deposit boxes for your old age. You also said that you're almost eighty years old. So I'm wondering, given your income and your simple lifestyle, what is it you expect to spend a million and a half dollars on in your old age?'

'Possible to live many years,' Martin Eng shot back at once. 'Do not know how much expense, every year. Life very hard. Deng Xiaoping, principal leader in China, say, "To become rich is glorious." ' He paused a moment and resumed in a more subdued tone. 'To become poor is not glorious. For old people, to become poor . . . very very hard.'

'*To become rich is glorious?*' Mahoney echoed. 'That's fascinating. Do you know about interest?'

'I do not understand.'

'Are you familiar with the idea of savings accounts in banks?'

'Yes.'

'And do you know that if you have your money in a savings account, then every year the bank pays you interest on that money?'

'Yes.'

'And do you know about U.S. Treasury bills and Treasury bonds, and that you can earn interest by keeping your money in that form? Similar to the bearer bonds in your safe deposit box?'

'Yes.'

'And to get rich is glorious?'

'So Deng Xiaoping has said.'

'Do you have any savings accounts?'

'No.'

'Do you own any Treasury bills or bonds?'

'No.'

'You say you have had this money for many years?'

'Yes.'

'Twenty years, say?'

'Yes.'

'Do you know what the interest rates have been over those years?'

'No.'

'Suppose I said they varied between about three percent and about fourteen percent. Does that sound familiar to you?'

'I don't know.'

'Do you know about compound interest?'

'I do not understand.'

'That's if you keep your money in the bank and you don't spend the interest, then you earn interest on the interest. And that makes your money grow faster.'

Martin Eng shrugged. 'I know that.'

'Suppose you could have earned only five percent interest on your money for twenty years. Then, with compound interest, you would have much more than doubled your money in that time, would you agree with that?'

A brief pause, then: 'Yes.'

'That's, let's say, two million dollars in interest, isn't it?'

Again Eng shrugged. 'So it may be.'

'At five percent.'

'Yes.'

'And interest rates have been much higher than five percent.'

'I do not know.'

'But you didn't put your money in the bank.'

'Many banks fail.'

That stopped Mahoney for a moment. 'Are you aware of the fact that bank deposits are insured by the United States Government?'

'I have much respect for Government of United States. But from days when I was young boy I learn – trust government protect money, same as trust tiger guard goat.'

At this, there was general laughter. Even Number Four snickered. Susan wanted to cheer.

'But you do own some bonds,' Mahoney persisted. 'Bearer bonds – certificates that can be cashed in by anyone who holds them.'

'Yes.'

'And you get interest on them.'

'Yes.'

'But you still kept most of your money in cash.'

'Only safe way.'

128

'Mr Eng, a lot of the money that was found at your apartment and in your safe deposit boxes was in hundred-dollar bills. Can you tell me how you came to have so many bills of that denomination?'

'From selling gold and jewelry and coins. Also, changed small bills for large ones. Easier to keep.'

'When did you change those bills?'

He shook his head. 'I do not remember.'

'Can you tell us which safe deposit boxes those bills were in?'

'Money all mixed together. Safe deposit boxes only two years old. Change bank many times. Count money, move money, change old money for new.'

'What about the bearer bonds? When did you buy those?'

'First buy, many years ago.'

'How many years?'

'Twenty?' He seemed to be trying it out. 'Around twenty years.'

'What money did you use to buy them with?'

'Money from gold, jewelry. Wife said, money too big.' His hands measured a pile of money over the table. 'Bonds small. Also, earn interest. Same as you say.'

'But you have much more in cash than in bonds. Why didn't you buy more bonds, make your pile even smaller, earn even more interest?'

'Not safe.'

'But you bought some bonds, even though they weren't safe.'

'To please wife.'

'Mr Eng, on some of the bundles of money there were Chinese characters written on slips of paper. Are you aware of that?'

He sat in blank silence.

'Mr Eng?'

'Yes. I know that.' His answer was slow, the words deliberate.

'And these characters match some of the writing in one of your ledgers.'

Again, no response.

'Are you aware of that?'

'Yes.'

'But you say these books are from long ago.'

'Yes. Use books long ago. Put away, many years. Take out again. Make new entries.'

'Then those entries *are* about the money in the safe deposit boxes.'

'Yes.'

'What do they mean?'

The witness leaned toward his lawyer, whispered a question, listened intently to the answer. He was silent a moment before he answered.

'For distributing money if not live to use in old age.'

'Don't you have a will for that?'

'Leave instructions.'

'And what do the instructions say?'

'Give some money to children. Some money for good friends and for poor people. Also, give to association.'

'Can you give the jurors more detail? Which friends? Which poor people?'

Visibly tired now, to Susan's eye, Martin Eng reached out for the ledgers, chose one and paged through it until he found what he wanted. Running his hand down a column, he read in Cantonese, each word or phrase followed by 'same as' and the name of a person or an organization, also in Cantonese. Each time, Mahoney made him stop and spell the words out for the stenographer. He was sometimes uncertain what English letters to use for the Chinese sounds.

'Why didn't you just write the names?' Mahoney wanted to know.

Martin Eng looked in the prosecutor's direction with an expression of disbelief.

'Secret,' he said as if it should have been self-evident. 'Also bad luck. Very bad luck.'

'But those same Chinese characters are also written earlier in the book,' Mahoney pointed out. 'Aren't they?'

'I don't know. Long ago.'

'Why don't you look?'

Dutifully, Eng paged through the book. Stopped and looked up, smiling. 'Yes. Same words.'

'And what transactions do those earlier entries represent?'

'I do not remember.'

'But the names are the same.'

Eng's smile had broadened. 'Yes. Very funny. Long ago use same code, names of Chinese years. Same words, mean different.'

130

Mahoney did not say anything for a moment. Susan thought he was finished with his questions, but then he said, 'Who gave you the shrine?'

The witness looked at him blankly.

'The shrine in your bedroom, the one with the heroin in it.'

The blank look was replaced with an indignant one. 'No heroin in shrine.'

'Who gave you the shrine?' Mahoney repeated.

'Friend of family visit from China. Bring shrine.'

'When?'

'Spring time.'

'Is it part of your religious observance?'

Eng hesitated. 'Old custom,' he said. 'Chinese people's custom.'

'Have you ever had a shrine like that before?'

'Old times, in China.'

'Not here in the United States?'

'Long ago.'

'Not recently?'

'No.'

'But you put this shrine on your bedroom dresser?'

'Yes.' He looked puzzled.

'How was the shrine packed when you received it?'

'Wrapped in red paper. Lucky color, good for gifts.'

'And you unwrapped it and set it up.'

'Wife unwrap and put on dresser. Gift for wife.'

'Were you there at the time?'

'Yes. Happy to see gift from friend.'

'What does your friend do for a living? The friend who gave you the shrine.'

'Business.'

'What kind of business?'

'Manufacture garments. Other business.'

'What other business?'

'Porcelain objects.'

'Like the statue in the shrine.'

'Yes.'

'He exports those objects to the United States?'

'Yes.'

'Along with some heroin.'

Martin Eng was silent. Mahoney did not press him for an answer.

The prosecutor came around to the front of the room. Susan thought he, too, looked tired.

'Any questions?' he asked them.

The first question was from the grand jury's alternate forewoman, who wanted to know about martial arts. Yes, Martin Eng acknowledged, he practiced Tai Chi as a form of exercise, as many Chinese did. Had he used it when the police came to his house? No. What happened when the police came? They broke down the door and knocked him down and put a gun to his head. Ruined a valuable antique work of art. Frightened his wife.

David, watching and listening to Martin Eng closely, had been uncertain about a lot of what he had heard, but this sounded like the truth. He hoped the alternate forewoman would not stop there, and she didn't.

'Do you know who knocked you down?' Mahoney asked on her behalf.

'A detective. I learn his name later. Detective Pullone.' He said the name clearly, without accent.

'A grand juror wants to know – did you resist?'

'How resist? Face on floor, gun press in back of neck. How resist?'

The corrections officer, Number Three, wanted to know, 'If it's not your heroin, whose is it?'

'Don't know. Many visitors. People from association. Many young people.'

What had happened to the rest of the heroin, since the package was more than half-empty?

'Never see heroin. Not my heroin.'

Number Ten, Manny Klein, the accountant, asked about how they could pay all their bills without bank accounts. His accountant paid the bills, Eng said.

'Did your accountant keep money in the bank?' Eng supposed so, but that was the accountant's choice.

'What's the difference between having the accountant put the money in the bank and putting it in yourself?' Klein had Mahoney ask.

'Give money to accountant,' Eng said with exaggerated patience, 'then accountant responsible for money.'

David wasn't sure what to do. He had pushed hard to hear if Eng had an explanation for the ledgers, and Mahoney had covered the subject thoroughly. David had expected Manny Klein to focus on it too, but he had let it go by. Maybe, given Martin Eng's determination to plead loss of memory about most of it, there was no point in pushing further. And Eng had given an explanation, of sorts, for the list that corresponded to the money in the safe deposit boxes. Or had he?

David raised his hand and, when Mahoney came over, said, 'If the list of gifts for after he dies is in some personal code, who's going to know what it means when he's dead?'

'Good question,' Mahoney said, and asked it.

'Friends know.'

'How? How do they know?' Mahoney's own question now.

'I explain.'

'Did they write it down?'

'Only remember.'

'Does your wife know?'

'Some. Not all.'

'And you're relying on this method to distribute well over a million dollars?'

'Yes.'

Norman Thompson, uncharacteristically silent up to this point, raised his hand. His first question launched a heated exchange with the prosecutor, and Thompson didn't let go until Mahoney finally asked a question for him. 'A grand juror wants to know if your wife examined the shrine when she unpacked it.'

'Not examine. Only admire.'

'The grand juror wants to know if she opened the drawer in the bottom of the shrine at that time.'

'Don't know. Didn't see.'

For a moment, Mahoney did not speak. 'The gang,' Thompson prodded audibly.

'Thank you,' Mahoney snapped. To Martin Eng, he said, 'A grand juror wants to know if your association is affiliated with a youth gang?'

Eng stared, then turned to his lawyer. As they conferred Mahoney once again made sure it was reflected in the record.

'Association to help members in business. Place to meet, have social talk.'

'A grand juror wants to know if you ever have gang members visit your apartment.'

'Young people come to visit.'

Abruptly, before Mahoney had a chance to ask for more questions, Eng turned and whispered to his lawyer. Mahoney, surprise in his voice, noted it for the record.

The lawyer said, 'We'd like to amplify that answer.'

'Go ahead,' Mahoney said.

'Young people in America today different from old days,' Eng said slowly, his voice weaker than it had been. 'Many young people wish to become rich with little work. Also, much trouble between Guangdong people in Chinatown and new people from Fujian province. Young people who come here wish to protect families, protect people from same birthplace, protect businesses. Make groups for self-defense. I do not know all things young people do.'

'All right, Mr Eng.' Moving back to the front of the room, Mahoney asked if there were any more questions. When it was clear there weren't, he dismissed the witness. To the grand jury he said, 'I know this is a lot for one morning, so let's take another short break. When we come back I'll have Mrs Eng for you.'

134

# 10

Mrs Eng – Meiling Cheung – arrived in the grand jury room in a pale-green silk cheongsam that made Susan think of her mother, though her mother had been at least a head taller. From a distance it was hard to gauge exact heights, but Meiling Cheung did not look as tall as the five feet Detective Pullone had reported. Age had not stooped her. Tiny as she was, she walked with an erect elegance that spoke to Susan of a heritage of privilege.

With her came the lawyer who had accompanied her husband, and a slender Chinese woman of about fifty in a neat gray suit a shade darker than her hair.

'Mrs Eng will be speaking to us through an interpreter,' Mahoney informed them.

He started by having the interpreter sworn in, then asked questions to establish her qualifications. Her voice was mellow, her English cultivated and without accent. Born in Hong Kong, she had been educated there in missionary schools and then at college in northern California. She had gone back to Hong Kong, and to China in the seventies to work as an interpreter, then returned to the United States ten years later. She had translated in hundreds of legal proceedings, in both state and federal courts. For the record, Mahoney declared her a qualified interpreter.

With her help he put Meiling Cheung through a series of questions like the ones her husband had answered, establishing that she voluntarily waived the immunity usually enjoyed by grand jury witnesses. Then he had the foreman swear her in.

Susan was feeling even tenser than she had before Martin Eng's testimony. She leaned forward in her seat, not just to listen but to judge how well Mrs Eng's story would match her husband's. That's what the others will be listening for, she thought. She wanted to be as impartial in this case as she had tried to be in all the others, but she doubted she could. For all his hesitation and uncertainty, Martin Eng had captured her sympathy.

As her husband had, Meiling Cheung began with a statement. After what sounded to Susan like several sentences of lilting Cantonese the interpreter began to speak.

'I came from a good family in China. It was a very prosperous family and it was accorded much respect. Among my ancestors were officials in the court of the Manchu emperors.

'My marriage was arranged by my family. My husband was a good and kind man from the first day we were married. He worked hard and studied hard. He was a scholar. His family, too, was a good one. The two families together made a business that they shared.' The interpreter was alternating listening and speaking with a subtlety that made the narrative seem almost uninterrupted. Her cultured voice seemed to Susan to fit perfectly Meiling Cheung's smooth and subdued Chinese and her self-contained presence.

'The Eng family was good at business. My parents were more interested in politics. In the days leading up to the revolution against the last Manchu Emperor, my family helped many outspoken young men to avoid trouble with the authorities. My grandfather and my father were friendly with Sun Yatsen and other political intellectuals. When Dr Sun was forced to go to Shanghai, around the time I was born, my grandfather went there to visit him and Chiang Kai-shek, the Nationalist leader. Because of these activities and these connections, the family business had some protection from the many battles that were fought over who would be in control of Canton and the regions around it.

'When the war with Japan came, many people in my family were killed. The conquerors took away our business. My father and mother took our family to Hong Kong rather than stay to work for the Japanese. I was twelve years old.

'The war quickly followed us to Hong Kong. We had nowhere to go, so we went back to China. In the countryside not far from our ancestral home, the Japanese had not come. The region was under the control of a local warlord who was allied with Chiang Kai-shek's Nationalist Army. Life was hard. We worked to make a small living and to help the war effort.

'Then, when the war ended, we reclaimed what was ours. Again we had to work very hard to restore it to what it had been. My husband and I were married. Then the Kuomintang came . . . the Nationalists. The soldiers took our business and made us work for them. They did not care that my grandfather had been friendly with Dr Sun Yatsen and Generalissimo Chiang Kai-shek. My brothers refused to cooperate. They were tortured and killed.

'Once again we escaped to Hong Kong. There, we had friends from before. They helped us start again. My husband and I worked hard and had success. Our first two children were born. After the Communists drove the Nationalists from the mainland of China we stayed in Hong Kong, because we were afraid of the Communists.'

Her version of the Chinese civil war story was new to Susan. Hordes had fled the Communists after their victory in 1949, but to flee the sometime brutality of the Nationalists and not join the Communists was not so common, and to flee the Nationalists and actively fear the Communists was even less so. A testament to the variety and subtlety of Chinese politics, she thought.

The interpreter was saying, 'Then Mr Mao said all Chinese people should come back to China and use their skills to make the country stronger. He said that the property of manufacturers and other business people would not be confiscated. My husband and I missed our place of birth. We wanted our children to see the country of their ancestors. We returned. We brought money from Hong Kong and established our old business again where it had been left to ruin after the Nationalists were driven away.

'We began to have success, but after a short time many of the old ways of doing business were declared illegal. We had to pay fines for things we had done when they were legal. Some of our workers became party officials and we had to be afraid they would inform on us. Still, we were spared the worst because my husband and I had some friends among the officials.

'Then Mr Mao said that the State would take over all business. He

137

offered compensation for the factories taken by the State. It was very little, but we thought life would not be too bad because of our friends. Our two younger children were still quite small, and we did not wish to subject them to the hardship of fleeing. For a short time my husband was in prison. During that time we could not leave.

'Then, after he was let out, we heard about Mr Mao's newest program. It was called the Great Proletarian Cultural Revolution. Many kinds of people were to be singled out and punished. Certain officials. Intellectuals. People who had been in business. Capitalist Roaders was the name Mao Zedong applied to such people. We understood that if we stayed we would be in much danger. Our friends could not help. They, too, were in danger.

'We took what we could. We dug up money from the back yard to pay people to help us escape. Many nights we walked, until we came to the mouth of the Pearl River and we paid for a boat. It was a small boat, old and not seaworthy. It sank in a storm before we could reach safety. We swam to shore but one son and one daughter were drowned. We felt a great sadness and we felt that we could not stay in that place.

'As soon as we could arrange it we sailed away with the other son and the other daughter, making the sea salty with our tears, until we came to the Golden Mountain – the United States. We came to New York and settled in Chinatown, where we found other people from the same region of China. We worked hard. We sold all the gold and jewels we brought with us from China and Hong Kong, a few pieces at a time. We had good fortune in our business. Our remaining son and daughter grew up straight and strong. They speak English like Americans, and we are all American citizens. Now Mr Mao is dead. Our son and daughter have returned to Hong Kong where they are working hard.'

As Meiling Cheung approached the end of her statement, Susan felt some of her own tension draining away. The story she had just heard was recognizable as a version of the one Martin Eng had told, only smoother and clearer. How much of that was Meiling Cheung and how much was the translator, Susan wasn't sure.

Mahoney spent no time on the story the witness had told. His first question was, 'Mrs Eng, do you have a bank account?'

She cocked her head quizzically at the question.

'Do you mean a personal bank account?' the interpreter relayed.

'That's right.'

'I do not have a bank account,' was the answer.

'Not now?'

'Not now.'

'Any time in the past?'

She shook her head as she answered.

'I have never had a bank account,' the interpreter reported.

'How do you pay bills?'

'I pay cash.'

'You pay cash for all your bills?'

'Our accountant pays some of our bills.'

'Does your business have a checking account?'

'I do not have a business.'

'Your husband's business?'

'My husband has no business.'

'Did he have a business in the past?'

'He was manager of some garment factories.'

'You just said you had good fortune in business in the United States. What business was that?'

'The garment factories.'

'To your knowledge did the garment factories have a checking account?'

'I don't know for certain. I believe they may have.'

'So you do believe in banks.'

'Banks are not necessary for a person. Only for a business.'

Mahoney came to the front of the room. 'Mrs Eng, have you seen these books before?' He put the ledgers on the witness table.

'I have seen them.'

'Do you know what they are?'

'My husband writes in them.'

'Can you read them?'

'They belong to my husband.'

'Yes, but can you read them? Would you open the top one, please, and see what it says.'

With a delicate gesture filled with reluctance she pulled the books

139

closer and opened the one on top. After a moment she looked up and spoke.

'This one says the names of animals,' the interpreter relayed.

Gently, Mahoney directed her to the last pages on which there were entries and asked if she recognized what was there and if it had any meaning that she knew of besides the literal meaning of the Chinese characters.

Susan had the impression that he was taking special care not to press her too hard and not to upset her, while at the same time keeping her firmly in the status of criminal defendant. Her age and fragility, and her inherent dignity, made it hard work for him, and it did not take long to become clear that on this subject he would elicit nothing more from her than increasing bewilderment.

Rather than continue, or start a new subject, he dismissed the witness for the day at a few minutes before one o'clock. As she and her lawyer left the grand jury room, relief and exhaustion were clear in Mahoney's face.

'The old man has balls, I'll give him that,' Mahoney told Estrada. 'And he was plausible, in a strange sort of way, as long as he stuck to his war stories. Even so, I gave him as much rope as I could, because every time he got to the details that mattered his story would get very foggy.'

'What did he say about resisting arrest?'

'He claims Pullone broke the door down, knocked him flat and held a gun to his head. Trashed the place and terrified his wife.'

'What do you think?'

'It makes as much sense as Pullone's version.'

'And the wife?'

'Quite a lady. It was like – *a million dollars? We made and lost a million dollars more times than I can count. We always keep that much money lying around, just in case we have to flee from the Communists.* I did what I could to bring it into the here and now, but I don't know . . .'

'How do you think the grand jury's taking it, so far?'

'One thing worries me. These really are old folks, and it doesn't look like they're doing that well in jail. They've got too much pride to milk it, thank heaven, but it's there and I can't tell how much the grand jurors are making of it.

'And this is a hard bunch to read, anyway. Number Eleven, the one who was such a pain in the ass, turned around and asked a terrific question for the home team.' Mahoney told Estrada about Eng's claim that the ledger was in part an informal will, in code. 'The guy really nailed him on that. He goes, if it's a secret code, who'll be able to read it when you're dead? Pretty sharp – I missed it completely.'

'And we know what a high standard that sets.'

'You know,' Mahoney reflected, 'long as it's been since I put a case into a grand jury, I forgot that standing in the back you can't really see a lot of their faces. It throws me off not being able to read the effect I'm having.'

'Never bothered me. I just always take it for granted I'm putting them to sleep.'

'Some of these, I'd rather they *were* asleep.'

'Yeah, there's that, too.'

'You know a defense lawyer named Ellen Hyams?' Mahoney asked.

Estrada took a moment with it. 'Nope, can't say as I do.'

'She took over from the guy they started with. Horgan doesn't know her either. Nice-looking, mid-thirties. Law review and a clerkship in the Southern District, then four years at the Department of Justice. I checked the firm she's with now, it's based in Washington, a couple of former Congress people on the roster, and a former deputy AG. Definitely heavy hitters. She probably made the connection while she was at Justice and then they decided to send her up here where she did her clerkship and knows the judges.'

'The *federal* judges.'

'Right.'

'Doesn't all that federal experience make her kind of an odd choice for a drug case in state court?' Estrada said.

'My thought, exactly. Rosen, the first guy, made more sense. Asian drug cases in state court is what he does.'

'Maybe she's good at fighting forfeiture.'

'Maybe. But her major experience would still be in the federal system.'

'Suppose somebody forgot to explain to her clients that the federal courts and the state courts aren't the same,' Estrada speculated. 'That they enforce different laws and use different procedures, little things like that.'

'Wouldn't you assume she'd tell them that herself, before she took the case?' Mahoney asked.

'You never know.'

'She'd have to.'

'And if she did, they hired her anyway.'

'That's what it looks like.'

Instead of going straight to the office from the grand jury, Susan let the car go and wandered through Chinatown. Watching the Engs testify for three hours had affected her more than she could have predicted.

As she walked the crowded streets she remembered her first childhood trips to Chinatown, a place her father shunned and didn't like to have his family visit.

Her mother had had a friend, close as a sister. The two had grown up together in China; separated by the Japanese war and out of touch for years, they had become friends again in America. It was a friendship Susan's father had not approved of, and trips to Chinatown to see Ann Lum had been a rare and much anticipated treat.

Then, during Susan's teenage years – perhaps as a counter to the Chinatown trips – her father had relaxed about Aunty Ann. She had become a regular at large family celebrations and had even been allowed to come to the Chans's house.

After Susan's parents disappeared, Aunty Ann was a constant presence, inviting Susan to tea-food brunches at Chinatown restaurants, sending notes, calling at odd hours. They did not have much to say to each other, but Aunty Ann clearly meant only to be comforting, and Susan suspected that she was, by this elaborate caring for the bereaved daughter, working off some debt she felt to Susan's vanished mother.

As time passed, Susan became convinced that the visits and ministrations were matters of duty and caused Aunty Ann considerable pain, so she had allowed, even encouraged, her mother's old friend to drift away. And Susan's brother Sandy had widened the rift by accusing

142

Ann Lum of having been instrumental in their parents' decision to make the trip to China from which they had never returned. Susan and Ann Lum had not seen each other in almost a decade and had not so much as spoken in more than five years.

When the heat and smells and crowds of Mott Street and Pell and Bayard began to be too much, Susan found a cab and went home. Out of curiosity she opened the antique roll-top desk she used for correspondence and bill paying to see if any of her old address books had a listing for Ann Lum. She found it in the oldest of them, from the beginning of her marriage.

She stared at the address and phone number. Oddly, her thoughts were not of her own childhood but of Meiling Cheung and Martin Eng. They were appealing people, and their stories bore out what Mrs Liu had said, but Susan was left feeling frustrated. Martin Eng's vagueness had been disquieting, if understandable – he was almost eighty and under enormous strain. In jail, probably living in circumstances that couldn't help his state of mind, much less his health.

Still, Susan wanted to know more. It occurred to her that Aunty Ann would be a good source. She'd always been social, a great mahjong player, a collector of acquaintances and casual friends. If only it hadn't been so long since they'd talked.

Late Friday afternoon, David's sister Alice called to say that she and her two children were at the airport.

'We're taking the bus into town. We'll be there in a couple of hours.'

'How long are you staying?' he asked but, Alice-like, she'd already hung up.

It was only the second time she had descended on him without notice; the other time she had come alone. Since the apartment was technically hers he didn't suppose he had much right to complain. He straightened away the worst of his bachelor mess, glad that the cleaning woman had been there only two days before.

When they arrived Alice announced that she was going to the beach for the weekend, leaving the twins behind with their Uncle David.

'I know it's last minute, but I haven't been to the Hamptons in for ever, I mean even long before we left New York, and there's a party at this old friend's house and there's going to be a major commercial director there who's about to make his first feature.' It was the first time in years that Alice had alluded to any hope of resuming her acting career.

'Is that why you came?'

'Somebody had these tickets they couldn't use, and I figured it had been too long since Jess and Zack were here anyway, not since Daddy died, and that wasn't very pleasant . . .'

It's her life, David reminded himself, but though he kept silent he could not help thinking that after all this time any notion that she might still suceed as an actress could only be a delusion.

'I only knew yesterday we could do it for sure,' she told him. 'And I promise I'll be back early Sunday, and then I'm taking the monsters to see something new, maybe up to Vermont or someplace, before we have to fly out again.'

He didn't tell her not to hurry back to get them, though he was tempted to. He had never really been comfortable with his sister, but right from the beginning he'd loved spending time with Zack and Jessica. Now that he was almost never with them, they were a source of wonder and discovery for him when he was. In the year or so since he'd seen them they'd grown amazingly. At just past twelve, each of them seemed to cram both an oversize child and a miniature adult into the same skinny, ravenous, constantly moving frame.

At the end of the afternoon, Susan was still debating whether to call Ann Lum, and what to say if she did.

There was a right way to do it, but it was all tied up in the part of her heritage that her American self had always had the least patience for: the social protocols, the circumlocutory phrases, the exaggerated politeness. They were forms of behavior Susan had breathed in with the air when she was growing up, unaware that they belonged to any particular culture.

Like the problem she was having now. A person simply *knew* that it was impolite to ask for anything directly, and bad luck besides. It was a precept that was out of synch with the America of assertiveness training into which Susan had emerged from her sheltered high school, and it was hardly calculated to serve her in the public relations business. Even so, she followed it almost by instinct, especially when she was dealing with Chinese people she knew from her childhood.

She went into the kitchen for a glass of water, telling herself she was being silly not just to pick up the phone. Aunty Ann would surely have moved by now, and if she was still there Susan would ask after her health and tell her some anecdotes about Richard. No, maybe not Richard – she'd always been sure Aunty Ann disapproved of him. The children, then. Lara was going off to college; her brother, on the verge of his last collegiate year now and already Phi Beta Kappa, was captain of the college squash team. As if Aunty Ann were likely to have the faintest idea what *squash* might be.

Ann Lum answered on the first ring and seemed not at all surprised to be hearing from Susan.

'I thought you might have moved,' Susan told her.

'Not this old lady.'

'Not so old.'

'Sixty-nine. Senior citizen.' Aunty Ann's English had always been spare, though she did not have much accent. Her apparently bland conversation was often full of irony. 'How is the great surgeon?'

'The same.' She really *didn't* approve. 'Greater than ever, I suppose. He's just finished developing a new procedure they're all excited about at the hospital. I couldn't begin to explain it.'

'These old ears aren't made for such things. How are your children?'

'Good. Fine.' Talking about them, Susan made sure to emphasize Charles – the all-important son.

Aunty Ann seemed pleased to hear Susan's stories, though Susan knew she had to be waiting to hear the real reason for the call.

'Aunty Ann, I have a question for you,' Susan said into an awkward silence. Too straight-ahead, but it would have to do.

'I'm always happy to be useful.'

'Do you still keep up with the juicy stories in Chinatown and read all the Chinese newspapers?' There were a half-dozen or more of them, dailies and weeklies.

'I try to fit them in, between parties.'

145

Susan smiled. 'Have you read anything recently about some people named Eng, Martin and Meiling Eng? Her Chinese name is Cheung Meiling. They were arrested for being involved in importing heroin from Hong Kong. There was a lot of money involved.'

'Ay! I hear these stories every day, now. The new business – laundering money. In my day, *shirts* were good enough. What do you want with people who do such things?'

A good question, Susan thought. 'It's a long story,' she said. 'I just wanted to know what kind of people they are. What their background is. I thought you might have heard something, or know someone who knows them. I know how popular you've always been . . . I'm sorry if I bothered you.'

'To help an old friend's precious daughter is not a bother. Maybe I do know something about these people. You have to give me time to think. My mind runs slower now than when your mother and I were girls in China.'

Susan waited through the silence.

'Here is an idea,' Aunty Ann said. 'Tomorrow is Saturday. You can meet me for tea and something to eat. There is a new restaurant we can try.'

'Oh, Aunty Ann, that's so nice of you. I wish I could.' She had so much to catch up on, at work and at home, and Saturday afternoon was one of Richard's chamber music concerts . . . She heard a small sound of disappointment on the other end, barely audible.

'Oh, I'm being silly,' she said quickly. 'Of course I can come. Saturday is fine. I'll be so pleased to see you again.'

'A pleasure for both of us. One o'clock is a good time.'

146

# 11

'How about we go exploring in Chinatown?' David suggested to Zack and Jessica on Saturday morning. The twins were both itching to be out of the apartment; they agreed almost before he named their destination.

They seemed amazed by the foreignness of it, the streets so narrow and dense with people it was sometimes hard to put one foot in front of the other. And accustomed as they were to manicured fruit-and-vegetable stalls near the Upper West Side apartment, the open-air displays here were not broccoli and grapefruit. Alien-looking roots and sprouts and sculptural green-and-white cabbages were piled either on pushcarts or virtually on the sidewalk, next to mounds of fish and shellfish – some recently dead, some still living. Even on a mild summer day the odors were arresting.

For a while, wandering the streets staring at the store windows and the people was diversion enough. As the novelty diminished, so did the kids' enthusiasm. Zack spied a video-game arcade and headed straight for it.

'I bet they have some cool games, Mighty Kung Fu Masters or something.'

David followed, with Jessica at his side; at the last minute some internal alarm told him this might not be a good idea. He put his hand on Zack's shoulder. 'Wait a minute, Zack. I'm not so sure about this.'

Zack rounded on him. 'What? What aren't you sure about?'

'About going in there. I don't think we should.'

'Yes, we should. Look, you can see, it's like, you know, it's a cool place.'

147

'There's a lot of crime down here.'

'It's only an arcade.'

'It's *their* arcade.' Saying it, David wondered if he would have made a comment like that anywhere else, and why he felt such a strong sense of not belonging here. 'There are some things that are meant for tourists and some that are part of the community. I think we have to respect that.'

'Then why did you bring us down here, if you won't let us explore like you said?'

The door of the arcade opened and a trio of teenage boys came out. They wore white T-shirts, black jeans and black boots, and their gait was a combination of strut and saunter; from behind dark, round-lensed sunglasses they glared straight ahead. Zack needed no urging to back out of their way.

'Okay,' Zack said, watching them cross the street. 'We don't have to go in there if you don't want.'

They set off down the street, past bakeries whose steamy windows were stacked high with unfamiliar-looking buns, and meat shops displaying whole glazed ducks and geese, hanging by their necks.

'Look!' Jessie was pointing. 'A museum. That might be fun.'

On the street corner they were approaching was an old building of red stone, mostly obscured by scaffolding. A sign like a church annunciator board listed the occupants: Chinatown History Museum in the largest letters, then, smaller, the names of other organizations, from arts groups to labor councils.

'It's in here somewhere.' The only door David saw gave every appearance of being impregnable.

'Over here,' Jessie called.

At the other end of the building she'd found an open door and was staring in. 'Come on.'

Beyond the doors was a room that might have been a school gym or cafeteria, high-ceilinged and almost as big as the whole ground floor of the building. It was filled with long tables, and the tables were filled with elderly Chinese people, men and women. On each table were arrays of domino-like tiles, white or green. The players sat grouped, each with a lined-up row of tiles shielded from the other players like a grand-slam bridge hand or a rack of choice word-game pieces. In the center of each group a pond of tiles lay on the table helter-skelter, like the ante in a casual poker game. Pervading it all was a din of conversation and the rapid-fire clack of tiles being slapped down on tables, one at a time in their hundreds all around the room.

'What are they doing?' Jessie wanted to know.

'I don't know for sure,' David said. 'Playing mahjong, I think.'

'What's mahjong?'

David waved a hand. 'This.'

'Some museum,' Zack could not resist saying. 'I bet this is another place that isn't for tourists.'

'You're right,' David agreed. 'There must a different way in.'

'Look, another door,' Jessie said, and began making her way along the front of the teeming room. Zack hurried after her, and David had no choice but to follow, making himself narrow to pass between the chairs of the players and the wall.

The door led to a wide stairway with an ornate wrought-iron railing. One flight up was a bright corridor. There were colorful posters for a Chinese dance troupe and for the exhibit at the history museum; neither they nor the gleaming wood floors diminished the indelible schoolness of the building. Except for details of size and layout it could have been David's own upstate grade school.

The museum itself was easy to miss, with an office door on one side of the hall and a door leading to the exhibits across from it. The locked door to the exhibits bore a sign telling visitors to stop at the office. The woman at the desk looked up at David when he stepped in, studied him for a moment, and covered her mouth to smile.

'Hello, Mr David.'

It was grand juror Number Six.

'Very nice to see you.' She came out from behind the desk. 'You come learn about Chinatown?'

'Yes, I did. It's nice to see you, too – I had no idea you worked here. I brought my niece and nephew to have lunch and walk around. We saw a sign for the museum . . .'

As he spoke she took a key from a hook by the door and walked with him into the corridor.

'This is Jessie and Zack. Kids, this is, um, I'm sorry, I don't think I know your name.'

'Big secret.' She hid another smile behind her hand. 'My name Mrs Liu. Welcome to museum.'

She bustled across the hall and let them in. 'Special tour, say thank you for help to bring Mr, Mrs Eng to grand jury.'

The exhibits in the three small rooms showed Chinatown in an earlier day. Built into the wall in one corner were file cabinets. 'Old newspapers, magazines, photos,' Mrs Liu explained. 'Come look here.'

Just past the file cabinets was a tiny room, not much more than three feet by eight, barely big enough to contain a short, narrow bed, a trunk, a small table and lamp, and a single chair. On the table was a steel-nib pen, an inkwell and some paper.

'This old Chinatown bachelor room. Old days, United States law say only China man, no China woman come to country. Man come here, work, wife in China. This room same from then, same furniture, one man live. You look,' she instructed them. 'Very interesting. Have question – come to office, I answer.'

She was right, it was all very interesting. David felt that he was, a step at a time, being led into a world he'd had no idea existed. First the Engs, now this. Thinking of the Engs brought a picture of Susan Linwood to his mind: hard to imagine her as a part or a product of the immigrant struggle depicted here.

Her image stayed with him as he studied the exhibits and then started to browse through the file drawers. He looked up to find Jessica standing by the open file drawer.

'Hello, Uncle David, you there?'

'Am I missing something?'

'This sucks, Uncle David. Not really, it's very educational, but we've had enough, okay?'

'Okay.' He put the folder back and closed the drawer. 'Let's go. Maybe there's something fun to eat.'

'I have a Chinese friend at school,' Jessie announced. 'She says sometimes her grandma cooks eels and sea slugs.'

'Yuck,' Zack said. 'Let's get some pizza.'

On the way out David stopped by the office, where he'd noticed a shelf of books for sale. He bought two recent books on Chinatown, one by a reporter and one by a college professor.

'Have good time?' Mrs Liu asked him.

'Yes, very,' David assured her.

'Good, good.' She nodded vigorously. 'Read book, come back, visit.' She handed him a brochure. 'Museum hours. Also, membership form.' Smiling. 'Join museum, make contribution.'

The restaurant where Susan met Ann Lum was one of the cavernous new ones people called Hong Kong style. At the entrance a young woman in a neat gray uniform blazer greeted them and directed them up a long escalator, calling ahead by walkie-talkie to another young woman in a matching blazer who led them endlessly through the restaurant. As they walked, Aunty Ann kept up a stream of rapid-fire Cantonese, to which the hostess replied with occasional polite grunts.

She led them past the round tables for six or eight that filled the huge room. Several of them had free chairs, and at each Susan expected the hostess to stop and seat them – with total strangers, as was the custom. Finally, at the side of the room, not far from one of the red-lined, private-banquet alcoves, the hostess offered them one of the few tables for four.

'How did you manage this?' Susan asked Aunty Ann. 'What did you say?'

'I told her you have bad trouble in your marriage and I did not want you to be shamed by talking about it in front of strangers.'

Ann Lum knew more about the Engs than she had let on in their phone conversation. Her impression of them corroborated both what Mrs Liu had said and their testimony in the grand jury. Martin Eng was indeed the president of a Chinatown benevolent association and he had been a successful garment manufacturer. He and his wife both came from good families in China and had suffered under both the Nationalists and the Communists. They had two children who were in Hong Kong or China now, and they might have had others who had been lost before the Engs reached America. And more: Martin Eng had been embroiled in some difficulty at the benevolent association where he had previously been a leading member. Election difficulty, Aunty Ann thought. She did not know the details but she understood it had involved some kind of treachery.

'I'm impressed that you know so much about them,' Susan said.

Aunty Ann busied herself with a dumpling before she responded.

'Do you remember that postcard from your mother in China? After . . . after the accident? It came from Shuntak.'

'Yes, I remember.' The card had been like a letter from a ghost, arriving months after the earthquake, even after the long-delayed message of condolence from Beijing.

'Shuntak was the hometown of your mother's family.'

'Yes, I remember that, too, now.' And something about the name, about the way it sounded in the older woman's mouth, was striking a chord for Susan, although she didn't yet know what or why.

'Your mother and I were friends in school there.'

It was an old story, how the two women, close friends in school, had been separated by the Japanese war and the civil war that followed it – one going to live in Hong Kong, the other in Singapore – and had rediscovered each other in New York.

'Shuntak is part of a region called Sam Yap. Three Districts. Shuntak, Namhoi, Panyu.'

Now Susan knew where she'd heard someone say Shuntak recently, though when Martin Eng had said it, sitting at the witness table in front of the grand jury, she hadn't recognized the name for what it was.

'Long ago I was a member of the old Sam Yap Association,' Aunty Ann continued. 'More than one time, I met Mr Eng there.'

'Did you know him well?'

'No. Met him, only.'

'Do you belong to the new association?'

'No. I joined a different association. A family-name association. Good thing, too. People join associations to get services, but also for feeling safe. Safety in numbers. How safe do you feel if the officers are using treachery to hold power?'

'Not very, I guess,' Susan said.

Aunty Ann waved down another of the young women wheeling stainless-steel carts around the restaurant. Aunty Ann pointed at three of the small bamboo steamers crowding the cart. The waitress put them on the table with her long serving chopsticks, then marked the bill with the cylindrical stamp she wore on a cord around her neck and rolled her cart away.

152

'The Chan Huiling I knew years ago was not so interested in people accused of crimes.'

'It's a new hobby.' Susan pretended not to have noticed Aunty Ann's pointed use of her Chinese name.

The older woman looked at her closely. 'Do you know Martin Eng and Milly Cheung?'

'Milly?' Susan asked, smiling. 'Is that what she's called? Milly, for Meiling?'

'I think that must be why.'

'It's cute.' People's English and Chinese names did not typically match that way. Susan's own Chinese name sounded not at all like Susan. Huiling meant something like bright and quick, and except for family occasions when she was a little girl she hadn't used it since she'd come to the United States.

'I've never met them,' Susan said.

'Then did you read about them in the American news?' Aunty Ann fished. 'I saw it only in Chinatown papers, myself.'

'I'm not supposed to say how I know about them,' Susan told her. 'I could get in trouble if I did. All I can say is I'm worried about whether it's right that they're being accused of this crime. If Martin Eng was the victim of some kind of treachery, I'd really like to hear more about it.'

'I do not know the whole story – it was after my time there.'

Susan wanted to press for more, to ask if there might be people who would remember. She had to struggle to keep her eagerness from overwhelming the need to be circumspect.

Aunty Ann Lum picked a translucent shrimp dumpling from one of the steamers with her chopsticks. She chewed it carefully and sipped sweetened tea.

'Perhaps I know someone to ask about this. I can talk to him, to ask if he will see you.'

'Will you?' Susan felt like a kid excited by a gift from a grownup. 'Thank you.'

Then she thought about the timing. Chances were, Meiling Cheung would be back in the grand jury Monday, and they would almost certainly deliberate and vote that same day. Improper as all this poking around probably was, if she was going to do it at all she ought to make sure it would be in time to mean something.

'Aunty Ann, I don't mean to seem ungrateful, but is there any way for me to see him today or tomorrow?' She did not have to say it was important to her: the mere fact that she was asking so directly established that, just as it established her rudeness.

Aunty Ann clucked her tongue. 'I am not sure I can speak to him, myself, by then.' She looked hard at Susan. 'For you, I will try my best.'

# 12

When Mahoney came back with Meiling Cheung on Monday morning, he brought a different interpreter: a stocky, round-faced Chinese woman in a straight-skirted navy suit a good two sizes too small for her. By contrast, Susan noticed that Meiling Cheung's cheongsam – pale buttercup yellow this time – looked slightly large, as if she'd lost weight since she had it fitted. As, come to think of it, had the one she wore on Friday.

Mahoney took his time qualifying the new interpreter. Like the earlier one, she was from Hong Kong, but she had stayed there through college before coming to the U.S. Her accent was thick, her credentials less impressive than those of the woman who had preceded her, though she, too, had years of experience as a court interpreter. The first chore she performed for them was to get Mrs Eng's reaffirmation that she had voluntarily waived the immunity accorded witnesses in New York grand juries.

'Now, Mrs Eng,' Mahoney began, 'did you ever know your husband to gamble?'

Meiling Cheung listened to the new interpreter's coarse rumble of Cantonese and then whispered to her lawyer.

'Could you try to ask that more specifically?' the lawyer requested.

'Sure. Mrs Eng, does your husband play mahjong or fan tan? Does he play cards, or roulette?'

'Not play mahjong,' the interpreter said, her delivery as rough as her voice. Susan could not believe both she and the previous woman did the same job.

'Fan tan?' Mahoney asked.

The witness shook her head.

'You'll have to answer aloud please.'

The interpreter told her. She answered.

'Not play,' the interpreter said.

'What about horse racing?'

'Not play,' came the answer.

'Did he ever play any of those games in the past?'

The witness spoke for a moment, her fluid voice a contrast to the harshness of the interpreter's.

'Yes.' The one sharp word was all that the interpreter had made of the answer.

'Do you know if he won or lost?'

For all the care Mahoney had been taking to avoid seeming to browbeat the delicate lady in the witness chair, Susan thought she heard a touch of impatience in his voice. The odd thing was that with this new, coarse and inept interpreter Meiling Cheung herself somehow seemed less fragile.

Again, her answer was long and complicated.

'Not tell results,' said the interpreter. 'Sometimes make offerings to thank gods for good fortune.'

'Offerings to the gods?' Mahoney's tone made Susan twist around to glance at him. She imagined she could see a gleam in his eye as he asked, 'Does he do that often?'

'Sometimes.' For once, the interpreter's curt answer echoed the tone of the witness's.

'Have you seen him do that?'

'Sometimes.'

'Can you describe that for us?'

Meiling Cheung hesitated and then answered fully, her voice returned to its melodious rise and fall.

'Go to shrine, burn incense,' the translator said.

'Is the shrine in your apartment?' Hot on the trail of an inconsistency.

'No.'

'Where is it?' Mahoney's tone had not changed but Susan imagined she could hear disappointment in it.

'In association building,' the interpreter said.

'Is there a shrine in your apartment?'

156

'Now?' the interpreter relayed.

'Yes, now.'

'No.'

'What about two weeks ago?'

'Two weeks ago, shrine in bedroom.'

'How long did you have that shrine?'

'Not long.'

'Where did you get it?'

'Gift. From China.'

'Whose shrine was it?'

Meiling Cheung gave another long and, to Susan, seemingly careful answer. 'Household shrine,' said the interpreter. 'Place to make offering to household gods.'

'You said your husband used to gamble,' Mahoney said, apparently deciding he'd had enough of the shrines. 'Do you know what happened to the money he won?'

'Some of it spent, some put away.'

'Where did you put it away?'

'In safe, in house, and also husband had other places.'

'What other places?'

'Sometimes in bank vault.'

'Safe deposit boxes?'

'Yes.'

'Did he ever invest money?'

'Invest in factory here, like in China.'

'The same garment factories he managed?'

'Yes. Same.'

'Can you describe the jewelry you took out of China?'

That was something Mrs Eng was willing to do, a piece at a time, in considerable detail. Susan thought some of the pieces sounded splendid, despite the clumsiness of the translation. Then, describing a gold brooch in the shape of a dragon inlaid with tiny jade scales and rubies for eyes, she faltered. Susan thought she might be on the verge of tears. Controlling herself, she spoke to the interpreter.

'I wish to apologize,' the interpreter told them for her. 'This jewel in family many generations, pass from mother to daughter, mother to daughter. Very precious to my own mother. I feel . . . sadness, I have no words for this. Sadness because I cannot enjoy to see firstborn daughter wear this jewel.'

Mahoney changed the subject in a hurry. 'Do you know what was in the safe deposit boxes that were in your and your husband's names?'

'No,' came the interpreter's abrupt answer before Mrs Eng had quite finished speaking.

'But the boxes were in your name, too: Meiling Cheung –' he mangled the pronunciation only mildly – 'that's the name you gave here today.'

'Yes.'

'And you visited the boxes yourself.'

'Yes.'

'Then how is it you don't know what was in them.'

'Money and gold jewelry.'

'But you said you didn't know.'

'Only not know how much.'

Again the interpreter's answer was sharp, almost impatient, though Susan didn't think the actual response had been anything like that. Yet somehow the interpreter's demeanor continued to impose itself on the witness. Susan, with her long-buried Hong Kong Cantonese, felt she had at least a faint idea of how Meiling Cheung actually sounded. She doubted the others could hear the nuances in the same way. She wondered why the defense lawyer was not upset.

After two more questions about the safe deposit boxes, she no longer had to wonder.

'Mr Mahoney,' the lawyer interjected, 'I'm concerned about this translator.'

'Counsellor, I shouldn't have to remind you that you're not here to participate in these proceedings in any way except consulting directly with your client,' Mahoney scolded. Then he said, 'In any case, I'm done.' He sounded relieved to be saying it, even more relieved than he had looked at the end of the previous day's testimony. 'The other interpreter was scheduled for a case in federal court, so I could only get her for one day.'

'The interpreters work half-hour shifts over there,' the lawyer said. 'If I can get her to come over on her break, will you use her for the grand jury's questions?'

'You're welcome to try,' Mahoney said, and: 'I see by the time that we ought to be taking a break about now, ladies and gents. Let's all be back in fifteen minutes so we can have as much time as we need.'

'What did anybody think of her, anyway?' Oswaldo Perez asked, out in the corridor.

'That was some story she told Friday,' Manny Klein said. 'A lot like the one her husband told, too.'

'Not much to do with the matter at hand,' Kelly observed. 'It's a wonder the man let her go on like that.'

'Once she was done he never came back to it,' David pointed out.

'True enough.'

'You think she's a dope smuggler?' Perez wanted to know.

'I think she's an elegant lady who's led a remarkable life that I wish I could hear more about,' Manny Klein offered. 'As for whether she's a dope smuggler, the jury's still out, as they say.' The accountant grinned at his own joke. 'Right now this juror is going to get a cup of coffee if he can get near the machine, and then he's off to the men's room before we have to sit down for another however long.'

Susan saw the four men standing together and hesitated before approaching them. She needed advice but she didn't want to advertise what she was doing to the whole world, just in case it was a worse transgression than she thought.

The white-haired accountant left the group, then David did. She intercepted him.

'Do you have a minute to talk?'

'Sure.'

She walked along the corridor to the stairwell he had shown her the first time they spoke: the way to the courthouse telephones. On the landing halfway down to the eighth floor she stopped and told him about her tea brunch with Ann Lum, leaving out the part about her being a member of the old Sam Yap Association when Martin Eng was, too.

'She called yesterday to tell me that the man she had in mind was out of town – the one who could tell me about Martin Eng and the

159

election treachery. I won't be able to see him for a week. I don't know what to do.'

'I don't see what you *can* do,' he said. 'We're only in session till next Monday.'

'Isn't there something in our little booklet about extending our term?'

'If there is I'll bet you'd need at least a majority of these folks to agree, and I don't see your convincing them. It was hard enough to get them to listen to the Engs. And you've already said you don't want to annoy them too much or they'll take it out on the very people you're trying to help.'

Susan listened with a growing sense of futility. He was only affirming her own thoughts. 'And I don't even know what this man is going to say.'

'Not to mention the question of whether you should be doing your own investigation at all.'

'I guess I don't think of it as an investigation, but I can see that you're right.' She sighed. 'I suppose I knew this was the answer all along. It's so frustrating, though, to think there's another part of the story we're not hearing.'

'But it may not be part of *this* story,' he reassured. 'And, as you say, you don't even know which way it cuts.' He smiled at her – a warm smile, his white teeth seeming whiter in the frame of red-brown beard and moustache. 'I have the feeling we'll have enough to do as it is, figuring out the evidence we have.'

Mahoney gave them five minutes more than the fifteen he'd offered before he reappeared with Meiling Cheung, her lawyer and the original interpreter. David thought the defense lawyer looked smug about that, though she seemed to be trying to hide it.

Mahoney reminded the witness and the interpreter that they were both still sworn in. 'And do you reaffirm that after consulting with your attorney you have voluntarily waived immunity in testifying before this grand jury?' he asked Meiling Cheung.

'I so affirm,' the interpreter said for her.

'All right. Does any of you have a question?'

Several of the jurors raised their hands. David kept his on the arms of his seat, waiting to see what the others would ask.

Mahoney went first to Number One, the car salesman.

'A grand juror would like to know if you recognize some names.' When the interpreter had conveyed that much, Mahoney read awkwardly from a list the car salesman had handed him. It took David a moment to realize that it had to be the list of names Martin Eng had given them when he deciphered his notebook code. Number One must have written them down at the time – note-taking being another of the things a New York grand juror could do that a trial juror couldn't.

Number One's list of names produced no immediate response. Mrs Eng whispered to her lawyer, who whispered back. Interesting, David thought: Mrs Eng must speak at least a little English after all, since there'd been no sign that the lawyer spoke Cantonese and this was at least the second time they'd consulted directly.

The brief conference, duly noted by Mahoney for the record, produced an exchange between Mrs Eng and the interpreter.

'I do not recognize the words you spoke as being names,' the interpreter reported for the witness. 'Perhaps if the interpreter were to try . . .'

Mahoney handed her the list. She converted it to Cantonese names and Mrs Eng responded to many of them: two were cousins of her husband's, three were people who had worked for him running the garment factories. Two more were officials of his association. One was the head of a day-care center she said was of great importance to him. The others she did not recognize.

Mahoney said, 'A grand juror wants to know if your husband spoke to you about giving any part of his money to these men when he died.'

Before she could answer, the lawyer touched her arm and whispered in her ear. She listened and then spoke a few careful words.

'I assert my marital privilege,' the interpreter said.

Mahoney was silent a moment before he said, 'Ladies and gentlemen, as your legal adviser, I should explain that when a witness testifies in a grand jury, with or without immunity, certain testimonial privileges remain. Among these is the privileged nature of confidential communications between the members of a marriage. Without commenting on the appropriateness of this assertion of privilege, one way or the other, I'm going to withdraw the question.'

He listened to another question from Number One and said, 'A grand juror wants to know if you can tell which of the notations in the book in front of you represents each of the men you just identified.'

This resulted in another consultation between Meiling Cheung and her lawyer before she answered.

'I wish to apologize,' the interpreter said for her. 'I recognize the importance of this occasion and I wish to answer all questions accurately. These concerns have interfered with my memory. I hope that the members of the grand jury will understand that this would not prevent me from carrying out any responsibilities my husband has entrusted to me.'

This clearly did not satisfy the car salesman. Though he was sitting in front of David, his words to Mahoney were audible only as a muted stream of indignant sound. The prosecutor, standing so he was between Number One and the witness table, his back to the witness, was facing David when he answered.

'I understand how you feel, but it's not going to help to bully her. Besides, I think you've made your point.'

Number One tried another question on Mahoney, who made a sour face when he heard it. 'You sure?'

The answer must have been yes, because Mahoney asked the question: 'How do the men you just identified help you in your heroin business?'

The response was completely unexpected. Leaning forward at the witness table, Meiling Cheung fired a volley of agitated words at the car salesman. Then she subsided, shaking, and stared at the table top.

The interpreter's delivery was as calm and courtly as ever: 'Why do you ask about heroin? I know nothing about heroin. Why do you wish to ruin my life and cause impoverishment and shame to my family?'

Mahoney gave the car salesman a look that said clearly: I told you so.

Mrs Eng's outburst cooled everyone down. The grand jurors had no more questions for her.

'I have the other witness you asked for,' Mahoney told them when Mrs Eng was gone. He went to the door and came back with a short, bald man in a rumpled navy-blue suit flecked with what looked like

162

cigarette ash. His name was Arthur Andrews and he was a police fingerprint analyst. Mahoney established that among his areas of expertise was finding and preserving fingerprints.

Mahoney first established that Detective Pullone had sent him an evidence bag containing a package of white powder, and that the evidence bag was identified by the voucher numbers corresponding to the package Pullone had found in the Eng apartment.

'Did you examine the package?'

'Yes.'

'Did you find any usable fingerprints?'

'No, I did not.'

'Is that packaging the sort of surface on which you might expect to find usable fingerprints?'

'That's possible, yes.'

'Was there anything about the package you examined that would allow you to form an opinion, with a reasonable degree of professional certainty, as to why there were no usable fingerprints on the package?'

'Not really, no. Anything I said about that would be pure speculation.'

'Thank you. Any questions from the jury?'

Kelly had one.

'A grand juror wants to know if you found any fragmentary prints, anything that was too small or broken or smudged to be usable?'

'No. There was nothing. The package was clean.'

Kelly had a second question: didn't that mean that the package had been wiped to eliminate fingerprints?

'I'd say it was wiped or washed or cleaned in some way, at some point. But whether that was to remove fingerprints or for some other reason, I can't begin to guess. Maybe it was dusty, or something spilled on it. There's lots of reasons why people wipe things off.'

There were no other questions for the witness; the prosecutor let him go.

'That's all,' Mahoney told them. 'That's our last witness. The rest is up to you.'

He wrapped it all up by reminding them of the law again and reading them a list of people who had testified since he had opened the case ten days before.

163

'I'm not expressing any opinions,' he said. 'Not as to the content or the importance of any of the testimony you've heard. It's your memory of those things that rules, and if you're having trouble remembering any of the details you have the record to refer to. I'll be right outside while you deliberate. If you need anything read back, or you have any questions about the law, buzz twice and I'll be right in to help.'

He thanked them for paying such close attention to the evidence and the witnesses – making eye contact with them all – and then he left the room. All that remained of the case they called 'Chinatown' was for them to deliberate and vote.

# 13

The grand jury's deliberations started with a surprise. For the first time in their weeks together, the foreman came to the front of the room to lead them. Susan thought he looked uncertain and not particularly happy to be there, and some of that was in his voice when he began to speak.

'I said right at the beginning I don't like to be telling people what to do. Only, my friends at the desk in the back convinced me we need to have more order in here for this one, and since I'm the one got picked out of a hat, I guess I don't have much choice.

'What we come up with – we thought to go right around the room and see what everybody's got to say, two minutes each, tops, then we can know where we stand and how much more time we need for talking before we vote.'

'Why don't we just vote now?' Number Four challenged. 'I say we've wasted enough time on this already.'

'And I say you're out of order, young man,' the foreman said quickly enough to forestall a chorus of protest. 'We're all grownups here, we can respect each other enough to talk one at a time and raise our hands before we do. Maybe doing it that way makes you feel like grade school, but that's the only way we could figure to do it. Anybody has a better way, I'm ready to listen. If not then let's get started. Number One?'

The car salesman stood up to face the others. 'I think we should vote for the indictment. They're guilty as hell, their stories don't make any sense. Number Eleven and some others wanted to know what they had to say about the ledgers. Okay, you heard it. It's ridiculous. They can't even tell a consistent lie.'

Number Two twisted around in his chair and said, 'I still say, what about the fingerprints? What's that cop think he's tellin' us – they *washed* their heroin? Nobody gonna *wash* no brick of heroin. Think about it. Nobody gonna wipe fingerprints off some heroin so they can shove it under some statue of some god right in their bedroom. Talk about no sense, talk about *non*sense, how about that? What I think is, I think these people bein' framed.'

Number Three, the corrections officer, said, 'My grandmother believes in some gods like that. Santería. She has shrines in her house, too. I've seen her do all kinds of things, make offerings and everything else. So if there's some reason in their religion they put the heroin there, it could be they washed it, too. Make it clean for the god, who knows what people do? But we don't need to know any of that. All of that comes out in the trial. All we need is to think somebody committed a crime, and it might be them. Number Four's right. Let's vote.'

'You all know how I feel,' said Number Four. 'Like Number Three was saying just now, this isn't a trial, it's a grand jury. I say vote yes and move on. And I want to reserve the rest of my time for the end.'

'I don't think so,' the foreman said. 'If you've got something to say, say it now like everybody else.'

'Listen old man, I don't come here to be pushed around.'

'Why don't you shut up and behave?' Norman Thompson yelled at him.

'Please, people.' The alternate forewoman had moved her chair from behind the foreman's desk to where the prosecutors usually stood. She was dressed more carefully than she had been, and her gray hair was brushed back and sprayed in place – as if, Susan thought, she'd anticipated today's deliberations and wanted to look more authoritative. 'If we can't get this far without an argument, we'll never finish. Young man, nobody's trying to take away your chance to talk. We're trying to make it easier for everybody. We'll go around the room however many times we have to.'

'Whatever,' Number Four gave in gracelessly. 'If it floats your boat to make a game out of it, knock yourself out.'

Number Five, the woman Susan thought of as the fashion plate, passed.

'Police make mistake,' Mrs Liu said. Susan was amazed she had decided to participate.

'Can you speak up, please?' the secretary called from the top of the room. 'We can't hear you up here.'

'Maybe if you turned around and faced us,' the alternate forewoman suggested.

Mrs Liu got up. 'Police make mistake,' she repeated, louder this time. 'Mr, Mrs Eng not sell heroin. Fat young woman make many mistake, try to say English for what Cheung Meiling answer to questions—'

'They told us we have to go by what the interpreter says,' Number Four interrupted.

'You're out of order again,' the foreman said. 'I'm sorry, ma'am. Please, go on with what you were saying.'

But Mrs Liu had had enough; she sat down. Susan wanted to scream at the macho idiot in the fourth seat who thought he knew better than everyone, and at the others, who tolerated him or let him bully them.

Number Seven was ready to step into the breach. She half-rose as she turned in her seat to face the grand jury, her headful of long, skinny extensions swinging as she moved.

'The way I understand it,' she said, 'we sat here two whole mornings listening to those folks, and the reason was, to set us straight about what was in those ledgers. Now, I ask you, do you believe what those folks said? All that about giving his money to his friends when he dies, only he couldn't put down their right names. If I ever saw a man lie, that was it. And his wife didn't have a clue about any of that. They couldn't even remember the whole same story. And something else – that money had heroin on it. I'm happy to listen to the rest of you all, but I already know how I'm voting.'

Number Eight, a dark, thick-necked, heavyset man Susan thought might be Dominican, barely looked over his shoulder to say, 'We're supposed to be here looking for the truth. I'm still looking.'

Number Nine, the redhead named Kelly, said, 'This is a hard choice. Too many questions, not enough answers. I'm thinking, suppose those people are telling just part of the truth. Suppose the money is their life savings, and their family's. It seems possible. Is it right to take it away from them based on the evidence that we've seen? Is it right to put two frail old people like that through the terrible ordeal of a trial because it's easy for us to vote yes and move on?'

Kelly's words underscored what was in Susan's mind. Whatever the whole truth was, she was increasingly sure that the Engs should not be made to stand trial, much less sent to jail.

Number Ten, the white-haired accountant, got up slowly and went to stand in front of the witness table next to the foreman.

'I'm going to talk about what I know. The whole business about the ledgers is guesswork. The police accountant was making it up as he went along, and if he got any of it right it's pure luck. In the first place, he never said there was anything in the Chinese words to indicate heroin, and the lady from the cultural center said loud and clear she didn't see anything like that.

'And he's guessing about what the numbers mean. All that business about significant figures is a way to hide the fact that he doesn't know what he's seeing.

'So that leaves us with what we heard about the ledgers from the defendants. And I have to say, that's just not as unlikely as it might sound. If I didn't say this before, I should have – the zodiac can be a handy-dandy kind of identification system, for the reason that it can work for anything that has to do with dates. When people use simple devices like that, they often use them over and over: it's easier than thinking up something new. And once you've started using the new meanings, your mind naturally gets rid of the old ones, because otherwise you'd be hopelessly confused. As for Mrs Eng, that poor woman was so nervous most of the time I'm surprised she remembered her right name.' He grinned. 'I know *I* don't remember it. But seriously, folks, I don't think we should hold it against her just because she was scared of us.'

Outside in the witness waiting area Mahoney was pacing the length of the old, unused counter at the front of the room, trying not to count the minutes. The hard oak benches did not look inviting.

Another A.D.A., not someone Mahoney knew, was sitting at the back with a couple of cops in streetclothes. Probably a subway chain snatching, Mahoney thought, cooling their heels until the grand jury got done deliberating about the Engs. He hoped they wouldn't have a long wait.

He'd been telling himself he could survive in the office if the grand jury didn't indict, but he was not convinced. Estrada was right: Kevin Horgan wasn't the only one who would notice if Dan Mahoney screwed this one up. So would all Mahoney's old colleagues in Appeals and, more important, the bosses in the eighth-floor executive suite. The office stood to come out of this with close to a million dollars after they paid Pullone's snitch and a share to the DEA as their partner in a bureaucratic dance Mahoney thought of as law-enforcement money laundering. Nobody at the D.A.'s office would take it lightly if they lost that much money, a distinct possibility if the indictment failed.

He extended his pacing so it took him to the grand jury warden's desk.

'Hear anything so far?'

'You mean like shouting and screaming, or somebody throwing the furniture around – that kind of hear anything?'

Tense as he was, Mahoney smiled. 'Yeah, that kind.'

'Not a peep. Listen – relax, take it easy, they'll be ready when they're ready. It's not a bad bunch.'

'Not so far,' Mahoney said skeptically, but he went and sat down.


David had not been sure what he was going to say when his turn came. He decided he should talk about a specific problem with the evidence, especially since he had no real conclusion to offer.

'I don't think we've been told all we should know, and I don't think that helps Mr Mahoney; it's important for us to know why the police decided to go to that apartment in the first place. How did they know they'd find heroin and money? I know they had a search warrant and that means somebody must have told them something. But that person must have had some reason to know about the money and heroin – assuming there really was heroin there to begin with, and nobody planted it. But we didn't hear about that reason, and we didn't see that person, and it bothers me that we didn't. Nothing against Mr Mahoney personally, but it makes me suspicious.'

'It's too bad you didn't say so before,' offered the normally retiring woman in seat Number Thirteen. 'Maybe we could have had him as a witness.'

'I did say so before. I asked Mahoney in one of those private sessions they make us have. He said it wasn't relevant and I didn't press the point, but now I think I gave up too easily.'

'Why? You think they're gonna bring their informants in here and parade them around?' the corrections officer put in. 'They'd never get anybody to tell them anything if they did that.'

'It seems to me I've heard about people getting bounties for turning other people in,' said Number Five, the stylish woman in the front row.

'The IRS does that,' Manny Klein said. 'They'll give you a straight fee or even a percentage of what they recover if you turn somebody in.'

'We don't know anything about that,' the grand jury's secretary reminded them. 'We just have the evidence we heard, that's all we have to go by.'

'We're supposed to use our common sense, too,' Manny Klein countered. 'And our knowledge of how the world works.'

'I don't know about all that,' the foreman said, 'but I think we're getting off the track.'

'Not really,' David said. 'Because that's my point. If somebody had a secret reason to turn these people in – like a bounty, for instance – I think that would make a big difference in how we look at the evidence. And because Mr Mahoney wasn't willing to make it clear to us that something like that *didn't* happen, I'd say we have to assume that it *did*.'

'Okay,' the foreman said. 'You've made your point and your time's up. Number Twelve?'

Next to David, Number Twelve shook her head – nothing to say. Watching her response and waiting for her to speak gave David a rare chance to look at his immediate neighbor without being too obvious about it.

She had an unorthodox kind of beauty that appealed to him: wide-set gray eyes and a slender nose in a long oval face, a broad mouth with a pouty lower lip. The first few days, he'd turned to her when it seemed natural because of something that had happened, when others around the room were commenting to their neighbors. But he had rarely caught her eye and when he had she'd turned away without responding to his ironic smile or whatever other expression he'd arranged on his face for the occasion. He'd told himself that it wasn't him, that she was aloof in an equal-opportunity sort of way, but it hadn't really helped.

Number Thirteen, it turned out, also had nothing she wanted to say. Number Fourteen passed, too – no surprise, since he often gave the impression of sleeping through the proceedings and had once actually been snoring until someone decided to poke him awake.

'I do community action work in the South Bronx,' said the woman in seat Number Fifteen, 'and I'm going to answer a question nobody's even asked yet. How can somebody who runs a community organization be dealing heroin at the same time? The answer is, I've seen that, and I've seen worse. And the heroin that comes into the country through China doesn't end up in Chinatown. One of the places it does end up is the neighborhood I work in, used by the people I'm trying to help. So it's not necessarily as if he was corrupting his own people. But saying that doesn't mean I know the answers.

'One thing that really bothers me is that the detective says that Martin Eng resisted arrest, and Martin Eng says the detective knocked him down and held a gun to his head. And I don't see how we can believe he resisted arrest, even a little bit. That old man, small and frail as he is – he even limps a little – resisting that burly detective?'

'If you believe that limp is real,' the corrections officer said. 'And martial arts can make a big difference about size. That's the whole point of martial arts.'

'Maybe karate or Kung Fu,' Number Fifteen acknowledged. 'But have you ever seen old people doing Tai Chi? And how about his squirming away? Isn't that what the detective said? That he was *squirming away*? I'll tell you what makes *me* squirm. I hate to say it, but that detective makes me squirm.'

'You ought to watch how you talk,' the corrections officer warned. 'The cops have a hard job to do. How'd you like to be waiting outside some apartment and you don't know if you're gonna get a handshake or a bullet when the door opens?'

'I'm not saying they don't have a hard job—'

'You're saying they don't tell the truth.'

'Sister's right,' Number Two joined in, emphatic. 'Happens all the time – cops lying in court, cops lying all over the place. Tryin' to put people in jail, guilty or not.'

'That's crybaby bullshit,' Number Four said. 'Cops are bad, home-boys are good. Well, bullshit. We don't have to listen to that.'

'Hey, we listen to plenty of *your* shit, white boy. So don't be sayin' I talk shit.'

'Folks! Please!' It was the secretary, a motherly woman with deeply creased brown skin and white hair. 'Let's not make this into something racial.'

'Maybe if we just moved on to the next,' the foreman said.

Next was Norman Thompson. 'There's been some talk about where the package of heroin might have come from,' he began. 'I was trying to get at that but Mr Mahoney wasn't very cooperative, just like he didn't cooperate with David, here. So I'm going to ask all of you to remember about youth gangs, and what Mr Eng said about letting the young people into his house.

'I do some volunteer work myself, at my church, and these gang kids are the same everywhere. You never know what kind of trouble they're getting into. And you heard what he said about how they want to get rich quick. It can be a horrible temptation for a young man, the chance to get rich quick by dealing drugs – you can ask this smart lady across the aisle from me in seat Fifteen – and it's especially hard when you don't believe you have any other prospects. These young men in Chinatown, a lot of them don't speak the language, and if they're undocumented maybe they don't have a good way to learn it quickly, either. And they may have a debt to pay off, too, to whoever got them here . . .

'And what's all that got to do with us? Well, suppose you're a young man and you've got some friends and you're trying out ways to make money. Maybe you come up with a drug deal. Not a big one, mind you. And you're living at home with your parents, maybe in crowded quarters, so what are you going to do with your stash? And suppose there's a man everybody respects and he invites you and your friends to his house now and then? What better place could there be to stash your heroin than the secret drawer under his little shrine? Just for a short time, because it might get discovered. But for a few days, it would probably do just fine.'

172

'You think that really happened?' The foreman was incredulous.

'I think it might have, yes. And I think it's something to think about when we're making up our minds if these people knew there was heroin in their home.'

'Maybe so,' the foreman said, still clearly disbelieving. 'Next.'

'I work in a beauty salon,' said Number Seventeen. 'You all know a lot more about this than I do. I don't even understand what some of you all are saying. So I'm just going to listen.'

'Well, Norman Thompson, aren't you a piece of work, makin' up all that about gang kids hidin' their stash.' The bus driver, grand juror Number Eighteen, was smiling and shaking her head. 'I'll tell you, though, no matter how you try to twist it around, these people are just as guilty as sin, and there's no two ways about that. Man got his training disrespecting the law once a week with that illegal gambling, and some other illegal recreations, too, I bet . . . I'm with Number Three and Number Seven. I vote yes.'

It was Susan Linwood's turn. David leaned forward so he could see her better, wondering how she was going to play it.

She cleared her throat. 'I'm finding this all very interesting, and I'm learning a lot by listening.' Her voice caught; she seemed to be having trouble breathing. 'I'm glad to see that at least some of us are trying to be open-minded and willing to listen. I thought Number Ten and Mr Thompson made excellent points just now, about how the police version of the ledgers is just guesswork, and how little we actually know about the way the heroin came to be where the police found it. I think we have to bear those things in mind. I think we have to ask ourselves seriously if we have enough evidence to add up to the crimes in the indictment.'

*Thank you, Number Ten and Mr Thompson*, David noted, but not Mr Clark. He tried not to feel slighted, even though the question he'd made so much fuss about had been hers to begin with.

'One other thing I want to say,' she continued, 'is I agree with Number Fifteen that those two old people couldn't really have *resisted* arrest. But I can believe they were afraid. I think we have to remember what kind of lives they've led – time after time having soldiers or police – people in uniform – take everything from them, put them in jail, torture and kill their relatives. We can't expect them to respond to

173

the police the way middle-class Americans do. Especially if the police introduce themselves by breaking down the door.'

A good point, David thought, and she'd made it well.

Number Twenty had nothing to say, nor did the grand jury's secretary. The alternate forewoman picked up on what Susan had said about not having enough evidence.

'I think Number Nineteen has the right idea. The first thing we have to be sure of is that we have all the pieces that add up to the crimes charged. If we don't have the crimes there's no reason to think about who might have committed them. And I don't think we have the crimes.

'Some of us seem to think it's open and shut on the charge of possession of a controlled substance. I don't think that's so. As I remember it, Mr Mahoney told us that possession has to be *knowing* and *unlawful* for it to be a crime. Well, I grant that the heroin was not in that house lawfully. Mr Mahoney also told us that if something's in your house and under your control, you possess it. That adds up to unlawful possession, but it doesn't say anything about *knowing*.

'The question is – did they know it was there? They say no. They claim they never saw the heroin before the police showed it to them.

'You might imagine that anybody who got caught with heroin hidden somewhere in their house would say something like that. *Who, me?* So you might think that's meaningless. But it's not meaningless. It's especially not meaningless because of the fingerprints – the *lack* of fingerprints, that is – and we should thank Number Nineteen and Number Two for pressing that point. The Engs claim someone else put the heroin there. What better evidence could there be of that than the fact that the package was wiped clean? Somebody was framing them and didn't want to get caught at it.

'Who? I don't know who. I don't know anything about what enemies they might have who might pick this as a way to hurt them or get even with them for something. And I don't know what gang members might have visited them, either. Because maybe it happened the way Mr Thompson described it, someone just parking their heroin supply there to keep it out of the way. I *do* know – and this is most important – I do know that I haven't seen any evidence at all that either of the Engs knew the heroin was there.'

174

'Yeah?' Number Four could not restrain himself any longer. 'Then what about the money, and the ledgers? If it's not their heroin, how did heroin get on their money, and what about all the testimony that the ledgers are about buying and selling heroin?'

'Exactly.' The alternate forewoman pushed her horn-rim glasses into place with an emphatic forefinger. 'You're admitting it's not an open and shut case about *knowing* possession. Even to indict them for criminal possession – never mind conspiracy to sell – you have to look to the ledgers and make a decision about what they mean.

'But Mahoney and the police are telling us the opposite. They're telling us they can decipher the ledgers because of the presence of heroin in the house.

'So . . . *you're* saying we know how the heroin came to be there because of what's written in the ledgers, and *they're* saying the fact that they found heroin there tells them what the words in the ledgers must mean. But it can only be one of those, not both. Because if it's both, it's completely circular. Which is to say, we don't *know* anything.'

'Okay, that's it,' the foreman said before Number Four could reply. 'Now, unless anybody who passed wants to say something –' he didn't give anyone much of a chance to say yes – 'then I think we ought to take a vote and see where we stand. And since Number Four has wanted most to bring this to a vote I'm going to ask him to suggest how we should do it.'

'Just *do* it. Both counts, get it over with.'

'All right. We can do that . . . vote on the whole indictment at once. That means if you want to indict them on both counts – possession of a controlled substance in the first degree and conspiracy to sell a controlled substance in the second degree – you vote yes. Otherwise, even if you want to indict them on one count or the other, don't vote yes this time. Only vote yes if you want to indict on *both* counts. If it passes, we're done. If it doesn't pass, then we can vote on the two counts separately, one at a time.'

175

# 14

There were eight hands in favor, and they all went up at once. No surprises as to who, David thought, except Number Twelve, the beauty next to him. For some reason he was disappointed that she had decided so quickly to indict. The real surprise for him was that there were only eight votes to indict, even though the foreman, his own hand aloft, gave ample time for others to join the *yeses*.

'Okay,' he said grudgingly. 'That means we have to vote on the two counts separately.'

'Not so fast,' said Norman Thompson. 'Maybe we just want to vote *no* on both together.'

'Not likely,' Number Four said.

'How do you know?'

'Let's not fight about it,' the foreman said. 'It's easier to vote. How many people just want to let them go free?'

Norman Thompson raised his hand, as did most of his usual voting mates – the beautician in seat Seventeen, the fingerprint kid and even Number Fourteen, who was as likely to doze through a vote as he was to sleep through testimony. So did Mrs Liu and Susan Linwood, Manny Klein and the alternate forewoman. And David himself, because a quick count told him it wasn't going to make an immediate difference and too many people would read too much into it if he didn't, not least Susan Linwood.

Number Fifteen, the community activist, and a frequent Thompson ally, was among the people who didn't vote either way, as were Oswaldo Perez and Jimmy Kelly.

'It looks like we haven't made up our minds,' the foreman said.

'Let's take a break, maybe talk among ourselves for a few minutes, then we can see what happens.'

'Are we going out in the hall?' the beautician asked.

'I think we're supposed to stay in here. But we have our waiting room, over in the back by the rest rooms, if you want to get in a huddle. That okay with everybody?'

Number Four was out of his seat immediately, headed for the small waiting room, motioning to the corrections officer and the car salesman to follow. Kelly and Perez and Manny Klein stood by their adjoining seats, talking intently. The alternate forewoman convened with Norman Thompson and Number Fifteen and some others at the witness table, which the foreman had left to join his former rules-of-order antagonist, Number Four. Susan Linwood was leaning over the rail between the rows to talk to Mrs Liu.

David sat where he was, watching the others. He was in no hurry to get up, because despite his vote he wasn't sure where he stood. But staying out of it didn't work, either. By now he was far too engaged in this not to participate. He went down to join Kelly and the others.

'We were just talking about you,' Manny Klein said as he came up.

'How's that?'

'I was trying to convince them to vote no, and Jimmy was saying how he wondered if he and Oswaldo were going to get pressured by the other side, too. I told them I was holding you in reserve for rebuttal.'

'I'm flattered,' David said. 'But I'm not that certain myself. I was surprised about you, Jimmy. You sounded like a solid no.'

'Being provocative, is all,' Kelly said. 'And this way I figured to keep everybody guessing what I'll do. Makes a lad popular.'

'What about you, Oswaldo?'

'I don't know, man, I really don't know. They seem like nice people and all, and I like what you and Thompson and Manny and that old Jew-lady had to say, but I still got to make up my mind.'

'So there we stand,' Manny Klein said. 'And Oswaldo, I forgive you for calling our alternate forewoman an old Jew-lady.'

'Oh, Jesus, man, you Jewish? I guess so, huh? I'm sorry, man, I didn't mean anything by it.'

'I'm sure you didn't. We're all like that in our own way. She's an old Jew-lady and Kelly's a Mick, and our defendants are Chinks . . .'

Susan had been hovering on the edge of the group, not really hearing what they were saying, waiting for a chance to break into their conversation. The word *Chinks* leapt out at her, especially coming from the white-haired accountant.

'I beg your pardon?' She let herself be indignant.

'Oh. Sorry. Really. I was just illustrating how the first characteristics we notice in other people are the ones that make them most unlike us. Oswaldo, here, just got three at one blow. But that's not what you came over to talk about, I'm sure.'

'I was talking to Norman Thompson and he thinks the vote is going to be close. I wanted to know if there's anything in particular that's keeping you gentlemen from making up your minds.'

Neither of them had a response.

'I didn't come over to pressure you . . . Well, really, I suppose I did. But these charges are such a travesty. It's interesting that you were talking about racial things. I don't want you to think that's what's motivating me in this. I've talked to Mr Clark about it—'

'David, please. No strangers in a foxhole.' He introduced the others.

'I've talked to David about this,' Susan resumed, 'and I'm willing to admit that at first I was more interested in this case because I'm Chinese. But now that I've seen the Engs and heard what they have to say, I see it as just a human issue. I don't see how we can participate in ruining what's left of their lives, not on such ambiguous evidence.'

'Can I ask you, did it make sense the way the old man acted about what was in those ledgers?' Oswaldo Perez looked embarrassed by his own question. 'I mean, make sense, you know, because of some Chinese thing?'

'That he was superstitious about writing down the real names because it was related to his death? I don't know a lot about it, but it does sound like the kind of thing a Chinese man might be concerned about. And we all make up our own versions of those things, don't we? Add a little here, subtract a little there.'

'It's hard, you know, because to be wrong . . . they might be drug dealers and we let them go.'

'They're old people,' Susan reminded him. 'And they don't look very strong. And, as Mr Kelly was saying, if they're *not* drug dealers and we put them through a trial for something they didn't do . . .'

'And take all their money,' the redhead added. 'Don't forget the money.'

Susan was going to ask what he meant, because she was not sure exactly what would happen to the money – Mahoney had dismissed the question from consideration. Before she could follow it up the foreman came back into the main grand jury room with the vanguard of the pro-indictment forces.

'It's getting late,' he said. 'I don't know what happens if it's one o'clock and we haven't finished voting, so let's try to get though this.'

'We can always keep talking tomorrow,' Norman Thompson said.

'They sequester trial juries if they're not finished.'

'We're not a trial jury.'

'Let's get started anyway.'

'Somebody sure put some iron in *his* drawers,' Kelly said as they separated to return to their seats.

'I think we talked enough about the possession count,' the foreman said. 'Let's move on to the conspiracy to sell. Do we think there's evidence that the defendants might have agreed with someone to sell a quantity of heroin greater than two ounces?'

The debate about the existence of a conspiracy to sell focused initially on the ledgers and the money. The battle lines were clearly drawn now, and the deliberations quickly wore a rut in the possibilities.

Susan began to wonder what they were accomplishing. The process had the feel of a pair of schismatic congregations each preaching to its own members. Whatever politeness had been part of it at the beginning was wearing increasingly thin.

'We've been over this ground a million times,' the secretary said. 'We're going around in circles, unless someone has something new to say.'

'There *is* one thing we haven't talked about,' David said. 'The biggest difference I can see between Mahoney and the Engs about those books is how old the books are. Maybe that can be some help.'

'Did anyone actually *say* how old they were?' asked the fashionably dressed woman in seat Five.

'The police accountant said he thought they covered about three years of transactions,' David responded. 'So he must think they're about three years old.'

'He said he was guessing about the time period.' The car salesman in seat One, always ready with a clarification.

'He was guessing about everything,' Manny Klein interjected.

'That's out of order,' the foreman said, giving every sign of enjoying his new officiousness.

'I was saying,' David resumed. 'The police accountant said three years. But Martin Eng was talking about decades.'

'Let's get a look at them, then, and see what we think,' Number Five suggested.

'What good will that do?' the corrections officer countered. 'We don't know anything about it.'

'You know if something looks old,' she said.

'I thought they had ways to know those things,' Number Seven said, playing with her braids. 'Testing the ink or something.'

'Maybe they'll do those tests for the trial,' Number Four told her. 'If anybody thinks it's important enough. This is only a grand jury, so they don't bother.'

'You keep saying that, as if what we do doesn't matter.' The alternate forewoman sounded angry. 'But it *does* matter. Grand juries are in the Bill of Rights. They've been around almost a thousand years, part of the very first ideas of democracy and individual freedom this country is based on. A grand jury is the people's protection against prosecutors who are too eager to put people in jail, and that's a worry that goes way back.'

'What does that have to do with anything?' Number Four challenged.

'I'm trying to put all this in some kind of perspective, so we do what we're really supposed to. We can't let ourselves be rushed through it for the wrong reasons. A chief judge in this state once said that a grand jury would indict a ham sandwich. Because it's so easy for a grand jury to turn into a rubber stamp for the D.A.'s office. And that's *not* how it's supposed to be.'

'How do you know all that?' the beautician asked her.

'I'm a history professor.'

'What kind of history?'

'European. I specialize in the Middle Ages, in France.'

'Great!' The car salesman. 'And that makes you an expert on American grand juries.'

'It's my profession to do historical research. And that's what I did when I found out I was going to be serving on a grand jury – historical research about the origins and function of the grand jury.'

'I don't know about your profession,' Number Seven said. 'But I hear you saying the police and prosecutors want to put people in jail if they're guilty or not. Why would they try that with two old folks if they didn't do anything? What could possibly be in it for them? You're not going to convince me they'd do it so they can have two more convictions.'

'How about – they're doing it for the sake of having a million and a half dollars,' Kelly suggested. 'Would that convince you?'

'What's that supposed to mean?' Number Seven wanted to know.

'What do you think's going to happen to that money?'

'I don't know. I never thought about it.'

'They keep it. The D.A.'s office and the police. And some goes to Albany. Or else the D.A.'s office splits it with the DEA or the FBI.'

'Who told you that?'

'You can read about it in the newspapers every week. They publish a list of what they're taking, a whole page of the smallest type you'll ever see. And there was a bunch of magazine articles and TV stories about it. They destroy the drugs and they keep the money.'

'For evidence.'

'And then after that they keep it for themselves. Not just money, either. They drive the cars and sail the boats and fly the airplanes – or sell them. And the cash goes into their budget.'

'That's crazy.'

'What did you think – they burned it with the drugs? Or gave it to the Boy Scouts?'

'So what?' the corrections officer said. 'What's wrong with having the Government keep it? You can't let drug dealers keep the money they earn that way, any more than you'd let a bank robber keep the money he stole.'

'Except a bank robber's money goes back to the bank he stole it from,' Kelly countered.

'Unlike Mr Eng's money, which never goes to the bank,' Manny Klein said. 'Except if his accountant deposits it for him.'

'You talk as if we can believe a word of that.' The car salesman again. 'The man talks out of both sides of his mouth.'

'I didn't hear it that way,' Manny Klein came back.

'You didn't? How about the whole question of banks and making money on interest? He *wants* to earn interest, he *doesn't* want to earn interest. He's afraid of banks and bonds, but he'll sink three hundred thousand dollars into bearer bonds to make his wife happy. Or so he wants us to believe.'

'Maybe that part makes sense,' the corrections officer speculated. 'Maybe she's the boss – I mean, that's one scary little old lady. Did you see, it was like she wasn't going to give Mahoney the time of day, this morning. She was like yes and no and screw you, Charlie. Then she got all sweet again, after the break, when she was answering questions for us.'

'But that wasn't her, that was the *interpreters*,' Susan protested. 'She didn't change at all, except at the very end, when she got so upset.'

'We're not supposed to question the interpreters,' the foreman said. 'Mr Mahoney made that very clear. We're supposed to take their word, even if we think we understand better.'

'I'm not challenging what either interpreter *said* – I'm saying we should remember what's the interpreter and what's the witness. That second interpreter didn't begin to reflect the emotional content, the spirit, of what Mrs Eng was saying.'

'Do you speak Chinese?'

Susan saw what was coming, but she had no choice except to play into the car salesman's hands. 'Only a little.'

'Then don't tell us what we heard.'

'I'm *not* –' Susan worked to get her frustration under control – 'I may not be able to make out all the words, but I could hear the emotion in them, and I can tell the difference between a short answer and a long one. I'm telling you, her attitude didn't change from beginning to end. She was being polite and helpful, not harsh and rude like that second interpreter. Why do you think the defense lawyer objected to her?'

'That doesn't have anything to do with us,' the car salesman said.

'And I have to say, I thought your friend the defendant was harsh and rude a *lot* of the time.'

'She's not my friend! I'm trying to do my duty here honestly, just like you are.'

'Look, lady,' said Number Four, 'we all know where you stand on this, so maybe you should just let us get on with our business.'

'Hey! That's no help,' David said sharply. 'Nobody goes around accusing you of having a soft spot for white defendants, or Italian ones. You *are* Italian?'

'Yeah, I'm Italian. You have some problem with Italians?'

'No. Do you have some problem with Chinese people?'

'Okay,' the foreman said. 'That's enough. We're talking about the crime of conspiracy.'

'We haven't said anything about an overt act,' the secretary said.

'Beg your pardon?'

'It's an element of the crime. Mr Mahoney read it to us several times. I took notes.'

'Good. Then you can remind us about it.'

'To have a conspiracy you need an agreement to commit a crime, but talking about it isn't enough. You need someone to do something to further the conspiracy. That's the overt act.'

'Anybody?' the foreman said.

The car salesman raised his hand. 'I'm going to figure possession of half a pound of heroin is enough of an overt act to further a conspiracy to sell two ounces of the stuff.'

'*Conspiracy?*' Norman Thompson was quick to divert the grand jury's attention. 'If this is a conspiracy, where's the rest of it?'

'We don't need it,' the car salesman said.

'Some conspiracy that would be, with just one side.'

'Mahoney said we don't have to know who the other conspirators are. All we need is evidence that makes us think there was somebody, anybody, who was a conspirator. Besides, there's two of them. That's a conspiracy right there.'

'That's only if you think she was involved,' said the community activist in seat Fifteen. 'I don't see anything that points to her.'

'What about the safe deposit boxes that were in both their names? The ones the bank officer said she kept going to.'

'But there was gold jewelry in those boxes. That's enough reason for her to share them and visit them.'

'If you want conspiracy, take any of the people in those notebooks,' the corrections officer proposed. 'Or whoever they got the heroin from. They didn't exactly go to the poppy fields and process it themselves. There's even a brand name on it, remember?'

'Conspiracy to *sell*, not *buy*,' the secretary scolded.

'But the woman from the DEA said that was way too much for their own personal consumption,' the corrections officer pointed out. 'It would kill them if they used it that pure, and if they diluted it they couldn't use it before it went bad.'

'Right,' agreed the car salesman. 'And Mr Mahoney said we could decide they were selling it if that's how the evidence adds up, even if no witness saw anyone make an actual sale. So . . . if they couldn't keep it for themselves, and it was going to spoil if they didn't use it or get rid of it, and if it cost fifty thousand dollars or whatever to buy and it's worth a whole lot more than that on the street . . . what more do you need?'

'You all keep saying *they*.' Number Fifteen sounded upset. 'What about her? Nobody answered that question. Even if you think it was him, what did she have to do with it?'

'It was her shrine where they found the heroin. They both said that.'

'That doesn't mean she knew there was heroin in it. He could have put it there.'

'Wearing gloves, right?' Number Two said acidly.

'Oh, shit, I'm tired of hearing about the damn fingerprints.' Number Four – being macho again, Susan thought. 'Maybe she likes to keep things clean.'

'Then there wouldn't be fingerprints *anywhere*,' decided Number Thirteen. 'We didn't ask about that.'

'Too late now.'

'Maybe we could get him back.'

'Oh, for chrissake.' Number Four was lashing out more frequently, Susan noted, and becoming more indiscriminate in his targets. 'Let's just get off it.'

'Hey, yo. Somethin' else,' Number Two said. 'Where's the scales 'n' baggies 'n' shit?'

184

'What are you talking about?'

'If they steppin' on the heroin like my man here said, they need weighin' scales, baggies to put it in . . . where's all that?'

'Didn't somebody say they keep the money and the drugs in separate places?' Number Seven asked, playing with her braids again.

'Not this time, they didn't,' Thompson came back, full of sarcasm. 'Not if you believe our prosecutor.'

'Maybe it was a sample,' suggested the corrections officer. 'For people they were making deals with to test before they buy.'

'You see that in the movies,' Number Twenty said, her first contribution to the deliberations. 'The bad guy's going to buy from the undercover policeman but they have to test it first to see if it's any good.'

'Oh, please,' Thompson said.

'Can we vote now?' Number Four tried again.

'That sounds right,' the foreman said. 'Time to vote.'

'Wait a second,' said Number Fifteen. 'Before we start, I think we should vote on the two people separately. Even if you think she knew about the heroin, there's not a single thing that ties her to any conspiracy.'

'There's no way to vote on him and her separately,' the secretary said. 'There's only one indictment, with two crimes charged, and there's only one set of boxes on the verdict sheet to check off the vote in.'

'Well, what are we supposed to do if we think one of them might have done it but not the other?'

'I guess you'd have to vote no,' the foreman said.

'That doesn't make sense. What does it say in the book?'

'Let's just get Mr Mahoney in here and ask him.'

Almost as soon as the secretary buzzed for him Mahoney came in, followed by a stenographer.

'Problem?'

'Suppose we only want to indict one of them?' the foreman asked him. 'Do we have to vote no on the whole indictment?'

Mahoney considered it. 'Well, we presented the indictment the way we did because we believe the evidence points equally to both of them. But if in good conscience you think you can separate what one of them

185

did from what the other did, there's no reason, in principle, why you can't vote on them separately. Just keep in mind that as to either count, once you find that the evidence establishes a reason to believe that the elements of the crime are present, then all you need is to form a *reasonable belief* that each or either one of the defendants may have committed that crime – *may* have committed it. You do not have to believe that their guilt has been *proved* in any sense.'

He waited a moment. 'Was there anything else?'

'I guess that's all,' the secretary said. 'Only we might need another slip to write down how we vote if we do it separately.'

'If you have to, you can use that one,' Mahoney said. 'Just drawn a line down the middle of the boxes and put the names at the top to show which is which. *If you have to*.' His tone left no doubt how he felt about it.

For a moment after he and the stenographer left, nobody said anything.

'All right, can we vote now?' asked Number Four.

'After we talk about Mrs Eng,' said the community activist.

'I don't see that there's any more to say,' the foreman announced. 'Either you believe her or you don't.'

Susan tried to reintroduce the issue of the translators, but the foreman and his pro-indictment allies shouted her down again.

'How can anyone not believe her?' Number Fifteen asked. 'What could have been more honest than what she said about being humiliated. I didn't understand the words, but I didn't have to. That came right from the heart. And these are people who understand about being humiliated. Isn't that right? *Face* – isn't that what it's called?'

'That's right.' Susan assumed the question was meant for her. 'Face is very important – your standing in the community, and how people think of you.'

'Anybody thinks that was real, I bet you think it was real when she choked up about that dragon pin, too.' Number Four was continuing his leadership of the wrecking crew for the other side. 'She has this pin, right, and it just breaks her up that she can't give it to her daughter. Let me ask you this . . . If it meant so much to her, why did she sell it? You going to tell me if they sold all that other shit she described – if any of it was real – they didn't have enough money so she could keep this precious dragon or whatever it was and give it to her daughter any time she wanted to? I mean, where's the sense in that? So they can put away a million and a half dollars and not spend any of it until they're eighty? If you ask me, the only thing that tells us is that the whole damn story is bullshit, just like I've been saying from the beginning.'

Nobody had an immediate response. Susan wanted to think of a justification for the story, but she couldn't.

'It does seem funny,' the fashion plate said. 'Some of those jewels she was describing must have been worth a fortune. I can't imagine why you'd have to sell every last one. And her husband said they sold them in the seventies, when gold prices were high. So they had them here and they held onto them until the market was right. That's pretty cold-blooded if they're heirlooms with so much sentimental value. I agree, it doesn't make any sense for her to be so upset.'

Mrs Liu stood up again and faced the others. 'Cheung Meiling say *firstborn* daughter.' Her tone was sharp. 'Firstborn daughter not wear pin because *drown*.'

'How do you know that?' the bus driver demanded.

'Cheung Meiling tell story. Say take boat from China, boat sink, number one daughter die in sea.'

'I didn't hear that, about the number one daughter. Anybody else hear that?'

'Say in Chinese language. Other lady not say, in English language.'

'We back to this again?' The car salesman's voice was harsh with impatience. 'We're not supposed to listen to anybody but the interpreter.'

'Suppose she made mistakes,' Susan said.

'How are we supposed to know that? That's the whole point. Is this lady here a qualified interpreter?'

'No, but she speaks Cantonese.'

'Yeah, well, maybe so,' the car salesman shot back. 'But she doesn't speak English so hot. How about you? You an expert at translating Chinese, too?'

'I've already said I don't speak enough Cantonese for that.'

'Then you can't vouch for this old lady, can you, sweetheart? So just butt out.'

'Hey!' David's angry response was immediate. 'Watch how you talk to people. Give us all a break.'

'What's your problem, buddy?' It was Number Four, coming to his ally's aid. 'You got the hots for that nice Chinese lady over there? I seen you going off together to have your little talks. And you do keep sticking up for her, don't you?'

Norman Thompson was on his feet in the second row, fists clenched. 'Listen, asshole, you keep this up, we're going to have real trouble, you and me.'

'Try me,' Number Four said, standing up to face him.

'*Stop!*' It was the woman in seat Twenty, the one in the floral dresses, who had barely participated. 'We're supposed to be doing justice here. People's lives are at stake.' She turned to the foreman. 'Please, please. All this yelling isn't going to accomplish anything.'

Mahoney heard the outer door of the grand jury waiting area open. He turned: it was Joe Estrada.

'I went by your office. They said you were up here.'

'Come to cheer me up?'

'Why, something wrong?'

'They've been at it an awfully long time in there. Shouting at each other. They just called me in to see how much I'd mind it if they only indicted one of my defendants.'

'And how much do you mind it?'

'I mind that they're even thinking of it. If they're not sure about one, who knows about the other?' Mahoney made a sour face. 'Looks as if I really bowled them over with my terrific presentation.'

'You figure the Mrs is the one they're having trouble with?'

'Most likely. I probably should've left her alone.'

'What happened, you make her cry?'

'Very funny.' Mahoney's voice betrayed the truth.

Estrada winced. 'How'd you manage that?'

'I asked her to describe some jewelry.'

'That's all? I mean, I know women like jewelry, but . . .'

Mahoney shrugged. 'Some days are like that. The thing was, I didn't want to leave a lot of questions for the jurors to ask. I figured I'd get the obvious stuff out of the way, and after that the questions would get asked how and when I wanted them asked.'

'Nothing wrong with that.'

'Except when the Grand Inquisitor here decides to ask a woman who looks and acts like she does to describe expensive jewelry in the hope she'll screw up.'

'You think she was involved?'

Mahoney looked at his friend. 'All Horgan said was get an indictment. I don't remember that thinking came into it.'

# 15

'All right,' the foreman said. 'Let's vote. Count one, Meiling Cheung
– criminal possession of a controlled substance in the first degree. All
in favor?'

Hands went up. It looked close to David, counting. He got eleven,
counted again. The whole grand jury was counting.

'Is that everybody?' the foreman asked. 'Everybody understand
that we need twelve or there's no indictment on this count?'

'Come on, get on with it,' Norman Thompson shouted.

'Hold your horses.' The foreman looked around one last time,
clearly unwilling to accept defeat. 'Everybody sure?'

'No. I'm not sure,' said Number Twenty, provoking groans around
the room. 'I don't know what to do.'

'We been at this a long time, Miss,' the foreman said, at the edge of
exhaustion. 'Can you tell us, please, what you're waiting for?'

'I'm just not sure whether I think they're guilty.' She was looking at
her lap, plucking at the filmy cloth of her skirt. 'I don't want to vote
yes if they're not, and I don't want to let them go free if they are.'

'It's not if they're *guilty*. Mr Mahoney just said that when he was in
here. It's just – is there reason to believe they *might* have committed
these crimes. If we indict them, all it means is there's going to be a
trial. That's when they decide about guilt. If we *don't* indict them they
go free right now.'

'All right. But I'm still not sure if they did it or not.'

The foreman stared blankly. 'I just *said* . . .' He stopped himself,
shaking his head.

'Would it help if we got the prosecutor back in here?' the secretary
asked her.

'I don't know. I think I understand.'

'Well, let's try it, anyway.'

Mahoney started with some of the same things he had said before. He wound up with, 'According to the law, indicted defendants are still considered to be innocent. And they stay innocent, in the eyes of the law, unless and until some prosecutor can prove to a trial jury that they're guilty. To do that requires a much higher standard of proof than we use here in the grand jury. Guilt in a trial has to be proved beyond a reasonable doubt. All we need here today is a reasonable cause to believe a defendant may have committed the crime. Just a reasonable cause to believe it *may* have happened that way, nothing more. Not being certain. Not beyond a doubt. Is that clear to everybody now?'

Nobody said it wasn't. The foreman said thank you.

'Why didn't somebody say that before?' Number Twenty asked when the door closed behind Mahoney.

'You ready now?' the foreman asked.

'Yes. Please, can we vote now?'

'I know it's unusual,' the foreman said, 'but I want to have a secret ballot. I think we need to, so some people can vote according to their conscience. Any little piece of paper is good enough. Write yes or no and our secretary can count them up.'

It took a while to straighten out the logistics, but once everyone had paper and something to write with, the voting went quickly.

On the charge of criminal possession of a controlled substance in the first degree, the grand jury indicted Meiling Cheung by a vote of twelve to eleven.

When the indictment was voted, Number Four and some of his allies cheered. Their glee enraged Susan. This wasn't a football game: people's lives would be profoundly changed by what happened here. She wanted to scream at them. No, it was more physical than that – she wanted to do them some kind of damage . . . saw clearly, for once, how some people could turn so readily to violence.

She was diverted from her fury by the need to vote on the next count of the indictment. She marked her ballot with a sense of futility borne out by the secretary's announcement of the tally: the grand jury had indicted Martin Eng on the charge of criminal possession of a controlled substance in the first degree by a vote of thirteen to eight, with two people turning in blank ballots.

This time it was only Number Four who shouted *yes!* The triumphant syllable echoed emptily in the room, as if the others had remembered why they were there.

They voted somberly on the charge of conspiracy in the second degree, indicting Meiling Cheung by twelve to eleven and Martin Eng by thirteen to eight to two, the same margins as on the possession counts.

'Shall I buzz?' the secretary asked into a distracted silence when the last vote was counted.

'No reason not to,' the foreman said. 'They know we're done. They must have heard the noise.'

'So what?' Norman Thompson said. 'I'd like some time to recover. They can wait till we're ready.'

'I'm ready,' said Number Four, without much passion. No one else joined in.

'It's almost one,' the foreman said. 'They won't start a new case anyway. Go ahead.'

The secretary buzzed once, the signal they were ready to report their action. The warden came in and conferred with her, made sure the right information was entered in the grand jury's log.

'I've got one more quick case for you,' he informed them, to a response of groans and muttering.

'They've been waiting out there more than an hour, and I promise you it's a real quickie.'

It was another chain snatching on the subway. The A.D.A. hurried his two cops through their paces and finished just after one. Sixteen people raised their hands to indict. The grand jurors emptied the room while the warden and the secretary were still making their notations.

David, glad he was near the door, got out before the people he did not want to commiserate with. Predictably, the elevator took for ever to arrive. He faced forward until it came and stared at the back of

Number Twelve's head in the packed cab, trying not to be too aware of how crowded together they were.

When he got outside, he saw Mahoney at the edge of the sidewalk talking to Number Four and Number One. He started to walk past, then decided not to. Instead, he hung back by the building entrance until the two grand jurors left and the prosecutor turned to go.

'Mr Mahoney?'

'Yes?' Mahoney looked at him. 'Number Eleven, right? What can I do for you?'

'You can tell me how the police knew.'

'Oh yes, I remember. That was one of those questions you asked that I couldn't answer for you.'

'*You're not here to satisfy your curiosity* – I think that's how you put it.'

'Did I? Not the way to win friends.' Mahoney smiled.

'You seem to have won friends where it counted.'

'Actually, we're looking for minds, not hearts, in there.' Now that he had his indictment, Mahoney was relaxed and expansive. David found it hard not to like him.

'You'd have done better with my mind if you'd let me know how the police found out about Mr and Mrs Eng and their drugs and their money.'

When Mahoney didn't respond David said, 'In the absence of information, my assumption was that someone turned them in.'

'Why did you assume that?'

'Because if it was detective work that did it, you'd have told us about it. I had the feeling you made sure to tell us about anything that showed how thorough and skillful you all were.'

Mahoney regarded him with greater interest. 'Okay, but tell me this . . . If you're that smart, why ask dumb questions?'

'So someone *did* turn them in. Some kind of informant.'

Mahoney said nothing.

'What was in it for him – what did he get out of it?'

'Wouldn't civic-mindedness be enough?'

'I'd be very surprised if it was, frankly. What happens to the Engs's money now?'

Mahoney checked his watch. 'You know, much as I'd like to stand here, I'd better go get myself some lunch while I have the chance. What happens to the money is a long process whose outcome will be determined in the courts.'

'And at the end of the process the courts will give it to the police and the D.A.'s office.'

'I really do have to go,' Mahoney said. 'Thanks for being such a concerned citizen. I know sitting up there isn't always a lot of fun, but it's really important and we all appreciate it.'

When Kevin Horgan was done in court for the day, he dropped in on Mahoney.

'I see you got the indictment.'

'Both defendants, both counts.'

'You had us all sweating there for a while.'

Mahoney stifled the impulse to explain.

'I'm still tied up in this damn trial of mine,' Horgan said. 'You'll have to keep after this Eng thing on your own for a while longer.' He pulled a cigar from his jacket pocket and peeled off the clear-plastic wrapper. 'At least now we don't have to worry so much about losing the money.' He crumpled the wrapper and flipped it through the mini-hoop over Mahoney's wastebasket.

'I was thinking,' Mahoney said, 'it couldn't hurt to have some more evidence. Maybe I ought to go over to the six-month grand jury and open a new investigation so I can start issuing subpoenas again. I thought maybe money laundering . . .'

Horgan was skeptical. 'Waste of time and effort, if you ask me. I'd just concentrate on what we have. We've already got money, heroin and records. If you tighten it up some, that should be plenty.'

'Horgan's tried a lot of these, so I have to figure he knows what he's doing,' Mahoney told Estrada. 'But I can't help thinking, a grand jury is one thing, guilt beyond a reasonable doubt is something else entirely.'

'You don't think the ledgers'd be enough, with a couple more months to get a solid handle on what they mean?'

'That'll help. But I'd be a lot happier with phone records . . . bank records if there are any, even if it's only the safe-deposit access lists we

194

don't have yet.' To get them he'd need to issue subpoenas, and to do that he needed an active grand jury investigation. 'Especially for the wife,' he said. 'When they asked to vote separately I was dead sure they were going to give me a no-true-bill on her.'

'What counts is you got the indictment,' Estrada said.

'Yeah, I'm a real hero prosecutor. But now that I managed not to screw up totally, I figure it's time to start thinking about the next step.'

'Horgan might not be that worried about convicting both of them, you know. He doesn't need to, to keep the money.'

'Maybe so, but that's not why I thought we were in business here. If I'm making a case that's worth twenty-five to life against a couple of people pushing eighty I want to know I've got solid proof. For my own peace of mind, if nothing else.'

# 16

The remaining grand jury mornings, Susan didn't participate in the deliberations: if she had a point to make, she made it through her questions. She was relieved when Friday morning had come and gone and there was only the following Monday before they would be done.

'I have a couple of announcements I've been asked to make,' the foreman said at the end of Friday's session. 'Mr Kelly in seat Nine is inviting us all to join him at his restaurant and bar on the Upper West Side for a farewell party Monday night after nine o'clock.'

'I'd make it earlier for you,' Kelly said, 'but my staff would kill me.'

'And grand juror Number Twenty has offered to bring in a cake for us to enjoy with our coffee Monday morning.'

'I can bring it to the party Monday night, if you want,' she said.

'You bring it in the morning,' Kelly said. 'I'll have plenty at the bar, and plenty for the teetotalers, too. This way we get two parties.'

At the Engs's arraignment, their lawyer made a new application for bail. Though Ellen Hyams's experience had been almost entirely in federal courts, she handled the details of state procedure with the ease of a veteran, Mahoney thought. Whoever had briefed her had done a fine job, and she was an exemplary student.

She presented a file of affidavits attesting to the Engs's good character and reliability and their deep roots in the Chinatown community. She had a doctor's report that claimed their health and mental acuity was suffering in jail and would suffer further if they stayed there.

'I need my clients' help in preparing their defense,' she argued.

'These are very old people. If they are too weak and tired as a result of their being incarcerated, they can't participate at all, much less participate adequately.'

'They're facing twenty-five to life, mandatory, your honor,' Mahoney countered. 'This is a very serious crime and the incentive to flee is enormous. They can have the requisite time with their attorney as guests of the State.'

The truth was, they looked terrible: gray and shrunken inside their jail garb. No accident that their lawyer hadn't got them all dressed up for this.

'We're offering to surrender their passports and airline tickets and to have them report in to the court every day, your honor,' Hyams said.

'We're talking about people who had a half a million dollars lying around the house. They had almost half a unit of heroin.' Mahoney made the arguments as if the Engs might flee, all the while wondering what the real point was of keeping them in jail. From what he'd seen of them, he didn't expect them to jump bail. 'People like this have access to money when they need it. If they're going to flee, surrendering their tickets or even their passports won't be much of an obstacle.'

The argument continued, theme with variations on both sides. The judge ended it by deciding to reserve judgment so he could study the defense's papers more carefully.

On his way back to the office, Mahoney stopped at the Asian Gang Unit, stuck off in a corner of the main court building, one of the scattered bits of real estate appropriated to accommodate pieces of the ever-growing D.A.'s office. The frosted-glass door still bore an etched-in sign identifying it as the entrance to the Corrections Department.

Mark Brattler came out to unlock the door and greet him. Brattler was a transplanted cowboy, born and raised in the South-west, a rarity in the New York County D.A.'s office. The two prosecutors had gotten to know each other three years before, when Mahoney had saved a conviction of Brattler's from being overturned on appeal. It had been Brattler's first big case in the downsized descendant of the old Jade Squad, and his success in that case had started him on the road to being the unit's boss.

'What brings you?' he asked Mahoney.

'You know I left Appeals.'

'Yeah, and I have to confess I felt a lot safer in court when you were there. You're in Special Narcotics now?'

'I'm working with Kevin Horgan, out of Rackets. Organized Crime Narcotics. We've got a heroin-and-money case with Chinatown perps.'

'Gang stuff?'

'So far, it's the over-the-hill gang.' Mahoney told him about the Engs. 'I wanted to see if you had anything on them, if they had any connections with the youth gangs.'

'Doesn't ring a bell, but let's take a look.'

Mahoney stopped in the doorway of Brattler's office to take in the blown-up photograph on the wall behind the desk. It showed the almost-empty interior of a bar. In the flash-whitened foreground, a middle-aged Chinese woman bartender looked up without visible interest at whatever was playing on the TV, out of range of the police camera, of which she seemed to take no notice. The long wooden bar itself was without patrons except for three men drinking peacefully on stools at its far end, almost obscured in the gloom beyond the reach of the flash. At the bar exactly opposite the unconcerned bartender, one red-topped bar stool had been knocked over. Next to it on the floor lay a man in a business suit, blood and brains leaking from a bullet hole in his head.

'Edward Hopper,' Mahoney said. 'In one of his grimmer moods.'

'That's why I had it blown up. I don't know whether I'm more fascinated by the woman or those guys down the end, just like nothing was happening.'

Brattler sat down at his desk, grabbed a pen from his desk set. 'Tell me those names again.'

'Meiling Cheung Eng. Martin Eng.'

'You know his Chinese name?'

'Didn't occur to me to ask.'

'It's important. I'll tell you, this whole name thing makes me nuts. There aren't that many last names, and the few there are aren't necessarily pronounced the same from one province to the next. And then some of them have more than one set of given names. It's not aliases, nothing phony – they have more than one actual name. Milk name, neighborhood name, grown-up name, professional name. Especially the Cantonese.'

'Like my people,' Mahoney said. 'Baptismal name, confirmation name . . .'

'Yeah, but you pick one and use it all the time.'

'Well . . .'

'Never mind, just you'd make my life easier if you could get me the Chinese name he goes by most. The one he uses for the criminal transactions would be best.'

'Right – I'll be sure to ask him. Also, he's president of something called the Guangdong Three Districts Association.'

'Don't know that one offhand, either, but we probably have it on the list somewhere.'

'And the Pearl River Garment Manufacturing Company.'

'You want to know if there's any gang connection.'

'Gangs, or drugs. Especially drugs. Or anything else you have.'

'I'll see what there is, but I don't expect anything much. What we've got, as far as associations, is mostly the big ones. There are too many associations and societies to really cover them all, new ones every day, and there are more and more unconnected gangs that freelance for whatever association needs them, or even for individuals.'

'Do what you can. Whatever you can get me is more than I've got.'


The cake Number Twenty brought to the grand jury remained untouched through most of Monday morning. At the break everyone gathered around to admire it.

Susan, not wanting to make herself prominent by her absence, stood at the back of the grand jury's waiting room. The cake, built out of three layers and meticulously frosted, was a model of the grand jury room, complete with curved rows of built-in seats and foreman's desk. Doll-house furniture served for the witness table and chairs. There was even an American flag in the corner.

'It's so beautiful it's a shame to eat it,' said Number Five, more stylish than ever on this concluding morning.

'Not if it tastes as good as it looks,' the bus driver said. 'Then it's a shame to let it be.'

'We don't have to vote on it, you know.' Number Twenty, in another of her loose, flowery dresses, was making a joke. 'I made it for us to eat.' She picked up the knife next to the cake – 'Courtesy of our warden,' she said – and cut a piece out of the front corner. 'There. Nothing to save. Please enjoy it.'

Before they could, the warden came in to tell them there was a case waiting. They dispensed with it even more quickly than had become their habit and returned to their waiting room, where Number Twenty handed out pieces of cake and people poured themselves coffee from thermoses she had brought. Susan, like Mrs Liu, did not join in.

At the end of the session the warden came in and made a little speech about what good sports and good citizens everyone had been. He said he'd had a lot of grand juries, some were grander than others, and he thought this one had been especially grand. He applauded them and invited them to applaud themselves. Then he said, 'I hear you've got some real good cake in here, and I sure want to catch a piece before it's all gone.'

That brought laughter and a flow of people to the waiting room to deal with the remains of the cake. Susan waited for the tide to pass and rose to leave. Kelly intercepted her on the way out.

'I hope you'll come tonight. I doubt Number Four and most of that crowd will make it, and it surely would not be the same without you.'

'That's very kind,' she said. 'But I do have plans with my family. I'm sorry. I'll promise this, though – I'll come to your restaurant for dinner one night soon.'

'I hope you will, but try to come tonight, too. Bring your family.'

Susan worked until after nine putting together a strategy for the second stage of the publicity campaign for Consolidated. In the hope that it would help her care about the job, she'd added something new: simultaneously with introducing their new estrogen implant, the company would underwrite an education program about breast-cancer detection and treatment. Convincing Shelby Portman in time to get his board of directors moving before the campaign-launch date would be no small task, but with luck the deadline would help her keep her mind focused on work.

She came home to an empty house. Richard was rehearsing with his chamber-music group and Lara was out with two of her friends who were leaving for college on the West Coast in the morning.

She unpacked the plastic containers she had picked up at a food shop on Madison Avenue and put together an attractive dinner plate for herself. She took it into the dining room with a glass of white wine and the morning paper, which she hadn't had a chance to look at. Sitting down at the table she realized she had no appetite and no real desire to read the news.

She got her briefcase and took out her planning notebook for Consolidated. She paged through it, reviewing what she had done earlier, and made herself pick up a fork to eat. The food and the Consolidated campaign were equally flat and without flavor. The wine, and it was good wine, tasted not much better.

She took her plate back into the kitchen and started to put each of the salads back into its plastic container. Halfway through, she stopped, opened the cabinet under the sink and scraped the plate into the garbage. She threw the plastic containers in, too – heedless of the niceties of recycling – pulled the garbage bag from its container and carried it out to the building's garbage chute.

She came back to the kitchen and put the empty plate in the dishwasher and sat down on the floor and cried. When the tears were dry she sat there blankly for a moment, then got up and went into the bedroom, where she stood by her closet going through her clothes. Nothing seemed right. She sat on the edge of her bed, afraid she was going to cry again and determined not to. She took a quick shower and put on the clothes Lara had picked out for her the night they went to the restaurant downtown, tucked some money in her pocket and headed out the door.

David was at the end of the bar at Kelly's Shamrock, next to the table Jimmy Kelly had set up for the grand jurors. Oswaldo Perez was at the bar with him, and nine of the jurors were crowded around the table, where Manny Klein was holding court. Norman Thompson was across the table from him, subdued and looking uncomfortable. The rest of the partyers were women.

The bus driver had turned out to be a two-fisted drinker and very funny. Number Thirteen, a retired schoolteacher whose name, if

David remembered it right, was Matilda Jackson, had lost all her diffidence after half a beer. Even the professorial alternate forewoman, who was drinking only mineral water, had loosened up. Number Twelve had stayed away – predictably, David supposed.

They were all having a good time but, as the bus driver had pointed out, tomorrow morning was back to normal schedule for everybody; by not much past ten, people were making going-home noises. Kelly, who had spent the late evening bouncing between his guests and his paying patrons, came over leading someone by the hand.

At first, in the dimness, David saw only an attractive dark-haired woman in jeans and a T-shirt and thought it might be Number Twelve: maybe he had been wrong about how aloof she was. Only when they were closer and Kelly was saying, 'Look who's here,' did David realize it was Susan Linwood. Given the way she had withdrawn from contact with the other grand jurors after the Engs were indicted, he was even more surprised to see her than he would have been to see Number Twelve.

Norman Thompson made a production of getting up to give her his chair. 'I was just going anyway. I've got a long trip home and I've got to be at work real early.'

David nursed his beer and watched the others fuss over her. The bus driver and the grand jury's secretary, a high-school speech teacher named Ethel Brown, both of whom had certainly voted to indict the Engs, were the most vocal in their greetings.

'Honey, you look so different dressed like that,' the bus driver enthused. 'I'd never have known you anywhere, and here we sat right next to each other for almost a whole month. It's like you're a whole other person.'

They pressed her to tell them all about herself, and though David thought her reluctance was clear, he had to admit she was charming in the way she held back information about herself while seeming to provide it. She lived across town with her husband, she said. He was a doctor, and she worked in public relations. She had two children, a boy in college and a girl on her way there. So she *was* around forty, after all, that hadn't been a figment of his preconceptions.

Kelly came back again, this time with two of his departing diners – a tallish, craggily good-looking man with gray hair and his somewhat younger wife, who looked to be about the size of Meiling Cheung. David didn't catch their names.

'My good, old friends and the source of my knowledge about the perfidious ways of prosecutors,' Kelly said as he introduced them around. They were both criminal defense lawyers, David gathered – prominent ones, or at least ones who had been involved in highly publicized trials. They seemed to know a lot about what had gone on in the grand jury – at least in a vague, anecdotal way. David wondered if it was all right for Kelly to have said that much about it. Both the judge and the grand jury warden had been very specific about keeping secret what went on in that room.

After two more of the former grand jurors left, Manny Klein urged David and Oswaldo to climb down off their bar stools and sit with everyone else.

'I gotta go,' Oswaldo said. 'Kids are gonna wake me in the morning, you know, first thing. And I got to get to work, too.' He said goodbye and how glad he was he'd had the chance to meet everybody.

'Come on, boychik,' Manny Klein urged David. 'There's a seat right here by me with your name on it.'

For no reason David could think of, he was reluctant to join them at the table. Still, he didn't want to be rude. He sat down next to Manny.

'That's more like it,' the accountant said. 'Too many pretty ladies at this table for an old man to handle all by himself.'

'Hey, Manny, I bet you're full of juice,' the bus driver chimed in. 'Don't you think so, ladies?' Then she reached over and gave David's beard a tug. 'But I do like this nice, soft, furry beard.' She laughed, enjoying herself thoroughly.

David, grinning, his face flushed, couldn't help looking across the table at Susan Linwood. She was watching with a faint smile. She held his eye a moment, then looked away.

Manny Klein did his best to keep the party's spark glowing, but the evening was past its prime, and one at a time the others got up to go. When the table was half-empty, Susan pushed her chair back and stood up.

'This has really been fun.' She meant it. She felt bad about having closed herself off in her anger and disappointment when the Engs

203

were indicted. 'I'm glad I came. We didn't always agree but in a way we were like a family, or some of us were.'

The bus driver laughed. 'Listen, honey, I don't know about your family, but mine argues a whole lot worse than anything in that grand jury, and we all love each other anyway.'

Susan came around the table and gave Manny a quick kiss on the cheek. 'I think you were very brave in there, and I thank you for it.'

'You're very sweet to an old man. I was just glad to have a captive audience like that. If I'd've known I'd earn a kiss from a beautiful woman, I'd've talked even more.'

David Clark stood to shake hands.

'Thanks again,' she said. 'I appreciate that you took me seriously. And you were very nice to come to my defense the way you did.'

'They were being jerks.'

'Not everybody would have stood up to them, though. I do appreciate it.'

'It's too bad it didn't work out the way you wanted,' he said. 'Are you going to follow up with that man you told me about, the one your aunt was going to introduce you to?'

'Oh yes. Now that the grand jury's over, I can investigate all I want.' She'd meant it to sound light but it came out serious. 'I still want to hear what he has to say. Very much.'

'Well, good luck with it.' He seemed about to say more; before he could, Manny Klein asked her if she had a business card.

'No, I'm sorry, I didn't bring any.'

Manny leaned forward to tug his wallet from his hip pocket and gave her one of his own. 'This is me. Send me a card or a brochure or whatever you have. I'm retired and all but I still keep in touch and people always need PR help.'

'You're the one who's sweet. I'm not really looking for clients—'

'You just send me something. You never know.'

'Well,' David Clark said. 'I ought to be heading home, too.' He shook Manny's hand and the bus driver's.

Susan realized she was standing there waiting for him to finish his farewells and turned to go.

'Not so fast,' said Kelly, reappearing out of the ambience. 'You can't leave without a proper goodbye for your host.'

204

'And a thank you.' She held out her hand.

He wrapped her hand in his big, square one. 'A pleasure. A great pleasure to know you. And I hope to see you in here again. Bring the family, we've always got a table for you.'

He turned to David Clark. 'As for you, my friend, you'll be sitting right down again. We've got business to talk, you and me.'

'We do?'

'From what you were saying there a while ago, yes, I believe we do. Computer business. You sit right here –' Kelly pulled out a vacant chair – 'I'll come back with my personal bottle and we can talk.'

Again Susan caught herself waiting. For . . . she didn't know what.

She waved a last goodbye and walked through the restaurant and out into the night, feeling an odd mix of warmth and sadness.

# II

## *CHINATOWN*

# 1

The man Ann Lum had arranged for Susan to meet was the former head of her family-name association. In the days when Chinatown had been at its most closed, before the opening of the immigration doors in the mid-sixties, he had been a pivotal figure in Chinatown's social and business structure, one of the leaders of a powerful umbrella organization called the Coordinated Benevolent and Beneficial Associations. His familiar name in Chinatown was Uncle Eight.

He met Susan and Aunty Ann for dinner. He was a large, athletic-looking man whose age Susan could not begin to guess, dressed in a beautifully tailored earth-toned suit she thought might be silk and linen. It fitted him as well as his immaculate manners. His English was polished in syntax and diction, colored with a noticeable Cantonese accent.

He started the meal with the story of how he had gotten his name. It dated back to when he was a young man and he had first tried to get the CBBA to oppose the gangsterish activities of some of its member organizations, in particular extorting protection money from Chinatown merchants.

Eight was a lucky number, he said, but for him it had almost been very unlucky. One day, just after closing time, he had been called to the front door of his family's large grocery store to receive a message from a young man he had never seen before. Without a word the young man had pulled out a knife and stabbed him eight times. He still bore scars, almost forty years later, where the knife had struck him when he put up his hand to defend himself.

When the police caught the hired assailant they had called Uncle Eight down to identify him in a line-up. Later that night the police had called him back to the precinct house. Why? Because the assailant – whose employer had told him only where to find his victim and what he looked like – had learned who he was and wanted to apologize.

'Sometimes,' he said, 'they also call me Uncle Sorry.'

The food had begun arriving soon after Uncle Eight had asked his guests if there was anything they preferred not to eat and then conferred with the restaurant's owner. After the soup, and scallops steamed in their own shells, came a series of platters: seafood, beef, chicken, fish. As they arrived Uncle Eight put a morsel on each of the women's plates before taking food for himself.

'Your aunt tells me you are interested in Martin Eng,' he said to Susan. 'In the past I knew Martin Eng. We were members of the same committees at the CBBA. That was long ago, and I have not seen him in many years. But I can tell you a story about him.

'For all the time I knew him, Martin Eng was a member of the Sam Yap Association. Sam Yap is the name given to three counties in China, in Guangdong province. Not many of those people came here to New York. Here, we have many many people from Sze Yap, Four Districts, a place to the south-west of Sam Yap, farther from the Pearl River but closer to the sea. And in Sze Yap – Four Districts – people speak the Toishan dialect, not the same as the Cantonese dialect people speak in Guangzhou or Sam Yap. So when people came here to Chinatown from the Three Districts area, they formed a Sam Yap association because they felt more comfortable with people who understood them, and they thought they could all help each other.

'There are many other same-birthplace associations, as you know, just as there are many same-family-name associations, like the one across the street which I have been happy to work for. The same-family-name associations have members from everywhere in China – north, south, west. This is the same for the merchants' associations, the ones most often called tongs, the ones that are famous from being in the newspapers for bad reasons.

'Of all these, the people in same-birthplace associations are often the closest to each other, because the other members may possibly know your relatives from their days in China, or their relatives who have remained in China may know your relatives who are also there. You may be familiar with the same temples and rivers and mountains in China as the other members. You may even have known them personally before you came here.'

'The way I knew your mother,' Aunty Ann said.

'The association for Three Districts people that Martin Eng belonged to was only a medium-sized one, but it was big enough to have some influence. This was because a large part of its membership came from the more prosperous part of the community, in China and here. Many of its members did not live in Chinatown, especially its more important members. Because so many of the members were successful, the association had a treasury that was large for the size of its membership. It was able to acquire valuable real estate – often when the market was low – in that way making itself both richer and more powerful. It was able to offer substantial loans to help its members start new businesses or improve the ones they had.

'All associations do these things, and there were many members of the Sam Yap Association who needed the same kind of services that we all provide to our members: help with immigration, advice on how to apply for a job, assistance dealing with the Government bureaucracies on things like drivers' licenses or whatever else they might need.

'Some years ago, Martin Eng, who had been a large donor to the Association and had risen to become a vice-president, worked very hard to raise money for a building to help the aged people in the community. It was intended first to serve the members of his society who had no other way to be supported in their old age, and then after that the employees of their businesses.

'This may seem an odd project for Chinatown, where we are all supposed to take care of our grandparents and parents for ever, but this is America and the generation that is born here –' he interrupted himself – 'you were born in Hong Kong, is that right?'

'Yes, but my children were born here.' The words were out of her mouth before she realized how careless they were. She had put Uncle Eight in the position of being about to criticize her children, even if only indirectly. Even a *jook sing* could see that it would not do for him to continue. But he had gone too far to back off entirely.

'Wonderful children,' Aunty Ann jumped in to say. 'Respectful of their parents. Not all children are like that today.'

'Sadly, they are not,' Uncle Eight agreed. 'They grow up in a different culture, they get good jobs, they marry, sometimes to people who are not Chinese, and they move away. They stay in touch, but it is not so common for them to have their parents come and live with them, and even if they want it that way, it is not necessarily good for the parents.

'I have seen it among my own members. They go to live in the homes of their children or near their children, in some suburban place. Once they are there, they cannot speak to their neighbors, they do not know where they are. They do not know how to drive a car and often they feel too old to learn, even if they know enough English to read the signs and pass the test. Here in Chinatown they have a home, friends, familiar foods, a language that they know. Out there they are strangers. Soon, they want to come back.

'Also, many are here from the old days. They came as young men, to work and make money to take back to China. They left their wives and children there. Then came a day when they could not go back. Their families could not come here. By the time the doors opened again, too late. They are alone.

'So, Martin Eng was going to build a senior citizens home. The Association had some real estate that might have been sufficient. It remained to raise money to do the renovations and to hire a staff. Also, in order to make all the plans and programs, consultants had to be hired. To do this he raised several hundred thousand dollars. He got grants from the State Government and the Federal Government and from private foundations. He convinced corporations to become sponsors. He negotiated a special health-care contract with an insurance company.'

Listening not just to what Uncle Eight was saying but to how he was saying it, Susan was sure that if there was treachery coming, Martin Eng was not going to end up the villain of the piece.

'When all this work was done,' Uncle Eight continued, 'it was time for the Association to elect its next president. In many benevolent associations, certain official positions are awarded to the men who have done the most for the organization in a financial way. This serves everyone. It brings in large donations to the association, and it gives the donors a title and stature in the community that can be valuable to them in business dealings in Taiwan and China.

'Though this is accepted practice, it is also expected that the president of such an association will be elected by the members. To be elected president is a mark of respect that must be earned. Martin Eng had been with that society more than twenty years. He had donated much money and brought it new members. Now he had struggled to create this home for older people that would serve the membership. He had many reasons to expect that he would be elected president. On the day of the election, he was told he had been defeated.

'His closest supporters were enraged. They claimed the election must have been stolen from him. He told them he had faith in the people of the Association, some of whose family members had suffered in China by his side.

'After some months, people came to Martin Eng and apologized to him for having sold their votes to his rival. Now they were afraid the new president was going to use the senior citizens home as a way to get rich from kickbacks and extortion.

'Martin Eng saw that his supporters had been correct about the election. At a meeting of the Association's board of directors he denounced the man who had defeated him. The man denied it. Martin Eng resigned from the Association. Another board member resigned with him. After that, news spread about the confrontation. Members began to resign.

'Martin Eng decided he would start another organization, also to serve people from that part of Guangdong. This was a course of action that might have been dangerous for someone else. But Martin Eng was a prominent man among the people from the Three Districts and he had a following. He formed the Guangdong Three Districts Association.'

'I knew he was president,' Susan said. 'but he didn't –' she caught herself in time – 'I didn't realize he had founded it.'

'You also may not know that after he resigned from the old Association and others resigned to join him, he suffered a severe beating. A man came to his house and broke in and beat him very badly. He was in the hospital for many months. When he got out, he went back to building his new Association. As you know, he succeeded.'

'Why? Why did they beat him?'

'People said that at first the man who had defeated him was not worried about the new Association. Martin Eng was too honest to compete with certain of the old Association's money-making activities. Later, as more people resigned from the old Association to join the new one, he may have seen Martin Eng as more of a threat, and this may have been the reason for the beating. An association's stature in the community depends in part on its wealth and size, and the two go together. If Martin Eng drew too many people away from the old Association, it would be weakened, perhaps mortally.'

'Do they leave him alone now?'

'They do not attack him personally. But in the years that the new Association has been operating, growing all the time, it has suffered many robberies.'

'What kind of robberies?'

'There is a room in the Association where members gather to pass the time. They play the sort of games that Chinese men play – mahjong, card games, sometimes fan tan. As you also may know, men in Chinatown often carry much money with them. Thousands of dollars. And to wear gold jewelry is a sign of success. Sometimes, when the Association is having a busy night, men wearing ski masks arrive, carrying machine guns. They make everyone lie down on the floor and empty their pockets, and they take all the money and watches and jewelry they find.'

'And they just leave?'

'They have machine guns. People say that once some officers of the new Association got up when the robbers left and ran to the office in the front of the building. They leaned over the desk of the Association's secretary while she sat there, so they could shoot their guns out the window at the robbers.'

Waiters were clearing the table; others put down fresh platters and clean plates.

'Dessert,' Uncle Eight announced. 'These are lotus-seed pancakes, and these others are filled with something special. You must try them.'

The delicate, rolled pancakes were delicious, sweet but not cloying. The other dessert was airy fritters filled with a fragrant paste of black sesame seeds. Susan was too preoccupied with the story of Martin Eng to be distracted even by food this good.

'It sounds as if Martin Eng is some kind of hero,' she said.

214

'I am sure some people call him that. I think, if these stories are true, that he is a man who sees what he believes it is right to do, and then he does it.'

'Do you think he's honest?'

'I believe every man is honest, deep in his belly. And I button the pocket where I keep my wallet.'

'Do you think he could be involved in the heroin business?'

'For many people in Chinatown the heroin business is no more than that – a business. Import-export. As long as it does not harm people in this community, they say, why care who it hurts among the *lo faan*? They do not see that trafficking in heroin harms people here even when they do not use the heroin themselves. It harms them because it makes the gangs stronger and it encourages illegal activity of a sort more dangerous than the gambling that was once our most serious transgression of the American laws.'

'And Martin Eng? Could he be involved in the heroin business that way?'

'About Martin Eng I have no idea. More tea?'

'I put out the word that I wanted to know about your Three Districts Association,' Mark Brattler told Mahoney. 'I didn't come up with much. The Association doesn't have a youth gang of its own, but it does have some connections with one of the freelance gangs. Some kind of security thing.'

Mahoney straddled a chair and crossed his arms over the back. 'What kind of security?'

'They've got some kind of problem. Robberies or something. We had some reports of shots fired out the windows a while ago. Probably part of the same thing.'

'Any word on what it's about?'

Brattler shook his head. 'Not so far.'

'What about the gang they use? Any connection with heroin?'

'These gang kids do whatever pays. The word I get is that this gang mostly does extortion, shaking down merchants on a couple of blocks they've marked out as their territory. Pretty standard. Plus they do enforcement for the snakeheads – the people who import illegals . . . strongarm stuff and kidnapping.'

'But not drugs.' Too much to expect Brattler to have a solution to all his problems.

'It's not like they're going to turn down a hot chance to make a dollar, but no, I'd say, not drugs. Sorry.'

'I appreciate the effort. If you hear anything else . . .'

'You'll be the first.'

Mahoney unwound himself from the chair.

'Before you go,' Brattler said, 'I've got some new pictures. Not as painterly as my bar shot, but interesting in their own way.'

Mahoney settled back onto the chair. Brattler flipped the switch on a slide projector next to his desk.

The first picture was the side of a road, somewhere out of town. 'This is part of a case we're working on, a guy we thought might testify for us. See the shoes?'

Mahoney looked. There was a pair of men's shoes at edge of the blacktop, by the grassy shoulder. The next slide was a closeup of the shoes. They were carefully placed, heels together, toes pointing apart.

Brattler advanced to a shot of a body in a shallow grave, in the ditch beside the road. The shirt was stained with blood from stab wounds, and the throat had been slashed.

'See the sticks?' Two sticks stood upright in the ground next to the body. Like the shoes, they diverged at an angle.

'The way I get it,' Brattler said, 'the killers are worried about being pursued and haunted by the spirit of the dead guy. So they put the sticks in the ground pointing in different directions like that to confuse the spirit. And the same with the guy's shoes. That way the spirit doesn't know which direction to go to follow the killers.'

'Does it work with the cops, too?'

'Sometimes I think so. But the part I like best is the egg.'

The next picture showed the corpse's head. The mouth and nostrils were obscured by a fried egg.

'It's some kind of custom to bury people with a whole egg in their mouth. Good luck, or nourishment, maybe, for the next world. So this has to be some kind of nasty, ironic version of that. Maybe even a curse.'

'Because the guy was going to talk?'

'That's what we think. This isn't local stuff. It's either a Triad hit or

216

meant to look like one. We don't see many of those.'

'Triad?'

'Chinese Mafia, sort of – goes back to sixteen hundred and some-thing, after the Manchus conquered the country. The Chinese formed these quasi-military secret societies, supposedly to protect the peas-ants – in the south-east mostly, Fujian and Guangdong – and over the centuries they turned more and more criminal. Just like the Mafia.'

'They operate here, too? Like the Mafia?'

'Depends on who you ask. There's a DEA guy in Washington who thinks they're masterminding major crime all over the world. Politics, too. Some say they're just friendly with the local branches of the tongs, and they confine their own operations to Hong Kong and the Asian side of the ocean in general. The Communists kicked them out of mainland China in the fifties, but they're moving back in there, along with capitalism. I hope they keep busy over there, too. We have trouble enough without them.'

# 2

The night after Susan's dinner with Uncle Eight, she and Lara went to a Broadway musical and then a nearby barbecue restaurant Susan knew Lara would enjoy. They talked about the show, but Susan found it harder to maintain her end of the conversation as the meal progressed.

Waiting for dessert, Lara said, 'Mom? Is something wrong?'

'No, it's this case I had in the grand jury. I can't get it out of my mind.'

'What was it about?'

'This is so silly. I've been wanting to talk about it but I'm not really supposed to, not to anybody.'

'Is it the one about heroin?'

Susan nodded.

'But this isn't about me and Charles again?'

'It's the people who were indicted. I just think it was so wrong. I wish there was something . . .' She looked at her daughter. 'That's what has me so bothered. I wish there was something I could do, and I know there isn't.'

'Do you think they're innocent?'

'I think they might be.'

'How come they got . . . indicted? I mean, if you think they might be innocent.'

'There were twenty-three of us. And in a grand jury, the majority rules.'

'When is the trial?'

'In the fall, I think.'

'But then they must have a lawyer or something, if there's going to be a trial.'

'Yes. They had a lawyer in the grand jury. They came and testified, and their lawyer came with them. They seemed so . . . so good, somehow. And they reminded me – the woman especially – they reminded me of your grandparents.'

'Really?' Lara laughed. 'That's so hard to imagine.'

'Why?'

'Well, I mean, like, I just get this picture of this tall, white-haired man in a three-piece suit and this society lady in pearls huddled together on a street corner going *Smoke?* or whatever heroin dealers say.'

Susan laughed, too. 'No wonder you thought it was funny. But I didn't mean Grandma and Grandpa Linwood. I meant *my* parents.'

'Oh.' Lara's expression grew sober. 'They were Chinese.'

'Yes. But that's really the only thing they had in common with Grandpa and Grandma Chan. Physically, they're much smaller than I remember my parents being. And much older – the man was in his late seventies. My mother and father were in their fifties when they died. Not a whole lot older than I am now.'

'Mom!'

'Well, I'm only exaggerating a little. I'm forty-two, after all. And sometimes I *feel* fifty-five.'

'Well, let me tell you, you sure don't look it. You remember Alan, from that restaurant we went to downtown?'

'Yes . . .'

'Well, he was telling me how he couldn't believe you were my mom, how sexy and good-looking you were.'

'I'll try to feel flattered.' Thinking how far from sexy she felt at that moment. Or at almost any moment for the last ten years. 'I guess this means your friend Alan is straight after all.'

'Not necessarily. Have you talked about any of this to Dad?'

'About Alan?'

'About these Chinese people in court.'

'I mentioned it to him once. That same night, in fact, the night we went downtown together. Because I was concerned about what you said about Charles.'

'I didn't say anything! What did you tell Dad?'

'Just that you asked if I'd talked to Charles—'

'Because you talked to me. It didn't *mean* anything. Anyway just now I meant have you talked to Dad since then, about how you want to do something for these people?'

'No, I haven't. I'm thinking of going to a lawyer, though.'

'Instead of Dad?'

'Your father's a doctor, not a lawyer.'

'But he knows about rules and things. And you're asking me.'

'Because I trust you to listen, and maybe that will help me find the right answer.'

'Not Dad?'

'It's different. He's a problem solver. He'd have an answer before I finished telling him the problem. I want to work this out myself. I need to understand why it bothers me so much. When I said I might go to a lawyer, I meant just for legal advice – to find out how much I can say in a more public way, and to whom. Talking to you helps me see what's on my mind.'

After a silence Lara said, 'Mom, how old did you say those people were?'

'The Engs? He was in his mid or late seventies. I think she was a few years younger.'

'And how old were Grandma and Grandpa Chan when they died?'

'In their fifties. Fifty-eight and fifty-two.'

'And how long ago was that?'

'Going on twenty years. But you know all that.' And then she saw. 'Oh. Very clever. They'd be about the same age now as the Engs, wouldn't they? But I remember them when they were much younger . . . I don't think I could imagine them in their seventies.'

'Just a thought.' But Lara was clearly disappointed by her mother's reaction.

'I didn't say it was a bad thought. In fact it's a good thought. I was being too literal. See – that's why I wanted to talk to you. I don't know if I would have let myself recognize that the connection to my parents was that strong. Thinking about them is still hard for me.'

Susan Chan Huiling had been a late baby for her mother, by the standards of the early fifties. Late and, she thought, probably not very welcome, not even in relatively cosmopolitan Hong Kong. After all, her father already had a son. Perhaps he'd thought he could repeat his good luck. Instead, he got little Susan.

How she had resented her parents for not treating her as well as they treated her older brother! She had no clear memory of the years before they had come to the United States, but growing through her girlhood in the late Eisenhower and Kennedy years had not provided any noticeable improvement in her status. The main difference from the old Chinese ways was that here she could expect to continue serving her own parents as well as her husband and his mother, whereas by Chinese tradition when she married she would have left her own family completely to become the property of her mother-in-law.

When the social rebellion of the late sixties erupted in the United States, Suzie Chan had been more than ready for it. Just entering adolescence, she had done her best to ape the dress and attitudes of her older schoolmates until her parents – worried by the times and by reported incidents of violence against Chinese people who had been mistaken for Vietnamese – had pulled her out of public school and sent her to a parochial high school for girls.

Up to that point in her life Susan had met few other Chinese girls. In the high school her parents had chosen, there were enough Chinese girls to form cliques.

Though the criteria that separated the groups were said to hinge on place of origin – north China or south China, east or west, U.S. born or not – Susan had quickly decided that the real glue was money. The very richest girls stuck together, and if some had ancestors from Shanghai, some from Fujian province, and some from Guangdong province, nobody really cared. And each of the lesser cliques was bound together by the ways in which its members approximated the twenty-four-carat attributes of that highest group.

In spite of the turmoil and experimentation going on outside the walls, her high school had been a sedate and conservative place, its social rules beyond challenge. Susan had found herself essentially shunned by the non-Chinese girls, and within the Chinese groups there was nothing to do but conform. Resistance, she could see, would get her nothing but isolation.

By the time she got to college the flower children were beginning to wilt, but the culture of drugs and sex was well-established. The conservatism she had brought with her from home and from high school eroded only gradually; to the end, it was durable enough to keep her from joining her classmates in their most extreme excesses. But she finally had something like freedom, and she used it.

It was a time of exploration and discovery for her – spent almost entirely with people she thought of as real Americans – and it had culminated, in her junior year, in her moving in with a boy from the Midwest who was a first-year student at the medical school. She remembered him now mostly for his ingenuity in devising ways to keep her parents from figuring out what was going on. For that, and for bringing her to the picnic where she first saw Richard, amidst a gathering of tired medical students and the girlfriends or wives who, in many cases, were putting them through school.

Her boyfriend had gone off to play softball and she was wandering around, looking for a place where the grass was not worn away so she could sit down and pretend to be out in the country. She had come around a thick-trunked oak tree and seen a group of women. Drifting in their direction she saw that there was a man at the center of the group, sitting crosswise on the end of a picnic table. How odd, she had thought, and walked closer. She had stopped when she had a better view of him. He seemed the best-looking man she had ever seen. She knew the phrase 'noble brow,' but she had never before seen anyone she thought it might apply to. Everything about him had seemed splendid.

She had wanted to join the group, if only to see him from closer up and to hear more clearly the deep, warm voice, but she was too shy. So she had stood watching until, to her dismay, he noticed her. He had smiled and called out a greeting. 'Hi, I'm Richard. Come join us.'

She could not have been more mortified, or more thrilled. Somehow, she had managed to speak, even to be entertaining – or so he had told her when, six months later, a month after their wedding, she had gathered the courage to joke with him about their initial moments together. Those first months, even the first years, had seemed idyllic. Richard had gone from being the medical school's star fourth-year student to being a star resident at one of the most prestigious teaching hospitals in the country. The move had forced her to change colleges, and she'd lost some credits, transferring as a senior; hard work had gotten her a diploma only a semester late.

After that she had basked in the glow of being Richard Linwood's wife. She had taken a clerical job in the public affairs department at the hospital, not because she and Richard needed the money – his small trust fund provided well enough for tuition and a modest standard of living – but because she wanted to be busy and near him. Impossible as it seemed with a resident's schedule, he was continuing his already well-established tradition of working twice as hard as anyone else. In those days he had been able to go without sleep altogether if he thought it was called for.

Her parents, predictably, had not been pleased. They had behaved in what must have seemed to them a civil manner, but to Susan it was clear they did not care about her happiness. The only thing that mattered to them was that their daughter had not married a Chinese man.

They were even more awkward about hiding their lack of delight at the news she was pregnant. Yet another loss of face for them. Even if they loved the child when it was born, the baby's mixed-race heritage would announce the fact that their daughter had married a barbarian white-ghost foreigner. And that would reflect badly on them – even, in their minds, to their non-Chinese friends. What had they done wrong, bringing her up, that she would turn her back on family, ancestors, community? And for themselves they would always wonder what aberration had led her to marry so far beneath herself, when she might have had a man of vastly superior Han Chinese heritage.

And so, in self-defense, she had stopped seeing her parents soon after Charles was born, and almost stopped speaking to them. Long overdue, she had thought at the time: they had given her nothing but grief for too many years. If they wanted a relationship with her, let them show it. By calling them once a month to say hello, instead of cutting off all communication, she had kept that opportunity alive for them. Her pain and resentment had only increased as, month after month, they had done nothing to avail themselves of it.

Almost two years after Charles's birth, when Susan had just become pregnant with Lara, her parents had gone to China to try to find the relatives they had left behind almost thirty years before. By that time the estrangement was so well-established that they did not call to say goodbye: she had learned about the trip from her brother. And it was from him she had learned that they had not returned on schedule and that he had not heard a word from them after they left Hong Kong for China.

Months after they had apparently vanished, after many futile attempts to find out what had happened, her brother had received a perfunctory official letter – a form letter, really – regretting to inform him that his parents had been killed in an earthquake of unprecedented severity. Along with thousands of others, the letter said, their bodies had been buried in a mass grave.

'Mom?' Lara prodded.

'Oh.' Susan pulled her attention back to her daughter. 'Sorry. I was just thinking about your Grandma and Grandpa Chan. These people really do make me think of them. And they even come from the same part of China.'

'No. Really?'

'The next county over, I think, but part of the same region.'

'Like, the Bronx and Queens?'

'Sort of. I'm not much of an expert on these things.'

'But if they really are innocent, won't it come out at their trial?'

'I don't know. There are all these rules about what evidence is all right for a trial and what evidence isn't. And I'm beginning to think a lot of really important evidence doesn't fit into the definition of what's all right.'

'Why do you think they're innocent?'

'Because of what they said in the grand jury, and because of the kind of people they seem to be. And what I'm learning about them. And, I guess, probably because they do remind me of Grandma and Grandpa Chan.'

'It's so strange to hear you call them that, and to think I never met them, and they died before I was born.'

'I'm sorry you never met them. They were very . . . interesting people.'

'Were they like you and Uncle Sandy?'

'More like Uncle Sandy than like me. But not like either of us, really. They were very Chinese, very formal in some ways, even though they tried very hard to be American, Grandpa especially. Grandma Chan had a friend you knew when you were little. I don't know if you remember her. Ann Lum. Aunty Ann, we called her.'

'A little round Chinese lady? She was always bringing me and Charles steamed buns and things and Charles would always throw them out when she wasn't looking? And she made faces a lot?'

Susan laughed. 'That sounds about right. She's one of the reasons I think these people are innocent – because of some things I heard from her and from a very well-respected man in Chinatown who told me something important about them.'

'What?'

'That they have a powerful enemy.'

'What does that have to do with it?'

'Somebody who might have a motive to frame them.'

Sitting there, her mind weaving painful, troubling memories of her own past with concerns about innocent people wrongly accused, Susan gazed across the table at her daughter. Susan thought she had not seen a person so alive with possibility and a kind of luminous power since that first time she had seen Richard. That Lara was beautiful she had been especially aware of for days now, but this was something more. Partly it was that Lara was on the brink of so much: about to go out in the world and discover what was there and begin to put her own mark on it.

That's me at her age, Susan thought. Me, not as I was but as I wanted to be. Only she really *is*. Unaccountably, the thought brought tears to her eyes. She blinked them away, hoping Lara hadn't noticed.

'But if there's somebody who might have framed them,' Lara probed, her attention on the puzzle, 'then why is there a problem?'

'I don't know who knows about it.'

'Like who do you mean?'

'Like the people who are trying to convict them.'

'Ask them,' Lara proposed. 'And if they don't know, you can tell them.'

'I like your instincts,' Susan said.

'Am I wrong? I mean, you're good at telling people things, that's what you do. So why shouldn't you tell this?'

'Maybe not to the prosecutor, though, not yet. Maybe I should start

225

with somebody who was on the grand jury with me, who knows the background. Just to make sure I'm not completely out of touch with reality.'

'This is so great.' Lara was full of adolescent enthusiasm. 'Saving innocent people from going to jail.'

'Well, I don't know if that's exactly what I'm doing.'

'That's what it sounds like. Lots better than teaching doctors how to make money for drug companies.'

'Where did you hear that?'

'From you. That's what you say about what you do, when you're not feeling good about it.'

'Do I really?' Susan had to smile. 'I guess I do.'

# 3

David Clark was the first person who came to Susan's mind, but the thought of calling him made her uneasy. Instead she called Manny Klein, because she had his card and because he had seemed like a nice, level-headed man she could trust to be honest with her.

'I think we should have some of the others hear your story, too,' he said when she called. 'The more heads the better on a thing like this.'

'Who else is there?'

'Jimmy Kelly. The professor. David Clark. Norman Thompson. There were eleven of us who voted not to indict.'

'Only eight, really, and we don't know exactly who all of them were. And Mr Kelly abstained on the first vote.'

'All the better. No point just preaching to the converted. You want somebody who'll ask hard questions.'

'I know you're trying to be helpful, Manny, but I'm really not looking for a debate. I just want to talk it out with someone. One other, but no more.'

'All right. But I still think Kelly's the right man for this. Bartenders make good listeners, and he's got relatives and friends in the business, if I remember.'

'What business?'

'Law enforcement.'

'All right, Kelly, then. Can you call him and see if he's interested? And if there's any problem about the date, let me know.'

David Clark was sitting in Jimmy Kelly's office going over the structure of the business with him and trying to make a first-draft flow chart of how it operated, when Manny Klein called.

227

The night of the grand-jurors' party, Kelly had lamented about his screwed-up computer system: it was supposed to do everything from transmitting dinner orders to the kitchen to keeping track of what food and drink needed ordering from his suppliers, plus all his receivables and payables. 'The trouble is, the damn thing is wrong more often than it's right.'

'You don't want me for that,' David had told him. 'You want the people who designed the system.'

'I already tried them. They made it worse. If I can't fix it, I'm going to have to junk it.'

A considerable amount of aged Irish whiskey and a stem-to-stern tour of the restaurant later, David had agreed to get the hang of how things worked at the Shamrock and sketch out the rough plan of something that might meet Kelly's needs. 'It'd be quick and dirty but it might give you a place to start, talking to the vendors about a new machine.'

When Kelly got off the phone with Manny Klein, he told David about the planned get-together with Susan Linwood.

'A little something to make life interesting,' Kelly said. 'Tomorrow evening.'

'I don't know, Jimmy.' This would be the follow-up on that Chinatown 'investigation' she had been worried about; he was not particularly eager for it. 'Nobody invited me, that I noticed.'

'No one said, one way or the other. Just she'd learned something important about the Engs and wanted to talk to some of her fellow grand jurors.'

'You'll all do just great without me.'

'She's a fine-looking woman.'

'No argument there.'

'So come along and spend the time looking at her, if you're not interested in what she'll be saying.'

Detective Mick Pullone walked into Mahoney's office without knocking. 'Kevin tells me you're looking for more from my snitch. I can tell you right now, as far as *you* talking to him, forget about it. He won't come in. That was our deal and he's not going to change it.'

228

'Isn't he worried about his money?' Mahoney asked.

'Yeah, he is. Calls me about it every third day. But he figures he already earned it.'

'How much have you worked with him before?'

'We have a history.'

'And all he told you was that these people were moving heroin money and if you hit them right away you'd catch them with a houseful.'

Pullone waved a hand at the case file open on Mahoney's cluttered desk. 'If that's what it says.'

'He didn't tell you whose money it was, who was moving the heroin, nothing like that?'

'This guy doesn't speak the best English, you know, so we kind of stick to basics. And we were in kind of a hurry on this one.' Pullone readjusted the leather belly pack that served him as a warm-weather holster. 'Look, counsellor, let me give you a piece of advice . . . I got my arrest, you got your indictment, that's what counts here.'

'I don't have anything against arrests and indictments, detective.' Fighting his own impatience. 'Right now, I'm worried about a conviction.'

'See, that's the best part – you don't have to worry about a conviction. That's Kevin Horgan's worry. All you have to do is get together whatever evidence there is. He'll do the rest. I've worked with him a lot. He delivers the goods.'

Mahoney knew that Pullone saw him as a temporary annoyance: the detective's connection was with Horgan, he had come today only because Horgan had said to. Attitude aside, everything he had said made sense, including how protective he was being of the informant. Cops didn't like to mess up their relationships with snitches by parading them around for bosses and prosecutors, even assuming the snitches were willing to be subjected to it. And yet Mahoney was left feeling uneasy.

His internal debate was interrupted by the telephone. It was an old law-school friend, but she wasn't calling to catch up on old times. As soon as Mahoney got off he called Joe Estrada.

'You have a minute?'

'I have a Bureau meeting in about twenty.'

'That's time enough. I'll meet you downstairs.'

They walked along the edge of the park that separated the courthouse building from Chinatown. The sun was hot in a clear sky; a breeze made the heat tolerable.

'You remember Mary-Lynne Gunther?' Mahoney asked. 'My law-school little sister, sort of?'

'The one you couldn't recruit for the office?'

'Right. She went to the Southern District instead.'

'I remember. Not your type, I thought.'

'That's not what this is about. She just called me.'

'I thought that wasn't what this was about.'

'She wants me to send her a copy of the Eng indictment.'

That made Estrada stop. 'Interesting. Why?'

'My question exactly. "Something we're working on might touch on it," she said.'

'That's vague enough. What do you suppose it means?'

'My very question . . . But she's not the type to give everything up on the phone, so I suggested dinner. You know – "It's been too long since we got together." And she was very quick to say yes.'

'Your animal magnetism at work once again. But didn't you say that's not what this is about?'

'You have a one-track mind, Estrada.'

They went over to a park bench and sat in the shade.

'You tell Horgan she called?' Estrada wanted to know.

'Not yet.'

'But you will, and soon.'

Mahoney shook his head. 'I don't think so.'

'You're not going to tell your boss that the United States Attorney's Office for the Southern District of New York is interested in his case?'

'I gather you think I should.'

Estrada looked at him.

'Okay. But I don't have anything much to tell, yet, so there's no point running to him with it. And I think Gunther is up to something. Somebody over at the Southern District is being devious.'

'All the more reason to tell Horgan.'

'I'm not so sure.'

'Why not?'

'Because as soon as he finds out there's federal interest in the case, he's going to jump in and deal with it himself and close me out. Unless there's a damn good reason to keep me plugged in. And I've put too much into this case to have him take me out of the loop.'

'How do you know he won't say, "You know her, go find out what she has on her mind?"'

'Because he doesn't like things to get to where he can't control them. And because he's been real unhappy with me since the judge let my defendants out on bail.'

'Maybe he'll have you wear a wire.'

'Very funny.'

Estrada checked his watch. 'I've got to get back. But first, since you seem not to be taking my advice, I'll give you some more. Going around behind Kevin Horgan's back might not be the safest way to travel. He's been in the office long enough to grow eyes back there.'

When Susan arrived at Kelly's Shamrock the hostess led her to a big round table in the far corner of the room. Kelly was there with Manny Klein. And David Clark.

She almost stopped short. This wasn't what she'd had in mind: with this many people she might as well be pitching a campaign to a client.

Kelly stood up to greet her. She tried for a smile as she accepted his hearty handshake.

'I took it on myself to ask David to join us,' he said. 'He was in the office with me when Manny called.'

'That's fine,' she said.

'Okay, we're all ears,' Kelly said when he'd filled drink orders all around.

She started slowly, uncertain at first how to proceed, framing her story with a description of herself and Ann Lum at the dim-sum restaurant. When she got to Uncle Eight, she had built up enough momentum to give a spirited account of Martin Eng's troubles with the senior citizens' home and the rival association president who had stolen his election and had him beaten up.

'That's quite a story,' Manny Klein said. 'Machine guns, yet. Looks as if they're not such quiet, retiring old people as they wanted us to believe.'

'That's one way to look at it.'

To David's ear, Susan didn't sound happy. He thought she deserved some help. 'It also means they have real enemies,' he pointed out. 'And that makes my question . . . excuse me –' to Susan – '*your* question about the informant seem much more important.'

'What question is that?' Kelly asked.

'I asked Mahoney, at Susan's suggestion, why the cops made the raid in the first place. He wouldn't ask it for me in the grand jury, but he more or less admitted to me later there was an informant of some kind.'

'He did?' Susan said. 'When did he do that?'

'I talked to him in the street. He wouldn't come out and say it in so many words, but it was what he meant.'

'*Snitches,*' Kelly said. 'There's always a snitch. If they can't find a rat who's been the poor defendant's bosom buddy since they were altar boys dodging priests together, then they get a junkie who'd rat out his old granny for the price of a fix.'

'But now that we've heard Susan's story,' Manny Klein ventured, 'we might be able to deduce something about this particular snitch. Like – he might have had a reason to inform on the Engs, guilty or not. Because it sounds like there are people who would be pleased as punch to see them disgraced and out of circulation. Too bad we didn't know that when it counted.'

'I should have thought of talking to my aunt about it sooner,' Susan said. 'We could have insisted on hearing from the informant.'

'Don't feel bad on that account,' Kelly said. 'I don't think Mr Mahoney goes around bringing informants to testify in the grand jury. Not likely most of them would live long if they did.'

'And they don't exactly make great witnesses,' Manny added.

'And even if the snitch did have some personal reason for turning them in,' Kelly said, 'they still did have heroin in the house.'

'But that's the point,' she said. 'The informant might have planted the heroin himself. That's what makes it so awful.'

'All right,' Kelly conceded reluctantly. 'Suppose, for argument, the snitch planted the heroin. What about the money and the ledgers?

232

Surely you don't think he planted it all.'

'No, I think the money is theirs, just as they said it was, and as far as the ledgers, I thought Manny and David got that out of the way in the grand jury. Why can't the ledgers be what Martin Eng said they were, too?'

'I was stretching things for effect, talking about them in the grand jury,' Manny said. 'The ledgers *could* be what he said they were, yes, but I'd believe they were a lot of other things first.'

'Are you saying you think they're guilty?'

'Not necessarily of selling heroin. But there are other reasons to keep coded lists of names and dollar amounts. Banks do it all the time. You've got an account number they use instead of your name, or in addition to your name.'

'But he said he didn't believe in banks,' Susan objected.

'He didn't believe in putting his money in the kind of banks you and I use,' David said, breaking his silence. 'But don't a lot of people in Chinatown feel that way?'

'Yes, I think so,' Susan said. 'At least it used to be that way.'

'And what did they all do with their money, then?' Kelly wanted to know.

'I suppose they kept it in a safe the way the Engs did,' Susan told him. 'If they could afford one and if they had a place for it. Or else under the mattress.'

'Only, keeping your money under the mattress isn't very secure if you live in a small room with a lot of other men as poor and hardworking and eager to make money as you are,' David said. 'Especially with a landlord happy to take rent from a dozen men living in a single room, sometimes subdivided, sometimes not. Which is how I understand a lot of men lived in Chinatown, especially in the old days.'

'How do you know all that?' Susan asked him.

'I took my niece and nephew to Chinatown last weekend. Wandering around, my niece saw an old school building with a history museum in it, so we went in. And you'll never guess who works there.'

'Mrs Liu.'

'Who's Mrs Liu?' Manny asked.

'Number Six,' Susan said. 'She works in the Chinatown History Museum.'

'She was very good about helping me to find out things about Chinatown,' David said. 'Going into the museum, I didn't have any real motive except curiosity and the idea it would be fun for the kids. Seeing her there made it seem a little like destiny, so I went back and learned some more, and I read a couple of books. I didn't know then that it would have any real-life application, but I'm beginning to think it applies here.'

'Like how?' Manny prompted.

'In the old days, men in Chinatown – and there were only men there until relatively recently – in those days, if you didn't want to carry all your money around all day every day, you gave it to someone you trusted to hold it for you. It might be a merchant you dealt with a lot but it might also be whatever benevolent association you belonged to – your same-family-name association or your mercantile association or your hometown or county association for people from the same place in China.'

'Like the Three Districts Association,' Susan said.

'Exactly. Like the Three Districts Association. And one thing that would look like those ledgers is deposit-account books. Just like a bank. Because if a lot of people are giving you money to hold, and they're going to want it back someday, you'd better keep good track of it.'

'If that's what it was, why didn't they say so in the grand jury?' Kelly challenged. 'Why make up a story about the family jewels and a coin collection? Though that would explain why Mr Eng couldn't do better telling what meant coins and what meant jewels – if all that about jewels and coins was blarney.'

'I don't know if he made up any stories. I'm just saying that kind of account-keeping would look a lot like Mahoney's so-called drug records but have nothing to do with drugs. As for why Mr Eng wouldn't say so in the grand jury – Manny's the one to ask about that.'

The accountant made a sour face. 'You're talking about people giving him cash earnings to hold, right? And expecting to get it back in cash?'

'As far as I know.'

'And how many of those men were properly documented immigrants? How many of them got paid on the books, with proper

234

deductions for federal and state income tax and social security? Not too many, right?'

'Say, none.'

'So if he told the police or Mahoney or us, "This money belongs to these other people and I'm just holding it for them," then the tax authorities would be all over him like a bad suit, and all over the people whose money it was.'

'And so would the immigration folks,' Kelly added.

'Except that most of what David's talking about happened a long time ago,' Susan said. 'Isn't there some limit on how long the tax people can come after you?'

'Not if these people never filed tax forms,' Manny said. 'The time limits you're talking about aren't always as much protection as people suppose. But don't you think we're getting way ahead of ourselves?'

'For a lot of reasons,' David acknowledged. 'As Susan just said, that was mostly long ago. *Really* long ago. The kind of thing I was talking about started in the days when Chinese women weren't allowed into the country and Chinatown was virtually isolated. For those ledgers to date from then, they'd have to be at least thirty years old, maybe a lot older. The Engs have barely been here thirty years, and it must have taken them a while to get established and build up trust. So they'd have to be reviving a practice from long ago for those ledgers to be that kind of account.

'And none of this has anything to do with Susan's story,' he continued, amazed that he had let himself be drawn into this so deeply. 'Wherever the money came from, the question she's raised now is how far would the head of that other association go to ruin Martin Eng and get his members back into the fold?'

'You might also ask what business it is of ours,' Kelly said.

'That's why when I heard the story from Uncle Eight I wanted to talk to you about it,' Susan said. 'We were on the grand jury that indicted them.'

'And we voted no,' Manny Klein pointed out, 'even without all this.'

'However we voted, this is new information. Don't we have some kind of obligation to let Mr Mahoney know about it?'

'Obligation?' Manny asked. 'Obligation to whom? Or to what?'

235

'An obligation to . . . well, to . . . the truth, or justice . . .'

'Don't you suppose the police already know about all this?' Kelly asked.

'If they did, why were they so eager to indict the Engs?'

'Maybe they don't think it means anything. Maybe Mr and Mrs Eng don't either. They didn't see fit to tell *us*.'

'But maybe that's because they weren't allowed to for some reason. Because it wasn't relevant, or something. There were times when Mahoney kind of shut them up.'

'Not much, though,' Manny said. 'They told their whole life story, all about the old country and the silk factories . . . This has to be more relevant to the charges than the Japanese Army.'

'I have a proposal,' Kelly said. 'That party we had, I introduced you to my friends the defense lawyers. How about I give them a call and ask them some of these questions?'

'But what about secrecy?' Susan sounded alarmed. 'Isn't it against the law for us to talk to an outsider about what happened in that room?'

'Not if it's our lawyer we're talking to. I took it on myself to tell my friends about this meeting we're having. I also gave them a crisp dollar bill as retainer so we'd have counsel to advise us what we can say and what we can do, in the world outside the grand jury room. And they assured me that in aid of that, we can tell them anything we want to.'

Kelly took them to his office to make the call.

'All right,' he started briskly when he was done on the phone. 'First off, there's no legal reason Mr and Mrs Eng couldn't have testified for us about their enemy in the other association. So we have to assume they had some reason of their own not to. My friend said if the Engs were his clients, he'd have told them go ahead and tell that story in the grand jury. So we have to consider the possibility they never told their lawyer.'

'Maybe they had a reason,' Manny said.

'Maybe so. Then he said, as far as a story like that goes, basically there's two ways the defense lawyer can play it, at this point. Take the information to the prosecutor right away and use it as an argument for him to drop the case. Or, develop as much evidence in favor of the theory as you can and reveal it at the last possible moment, at trial. The strategy there being, the less time the prosecutor has to find ways to poke holes in your theory the better off you are.

'Now this next is more than just what they were telling me right now,' Kelly went on. 'It's something I've heard a lot over the years, from the lawyers in my bar, and these days on the TV.'

'Plenty of that, isn't there?' Manny said. 'We're all courtroom buffs now.'

'We are that. And one thing you hear often enough is that your defense lawyers are fond of putting forward an alternate theory of the crime to the prosecutor's. And that's what my friend brought up just now. If this lawyer is building a defense on the theory that someone had a motive to frame her clients, then if you tell the prosecutor this story about the stolen election and so on, you might be taking away the defense lawyer's chance to use it the way she wants to.'

'I never thought of that,' Susan said.

'That's why I called my friends.'

'I appreciate it. I don't want to spoil anything for anyone.' She sounded bewildered, David thought, and not happy. She stood up. 'Thank you, Jimmy. Thank you all. I hate to think I might have gone off and done exactly the wrong thing.'

'It's a pleasure to help somebody as nice as yourself,' Kelly said. 'And beautiful, too, if I'm not out of line to say so.'

She smiled briefly. 'You're not out of line at all. That's a very pretty compliment, both parts of it, and I thank you for it.'

They were all standing now. Kelly came around his desk to show them out.

'Before we all go home,' he said, 'there's one thing occurred to me. Some of what Susan was saying sounded like getting herself into the middle of a feud in Chinatown. I'd say you might like to think twice about that. This fellow you're getting ready to accuse of a frame-up – didn't I hear you say this same fellow ordered a brutal beating of an old man, and a bunch of nasty armed robberies? If I was him, whether I framed these people myself or I didn't, I don't expect I'd want to be hearing that people were going around saying I did. And this fellow doesn't sound like the kind you want to be on the wrong side of.'

★ ★ ★

'I guess that didn't go too well,' Susan said to David Clark outside Kelly's after they'd said goodbye to Manny Klein. She stepped into the street to hail a cab.

'I don't see why,' he responded. 'That's an important piece of information you came up with, and I thought the lawyers' advice sounded smart, as far as what you should do.'

'*Nothing*.' She let a cab go by without hailing it. 'Isn't that what they said to do? Nothing.'

'They said that going to Mahoney might hurt the Engs's defense.'

'And Kelly said it was dangerous to get involved in Chinatown feuds.'

'Yes – and that does sound like good advice.'

'But what does it leave?'

'I suppose you're right, it leaves just letting it go. Giving the Engs and their lawyer credit for knowing what they're doing.'

'Is that okay with you?'

He looked away for a moment. 'I'm not sure what's okay with me.'

She let another cab go by. 'Where do you live?'

'Not far.' He gestured vaguely uptown.

'Oh. I live the other way. Do you want to walk for a minute?'

'Sure.' He headed downtown with her.

'What *do* you think? About the Engs?' she asked him, suddenly feeling lost.

He walked in silence a while before he answered. 'I'll make a confession. I'm not as convinced about all this as you are. I voted against indicting Mrs Eng because Mahoney didn't convince me she was anything more than Mr Eng's wife. But I was one of the people who abstained on indicting him.'

'Oh. I wouldn't have guessed. But at least you didn't vote yes.'

'No, I didn't,' he said. 'I was too uncertain to be the deciding vote, either way, unless I had to.' After what had happened with Number Twenty he'd assumed there'd be another vote if one side or the other didn't muster a clear majority.

She paused to face him. 'I'm glad you told me. I respect that. I appreciate it.'

Before he could think of anything to say she had started walking again.

238

'I feel so bad about not having found all this out sooner,' she said, almost to herself.

'What could you have done if you had? And the Engs could have brought this up themselves if they'd wanted to.'

'Maybe they just haven't thought of mentioning it,' she said. 'Not even to their lawyer. I mean, why would they? What does one thing have to do with the other?'

'Everything, I'd think. If you've been framed, what's the first thing you ask yourself? *Who did this to me?*'

'And my answer to that is, first, the head of the Sam Yap Association, and second, the police.'

'The police?'

'For the money. Because they get to keep it.'

'Assuming Kelly's right about that. But you see, you did think of the rival association president . . .'

Susan stopped walking again. 'This whole thing makes me want to scream. I'm so sure they're being railroaded.'

'Why so sure?'

'I don't know. I just am.'

She thought she saw why she felt so strongly about it, but how could she say it . . . *Because I've been afraid for years that the Government in China did something horrible to my parents. Because these people make me think of my parents. Because the Engs have already suffered so much at the hands of other governments, and I don't want to think that now they're suffering at the hands of American officials.* She couldn't say any of that. None of it was rational.

'Don't get me wrong,' David said. 'I'm not completely satisfied, either. For one thing, I don't think we ever got to the bottom of what happened when the police went to the apartment. The detective – Pullone – told that story about martial arts, which I have a lot of trouble with. I have trouble with him, anyway, something about him . . . But that business about martial arts was like he was pulling out the first stereotype that came to mind.

'Meanwhile, Martin Eng said Pullone knocked him down and put a gun to his head, and I can definitely see Pullone doing that, no trouble at all.' He shook his head. 'But even if he did, maybe in the big picture it's only a minor detail . . .' Frustration clear in his voice. 'I don't know, maybe Kelly said it best – when you come down to it, what business is it of ours?'

'I'm so tired,' Susan said, because suddenly she was, and she didn't want any more of this conversation. 'I ought to get a cab.'

She raised her hand and a taxi pulled to the sidewalk. 'Thanks for putting up with me.' She got into the cab before he could reply.

He stood watching the cab drive off.

*You're very direct*, he remembered her saying the first time they'd talked. Direct, and clumsy, once again.

Not that he thought he was entirely wrong. Asking what business it was of theirs didn't mean the only answer was 'none.'

Maybe – for her, at least – participating in the case had thrust her into the lives of Martin Eng and his wife past where she could stand back and let things take their course. Tentative as she had been when she offered the notion that she and the others might have an obligation to truth or justice, she had sounded like she meant it. He wondered where that feeling would take her.

Not that it ultimately mattered to him, he reminded himself. She had her life, and he had his – such as it was, these days.

# 4

Susan kept thinking about the difference it might have made if she'd called Ann Lum sooner. Could people's lives hang by such slender threads? It seemed grandiose to think the Engs's fate had been in her hands, and yet in a sense it had been.

She tried to comfort herself with the idea that the grand jury was supposed to decide solely based on the evidence it got from the prosecution, but then she thought of what the history professor, the alternate forewoman, had said about how grand juries had developed, how the value of grand jurors had originally depended on their bringing with them their knowledge of the community.

And while Kelly was waiting for his lawyer friends to get on the phone, he'd repeated something even more interesting that he'd learned from them. Grand juries had the power go in directions different from what the prosecutor wanted. The grand jury he'd talked about, a federal grand jury in the South-west, had voted indictments against some environmental polluters when all the Government wanted to do was fine their company. And when the prosecutor refused to sign the indictments, the grand jury had done its best to indict the prosecutor himself for failing to do his duty.

So she couldn't hide behind the idea that she'd done as she'd been told, or that Mahoney would have been reluctant to call the informant as a witness. She could have done more – in a sense, there was no limit to what she could have done – but she hadn't.

She had gone to Kelly's in the hope she might find some support for her desire not to let the Engs be railroaded. They had all taken her seriously, even though they didn't all agree with her. David Clark in

241

particular had seemed to be with her – at least until the very end. How interesting that he had done research of his own. Somehow that seemed like him, she thought, and then had to laugh at herself for the notion that she knew him at all.

*An obligation to truth and justice*, she had said at Kelly's, not words she had planned. She had no idea where they had come from, and in the light of day they seemed overblown. And yet she felt there was more she could do, now, even though the indictment was in and the grand jury session over.


The Council on Violence Against Asians was farther east than Susan had ever been in downtown Manhattan, almost as far as a person could go. Its office was partitioned into an area for desks and a smaller area that seemed to double as a sitting area and a mini-meeting hall. Three of the desks were occupied by young people working at computers: a Chinese woman, a Vietnamese man, and an Indian man – college kids or graduate students. They were all busy, and she did not interrupt them.

She browsed among the racks of literature: handbills, newsletters, photocopied reprints of newspaper and magazine articles, all with one subject – prejudice and violence directed against Asians. On one wall a poster announced a long-ago rally to protest the beating to death of a Chinese auto-worker mistaken for Japanese by his factory-mates at a time when Detroit was suffering most from America's hunger for cars made in Japan.

Odd, how time and place could change allegiances and loyalties. Her parents, and certainly her grandparents – like the Engs and millions of others – had been victims of the brutal Japanese occupation of China, not that long before Susan's birth. But in an America that had fought successive wars with Japan and Korea and Vietnam and had intermittently feared and continually demonized Communist China, anyone from East Asia was seen by too many people as strange and dangerous. So there was a peculiar logic in making common cause here with the descendants of people who had raped and pillaged and slaughtered among your own ancestors, only a single generation ago.

★ ★ ★

242

'Hi, can I help you?' It was the young Vietnamese man, in trim black jeans, a white business shirt and black vest. Round, steel-rimmed glasses and a sparse goatee accentuated his air of intellectual hipness.

'I'm Susan Linwood,' she said. 'I have an appointment.'

'You're . . .' He was at a loss. 'Oh. Right. Just a second.' He hurried off in the direction of the desks and returned with the young Chinese woman.

'I'm Phoebe,' she said, extending her hand to shake Susan's. 'I'm sorry if I kept you waiting. I thought you were just browsing. We weren't expecting . . .' She let it trail off.

'A Chinese woman,' Susan filled in.

'It's awful, isn't it? And I don't have any excuse. It's not like Phoebe is exactly a Chinese name, either.' She sounded just like the American-born college student she was.

'Let's start again,' Susan said. 'I'm Susan Chan.' She held out her hand and they shook again.

'Chan. That's my name, too.' Phoebe smiled broadly. The humor lit her eyes and transformed her round face. 'And my boyfriend's name is Zvi Asher.' Another quick smile. 'But if we get married I'm going to keep Chan.'

'The Chinese way.'

'I think of it as feminist,' Phoebe said. 'How can we help you?'

Susan started with questions about the organization's purposes and activities. Gradually she led the conversation away from the subject of physical violence – the beaten auto-worker, a Japanese student shot dead asking for directions, organized violence in the South and South-west against Vietnamese shrimp fishermen – toward other forms of prejudice against Asians in America.

'We're most concerned about people getting beaten and killed,' Phoebe told her. 'But verbal violence encourages physical violence, so that's part of what we watch out for, too.'

The CVAA was hampered by a small budget but not by a lack of enthusiasm. It helped distressed Asian-Americans find volunteer legal help and medical assistance, but its chief function was cataloging and documenting racial incidents as a tool for people interested in fighting prejudice in general and anti-Asian prejudice in particular.

'I'm impressed,' Susan said.

Again, a smile, this one full of commitment. 'It's a dirty job, but somebody's got to do it.'

'What about the police?' Susan asked. 'And law-enforcement people in general? Are they helpful?'

'Why? Do you have something in mind?'

Susan took a breath. 'Well –' *never ask for anything directly* – 'I know that other minority communities often complain about how the police respond to them. And you hear a lot these days about police who are actively prejudiced.'

'Sure. Asians have that problem, too. Like, the street vendors. The cops rip them off all the time. Somebody – a Vietnamese woman, say – is selling T-shirts or whatever, and this big guy comes up, a detective, maybe, and he gives her some piece of paper that's too legal and complicated for her to read even if she reads English, and he tells her he's confiscating the merchandise for trademark violations. And the poor woman is so scared she can't say boo, because where she comes from, the police are dangerous people. And he scoops up all the merchandise into his unmarked car and drives away, and before long the merchandise shows up on a pushcart somewhere else, one where the cop gets a kickback. And meanwhile the woman's whole investment is gone – stolen, really – and she's totally terrorized.

'And then there's the whole business with youth gangs. Any time you see two or three Asian boys or young men together, as far as the police are concerned they're gang members. The police make sweeps, just pick people off the streets and photograph them and put their pictures in mug books. And then when people tell the police they're victims of a crime by some man who might have been Asian, out come the mug books. But a lot of the pictures are people who were just walking from the game arcade to the restaurant with a friend when there was a cop on the same street. One case we know about, it was four guys home for Christmas from prep school, on their way to church.'

'Do you keep lists of incidents like that?'

'Sure.'

'Do you ever get the names of the cops?'

Phoebe looked at her. 'You *do* have something in mind.'

Now or never, Susan thought. 'I have some*one* in mind. A specific

244

policeman. I want to find out if he has any history of . . . anti-Asian behavior. And if he does, what kind.'

'Is this someone you've had trouble with?'

'Not me, not exactly. I'm not sure how much I can say about specifics. I know about a situation in which law-enforcement people may be mistreating a Chinese-American couple. And the person most likely to be responsible for it is this particular detective I want to know about.'

'Is this something we can follow up on for you? If there's a cop doing bad things . . .'

'I'll be happy to give you more information when I can, but I don't know how much the victims, if that's what they really are, are going to want me to reveal.'

'I guess I can understand that . . .'

'For now, if I give you the detective's name, could you just check him out for me?'

'Sure. Only, the guy who manages that list is out of town and he's the one who's got to massage the database to see what comes up.'

Susan wrote Detective Pullone's name on a piece of CVAA stationery and gave Phoebe a business card. 'I'll be grateful for anything you can do.'


Mary-Lynne Gunther gazed steadily at Mahoney from across a table at the back of the restaurant she had picked for their rendezvous. She looked even thinner than he remembered, and sharper.

'All I can tell you is that these people are of interest to us,' she said.

'You said that on the phone.'

She regarded him in silence.

'I bet you do real well with interrogations,' he said. 'I always thought that was going to be one of your strengths. But if that's how you want to play this, we'd better just drink our beer and eat our dinner and trade some light gossip. I didn't come here to play prosecutorial head games.'

'All right, that's fair.' She drank some beer. 'I heard you and Kath broke up again.'

'Old news.' He went along with the change of subject, though he knew neither of them was giving up that easily. 'I'm a great one for

245

making the same mistake any number of times. It's not a style I'd recommend.'

'Is there a hidden message in that?'

'About our professional conversation? I didn't think of it that way.'

'You know I don't make the rules.'

'No, and I don't make the rules in my office, either. But I think maybe I ought to let you know where I stand on this.' Because otherwise they were never getting off the dime: he had to offer her something and count on her giving something in return.

'On paper this is Kevin Horgan's case,' Mahoney said. 'And he's going to be the one who presents it to the jury. But on the sweat-equity scale it's mine, at least so far.'

'I know how that can be.'

'And I need to make this case work for me, because I need to convince a lot of people, myself included, that I didn't make a mistake leaving Appeals.'

'And if you can be the point man for your office where we're concerned . . .'

She stopped talking while the waiter put their food in front of them.

'Something like that,' Mahoney said.

'That's not why I'm here.'

'No. You're here to learn from me. But there's no point in my talking to you if you can't tell me what we're talking about.'

She sat thinking. 'All right,' she said finally. 'We've got something going. It's fairly big and these defendants of yours are right in the middle of it.'

'Heroin?'

'I'm not supposed to say.'

'If it's heroin it should be easy enough for us to get together on it, as long as you're not looking to take over. I'm guessing here, but if you're bringing something to the picnic we can share, we might be willing to throw in what we've got.'

'It's not like that.' She poked her fork around in her dish, but she didn't eat.

'Not heroin, or not something we can share?'

She put down the fork and picked up her beer. 'Both.' She said it into her glass, so muffled he almost didn't hear her.

'Then what is it?' His mind still working on the fact that it wasn't heroin the federal prosecutors were pursuing.

'I'm not supposed to say as much as I have.' She picked up her fork again and this time started to eat. 'This is big,' she said between bites. 'And they care about it a lot at main Justice in Washington. We're only a piece of it up here.'

Mahoney was hungry, but he didn't move toward his food.

'These defendants play some role we don't understand yet,' she continued. 'But it looks like they're central in whatever it was that caught Washington's eye. We think getting them to cooperate could be –' she cut herself off – 'I'm talking too much. All I know is, your case could give us the leverage we need to move them. We know it's not all sweetness and light between your office and ours, we know there have been some big ones over the years where Manhattan D.A.'s have ended up feeling burned by the Justice Department or the Southern District.'

'Feeling burned hardly begins to describe it.'

'But this one heroin bust can't mean that much to your office, can it?'

She did a fair job of making it sound like a throwaway line, but Mahoney knew it had to be the crux of her assignment.

'I don't think you should count on that,' he said. 'For starters, it's a lot of money.'

'Okay, but suppose we could work out the money part.'

Now she was making it up as she went along, Mahoney was sure. If the U.S. Attorney's office was ready to deal, they would be approaching this at the level of bosses, not line assistants at the bottom of the case's hierarchy. So maybe this wasn't an assignment, maybe this was Gunther doing a little freelance spying: she'd seen his name on the unit's roster and volunteered to get a copy of the indictment, hoping to pick up more along with it. On her own. Which meant they were both playing the same game.

'This would be a whole lot easier for me if you could tell me more,' Mahoney told her.

'I can't. And you haven't told me much, either.'

'Enough for you to know I'm interested to hear you're not after them for heroin.' And eager to know what that might imply, though he was not about to say so.

'You didn't hear me say that, about heroin.'

Mahoney finished his beer. 'Another one?'

'I shouldn't. Maybe I'll have a brandy with coffee.' She leaned toward him, her wide hazel eyes on his. 'We want these people. We need this case to get them. What I'm asking is how can we approach Horgan so he doesn't just flip us the bird and tell us to fuck off?'

'That's colorful.'

'I'm serious.'

'Seriously, you just predicted what's going to happen, unless you unbend a little. Here's what I can tell you. Horgan has to think he's coming out ahead, because otherwise he's going to be sure he's coming out behind. When I say ahead, that's not necessarily ahead of you, it's more . . . ahead of where he was before you complicated his life. Play it straight and keep his real needs in mind. Then, maybe.'

David rode out to the airport with his sister and the twins, to see them off. Alice had been sullen and uncommunicative when she'd returned from her weekend in East Hampton, and her mood hadn't been improved by the promised trip to New England with the twins. David didn't need an encryption key to decode the message she'd been sending: whatever she'd expected to achieve out at the beach, she hadn't succeeded.

Back home, David had a new sense of the apartment's emptiness, and his own. It wasn't only that he craved human companionship, though he wouldn't have minded it. It was being without a sense of purpose, a direction. For more than a year he had felt drained of inspiration. He tried to get excited about the magic e-mail words that his ex-partner Jon Levi still sent him regularly; each time he was stopped by thoughts of what had happened to them when they'd last put their sweat and talent and their hearts into a grand plan.

He sat down at the computer and pulled up his latest contract job. The problem involved maintaining multiple levels of security on an interlocking complex of local computer networks. The company had kludged together a bundle of commercial applications to do the job but the result was predictably clumsy to use and only spottily effective. It hadn't taken David long to see why the current approach didn't work; coming up with a solution was proving harder.

His headhunter was after him to get the job finished; David had told him it would be done when it was done. That had produced a barrage of e-mail, more relentless than Jon Levi's, only without his sense of humor. David finally put a filter on his e-mail box to screen out the headhunter's messages.

Predictably, the headhunter called him on the phone. 'I expect an answer when I send a message.'

'You want me to do the work or play your games?' David asked him.

'I don't notice you doing either.'

'My muse fails me when you're on my back all the time.'

'I told you when you took this job, the client was in a hurry.'

'They can have it soon, or they can have it right. I made that clear when you first told me about the hurry.'

'Listen, Clark, attitude is not a valued commodity in this business. You want to be an artiste, get somebody else to find you work.'

'You've got it,' David almost said, but as things stood there was nothing to be gained by it. 'Maybe I should think about that,' he said calmly and hung up.

Two days after her visit to the CVAA office Susan got a call from Phoebe Chan.

'I don't know where you ran into that detective,' she said. 'But as soon as I mentioned the name to our guy who deals with incidents involving the police and prosecutors he knew right away who it was.'

'Really?' Susan allowed a silence; this was not the time to be too eager.

'Detective Pullone does big drug cases now, according to our information, but he used to do all sizes and all kinds. He comes and goes in the Asian community, but when he's around the word is, watch out.'

'Why?'

'He bends the rules. It's not so much that he's brutal, though apparently he can be that, too. It's that when he wants to make a case he'll do whatever it takes.'

'What does that mean?'

'The police aren't my specialty, so I couldn't tell you exact things he does. But people are scared of him.'

'Does he manufacture evidence?'

'That's one of the things people say.'

'Do they say how?'

'The people we talk to don't always get too specific, but if it comes to like planting drugs on somebody, there are a few stories. When he was working the street he'd stop someone, or sometimes two or three kids at a time. He'd always come up with little glassine bags of heroin. Three bags, maybe four. And sometimes a gun. And all the while, the kids say they were clean – it was his heroin and his guns.'

'Does he have . . . informants . . . in the community?'

'He must.'

'Do you think he'd pay them to lie? Or scare them into it?'

'I'd have to read between the lines to answer that. As I said, the word is – he makes his cases, whatever it takes. And he definitely has no soft spot in his heart for Asian-Americans. I hope that helps.'

'Oh, yes. It helps enormously. I can't thank you enough.'

'You could tell us what this is about.'

'I'll try to. For now, though, I really can't. Not yet.'

'Well . . . When you can, we'd appreciate knowing more.'

On the days when Kevin Horgan's trial had a morning off for the judge to attend to his calendar, Mahoney knew Horgan would come in and check on the Eng case. He tried to be prepared.

'Progress?' Horgan opened, as he usually did.

'Not much. I've got subpoenas out, same list I already gave you – phone companies, accountant, bank, garment company, credit bureau just in case they weren't being honest about credit cards and such. Nothing's come in yet. Nothing new from the Asian Gang Unit. I still think we'd be a lot better off if Mick Pullone could get something from his snitch, but Mick already more or less closed that door, and since then he hasn't exactly been jumping to answer my phone calls.'

Horgan walked around Mahoney's desk to stand, arms crossed, by Mahoney's chair, looking down at him. It made Mahoney feel crowded and overtopped – an unusual and uncomfortable feeling for someone who'd left the six-foot mark behind at fifteen.

Horgan said, 'You don't want to start relying on snitches for too much, anyhow. A snitch is a snitch, not Sherlock Holmes. He hears something on the street and passes it on, what does he know what the background is? Or maybe he got it peepin' in the window. All we care is, does what he gives us pan out?'

'Granted. But it seems weird to me that we haven't got more by now. The grand jurors had questions the evidence didn't cover. I have to assume the trial jurors will be bothered by the same things.'

'I told you before,' Horgan said. 'You have the heroin and you have the money and you have the ledgers. Concentrate on that and stop trying to poke holes in my case – you're not a fucking Appeals-Bureau assistant any more. When I go into the courtroom I have to make the jury sit up and take notice. So I need you to be a mad-dog prosecutor, not some fucking appellate lawyer. Seamless logic is not what this is about.'

'I hear you,' Mahoney said. 'But when my friend at the Southern District said they weren't looking at these people for drugs—'

'*The Southern District.*' Horgan said it with infinite contempt. 'I got that call from them you warned me about. They must be even crazier than I thought.'

'What'd they say?'

'They want me to give them my case. Just like that. You know what the asshole told me? For the umpteenth fucking time in my career? That we had to *accommodate the prerogatives of federal law enforcement*. I thought you said they were prepared to deal straight.'

'That's what I told her they'd have to do, and I thought she got it.'

'Then *somebody* over there didn't. And I've been screwed too many times by those people to lie down for them again. You may be a virgin in these things, but I sure as hell am not. Assholes! Since when do we fetch and carry for them? I mean – what the holy hell have they done for *us* lately?'

Inevitably, as David was finishing the computer-network security project, he caught what looked like an error in the programming code he was submitting. Debugging it meant he would be even later delivering the finished product.

It was no surprise that the news would make the client unhappy. The call shouldn't have bothered David, but it did. He went over to Jimmy

251

Kelly's. It would be diverting to do the unpressured, conceptual kind of work that was waiting for him there, and when he was done he'd have a beer.

'Looking kind of glum,' Kelly said when David closed up the office and came to sit at the bar. As was Kelly's custom at least two nights a week, he was tending his own bar.

'Professional problems. The world's too full of self-important idiots.'

'Ain't that the sad truth.' Kelly poured a shot of his good aged Irish to go with David's beer. 'On the house, my friend.'

David protested, but Kelly held up a hand. 'This is a place to put those cares away. Not, mind you, that I'm talking about drowning them in a bottle. That's not how I like to make my profit.'

David raised his glass. 'What was that toast, the other night?'

'*Slainte*. Means cheers, basically. I've got another one for you.' He poured himself the shortest of shots and lifted it. 'Confusion to our enemies.'

'Perfect. Confusion to our enemies.' The whiskey tasted good – pungent and spicy, and smooth on the way down.

Kelly went off to see to his customers at the other end of the bar, leaving David to mull over his problems, principally his need to straighten out his own life. He knew he was good at what he did, but he could feel himself getting stale and frustrated, unhappy at the idea of having anything to do with computers. He didn't know if that was because of his current situation or the way the technology was developing or just the effects of age.

The teams he'd been on when he was doing his best work had topped out at about age thirty-four, his own age now, and most of the key players had been in their mid to late twenties. That was how old he and Jon had been when they'd started on the road that almost led them to the top. It was the perfect age, experienced enough so the unfamiliar didn't scare you and you didn't make obvious mistakes, young enough not to have lost the sense that you could do anything you set your mind to, and to be willing and able to work day and night accomplishing it. He wasn't sure he had that kind of fire any more.

Kelly came back with a fresh beer for him. 'Not to intrude on your solitude, my friend, but there's a fine lady down the other end of the bar who could use a little companionable conversation, and sadly I'm too busy myself to be much company for anybody tonight, you or her. So I was thinking you two could talk to each other, take the responsibility off my shoulders.'

'It's okay, Jimmy, really. I'm not much in the mood for conversation . . .'

'Tell you the truth, there's kind of a jerk down that end who's getting on the lady's nerves. If he keeps it up I'll have to heave him out, and he's not such a bad sort, most nights. So you'd be doing a lot of people a favor if you'd let me bring her over here and sit her down next to you.'

David shrugged. 'Sure. Why not?'

She was tall and athletic-looking, with a tumble of curly chestnut hair and a deep suntan. Her name was Paula.

'Hi,' she said. 'Thanks for rescuing me.'

'Glad to be helpful.'

She raised her wine glass to him and then clinked it against the beer glass in front of him on the bar.

'Cheers.' She took a hearty swallow of wine. 'So tell me, what do you do when you're not playing knight in shining armor?'

'I'm a computer nerd.' He said it flatly, without the smile that might have made it seem a jokey invitation.

'Well, excuse me. Maybe I should go back where I was.'

'Sorry, I don't mean to be rude. Jimmy means well, but the truth is I'm in a major funk. I don't think I'll be very good company.'

'Oh, listen, I know all about being in a funk. Sometimes the best thing is to get your mind someplace else entirely. So how about I promise I won't ask you about your life and you don't have to ask me about mine. We're sophisticated New Yorkers –' she leaned heavily on the adjective to make it ironic – 'there's got to be lots we can talk about.'

*Sex*, David thought: Sex and warmth and the comfort of another body in the night – that's what we both want to talk about. But they wouldn't, because it was too risky just to name it for what it was, because you started out with your pride already naked and bruised just by the fact of being alone in a bar late at night.

They talked about movies and books and museums. Paula had an interest in art: on weekends when she had free time she did watercolor landscapes. Except for a mutual appreciation for Buster Keaton, they had very little in common, but by the time they were sure of that they both knew it didn't matter.

Kelly came over when Paula was off in the ladies' room.

'Going okay?'

'Sure. Thanks.'

'She's real sweet,' Kelly said. 'Had a hard time with her last boyfriend.'

'Story of my life,' David said.

Kelly looked at him, not quite sure how to read that. Paula reappeared before he could follow it up.

'I'm kinda ready to leave,' she said, opening her purse to pay for her wine. 'You know how it is, the alarm always goes off way too early, just when you really want to be all cozy in bed.' Her voice and her eyes put an invitation in the words.

'Yeah, I'm pretty tired myself,' David said.

'Oh. Well –' she snapped her purse shut – 'Nice meeting you, I guess.'

Something about the moment made David change his mind. He climbed off the bar stool and dug for some cash. 'I was thinking, I'd be no proper knight in armor if I didn't at least see you to your door.'

She looked into his eyes, trying to read . . . something . . . then she smiled. 'Okay. I'll take you up on that.' She hooked her arm in his. 'Let's go, Sir Galahad.'

David woke up in the middle of the night atop rumpled sheets, his skin tight with sweat dried by the chill breeze purring from the air conditioner. Next to him, Paula was an undulant shape and a mass of curls, black in the faint light.

In the bathroom he looked in the mirror, splashed water on his face and neck, thought about staying. He discovered that he couldn't visualize how the morning might go. Couldn't, or didn't want to. He prowled through the small apartment looking for something to write a note on.

254

*'You're beautiful asleep,'* he wrote. He signed it *'Galahad.'*

When he got home he found a message on his answering machine from Susan Linwood, an invitation to lunch at a midtown restaurant. She'd left a number for him to call if he couldn't make it.

# 5

The restaurant, just off Fifth Avenue, was grander than any David had been in since his dream deal went south. Even then, it had been the kind that he went to only on special occasions. Waiting by the bar, he wondered if Susan Linwood ate here often.

'I hope I'm not late,' she said, bustling in from the street. She was wearing a creamy jacket and skirt with a blouse almost the same color, and more gold jewelry than he remembered.

'You're not late, I was early.'

'Let's sit down.' She gave her name to the hostess, a tall slender woman in black with the cheekbones and posture of a high-fashion model who appraised them each in an instant.

'Oh, yes, Mrs Linwood. This way, please.'

When they were seated, Susan asked for a glass of white wine. David ordered a beer.

They sat across the table from each other in silence. David supposed small talk was in order but he had none to make under these circumstances and to come right out and say 'Why are we here?' was too direct, even for him.

'Well,' she said in a strained voice. 'I guess you're wondering why we're here.'

He had been sitting with his hands folded on the starched white tablecloth, studying his knuckles. At her words he looked up, and she thought she saw a sparkle of amusement in the cool blue eyes.

'You could say that. I mean, besides assuming that it's about the Engs.'

'Which it is,' she said. 'I've learned something new. It might be even more important than what I learned about the benevolent associations. It's about the detective.'

The blue eyes widened with interest.

She said, 'It was because of you, really. That night outside Kelly's, you reminded me about him, the whole story he told about martial arts and tackling Martin Eng. And I've said before that if the Engs were innocent I thought the police had to be involved somehow. So I did some research.' She paused while a captain opened menus for them and a waiter gave them their drinks.

'Let's look at the menu, and then I'll go back to my story.'

The captain told them about the specials and withdrew. Susan allowed herself another minute's perusal of the menu before she offered some main course suggestions, hoping to make David comfortable with ordering the food, not the prices.

She had judged, from his standard-issue summer suit and his look of going slightly green around the gills as he first glanced over the menu, that he was worrying about the damage this meal was going to do to his wallet. She considered saying up front that she was paying, just to get it out of the way, but she wasn't sure if that would make him more comfortable or less. The last thing she wanted was to start out by giving him the impression she was undermining his manhood.

'I think I'll start with the field greens salad,' she said. 'The one with portobello mushrooms, though I have to admit the appetizer special sounded good, too.' Hoping he'd take the hint. 'And then I'll have the salmon.'

'Sounds good.' He continued to study his menu. 'I think maybe roast chicken for me.'

'It's very good here.' It was, and it was also the cheapest thing on the menu. 'What about something to start with?'

'I think the chicken's enough.'

'You sure?'

He closed his menu. 'It's fine.'

She let it go. Too late now to tell him she was going to pay: there was no way he could change his mind based on that news without either admitting he'd been counting dollars or seeming eager to take advantage of her. Face, she thought. So much was about saving face. A person didn't even have to be Chinese.

'Well, I hope you won't mind watching me eat.'

'No problem.'

She motioned for the captain, who came over and took their order. 'An appetizer for you, m'sieu?' he pressed.

'Is this a conspiracy?' David smiled. 'The chicken will be plenty, thanks.'

Maybe it really is all he wants, she chided herself.

He drank some beer. 'You have news.'

She told him first about the CVAA. She wanted him to have a clear picture of the source of her information. While she was talking, her salad arrived.

'Are you sure you won't at least have a little of the salad with me? Otherwise you really will have to sit and watch, because it would hardly do for me to talk with my mouth full in a place like this.'

He was smiling again, showing an even row of very white teeth between his auburn moustache and the top of his beard. 'Okay. Just a little, so you won't be eating alone.'

She motioned to the waiter hovering nearby. 'Can we have a small plate, please?'

He returned with a plate the size of hers. 'Do you wish to split the salad?'

'Please.'

The salad proved to be far better than anything David could find at his local greengrocer. He revised his opinion of the restaurant: it was not like the places he'd been to on special occasions, it was a lot better. He could almost understand why the prices were so high.

Susan resumed her story. David was intrigued by the idea of an organization monitoring violence against Asian-Americans and not at all surprised that one existed.

'The point is,' she said, 'they know Detective Pullone at the CVAA. He's on their list.'

He raised his beer glass in tribute. 'That definitely qualifies as news.'

The waiter returned, followed by a second man in a white jacket carrying their food – a runner, Kelly called such people. In addition to the two main courses, there were tiny roast potatoes and long, very thin green beans for both of them.

Susan tried her salmon and pronounced it good. David did the same with his chicken. *Monkey see, monkey do*, he thought, but he realized he was having a very good time. The chicken was as good of its kind as the salad had been – maybe better. Even the potatoes and truly string-like string beans were special.

As for the company . . . well, she was beautiful, that was for sure – in her gilded-lady way. Strange, he thought, that he saw the perfect clothes and the heavy gold jewelry and the upper-class bearing and manners more clearly than he saw that she was Chinese – that her eyes were not just wide and deep brown and penetrating but shaped differently from his, that her hair was not just richly black and long and sleek, but a different texture, that her lips were not just gracefully, precisely shaped, but fuller and softer-looking than any he had ever kissed.

Beautiful, no question about it. Beautiful and strange. Apart from the fact that she was so much of a different class from his own, she sent so many inconsistent messages he could get no fix on her. He was seeing it again now. Though she was clearly at home in these sur-roundings, she also seemed stiff and tentative, as if she was nervous about something.

After she had eaten some salmon and given David a chance to have some of his chicken, Susan went back to talking about Detective Pullone. She repeated everything Phoebe had said about him.

'It's potentially so damning,' she concluded. *'He'll do whatever it takes to make his cases.'*

'It doesn't sound good.'

'I remember reading not so long ago about a New York State Trooper who had won all kinds of medals for heroism and arresting more people than anyone else. He ended up in jail because someone discovered he'd made up some of the most important evidence in his big cases. I think it was fingerprint evidence. Apparently he just lied about it. Made it up out of whole cloth, and he wasn't the only one doing it, either. And then there were the city cops who were shaking down drug dealers and peddling the drugs themselves – in Brooklyn or Queens, I'm not sure which. And that report about police corruption that said for some policemen lying on the witness stand was a regular thing.'

'I remember that.'

'So if the CVAA is right about Pullone, it could be that none of what we heard in the grand jury is the truth.'

'You're saying Pullone lied about more than just that the Engs resisted arrest.'

'I'm saying he could have lied about everything.'

He had been about to eat the piece of chicken on his fork. Instead, he laid it carefully back on his plate. 'Okay. Let's take this one step at a time. He lied about finding the money?'

'No, not that. I still think it was their money. Or at least it was really in their apartment and their safe deposit boxes. They might have been holding it for other people, the way you were saying at Kelly's.'

'Then . . . he lied about finding the heroin.'

'Yes.'

'How? What lie did he tell, exactly?'

'I don't know.' Something about the question, or perhaps the clinically probing way he asked it, suddenly filled her with despair. She took refuge in flaking off a piece of salmon and pushing it onto her fork.

'Hey, remember me?' Smiling. 'I'm the guy who's always being direct. I'm not arguing with you, I think you're onto something interesting. But I think it's a good idea to be as precise as possible when you're putting together a theory like this, especially if you're going to base any kind of action on it.'

She tried to return his smile. 'It's not like me to go charging off on my own in uncharted territory – my crusades tend to be carefully mapped out, and officially sanctioned. So I kind of expect people to pat me on the head about this.'

'I'm taking you seriously.'

'I know you are, and I appreciate it.' He's not Richard, she reminded herself. 'Go ahead, what were you going to say?'

'I was trying to understand what kind of lie he could have been telling about the heroin. I think we have to assume that there really was heroin in that apartment. They put it into the evidence bags right there, and there were too many cops involved for Pullone to have been able to take it out of his pocket and plant it during the raid. Unless they were all in on it with him, but that seems like too much to believe. So let's assume the heroin was there.'

'But it wasn't theirs,' she insisted.

'Okay. Whose was it?'

'Pullone's. Or else the man who stole the election from Martin Eng.'

'That's what I was leading up to. I think you've got two different theories here – Pullone framed them or Martin Eng's Chinatown rival did – and I don't see how they go together.'

'Maybe they're connected by the informant,' Susan guessed.

'How?'

'I'm not sure.' She looked down at her plate, then up at him. 'Truth? Until you said it, I was too excited, learning about Pullone, to ask myself how it all fitted together.'

David picked up his fork. 'Let's eat some more and just let this sit for a moment. We can get back to it later.'

They ate in silence until she said, 'What kind of work do you do with computers?'

'Basically, I try to figure out how to make computers do things they haven't done before, or do the same old things better.'

'You're a programmer.'

'I think the official designation these days for what I do is computer systems engineer. Part of it involves writing instructions for computers in specialized languages they understand, so in that sense, yes, I do program computers. But if I design something that takes a lot of straight programming I'll hire somebody for that, or whoever I'm working for will.' He waved it away. 'It's not very interesting, really, not unless you're really into computers.'

'Actually, when it comes to computers I'm more likely out of it than into them.' He thought she was holding back a smile. 'I mean, I need them in my work, but mostly I just use the word processing. My associate does all the spreadsheets and those things.'

261

'Your work? Public relations? Is that what you said at Kelly's?'

'Did I say that? Well, it's true. Medical public relations.'

'And what's that involve? Hospitals? Drug companies? The A.M.A.?' It was not a subject he had thought of before. 'The possibilities must be endless. All the different diseases and their information organizations and charities, medical relief all over the place, nursing homes . . .'

'And that's just the beginning.' Now she was letting the smile happen. He liked it.

'You already understand it better than most people,' she told him. 'Most people don't get it at all.'

That seemed to be all she was going to say, for the moment. They ate some more.

'You haven't told me what kind of medical public relations,' he prompted her.

'Oh. I've done all kinds. I started out at a hospital. My husband's a surgeon, or did I say that, too?'

'A doctor, I think you said.'

'He's a neurosurgeon, actually. I did my first PR work for the hospital where he did his residency. Then when the kids came I gave it up. I just got back into it again about ten years ago. I did mention the kids?'

'One in college, one about to be.'

'You have a good memory.'

'For some things.' In fact, he hadn't known he remembered about her children until he said the words.

'Anyway, when I started out again, working for a small company, I had all kinds of clients. But my experience was in medical PR, and of course my husband has all these connections – he's fairly famous at what he does – so it looked like medical was the place for me to be. Once I had some fresh experience and a portfolio of recent work, I went out on my own. Now I've got a secretary and an associate. Most of my clients are pharmaceutical-related, but I also get overflow work from hospitals and medical associations, when they've got something their in-house people can't handle. The part I like the most is public-information work, where we're trying to raise the health-consciousness of the population at large on one issue or another.

'I've got a campaign I'm pushing now with a company that makes hormone patches and implants. I want them to do a major breast-cancer awareness campaign. Early detection, of course, but also treatment and post-op implications, support groups, everything. I think they're going to go for it.'

The rush of words stopped abruptly. 'How I do go on. You're a good listener.'

'Shall we get back to Detective Pullone?' Susan proposed while they waited for their coffee.

'That's what we're here for.'

'We were trying to figure out how the two separate bad guys we know about could both be responsible for railroading Mr and Mrs Eng.'

'Even though our bad guys have nothing in common.'

'Nothing that we know about,' she countered.

'Granted. Nothing that we know about. And you have information that Detective Pullone is hard on Asians.'

'That's a reason for him to plant the heroin.'

'Well . . . I suppose,' he conceded. 'But why plant it on these particular people?'

'Maybe the Engs's enemies put him up to it.'

'But if he doesn't like Asians, why pick the head of the Sam Yap Association as an ally?'

'We can assume he's got Asian informants, and that could be the connection. I still think the key to this is the informant.'

'About whom we really know nothing.'

'You like to make things difficult, don't you?' She was only half-kidding.

'Just the facts, ma'am.'

It made her smile. She had the feeling he liked it when she smiled. 'Isn't that before your time?'

'Reruns. Before yours, too, I'd think.'

'Not really, I'm afraid. But we're talking about the informant.'

'Only if we want to play guessing games.'

'What's wrong with that?'

'It depends on what you want to accomplish.'

She looked at him. Not just as someone who happened to be across the table, but in an attempt to see who was there. He was regarding her with patient interest, waiting for a response. Midday light from a high window to his right brought out red highlights in his hair and beard and made his right eye look lighter than his left.

How odd, she thought, that I want to keep talking to this man I don't know, a man who wears clunky, rough-leather boots with a suit and looks like he spends his spare time hiking in the woods in those same boots. Whose worklife is about talking to machines. But of all the people who knew the background of the story, whom she could talk to without worrying about breaking secrecy laws, he was the one who *listened*, and he had a way of getting to the core of things. As he had just now.

'You ask good questions,' she said.

'It's my training. Until you make the problem clear there's no way you're going to solve it.'

'I'm not sure I can do that,' she had to admit. 'Make the problem clear.'

'Well, maybe that's what we should work on first. Starting with, what do you want to accomplish?'

Their coffee arrived. While the waiter poured it for them she tried to think of something clever to say, with no success.

'The best I can do is – that depends on what the truth is.'

'Nothing wrong with that answer. What are the possibilities?'

'The Engs are innocent or they're guilty. But I don't think they can be guilty.'

'All right, let's say they're innocent. Then what do you want to accomplish?'

'To help get them off?' She answered her own question: 'I suppose that's what I'd want ultimately, but I don't think it's a useful goal to start with. It doesn't suggest an immediate course of action.'

She was at a loss. She felt something like a compulsion to find out more about the Engs, about how they had been put in this awful position . . . but she didn't know how to describe it and even if she had she was far from sure she would have voiced it – not to this logical and analytical man whose opinion of her she was surprised to find she cared about.

'I want to know what really happened,' she ventured. 'I want to know who planted the heroin and why. That's what I really want.'

She thought about what she'd said. It sounded almost right, but it bothered her.

'You know what I'm afraid of,' she said, about to go further than she'd intended. 'I'm afraid I'm just plain curious. I just want to *know*.'

'Nothing wrong with that.'

'Isn't there? Isn't curiosity what killed the cat?'

'I'm not sure it is. The part of that one I never got was – what was that cat so damn curious about? And exactly how did being curious about it kill him? I think curiosity's fine. How else would anybody learn anything?'

'I think curiosity's fine, too, if you're discovering the theory of relativity,' Susan said. 'I'm talking about poking your nose in where it doesn't belong.'

'Are you doing that?'

'I don't think I am. Though I suppose being careful is a good idea. As Mr Kelly said.'

'So far, you've stayed away from the principals. I think that's important. Learning what you can from a distance.'

'What about you?' she asked. 'Are you curious, too?'

He ran a finger around the edge of his coffee cup. 'I suppose I am,' he said without looking up.

He glanced at her. 'You know what I've been thinking about? I imagine them not being guilty – and they get here after all they've been through, war and tyranny and death, thinking that finally they're safe and sound, only to find themselves done in again, this time by the State of New York. So . . . yeah, I want to know what really happened, if only so I can stop having thoughts like that.'

What he was saying about the Engs was so close to how she felt herself, and brought her such a strong image of her parents, that for a moment she didn't trust herself to speak. She paid attention to her coffee until she felt in control of her voice.

'What you said before about learning things and keeping at a distance? That's one of the things I wanted to talk to you about.' She was glad to have such a direct lead-in. 'I think we can learn more about Pullone and the kinds of things he does, and we might be able to

265

learn more about the dispute Mr Eng had with the other benevolent association – the beating he got and the robberies and all of that – if we can search all the newspapers and news magazines to see what kind of coverage there's been.'

'That sounds right.'

'I know there are news-database services where you can do that. I've never used them myself, because we deal so little with the mass media and we have a service bureau that handles that kind of research for us when we do. Only, I wouldn't want to do this through them. But I think you can have your own computer hook into some of those same services by modem.' She let herself grin at him, only slightly self-conscious. 'See, I'm not a complete dunce when it comes to computers.'

'I never thought you were.'

'Anyway, I was hoping you might have access to some of those news-database services.'

He shook his head. 'Not really. In the kind of work I do, there wouldn't be much sense to it. And I think the serious ones are kind of pricey just to belong to for the heck of it.'

As if on cue, David thought, precisely on the word 'pricey' the waiter slipped a dark red, leather-look folder onto the table midway between them.

Reminding himself that by the standards of his youth he was a semi-rich man, David reached for it. Susan covered it with her hand and pulled it slightly away. Briefly, he felt her fingers overlap his.

'Please, David,' she said. 'I'm the one who insisted on this lunch, I spent it picking your brain, and I chose the restaurant. This is my party. I insist.' She sounded as if she meant it.

'Well, I suppose if you put it that way I can't fight too hard, though I must say it's been a pleasure for me, beginning to end.' He was trying for a smile, doing his best to contrive a façade of gallant reluctance. 'I'll yield this time, but only on the condition that you let me get the next one.'

'We'll worry about that then.' She slipped a platinum-gray credit card into the folder with only the briefest glance at the check. 'When I first thought about the news services, I thought David Clark's a computer person, he'd know how to do that. So this lunch is really kind of a bribe – not that I didn't enjoy it, too,' she added quickly. 'And I did want to talk to you about all this. But I was also hoping I could interest you enough in what I found out that you'd want to put your good computer skills to use finding out more.'

'I'm flattered, but I'm not sure I'm the right person for the job, not in the way you think.' He could sense his resistance to getting involved in this, despite his desire to know the truth about the Engs. True, he found her intriguing – compelling, even – but at the same time her glossy surface continued to make him feel she knew things he didn't, belonged places he couldn't. Getting himself past that was something he recoiled from instinctively, not least because of how badly he'd been betrayed by the only woman remotely like her he'd ever let himself get close to.

'I'd love to help,' he told her. 'But this is really not the best time for me. I've got a big job I'm trying to finish, and I promised Kelly I'd give him a plan for his new computer system so he could start looking before the summer was over. But I think you have the right idea, and I'm sure you can do just fine on your own. If you can use a word processor, you can use an online database.'

'Well, perhaps,' she said. 'But I can't help thinking you'd be better at it than I would.'

She signed the credit-card slip and put her copy of it and her card in her wallet. 'I suppose we should go. You've given me a lot to think about. I really appreciate it.'

'It was a pleasure, really. I'm sorry I couldn't be more help.' He wanted there to be more for them to say, but there wasn't. 'And thank you for the delicious lunch.'

'My pleasure.' She paused, putting her wallet in her purse. Handed him a business card. 'I know you're busy. But if you get some time, or you're *curious* –' a smile accompanied the word – 'curious to know how I'm progressing, you can give me a call.'

'Well . . .' she said when they got outside. He had the feeling she was searching for something to say. If she was, she didn't find it. She held out her hand. 'Goodbye.'

Her hand was smooth and warm, her grip firm. 'Goodbye,' he said. 'And thank you again.'

'Oh, no. Thank *you*.' She turned and went up the block.

He turned the other way and started walking. He didn't yet know where he was going, but it seemed like the right thing to do.

# 6

*I just want to know.*

Susan kept hearing the words in her mind, and they seemed less and less an unworthy motivation. David Clark's comfort with the idea of being propelled by the pure desire to *know* had been surprisingly freeing.

And, she realized, not knowing the truth – *wanting* to know the truth though she had not allowed herself to be aware of the need – was at the heart of the two events that had done the most to form her emotional existence since her marriage.

For more than ten years she had been tormented by not knowing what was in her son's mind and heart. And for almost twenty she had been telling herself not to question the story that her parents had died in an earthquake in northern China, at a time when there was so much between them that was unresolved.

The truth about all that was beyond reach – locked in the past partly because of her own inaction when she still might have learned more. What a bitter joke of fate it was that when it came to the Engs she had so much less at stake personally and yet it was so much easier for her not to be paralyzed.

It was too bad that David had taken himself out of the search for the truth about the Engs. Not because she was intimidated by the news databases, she could deal with that. Talking to him was thought-provoking at a level most people couldn't provide.

He was sharp – maybe as sharp as Richard – but without Richard's hard, polished exterior and unremitting drive. David's analytic powers did not seem to be so much a weapon for him as Richard's had always been.

David was edgy in his way, and she thought he often seemed nervous around her; still, there was something reassuring about him. An absence of obvious striving, or maybe just obvious competitiveness – he seemed self-contained in a way that she liked. And when he was paying attention, he was truly paying attention. Not like Richard and his friends, who never attended more closely to anything than they did to their own brilliance.

Thinking about it only increased her disappointment that David wouldn't help. She wondered if he had told her the whole truth about why.

In the end, though, it didn't matter why. If she was going to follow this up she'd have to do it alone. As soon as she could find some time. For now, it was out of the question.

There were only a few days left to get the main Consolidated campaign into shape *and* put together a final proposal for the breast-cancer-education program. If she was going to get the program funded, she first had to convince Shelby Portman it was worth pushing for at Consolidated's pre-Labor-Day executive retreat.

And Lara. There was her going-away party and all the shopping they still had to do. Lara was talking about spending the weekend at the beach house so she could say goodbye to her friends out there, though Susan could not imagine how they could do all they had to in the week that was left and go out to the beach, too.

But that decision would not be entirely up to her and Lara. Richard would have an opinion, and that would depend on Charles, who was due home the day after tomorrow. There would be a welcome-home dinner – the immediate family plus her in-laws. And then Charles and Richard would go off on their annual fishing trip.

For David, the relief of finishing the network-security job and being free of the headhunter he had come to hate wore off all too quickly. The freedom was fine, it was feeling directionless again that bothered him. He couldn't fool himself that the job he was doing for Jimmy Kelly, diverting as it was, was anything like a rewarding piece of work.

As a substitute for more satisfying activity he firmed up the details of his September whitewater trip and began reading through adventure-travel catalogs. The traveling he had done so far had all been in the

270

lower forty-eight states. When he was younger he hadn't been able to afford anything more exotic; in more recent years he had been working too hard on the dream project to go anywhere, anticipating that he would have the world at his feet when it was done. Life hadn't worked out quite that way, but that didn't mean he couldn't expand his horizons: he'd just have to be a little more selective.

As if sensing the void in David's schedule, Jon Levi barraged him with e-mail reminding of him of what they had been doing when they met, working for a company that got classified Government contracts for keeping electronic communications secret and for finding ways to break the secrecy of other people's communications. The time was ripe, Jon was arguing, for them to get back into that business – on their own this time.

David had resisted at first, the way he had been resisting Jon's new ideas for almost two years. But now he found himself more willing to remember the good parts of their collaboration instead of focusing on the final débâcle – Jon's endless energy and insatiable need to explore hidden byways, the glee he took in accomplishing something no one else ever had . . .

For variety, and to restore his sense that computers could be fun, David jacked himself into cyberspace – using his computer's modem and the phone lines to make himself part of the worldwide fabric of interwoven computers – just to see what of interest was happening. His attention was quickly drawn to an area he had not previously had any reason to notice – the law servers, computers stocked with Supreme Court decisions and the texts of statutes and other legal information. As he browsed among them he wondered how Susan Linwood was progressing in her attempt to learn about Detective Pullone and the Engs.

David had never spent much time on the computer-snooping activities that went with the media-name 'hacker,' but his increasing e-mail correspondence with Jon was reminding him of all the things he knew about finding his way around unfamiliar networks. And if he was going to stretch his computer-security muscles, why not begin by seeing how good he was at getting past some commercial security setups?

As a motivator for picking which systems to get into he chose Susan

Linwood's request for news stories about Detective Pullone and his informant. He didn't find anything worthwhile on the detective, but he quickly got wrapped up in following a related path.

'Jesus fucking H. Christ!'

Mahoney had heard Kevin Horgan in a fury before but this sounded like something special.

'Motherfucking feds!'

Horgan burst into Mahoney's office. 'Playing straight! Is that what they told you!'

Mahoney waited for what was coming next.

'The motherfuckers threatened me. I don't believe their fucking balls. I tell them this is *our* case and I'm not interested in their song and dance, and they turn around and *threaten* me! They're going to subpoena my evidence. They're going to subpoena my detective. They're even going to get a goddamned subpoena out on the informant. John Fucking Doe.' Horgan sank onto the visitor's chair. 'Some curly-headed prick wears a skullcap held on by a bobby pin standing there in my office threatening me! What the fuck do they think they're pulling, answer me that.'

Mahoney took a long breath. 'I don't have a clue. This is as big a surprise to me as it is to you.' More than that, he felt betrayed. Gunther should have warned him. This had to mean that the Engs were a lot more important to the Justice Department, or at least to the United States Attorney for the Southern District of New York, than Gunther had let on.

'A surprise, huh? Yeah, they're full of surprises over there. I'll tell you what. We're going to have a surprise for *them*. We're going to have this thing all tried and over with so fast they won't know whether to shit or turn green.' Horgan subsided, the fury temporarily gone out of him. 'And what did they suppose they were going to do, anyway? Send some FBI over here to execute their subpoenas? Sure – like the guys who work for us don't carry guns, too. Arrogant, shit-for-brains assholes.'

He hauled himself to his feet. 'Christ, this bullshit makes me tired. Bad enough I have this trial that's taking a lifetime and a half.' He pulled a cigar from his jacket pocket, pointed it at Mahoney. 'Your job is to get this thing ready for trial and on the calendar. No more screwing around. When's our next court date?'

'Right after Labor Day.'

'Okay. I want to be be ready to go in there and press for a firm trial date. This damn trial of mine can't last for ever.' He patted his pockets distractedly, came up with a book of matches. 'All right, I'm going to go take a leak and smoke a cigar. Why don't you get on the phone to your buddy over there at the Southern District and find out what the fuck they think they're doing.' He stalked out, turned just past the door. 'If I'm not in my office in ten minutes I'll be on the eighth floor, seeing if I can get one of our sainted bosses to give me a minute of his golden time.'

Mary-Lynne Gunther wasn't in her office when Mahoney called. Or, more likely, she wasn't answering her calls, or maybe just her calls from people named Mahoney. He left a message.

On an impulse he called his answering machine at home. There was a message from his brother about a birthday party for his six year old, and then there was one that began with a brief silence and then, quickly, almost whispered, 'Sorry. I told them not to.' Gunther – it had to be. And 'sorry' was the right word, given the new pressure this had put him under from Horgan.

Mahoney wadded up balls of paper from a legal pad and lofted them across the room toward the hoop over his wastebasket. With each shot he tried to convince himself that it was okay to live with the holes in the Eng case, that it didn't matter that the U.S. Attorney's office didn't see heroin as part of what they were involved in.

He went five for fifteen at the wastebasket. That they were all three-pointers was no solace.

Charles emerged from the airport gate looking taller and more gangling than Susan remembered. He had a knapsack over one shoulder and a suede jacket over the other and a cowboy hat on his always-unruly black hair. As he got closer she saw he was wearing cowboy boots, too.

She stepped away from the crowd of welcomers to greet him. 'Hi, cowboy.'

He seemed surprised to see her. From his expression she judged that she shouldn't have commented on his new boots and hat.

'Hello, Mother.' He saw Lara and reached out a long arm. 'Hi, there, squinty.' It was a childhood taunt turned affectionate; he was the only person in the world who called her that. They hugged each other.

'Where's Dad?' he asked.

'He had an emergency. He said he'll be done in time to meet us for dinner.'

'We having the usual deadly crowd?'

'The four of us and your grandparents, if that's what you mean by deadly.'

'There's something about Gram and Gramps that casts a pall.' Charles started loping along the airport corridor at his usual agitated pace. Susan hurried to keep up.

'They're good at being stuffy,' Lara said. 'They've been practicing all their lives.'

'Did you check any luggage?' Susan asked.

'Nope. Alex's dad is sending everything by one of the company planes. It'll just come to the house in a couple of days.'

'That's nice of him. Did you have a good time?'

'Yeah, great.' He turned to Lara, on the other side of him. 'So, squinty. Lose it yet?'

She punched him. 'You have a disgusting mind.'

'Get used to it. You're about to be a college woman.'

'You're so right. And I intend to take zero crap from college *boys*.'

'Don't worry, squinty, that isn't what they're waiting to give you.'

'All right, you two,' Susan said. 'We're in public.'

In the car, Lara pressed her brother for stories of living on the horse ranch in Wyoming where he'd spent most of the summer. Charles was in a particularly relaxed mood, less brusque and withdrawn than usual, full of taunts and small jokes with Lara. But in her direction Susan felt the familiar reserve.

Charles was a dutiful and respectful son, even sometimes warm and affectionate with her. But he always pulled back, and there was a line she had learned not to cross because if she did he was certain to close her out. She took refuge now, as she always did, in being the efficient mom, reviewing the program for the evening and for Charles's first days home.

'Doesn't a person get to have any fun?' he asked sourly. 'Sounds like you've got me scheduled every minute.'

'You have your fans, Charles. They'll be disappointed if they don't see you. You're around so little.' She wanted to sound welcoming, but apparently she came off more like a conductor announcing a railroad schedule. 'I thought it would be easier for you if you could see people in small groups, and if they came to you, instead of your having to make a lot of duty calls.'

'Isn't it possible for me to outgrow some of these people? They're your friends, not mine.'

'That's true. If you don't care for them there's no reason to see them at all.' She felt an impulse to apologize that was harder to stifle than she wanted to admit to herself.

*Heritage*, she thought. He was the oldest son, the incarnation of heaven on earth – everything revolved around him. And she had lost the ability to make real contact with him years ago. There had been a time – too long after the fact, she knew now, when it was already too late – when she tried talking to him about the incident she was sure had caused the distance between them. Tried more than once, to no avail. Each time she had approached the subject he had reacted as though he didn't know what she was getting at. She couldn't tell if that was because talking, or even thinking, about it was too painful for him, or if he genuinely didn't remember.

Finally, there seemed to be no choice but to resign herself to their being beyond the kind of trust and love she longed for with him, though she had never quite surrendered the hope that she could somehow please him enough to get by the barrier he had erected between them.

When David saw that he was accumulating too much information to deal with, he called Susan. She seemed surprised to hear from him.

'It's my turn to have some news,' he told her. 'Assuming you're still interested.'

'Yes, of course I am. What is it?'

'It's about the money, and informants.'

275

'Informants? Do you know who—'

'No. Something else. You remember what Kelly said about the police being greedy for money they could seize from drug dealers?'

'Yes . . .'

'Well, it turns out that seizing money from people is a whole branch of law enforcement these days, complete with its own vocabulary. It's called asset forfeiture, and it comes in two flavors, civil forfeiture and criminal forfeiture.'

'How did you find this out?'

'I tried some of those database services you were talking about.' True enough, as far as it went.

'I thought you weren't going to.'

'I wasn't but then I tried it, and once I got going I couldn't resist.'

As he had gotten deeper into it he had begun to wonder exactly what it was he couldn't resist. He didn't want the answer to be Susan Linwood. His life was uncertain enough without his becoming point-lessly fascinated with a woman who represented everything that was alien to him and beyond reach, who had a marriage and kids and a career. And was old enough to have answered for herself the questions about life he was still struggling with.

He said, 'I have a whole stack of printouts, and I have the citations for a lot of material I didn't actually download. You won't believe it.'

'Like what, for instance?'

'Like not only does the Government really keep the money, it's a whole major part of the law-enforcement budget. Billions of dollars every year.'

'Billions? That can't be.'

'Billions. Not just for drug crimes, either. Almost any kind of crime at all, the Government can take the proceeds of the crime, cash or whatever else, and they can take whatever you used to commit the crime. They can even take the *place* where you committed it. It gets crazy. One guy sold two grams of coke at his auto-body shop, and they took the shop. All of it – the building, the land under it, all the tools and paint and everything. He had to go to the Supreme Court to get it back; it took him years.'

'I don't believe it.' She paused. 'No, I guess I do.'

'The worst part of it is how many times cops and prosecutors don't

276

seem to care if the tips they get are true or not. One story, in California, somebody told the sheriff this guy had marijuana on his farm, so first thing in the morning this army of cops and federal agents rousted him, half-asleep and half in the bag from a hard night's drinking. He heard a commotion so he went to the door with a gun. They shot him dead. Turns out there was no marijuana on the farm. Two hundred prime acres near a state forest. Seems like somebody was eager to add it to the state's land-holdings.'

'And they killed him.'

'Right.'

'Good thing Martin Eng didn't have a gun.'

'Amen. But killing's unusual. Mostly, they ruin people financially, on the word of paid informants.'

'*Paid?*'

'That's what I said. Remember, Manny Klein mentioned something about it, about the IRS paying bounties? Well, it's not just the IRS. The Drug Enforcement Agency pays ten percent of what they seize based on the tip, or at least they used to.'

'But that's hundreds of thousands of dollars for turning somebody in.'

'In the Engs's case, yes – a hundred and thirty thousand dollars for the informant. That's if the DEA took the money – they're federal, like the IRS. Not everybody pays that much. But I checked, and from what I read, both New York State and New York City law enforcement pay finder's fees for special cases. Finder's fees. I couldn't believe it.'

'I wish *I* couldn't.'

'You'd think it would make them awfully careful about which informants they trust, but apparently that's not the first concern. One article I found had Justice Department memos, from Washington, giving major grief to the prosecutors in different U.S. Attorney's offices around the country for not making their quotas, saying they ought to shape up and bring in some more money before the fiscal year ended.'

'Law and order.' She was sounding increasingly dismayed.

'I can get all this material to you if you want it.'

'Yes, please.'

'If you have a doorman I can just drop it by.'

'Oh, you don't have to do that. The mail will be good enough.'

'No problem. I like going for walks.'

They were both silent for a moment.

Susan said, 'I didn't know it would turn out this way when I asked you to help, but this is exactly what I was looking for. Now I don't have to wonder about the informant's motive for lying or even for planting the heroin. Or the detective's motive for condoning it if he knew what was going on. Not if the police are giving big cash rewards to informants who turn people in, and if the police and prosecutors are so hungry for the money they listen to whatever the informants have to say.'

David had had the same kind of reaction, but he still found it hard to take it all the way to planting the heroin.

'I wonder if Tony Ching got any of the blood money,' Susan said.

'Tony who?'

'Oh, didn't I tell you? I found out the name of the man who stole that election from Martin Eng. He's called Tony Ching. He's still president of the Sam Yap Association, and I've been thinking more and more that he could have been the one who put the informant up to talking to the cops, the way we were saying at Kelly's.'

'Why would anyone have to put him up to it, if he had all that finder's-fee money to look forward to?'

'Whoever the informant was, he still needed a reason to pick the Engs to inform on, out of all the people in Chinatown. And remember, if I'm right, the informant didn't just go to the police, he planted the heroin, too.'

'Skipping the heroin for a minute, why would he need a better reason to pick them than all that money? Though I guess that leaves the question of how he knew about it.'

'Actually, Tony Ching would be in as good a position as anybody to know they had money.'

'I thought Ching and Eng were enemies. Do people tell their enemies how much money they have?'

'He'd have known from before they were enemies. Maybe not exactly how much, but that they had plenty. If nothing else, he'd have seen Mrs Eng wearing her jewelry in the old days, when they were all part of the same Association.'

'Would she have worn it in public?'

'When they first got here, and they were establishing themselves, I think she would have. The kind of jewelry she described, and the piece in that picture – those are powerful signs of success and status. And I remember when we got here from Hong Kong, I was very little, but I remember there was a lot of tension in the house, for years, about what people thought, and establishing the proper position. When you just arrive you want to make sure people don't put you in a lower status. The proper display of wealth can be very important.'

'But then other people must have known about their money, too. A lot of people would have seen her in her jewelry, just like Mr Ching did.'

'But other people don't have the same kind of grudge against her husband, and he isn't a threat to them the same way.'

'Maybe somebody just wanted the bounty. Maybe it's a person who traveled in those circles in the old days and fell on hard times and now he's turning in his old friends for finder's fees.' David realized belatedly that he was talking about this as if he accepted her premise – that the Engs had been framed.

'I suppose I can't say you're wrong, not for sure,' she said. She was silent again.

'I can't get over it,' she resumed. 'All this about paid informants. Can you imagine how different it would have been in the grand jury if we'd only known that people can have everything they've worked for all their lives taken away just because they've been denounced to the authorities by somebody with a grudge? And be in danger of spending the rest of their lives in prison, even though they're old and frail?' She was sounding more and more incensed as she spoke. 'And whoever denounces them stands to make money from the accusation. At least in China under the Communists people denounced each other because they thought it was patriotic – however misguided that was – not out of greed.'

'Are you sure that's better?'

'I don't think it's any worse. It bothers me that all this isn't better known. Don't you think people would be outraged?'

'It sure is outrageous.'

'I think after I read what you have for me, I'm going to put on my

279

PR-lady hat and see if I can't get some people to cover this.' He heard the excitement in her voice. 'Newspapers, magazines, maybe even TV. And maybe I can slip in a word about the Engs, as an example.'

'Are you sure that's smart?'

'When you and I talked about it we said we wanted to know the truth. As long as the police can keep this case quiet I think we've seen all the truth we're going to.'

'I guess you know what you're doing.'

'That doesn't sound like you,' she said. 'What happened to the direct Mr Clark?'

'I thought he was right here.'

'I might be misreading your voice, but that sounded more like you meant – you *don't* know what you're doing.'

This was more than he'd bargained for. 'Take it however you want.'

What *had* he bargained for? Why had he called? Why had he done all that research? Could it be, as he already suspected, that he just wanted an excuse to stay in touch with her? And if that was it, why was he working so hard to alienate her?

'I'm not looking for a fight,' she said. 'You're my only ally in this, and I'm glad you called.'

'If it was helpful, I'm glad, too. Let me know how it comes out.'

'If what I'm thinking of doing works, I won't need to let you know. You'll be able to see it for yourself with no trouble.'

There was an awkward silence.

'Thanks again,' she said.

'My pleasure.'

# 7

Busy as Susan was, she found David Clark's information irresistible. She scrapped her morning's work plan and instead combed through what he had dropped off, looking for material she could craft into a release strong enough to prompt an editor to assign a feature story.

Susan's business depended on her being able to persuade people to spend their own professional time doing what was good for Susan's clients. But advocacy that was too blatant was sure to fail. It took her three drafts before she was ready to have Mona take it to be copied.

She thought about letting David Clark read it before she sent it out, decided not to. As sharp and logical as David could be, this kind of thing was completely out of his realm. But she would send him a copy. His research had inspired it, so she owed him at least that.

'It was all a misunderstanding,' Mahoney told Estrada. 'At least, that's what the feds were trying to sell. They sat there in the conference room with Horgan and me – the Assistant U.S. Attorney who made Horgan so crazy and his boss, the one who's running the case – and they both kept a straight face right up to the point where Horgan got so mad he walked out. So then they were up to the next level, our Bureau chief on the phone with their unit chief, making the right noises and getting nowhere.'

'That's par for the course. Who do they say misunderstood whom?'

'They claim Horgan didn't hear the guy right, or else he didn't make himself clear. What the guy really meant to say was, since the minions of her holiness, the U.S. Attorney for the Southern District of New York, have a grand jury investigation underway with the Engs as subjects, it's a natural part of their investigation to develop

281

information on *any* criminal activity the Engs might have been involved in, including distributing heroin and laundering drug money. And a natural way to develop that information is to subpoena the people who have direct evidence of that criminal activity. Such as, for instance, the arresting officer – along with his principal evidence, of course – and maybe also the sources of information who alerted him to the criminal activity. Which is to say, the snitch.'

'In other words,' Estrada deciphered, 'they threatened to strongarm Horgan to get the case away from him. Just the way Horgan said. And basically all the guy did at the meeting was repeat the threat.'

'More or less.'

'No wonder Horgan walked out.'

'And they could have pulled it off, too. If they'd just gone ahead without that clumsy warning – calling Horgan to tell him what they were doing – they might have got the evidence before we knew what was happening.'

'Not with a subpoena to Mick Pullone. He's got to be smarter than that.'

'Suppose they had subpoenaed the police property clerk first,' Mahoney speculated. 'Send an FBI agent down with the papers. *Here's the subpoena, need the evidence right away, here's a receipt, thanks a lot.* Hit it right, and it's all over before anybody knows it. Then all they need is to subpoena our grand jury minutes. Because grand jury minutes may be only hearsay in New York State, but in a federal grand jury they're actual evidence. Hearsay being how they do their business over there.

'And then we're in a real race, because once they have a guilty plea, we're out of the game.' The state constitution prohibited, as double jeopardy, any prosecution by the D.A.'s office based on the same facts which had already produced a guilty plea or a trial verdict, whether in state or federal courts. 'And *they* know that *we* know that we can't do the same to them, because the federal courts aren't so quick shutting the double-jeopardy door on a prosecutor as the state courts are.'

Estrada shook his head. 'I don't want to think about the kind of war it would start if they really tried to double-jeopardy us out of the case. The Boss may be an old-school gentleman, but he wouldn't take a

282

stunt like that without hitting back as hard as he could.'

'You'd think, in a country with fifty-one different systems of criminal law –' one for each state and one for federal law enforcement – 'we'd at least learn to work and play well with each other.'

'You'd think . . . but you'd be wrong. What's next on the agenda? Are they up to the meeting with the real bosses?'

'I see you've been here before.'

'Oh, yeah – the never-ending story.'

'Well, that's just where we are. Ned King –' Chief of the D.A.'s investigation division – 'is bringing our team over to the federal building to talk to the head of their criminal division and his team. Presumably they think the bigger bosses can do a calmer, saner job of making sure everyone is singing from the same page on this. The question right now is, who goes to the meeting and who doesn't? Horgan made the cut, but that's all I'm sure of right now.'

'They bringing Pullone?'

'Lawyers only.'

'You?'

'I'd damn well *better* be going. This case may have started with Horgan's name on it, but I'm the one who's doing the work. And with Horgan pushing me harder than ever to get it on the calendar for trial, my sweat-equity stake is getting bigger by the hour. Not to mention my fascination with it. The more I see of this case, the surer I am it's not what it looks like.'

Unexpectedly, Richard announced to Susan that he had arranged to get away from the hospital early. He and Charles were leaving for the Canadian wilderness a full week sooner than planned. 'That way you two girls can have a couple of days alone together before Lara has to go to college.'

Susan wanted to believe that had been some part of why they changed their plans, but whether it had or not, she was happy to have the time with Lara. The days were full of shopping and packing and seeing friends, busy enough so that Susan went long stretches without wondering how her backgrounder on asset forfeiture – and the Engs – was being received by the editors she'd sent it to.

283

As Lara's departure neared she became increasingly tense and snappish; she and Susan found previously untried ways to annoy each other. Mostly, Susan managed not to take it personally. Lara had to be nervous about the new world she was about to enter, full of strangers and unfamiliar customs and new kinds of academic demands.

They loaded the car up with help from the apartment-house porter. Susan, whose driving was limited to summer weekend trips to the beach house, navigated the narrow crosstown streets with more than her usual caution. Even the ride down residential West End Avenue was a trial, worse when it became Eleventh Avenue and she had to contend with trucks as well as taxis and passenger cars.

Emerging from the Lincoln Tunnel in New Jersey, the confusion of finding the correct lane kept her busy. It was only on the New Jersey Turnpike that she realized her hands hurt from gripping the steering wheel.

'Mom, are you okay?' Lara asked.

Susan glanced quickly across the car at her daughter. 'I'm fine.'

'You haven't said a word.'

'I haven't?'

'Not except "Which lane should I be in?" '

'Oh.' Susan flexed one hand to get it back to feeling normal. 'I guess I was worried about getting lost.'

'We're okay for the next hour or so.'

'Except for the traffic.'

'I meant getting lost.'

'If you left anything behind, all you have to do is call. It's no trouble to send it—'

'Mom! It's only fifty miles. You act as if I'm going to Mars. Or China.'

Lara leaned forward to turn the radio on. Glancing over at her, Susan caught a thick gleam of gold between Lara's shirt and her neck.

'What's that?'

'What?' Lara sat up abruptly.

'Around your neck.'

'Oh.' She fussed with the heavy chain to get it tucked out of sight under her shirt. 'Daddy gave it to me,' she said.

'When?' Susan fought to keep her voice level.

284

'We had a goodbye lunch, that day you had to stay at your office.'

'Oh? Where'd you go?'

'You know, the restaurant Daddy likes so much. The one way downtown.'

Susan knew. She'd last been there with Richard three anniversaries ago. 'Did you enjoy it?'

'Yes.'

'Did Daddy give you anything else?'

'Some extra allowance.' In a small voice. 'For clothes or anything.'

Susan held her peace. How like Richard. She had wondered why he had so casually let her monopolize Lara's departure for college. The answer was, he hadn't.

But this time Susan was determined not to react, because to react was to let him win. No matter how he tried to get between her and Lara, this was her last pre-college time with her daughter and she would not let him spoil it.

Lara was fiddling with the radio again, searching through the stations. She didn't find anything she liked.

'What's happening with your grand jury people?' she asked. 'Did you ever talk to anybody about it?'

'I had a meeting with some of the other jurors.'

'What'd they say?'

'The way it turned out, it wasn't so much what they said as how I responded to it. Since then I've talked to one of the other jurors again and I've learned a lot more. Some very interesting things.' She told Lara about asset forfeiture and how the Government used paid informants.

'That's horrible. Are you going to do something?'

'I already have. And I think it might even make a little difference.'

'Yay!' Lara leaned across and gave her a quick kiss on the cheek.

'What was that for?'

'I said before, I think it's cool that you're doing something to help innocent people.'

The street that ran alongside the campus was a two-way procession of station wagons filled with arriving first-year students and their parents and all the clothes, music tapes and CDs and computers the cars could hold. Now Lara was looking eagerly out the window at the Gothic buildings and the grassy quadrangles and at the passing cars and their occupants, their faces obscured by reflections of sky and trees and gray stone on the car windows.

Susan drove like an automaton, following the signs and directions Lara gave her from a campus map. Unpacking seemed to be over at once. Susan had a vague impression of wood floors and walls of plaster and brick, of communal bathrooms, and of a stream of students and parents staggering under heavy boxes. Already, Lara was meeting her dormmates, seeing who was in which room and where they were from.

Susan could tell, through the haze that surrounded her, that Lara wouldn't want to have her mom hanging around. 'I'd better be going,' she said. 'Walk me to the car?'

Lara came with her and submitted to a much tighter and needier hug than Susan had expected to give her.

'I'll be fine, Mom. Don't worry.' Lara gave her a kiss on the cheek. 'You going to be okay?'

'Me? Don't be silly. I'm the mother. I'll be fine.'

They smiled at each other, hugged again quickly. Susan got in the car and watched her daughter walk away, turning at the dormitory door to wave before she disappeared inside.

Susan navigated carefully back the way she had come. At the first place on the turnpike where the shoulder was wide enough she pulled the car over and sat and cried.

When she thought she was ready, she turned the ignition key and realized that the world was a blur. Somehow, in the flood of tears, and intermittently wiping her eyes, she had popped out her contact lenses.

She made herself frantic, looking; she couldn't find them. Behind her, the sun was setting. Driving in the daylight without her glasses was a questionable proposition, driving at night would be impossible. She put the car in gear and started for home, keeping to the middle lane among the colorful blurs of the cars around her – concentrating hard to avoid the cars speeding by on both sides and traffic merging ahead, working out in her mind how she would recognize the exit to the tunnel.

★ ★ ★

Kevin Horgan came by to collect Mahoney first thing in the morning. 'Showtime. Let's go.'

Their first stop was the eighth-floor executive suite. The long, pale corridor beyond the security-locked entrance door bore the usual No Smoking sign; the air reeked of cigars, as no doubt did the carpet. Mahoney was sure the sepia-tone portraits of all the previous New York County District Attorneys had absorbed the smell, too.

During his years in the Appeals Bureau Mahoney had gotten to know a lot of the trial A.D.A.s, filing appeals to preserve their convictions; Ned King, Chief of the Investigation Division, wasn't one of them. Mahoney knew him only as a boss. He had risen rapidly through the ranks to the office next to the Boss's, and he had a reputation to fit: tough and smart, with a nose for what was important and what worked. Only his enemies went so far as to call him ruthless, but nobody wanted to be on his wrong side.

They were shown right into his office. Mahoney found himself sitting next to Horgan on a vinyl-covered couch, much bigger and newer than Estrada's wreck. Ned King was behind his desk, across the room – a long-limbed man with deep brown eyes and a strong jaw and a rich suntan – from hours on the golf course, judging by the trophies on the window sill. Mahoney noticed a basketball hoop and mini-backboard, the same as Mahoney's own, clipped to the wastebasket; seeing it relaxed him a little.

'What have we got here?' King opened. He leaned back in the tall desk chair. 'I know Chinese heroin and a million and a half dollars, and I know they're climbing up on their high federal horse over at the Southern District, trying to grab this for their very own.

'We're about to go over there and try to keep them from screwing us blind, and frankly I have no desire to be stomped into the underbrush in the process. So if you gentlemen will bring me up to speed so I can decide if this is worth going to war over, I'd greatly appreciate it.'

Horgan started, as he'd told Mahoney he would. He ran down a quick outline of the case's history and the highlights of the evidence. 'It's a lot of money, and we're working it through the DEA, so we'll end up with close to eighty percent of it. And it's a good, strong case.'

'It seems to me this is the case where the grand jury asked to hear the defendants, or am I wrong?'

'No, this is the one. Dan can tell you about that. I've been on trial on another case, so he's been doing the legwork and he had it in the grand jury.'

King looked in Mahoney's direction.

'I can't say for sure whether it was something about the case that got them going or if it was just that particular grand jury,' Mahoney said. He'd given a lot of thought to how he was going to present this: he wanted to be able to keep working on the case and didn't want to lose it to the U.S. Attorney's office, but the more he'd reviewed it the uneasier he'd become, and he didn't think he could hide that completely. It was a fine line to walk, but ultimately he didn't think anyone would be served if he papered over the case's problems.

'The grand jury had heard from a defendant before, and they'd no-true-billed the prosecutor on that one,' he began. 'So they might just have been feeling their oats. But I'm reasonably sure they had some trouble with the evidence, too. They took a long time to vote, and according to the warden they were really going at it – a lot of shouting. And they had some serious questions to ask.'

'That's what I want to hear about.'

'They didn't like it that the defendants were so old, for one. And some of it . . . Without the specifics, I'd say it added up to their being frustrated there was nothing to connect these people to anybody else. At least one of them thought maybe the heroin was planted, and the package was wiped clean, so that didn't help.'

'Wiped clean?'

'That's what the lab said.'

'Anything else?'

'The record books gave them some trouble.'

At that, Horgan jumped in. 'Yeah, but the accountant and the translator only had, what, four days with them by then. That part ought to be a lot stronger by now.' He turned to Mahoney. 'Right?'

'I talked to the accountant,' Mahoney affirmed. 'He says he has a clearer picture. He also says he's still not a hundred percent sure by any means. The one thing he's sure of is that it's a payment record. Money in, money out. He thinks heroin, he says there's nothing

288

inconsistent with heroin. But if there'd been no heroin in sight—'

'Dan still has his Appeals head working, some days,' Horgan interrupted. 'I'm the one who's going to put it in front of a jury, and it looks real solid to me. I'm going in there with the heroin and the money and the records to tie them together.'

'You say there's no connection to anybody else?' the Chief asked Mahoney. 'No source, no buyers?

'None that we can find so far. I'm waiting for the phone records, that's my best hope. I've been checking with Mark Brattler at the Asian Gang Unit. So far his people don't have anything useful.'

'You got this case from a snitch.'

'Right,' Horgan said. 'One of my detectives brought it in.'

'What does the snitch have to say?'

It was a chance for Mahoney to talk about his frustration with Pullone, his doubts about the snitch . . . He glanced at Horgan. There was no mistaking his expression: *All right, Mahoney*, it said, *here's where you show how loyal to me you are*.

'It doesn't look like the snitch has anything more than the initial tip,' Mahoney said. 'But we're working on it.' Satisfying Horgan, he hoped, while leaving the door open a crack.

'Anything else I haven't heard yet?'

'Just, I got an early warning of this federal interest,' Mahoney said. 'I have a friend over at the Southern District who said they wanted us to let them use our case for leverage. All she told me was that whatever case they were making it wasn't heroin, and it wasn't something they were likely to share.'

'Based on the roster for this meeting, I'm not so surprised about the heroin. I'm more interested in the part about them not being likely to share.'

'That's pretty much what she said.'

'That sets the terms of debate, doesn't it?'

King glanced up at the clock on his wall. 'Okay, let's go over it once more, top to bottom, and then we've got to get over there.'

The three of them, plus the head of the Rackets Bureau, walked over to St. Andrew's Plaza. The building was new and luxurious by D.A.'s-office standards, but it still bore unmistakable signs of being used by busy prosecutors. The hallways and offices were randomly stacked with cardboard boxes of court papers, evidence charts, and reams of paper waiting to be fed to the copying machines.

Their meeting was in a room that clearly doubled as library and conference room. The long conference table occupied the center of the room; the walls were floor-to-ceiling bookcases.

Mahoney recognized the two line assistants from the meeting Horgan had walked out of. With them were two men around forty, one thin and bald, the other round-faced, ruddy and wiry haired, with owlish glasses. As a group the federal prosecutors looked more prosperous and, Mahoney thought, more self-satisfied than the ones from the D.A.'s office. On second glance, Mahoney amended that to *smug*. They were also, on average, about four inches shorter than the state prosecutors.

As Horgan had predicted when he briefed Mahoney, the proceedings began with the subordinates sitting in polite silence while the bosses made noises establishing that they were connected by long familiarity and above being distracted from their mutual goals by the petty squabbles of underlings. They batted around puffballs like . . . Great case you just made . . . How did your boy do at his soccer championship? . . . I see where you just won another golf tournament . . . We ought to get out on the course so I can see that famous swing of yours . . .

With that out of the way they got down to business. Ned King told a concise tale of a strong case against two people who were all but convicted of heroin possession and conspiracy to sell, and of money-laundering as well, though that indictment had not yet been presented for a vote. He managed to seem complete in his description of the case without revealing anything more than the essentials.

The federal boss pushed his round glasses up the bridge of his nose and cleared his throat.

'I don't want to belittle any of what you've just said. A million four is a lot of money and distributing heroin is a serious crime. I do have to say that what we're looking at is many orders of magnitude greater. These defendants are central to it, essential to our case. But they're small players on a big stage. And –' he made what came next a pronouncement – 'what we're looking at these people for has nothing to do with heroin.'

In the pause, Ned King said, 'Seeing as you're sitting here with your head of Public Corruption and nobody from Narcotics, that's hardly a major piece of information. I'm doing my best to lay my cards on the table here, and frankly I expect you to be as forthcoming.'

The Criminal Division head smiled and Mahoney was surprised to see that it looked real. 'I guess I was sounding sort of pompous, there, but it's only because this really is so important. We're talking about international monetary transfers, with wide implications. These people you arrested just showed up on our radar. The main case is being built at the Department of Justice in Washington – we're on the fringes of it here in New York.

'Because these people are essentially middlemen we think they could hold the key to the whole show. The difficulty is that our case is almost completely stymied by this arrest of yours, because they're out of action now. Our best hope of salvaging many person-years of work on a very significant case is to use *your* case as a lever to get them to talk to us.'

'That all sounds very imposing, but it doesn't tell me anything,' King countered. 'I'd have a lot easier time not stepping on your toes if I knew what territory you were in.'

The federal boss smiled again, less genuinely this time. 'I know you'll understand that I'm between a rock and hard place here. I've got grand jury secrecy to worry about, and I have no permission from DOJ to share anything with you beyond what I already have.'

'You're looking for us to give you our case, based on no information,' King said. 'Giving you our case means giving up our informant, and you know I can't do that.'

'I understand the difficulty that presents.' The Federal Division chief drew himself up even more pompously. 'But I think we all have to keep uppermost in our minds that what matters here when we look at the situation as a whole is what is in the best interests of law enforcement.'

'Well, yes, that's always the question, isn't it? I've got a fully developed case here, and the exposure for these defendants is life in prison. The way *I* understand the interests of law enforcement, a case of that seriousness demands full respect.'

'I'm not saying it doesn't. I'm saying what we're looking at is

291

bigger than just two defendants. A lot bigger.'

'One thing puzzles me,' the D.A.'s-office chief said. 'If these people just came on your radar, how can you be so certain they don't have anything to do with heroin?'

The answer to that came slowly. 'I am not saying definitively these people have nothing to do with heroin. Just that our case doesn't. I notice, though, that the conspiracy count in your indictment is silent on the subject of co-conspirators or specific acts of conspiracy. Do you know who they're involved with?'

Mahoney, sitting in enforced silence, wondered how his side would respond to that one. He didn't have long to wait.

'I don't see where that's an issue – we don't usually name the co-conspirators in the indictment,' Ned King said. 'We've given you a good, clear idea of our basic evidence, and I haven't heard you offering anything in return.'

The meeting went on in that vein for another twenty minutes, with no ground given on either side. In keeping with the early show of collegiality, no voices were raised. It ended with mutual protestations of the great value of cooperation. The bosses promised to take the issue up with their respective Bosses – the D.A. and the U.S. Attorney. A later meeting was mentioned but not scheduled, and both sides agreed not to interfere with each other's case in the meantime. At the end they shook hands all around.

'What a crock,' the Rackets Bureau chief said on the way back to the D.A.'s office. 'The best interests of law enforcement! Translation – what's good for them.'

'Right,' said King. 'We all said all the right words, now the only question is who's going to screw whom first, and how? Anybody have any ideas what their case might be about?'

Apart from a consensus that the federal case was more likely to be a molehill than the mountain they had tried to paint, the speculation didn't get very far. The fact that it was a Public Corruption case for the feds made everybody think of bribery. That it was Chinese and federal and allegedly not heroin brought up illegal immigration and commercial smuggling – bribing consular officials for visas, or Customs or the Coast Guard to let illegals land or contraband come in.

'You think they're being straight when they say their case isn't about heroin?' Ned King asked.

'I don't think they're being straight about anything,' Horgan said.

'If it's bribery they're after, that doesn't necessarily mean it's not heroin,' the Rackets Bureau chief speculated. 'If somebody in Public Corruption opened the case, it would stay there even if it turned out that narcotics was the subject matter – say, if they're bribing somebody in Customs to let drugs in.'

'It fits best with what we have, if that's it,' Horgan was quick to say.

'Our own case is what I'm worried about right now,' King said. 'We're going to have another meeting with those folks by and by, and I'm going to need some cards to put on the table. This time I got away with a bluff –' Horgan started to protest but King cut him off – 'I'm not saying you couldn't convince a jury. What I'm saying is, at the end of the day this is going to be a pissing match between us and them, and what's going to count is who has the goods. If we're going to divide this up between the offices on results and sweat equity, I want to be ahead in both columns. We've got some running room here, a little inter-office peace treaty. But it's not going to last for ever, so let's make the most of it.'

Outside the D.A.'s office entrance, King said, 'One other thing. While we're making this case as strong as we can, let's not forget to keep our eyes open for whatever it is the feds are after. I'm mostly out of the office until Labor Day, but they know where to find me, even if I'm on the golf course. Don't hesitate to call.'

David called Susan as soon as he'd gone through her package of press material on asset forfeiture and the Engs. 'I'm glad you decided to send it to me. That's one impressive piece of work.'

'Thank you.'

'Where else did you send it?'

'Mostly to newspaper and magazine editors, some TV and radio news and some journalists with a good track record in investigative work.'

'Quite a list.'

'The hard part is doing the research and the writing. After that it's only photocopying and postage and the fax bill. And David Clark gets credit for the research.'

The acknowledgment pleased him, but he let it go by. 'I was interested to see that you included some points for the other side.'

'I had to. Those stories about how the D.A.'s office has cleaned out whole buildings that used to be drug supermarkets so local people can use them for housing and community services – what could be more admirable?'

'True. It's too bad that's not all they do.'

'But it's what they're bound to come back with any time they're criticized, and I don't believe in hiding from the other side's arguments. I think it makes me stronger to show that I'm comfortable with the best face they can put on it.'

'And where did you find that business about the speed trap down South? I don't know how I missed it.'

'My associate remembered reading it in a Sunday news magazine,' she said. 'For me, it's the one that seems scariest, because it's so random and everybody is at risk. The very idea of those redneck troopers stopping anybody they think looks wrong, searching them, and confiscating any large amount of cash they find. And doing it on an interstate highway.'

'And once they have your money it's up to you to prove that you got it honestly, and that you don't plan to buy drugs with it.'

'That's what so terrible about all of this forfeiture,' Susan said. 'That once they have a basis to seize something, the victim of the seizure has to prove they didn't get the money or whatever it is illegally, didn't use it for anything illegal, and don't ever intend to. It's the opposite of innocent until proven guilty.'

'You do a great job portraying it. I don't see how anybody could read some of those pages and not have their blood boil.'

'Thank you again. You're not just my most important source for this, you're my most important audience, too.'

'There's one thing you wrote that I wondered about,' he said.

'What's that?'

'Where you talk about the Engs and you say the evidence barely convinced the grand jury. Isn't that violating grand jury secrecy?'

'Is it? I assumed that meant revealing testimony or evidence. I wasn't specific about why, or anything about the argument or the exact vote. What harm can there be?'

'Maybe I'm being alarmist, but I think that little white booklet they gave us says we can't disclose *anything* about grand jury proceedings.'

There was a long silence.

'Is there anything else like that?' she asked in a thin voice.

He knew she was upset, but he had something else he thought needed saying.

'There is one other thing, and I'm sorry I didn't raise it as soon as you said you might try to do some kind of PR work based on what I dug up. I just wonder if it's what the Engs would want, putting the word out this way. They still haven't done anything themselves to publicize this – not that I can see. Doesn't sending this out amount to making that decision for them?'

'The only decision I'm trying to influence is some city editor's about what to run in the paper or show on the news,' she responded with some heat. 'If the news organizations in this city were worth a tenth of what they're cracked up to be, we wouldn't be having this conversation. Think about it – the police seized a million-plus dollars and some heroin from two elderly Chinatown people who run a community organization. Wouldn't you expect more than just reporting the arrest? Even if they just picked up a fraction of what Mrs Liu said was in the Chinatown papers, that ought to have put them onto this. It's disgraceful.'

'I'll admit it seems kind of odd. Except the police are seizing drugs and money all the time, now. Maybe it wasn't a big deal for them.'

'You're right that the only way the press would have picked up on it was from the police. And all the police seem to have done was issue a minor press release about the money, with almost nothing about the Engs but their names. So the news media reported the money and let the *human* part of the story go by. I'm just trying to get their attention, so they'll do what they should have done in the first place.'

'Maybe they have a reason for not getting into all that.'

'Of course they have a reason. They're lazy. They want somebody to feed them the story. If it's a controversy they're in heaven, because then they've got people on both sides feeding them.'

He was impressed by how passionate she was about this.

'I've never been focused on getting coverage in the mainstream news media,' she said. 'I do more conferences and informational programs – but I'm always having to write news releases for my clients anyway. And you don't want to know how many of them run almost exactly the way I submitted them. Word for word. Some days I think I get more in print than I would if I were a reporter.'

'I always assumed reporters went out and talked to people,' David said. 'That they had sources they went to who gave them inside information.'

'Sure they have sources. Like *me* – I'm a source. And that's all I want to do with this. I want to be a source. And it's not just the Engs. This whole business about the Government taking people's property makes me furious, especially when it's on the word of some lowlife who's getting paid on a percentage basis.'

'*The police rely on informants more and more, because a well-placed informant can learn a lot more than the best-trained under-cover officer,*' he quoted from her release. 'That really says it – we've got a legion of criminals and snitches out there doing police work.'

'Would you like to have the icing on the cake? The detective who inspired that quote, right after he'd just made a huge drug bust based on what he'd learned from his informant – do you want to guess who it was?'

'If you're about to tell me it was our old friend Detective Pullone it won't exactly make me happy.'

'Then I'd better not tell you,' she said.

# 8

In the late afternoon, Susan got a call that she had been both hoping for and dreading.

'This is Ellen Hyams. I'm a criminal defense lawyer, but I think you may know that.' She left Susan no room to comment. 'I've been getting phone calls about some clients of mine. Press interest. When I pushed to find out why, I started hearing about a press release dealing with asset forfeiture in which my clients are used as an example. And my people trace this press release to you. Is that right?'

'I wrote a backgrounder on that subject.'

'If it's the one I've seen you have my congratulations. It's a pernicious thing, the way law enforcement policy is being twisted by the greed for forfeiture revenue – and citizens' rights are being trampled in the process. And you've done a fine job of capturing the dangers.'

'If it is my release you're reading, I appreciate the compliment.' Susan had the distinct feeling the lawyer had not called to praise her.

'One thing I was wondering about . . .' Ellen Hyams's tone conveyed only casual curiosity.

'Yes?' Here it comes, Susan thought.

'Who did you talk to at the D.A.'s office?'

It was not a question Susan would have anticipated; she was sure that if not for David's warning she would have handled it badly. As it was, it made her very nervous.

'I'm not sure what you mean.'

'To get your information.' The lawyer was still playing casual.

'It was all secondary sources. Public record.' Susan named some of the news organizations and interest groups David had tapped for the forfeiture information.

'I was thinking more about what you wrote about my clients.'

'Your clients?'

'You seem to know who they are. You wrote a good deal about them.'

'If it's the people I think you mean, a lot of people know about them.'

'But I'm particularly interested in you.'

'I heard about them from Chinatown people. They've been in the Chinese language newspapers.'

'Only in passing. I'd be very interested to know what prompted you to send out those releases. Who's your client?'

'You don't expect me to answer that.' Susan's apprehension made her answer sharp.

'Don't carry on as if you have a confidentiality privilege.' Hyams's tone had sharpened in response. 'You don't.'

'I'm not sure what that means, but I know I have a professional responsibility not to expose any client who would prefer it that way.' Susan was keeping her voice strong and level, but her palms were sweating and she could feel perspiration running down her sides.

'Well, my message to you and your client is that we would prefer you didn't do this at all.'

'Why?' popped out.

'*Why* isn't really the important question.'

'How can a release about a bad Government law-enforcement policy hurt anybody but the people responsible for the bad policy?'

There was a momentary hesitation before the lawyer asked, 'What's your interest in all this?'

'The interest of an ordinary citizen who's worried about what her Government is doing. And I like to pick out issues to experiment with.' It was the story she'd decided to tell if she was ever challenged like this. 'I check the reaction to various kinds of presentation, in various media.'

'Practice on somebody else.'

'Maybe if I understood better why you – why your client objects.'

'I repeat, what's your interest in that? No, on second thoughts I think I'll just call this conversation closed. If you have any concern for my clients, and I can only imagine you must, please don't carry this any further.'

'I have plenty of concern.' Susan was suddenly angry. 'You'll notice there's nothing in that release about Tony Ching.'

'Tony . . .' The phone went briefly silent. 'Who *are* you?'

'Just a PR lady.'

'And just what is it that makes you bring up this Mr Ching?'

'I've heard that he has reason not to be displeased by Martin Eng's difficulties.'

'Can I ask where you heard that?'

'From a reputable source.'

'And did you hear only that statement, or was there background?'

'There was considerable background.'

'And you found it credible?'

'Shouldn't I have?'

'Oh, no, you should have. It's quite a story, isn't it? But I'm not sure why you would think that leaving it out of your release was a sign of concern for my clients.'

'I was advised that publicizing it might not be consistent with your defense strategy.'

'Really?' Ellen Hyams said after a moment. 'Who told you that?'

'It's not important.'

'It was a thoughtful impulse,' the lawyer said. 'But the police know the story, or if they don't they will soon.' She paused, and when she resumed the steel had gone out of her voice, replaced by a soothing tone. 'You seem to have gone to a lot of trouble over this.'

'I said I'm a concerned citizen.'

'A concerned Chinese citizen?' Lightly.

It was Susan's turn to be silent.

'Never mind,' the lawyer said. 'I withdraw the question. Let me tell you what my problem is now, and maybe you can help. My problem is, you know too much for it all to have come from the Chinese newspapers.'

'I said I have reputable sources. In the community.' True enough, and perhaps it would divert her from thoughts of the D.A.'s office.

'And these sources gave you enough information to imply that the prosecution case might be manufactured.'

*Careful*, Susan warned herself, this is slippery ground. 'That doesn't take a genius. Two old people with their history in the community aren't the best candidates for Heroin Distributor of the Month. Especially if you factor in all those stories about how cavalier the police and prosecutors can be when they have a chance to seize a lot of money.'

'And is that why you wrote that the grand jury almost didn't indict?'

'Yes. Yes, you can call that a . . . a guess. Is it wrong?'

'I don't know. Grand jury deliberations are secret, as I'm sure you're aware.'

Susan's mind froze: she could not think of a safe response.

'Well,' Ellen Hyams said. 'I will say I appreciate your support, though I do wish you had called me before you sent this out. My clients have specifically asked me to limit the amount of publicity they receive.'

'Do they think you have control over that?'

'I admit it's wishful thinking, to a degree – ultimately the press will do what it wants. And I'm ordinarily eager for any positive publicity I can get – Lord knows, the prosecution will do what it can when it thinks the time is right. But nevertheless my clients are quite adamant. No publicity.'

Again, Susan thought of her conversation with David. Could she have done the wrong thing? It didn't make sense. With the arrest and accusation already reported, where was the harm in a press release that implied you'd been falsely accused?

'I'd like to hear that from your clients directly,' Susan was surprised to hear herself say.

'Oh, no.' The lawyer sounded startled. 'I don't see how that would be appropriate. They were very explicit in their instructions about publicity. I don't see why they would have any desire for personal contact, and I wouldn't advise it.'

'Why? What do you, or they, have to lose by letting me talk to them?'

'I don't know how you get your jollies, Ms Linwood, or what part this all plays in it. I can tell you that I'm going to do what I can to find out about that. But whatever I learn about the purity of your professed

300

good intentions, personal contact with my clients will still be out of the question.'

'What do you mean you're going to do what you can to find out?'

'There's nothing personal in this,' the lawyer said. 'But under the circumstances I'm going to have to talk to my investigators about checking you out. It would be irresponsible not to.'

'You don't have to threaten me.' Susan was shaking now, but her voice was still under control. 'That's a peculiar way to treat someone you've just thanked for her help.'

'I said it wasn't personal—'

'How do you know what you're passing up by not letting me talk to them? How do you know what help I might be?' Susan heard the tension creeping into her voice, sensed how close she was to saying something she would regret. She told herself to calm down.

'What kind of help do you have in mind?' Again the lawyer had turned on her soothing voice.

'None. Nothing.' Susan was suddenly exhausted. 'Let's just forget it. I meant to be helpful. Let's leave it at that.'

'Good. I think that's best.'

Susan hung up and sat by the phone, unmoving. I provoked that, she thought: I could have let it go, and maybe Hyams would have accepted the idea that it was a coincidence. But no, she told herself – you had to keep pushing, waving a red flag in her face. And now she's wondering exactly who Susan Linwood might be, and how she got her special knowledge. What would Hyams do if she learned that Susan had been on the grand jury, had leaked secret information?

But who was Ellen Hyams to take the attitude she had, anyway? As if Susan were some kind of nut, trying to find a way to get near accused criminals for the thrill of it. *I don't know how you get your jollies!*

She had to talk to somebody about this, and there was really only one person who had been through enough of it with her to understand.

She got an answering machine when she called David Clark. She hesitated over whether to leave a message, decided not to.

Her frustration mounted. She paced around the office, straightening things that were already where they belonged.

She picked up the phone again. This time, she called Ann Lum.

301

★ ★ ★

Mahoney glanced over the front page of the *Times* the way he always did with his morning coffee. There was nothing much different from the day before. An article about political turmoil in China and awkward U.S.-China relations that he might not have noticed if he didn't have a case set in Chinatown and if he hadn't been talking to Mark Brattler and looking at his photographs.

He turned to the letters to the editor. Most days there was something he found thought-provoking, which was more than he could say for the rest of the paper. As he folded the paper his eye was caught by a headline on the op-ed page: STAND AND DELIVER.'

He started out skimming the column. It cast law enforcement as a modern highwayman, holding up the citizenry at the point of the forfeiture laws. There were three of the usual examples people cited to show how the system was abused, and one he had never seen before. Nothing about the positive aspects of the system. The column closed with a paragraph about Martin Eng and his wife.

*'We do not pretend to know what Mr and Mrs Eng did or did not do,'* the columnist wrote. *'We know that they have been leaders in their community and we know that they have a history of philanthropy. We know that though they have been indicted the law says they are innocent unless proved otherwise, and we know that they have been deprived of all their financial assets. We also know that given the current state of the law they are not likely ever to get their money back, not any of it, even if they are never convicted of any crime, even though the evidence presented to support their indictment barely passed the scrutiny of the grand jury.'*

Mahoney read the last part again. It said what he thought it did: either the columnist was making irresponsible guesses or someone had violated the secrecy of Daniel Mahoney's grand jury.

He went back and read it all again. His intention was to look for clues, but instead he paid closer attention to the anecdotes of law-enforcement rapaciousness.

It stayed with him in the shower. His mind kept coming back to the question of what people would do for money – good people and bad, cops and robbers – and if not for money, for power. He thought about the Engs, and the grand juror who wanted to know why the police had raided their apartment in the first place. And about all the things that bothered him about the case.

The trouble was, this wasn't just any trial he was preparing, now. This was a case that was under a special kind of scrutiny because it was the subject of a turf war between state and federal prosecutors. If the case was rotten at the core – as, off and on, he had suspected it might be – that was no longer something that could simply be hurried past a jury by a showman like Kevin Horgan. More critical eyes would be watching: Ned King was going to be putting the office's reputation on the line, based on the idea that this was a case worth fighting for.

When Susan next reached for the phone to call David Clark, her mood was very different. She had a favor to ask him, and the call suddenly seemed daunting. Suppose he said no, where would she be then? But why should he say no? He'd been interested enough to begin with. Surely he'd at least want to know what she was planning.

And there was more. She suspected he might be interested in her. Not that he'd done something overt, or said something to make her think so. If anything, he'd seemed somehow intimidated, for all that he was a man who spoke his mind without worrying too much about being tactful.

But even if he was interested in her, that didn't mean he'd be willing to spend another minute on the Engs. And she was probably exaggerating whatever interest he had in her, or making it up . . .

After all these years, she still had no real grasp of her appeal to men – she couldn't predict which ones would be drawn to her, which would not. She suspected that little of it had to do with Susan Chan, the person, or Susan Linwood, as she had been for twenty-odd years. She understood in an abstract way that in some eyes she was what might be considered beautiful, and she accepted, without understanding it, that Asian women had a special allure for certain non-Asians. How much, if any, of this applied to David Clark she couldn't guess.

She decided she was being silly and dialed the number.

A woman answered. 'Hello?'

'Hello,' Susan began tentatively. 'I'm calling for David Clark. My name is Susan Linwood.'

'Just a minute.' The phone clattered on a hard surface. There were voices in the background: the woman, calling *David*, and one or more high-pitched voices that had to be kids.

So much for the idea that he was interested in her. Not that his domestic situation precluded it; she was no stranger to passes from married men. But for whatever reason she had not seen him as married, and somehow that picture of him changed things.

'Hello,' he said.

'I hope I'm not disturbing you. It's Susan Linwood.'

'No, it's okay. My sister and her kids just flew in unannounced, we were talking about what to do for dinner.'

*Sister.* 'Oh. Well, I can call back.' Of course – he'd once said something about a niece and nephew.

'No, go ahead. What's up?'

'I had a call from the lawyer who represents the Engs.' That wasn't why she had called him, but it was a start.

'Their lawyer? Why?'

'About the press release I sent out.'

'I saw the op-ed piece today. Very exciting. You were right, they hardly changed what you wrote.'

'The sincerest form of flattery, though it's the only one so far.'

'I should have called to congratulate you. I've been so busy, finishing up with Jimmy Kelly . . .'

'Did you figure out how he could make his computer work?' She was glad to have another subject for a moment.

'I think I gave him the kind of information he needs to do better with the next one. But what's this about the Engs's lawyer?'

'She wanted to know why I sent out that release.' She told him a little about the conversation.

'Does she know who you are?' David asked.

'If you mean about the grand jury, I was worried about it but I don't see how she could. All she knows is that I'm interested in the Engs and I've talked to people in Chinatown.'

'She knows your name, and what you do.'

'Yes.'

'Then she probably knows more about you than that.'

'She said she was going to have an investigator check me out and it scared me, but then I thought why would she bother? It didn't occur to me that she'd already started. I guess that was naive . . . But I don't see how she can find out I was on the grand jury, not unless she taps my phone.' It was meant as a joke, but the idea gave her a chill.

'There's something else,' she made herself say. 'I have a favor to ask you.' She hurried ahead with it. 'Those Chinatown friends who told me about Martin Eng's problems – Ann Lum and Uncle Eight? I've asked them to arrange a meeting for me with the Engs. I was hoping you'd be willing to come along.'

There was a long silence.

'It seems to me we talked about how it might not be safe to get involved in this too deeply,' he said.

'But this isn't like that. It has nothing to do with his fight with Tony Ching.'

'You know that, and if you tell it to me, I believe you. But Mr Ching doesn't know it.'

'Why should he care whether I visit Mr and Mrs Eng? Or whether you come with me? How would he even know?'

He was silent again. She fought the impulse to urge him to come.

'What's it all about? This visit, I mean.'

She told him about Ellen Hyams's insistence that the Engs wanted no publicity. 'I want to hear it from the Engs themselves. And I want to ask them some things, too.'

'Why bring me?' he asked. 'Why bring anyone?'

'I don't think it's a good idea to go alone. I want somebody there who can see what's happening from a different perspective. Some-body who knows what it's all about.'

There was more silence on his end.

She said, 'I thought . . . you seemed interested before. I know it's an imposition, but it would be a great favor.'

'When is this going to be? I'm not saying yes, I just . . . Do you have an appointment with them?'

'Not yet. My friends are calling them for me.'

'If you call me again when you know what's happening, maybe I'll have had a chance to give it some thought.'

'Sure, that's great.' She got off the phone, absurdly relieved.


After lunch Mahoney and Horgan answered a summons from Ned

305

King. There was a copy of the *Times* on his desk. Mahoney didn't have to look to know what it was open to.

'I assume you've seen this.' The Chief of Investigation waved the op-ed piece at them.

'We've been talking about it,' Horgan said.

'And what have you been saying?'

'For one, I'll bet that asshole reporter who weeps so much for those people never had a kid of his strung out on drugs. It's hard enough doing our job without having to fight bullshit like that.' Horgan seemed to detect King's impatience. 'And we've been saying somebody has to be leaking that stuff about the grand jury.'

'Any ideas?'

'It smells like the defense to me.'

'And where do they get their information?'

'A court officer, maybe, or the grand jury warden, something like that. Everybody knows somebody in the courthouse.'

'Who's the defense lawyer?' King wanted to know. Mahoney told him; he didn't recognize the name.

'She was at the Southern District for a while and then down at the Justice Department. She works for a D.C. firm, in their New York office.'

'Not one of the usual suspects around here.'

'No.'

'So maybe she doesn't have such great contacts in the courthouse.'

'She could have co-counsel who does,' Horgan suggested.

'She could. Could it be a grand juror?'

'Sure, why not?' Horgan was easy on the subject of who had done the leaking. His first opinion had been, who the fuck knows?

'Any thoughts?' the Chief asked.

'There were a lot of grand jurors who didn't like the case,' Mahoney said. 'Including two Chinese women, one very prosperous and well put together. The kind who knows people.'

King put his hands behind his head and stared at the ceiling. 'All right,' he said after a moment. 'This stops right here. We're not going to start investigating our own case, because we've got better ways to spend our time and money and I surely don't want to end up finding out there's something wrong with our indictment. And we know we're

306

not going to investigate the reporter. If it's the defense, well . . . maybe I can get somebody to give the court officers a pep talk about keeping their mouths shut, for whatever good that'll do.'

Mahoney was expecting that to be it, but King leaned forward in his chair and fixed them both with a serious stare. 'The Boss was in here about this, this morning. It got him good and interested – in the case and in this whole business with the Southern District. And the trouble is, shit like this –' he waved the paper at them again – 'is not going to help me when we have our next meeting at the Southern District. Our point over there is, we've got a strong case. Newspaper pieces that say we squeaked by on the indictment are not what we want to see. If you have holes in your case, fill 'em. Fast.'

David had not been ready to find Alice and the kids in the apartment the evening before, when he came home from celebrating the conclusion of his work for Jimmy Kelly. The bar owner had been pouring his special Irish whiskey, and even being careful David had headed home with the knowledge that before long his head would begin to pound.

In the morning, standing in the kitchen drinking his morning coffee, head truly pounding, he had gotten the story, or as much of it as Alice was going to give him.

The meeting with the movie director her last trip out had not been the disaster she'd imagined, she told him while she assembled tuna salad from ingredients that had not been in his kitchen when he'd left for Kelly's. Walter – the sometime boyfriend who'd introduced them – had called her in Colorado to say the director had decided to audition her for a small part in the movie he was about to make.

'If I get it, I'll have to come back in three weeks or a month and stick around so I can be on call. And I'll have to be away for at least a week, on location.'

'I thought you'd decided all that was a closed chapter.'

'Did I say that?' She looked up from the celery she was chopping. 'Well, let me tell you, little brother, there's no such thing as an ex-actor, only a recovering one. We're all hooked for life. So if they'll have me, I'm going.'

'How did you pay for the trip?' he couldn't help asking.

She put down the knife and leaned into the kitchen counter. 'Oh hell, Davey. I went into hock, all right? I borrowed from my friends out there, and I took money from Walter. And if this doesn't come through I don't know what I'll do.' She started to cry.

David reached out and gathered her in. 'It's okay,' he said. 'Don't worry about the money.'

Sniffling, she pulled away from him. 'I can't take money from you. I don't take money from family.'

The twins came into the kitchen. 'What's wrong?' Jessica wanted to know.

'Nothing, I'm peeling onions,' Alice said. David could barely tell that her grin was forced.

She pushed David away. 'Go on, let me make lunch in peace.'

'Okay. I'm going to get some air,' he said. 'And don't worry about the other, we'll work it out.'

'I'm going to need you to stay with these two,' she said.

Out in the air, he began to feel better. The day was relatively cool, a break in the summer's record heat, with a fresh breeze coming up off the river. Walking along the river, he marveled at his sister's resilience. She'd had more than her share of reversals, but she kept coming back for more. He wished he was surer it ran in the blood.

He thought about Susan Linwood's asking him to go with her to see the Engs. Did he want to do that? He couldn't envision the event itself, but he had a clear image of Susan Linwood. No, not that clear, he realized. He could see the thick, shining black hair, the brown eyes and the glowing skin and lips that looked so temptingly cushiony; he could see how much younger and more sensuous she'd looked in jeans and T-shirt the night she came to the grand jury party. And there was her enthusiasm for learning the truth about the Engs, her fierce reaction to the stories about irresponsible law enforcement. But those pieces still clashed with his other images of her: the rich-lady clothes and manners and the massive gold jewelry, the way everything about her had seemed calculated.

It would be interesting to see what she would say and how she would act talking to the Engs. And it would be interesting to see how they responded to her, too.

He and Susan had talked about wanting to *know* what had happened. He was sure that was a stronger motivation for her than for him, but the idea of seeing the three of them together definitely piqued his curiosity.

He'd warned her that it was dangerous to get involved with the principals – he was skeptical of the conventional wisdom that the violent criminality of Chinatown was confined to Chinatown people and that outsiders were rarely targeted. And even if that was true, it didn't begin to cover outsiders who intentionally involved themselves in Chinatown feuds.

On the other hand, he couldn't refute Susan's argument that Tony Ching had no particular reason to think they were a threat to him – no more than anyone else who visited with the Engs.

He could feel curiosity overcoming caution. It would be a couple of hours at most . . .

'I have an appointment to see them the day after tomorrow at three,' she said when he called. 'Can you make it?'

Though he'd already made up his mind to go he still hesitated before he said yes.

# 9

Richard and Charles came home early from their fishing trip. With Lara gone, Susan had thought she'd be spared the inevitable dinner of fish caught in some wilderness stream and flown back to New York, but there it was – the cooler of dry ice holding a substantial quartet of blindly staring Canadian trout.

It was part of the ritual for the men to cook the fish, but this time Charles went to his room and Richard cooked alone. Susan stayed in the kitchen with him and blanched some asparagus. The fishing trip had been fine, Richard said, but they'd agreed to cut it short. There was a tenseness about him that worried Susan, especially coupled with Charles's retreat to his room.

They ate in near silence. Charles seemed vague and distant, and his movements were slow. The food didn't seem to interest him. Susan noticed Richard glancing sharply at him from time to time. Charles gave no sign he was aware of the scrutiny.

When the coffee was on the table, Richard asked Charles to pass the milk. Charles kept stirring his own coffee as if he had not heard. Richard repeated the request – sharply enough to make Susan wince.

Charles did not look up. 'Sure,' he said and dreamily reached for the pitcher.

'Just a minute, young man,' Richard snapped.

Charles stopped moving, his hand on the milk pitcher.

'I'm talking to you, son. I expect you to look at me.'

Charles remained immobile, staring at the table. Susan felt the tension building.

'I said look at me.'

310

Charles shook his head, his eyes still on the table.

Richard half stood, leaning over the table.

'Richard!'

'Stay out of this, Susan.' Richard took Charles by the chin, tried to raise his face. Charles twisted away and got up, bumping the table hard enough to rattle the plates, headed for his room.

'Richard, what's going on?'

'Our Charles is high as a kite. Couldn't you see?'

'I saw that he was acting strangely, but I thought he was tired.'

'Stoned, I think, is the word.'

'On what?'

'Some kind of opiate, I'd say, by the symptoms. Contracted pupils, general dreaminess and apathy. Slurred speech.'

'I didn't notice any slurring. He hardly said a word.'

'Slight, but it was there. I saw the same things on our trip. That's why we came back early.'

She remembered her downtown dinner with Lara: *Have you talked to Charles about this?* 'Did the two of you talk about it?'

'I tried. He decided that the right response was to go sullen and uncommunicative.'

'I'm frightened, Richard.' She put her hand on her husband's arm. 'What are we going to do?' She was beyond thinking.

'One thing we're going to do is in the morning Charles Linwood is going to contribute a sample of his urine to the cause of scientific knowledge.'

'You're going to have him tested? But that's so . . .' She didn't have a word for it, but her instincts told her that confronting Charles so directly was not a good way to handle this.

Richard was adamant. 'If he *is* involved with drugs we have to know about it.'

She wished Lara wasn't gone. Lara, she was convinced, knew something about all this.

'He didn't say anything about it when you asked him?'

'As I said, he became very uncommunicative. And defensive. Why was I accusing him? Didn't I trust him? That sort of thing.'

'So he's made it a matter of face.'

Richard gave her a sharp look. 'I don't think he thinks that way.'

311

'I don't mean it in some exclusively Chinese sense. Kids have their own version of that. You're disrespecting him by asking the questions.'

'I'm his father. He's disrespecting me by not giving me a straight answer on an important issue.' Richard's expression hardened. 'That's the kind of disrespect that matters here.'

'Who's going to do the test?'

'I'll make arrangements at the hospital lab. Discreet arrangements, if that's what you're worried about.'

'I'm surprised you're doing it there.' It was Richard who would be most worried about that kind of discretion.

'It'll go through the lab with a number and no name.'

Susan's first impulse was to keep silent, the way she always did when it came to Richard and Charles. The realization came quickly that this time she could not.

'Are you sure this is a good idea?' she said. 'Forcing him to—'

He cut her short. 'Don't teach me how to practice medicine.'

'It's not about medicine, it's about being a father. What kind of message does that send to your son?'

'I'm hoping that Charles has the sense to realize that my involvement means I care. I'm not sending him off to some stranger.'

He bridged his forehead with his strong, graceful neurosurgeon's hand, pressed his temples with thumb and forefinger. For an instant he looked as close to defeated as Susan had ever seen him.

'This isn't like you,' he said.

'Yes, I know. I've let you deal with Charles without interfering, for too many years. Don't think it hasn't bothered me. I'm beginning to think I made a mistake.'

He pushed himself back from the table. 'I'm going to attribute that to how worried you are.'


'I'm on the spot,' Mahoney told Estrada. 'Horgan's really after me to wrap this up for him so he can try it as soon as he's free. But Ned King wants us to cover every aspect of the case. And he was talking to *me* when he said make the case as strong as possible. Now it shows up in the papers as an example of how we're stealing people's money, so the Boss is interested in it, and he's after King, and King is doubly after me.'

'Makes life interesting.'

'Yeah, but if I have reason to think there's something wrong with the case and I don't give them some kind of heads-up . . .'

'It's a lot to take on yourself,' Estrada warned him.

'Sure it is, but I don't see how I can turn my back on it.'

'That depends on what you think you're seeing.'

'And that, exactly, is my problem, doctor. I don't know how far to trust my instincts on this. All that Appeals work I did was about law, not facts. I trained myself to make sure every assertion was supported six ways to Sunday and nothing was left out. That kind of thoroughness is a luxury in a trial. Horgan said it himself – I'm not in the Appeals Bureau any more. But damn it, right now I don't see any case at all that makes any sense. It's all circumstantial, and there are no *people* in it. We don't have a hint about the suppliers or the customers. Just these two old folks and their money and their ledgers, and what the hell are they doing with eight ounces of heroin hidden under the god of prosperity, for heaven's sake? A third of a unit – I mean, what sense is there in that if the accountant is right and they did twenty-five million dollars' worth of deals in three years? It's way too much for a sample and, anyway, who wipes off their own stash? Plus the feds were very strong that whatever they have on these folks isn't heroin. So if the Engs are into something big enough for all this interest at the Justice Department – not just the Southern District, mind you, the *Justice Department* – and if whatever it is isn't heroin, then why are they fooling with heroin at all?'

'For the money?' Estrada tried.

'It's too dumb. Suppose they really are up to something the feds would consider major – assuming it's even close to as big as the feds make out, which nobody here is willing to concede. But suppose. Then why jeopardize it just to pull down a few dollars selling dope?'

'For starters, you might remember that dumb is an occupational prerequisite for felons. Dumb and greedy. And a million four isn't a few dollars.'

'Maybe so.' Mahoney was not convinced. 'But the feds said international monetary transactions, so maybe that's what the money's for. And what about Mick Pullone, pushing too hard in the grand jury, as if

313

he wasn't sure the defendants would sound evil enough unless he said they gave him trouble?'

'If I'm not wrong, this is a guy with a reputation for pushing extra hard, in the street. Why expect moderation when he's testifying?'

'Okay, I can believe he gilds the lily whenever he testifies, just on general principles,' Mahoney conceded. 'But I can also believe that maybe he had a bad conscience.'

'What kind of bad conscience?'

'Who'd know better than Pullone how dirty these people really were, or weren't? So he threw in a little extra to make them look worse – not enough for a phony resisting charge, just a little extra dirt. And he got caught at it and he had to come up with something in a hurry.'

'You're saying he did it because he knew they weren't dirty enough.'

'Right.'

Estrada studied Mahoney. 'Do I begin to sense that you have a theory on how the nasty detective came to arrest these nice old people?'

Mahoney wasn't about to be slowed down by sarcasm. 'Suppose he cooked this up with his snitch – find some people with money, plant the powder on them, go running to Horgan with it like it's a fire drill – now or never . . . That part especially makes sense. If the snitch planted the heroin, Pullone would want to hit the place in a big hurry, before the heroin got discovered by accident and moved or disposed of.'

'Why do it at all?'

'For the score. Horgan keeps a running tally of forfeitures. The more money, cars, houses you bring him, the better he looks, and the better he likes you. And Pullone's looking to make First Grade. The informant's motive we know – he gets a big piece of change. Who knows, maybe Pullone gets a taste of the informant's fee, too. Everybody comes out ahead.'

'Boy. What have you been smoking? Or should I say snorting?'

'I'm not saying it happened that way.'

'What *are* you saying?'

'I'm saying I want to see some evidence it *didn't* happen that way.'

Estrada considered it. 'Well, I don't have any evidence, but I have a

314

question. If that's what they were up to – building up the forfeiture numbers – why not just hit the place and seize the money and forget about the arrest? Isn't that how it's done these days?'

'Sure that's how it's done, assuming the perp is willing to walk away from the cash.'

'As mostly they are. "*Money?* What money, officer? I never saw no money before. Must belong to some other dude." '

'But not these folks,' Mahoney pointed out. 'These folks came into the grand jury to claim that the money is theirs. Is, and always was, going back generations. The money matters to them. So Pullone had to make the arrest, even if maybe he didn't want to.'

'Not so fast.' Estrada was shaking his head. 'When Pullone was deciding to make the arrest, how would he know one way or the other if they'd walk away like everybody else or not?'

'That's easy . . . The people who walk away, walk away from drug proceeds. But if Pullone knew, going in, that it was their money – *really* their money, not drug money – then he'd have to assume they'd try to keep it, and he'd know he had to make the arrest.'

Estrada had no comeback for that. 'Okay,' he said. 'It makes sense, but you need more than suppositions. You can't go waltzing into the Chief of Investigation's office with this kind of craziness.'

'No, but now we've talked about it, I can see I've got to do *something* – craziness or not. Let me ask you a question.'

'Be my guest.'

'Who do we know in Official Corruption?'

Estrada looked at him a long moment before he answered. 'You mean who do we know who we can trust?'

'Right.' Official Corruption was the unit that prosecuted bad cops and other rotten apples in law enforcement. They kept a running record of complaints filed against law-enforcement personnel.

'Remember Laurie Jordan?' Estrada asked him.

'Hard to forget. I've lost track of her, though. The last time I saw her was at the farewell racket for Loco Izqierda, when he left us for fame and fortune.'

'That was some party.'

'When we lost Loco we lost our best party animal. When did Laurie go to Official Corruption? I must have missed it.'

'About that same time, a year or so ago. If I remember, she was kind of sweet on you.'

'We were just friends, actually, which was about all I could handle. I used to have to defog the windows when she left the office. Anyway, isn't she engaged to a stockbroker who buys her Porsches?'

'Investment banker. And it's a Jaguar, I believe. You maybe going to ask her for help on this?'

'I might.'

Estrada whistled. 'Well, all I can say is, keep your powder dry.'

The evening after the night of the fish dinner, Richard came home earlier than usual.

'Charles in his room?'

'I haven't seen him.'

Richard stormed down the corridor. 'Charles!'

He was back almost at once. 'Do you know where he is?'

'I haven't seen him since the two of you left this morning. I presume he had things to do.' In truth, she had been hollow with fear all day. Richard had been in the operating room, beyond reach. When they spoke, briefly, he'd said, 'We'll talk when I get home.'

'He's twenty years old, Richard,' Susan said now. 'He doesn't report his comings and goings to his mommy any more. Not that he ever did.'

Richard glared at her, then turned away.

'Did he know you were going to have the results tonight?' she asked, knowing the answer.

'Of course he did.'

'Well, then . . .'

'Yes, I've thought of that, thank you. It doesn't exactly make me happy.'

'Are you going to tell me?' she said finally.

'Oh. Didn't I?' He seemed genuinely surprised. 'Heroin.'

She waited for a reaction but she just felt blank.

'Can you tell how much, how often . . .' How badly he's addicted, she could not make herself say.

'Not really. The amount in this sample wasn't staggering, but that doesn't tell us anything useful. He'll have to go into detox, of course.'

'Isn't there another way?'

'I don't see one.'

'If it's not bad, if he's only just started . . .'

'It won't help to be unrealistic, Susan. We have to face this for what it is.'

'Richard, please . . .' She started from the room. 'I'll be in the study if you need me. And please let me know if Charles comes in.'

As soon as the door was closed Susan picked up the phone and dialed Lara's number at college. There was no answer.

When morning finally came, she had no idea how she'd made it through the night. She felt as if she hadn't slept at all. Richard, too, looked uncommonly haggard. She put up a pot of coffee for him.

'What are we going to do?'

'For now, we're going to go about our lives. As you pointed out yesterday, Charles is a grownup, so there's not much else we can do.'

'We can report him missing.'

'It's too soon for that. A twenty-year-old college boy who stays out all night during summer break is not going to get anyone's attention.'

'I suppose not.' She didn't have the spirit to argue with him.

'Where will you be today?' he asked.

'I can stay here.' Then, 'Oh. I have an appointment this afternoon. I'll cancel it.'

'There's nothing to be gained by sitting around waiting for him,' he said. 'He's just doing this because he knows how hurtful it is.' He gave her a kiss on the forehead. 'It's going to be all right. He's just being difficult because I caught him doing something he knows he shouldn't. And he knows he'll have to take the consequences.'

She took a nap and woke up just after noon. She called four of Charles's friends and reached none of them. She decided not to leave messages. She spoke briefly to Lara's roommate, asked her to have Lara call home.

She realized she was hungry and made herself a belated breakfast of coffee and eggs and half a grapefruit. The food made her feel stronger. Maybe it was best to go through with meeting the Engs this afternoon, she told herself. Better than sitting here, waiting. She went to the phone to arrange for a car and to tell David Clark when to expect her.

317

★ ★ ★

The Official Corruption Unit had offices of its own in a loft building in Soho, where the comings and goings of potential witnesses and informants would not be visible to the crowd of cops and lawyers at the D.A.'s office in the criminal court annex.

Mahoney had heard about it, but the reality of the vast, bright, open space with its double-height ceiling and floor-to-ceiling windows filling one long wall was unexpected enough to make him gape like a rube. The sense of light and airiness was heightened by the fact that most of the office spaces were created by partitions that, though they were well over head-high even for Mahoney, lacked a good seven feet of reaching the ceiling.

'Hi, Dan,' Laurie Jordan breathed when Mahoney walked into her office. 'Long time.'

'I guess we both got busy.'

Languidly, she pushed a wing of dark hair back from her forehead. 'It's a shame. I miss our lunches.'

Mahoney was at a loss for a response. When they'd been friends – and almost more – he'd wondered if she turned on the heat intentionally, or if it was just her natural style. He'd never reached a conclusion.

She smiled. She had a generous mouth and perfect teeth. The tip of her tongue touched her upper lip for an instant. 'I was glad to get your phone call.'

'I appreciate your helping,' he managed.

'I don't know how much help I'll be. I don't have that much for you.'

'Every little bit counts.'

She favored him with another slow smile. He half-expected her to turn what he'd said into a cue for a suggestive remark. In the old days that had been a regular part of her act.

'Did I hear that you and Kath broke up?' she asked instead.

'I don't know if you heard, but we did.'

'I'm sorry.' She didn't sound it. 'I know you wanted to make it work.'

They caught up on each other's personal lives for longer than made him comfortable. He was increasingly aware that her blouse wasn't buttoned quite high enough, and he could hear the whisper of cloth as

318

she crossed and uncrossed her legs under the desk. She was still with the banker, she told him, but complained that his work kept him traveling all the time.

'He's making himself an expert on emerging markets . . . flying off to Asia or South America or someplace else every minute. I get lonely.'

'We all get lonely,' he said. 'Tell me about Mick Pullone.'

Her report was not a lot different from what he'd expected. Still, it was not what he wanted to hear.

Pullone was not at the top of the Official Corruption Unit's statistics, but he was close. A larger than average number of his arrests resulted in allegations by the defense attorney that the warrant had not been good, that the search had exceeded the terms of the warrant, that the detective had roughed up the defendant prior to, during or after the arrest, and sometimes all three.

'The actual number of complaints isn't that high, but bear in mind that a lot of complaints get made but not reported. The A.D.A.s at arraignment forget to note it, or they figure it's just the perp trying to weasel out or make trouble for the cop. They're not supposed to make those judgments, but they do.'

'I remember. I remember being too tired to write my name, much less some skell's ranting about how the cop did him wrong.'

'Those were the days, weren't they?' This smile seemed to contain only pleasure at her memory of the years when they were starting out as prosecutors together.

'One thing interesting about Detective Pullone's complaint record – the numbers have been on the increase,' she told him. 'Nothing but drug cases recently, I notice.'

'He's working with Kevin Horgan. It's a new unit that works out of Rackets, with connections to Special Narcotics and Asset Forfeiture. Not quite the same as the old Organized Crime Narcotics, but that's what they're calling it.'

'That sounds like his kind of assignment. Is that where you know him from?'

'Yep. I'm the new boy on the block.'

'Want to tell Mama what this is about?' She had let the hair fall back over her eye; she looked at him slantwise from under it. It was almost self-parody, but steamy, nonetheless.

*This is business*, he reminded himself. 'It's a little premature to go into much detail.' He knew that wasn't good enough. She'd already given him something worthwhile and if he wanted more from her, he owed her at least not closing her out entirely.

'Mick Pullone is the arresting officer on a case I'm putting together for Horgan. Putting it in the grand jury, I saw some things that made me uneasy, and since then I've learned other things that make it worse.'

'From what I know of his record, I can't say I'm surprised. You said Asset Forfeiture. Is there a lot of money riding on it?'

'Enough.'

'I'd like to keep up with you on this one.' No flirting now.

'If there's more I'll let you know.'

'*As soon* as there's more.'

'It's a deal.' He got up to go. 'One other thing. Was there anything about planting evidence?'

'This *is* interesting.' Her smile this time was cold. 'I think there might have been one or two, but it wasn't what you told me to look for. I'll check it out and give you a call.'

# 10

The weather had turned brutally hot again, as if in revenge for the previous day's pleasant breezes. Until Alice knocked on David's study door to say his friend was downstairs he took advantage of the cool dry air he was careful to provide for his computer. On his way out, he carried the jacket of his summer suit.

Susan was waiting in the back of an air-conditioned black sedan like the one he'd once seen her get into after the grand jury. She seemed unfocused; he attributed it to anxiety about the upcoming meeting. He settled in for the ride, content that she did not seem eager to chat.

'Do they know I'm coming?' he asked as they turned onto the Bowery.

'My friends told them I might bring someone.'

'Do they know we were on the grand jury?'

'Yes.'

'What about the lawyer? Does she know we're doing this?'

'I didn't bother to tell her, for obvious reasons.'

'Do the Engs know she doesn't approve?'

'I didn't talk to them about that. I didn't think it was my business.'

After a silence he asked if she knew what the Engs thought this meeting was for.

'My friends said I want to tell them some things that may be helpful to them and ask some questions.'

'That sounds simple enough.' And opaque. 'Do you have a strategy?'

'Just that – what I just said.'

The driver was threading his way through the narrow, winding streets of Chinatown, spending more time stopped than moving. If not for the heat, David would have suggested they get out and walk.

When traffic halted them on one especially crowded street, the driver twisted around to say, 'This is the block. You want four buildings up. I don't see any place to pull over up there.'

'We'll get out here,' Susan said. 'Thanks.'

David slid across the seat to follow her out. She was standing between two parked cars, watching the people pass on the crowded sidewalk.

'Are you okay?' he asked.

'Not really. I didn't sleep very well, and I'm preoccupied with other things. In fact –' she put a hand on his arm – 'if you could take the lead sometimes, it might help. Or at least be ready to come to the rescue if you see I'm having trouble.' She looked away. 'Just like in the grand jury.'

The building that housed the Guangdong Three Districts Association was six stories high, faced in white tile on the lower stories with tan brick above it, grimy top to bottom. Two stories up, a balcony of white-painted wrought iron that made David think of New Orleans ran across the face of the building. Above it, between the third- and fourth-floor windows, was a row of large red Chinese characters.

The main doors led to a broad, red-tiled stair with pale-green tiled walls. On the first floor, a gray metal door on each side of the stairway barred access to the rest of the building. Susan tried them; they were locked. David looked a question at her; she shook her head – don't know – and they went up another floor. Here, too, they found locked metal doors on both sides of the stairs.

'Let's try one more,' Susan said.

They started up. David had made the mistake of putting on his suit jacket when they came into the building. Now he could feel his shirt adhering to his back and beads of sweat collecting under his moustache and in his beard.

On the third floor one of the metal doors was open. Just to the right of the doorway was an open office where three woman sat at desks behind a counter that divided the room in half. One of the women got up and said something to Susan in Chinese.

'We have an appointment with Martin Eng at three o'clock,' Susan said.

322

Flustered, the woman turned to the others and spoke in rapid Chinese. After an extended dialogue one of the others said, 'Please follow me.'

She brought them down a corridor to a large room – something like thirty by forty, David thought – with polished dark wood floors and dark wood wainscoting up to about five feet of the room's nine-foot height. Against the off-white plaster above the wood were pictures of old Chinatown and portraits of august-looking men in high-necked, embroidered jackets and black pillbox hats, some with single, long braids of dark hair. Two large air conditioners made the room feel chilly compared to the muggy corridor. The center of the room was filled with rows of graceful, tall-backed wooden chairs.

'Scholars' chairs,' Susan whispered. 'Because the wooden crosspiece at the top looks like the kind of hat Chinese scholars used to wear.'

At the front of the room a red banner with gold Chinese letters covered the wall behind a long table. The woman from the office offered them seats at the table facing the rows of chairs.

'Like being at the witness table in the grand jury,' Susan said.

'I was just thinking the same thing.'

A door opened at the front of the room and Martin Eng and Meiling Cheung came in, dressed much the same as they had been as witnesses. David stood, as did Susan.

David felt suddenly as if he'd stepped through the looking glass. In the grand jury room he'd been essentially a spectator in their drama – separated from them not so much by distance as the clarity of his role. Now, up close, he felt like a participant in a way he hadn't anticipated.

Susan introduced them.

'I am Martin Eng and this is my wife Meiling. As you know. She is also called Milly, as I am called Martin. Please sit down.'

Martin Eng looked less frail than he had in the grand jury, though it was hard to be sure, because now, as then, David's dominant impression was formed by the man's large head and the compelling intelligence in his wideset eyes.

One of the women from the office came in to put a tea service on the table. Meiling Cheung poured tea for them. David said thank you, though he didn't think Susan did. Turning in her direction he caught a quick motion of her fingers on the table before she raised her cup and held it in both hands poised in front of her chest. When they all had their cups raised they drank, beginning with a small lifting of the cup in both hands, like a toast.

'Welcome,' Martin Eng said. 'It is kind of you to come so far.'

'It is our pleasure. We thank you for taking the time to see us,' Susan said. 'This is a beautiful room.'

'It is kind of you to say so. It is our main meeting room. You see that we have many pictures of the history of our members in Chinatown. Also on the other side are pictures of some leaders from China and Taiwan.

'The politics of Chinatown have changed. Once there would only have been pictures of Chiang Kai-shek, when he was dictator in Taiwan after he fled from the mainland of China. Chiang Kai-shek and other Nationalist leaders. Never Mao Zedong or any Communist leaders. Today, we display a picture of Hu Yaobang, important Communist official, famous for supporting liberalization and democracy. To commemorate his death students demonstrated in May and June, 1989, in Tienanmen Square. Until then we also had a picture of paramount leader Deng Xiaoping. After June fourth our younger members insisted we remove it. Now, no more Deng Xiaoping.'

'It's a difficult time for China,' Susan said.

'Yes, and also exciting. There will be much change now that there must be a successor to Mr Deng.' He waved a hand. 'You did not come here to speak of politics.'

'China is always interesting to me,' Susan said.

Martin Eng sipped some tea – to punctuate the change in subject, David thought.

'I have heard that your parents were from the Three Districts. From Shuntak.'

'Yes, I've only heard that recently, myself. It's an interesting coincidence.'

Interesting coincidence, indeed, David thought. He understood a little better why Susan was so caught up in these people's story.

'Have you ever been there yourself?' Martin Eng asked her.

324

'No, I haven't. I was born in Hong Kong. We came here when I was six, and I've only been back to Hong Kong once.'

'And did your parents go back?'

'They are –' she seemed to be searching for a word – 'no longer alive.'

'I am sorry to hear. Long time?'

'Soon it will be twenty years.'

'You were very young.'

'They were on a trip to China. They never came back.'

'I am so sorry. Is it unpleasant to speak about this?'

'I never have. I don't really know how they died. The Government said it was in the earthquake at Tainjin in 1976. But they had no reason to visit Tianjin.'

Martin Eng nodded. 'You would like to know more.'

'Not in the past. Now, though, I think I would. And now it's too late.'

'Milly and I did not go back for many years,' Martin Eng said after a pause. 'Not to China or to Hong Kong. But we have visited Hong Kong not long ago. Very different from Hong Kong when we left there. Now New York is slow next to Hong Kong.'

'Yes, I have a childhood friend there who writes me letters. She tells me the pace is amazing. Did you enjoy your trip?'

'We went there to see our children. To see children healthy and prosperous is always good.'

David thought he saw something change in Susan's expression.

'Children,' she said. 'In the grand jury you talked about your children. It was a very moving story. There's no greater sadness than losing a child.'

'You are very kind.'

'I have a son. He's in college. He's a scholar, if I may presume to say so – just as I understand you're a scholar.' Her voice had taken on a tense, brittle quality.

'You are kind to call me that.'

'It's what people say. It's what your wife said in the grand jury.'

'A son is the center of every Chinese family.' Turning the conversation away from himself.

'Yes, sons are so important. And I'm very proud of my son.'

325

David could hear a tremor in her voice. She stopped talking and sipped tea. Was this what she'd meant about his having to rescue her?

'I mention my son for a reason,' she resumed before he could change the subject. 'I mention him because I am learning that even the young people in the best universities in this country are not safe from heroin.'

'It is a terrible problem,' Martin Eng acknowledged.

'I'm worried about my son.'

David was as unprepared for this as Martin Eng evidently was. It had to be what was preoccupying her.

'I truly feel sorrow for you,' Martin Eng said. 'If you are worried about your son and heroin, I think you must also feel anger. Much anger.'

'Yes, I do.'

'Please do not feel anger at us. Heroin the police find in our apartment, not our heroin. We say so to grand jury, say same thing now. We have no business with heroin. Not now, not ever.'

'I would like to believe that,' Susan said. 'When you came to testify in the grand jury I believed it. When I asked Uncle Eight to speak to you about this visit, I believed it. Now I'm afraid I must ask you to help me believe it again.'

'It is quite difficult to prove a negative proposition,' said Meiling Cheung.

David stared. So did Susan.

'Forgive me for being rude,' Susan said. 'But I didn't realize you spoke English so well.'

Meiling Cheung covered her smile. After a moment she said, 'I can speak English, slowly. I need time to translate my Chinese thoughts.' Pausing slightly between phrases, she continued: 'I can never speak English when a person asks me difficult questions to answer quickly. That is why to participate in the grand jury I needed to have a translator.'

'Did you need her to tell you the questions, too?' David asked. 'Or did you understand?'

'I welcomed having extra time to think about answers.'

Very clever, David thought. 'What did you think of the two trans-lators?'

'The first, quite good. The second . . .' She shook her head and rolled her eyes heavenward. Covered another smile. David thought he heard her giggle. 'I was pleased when our lawyer complained.'

'I interrupted you,' Susan said. 'I apologize. You were saying . . .'

'My thought is, we can say, the heroin is not ours. We cannot say, the heroin belonged to one certain other person. We cannot tell the name of that one other person. We can tell you only, the heroin is not ours. We ask you to believe that. We can do no more. Is that enough?'

'You're right. It's difficult to prove that kind of negative.'

'May I ask you a question?' Martin Eng said to Susan.

'Yes, of course,' she said.

'What can lead you to the thought – Martin Eng and Milly Cheung are in business to sell heroin? Martin Eng and Milly Cheung sell this poison that kills children?'

'For the money,' David said, thinking: that's probably rude of me by his standards, but he asked for it.

'Yes, for the money. Sometime you come see how well we live.' He smiled to emphasize the irony. 'Like rich people, in Chinatown tenement building.'

'You might want to live better.'

'Or the money could be for your children,' Susan said. 'We were talking about how important children are.'

Meiling Cheung said something to her husband in Cantonese.

'My wife says, tell you about our children. We have remaining one son, one daughter. They are living now in Hong Kong. Also they do much business in China, Guangdong province.'

'Are they in the garment business?' David asked.

'Yes. Garment business and also real estate and . . . what is the other business called?'

'Infrastructure development,' his wife supplied, with some effort. 'Highways and electric-power generating plants.'

'Yes. So. From these businesses, they make much profit. In five years they make more money than I earn, whole lifetime. Not necessary to do heroin business in order to make money for children.'

So you're not in immediate danger of starvation, after all, David did not say.

'According to what I read, there are people in Hong Kong and China who are billionaires,' he remarked instead. 'I don't have the impression any of them is slowing down, or turning away from a chance to earn more money, for themselves or their children.'

Martin Eng nodded. 'That is true.' His hands were steepled in front of his face. David thought there might be a smile behind them.

'In the grand jury you said it was wonderful to be rich.'

'To become rich is glorious,' Martin Eng corrected. 'It is a saying of paramount leader Deng Xiaoping. With this saying he started the new economic era in 1984.'

'I notice,' David said, 'that he didn't specify a method.'

'I am sorry,' Martin Eng said. 'I do not understand.'

'Deng Xiaoping didn't say to become rich is glorious, except if you get rich by selling heroin.'

There was a tiny silence in which Martin Eng's brow furrowed, and then he laughed. It was a sudden, explosive sound, deep and hearty. His wife laughed, too.

'No, no, no. You are right, young man. Deng Xiaoping did not say, except if you get rich by selling heroin.'

'Perhaps if you had asked him he would have said that,' said Meiling Cheung.

They sat quietly a moment. Meiling Cheung leaned forward to pour them more tea.

'Thank you,' David said. Susan tapped the coffee table with her first two fingers. It was the second time he had seen her do that – he thought it might mean she'd had enough, but she picked up the cup carefully in both hands and sipped from it.

'I think we are at stalemate,' Martin Eng said. 'We can only make the same moves again and again. We are happy if you believe us. If not, we can do nothing. I do not wish to be rude to a guest, but I must wonder – why come, if you do not believe?'

David, like Susan, took refuge in his tea. As soon as he put his cup down, Meiling Cheung filled it again. He tried tapping with his fingers.

'Ah,' she said. 'You know the story?'

'I'm sorry,' David replied. 'What story?'

'The way you tap with your fingers. Story about an old Emperor, long ago. I will tell.' She took a breath. 'Long ago, the Emperor of China went out among the people to see if his reign was good for them.

328

He knew all people would be afraid to tell the truth to the Emperor, wearing imperial robes with many soldiers and servants. Instead he dressed in ordinary person's clothes and took with him only two retainers.

'When the Emperor and retainers stopped at an inn to eat, the Emperor poured tea. The Emperor pouring tea for his retainers! It was necessary then for them to bow very low and touch their heads to the ground. They could not do this, because no ordinary person would bow so low to another ordinary person, and they were commanded to help the Emperor in his deception. So instead, they made their fingers into legs, and so these two first knuckles were knees. They bent their finger-legs to touch the table with these two knees. That way they bowed to the Emperor and no one saw to spoil the Emperor's disguise.

'So,' she concluded, 'when someone pours tea for you, you bow to them with your fingers, the same way the emperor's retainers bowed to him. It is a sign of respect.'

'What a great story,' David said. 'I saw Ms Linwood doing it, and I thought I should, too. I'm glad I did.'

'I can't speak for Mr Clark,' Susan said into the moment of warmth, 'but I'm very grateful to you for taking the time to see us, and I hope you will forgive us if we seemed rude. With your permission, I'll tell you something about myself.'

'Please,' Martin Eng said.

Susan shifted in her tall-backed chair. Sitting up straighter, David thought at first but it was more than that: everything about her seemed more formal. When she spoke, her tone and diction matched her posture.

'I work in a business sometimes called press relations. Most of my work is in the field of medicine. One of my jobs is to take complicated information and try to make it interesting to editors of newspapers and magazines, and to television news producers.

'Recently, with much help from Mr Clark, I learned a great deal about how the Government takes money away from people they accuse of crimes. I learned that these accusations are often based on the word of paid informers who are in a position to profit from their lies. It seems likely to me that such an informer could have been involved in your case.

329

'It seemed important to me for the public to know about the abuses of this system and so I wrote and circulated a press release about the bad things that could happen to innocent people. I took the liberty of using your case as an example. As a result there have been three newspaper articles that I know of dealing with the problem and mentioning your case, and I think more may be coming.'

The Engs were paying close attention, David thought, but they kept silent.

'Mr Clark and I have also found out other things that bear directly on your case. Detective Pullone, who arrested you, has a history of brutality against Asian people. And I know that you have had trouble here in Chinatown with a man named Tony Ching, who might be pleased to see you have trouble of the kind you have now.

'I could publicize what I know about the detective and about Mr Ching the same way I publicized the seizure of your money. I would be happy to do that. But recently I had a phone call from your lawyer. She told me you don't want to have publicity, not even if it's favorable to you. I thanked her for the call and explained that I would respect your wishes if I heard them in your own words. She said it was not possible for her to arrange that. It was very important to me to hear what you want directly from you, so I arranged to meet you another way. I apologize for my presumption.'

Martin Eng said, 'We thank you for your concern and your good intentions. We are grateful to you for this work that you have done for people who are not your relatives. Now I can say this to you – what you have done until now is more than enough. We cannot ask you to do more.'

'You don't have to ask me,' Susan said. 'I'm volunteering—'

She stopped herself abruptly, looked down at the table. 'Forgive my clumsiness,' she said. 'I certainly do not wish to do more than what you tell me is enough. But it would put my mind at rest if you could talk to me about how you have come to that decision.'

It was Meiling Cheung who answered her. 'We see many people who defend themselves in the press. We do not wish to turn a light on ourselves. If the press is interested in a person, all of that person's life is their playground. Nothing is spared. We will not encourage that to happen.'

'I can understand that,' Susan said. 'But not everything I might write about concerns you directly. Detective Pullone, for instance. His record of bad behavior involves many people besides you.'

'Sometimes life holds dangers we do not anticipate,' Martin Eng said. 'So we are grateful to our good friends for respecting our wishes completely.'

'We are interested to learn more about the detective's history,' his wife said quickly. 'Information is helpful to us.'

'I learned about him from an organization called the Council on Violence Against Asians. I am sure if you or your lawyer contacts them, they will be happy to help you.' She gave them the address and phone number.

David sensed that the meeting was about to end. He said, 'There was something I wanted to mention. In this country, not many people keep their money in cash or actually own gold. It can be hard for some people to understand how the million dollars in your safe deposit boxes could be the result of two families' hard work for generations.' He was being careful not to specify that anything he was saying had come out of the grand jury. 'But some of us had a conversation recently about old Chinatown customs, and people seemed more ready to believe that you might be holding money for members of your Association, the way some merchants and some benevolent associations have in the past.'

'That is very interesting,' Martin Eng said. 'It is true – many well-respected people in the old days of Chinatown acted in that role. Some people, still.'

'But not you?'

Martin Eng shrugged and made his mouth into a close-lipped smile. 'We have said where our money comes from.'

'We've taken enough of your time,' Susan said. 'You were kind to see us. I appreciate your being so honest with me about your wishes.'

'We are grateful to you for your help and understanding,' Meiling Cheung said. 'We hope to enjoy the pleasure of seeing you again.'

Martin Eng escorted them downstairs. At the sidewalk he shook hands with them. 'Please come back. The door is always open.'

'You did fine,' David said. 'You didn't need anybody's help. But I guess you're disappointed.'

She shrugged it off, looked around. 'Do you know where there's a subway?'

'A subway?'

'Well, yes. I didn't keep the car, because I didn't know how long we'd be or where the driver could meet us. And it's rush hour, so we'll never find a cab.'

'It's rush hour down there, too.'

'I know, but at least that means they'll be quick.' She checked her watch. 'I'm in a hurry to get home.'

He had forgotten for the moment how preoccupied she'd been. Her son and heroin. 'You want the East Side, right? There's a station in Foley Square, by the courthouses. We can catch the express there.'

Susan was silent on the way to the subway.

'I was impressed,' David remarked, as a way to maintain contact with her. 'They're impressive people.' He paused. 'That doesn't mean they don't sell heroin.'

'It seems unlikely,' Susan said in a flat voice. 'In a way I'm surprised he even sells clothes.'

'Manufactures clothes.'

'It's more or less the same to them, I'd think. Merchants were a low class of people in imperial China. Scholars and public officials mattered.'

'You're saying you think he's too refined to sell heroin.'

'Yes, in a way.'

'They're definitely refined in their attitude toward the press.'

'I suppose I should have expected that.' She sounded resigned. 'Standing out from the crowd and being noticed aren't exactly positive cultural values in China.'

'I can see where they wouldn't want the press digging too deeply into their personal fortune.'

'I wasn't ready for that question you asked at the end,' she said. 'I don't think they were, either.'

'It didn't get me much. But, you know, if they were holding money

332

for other people that would go a long way toward making them shy of the press. They'd really not want to have reporters checking into where the money came from, then.'

'Either way,' she said, 'they couldn't have been clearer how they feel about it.'

She fell silent again. He left her to her thoughts.

They sweltered on a platform made intolerably stifling by the waste heat pumped out of the very subway air conditioners intended to cool them. The train came quickly, one of the new steel ones with a recorded voice to announce the stations and warn that the doors were closing. Once they were in the car, it was blissfully cool.

Susan did not speak again until the train was on its way uptown.

'I can't believe I talked to them the way I did, especially at the beginning.'

The car was crowded and David was very aware of her closeness. 'I thought it went all right.'

'It must have sounded like I was accusing them of something, but that's not what it felt like to me. Sitting there, it was more like I was with my parents, and I was asking them for some kind of solace.' She rested her forehead briefly against the cool metal of the grab pole. 'I knew I was worried, but . . . just to let it run away with me like that . . .'

'Worried about your son?'

'Yes. Very.'

'It must be –' he couldn't think of a word, just shook his head – 'to be worried about something like that. I don't have anything to measure it by.'

'Don't you have kids?'

'Never married. I've spent some time with my sister's kids, though.'

'How old are they?'

'Twelve, now. They're twins.'

'Do you like living with kids?'

'It's never been more than a week or two at a time. I work in the apartment, too. That makes it hard.'

'You have to tell me more about that, some time.'

The train stopped and a carful of high-school kids piled on. Strap-hanging, they crowded close to Susan and David. He smiled at her. She smiled back, weakly.

At Forty-second Street most of the kids pushed their way out the doors.

'A lot of energy,' David said.

'And they have their own thoughts and their own lives. You think you know them, because once upon a time you could see them as not much more than helpless extensions of yourself. But they're separate, real people. It can be a big shock to learn who they are.'

David could hear the pain behind the matter-of-fact words. He had nothing to say, nothing he could do but listen.

'When that happens,' Susan went on, 'you hope and pray that it isn't too late. That you can be some help.' She closed her eyes. 'I don't know why I'm saying these things. He's a fine young man, a good scholar and an athlete. He's kind to his sister . . . It's probably all right . . . I'm sure it's all right. This is just my imagination making me crazy.'

'Are you sure you're okay?' It took no expert to see that she wasn't.

'You're very kind to ask,' she said. 'And the obvious answer is, no I'm not okay. But it's something I have to deal with.'

She looked around. 'We don't seem to be going anywhere.'

The train was still in the station. 'No, we don't.'

The loudspeaker in the ceiling above them popped and crackled. A too-loud voice overloaded the system to incomprehensibility.

'Did you get any of that?' Susan asked.

'Something about an interruption of uptown service on this line, I think.'

'Did they say how long?'

'I'm not even sure about the first part. But it might have said indefinitely.'

She looked at her watch. 'I can't wait, and it's Grand Central, so I can probably get a cab here. I hope you don't mind if I try to find one alone. I need time to compose myself and do some thinking.'

'Sure. It's better for me to go across to the West Side, anyway.'

They got out of the car together and he bulled a path for them across the jammed platform to the stairs.

At the exit, they paused.

'Are you sure you'll be okay alone?' he asked her.

She nodded. 'Thanks.'

He put a hand on her shoulder. 'Take care of yourself. And if you hear anything more from these people, let me know. We've come this far together . . .'

'I'll do that. Promise.'

He watched her push through the turnstile and rush out of sight up the stairs to the street. Then he turned and walked through the station toward the crosstown shuttle.

# 11

Susan returned home to find no Charles and no sign he'd been back. No messages on her machine except two from Richard asking if she'd heard anything, Richard who never called during the day. So he wasn't as unconcerned as he pretended. She called the hospital. He'd had no news since his last call to her.

'Are you going to your rehearsal tonight?'

'If nothing happens, I don't see why not.'

She wondered if it had even crossed his mind to come straight home so they could comfort each other. 'Call before you leave.'

Richard called at seven-thirty to say he was leaving work and again at nine to check in and at ten to say he was on his way home. In the meantime Susan sat alone, trying to control her imagination.

At five after ten the phone rang. Susan did her best to calm herself as she rushed to answer it.

It was Lara, finally responding to the message Susan had left for her.

'Hi, Mom, is everything okay?'

'I'm not sure, sweetie.' Susan caught her breath, tried to keep her voice light. 'Have you heard anything from your brother?'

'No. Why? Should I?'

'I don't know. He seems to have gone off somewhere and your father and I are a little concerned because he didn't tell us anything about it before he left.'

'Oh.' Silence. 'No. I don't know. He didn't say anything to me.'

'If you hear from him, will you let us know? And tell him we'd like him to call. We don't care what he's doing, we'd just like to know where he is.'

'Mother! Something *is* wrong.'

'I don't know, sweetheart. It may be nothing.' Susan didn't want to put Lara in the middle. Her behavior had already made it clear she felt pulled in both directions on the question of her brother. 'You have college to pay attention to, and I don't want to upset you.'

'For God's sake, Mother, it's only orientation. Classes don't start for days. If something's wrong . . .'

'Your brother and your father had some difficulty – about that subject you and I were talking about.'

'What subject?' And then, almost immediately, 'Oh.' Another silence, deeper than the first. 'Mother, what's happening?'

All right, a little at a time. 'Your father was a bit stern with Charles. You know how he can be. He had Charles take a test—'

'A test! Oh, Mother, no.'

'Why? If you know something—'

'Not about that. Not about *using*.'

'I don't understand.' She heard the door opening. 'Wait a minute, I think your father's home. He'll want to talk to you, too.'

'No. Mother, please.'

Susan hesitated, torn, but there was really only one answer. 'All right.'

Richard came into the room. 'Lara,' Susan mouthed to him. He started for an extension phone.

Susan shook her head vehemently and waved a finger no. He paused only an instant, then reached for the phone.

*'Richard! No!'*

He stopped.

'I'm sorry, sweetie,' Susan said into the phone. 'You were saying . . .'

'Nothing, really,' Lara said. 'I don't know anything about it. Charles doesn't exactly confide his darkest secrets to me.'

'Do you think he has some?' Even as she asked, Susan knew that whatever Lara had been on the verge of saying was closed off now.

'It was just a way of speaking, I don't know if he does or he doesn't. I'm sorry, Mama –' Mama, she hadn't called Susan that in years; it brought back memories of little Lara, clinging to her in the night, terrified of dream demons – 'If I hear from Charles I promise I'll let you know. I have to go now. Say hello to Daddy for me.'

337

★ ★ ★

'Well?' Richard said as she sat there unmoving with the phone in her hand.

'She knows something.' She wished the phone were a club, she wanted to hit – hit hard, do damage. 'She was going to tell me, but you had to insist on getting on the phone.'

'And you had to insist on screaming at me.' He sounded uncommonly tired. 'There's no profit in our blaming each other for ruining something that might never have happened.'

'God, you're so *rational*. Do you ever stop being rational?'

'*One* of us has to be.'

Susan stared at him. 'You bastard!'

She ran from the room and threw herself on her bed and cried. After a time she was aware of a weight on the bed, and Richard's smell – a hint of woodsy cologne over the sharp tang of antiseptic soap.

For what seemed to her a long time he sat in silence, motionless, while she sobbed. Then he began to stroke her head and rub her back. 'I'm sorry, Susan. I know how frightened you must be. I know how frightened I am.'

She rolled over to face him and he took her in his arms.

'I'm so sorry,' he said.

She clung to him as she hadn't in many years. They held each other and she felt his body shudder and knew that he was crying, too, or as close to crying as he could come. She fell into a dreamless half-sleep holding him and woke to the realization that she wanted him, and that he wanted her, too. Wordlessly, they pulled at each other's clothes and came together with savage energy, both pushing, pushing . . .

She did not know how long she slept or how long the phone rang before she became conscious of the harsh, insistent bell. Richard untangled himself from the bed sheets and sat up in the darkness to reach for the phone.

'Yes, this is Richard Linwood,' he said. The rest of his side of the conversation was a mix of short, clipped responses. 'Yes,' he said, and, 'When?' and, 'I see.' Susan did not have to hear the other side of the conversation to know it was something bad.

338

He hung up and sat immobile, staring into the night. She sat up beside him.

'Richard, what is it?'

'We've got to clean up and get dressed.' He stood up and headed for the bathroom. 'Charles is in the hospital.'

'What is it, Richard?' Her voice had gone up an octave. 'Is he all right?'

'He's alive.'

She intercepted him, grabbed his shoulders. 'What is it? What happened?'

Immobile again, staring past her, he did not speak.

'Richard?'

She could feel him gathering himself. He took her hands from his shoulders. 'It seems he took too much heroin.'

Masked and gowned, Susan and Richard stood in the intensive care unit watching their unconscious son. They stood side by side, but they did not touch.

A nurse came in to check his I.V. Susan did not want to believe how drawn and pale he looked, how much older than his years. *Wasted* was the word that came to mind. Her eyes avoided the tracheotomy tube.

The nurse finished with the I.V. 'All right, folks, you'll have to leave now.' Susan could almost hear the unvoiced: no matter how much pull you have.

Movement at the open door of Dan Mahoney's office cubicle made him look up from a list of Martin Eng's local phone calls. Laurie Jordan was leaning against the doorjamb, her suit jacket slung over one shoulder. In the gray afternoon light filtering through the dirty window he thought she looked like Lauren Bacall vamping Humphrey Bogart.

'Hello,' he said.

'Hello, yourself.'

'Come on in.'

'Can't, I'm on my way out – big weekend. I just stopped by to say I found something you might want to know about. Last we talked, I'd checked the statistics on complaints from outside. Since then I've had a chance to look for charges generated within the system. Michael A. Pullone pleaded guilty to command disciplines twice in the last three years. He took ten days suspended pay each time, for using – and paying – an unregistered informant. And on one of those, on the same case there was an allegation of planted evidence . . . in case it's relevant.'

He nodded, digesting it. There were systems for registering confidential informants. You could do it with the police department, or you could it with the D.A.'s office. Either way, the informant's identity was protected but the system had a chance to consider his reliability, and a way to keep track of how much he got paid and how his information panned out. Using an informant who had not been registered was okay in a rare emergency, but the need had to be clear. And an unregistered informant plus planted evidence made a nasty combination.

'Oh yeah, I think it might be relevant. Thanks.'

'Glad to help.' She hesitated before leaving. 'It's getting to be past time for you to bring me in on this with you.'

'Soon.'

'You know, I'm already far enough into this that it's my –' she showed him her perfect teeth – 'my ass on the line with yours. If I don't know what you're doing I don't know when to duck.'

Mahoney smiled back at her. 'If you don't know what I'm doing, I'd say that's your best protection, at least for now.'

'Okay,' she agreed grudgingly. 'For now.'


It was more than a day before they were sure Charles would not die. Richard seethed with impatience at not being able to move him to a hospital where he could exercise more control. Susan's main worry – once she could banish her lingering fear that Charles might not live – was that he would have some sort of permanent brain damage. The sessions they spent with his doctors were largely incomprehensible to her: everything was geared toward Richard, whose fame, after all, was based on his knowledge of the human brain.

As he interpreted for her, the issue was a simple one: how badly had Charles's brain been deprived of oxygen and for how long? It was information they could not have, at best could deduce by observing the symptoms.

It was a good sign, Richard reported, that Charles's initial period of unconsciousness had not been very long. He was keeping his eyes open now for longer and longer, showing some signs of purposeful movement.

As time passed Susan felt as if she were being dried down to a husk by constant worry and watching. Her eyes ached from looking at her son and not looking at him. From trying to decipher the words he was mouthing while the tracheotomy tube kept him from making sounds. From hoping to find some sign of sentience in the blank gaze he turned on the world when his eyes were open.

*Anoxic encephalopathy.* Who would have thought that such an awkward, bumpy phrase could contain at once so much hope and so much terror. She kept repeating to herself the reassurances she'd heard from the doctors and from Richard. This was to be expected: *diffuse cognitive deficit*, they called it, *flat affect*. It would improve. But it might not go away entirely. At this early stage there was no way to know for sure. The CAT scans were encouraging, they said. Give it time. A period of weeks, they said. She was not sure she could stay sane that long. At least Richard could occupy himself with the illusion of control.

'Do you think it could have been intentional?' Susan asked the hospital's social worker. Richard was off talking to Charles's neurologist. The two women stood alone in the cold blue light of the hospital hallway.

'He didn't leave any note, not that I was told about.' The social worker, not much older than Susan, exuded an institutional motherliness. 'Unless there's something you know about his state of mind, there's really no reason to think he did it intentionally. Especially with a beginner, and my understanding is there's no sign he was a regular needle user. People –' she seemed to search for a way to say it – 'make mistakes. Every now and then there's a new shipment of heroin, especially from China, that's more potent than what the market is used to. And sometimes it gets out onto the street with less than the usual amount of inert substances, so it's got even more kick. And people don't know what they have and they overdose without ever meaning to.'

341

★ ★ ★

That Kevin Horgan had spent his Labor Day break preparing his rebuttal witnesses and sketching out his closing argument for his interminable trial had done nothing to improve his mood. Mahoney approached Horgan's office at the end of the day with a large measure of unease.

'Another smiling face,' Horgan said when Mahoney came in. The unit chief was in his shirtsleeves, feet up on his desk. 'Sit down, relax.'

Mahoney sat, but he didn't relax.

Horgan removed the dead cigar from the corner of his mouth and sipped from a waxed-paper water cup. 'The damn trouble with this place is, we all work too hard.' He took another sip, replaced the cigar in his mouth. 'It gets to me sometimes. Like today I spent the day yelling at people who were just trying to do their job. You get so the result is all you care about.'

This side of Horgan was one Mahoney had not yet seen, though he'd had hints of it. There were stories around the office of all-night pub crawls after a hard trial, and occasional references to a major party Horgan had thrown the previous Super Bowl Sunday. Work hard, play hard seemed to be the theme, and this gruff camaraderie had to be part of it.

'So,' Horgan said around the cigar. 'You getting anywhere with that piece-o'-shit?'

'I feel like I'm beating my head against the wall,' Mahoney told him. 'That much hasn't changed. If anything it's gotten worse. I'm not coming up with the kind of cards Ned King wants to play against the feds, and it's not for lack of trying.'

Mahoney took a moment. This was the hard part. He had to talk to Horgan about what Laurie Jordan was learning about Pullone, but he had to approach it carefully.

'I'm looking for some guidance here,' he said. 'Because I'm beginning to think there may not be any cards for Ned to play.'

'And what does that mean?'

'I still think Mick Pullone's snitch has to be the key to this, if there is a key. I remember you said snitches aren't Sherlock Holmes, but I still think I could learn something talking to him.'

'We've been over this. Here's what's gonna happen . . . You're gonna ask him, "How do you know about these Eng people?" And he's gonna say, "I heard it." And you're gonna say, "Where?" And he's gonna say, "Around." '

'But he might not. And if he does, there might be other things I can get from him.'

'Like what?'

'Well, talking about snitches – if I have it right, they talk to us because they're looking to cut a deal on some beef they're jammed up on, or else they're in it for the money. And where there's a lot of money involved—'

'Is this more *it's a bad case* bullshit?' Horgan pulled the cigar from his mouth and spit out a crumb of tobacco.

'Don't we have to take that into account?' Mahoney couldn't stop now, had to get through this. 'I'm thinking this is a lot of money. I don't know what the snitch is getting, but even if it's only five percent, that's more than fifty thousand dollars. If he smelled a score like that and if maybe Mick got a little eager, cut some corners, didn't look close enough—'

'Whoa! Stop right there.' Horgan swung his feet off the desk, the better to glower at Mahoney, a thick finger pointed at his head. 'I don't want to hear a word about Mick Pullone. Mick Pullone works his ass off to get the bad guys, and there's nobody does a better job of catching them with the goods. I've worked a lot with Mick Pullone. He's as straight as they come, he doesn't cut corners, and I'm here to vouch for that one hundred percent. So stop looking for excuses not to do your real work.'

Horgan drank off whatever was in his paper cup and put the dead cigar in his mouth again. 'I'm going to be off this fucking trial of mine in a week or two, and as soon as that happens I'm taking *People v. Eng* off your hands. We have a calendar date coming up, don't we?'

'Friday.'

'All right, we'll have to get the judges coordinated on scheduling it so I can be there.' Horgan smiled. 'Hey, who knows – maybe my trial will have gone to the jury by then.'

# 12

No one at the hospital wanted to let them move Charles, but ultimately Richard prevailed. If they could move him to the neurology floor, he insisted, they could move him a mile by ambulance to another hospital. Finally the administrators and physicians gave up. Susan had the feeling they would be more than glad to be rid of the Linwood family.

She and Richard went in to see Charles and tell him about the move. He had reached the point of speaking occasional words, though he couldn't stay on track for more than a short sentence. After they'd given him the news, he rasped something almost inaudible.

Richard stepped closer to the bed. She moved with him.

'Knew . . . make me . . .' Charles said, his voice thin and shaky, the words extruded one at a time. He seemed to lose whatever had been the end of that thought. Then he focused again and as if out of another conversation he said, 'Detox.'

He paused, as if the effort to speak was exhausting. He was flat on his back, facing the ceiling, his eyes blank, but Susan knew he was talking to his father.

'Knew . . . wouldn't believe . . .' He stopped. His eyes wandered over the ceiling. His mouth worked, without sound, then produced a whisper: 'Once . . . twice . . .'

'I saw how you were behaving on our fishing trip,' Richard said evenly. 'That was more than once or twice.'

Charles said nothing. She wondered if he'd heard.

A spot of color touched his cheeks. 'You. Never. Saw.' The barely audible words had the force of a shout.

'I am not in the habit of lying, young man. And I don't put people

344

who love me in jeopardy by keeping illegal substances in their houses.'

Susan put her hand on her husband's arm.

He stiffened, turned his head. 'I'd like to be alone with Charles, please, if it's all right with you.'

'No, it's not all right.' She said it softly but clearly.

'Charles, your mother and I are going to go outside for a moment. I'll be right back.'

In the corridor he said, 'He won't be himself in front of you. I can talk to him better alone.'

'How can you talk about his being himself! He can barely put one thought after another. That's the best he's done so far.'

'You know that's not what I meant.'

'I saw you talking to him, Richard. You browbeat him, the way you browbeat everyone.' She was past calculating her every phrase. 'Don't you see he can't take that now? I won't let you do it.'

'What is that supposed to mean?'

'I'm his mother. I'm not going to be shut out of this.'

'Because you've been such an exemplary mother all these years?'

'What is *that* supposed to mean?'

He glared at her, then without a word turned back toward Charles's cubicle in the ICU.

'Wait,' she said. 'What was that about illegal substances in the house?'

'When I found them I thought I'd spare you. That first night he was gone I looked through his things. He had a stash of little glassine bags of white powder with Chinese writing on them. And some meaningless English.'

'Double UoGlobe,' she said.

'Something like that, yes.' A suspicious glance. 'But how did you . . . No, never mind. That's in the past now.'

He went to Charles's side. She followed him.

Charles's eyes were closed again. They went back into the corridor.

Richard said, 'I've talked to Myron Morris about detox.' Morris was the head of the psychiatric services at Richard's hospital; Susan knew him from fund-raisers and board gatherings. 'He's going to arrange it for us. Someplace in the Midwest, I think.'

*The Midwest*. Not close by, where he might be a constant reminder to your precious colleagues that Richard Linwood isn't perfect.

'Whatever's best for Charles,' Susan said quietly, eyes on her son, beyond the observation window. 'But I won't be presented with a *fait accompli*. I'm part of whatever decisions have to be made.'

Richard regarded her steadily for a moment. 'Of course.'

She stood watching Charles after Richard walked off down the corridor. How had things gone so wrong? She was afraid to let herself think about it, she had to keep her mind on the present, at least until Charles was through the worst of it.

She found a pay phone and checked her voice mail to give herself something to do. Among the others there was a message from David Clark: 'I just wanted to be sure you were okay,' he'd said. A nice gesture. You ought to acknowledge it, she told herself. But she wasn't okay, and what would she say to him?

At least *he'd* really listen, she couldn't help thinking.


The morning after his conversation with Horgan, Mahoney pried Estrada away from his desk.

They walked slowly along the periphery of the park. Estrada was silent while Mahoney filled him in.

'I can see why you didn't want to talk about this in the office,' Estrada commented when Mahoney finished. 'What do you think?'

'I think Horgan decided long ago I'm not a guy he's going to listen to very much. And I think I can either let this whole thing drop right now or I can go for a reality check with somebody who knows about these things.'

'You have somebody in mind?'

'Yeah. My former boss at Appeals.'

Estrada whistled. 'That's serious.'

'I don't know who else to talk to.' Max Straus, the former Chief of the Appeals Bureau, had been moved into the eighth-floor executive suite as Counsel to the District Attorney. By position and reputation he was the unofficial office ethicist for more than six hundred lawyers.

'If you're going to do it, there's nobody better,' Estrada said. 'The good thing is, you know him well enough for it to be a personal visit, not an official one . . . in case anybody wonders why you were there.'

346

'That's what I was thinking. But it's a big step anyway. Because if I'm questioning how Horgan's dealing with this, then I'm inviting Max to look at *him*, too, not just Pullone. In effect I'm taking the first step toward bringing down my own supervisor.'

'That's kind of a perverse way to look at it.'

'Because it might not work out like that? Sure, but what counts is, the possibility exists and Max is going to see it right away. And one thing I know is, you want to be real careful bringing down your supervisor, because you can't do it without help from other supervisors. And supervisors don't like to encourage that sort of thing.'

For Susan, the days that followed Charles's transfer took on a deceptively simple form. Charles's room in the recently constructed luxury wing of the hospital where Richard was on the board of directors was almost as big as their living room at home, with real living-room furniture and space for two visitors to spend the night on rollaway beds, and room-service catering the caliber of an above-average restaurant. Susan moved in, and Richard spent half the nights there with them. Lara, up from college, stayed the nights Richard didn't.

Charles was conscious more of the time but only minimally communicative at first. He still spent much of his waking time staring vacantly, and he needed help walking up and down the marble-floored hallways. As soon as possible, his doctor scheduled him for regular visits to the Physical Therapy Department.

Richard had softened slightly where Charles was concerned. Susan thought the change must have been prompted by his all-too-obvious horror at Charles's difficulty concentrating, the sluggishness with which he processed even simple questions, the trouble he had organizing his thoughts. This, in the son whose mental acuity had been a source of pride and a badge of honor to Richard.

Susan herself lived in a limbo of uncertainty. At some point early in the ordeal, along with the broken cadence of *anoxic encephalopathy*, a phrase from a college Shakespeare course had come to live in her mind. *O what a noble mind is here o'erthrown*. She could not shake it off.

Only Lara seemed to accept what Charles was going through as a kind of process. She sang him songs, read to him, and played games

347

with him, tolerant of his mental wanderings, his frequent complete abandonment of whatever thread she was attempting to establish. She walked up and down the hallways with him, and made his physical-therapy exercises into a kind of sport. Unlike her parents, she ministered to Charles without the slightest outward sign of concern, being encouraging without a hint of anxiety or pressure on him to do any better than he was doing at a particular moment.

Mahoney stopped at the security desk outside the D.A.'s office executive suite.

'Dan Mahoney for Max Straus.'

The cop on duty looked up a number and called in. 'Okay.' He clicked the door open and Mahoney went in.

A petite African-American woman with huge round eyeglasses met him halfway down the corridor. 'Mr Mahoney? Mr Straus is over this way.'

They made a left past the door that led to Ned King's office and the Boss's and she showed him into a small anteroom. 'He'll be right with you.'

Max Straus came out to greet him. A stocky man with thinning gray hair, he wore the same style of generously cut trousers, held up by suspenders, he'd always worn as Appeals Bureau Chief. As then, his tie was loosened at the neck and the sleeves of his striped white shirt were rolled up.

'Well, Daniel, it's nice to see you.' He shook Mahoney's hand warmly. 'I don't suppose this is a social call, though.'

'No, not really. I don't think of you as having a lot of time for social calls.'

'That's what happens, a man gets moved to an office within sight of the Boss's and suddenly nobody stops in to say hello any more.' Straus's grin was all tobacco-stained teeth. He led Mahoney into an office cluttered with the typical Max Straus piles of law journals, file folders and books.

'What can I do for you?' he asked when they were both seated.

'I'm here for a reality check,' Mahoney began, uneasier than he'd anticipated now that he was actually here, doing this. 'This may all be foolishness, but I have a lot of pieces and either they don't relate to each other or they're all part of the same puzzle.'

'Foolishness?' Straus leaned back in the tall leather chair, hands behind his head. 'I don't think of you as being prone to foolishness. Irreverence, maybe, but not foolishness. Give me the pieces.'

Mahoney told him about the Eng case, about how he'd not been able to make any headway with it. Without referring to any source he talked about his concern that Mick Pullone had a high quotient of complaints for bad warrants and brutal arrests. That there were rumors of his having been disciplined for using unregistered informants and maybe having been accused of planting evidence. Straus listened without comment.

Mahoney described the flap with the U.S. Attorney's office over the case. 'They say their case has nothing to do with heroin, though I suppose there's a possibility that's just a smokescreen.'

Straus considered it all. 'I can see where you might be thinking in terms of all this fitting into a single puzzle. But wouldn't the first step be to go to your supervisor?'

'I did.'

'And what does Kevin Horgan have to say about it?'

'He didn't let me get very far into it. Basically he told me I was dreaming and I should get back to work.'

'That's all? Not that he'd follow up on any of it?'

'He dismissed it out of hand. He said he's worked with Pullone for a long time and he vouches for him totally.'

'And to what do you attribute his brusqueness with you?'

'He and I don't get along that well. He's a hard charger – full steam ahead, take no prisoners – and I'm an analyzer. I think he thinks I'm soft, or not definite enough.'

'You and I both know that you're capable of being quite definite. And your analytic talents served us all very well in our Appeals Bureau days. I can't say I agree with Mr Horgan. And the fact that you're here makes me wonder if what you said just now doesn't downplay your own feelings about it.'

Straus stopped talking; his expression turned vacant. Mahoney knew better than to interrupt him while he was thinking things through.

'Have you talked to anyone in Official Corruption?' Straus asked.

Mahoney hesitated.

'Not officially,' his mentor supplied. 'And what about Asset Forfeiture? Have you checked to see how these bad cases of Detective Pullone's fit with the money he's brought in, if at all?'

'I didn't take it that far in my own mind. That's why I'm here.'

Straus went off into thought again.

'All right,' he said. 'This is not something I can ignore. If there's anything to the connections you're implying, there are too many ways it could touch this office. Especially if we're already in a war with the Southern District about the case.' He rubbed his face with both hands as if to scrub away his unpleasant thoughts.

'The best thing you can do right now is keep working on the case,' he told Mahoney. 'I want you to work on it as hard as you can. If you do come up with drug connections, let me know right away. If you come up with anything else, let me know that, too. I know you'll keep your eyes and ears open, but the most important thing is to know everything you can about the defendants and the case against them.'

After their meeting with the Engs, David had worried about Susan Linwood. She had looked so beleaguered and so – courageous was the word that seemed to fit best – as she left to face whatever terrors awaited her that day. He hadn't known whether he'd hear from her or not; he'd called once, just to make sure she was all right.

As time passed with no response to the message he'd left her, he felt a growing disappointment. He decided that her problem with her son and heroin must still be occupying her. It was either that or she was done with the Engs or she'd decided that, after all, he wasn't the ideal person to have along on that mission. Whatever it was, he told himself, the next move was up to her. There was no point sitting around waiting and wondering.

Jon Levi was after him again, and this time David responded by flying up to see if they could actually come up with something together. It felt good to be back in the Boston area; he'd been missing his old haunts more than he'd let himself know. Jon, too. But there were other memories here, not so welcome. He banished them by burying himself in work.

He found it exhausting, trying to recapture the old collaborative spark that had animated them in the dream-project days. Nothing went the way he intended. It was Jon who first called a halt.

'Let's go out and party. We're working at this too hard.'

The partying was easier than the working but David couldn't generate much enthusiasm for it.

'Something on your mind?' Jon asked him over the din of mediocre country-and-western music.

'Unfinished business.' He didn't say more. Jon would be too quick to read sex into any mention of Susan, and David wasn't in the mood to hear that.

'Unfinished business? Tell me about it!' Jon responded. 'We've got a pile of that in our collective history.'

'And some of it's damn well going to stay unfinished,' David reminded him.

'Right you are, right you be.' He waved to the bartender for two more beers. 'Listen up, O mighty bearded one, what I'm looking for here is some *new* business to finish.'

David leaned back against the bar and watched the engineers and programmers trying to two-step in their shiny new cowboy boots.

'I think our problem is we're looking too hard,' he said in an unexpected moment of clarity. 'It's as if we're desperate to find the magic wand.' And *desperate* was the right word. He kept having the fear that he'd lost his creative spark altogether. 'Why don't we just poke around easy for a while. This is kind of fun stuff we've got ourselves into. Let's enjoy it.'

Jon pointed the top of his empty long-neck at David. 'You, sir, are a proper genius.'


The story of what had happened to Charles remained lost with his memories of that day, memories that had not had a chance to take hold before the lightning bolt of heroin had blasted clean his short-term memory. He added detail to the story each time he told it, but it remained basically the same. In the recent past, he admitted, he had experimented with heroin. He knew from their arguments on the fishing trip that his father suspected him. He knew, too, that no matter what he said his father would insist on sending him to detox. While they were still on the trip he had thought about having a last fling, because he was sure that once he'd been through detox he would never experiment like that again. He remembered coming home from the trip, but he had no clear memories since.

The last fling – if he had taken it, and the evidence surely was that he had – must have been wilder than he'd intended. He had never injected any drugs before, he insisted. He had always thought it was a dumb thing to do, and needles made his skin crawl. He couldn't imagine why or how he had come to use one this time.

'Who were you with?' Richard asked him repeatedly, and just as repeatedly Charles said he didn't remember.

'But you know who your drug-taking friends were.'

'Didn't have any.'

It was a position from which Charles would not budge, and when Richard pushed him on it, he got vacant and distracted. Finally the social worker who was working with them told Richard that if he didn't let it go he might interfere with Charles's recovery.

'He's got to want to work at it. He's got to believe you support him,' she said.

This woman was nothing like the artificially maternal social worker at the other hospital. She was in her mid-thirties and her manner was at once open and firm. Susan was sure that Richard endured what he had more than once called her 'meddling' only because Susan insisted. For Susan their sessions were the only time she had a chance to explore her thoughts without Richard simply overriding her.

There was one fear that she could not share with the social worker – the fear that somehow her own actions had precipitated Charles's overdose, that his protestations that he would never have injected the drug were the truth, that someone else had forced it on him.

She told herself it was crazy to think that way, yet she couldn't get it completely out of her mind. Double UoGlobe heroin, *in her house*. And she had already sent out her press release and done her follow-up calling before Charles disappeared. If Ellen Hyams could trace the release back to her, why couldn't Tony Ching? Or someone else who wasn't happy about her trying to help the Engs. Charles's overdose hadn't been administered until hours after she'd left the Three Districts Association.

Much as she hated it, she couldn't avoid the thought that someone

352

had known what she was doing and had struck at her through her son –
a form of intimidation or revenge that was by no means un-Chinese.

But if that was how it had happened, why hadn't anyone warned her
off, or told her to mind her own business? The Engs had, in a way, but
there was no logic in their being behind this – none that she could
imagine, not even in the light of Martin Eng's odd remark about life's
being full of unanticipated dangers.

# 13

'Remember those robberies at your defendant's benevolent association?' Mark Brattler asked Mahoney. 'The ones that turned into kind of a shooting war? I may have found out who's behind it all. It's the head of a rival benevolent association. They had a feud going for a while.'

'Benevolent? And they shoot at each other?'

'They use the local definition of benevolent.'

Brattler told him about Tony Ching and the contested election and the beating that had preceded the robberies. 'Things seem to have cooled off some, though. It's not a hot war between them the way it was a while ago.'

'You think he'd frame my defendants?'

'These people usually settle their quarrels themselves. Letting the police and the courts do their work isn't their style.'

Mahoney put a thick envelope on Brattler's desk. 'A present.'

Brattler hefted it. 'Generous.'

'Phone records for the Eng household, with names and addresses. Needless to say they're mostly meaningless to me.'

'I'll give it to my investigators and see if they find anybody they know.'

'Appreciated.' Mahoney told him about the meeting at the Southern District, asked if he could make anything of what the feds had said about their case.

'It's kind of vague.'

'I think that's what they had in mind.'

'If it's really not drugs, immigration makes the most sense. Something like bribing consular officials in out-of-the-way places to issue

354

visas . . . I don't know. I'll give it some thought.'

'Thanks.' Mahoney turned to go, stopped at the door. 'No picture today?'

'I was going to spare you, but now that you ask . . .' Brattler opened a file folder and pulled out a color eight-by-ten. 'Something special.'

It was a naked man lying on his back. Mahoney recognized the characteristic shape of a slash wound, like an elongated football or a cigar pointed at both ends, an effect caused when the tension in the skin pulled the wound open. If he had seen slash wounds before, he had never seen this many. They ran straight across the man's body and limbs, parallel to each other – some long, some short – horizontal slashes covering him from head to foot.

Mahoney looked away.

'Something, isn't it? I don't think I'm going to get this one blown up for the wall.' Brattler put it away. 'Another Triad-style hit.'

'Didn't you say they were keeping busy on their side of the ocean?'

'I said I hoped so. And even if they do, there's an increasing business lately importing killers from Hong Kong for single jobs. You hire a guy over there – usually through the Triads – and ship him here. And I mean sometimes they *literally* get shipped, inside a freight container. The guy gets off the boat, does the murder, gets right back on the boat and goes home in the same container he arrived in. Going price last I looked was transportation plus around two hundred Hong Kong dollars. That'll buy you a mediocre dinner for one, over there.'

'And that poor bastard you just showed me is an example of how they operate?'

'Could be. Funny thing is, that's a traditional Chinese method of judicial execution for criminals, goes back centuries – they actually sentenced people to be *sliced*. "Death of a thousand cuts," some people call it.'

'You know what this guy's crime was?'

'Looks like he might have talked too much.' Brattler took the picture out again. 'See where it's scorched, by his throat? Best guess is they poured lighter fluid in those cuts and lit it up. That's a modern wrinkle, I'd say.'

Mahoney didn't look.

'Or else maybe he took something that didn't belong to him. Maybe you noticed, his hands are gone.'

'I missed that detail,' Mahoney said. 'I really ought to come by more often.'

'Oh, yeah. Barrel of laughs. I'll call you when my guys have been through the phone records. Or if I learn anything else.'

When Charles was strong enough to get around unaided and Richard had arranged for him to fly to the Midwest for a stay of undetermined length, they had a final family conference with the social worker about what the family could do to provide emotional support for Charles, and for each other, while he was in detox.

'I've been talking to the people out at the Center,' the hospital social worker said. 'They try to fit their policy on family participation to each situation. You can expect them to tell you that they feel in this case – and I must say I agree very strongly – that for the first six weeks there should be no contact at all between Charles and the rest of the family.'

'We'll see about that,' Richard said.

'I don't think you will,' the social worker responded calmly. 'Not in the sense you mean. The staff out there will be quite adamant about it.' She sighed. 'You know, I've said it before, this kind of thing is often largely a matter of family dynamics. If you want Charles to stay clean you'll have to do some work on that part of it.

'There's no question he's going to need support from all of you. But he also needs to be his own, autonomous person. If that means he has to suffer for his behavior, and face his pain and fear alone, it's for the best. This may seem arbitrary and painful to you, but it's the best treatment. For Charles and for the rest of you.'

Later, she took Susan aside. '*You* need the time, too, and most of all you need to protect yourself. I know your impulse is to help, but Charles has to take the first steps toward healing on his own. My feeling about you is, you have a lot of guilt you need to deal with. Take some time. Don't sit around worrying about Charles or blaming yourself. The best way for you to help Charles heal is to help heal yourself.'

The walk down the eighth-floor executive corridor seemed longer to

356

Mahoney than it had the last time. Then, he'd been preoccupied with what he was about to say to Max Straus. Now he was here to listen and his thoughts were dominated by the unwelcome possibility that he might run into Ned King. *Just stopped by to see my old Bureau Chief,* he rehearsed.

He made it into Max Straus's office without running into anyone.

'Well,' Straus said, 'you've given me an interesting few days. I had a chance to catch up with some people I hadn't spoken to lately. I even got to have a pleasant lunch.'

This was Straus's style. Mahoney waited.

'You understand, of course,' the D.A.'s counsel said. 'I was concerned that we not be going to war with ghosts, so I talked to some people here and there and I learned that our Detective Pullone has built himself something of a reputation, and not a good one. And considering that he's so close to so much money so much of the time these days, what I've been hearing makes me very uneasy.'

Mahoney thought he should be relieved: at least he hadn't been imagining things. But relief did not seem to be in sight.

'What I'd like you to do for me now is this,' Straus said. 'Tell Kevin Horgan you really need to talk to Pullone's informant. I'd like to see Horgan put some pressure on Pullone to bring the snitch in for a chat. Then we can see what happens.'

Mahoney shook his head. 'I don't know . . . That snitch has been a sore spot between me and Horgan for a while now. I doubt the request would get as far as Pullone. If I bring it up, Horgan's just going to shoot me down again.'

'Do your best. I notice that they haven't paid the snitch yet, so you might suggest using the money as a lever to bring him in.'

There was no point saying he'd already tried that with Pullone. Mahoney knew Straus well enough to gauge when an opinion was appropriate and when to keep his mouth shut and just charge out of the trenches and into the cannon fire.

'I'll try it,' he said.

'Good. And bear in mind – whatever Horgan's reaction, I'll be interested to hear it.'

'Okay.' So he already had Horgan in his sights. Again, Mahoney was not relieved.

357

Straus shook his hand at the door. 'I'm glad you came to me about this, Dan. It was the right thing to do.'

With Charles getting ready to leave for the clinic, Susan urged Lara to go back to college. After she had said goodbye to her brother, Lara asked Susan to come downstairs with her and take a walk.

They walked into the small conservatory park at the edge of Central Park. Except for a few people on benches under the bowers they had it to themselves.

'I feel like it's my fault,' Lara said.

'Join the club.'

'No, really. I knew things, and I didn't know what to do about them. I heard rumors. My friends in school went on weekends sometimes, you know, to Charles's college. And they'd come back and say how wild it was, how everybody did everything. Remember you asked me if I knew people who did heroin? The first people I knew who did, got it there. And once or twice I'd hear about this cool guy and he wasn't, like, a *dealer* but if you were lucky you could catch him when he had some heroin to sell, and it was always the best. And people called him Chuck the Chink.'

Susan started to interrupt, but Lara didn't let her. 'No, wait. First I thought it couldn't be him. He's so regular. But then I would hear Chuck the Chink had a 4.0 and he played sports and it was so funny because everybody thought he was Mr Straight. And then one of my friends actually met him and so I knew it was true, it was really Charles. She was a really good friend and I swore her to secrecy and then she moved away anyway.'

Susan put her arm around her daughter. 'Oh Lara, what a hard secret for you to have.' She pushed her own horror aside. Whatever had been was over. All she could do now was be here for her daughter.

'I didn't know what to do,' Lara went on. 'I was crazy afraid he'd get in some kind of really bad trouble. But then, you have to understand, it's not like everybody thinks dealing is such a terrible thing. Not as long as you don't do it every day like it's your *job* or something, you know. Lots of kids deal, now and then. It's like a way to supplement your allowance? Not heroin, but other things. Pot, and pills, mostly. And the thing is, almost always the kids who deal don't use.

358

They figure, "Hey, I can make some money off these kids who are dumb enough to use this stuff." Not pot, I mean, lots of kids smoke. But the pills. And coke, if they deal that, and heroin, for sure.

'It made me worry so much that Charles was dealing that I just wanted him to stop, even if some people thought it was cool, or okay. But I never thought he was *using*. I talked to him about it last Christmas, about dealing, and he laughed at me. He said, "Where did you hear that silly story?" So I told him the really silly thing was if he kept doing it, because what if he got caught, and he told me to mind my own business and not to worry, he had everything under control, and he wasn't going to do anything stupid or dangerous.'

They were alone under the arching branches of a very old tree. Susan sat them on a bench next to each other and put her arms around her daughter.

'Oh, Mama,' Lara said and buried her head in her mother's shoulder and cried. 'I didn't want to tell on him. I was so scared but I didn't want to tell on him. I didn't know he was using it himself.'

'Of course you didn't, darling.' She hugged her daughter tight. 'Of course you didn't. And you did alert us, without ever saying anything bad about your brother.'

Lara sat up. 'But that's the worst part. If I hadn't said that, and if you hadn't told Dad, then Dad wouldn't have made Charles take a test and this might not have happened.'

Susan took both Lara's hands. 'This is the best thing that could have happened.' She had been convincing herself of that for days. 'Something like this, or worse, would have happened, eventually. If you hadn't said anything, if we hadn't known to be concerned, if your father hadn't known what Charles's odd behavior on their trip might mean . . . Charles might have hidden what he was doing long enough to get himself much more seriously addicted. He could have ruined his health, and he might have gone to jail for years. He could have ended up using needles, maybe some that weren't clean. At least now he'll go to detox and get straightened out, and we all have a chance that this will be the end of it. We all owe you a lot.'

'Don't ever say so!' Lara's reaction was immediate. 'You don't owe me anything. I had nothing to do with it.'

Susan hugged her again. 'It's our secret.'

Lara pulled back. 'No. There's no secret. I didn't do anything.'

Susan looked straight into her eyes. 'Okay. You didn't do anything.'

'That's better,' Lara said and pressed herself back into her mother's arms.


Mahoney decided the only way to tackle Horgan about the snitch was head on. He picked his moment: on the way back to the office after their court date on the Engs. Ellen Hyams had asked for extra time to file defense motions, and over Horgan's argument that the prosecution was ready and eager to proceed, the judge had given her the extension.

It meant Horgan was angry, but at least he was angry at the judge and the defense. And the delay also provided a pretext.

'Looks like we're not going to get this over with before we have to worry about the feds again,' Mahoney opened.

Horgan looked at him but said nothing. He puffed savagely on his cigar as they crossed the street from the civil court, where a fair percentage of the courtrooms now housed criminal trials, including *People vs. Eng*.

'I really need to talk to that snitch if I'm going to get anywhere with this,' Mahoney went on. 'And if he doesn't want to come in, let's hold his money until he does.'

Horgan stopped dead in the middle of the street, oblivious of the traffic being released by the changing stoplight. 'Damn it, Mahoney, how many times do we have to do this? I swear, I don't get it.' He flipped the bird to a driver who veered past them, horn blaring.

On the sidewalk, he said, 'Look, I'm trying to make allowances, but I'm flat out of patience. I think you just don't belong in this kind of work. You tried it, it didn't fly. I'm sure they'll be real happy to have you back in Appeals.'


Mahoney was still fighting to contain his fury when he got to Max Straus's office.

'Don't worry about that,' Straus told him. 'He was being dramatic. He'll forget he said it.' The D.A.'s counsel stared off into space, thinking. When he returned he said, 'I want you to be careful about annoying him again. From now on you want to be a good team-player, keep your head down, do what you're told. You've attracted his attention enough.'

Amen, Mahoney said to himself.

'Now, harking back for a moment to an earlier conversation,' Straus went on. 'If I were to go over to Official Corruption and hope I might find someone who already knew a little about Detective Pullone's record, who do you suppose that might be?'

Mahoney felt a surge of apprehension. They were at the Rubicon now. He had started the process in motion, and now they were crossing into territory where it would proceed on its own, with or without him. If he was wrong – and he still might be wrong – the best he could hope for was embarrassment. At the worst, he had spiked his career at the D.A.'s office.

'You might try Laurie Jordan,' he said.

'Really.' Straus allowed himself a small smile. 'You have good taste in allies. I've always thought she was as smart as she is pleasant to look at.'

'Just one favor,' Mahoney said. 'Before you call over there I'd like to give her a heads-up on this so it doesn't take her by surprise.'

'Fine. Why don't you talk to her today, and in the morning I'll call her unit chief and tell him I have an investigation to discuss with him, and he might want to consider assigning her to work on it. Then we can all get together and have a chat.'


Mahoney's apprehension about how far things had gone was not eased by the meeting with Straus and Laurie Jordan and her unit chief, a deceptively sleepy-looking man with hooded eyes and hair an oddly metallic orange. He was known around the office as Copperhead, a nickname that brought to mind not just his hair but – not incidentally – a poisonous snake.

He listened in silence to what the others had to say, interrupting only to ask Mahoney what subjects he had covered with Pullone in the grand jury.

'All of it, I'm afraid. I took him through the raid and the arrest a step at a time. Including finding the heroin.'

'You didn't have him waive immunity?'

The question went straight to the pit of Mahoney's stomach, though he knew it was coming. 'It all looked straightforward when I got it. There was nothing to suggest I needed a waiver.' As a general matter, cops were only asked to waive immunity before their grand jury testimony if police weapons had been fired, in which case a grand jury investigation was routine.

'How about perjury?'

'I checked the transcript. I didn't see anything chargeable.'

The shadow around the Official Corruption chief's eyes seemed to darken. 'Damn shame. Not only because it puts him out of reach—'

'Except for departmental charges,' Straus pointed out.

'I'm thinking what leverage we have on him if we want to look higher.'

Which had to mean Horgan. 'Even if we can't prosecute Pullone,' Mahoney hastened to say, 'I'm worried about these defendants. These are old people, and from what I saw they weren't doing well in jail. They're looking at mandatory prison time, and for them that might as well be a death penalty. If this is a bad case . . .' He didn't say the rest.

'Nobody's talking about backing off,' Straus said.

'Damn shame, though,' the Copperhead repeated. 'If the guy's dirty I'm going to hate to see him walk.'

# 14

Susan and Charles spent the flight to the clinic in silence. Richard had said his goodbyes that morning before leaving for the hospital; having accepted with unexpected grace the clinic's plan to separate Charles from them, he had immediately gone back to his normal schedule.

Charles kept his headphones on from takeoff to landing and flipped through the magazines he kept asking the attendants to bring him. Susan tried not to be worried by his apparent inability to concentrate on a single article or even a single magazine.

The drive to the clinic made no impression on her, and by the time she was in the same clinic car headed back to the airport she had forgotten what the grounds or buildings looked like. All she remembered was Charles, still looking dazed in a way she had never seen before all this, saying goodbye to her in a large reception area paneled in wood, at the foot of a grand circular staircase, and the sting of tears rising in her eyes as her son's blank face began to register that she was leaving him there alone.

She had hugged him then, with as much as she could bear of the love and longing she had kept carefully in check for a decade and more, her tears flowing freely when she felt his return embrace, wetting his shoulder as baby Charles's tears had once wet hers.

'Don't cry, Ma,' he had said, and kissed her forehead. 'I'll be okay.'

Mahoney sat at the conference table listening to Horgan conduct the weekly unit meeting. Horgan's own trial got the most time and attention, as always. It was grinding through its final stages and – the way Horgan reported it – his rebuttal witnesses had the defense on the run.

With a happy ending apparently in store there, Horgan was

concentrating more on what came next. The unit had two other matters in active preparation for trial, *People v. Eng* and a multi-count indictment against a Colombian money launderer named Ocampo. The unit's other cases were still in the investigative stage, evidence building up in the long-term grand jury preparatory to indictment and arrest. The way it should have been with *Eng*, Mahoney thought, if it had been a righteous case.

When Mahoney's turn came, he gave the progress report on the Eng money-laundering investigation – a pretext for collecting more evidence against the Engs, necessary because using grand jury subpoenas for investigation after indictment was abuse of process. He talked about the follow-up on bank records and other documents he had subpoenaed but not yet received. He was still waiting for the Asian Gang Unit investigators to report on the Engs's phone records. The ledgers were fully translated now, with nothing that spoke more directly of heroin than the zodiac animals they already knew about. Nothing that corroborated Martin Eng's self-serving description of the ledgers' contents, either.

Giving his report, Mahoney let his eyes travel across the eight people at the long table, not avoiding Horgan but not addressing him any more than the others. Part of Mahoney's mind watched his own performance, wondering how a polygraph would react to his faster heartbeat and drier mouth when his eyes were on Horgan, or the sweat on his palms. Knowing that Max Straus was checking up on Mick Pullone, with help from Laurie Jordan, knowing that an unspoken part of that investigation was pointed at Kevin Horgan.

At the end of Mahoney's presentation, Horgan announced that he had some news about the dispute with the U.S. Attorney's office over the Eng case. When the anti-fed hooting and jeering had died down, he took a manila folder from the pile of papers in front of him and pulled out a stack of photographs.

'They've decided to do us the favor of sharing their surveillance photographs. If they get some mugs they don't know they send them over – maybe they're the heroin connection we're looking for. Ask me, it's a way to give us the finger, but I want everybody to look through them – detectives and any active Chinese snitches, too. You never know.'

He passed the photographs around the table. Everybody shuffled through them, with the predictable rude remarks, particularly about one subject – an attractive Chinese woman from the sound of the comments, which were only slightly tempered by the presence of two women in the room.

Mahoney glanced through the photos quickly, too preoccupied by his double game to pay much attention. There was no point in his studying them, anyway: he was too new to narcotics prosecution to recognize any of the players. His eye stopped briefly on a telephoto shot of a woman likely to be the one who had provoked all the reaction. She was talking to Martin Eng at the entrance to a building; another man – Caucasian, probably – was an out-of-focus presence beside her. Even in the grainy surveillance photo she was worth looking at. And tantalizingly familiar – a model or a movie star or . . .

He shook off the feeling and passed the photos along. All he wanted right now was for the meeting to be over so he could stop feeling like a double agent.

Susan made herself go to work the day after she got back from the clinic. With Charles in the hospital fighting for his life she'd had no time to notice that Labor Day had come and gone – and with it Shelby Portman's pitch to his board of directors for her breast-cancer education program. He had warned her not to expect a decision immediately, but she still flinched every time the office phone rang, and she was having trouble focusing on the work she had to do for other clients.

At home that night she tried to eat dinner, but she could not bring herself to put the food in her mouth. Her very aloneness made her think of Charles, banished to an unfamiliar place with only unfamiliar people for company.

Over and over she had to remind herself of the social worker's warning that for her own sanity she needed to let Charles heal himself. Finally she picked up the phone and called Lara.

'Who's this?' Lara's roommate asked.

'It's her mother.'

'Is everything all right?'

'Everything's fine. I just want to talk to her.'

'Oh. Well, um, she's at the library. You know, studying?'

'I thought classes didn't start till Monday.'

'Oh, yeah, well, no they don't, not classes. It's for this like freshman orientation thing? World Civ? And we have a reading list?'

'Well, tell her I called.'

'Okay, sure.' Sounding relieved. 'Bye.'

I wonder where she really is, Susan thought. Accustomed as she was to hearing Lara's friends put an upward inflection at the end of every sentence, this set of questions had sounded more like *Do you believe me?* than the usual *Are you listening?* or *Do you get it?* And if Charles had been dealing heroin and snorting it, too, doing it off and on for months without either parent's knowing it, who could say what Lara might be up to?

It took Susan a frantic few minutes to calm down enough to see that if she wasn't careful she'd truly make herself crazy with thoughts like that. This night was only one of many years of nights she would be spending by herself, in a way that felt far more desolate than the solitary nights she had lived through in the past.

She slept badly. In the morning she called a car and had the driver take her to the Brooklyn Botanic Garden in the hope that wandering among the trees and flowers might remind her the world was still full of beauty and variety.

Instead she thought about Charles. About the things she could have done and about the things she had done. All the ways she could have been a better mother. Again, she wished there was someone she could talk to about this. Not Richard, certainly. None of the women she thought of as her friends, either.

She turned a corner, walked along a row of Japanese cherry trees that in spring would be glorious with blossoms. The sun slanted past their leaves, dappled the ground. It brought back a memory of David Clark, sitting opposite her at their lunch together, a bright slant of sunlight in his hair, his eyes intent on her, completely focused on what she was saying. And that made her think of him in the subway on the way back from the Engs, concerned but not intruding . . . There was something about talking to him that made her feel more clear-headed, that made problems seem less dauntingly complex; she missed that,

366

and yet as her life stood now she had nothing to say to him, really. Even if she returned his call – unpardonably late, now – what would she have to tell him? It would only be awkward for both of them.

She thought about the Engs, too. It no longer made sense to her that they might somehow have been responsible for what had happened to Charles – they or their enemies. That was too simple a view, too external. Blaming herself in that way – as if by some thoughtless act of meddling she had brought this on – stretched her guilt too far. And she could not escape her own true responsibility by blaming evil strangers for choices Charles himself had made. If having her as a mother had influenced his behavior – as it must have – she had to accept the pain and sorrow that came with that fact.

The Engs had been through so much more than she had. Did *they* blame themselves, she wondered, when their two children drowned, laden with gold? Recovering that gold, had they felt guilty spending it – or hoarding it, as they claimed? They had expressed sorrow, but there was nothing in what they had said that spoke of responsibility. Did that mean her own feelings of guilt were the product of something foreign – her church-school girlhood, her carefully cultivated Americanness? Or were the Engs simply being private in their grief?

She wondered if they had followed up about Detective Pullone, regretted that she hadn't told them more when she had the chance to, even if it might have meant violating the secrecy of the grand jury far more seriously than she had in the press release.

David pushed his chair back from the long worktable Jon Levi had rigged up for them out of an old door and a couple of sawhorses.

'Did I hear somebody say this was fun?'

'Hey!' Jon said. 'Don't go changing your tune on me now. I was getting to like it.'

'I'd like it better if I could see it leading somewhere.'

'Now, where's the man who said let's stop trying to build a killer application and just smell the roses?' Jon got up and went to the fridge. 'How about a jolt of caffeine?' He held up a frosty bottle.

'I'll take mine hot, thanks.'

He poured himself inky coffee that had been kept just short of boiling for hours. Sipping it, he thought of the time with Susan

367

Linwood when he had been less careful about hot coffee.

He wondered yet again how she was, what she was doing. He missed the sense of discovery he had, belatedly, realized she inspired in him—

'How about this?' Jon said with sudden enthusiasm, cutting into David's musings. 'Could it be we're going at it backwards? The way we've been looking at it, we start with – I want to send you something so nobody else can understand it, not even my good friend Joe, to whom I also send encrypted messages. Plus I want you to know for sure it came from me, not some other dude using my name.'

'Right. So I have a translation key and you have a signature key and all the communication from you to me needs both those keys to encode and decode it properly. But if I want to send a message back, I can't use those same keys – I need *my* signature key and *your* translation key.'

'And Joe has a different translation key and when I send him a message, I have to use *his* key. And that's how everybody is approaching this, and doing it that way has the kinds of problems we're sitting here to solve.' And Jon was off and running with his new idea . . . imaginative as always and absolutely determined to get to the end of whatever road he'd set out on.

David paid as much attention as he could, with a growing sense that Jon was heading down another blind alley, Jon's main problem being that he was as tenacious in pursuit of a bad idea as a good one.

From the Botanic Garden Susan went to the office. Mona and Annette were frantic.

'Where did you go? We were trying to find you all morning. You got three calls from Shelby Portman.'

Portman's first words after they said hello were: 'Susan, it's not like you to go off without telling someone where to find you.'

'Life's been a little complicated lately, Shelby. I'm sorry if I inconvenienced you.'

'No, it's not that. It's just, I heard from the board, and I was hoping you might be around so we could try to get some time to talk to them, change their minds. I was being foolish, really. It wouldn't have done any good. The decision is made.'

'I gather it's not good news.'

'No, I'm afraid not. I'm sorry, Susan. I thought public-health education was a good idea. I still do.' He mumbled something about the new chairman's enthusiasm for the arts . . . making the company visible outside the medical field . . .

She couldn't make herself listen to it. 'That's such bullshit. It's a medical supply company!' She could see Annette staring at her: she never raised her voice, never ever used profanity. 'You need to give an impression of caring and compassion, to show you're not just in it to make money on people's misery. What's the point in hiring somebody like me if they're going to go off and make stupid decisions anyway?' There . . . said it.

Portman seemed to take a long breath. 'I don't blame you for being disappointed. Why don't you take a week or so and then call me and we can get back to the real work?'

She slammed the phone down. The real work!

She didn't have to interpret for Annette and Mona. 'We all worked hard on this,' she said. 'We deserve better.'

'We sure do,' they agreed.

'Tell you what – let's wrap up what we're doing and take the rest of the day off.'

The phone rang. 'I'll get it,' Susan said. 'You two finish up.'

She picked up the phone. 'Linwood Associates.'

'Hello?' said a woman's voice. 'May I speak with Mrs Linwood?' A slight Chinese accent.

'This is Susan Linwood.'

'Oh. Hello. This is Milly Cheung.'


'The nice thing about this job,' Mark Brattler said on the phone, 'there's always something new.'

'What now?' When Mahoney saw the message slip from Brattler he'd decided to call instead of stopping by. He wasn't in the mood for pictures.

'We just raided a snakehead safe house. The way it works, they bring these people into the country and sometimes they hold them prisoner, let them out to work while they're paying off their passage money. Or else, if they've been living out in the community and

369

they're not paying up on schedule, they kidnap them and hold them for ransom. The kidnapped ones they don't let out.'

'Then how do they pay?'

'The gang members make them call their friends and relatives and beg for the money. The place we just raided, there was a fax machine and a phone – they pay the bills with stolen credit cards – and next to the phone was this hammer with the handle broken in two right near the head. The way I get it, they had this guy on the phone with his people in China and they were hitting him on the back with the hammer while he was talking, so the folks back home could hear him scream. Kind of to show they were serious. And they hit him so hard the hammer broke.'

'Holy . . .'

'You bet. The trouble with using the gangs for kidnappings is they get carried away. They do too much damage. Break bones, kill people, rape the women for sure. But that's not why you called. You want to know what I have for you . . . First, on the phone records. Nobody we know from the drug world is on those lists you gave me. It could be that every one of them is a drug dealer we don't know yet, but the ones we do know aren't there.'

'Well, thanks for looking, anyway.' Mahoney knew he shouldn't be relieved, but he was.

'There was one interesting thing, could be just a coincidence. The biggest activity on the LUDs –' the telephone-company phone-call lists known as Local Usage Details – 'was a bunch of calls, pretty much every weekday, to a mid-town office location listed to a guy named Wu.'

'And?'

'Well, the thing is, your guy is named Eng, right? That's a Cantonese pronunciation of the name. And the same name – the same written character – in Mandarin you pronounce it Wu. So Eng, Wu – it's the same name.'

'What was Mr Wu's first name?'

'Initials. M.C.'

'My guy is Martin. That's M.'

'But M.C. could stand for a Chinese name, too, and if it does there's no way to know if the C or the M is for his personal name. And there's

370

no consistent pattern between Chinese names and American ones – a guy named Fong might call himself Harry. So it *could* be the same guy – or it could be his brother, or his cousin. Or not. Remember, this is a billion people and altogether they have maybe a thousand last names, tops. So that's a million or so Engs or Wus.'

'I see what you mean.'

'However,' Brattler said in a celebratory tone, 'I do have some actual news. Good news.'

'Such as?'

'One of my investigators was following up on some things he heard from a snitch, and he came up with a couple of people who maybe can give you what you need on your money laundering.'

'Tell me more.' For a moment, Mahoney wasn't sure what Brattler was talking about.

'You've still got a money-laundering investigation open on Mr and Mrs Eng, right?'

'Yes.' He'd just stopped expecting it to produce anything.

'I assume you would want to hear from two gentlemen who were making large cash deposits for an elderly couple named Eng, on a regular basis.'

'*Large* deposits?'

'That's what I hear. I think we can get them to talk, but you're going to need an interpreter. Toishanese.'

'Sorry?'

'I know the feeling. Life would be so much easier if they'd all just speak the same language. Toishanese is the main language for the Cantonese old-timers in Chinatown. But it's a different dialect from actual Cantonese. Anyway, I'll get back to you on this. It shouldn't be more than a couple of days.'

Mahoney put the receiver back in its cradle and stared at the ceiling, willing himself to believe this was good news: if it was for real, it meant a chance to remove the doubts about the Eng case and it would give Ned King plenty to use against the feds.

But then where did that leave the theory he'd raised with Max Straus, that Pullone had invented the case?

*Great work, Mahoney*, he told himself. You've got the Official

Corruption Unit and the Counsel to the D.A. on the trail of what may well be a figment of your own overheated imagination. If it turns out the Engs really were laundering heroin money, you're going to look like a hundred percent pure asshole. And the longer you let it go the worse it's going to be.

On the other hand, if you do call them off now, and Brattler's lead doesn't pan out, then you'll have to go back and convince Max to get underway again – that you were wrong to think you were wrong and now you realize you were right all along.

By reflex, he picked up the phone to call Joe Estrada for a second opinion, then put it down again. Estrada was off somewhere in Mexico, visiting his grandfather. Besides, it was Daniel J. Mahoney's career at stake, and if anybody was going to screw it up, it ought to be Daniel J. Mahoney. He went to see Max Straus.

As soon as she got off the phone with Meiling Cheung, Susan called David Clark.

'He's out of town,' his sister said.

'Do you know when he'll be back?'

'He didn't say. He's up in Boston doing some work. You want him to call you?'

Susan hesitated. 'Thank you, that's all right. I'll try him again.'

'Toward the end of the week, maybe.'

'Thanks.'

She told herself she had no right to expect him to be there the very moment she needed him. He had a life to live, too, and she had disappeared on him without word or warning, without even returning his call. She'd had ample reason, but he couldn't know that.

It didn't matter that he was away, she told herself – she could do this without him. She dialed the number Meiling Cheung had given her, got an answering machine.

'This is Susan Linwood,' she told the machine. 'I'll be happy to accept your gracious invitation.'

It wasn't Max Straus's style to rant at news like Mahoney's the way Horgan would have. In a way, Mahoney would have preferred a noisier response.

Straus just looked off into the distance the way he did when he was thinking. After an interminable silence, he let his eyes come back to Mahoney.

'Follow it up, see what it is. You may have been wrong about this Eng case being bad, but that doesn't necessarily mean you were wrong about Detective Pullone. I'll pass this on to our friends at Official Corruption, because I do think it's best for us to slow down until you resolve this. But I want you to keep me posted.'

Mahoney made his way back to his office. He didn't fool himself that the ax hadn't fallen. Straus had just brought it down very gently until it rested on his neck. Time and events – and Daniel Mahoney's next moves – would determine whether it cut through. Or maybe the right word wasn't *whether* but *when*.

# 15

Martin Eng opened the apartment door for Susan. Again, he was wearing a shirt and pants like the ones he had worn in the grand jury. He led her down a short entrance corridor. At the living-room doorway they detoured around a black wooden screen: four angled panels adorned with mountains and trees painted and inlaid in a traditional Chinese style, surrounded by a carved wooden dragon.

Susan looked quickly around the narrow living room to take in as much as she could without being rude. There were clean-lined Chinese chairs and tables of dark wood, antiques or good reproductions. Blue-and-white porcelain vases stood in a cupboard against one wall; a second cabinet held porcelain decorated in red. In a massive fish tank swam what looked like large, exotic goldfish. Mirrors had been hung diagonally across some of the angles of the walls.

Screen and fish and mirrors were all signs that, long as the Engs had been here, they had not abandoned the centuries-old Chinese concern with wind and water, with the vital energy called *qi*, with the dragons that lived in the earth. That much of the old lore, Susan knew about.

Meiling Cheung was sitting on a couch by a long coffee table. There was a porcelain tea service at her end of the table. She was wearing, again, a silk cheongsam. And, again, she reminded Susan of her mother.

'Welcome,' Martin Eng said. 'We are happy to see you.'

'It is a great honor to be invited to your home,' Susan replied, keeping the acknowledgment a formal one.

'An American custom we follow, not often. But you have been as kind to us as family, so we are happy to see you in our home.'

'A very beautiful home,' Susan said. 'My parents brought some

374

porcelain from China but none so exquisite as yours.'

'You are kind to say so.'

Meiling Cheung poured tea for them and they drank in silence.

'When you came to visit us before, you were worried about your son,' Martin Eng said. 'Is he well?'

'It's thoughtful of you to remember. He's fine, thank you.'

'I hope you do not think we were rude not to be eager for more of your generous help.'

'I think I understand.'

'We do not wish anyone to think we encourage reporters to be interested in us,' his wife said.

Susan smiled. 'Some of the people who pay me to get them noticed say the very same thing. But I respect how you feel.'

They both looked robust and energetic, she thought – far healthier than when they testified in the grand jury or even when she saw them at the Three Districts Association. The difference emphasized how badly even a couple of weeks in jail must have affected them. How they would suffer under a long prison sentence did not bear thinking about.

'When I first arranged to see you,' she said; 'I asked Uncle Eight to tell you that I was on the grand jury that indicted you. But when it came to talking about that, I hesitated. There were many reasons.'

She paused. She wished David were here. She wished she'd waited to talk to him about this before she accepted the invitation, before she decided she was going to tell them the things she hadn't last time.

She cleared her throat and began again. 'One of the reasons I hesitated is that it's a crime for me to tell you about what happened in the grand jury room. What happens there is secret.'

'We know from our lawyer, no one can tell what we say in grand jury,' Martin Eng said. 'Only we can tell. Not like trial.'

'Yes, that's true. But it's not just your testimony. It's anything that happened in the grand jury room. It's all secret.'

His wife said, 'We did not invite you to our home in the hope you would break this law. We are happy only to have your interest and your concern. Your friendship. We wish only to express our gratitude for that.'

The words, and the simple and earnest way she said them, softened

Susan's inhibitions. 'I can tell you this much. I never fully believed the police story about you. There were others on the grand jury who felt the same way, that the evidence wasn't convincing.'

She paused – she needed to know more before she went on. 'Have you told your lawyer about my previous visit?'

The Engs looked at each other. 'We did not speak of you,' Martin said. 'We understood it was what you wished.'

'I'm grateful for your discretion,' Susan said. 'Some of what I'm going to tell you now is useful to you only if your lawyer knows about it. So, of course, I expect you to tell her those things. I have to ask you, though, not to tell her how you learned them. She may press you quite hard for an answer.'

'We respect your privacy.'

'Thank you.' Susan was surprised to find that she was nervous. 'I can tell you that to make their case the prosecutors are relying on the heroin and the ledger books the police took from here. About the heroin, many of the grand jurors were bothered by the fact that the police found no fingerprints on the heroin package. This could only happen if someone wiped the package off and put it away without touching it, perhaps by wearing gloves. Some of us on the grand jury could not understand why you would do that in your own home.'

'Wearing gloves?' Meiling sounded amused. 'When do people wear gloves inside in summer?'

'Yes, that's one reason people were bothered by it.' Close enough. 'I don't know if your lawyer knows that particular fact yet, that there were no fingerprints on the heroin package. It might be important to her.'

'We will ask,' Meiling said. 'You are kind to tell us.'

'The detective who arrested you also claimed that Mr Eng resisted him by using martial arts. That's why the grand jurors wanted to ask questions about your practicing martial arts.'

'I see,' Martin said. 'You spoke of him when we met at the Association building. That he has a record of dishonesty.'

'So I've heard. That he bends the rules, and that he has been brutal toward Chinese people. The things I said about him weren't secret grand jury information. As I told you then, your lawyer can call the CVAA to learn more about that.'

'We appreciate your concern for our difficulties,' Meiling said. 'We understand the need to be careful. We will not reveal that we learned secrets from you.'

'Both of us promise you that.' Martin checked his watch. 'I must apologize for my rudeness. I received word this afternoon of an important matter at my Association I must attend to. I agreed to be there in fifteen minutes from now. It is my loss to miss the pleasure of your company. Please, stay, talk with my wife.'

When her husband was gone Meiling came to sit on the couch with Susan. 'Now we are two Chinese ladies gossiping together.'

'This must be so hard for you,' Susan said.

'We live long, we see much sadness, we experience much treachery. Before now, our homes and our businesses and our money have been taken from us.'

'But still, to be brought to court on a false charge . . .'

'When Japanese soldiers come to China, take away house, put people in prison, they do not say you commit this crime or that crime. To be Chinese is enough crime. When Nationalist soldiers come, also no crime necessary. They take property, throw people in prison. For Communists and Red Guards in the Great Proletarian Cultural Revolution, big crime is to own something, to sell something.' The older woman's agitation was clear in the way her command of English had diminished. 'That time – bad, bad crime only to *know* something. My husband suffer in jail because he own books.'

Susan thought about her own privileged, protected existence, the petty prejudices she'd had to endure. 'It's hard for me to imagine what all that must be like. I only wish I thought what they're doing to you now was very different.' Even as she said it, Susan had a moment's doubt: was she going too far, being too trusting? 'Just when you thought you were in a safe place.'

'Never safe. Life teaches that lesson. You asked before is this hard? Yes. Hard is to worry about children. We are here, children are in Hong Kong, sometimes in China. Children get news, mother and father in jail. Want to come here, interrupt important business. We call, say, out on bail, no need to come now.' She looked quizzically at Susan. 'Is that right? Out on bail?'

377

'That's right. How did that happen?'

'Lawyer arrange. We give passports, airplane tickets to judge. Make phone call every day to say yes, here at home.'

'House arrest.'

'No. We can go anywhere in island of Manhattan.'

'Still . . .'

'Now our children are waiting for the trial.' She was speaking more slowly and carefully again. 'We cannot talk to them openly. Telephones cannot be trusted. Many people listen.'

'You think your phone is tapped?'

'Our phone, many phones. We are sad that when our children speak to us we can say so little to them. They speak to our lawyer, but our lawyer can say even less. Also, our children cannot hear from other people, to know what is happening to us. They do not see you come here to say you believe our story. That is hard – to be children in a distant country and know you cannot help your parents.'

Thinking of her own parents, Susan felt a chill. 'I know how that feels.'

Meiling poured tea. 'Yes, it is like what happened to you.'

'Except I only began to worry seriously about them after it was too late.' Susan sipped her tea. 'You remind me a lot of my mother.'

'I am honored to hear you say that.'

'She was an elegant woman, and very intelligent. I'm sorry I didn't know her better.'

'Sometimes it is hard for a daughter to know her mother. Just as it is hard for a mother to know her daughter.'

Susan laughed with recognition. 'Truly.' Then, sadder, 'And even harder to know sons.'

'Sons are different. For a Chinese mother, in my generation, a son is as important as the emperor. In a daughter, a mother can see herself.'

'Yes.' Susan thought of the moment in the restaurant when she had felt that way about Lara, so strongly and immediately. 'People say all the time that parents see themselves in their children. I always took that to mean a kind of vague, general feeling. Now, with my own daughter, I see it so much more clearly. As if she were a new version of me, starting all over again.'

'Your mother the same, too, I think. To see herself in you.'

'I don't know. I didn't know enough then – when she was alive – to have a thought like that, that she might see herself in me the way we're talking about.'

Susan settled back on the couch. She felt comfortable here with this small, precise woman whose deep brown eyes seemed filled with experience. 'Do you think your daughter knows you feel that way?'

'I tell her. Some things people only know if they hear the words.'

'I don't know how my daughter would take it. I'm not sure she would understand.'

'Depends how you say, when you say.'

Talking this way to Meiling Cheung about mothers and daughters, Susan felt disoriented. Even as she was discussing with this near-stranger their common experience of being a mother to a daughter, she knew that she herself was no older than the daughter Meiling was talking about.

The phone rang. Meiling excused herself to answer it and returned quickly. 'Mr Eng says that he will be detained at his office past dinnertime. We planned to eat in a restaurant near here, but he cannot be there. Can I ask you to dine with me in his place?'

'Thank you. I'd be pleased to do that.'

The restaurant Meiling took Susan to was small, and formal for Chinatown; it reminded her of the place where she'd had dinner with Uncle Eight. Crossing the restaurant to a small private banquet room, Susan saw people turn to stare.

'You see,' Meiling noted when they were alone. 'Even in China-town some have learned the American habit of open curiosity. We cannot live the same lives we did before.'

As had happened with Uncle Eight, the waiters brought food without Susan noticing that anyone had ordered it. Over a delicate steamed fish, Meiling brought the conversation back to Susan's parents. 'You said they were on a trip to China, and they did not return? That they were caught in that horrible earthquake in Tianjin, the one they say killed half a million people.'

'That's what we were told, but not until months later.'

'You did not hear for months? How difficult.'

'My brother never believed it. He's convinced they got in some kind

379

of trouble and the Government made up the story to cover up what really happened. It's convenient to have an earthquake that big, he says – it saves a lot of explaining.'

'And you? Do you believe?'

'I don't know. I don't think my parents were political. They went to find the members of the family they had left behind, to visit with them. To see how well they had survived the Cultural Revolution.'

'Such an unpleasant time.'

'Were you there, then? I don't remember from your testimony.'

'We stayed only until we could escape. A short time. Your parents went there afterward?'

'In the spring of seventy-six. They were there during the big demonstration in Tiananmen Square after the death of Zhou Enlai. My brother thinks it has something to do with all that.'

'My husband and I have seen terrible things happen at such times. These things happen to citizens of China. They are more careful about foreigners.'

'Both of my parents were born in China, and they went back as returning citizens. They thought they would have more access to places and people that way than traveling as Americans.'

'Ah.' She clicked her tongue and shook her head. 'But you do not agree with your brother?'

'As I said, I don't know. I wish there was a way to find out.'

'Were they in Beijing at the time of the demonstration?'

'I don't know. I last heard from them in a postcard they sent from Shuntak. It was postmarked before the date of the demonstration, but by the time I got it, the demonstration was long over and so was the earthquake, and they were already dead.'

'So sad.' Meiling Cheung sat with her eyes downcast for a moment. She looked up and said, 'Shuntak. So close to where I was born. I used to go there to visit. I wonder if I met your relatives. Did you tell me your mother's family name?'

'Wong.'

'Ah. Wong. I knew many people called Wong. And people named Chan, too.'

Susan smiled. 'Yes, they're very popular names, aren't they?'

380

Bob Marion, investigator from the Asian Gang Unit came into Mahoney's office with the Chinese waiters his snitch had turned up. The interpreter brought up the rear. She was the second of the two who had translated for Meiling Cheung in the grand jury. Mahoney would have preferred the other one, the one the defense had insisted on, but she'd told him she wasn't comfortable translating Toishanese.

It was too bad, because this interpreter's curt, abbreviated translating style left Mahoney certain he was missing a lot. He wanted all the words, not only the gist, but the other Chinese interpreters the office used weren't available and he couldn't afford to delay interrogating these men.

Despite his request that she be as complete as possible, her translations had the same skeletal quality. This time, though, Mahoney had the feeling that the witnesses weren't being much more complete than the interpreter.

Skinny and nervous, both of the waiters looked over forty and undernourished. They had been recruited to make bank deposits by a man who worked at the same restaurant they did. He was the representative of another man to whom they owed a great deal of money.

Mahoney had learned enough from Mark Brattler to decode that: the intermediary had to be a collection agent for the snakehead who had smuggled them into the country – the unpaid debt could be as high as thirty-five thousand dollars each. Mahoney had to hand it to Marion and his snitch. It wasn't every day you got undocumented aliens to come in and offer testimony.

The deal, the waiters both said, had been simple. They were introduced to a man they later learned was Martin Eng and told they should do errands for him. The errands involved bringing amounts of cash to different banks for deposit. They were taught the English words they needed, though mostly they didn't need to speak at all. Each deposit was around five thousand dollars. Each time they went, two hundred and fifty dollars was paid toward their debt. One had made over a hundred such deposits, the other had made about seventy-five. A few months ago, the errands had stopped.

Did they remember which banks they had gone to? Only some of them, there had been very many. Did they remember anything about the names or the numbers on the deposit slips? Predictably enough, they didn't.

That was all. It was enough. So much for Martin Eng's aversion to banks. So much for there being no visible connection between Martin Eng and drug or money-laundering activities. Mahoney thanked the investigator and checked the clock.

'You can take a break, let them get some tea or whatever. We're due upstairs in the grand jury in fifteen minutes.'

# 16

'Your friend from the grand jury called,' Alice told David when he got home from his stay with Jon Levi.

'Really?' So she hadn't forgotten him completely.

'She sounded disappointed, like she expected you to be here. Then she said she'd call back.'

'Did she?'

'Yesterday and then again today. Kind of on edge, I'd say. Upset, or excited, I don't know.'

'Why didn't you tell me?' It came out harsher than he'd intended.

'Hey, now – back off, buster. The first time, the lady said she'd call back. Then I got that message from you on the machine that you were going to be busy at a conference all day yesterday and on your way back today, so what was the point giving you messages?'

'Okay . . . Sorry I snapped at you.'

'I expect no better.' Mollified.

'Anything else new?'

'Indeed there is, if you truly must know.' She was being theatrical now. 'I heard from the director. He definitely wants me.'

'Terrific!' Much as he thought it was exactly what she and the twins did not need, he couldn't resist her joy. 'That's really great. Congratulations.'

She bowed deeply. 'We thank you.'

'When do you go?'

'Next week. Off to Toronto.'

'That soon?'

'Yep. And the sooner the better, too. We've got to come to rest someplace – the monsters are already late starting school.'

'I'll bet they hate that.'

'It's not so great with their friends busy all the time. They're at a party now, but today was not our best. You know, it's amazing how they make new friends. Their mother's a loner and they're some kind of people magnets. And speaking of new friends, shouldn't you go call Ms Grand Jury?' She gave him a look. 'What's up with her? Do I smell a romance here?'

'She's a forty-plus, upper-crust Chinese lady with two college-age kids, married to a world-famous neurosurgeon.'

'Oh, yeah?' Alice grinned mischievously. 'And which one of those is the disqualifier?'

'Always looking for trouble.' It was not a question he wanted to deal with.

'No, really,' she goaded. 'I didn't hear stupid or nasty on that list. Or unwashed.'

He called Susan; she wasn't home. He took a shower to get the road dust off, then tried Susan again. She still wasn't home.

It bothered him not to be able to get through. Alice wasn't a particularly accurate message-taker, so he couldn't be sure about Susan's agitation, but he found that he was worrying about her.

The twins came home at six. He heard them in the hallway outside the apartment, still full of the day's high spirits. When they crossed the threshold they turned quiet, as if they'd passed through an energy-sucking force field.

'Hey, guys,' he said, trying not to be too artificially cheery.

'Hello, Uncle David,' they chorused.

'Welcome back,' he said to them.

Zack stared at him. Jessie said, 'Oh, right. Welcome back, Uncle David.'

'Brought you something from Boston,' he said. That brightened them a little.

'Look who's here,' Alice said, coming in from the kitchen. 'The mini-tyrants of southern Colorado and West End Avenue.' She mock-bowed to them.

'Oh, Mom,' Jessica said and went off toward the room the twins

384

were reluctantly sharing. Zack followed, without comment.

Alice rolled her eyes. 'Oh, boy.' She started after them. The phone rang. 'Get that, okay? Whoever it is, I'll call back.'

'Even if it's Walter?'

'Especially if it's Walter.'

It was Susan. 'David. I'm so glad you're back. Can we get together?'

'Sure.' He was keeping his questions for later. 'When?'

'How's right now?'

'I was thinking more like tomorrow.'

He heard her take a quick breath to speak and then hold back. 'Something's come up,' she said in a more controlled voice. 'If it's waited till now, I suppose it can wait until tomorrow. But I really want to talk to you about it. I have an important decision to make – *we* do, really, and I'd like at least to get the conversation started. I'll come to you – name a place.'

'Kelly's.' It was the first thing that came into his mind.

She barely hesitated. 'Fine. Kelly's. Twenty minutes. No, make it fifteen. See you at Kelly's in fifteen minutes.' She hung up before he could object.

'I've got to go out,' he told Alice.

'Now?'

'Just for a few minutes.'

'Don't be long, okay? We've got plans to make.'

Dinner-time at Kelly's Shamrock was just getting started when David arrived; a few of the tables were occupied by the early crowd – mostly older people from the neighborhood – and there was a small after-work gathering at the bar.

Kelly greeted him heartily. 'I took that wish-list you made for me to the restaurant-tech show and went around the booths with it. You never saw so many brave men duck for cover. Women, too.'

'I kind of hoped they'd jump to meet the challenge.'

'I'll tell you, if not for your good work on this I'd not have seen it, but those people exist on mystification. It's a right bloody priesthood they've got themselves. Tighter than the blessed Jesuit Brothers who taught me high school.'

'Knowledge is power,' David said. 'And people do love their power.'

'And thanks to David Clark I had power on my side this time. It took me all day tramping around among the exhibits, but in the end I found a man who claims he can do everything on your list.'

'I'm glad it worked out. I was kind of concerned about coming in here.'

'You're always welcome, my friend, even if the new computer sends out mud cake for starters and Parma ham for dessert.' Kelly cocked his head. 'Though in that case it might be smarter to stay away a day or two. What brings you in, this fine evening?'

'I'm meeting a lady.'

'Oh? And might it be a lady I know?'

'It might. We can use some privacy, I think.'

'Can you, now? Would my office suit you?'

David was going to decline but thought better of it. 'If it's not an imposition—'

'Not for a minute.'

'And if we can get a drink back there.'

'I'll serve you myself.' He looked over David's shoulder then winked at him. 'You dog. I believe that's herself just walked in the door.'


'This was a good idea,' Susan said when they were settled on the couch and easy chair in Kelly's office with a mineral water for her and a beer for him.

'It was Kelly's. I said we might need some privacy.' David was trying to keep it businesslike, to get himself past thinking how desirable she was. Had he forgotten, or had he just never let himself see it fully?

As she had at Kelly's grand jury party, she was wearing a white T-shirt and jeans and a broad belt that emphasized her long, narrow waist and the curves of her hips and her full breasts. Her hair was down – thick and dark . . . He made himself look into his beer glass. 'What's happening?'

'I went to see the Engs.'

He looked at her. 'Oh?'

'They invited me to visit them at home. It's very unusual for Chinese people to do that. I called you to come with me but you weren't there, so I went alone.'

'What did they have in mind?'

'They said they wanted to thank me for what I'd done. That they were afraid I'd misunderstood when they told me to stop.'

They could have sent a card, he didn't say.

She said, 'I told them I thought they were innocent and I still wanted to help if I could. And I said you'd been called out of town and you sent your best wishes.'

'Did you say what I thought?'

'No.'

'Okay. Then what?'

'We talked, and then Mr Eng had to leave. I stayed and talked to Meiling.'

'Meiling?'

She drank some water. 'Meiling. Yes. Meiling. We talked for a long time and then we went out to dinner.'

'The two of you.' He wanted to be sure he got the details right; he had the feeling he'd be needing them.

'The two of us. We talked about a lot of things.' She finished the water he'd brought. 'I didn't know I was so thirsty.'

He got up and took her glass. 'I'll be right back.'

'Thanks. Only I think maybe white wine this time.'


'A fine lubricant,' Kelly said when David asked for the wine. 'Better than that fancy water she started on.' He poured a generous glass. 'On the house. Anything for you?'

David shook his head no. 'Thanks.'

'Good luck,' Kelly said after him.


Susan took her wine glass in both hands and raised it – a silent toast. His eyes met hers as he lifted his glass in response.

'They want us to go to Hong Kong,' she said.

'They *what*?'

She laughed. 'I'm not laughing at you,' she said quickly. 'Maybe I'm laughing at me.' She put her glass on the end table between the couch and the easy chair. 'They want us to go to Hong Kong.'

'Just like that.' At least it was a reason for their invitation.

'They want us to talk to their children for them.'

'I guess they don't like the telephone.'

'They think their phones are tapped, so they can't really talk about what's happening. I don't think they even trust pay phones. And they think it will mean something extra to their children if we tell them in person what we saw. More than a letter from their parents.'

'So much for the world-wide electronic village,' David said. 'Though, the truth is, I just made a couple of trips to Boston because being in person is still so much better than all this action-at-a-distance everybody is so hyped on.'

'You see?'

'Okay, we agree on that. I'm not sure it justifies springing for a fast flight halfway around the world.'

'I didn't say we should do that.'

'I must not be hearing right. They want us to go to Hong Kong, isn't that what you said?'

'They're offering to pay for the trip.'

Speechless, he drained his beer glass and took a long breath. 'Now correct me if I'm wrong – you just said that our old friends Marty and Milly want to pay for us to go to Hong Kong to have a chat with their grownup children, to the effect that we – or you, anyway – think their mom and dad might not be guilty of the crimes they're accused of. Is that more or less it?'

'More or less. I got the impression from Meiling that they care very much about their children, all the more because they lost a son and a daughter. They're afraid their children are more worried about all this than is really necessary. They're also very concerned about the image their children have of them. That's why an outsider's view counts so much. They want us to tell them about how close the vote was, and some of the reasons.'

'The holy secrecy of the grand jury aside for a moment, didn't the police take all their money?'

'Their children are going to pay.'

'Does their lawyer know about all this?'

'Sort of.'

He looked a question at her.

'She knows that we're sympathetic grand jurors who have volunteered to help. She doesn't know about the offer to pay for our tickets.'

'And?'

'At the beginning she didn't exactly love the idea that we'd become friendly with them. But once she got used to it she didn't have much more to say. I think she's actually pleased about what I told them – although she doesn't know it all came from me.'

'What you told them,' he echoed. 'What did you tell them?'

'About the fingerprints, for one thing. The no fingerprints.'

'Isn't that one of those holy secrets?'

'I'm sure they'd have found out eventually.'

'Then why did you need to tell them?'

'Why are you arguing with me?'

'Am I? I didn't know I was. I thought I was being direct.'

'It feels like arguing to me.'

'I apologize.'

'Maybe this was a mistake,' she said.

'Maybe what was a mistake?'

'This. Coming here. Maybe there was a better way to talk about this . . . or not talk about it.'

David felt stymied. 'I thought we were doing all right. You just dropped some moderately heavy stuff on me. I ought to get some time to process it, don't you think? Including a certain number of shouts of amazement and some huffing and puffing of various sorts.'

She laughed. 'I suppose so. Now that you put it that way.'

'All right,' he said. 'Now. Do we have a problem here? And if so, what is it?'

'For one thing, we have to decide whether we're going.'

'Right. Well. I think I'll get myself another beer.'


'I've hardly been back to Hong Kong since I left, when I was six,' Susan said when David returned. 'For a long time all I wanted was to be an American. And then I was too busy being a new wife, and I had my children to raise and . . . I went back once and after that I didn't want to go back again.'

'What happened?'

389

'It was almost twenty years ago. After my parents went to China and didn't come out, I went back to try to learn what happened.'

'Yes, I remember you talked about that at the Engs's but didn't you say they died in an earthquake?'

'They just disappeared. Months later, after my brother had been in Hong Kong for weeks without finding out what had happened, I went to take his place. The Chinese Government claimed the whole time they didn't know anything. It was only later that they decided to tell us about the earthquake.'

'That's awful.'

'You can see why I didn't want to go back. Being there was so closely connected to my parents' disappearance.'

'But you want to go back now?'

'Very much. It surprises me, but . . . Hong Kong is still my home town, and I do think about it, more and more as time passes. And this may be my last chance. For my whole lifetime Hong Kong has always been the place that changes faster than anywhere else. It keeps growing and getting more prosperous. Buildings go up and then before you know it they come down so bigger buildings can go up in their place.' The city's dynamism was mirrored in her voice.

'But a different kind of change is coming now,' she said, more subdued. 'For the past hundred and fifty years, Hong Kong has been run by the British. And now, in no time at all, they're going to turn it back over to China. They've been working on the transition for over a decade and some people say most of the changes have happened already, but I think it's going to change a lot more, and not for the better. I'd like to see it one more time before that happens.'

'Then this couldn't be better for you,' he said. 'An all-expense-paid trip back to the place you were born, where you almost haven't been since you were six, just when you want to go.'

'Yes. It's hard not to see it as fate.'

'And all you have to do to earn it is have a chat with some people when you get there.'

He drank some beer, wondering how far to go. And thought, *who do I help, holding back*?

He said, 'If it were my decision I don't know how I'd feel about the money. It's easy for them to say it comes from their kids, but the only money of theirs I know about had heroin powder on it.'

'Yes, I've thought of that.' She seemed to regret having to acknowledge it. 'I've already decided that if I go I'll pay my own way. But I didn't want to tell you that because I want you to come, and I can't ask you to spend thousands of dollars . . .'

'Well, I appreciate the thought, but I'm not about to take any of their money.'

'I understand.' She studied him for a moment. 'Actually, I think it's best if neither of us does.'

He felt a sudden need to get up. He stood and rolled his shoulders, kneaded his neck. 'Excuse me, just trying to get the kinks out.'

She smiled. 'It's making me tense, too.'

'Now look who's being direct.' He smiled back. 'Tell me something. You said they want *us* to go. Why *us*? Why not just you?'

'I think they'd be happy to have as many people as possible tell their children about this. But I was the one who made sure you were included.'

'That's very kind of you, but under the circumstances I think you should consider going without me.'

'I'd really rather not.' She seemed about to say something else, but she stopped herself.

He sat down again, shifting forward to keep from sinking into the softness of the easy chair. 'I was happy to go with you to see the Engs, but this isn't a car-service ride to Chinatown we're talking about . . . What about your husband? Wouldn't your husband want to join you?'

'I never thought to ask him.'

David didn't ask any of the questions that came to mind.

'This has nothing to do with him,' she said. 'And he'd never be able to get away from his obligations at the hospital.'

'Well, you see – there's something your husband and I have in common. We've both got obligations. My obligations right now are to my career and to my sister and her kids. Plus, I have a trip of my own scheduled, with a bunch of friends.'

'You must think I'm very selfish and high-handed.'

'I didn't say that.'

'Some things don't have to be said.'

'Here's what I think,' he said. 'I think I don't understand much

391

about you, or about your life. I know that you've just been going through something very difficult, which you've told me very little about. As for selfish or high-handed, it never crossed my mind. But I have my own plans, and my own problems to deal with, minor as they might seem by comparison.'

'I guess I deserved that,' she said quietly.

'Deserved? I don't . . . I was just telling you how this seems to me.'

'I understand that you have problems, too,' she said. 'I understand that it would be disruptive. But having you come along is important to me. Important enough that I'll be more than pleased to step into the role you don't want to have the Engs play, if that makes a difference.'

He didn't get it at first. 'You . . . oh. No. Thank you, but . . .' He stood up again, walked to the barred window next to Kelly's desk and stared out into the alley behind the restaurant.

'I think we have a misunderstanding here.' He turned to face her. 'I mean, I let you pay for that lunch, you seemed determined to, but when I go places I pay my own way.'

'I didn't mean to offend you,' she said. 'I'm asking you to do me a huge favor. I understand that. It's one thing to give up time and effort, and disrupt your schedule – it's entirely another thing to have to pay for the privilege. I'm the one who benefits.'

'And your husband wouldn't mind your subsidizing some man to travel halfway around the world with you?'

'I'm not sure what you mean to imply by that, but people go on business trips all the time. And it's not his money.'

'Okay. My turn to apologize. But didn't you mention a brother?'

'He won't come, either. After all those weeks in Hong Kong trying to learn what happened to our parents, he swore he would never go back. And I know his wife would hold him to it even if he was tempted to waver.'

'And there's no one else?'

'It's not a question of no one else. I want it to be you. You're the best person I know to bounce ideas and impressions off of. You listen, and you say what you think.'

'Well, thank you. But there's something you should bear in mind about what I think. As I told you after that first conversation we all had here, I was never fully convinced the Engs were wrongly accused.'

'I thought with all your research since then, your opinion might have changed.'

'Granted, I've learned a lot. But I'm still not as convinced as you are they're not guilty of anything. So if I were to go, I'd go skeptical. Which isn't to say I'd go,' he hastened to add.

'I don't know what to say. You argued so persuasively for them in the grand jury. And you helped me so much.'

'All I ever argued for was getting more information. Not everything I heard was persuasive. You can hide a lot behind a colorful story of war and oppression.'

'I suppose,' she said in a tight voice.

'That doesn't mean I'm convinced they're out-and-out liars. And I'm still intrigued by that theory we talked about, that the money might actually belong to the Association's members. I'm just very skeptical where they're concerned.'

'Well, maybe that's a good thing.'

'And you really think it makes sense to go there to talk to their kids?'

'When my parents were in China – who knows, maybe in some kind of trouble – no one came here to help me understand. Not even after they were dead. I have a chance to do that for the Engs.'

He went back and sat down. 'Okay, but still – Hong Kong – that's got to be at least two days just traveling, there and back. And your mission takes – what? – a few hours? So I have to assume you're planning a lot of sightseeing.'

'It's more than that.'

He waited.

'Our old friends Marty and Milly, as you called them, think they can help me find out what my brother and I couldn't learn, all those years ago – the truth about how my parents died.'

'Really?' So her eagerness to go wasn't just about checking out the latest Hong Kong construction, or delivering a reassuring message. 'How can they do that?'

'My parents were originally from the Three Districts. The Engs think they may know people I can talk to in Hong Kong who might be able to get some information for me.'

How convenient for the Engs, that they know such people, he did

393

not say. Instead, he said, 'That's terrific.'

She didn't respond.

'Isn't it?'

'I don't think I can go if it has to be alone.'

'Now I *know* I'm missing something. Isn't learning about your folks reason enough for your brother to break his vow not to go back?'

'He says he knows all he needs to know. For years he's said the Communists killed them for something political.'

'Is that what you think?'

'I don't know what to think.' She paused, obviously upset. 'Will you consider coming?'

It was his turn not to respond.

'At least that – just think about it?' she persisted.

'You must have people there your family knew before they left. And your friends from those days who are grown up now. That pen pal you mentioned.'

'Yes. There are people like that.'

'So you won't be alone.'

'It's not the same.' She picked up the wine glass, put it down without drinking. 'I don't know what I'm going to be hearing about my parents. It would make a big difference to have someone there with me I really trust, to help me see things clearly.'

'I appreciate the compliment.' He said it breezily to avoid having to think about it. *Trust* could be a dangerous word.

'I told you once that I'm not good at charging off on my own into uncharted territory. That's really what this is for me – uncharted, and scary.'

'Scary?'

'It doesn't make a lot of sense, I suppose, but I have this feeling that I shouldn't go by myself. I mean, besides the fact that traveling alone – this kind of traveling – is not something I've ever done, or ever planned to.'

She picked up her wine glass again and this time she drank. 'It's true, I'm not going to *China*, so it won't be quite the same as my parents. But now Hong Kong *is* China, or it almost is.' She grimaced. 'It's like something my brother said – it's not a stable place, and you never know whose toes you're going to step on. And if it *wasn't* the earthquake, there must have been people who didn't want the truth to come out. And if they *still* don't . . . you only have to read the papers to see what they do in China if you poke around where they don't want you to.'

'But it *is* Hong Kong you're going to. And things have been bumpy enough this summer that I'd think Beijing would be on its guard about its relations with the U.S.'

'Maybe . . .' She took another sip of wine. 'I have to admit that I've come to feel very close to Meiling, and to Martin, too. And yet I can't help being a little skeptical of their story, myself. I keep thinking there's more going on with them than we know about. It's not heroin – I truly don't believe they're drug dealers. I don't even think it's just that they're holding money for their Association members. It's something more. I think I'm even more frightened about that than I am because of what happened to my parents. Frightened *for* them, not frightened *of* them.'

'Either way, why go if it frightens you?'

'I don't know if I'll ever have a moment like this again, for so many reasons. Because of what's happening in Hong Kong, but also what's happening in my life. For now, my son is at a stage where there's nothing I can do for him but wait . . . I was just liberated from a big project I was hoping to land, at work . . . and this may be my only chance to learn more about my parents. It's all coming together at once.' She fell silent – looking inward, he thought. He finished his beer and waited.

'How is your son?' he asked when she looked up. 'I called, I don't know if you got the message.'

'I did. I'm sorry, I know I never returned it. Things were . . .' She was silent again, her expression dark. It took her a moment to recover. 'He's getting better.' She tried to smile. 'It was an ordeal for all of us, but I'm hoping we'll be better off for it in the long run. And I think that's part of this, too – I think going through all that taught me something about facing hard choices head on . . .'

She took another moment for reflection, sighed. 'It's true that all this about Hong Kong scares me. But at the same time, it seems so important. I know I have to go through with it if I can. That's why I'm selling you so hard, even though it's uncomfortable for me.'

'Well,' he said. 'I appreciate your trying to make it clearer.' Although he had the feeling there was more, that she was holding something back.

'I made it clearer for me, too. Talking to you always makes things clearer for me.' She looked at her watch. 'You said you had to get back. I'm afraid I've kept you a lot longer than either of us expected.'

She stood, held out her hand. It was as he remembered it, warm and smooth and firm.

'I really do appreciate how patient you've been, and how much time you've spent with me on this.' With the words there was an extra pressure in her handshake.

'No thanks necessary.' He let go reluctantly.

'I do hope you'll consider it,' she said as they left the restaurant, 'even though I know it's a lot to ask.'

The evening had turned cool and damp; there was a cloud of mist in the air. He stood looking at her – moisture glistening in her hair, her deep brown eyes turned on him.

'I promise,' he said. 'I'll consider it.'

But he knew as he heard the words that he did not mean them. He would not consider it. There was nothing to consider. He was going with her.

He would find a way to make it up to Alice and the twins somehow. At the least, he could give Alice money to hire someone who'd look after Zack and Jessica while she was away. It was time to stop hoarding his hummingbird-size nest egg, anyway, relying on it for a false sense of security.

He sensed that he was poised on some unforseen cusp of his life: he could either leap into the unknown or slide back down to where he had been stagnating, where he would continue to stagnate, sustaining himself on illusions of renewal.

So he would follow this woman he did not know to a place he had no reason to visit, on a quest he knew nothing about. There was nothing else he could do.

# III

## *HONG KONG*

# 1

They left New York not long after dawn. Susan had been up almost the whole night before, too agitated to sleep. Though she didn't usually sleep well on airplanes, she quickly discovered that staying awake would be a bigger trick than sleeping.

In Los Angeles they changed to a Hong Kong airline. They had seats in a small business-class compartment upstairs in the jumbo jet's bulbous nose. The cabin attendant gave them cloth bags that held socks with slipper bottoms and an eye mask to make sleeping easier.

'I could have used one of these this morning,' David said. He looked at the entertainment schedule he'd taken from the seatback pocket. 'Three movies.'

'Fifteen hours.' She settled herself in her seat and accepted a glass of orange juice from an attendant.

'I have a bunch of books about Hong Kong, if you're interested,' David offered. 'I don't know – maybe you already know most of this.' He had one that combined Hong Kong history and travel memoirs, an economic study of the Colony since 1950, and a policy pamphlet from the China Society about the effects on the U.S. and Japan of the coming transition of power in Hong Kong.

'That's way past the kind of gossip I get,' she said. 'I ought to take a look, if you won't be reading them.'

'I can't read them all at once.'

My God, she thought, we're going to be together for days and we can't find a way to relax with each other. She wondered, as she had off and on since pushing him to join her, if she wouldn't have been better to let it be.

399

★ ★ ★

Mahoney found an envelope of photographs waiting in his IN box, with a note from Horgan that said, *'More pix from the Southern District.'* Most of them were as meaningless as the first batch had been.

The beautiful Chinese woman was back, he noticed: leaving the Engs's apartment building with Mrs Eng, walking through Chinatown to a nearby restaurant, out of the restaurant again and back to the apartment.

There were a half-dozen pictures in the sequence, all from different angles, and suddenly he knew who she was. Once he made the connection it was hard to see how it had eluded him the first time. He called the paralegal he'd been working with and asked her to chase down the earlier batch of pictures.

An hour later he was looking at photographs showing not one but two of his grand jurors, visiting the defendants their grand jury had recently indicted. What the hell was going on? He put the pictures in his briefcase and went to see Max Straus.

Straus was intrigued. He called Laurie Jordan and suggested she draw up a subpoena for the grand jury warden.

Jordan delivered the grand jury contact list to Mahoney before the day was over.

'That was quick,' he said.

'We aim to please.' In case he had missed the double meaning, she leaned over his desk to put the list of names and phone numbers in front of him.

To hell with playing dumb, Mahoney thought, and let himself enjoy the view. He looked up, not quickly but soon enough to be sure to catch her catching him, so there would be no doubt. She smiled.

'I also learned that on their last day one of the grand jurors brought a cake shaped exactly like the grand jury room. And there was a party that night at a bar called the Shamrock on the Upper West Side. Owned by one of the grand jurors.'

'You didn't get that with a subpoena.' He remembered now that there'd been a party – the warden had passed along an invitation.

'Charm,' she said, perching on his desk, her skirt hiked up on her thigh.

400

'Hey,' he protested. 'People are going to talk.'

'I hope so. Then they won't wonder why we're seeing so much of each other.'

'Oh.' The disappointment in his voice was not entirely a game. 'And I thought you cared.' He grabbed the grand jury list and swiveled his chair to face his computer so he could pull up the reverse phone directory.

'The Chinese woman was in Number Nineteen,' she told him. 'The beard was in Number Eleven.'

As he'd remembered. He ran their phone numbers. David Clark – same number for home and business, was listed on the Upper West Side. Susan Linwood – odd name for a Chinese woman – showed up as Linwood Associates, in an office building on Park Avenue in the fifties. Her home number was unlisted – they would have to subpoena the phone company for that. For all the unlisted Manhattan Linwoods, to be safe – in case Susan Linwood had no phone in that name.

He offered Laurie Jordan the list. 'You want to see if the lady's in?'

'Sure.' She reached for the phone, this time making a comedy of putting a hand modestly over her blouse.

She dialed. 'Is Ms Linwood there, please? My name is Laurie, she doesn't know me but I was referred by a friend of hers from college.' She listened. 'Oh, okay, I see. Do you know where, and when she'll be back?' Listened again. 'No, that's okay, I'll call back.'

'Out of town,' she told Mahoney. 'Wouldn't say where. Won't be back for at least a week.'

'Shit,' he said with feeling. He tried David Clark and got an answering machine, hung up on it.

'Zero for two. Maybe I'll try to find the Shamrock, see what the bartender can tell me.'

'You want some company?'

He thought about it. 'I'll probably learn more alone.'

'I could go off to the loo at the right moment.'

'Next time.'

'Killjoy.' She leaned close and kissed his cheek. 'See ya.'

Susan tried to sleep as much as she could at the beginning of the flight from Los Angeles, the best approximation to Hong Kong's night. She made herself get up when she calculated morning was well-established in Hong Kong, though it was late evening in New York, where she had started her day.

The cabin was dark and everyone else was asleep, including David. She tried to read his books, had trouble concentrating. As the Hong Kong day progressed in tandem with New York's night, she forced herself to stay awake. By the time David woke up she was falling asleep, in spite of herself.

Mahoney stood outside the restaurant and bar: KELLY'S SHAMROCK, according to the neon sign. It looked like a nice enough place.

He'd hoped to let his grand juror discover him; after half a slow beer, he was thinking he should give up and ask for the owner, if only to be sure he was actually on the premises. While Mahoney pondered, the man sitting next to him got up and a woman with curly chestnut hair took the vacant stool.

'Hi,' she said. 'You're a new face.'

He smiled. 'I was in the neighborhood and I got thirsty.' She had blue eyes and a narrow nose and mouth in a face a police artist might call heart-shaped. Freckles.

'I'm Paula.'

'Dan.'

She held out her hand to shake. 'You're a big one, aren't you? Play ball?'

'A little.' This wasn't what he'd come here for, but it would give him some protective coloration if the owner did show up.

They were ready for refills and Mahoney was thinking it was time to leave – though Paula was fun, and sexy, if no match for Laurie Jordan – when a hearty voice with a touch of brogue said, 'Well, now, if it isn't my old friend Mr Mahoney.'

Mahoney turned: there behind the bar was grand juror Number Nine.

'I'm Jimmy Kelly.' The former grand juror held out a big, square hand. 'Glad you came by.'

'I am, too. Nice place you have here.'

'Thank you. I guess you met Paula.' To her, he said, 'Better watch what you admit to. You're sitting next to one tough prosecutor.'

She looked at him. 'No. Really?'

'I'm afraid so.'

'Puts on a fine show, too.' And to Mahoney, 'That was a tough crowd you had, made it a real squeaker, if that's not revealing more than I ought to.'

'I don't think that much is a felony. But I will say, I thought your grand jury was a smart group. Not every grand jury is.'

'A good group, indeed,' Kelly affirmed. 'Even some I thought were kind of a pain turned out all right.'

'They certainly made me work hard.'

'Didn't they, though?'

'You see any of them since?'

'Some of them come in now and again,' Kelly seemed pleased to say.

'I'm sorry I had to miss that party.'

'We had a good time. Odd way to make friends, don't you think – serving on a grand jury?' Kelly was warming to the subject. 'I had one of them in here helping me redesign my computer system.' He grinned. 'One of them as gave you a hard time, I might say – the fellow with the beard. Number Eleven, I think he was.'

'You know, it's funny you should mention that,' Mahoney said. 'I could use a guy who knows something about computers.'

'I don't think he does much with home computers. He's kind of high-powered.'

'This is for work,' Mahoney improvised. 'We have a regular information-systems department, but they're always too busy, and they hate to work on anything they didn't think up themselves.'

'Well, anyway, he's out of town.'

'Too bad. For long?'

'I don't know. He's gone clear out of the country.' Kelly winked. 'In fact, talking of my fellow grand jurors as we are—' With a glance at Paula, he stopped abruptly. 'Listen to me, will you? I ought to shut my big mouth and go tend to my other customers, leave you two in peace.'

He refilled their glasses. 'You enjoy yourselves. If you need a refill tell John Moore – that's the bartender – tell John Moore that Jimmy says your tab is on the house tonight.'

★  ★  ★

403

Susan and David landed just after seven in the evening, Hong Kong time. The plane's glide-path took them below rooftop level past solid rows of apartment buildings that seemed within reach of the wings. It was almost precisely twenty-four hours after they had left New York, thirty-six hours on the clock. By the time they collected their luggage and went through passport control it was close to eight, and dark.

David wheeled the cart with their bags on it through sliding glass doors into the stifling Hong Kong evening. A row of men and boys and young women held wooden or paper plaques bearing the names of hotels. The sign Susan had told him to look for was borne by a tall man in a dark blazer. He checked for their names on a clipboard and when he found them assumed an instant air of refined deference.

'Oh, yes, Mrs Linwood, Mr Clark.' He had a crisply British accent. 'Welcome to Hong Kong. I'll have a car for you at once.'

The car was driven by a man in livery wearing white gloves; its interior was icily cool. As they idled in the dense airport traffic the chauffeur handed them a small silver tray holding sealed bags with damp, citrusy washcloths.

'Not bad,' David said. 'Does everybody rate this treatment or did somebody lay it on for us?'

'As a matter of fact, *I* did,' Susan said.

'How'd you manage that?'

'It's kind of professional courtesy,' she said. 'I have a friend who works for the company that handles the hotel's PR in New York. It isn't quite their high season, so we're getting a touch of V.I.P. treatment. And down the line, I'll try to find a way to return the favor.'

'Very nice,' he said. 'One hand washes the other.'

'Minor, by Chinese standards.'

The car took them along a freeway past massed high-rise apartment houses, a glittering skyline of thin towers.

'Public housing,' the driver said.

David whistled. 'Looks like fairyland.'

'Different in daytime,' the driver said.

They had a glimpse of the harbor and Hong Kong Island's skyline before they went through a tunnel. They emerged on a road that ran along the water past some of the fantastically lit skyscrapers they had seen from the other side; then they turned toward what seemed a less-populated part of downtown. They pulled into a taxi queue in front of a medium-size, squarish building.

While bellhops dealt with their bags, a man in a cutaway coat minimized the registration formalities and escorted them through the black marble lobby to the elevators. He showed them to their rooms, which were in the back of the building, two doors apart.

Susan took a shower and lay down on her bed, trying to let the vibrations of travel drain away. After an hour she dressed and went downstairs to meet David for a light supper in the coffee shop.

'It's nice to be here,' she said. 'I was afraid of the memories.' In response to his polite incomprehension, she added, 'This is where I stayed when I came to see about my parents. It was only for a few days, and a lot of the décor was different, but it was the same hotel. Have you been out on your balcony?'

'Yes.'

'Well, when I was here last the building right across the street was there, but not any of the other tall buildings. If you looked to the left you could see the hills, with a few tallish buildings off in the distance.'

'And now it's solid tall buildings. In every direction.'

'And I don't remember *any* of what we saw on the way in. The public housing is all new, and all those skyscrapers along the harbor. It's disorienting. I think it must be much worse than for someone who comes back to New York after twenty years.'

In the morning they met in the coffee shop again. The bright light of day made the room's slightly incongruous combination of casual and formal more apparent, Susan thought, or else she was just more awake.

'How'd you sleep?' David asked her. They were seated side by side on a love seat that served for a banquette.

'Better than I expected. I almost feel normal.'

'Could be your strategy worked, then. I was up more than I slept.'

Precisely on time, a hostess led a woman to their table. She was small and round-faced, with faint tracks of acne scars on her cheeks. Like her father's, her head was large for her body, her pale skin drawn tight.

405

There was intelligence and humor in her eyes.

'Hello,' she said, her hand extended assertively. 'I'm June Eng. You must be Susan.' Her accent blended American with a faint flavor of something else – not identifiably British or Chinese. She shook Susan's hand with an insistent warmth. Susan liked her at once.

Susan introduced David and signaled a waiter. Susan and David ordered breakfast; June Eng demurred. 'I'll just have coffee. I had my breakfast ages ago. But please don't let that stop you.

'Thank you so much for coming all this way,' she went on, 'My parents are very old-fashioned when it comes to their children, especially because they lost two.'

'Yes,' Susan said. 'That's so sad.'

'It happened to a lot of people in China. It's almost the national story. There was so much upheaval in that generation. A long civil war, the war with Japan, and then all the disruptions under Mao. Much grief. But here we are, on the verge of a brave new world, as they say.'

'New, certainly,' Susan said. 'I left Hong Kong when I was six, and I've only been back once, for a few days about twenty years ago. Even from what we saw on the way in from the airport, it's changed enormously.'

'Yes, it's amazing for us, and we come regularly. But to see change you have to see China itself. Modern cities where ten years ago there were only small, old villages. From the border to Guangzhou there's a toll highway, now, just like in the U.S.'

'I'd love to see it. I don't know if we'll have time. But we should tell you about your parents.'

'Yes. I want to hear. But you mustn't tell me everything, you'll only have to repeat yourself when you see my brother. The crucial thing is that they're all right. It's so hard to know the truth about that from what they say.'

'They seem fine,' Susan said. 'They look strong and healthy and seem to be in good spirits. I hope I'm as active and alert at their age.'

'You're very kind to say so.'

'Of course,' David said, 'we can't tell you how they compare to how they were before this ordeal started. The first time we saw them, they'd already been in jail for several days.'

'But they tell us they are no longer in jail.'

406

'No, they're not,' Susan said. 'And they look noticeably better since they've been out.'

'My father's been in jail before, you know. In China, for years. For political re-education.'

'It's so hard to accept,' Susan said. 'That people who went back to China to help build the country could be put in jail only a few years later because of something political they'd done or said years and years before.'

'China has a long memory. How was your trip?'

'It was comfortable, thank you.'

'And the hotel?'

'It's very nice.'

'Susan has some friends here,' David said. 'They're treating us extra well.'

June Eng looked at her. 'Really? That's a bonus, then. It always helps to know somebody.'

'Yes,' Susan said. Unsure whether to play up the connection or minimize it, she left it at that.

'My real concern this morning was to greet you and make sure that you were comfortable,' June Eng said. 'Since that doesn't seem to be a problem, I'll let you have your breakfast and the rest of your day. I hope you can join my brother and me for dinner. We thought it would be better if you had the day to recover from your trip.'

'That's very considerate,' Susan said. 'But we shouldn't keep you waiting for news of your parents.'

'You've given me the most important news, that you have seen them and they seem healthy and not unduly distressed.'

'Oh, and there's one other thing,' Susan said. She got her purse from the couch between her and David and took out the small, gift-wrapped package Meiling Eng had asked her to deliver. 'From your mother.'

'Oh. Thank you.' June Eng seemed pleased, if not particularly surprised.

'A spoken letter, your mother called it.'

'Yes, they do that now and then. It's not the same as having them here, but it's so much better than reading a letter, and they don't trust the telephone. Thank you, for me and for my brother.'

★ ★ ★

'What was that?' David asked when June Eng had left.

'What was what?'

'What you gave to June Eng.' It didn't help that she was playing innocent.

'Oh. It was nothing. A cassette tape.'

'From her parents.'

'Yes, from her parents. What's the matter? Why are you taking that tone?'

'Am I? Maybe because I'm angry.'

'What right do you have to be angry with me?'

'You brought something from the U.S. to give to June Eng. You didn't tell me about it.'

'It didn't seem important.'

'You act as a courier for people you know may be distributing heroin, and you make me your accomplice without so much as a by-your-leave – and that *didn't seem important*?'

'David, I honestly don't see anything wrong. It's a cassette tape, that's all. But I'm not going to talk to you about it if you keep up with that accusatory tone.'

He stared at her in silence. Couldn't she see the danger in what she'd done? But he was not going to convince her of that unless she was willing to listen to him.

'Okay, maybe I should slow down,' he conceded. 'It's just that you took me by surprise. Let's go somewhere a little more private and we can talk about it.'

'I want to get out and see the city. We can talk on the way.'

There was a harbor-ferry terminal just across the road from the hotel. From there the green-and white ferries crossed the harbor to Kowloon, ten minutes away on the tip of the peninsula that made up the bulk of the territory collectively called Hong Kong. The day was hazy, the sun bright, and already the heat was oppressive.

On the way out, they bought first-class passage for the Hong Kong equivalent of about a quarter, American, and boarded the enclosed upper deck. Most of their fellow passengers had the look of tourists; they crowded close to the windows at the bow end. David pointed to a

408

long bench at the aft of the enclosed part of the deck. Reluctantly, Susan joined him there.

As the ferry maneuvered its way out past the pier, David watched Susan. She was looking eagerly out the spray-dashed window, captivated by some mix of the familiar and the new.

He supposed it was an interesting view – busy harbor and teeming shores – but he couldn't, for the moment, bring himself to care. He realized that part of his anger stemmed from a kind of retrospective fear: How certain was she that it was a real audio tape? Even if it was, he had no doubt that plastic explosives could be shaped into an audio-cassette shell . . .

But that was going too far – they were alive, and what sense would it have made to use them as patsies for a terrorist attack? Whatever the Engs were up to, that wasn't it. Still, there were other things the cassette could be that were not as innocent as she thought, and suppose they had been caught . . .

'Are you going to tell me about it?' he asked her.

She turned from the window to face him.

'They told me they wanted to let their children know about their legal strategy, and they were afraid their phone lines were tapped by the police. And they had personal things to say, too, that they wouldn't want the police to overhear. They're private people – I can understand that. And this way they could add a few words introducing you and me more completely, without having everybody in the universe know that a couple of grand jurors are consorting with them.'

David looked past her, out at the harbor and the swiftly receding skyscrapers on the Hong Kong side.

'Did they play it for you?' he asked.

'No, I . . . They offered, but I said they didn't have to. I didn't think it would be polite to say yes.'

'Did you listen to it yourself when you got home?'

'No . . .' Again she hesitated over her explanation. 'It's private, David. I wouldn't read their mail, so why would I listen to the cassette? Even assuming I could understand it.'

He didn't know what to say. He had to believe she was sincere – that a combination of whatever faith in the Engs she had talked herself into, and whatever strain she was under about her son, and whatever apprehensions she had about her parents' true fate had combined to make her uncritically accepting.

'I don't understand what's wrong,' she said. 'What could be on the tape that's so bad?'

'I don't know,' he answered. 'That's the problem. Magnetic tape is a classic storage medium for computers. A tape like that could hold a huge amount of information that only a computer could read. Far more than in those ledgers we saw in the grand jury.'

He stopped talking while some Chinese children ran past them laughing and shouting, playing a game indecipherable to adult, Western eyes. They ran back past in the other direction, shouting louder.

'The trouble is,' he resumed, 'we don't know anything about these people. If they *are* distributing heroin, that tape could be a record of everything they've done, a catalog of all their contacts, and a blueprint for how to carry on the business after they're out of circulation.'

'They're not heroin distributors.'

'I hope you're right. But we still don't know who these people really are or what they really do. I hope they are what they say they are and no more, and I suppose they could be, but so far I don't have any good reason to believe it. And I don't believe that tape is just a way to send the very best.'

Susan was silent, considering what he'd said.

'Could the tape have all that computer data on it, with room left over for a regular recording?' she asked in a more subdued tone.

'Depending on how they did it. The data might show up as noise, like a kind of wobbly humming sound—'

'Then it wouldn't have helped for me to listen to it.'

It might have helped if I'd been able to try, he didn't say. 'I just wish you'd told me.'

She smiled ruefully. 'I do, too, now. I'm sorry.'

The ferry bumped up against the wooden pilings of the pier. 'This is it – Kowloon,' she said.

'What do you want to do next?' he asked as they walked up the steep gangway with the rest of the crowd from the ferry.

'Turn around and go back. This ferry ride is one of my favorite things in Hong Kong, and I barely got to look at the Hong Kong-side

410

skyline on the way here. I want to study it. I want to revel in it. It's amazing, isn't it?'

'Yes, it is. I don't have anything to compare it to, in terms of what it used to be like, but it's amazing enough seeing it for the first time.'

They turned around at the terminal end of the gangway and fed coins into the turnstiles, but by the time they were at the entrance gate it was closing.

'We can wait for the next one,' she said.

They went to stand at the back of the waiting area, away from the gate and the benches along the walls where people congregated.

'When you and I were talking at Kelly's,' David said, 'and you were convincing me to come here with you, did you know about the cassette then?'

'No.' She put her hand on his arm. 'David, I do see why you're upset, and I understand. I should have told you . . . But I honestly don't think it's what you're worried it might be. It's just a more intimate way to send a letter. A lot of people do it.'

'I hope you're right,' he said.

They traveled second-class on the way back, standing by the rail of the open lower deck, where the harbor's choppy gray water was palpably close and David had a sense of being immersed in the traffic of motor junks, police launches, water taxis, and pleasure craft.

Susan leaned on the rail, rapt in the vista of the approaching island.

David saw a shoreline from which skyscrapers seemed to grow out of the water like cattails at the edge of a pond. Behind them rose steep green hills, and on the flanks of the hills were row on row of towers. Some, especially the ones higher on the hillside, were unremarkable except for how tall and thin they were. Closer to the shore, all manner of architectural whimsy seemed to be at work. Reflective glass was common, in a spectrum of colors, many of them metallic. The buildings were angular or cylindrical or a combination of both, with pointed roofs or slanted ones as counterpoint to the more usual squared-off tops.

'I just don't believe this,' Susan said. 'Most of those buildings look as if they went up last year, or last week. They're immense, and so many and so close together. How do they do that?'

'Excuse me, is this the Susan Linwood who lives on Park Avenue, in Manhattan?'

'It's not the same. Some of those buildings are built right on the mountainside. Or right on the water. And they're still building, everywhere. Look at it. Dredges in the harbor, landfill over there.'

She was so captivated she insisted on taking the ride all over again. David, his shirt already stuck to his body with perspiration, agreed. The third time, he said, 'Enjoy yourself. I'm going back to the hotel to dry off and take a nap.'

She wasn't ready for him to go. She felt she had let him down somehow, about the tape. He was right, she couldn't be sure it was innocent, yet it was vital to her to think it was.

'We should make some plans,' she said. 'I took your advice and called my friend Sunny. I'm having tea with her this afternoon. Would you want to join us?'

'Sure. I've got a call to make myself – a possible appointment. I don't even know if he can see me today, but I'm sure I'll be free by tea-time. That's four?'

'Four is fine.' She was intrigued by his news, intrigued and something else: annoyed or disappointed that she wasn't his only reason to be in Hong Kong. 'You didn't tell me you knew people here.'

'I don't. I got in touch with someone who posts jobs that sound sort of interesting.'

'Are you thinking of taking a job here?'

'I was curious. This guy runs computer operations for something called the Royal Hong Kong Racecourse Association, and his internet address is care of Hong Kong Institute of Technology. Seemed like an interesting combination – race horses and student engineers.'

'The Racecourse Association? I think that's the serious big time, here.'

'Is it? All I've seen about it so far is that it does a phenomenal volume of betting. Something amazing like a billion American dollars from seventy days of racing.'

'Well, this is Hong Kong, after all. Money is power, here. We can ask Sunny about it this afternoon.'

# 2

Sunny Wong was taller than June Eng and shorter than Susan. She had very large brown eyes set wide on either side of a petite, symmetrical nose. She was wearing a tailored jumpsuit – very expensive, David thought – and carrying a large, soft-leather shoulderbag; heavy gold bracelets weighed down both of her wrists.

She and Susan hugged. 'I'm so glad you came,' Sunny said. 'After the last time, I never thought I'd see you here again.'

'I didn't think so either. Let me introduce David Clark.'

'Hi.' Sunny shook his hand. 'Susan only told me a little about why you came. I think it sounds crazy, but I'm glad it got her here, anyway.' She spoke rapid-fire English with enormous enthusiasm and only a hint of accent. 'I hope you'll excuse us if we trade some gossip about people you don't know.'

'I don't really know most of them either,' Susan laughed. 'Except what I hear from Sunny.'

'Seven of us started out as great friends in nursery school,' Sunny told David. 'Except for Susan, we all went through at least grade school together. Five of us stayed in Hong Kong, or else left and came back, the way I did, and we're still great friends. When Susan left, all those years ago, I made her promise to write or I would put a curse on her.'

'And by the time I figured out I didn't believe in curses I was too hooked on Sunny's letters to stop.'

'It's her prurient curiosity. I keep Susan posted on everybody's sordid doings.'

Listening with half an ear to Sunny's stories about husbands and children and shopping trips to Paris and Rome, David watched the

413

traffic of American businessmen, rich Chinese ladies and wealthy tourists who had come to enjoy a leisurely tea and do business, or gossip about men and children and shopping, or whatever else they were here to do. He thought about his first impression of Susan – wealthy and forbidding. Most of the women here were considerably more polished and done up than he had ever seen her.

A waiter stopped to see if they needed anything. Sunny asked for another pot of water for their tea, which had been served in what David supposed was the traditional British manner. This didn't seem the kind of place where people would be tapping their fingers on the table in thanks.

'How is everybody feeling about the transition?' Susan asked her friend. She turned to David. 'You might find this more interesting than ruined marriages and precocious children.'

'Ah, the transition.' Sunny was slightly subdued now. 'Everyone is pretending to carry on as if it were nothing. But there's a tension in the air and everyone is just the slightest bit frantic.' To David she said, 'You know that the British are leaving – after ruling here for a hundred and fifty years they're giving Hong Kong back to China?'

'So Susan told me. And I've read a little about it.'

'Well, the question of the hour is this: Hong Kong is one of the most capitalist places on earth, and it's about to be taken over by the world's last major totalitarian Communist power. You must admit, that doesn't announce itself as a comfortable combination.'

'Are a lot of people leaving?'

Sunny turned to Susan. 'You friend's a quick study.'

'He's very direct,' Susan said, with a small smile for David.

'People are preparing to leave,' Sunny told him. 'Or reassuring themselves that they *can* leave. The problem is, we've all been living here as British colonial subjects, with no citizenship or right of residence in Britain. When the transition comes we'll be Hong Kong residents, period. Citizens of the Hong Kong Special Administrative Zone. Except for the people who already have foreign passports.'

'Is that common, to have a foreign passport?' he asked.

'I've got a Canadian passport. So does my husband. Our son was born there, so he's Canadian by birth. People make all kinds of arrangements. If you have the money to invest in a new business,

414

you can get permanent resident status, and then a passport, in a lot of places. Including the U.S. But it takes hundreds of thousands of U.S. dollars – more in the U.S. than in Canada or Australia. And in the U.S. it's not enough to invest all that money in some new business. You have to create employment there for a certain number of U.S. residents.'

'Citizenship for sale.'

'And why not? If a country is going to have immigrants, shouldn't they be people who are bringing in capital and creating jobs?'

'Do you think all the Hong Kong people with foreign passports are going to leave?' David asked.

'Never mind *all* the Hong Kong people,' Susan interjected. 'What about you?'

'Well, because we have somewhere to go if we leave, we also have the luxury of being able to stay here until there's clear reason to go.' Sunny sipped her tea. David had the feeling she was deciding how much more to say.

'It could be that the people who claim that nothing will change are right, because Hong Kong's prosperity is too important for China to fool with it. I mean, obviously some things will change. Some already have. Journalists, for instance – there's a lot of self-censorship going on, already. Outspoken people are being fired. I'm glad I don't have to be a reporter. But the big things may not change. In the meantime, there's nowhere in the world where I can make as much money as I can make here. So I'm staying as long as I can.'

'Wouldn't everybody want to do that?' David asked her.

'There are a lot of people here who ran away from China after the Communists took over at the end of the civil war,' she said. 'Some of them are people who were connected with the Nationalists but didn't go with them to Taiwan. Some of them had nothing to do with the Nationalists but they opposed the Communists, or the Communists made them flee for one reason or another.' She stopped to spread jam on a piece of scone. Unobtrusively, she glanced around before she began to speak again. 'Many of them had already suffered badly under the Communists before they left.

'Most of these people are no longer young, but in many cases they have small businesses, and families who have grown up here. They're prosperous, or comfortable, but they don't have enough money to buy residence in some other country. These are the people who are most frightened, I think – because they know first-hand what the Communists can do, and leaving here is difficult for them. They're frightened and they're not visible. I couldn't guess how many there are.'

'I knew there was a lot of scare talk after Beijing crushed the democracy movement in Tiananmen Square,' Susan said. 'But I thought that now everyone was acting as if it never happened.'

'When I say frightened I don't mean they're necessarily frightened of what will happen tomorrow or the next day,' Sunny amended. 'Though as time passes even present times have been looking gloomier. But these are people who have learned to take the long view. They've seen policies come and go in China, velvet gloves replaced by mailed fists. They remember the period of One Hundred Flowers, when everyone was encouraged to be critical of the Government and then the leaders turned around and purged all the people who had accepted their assurances that to speak out was patriotic. They remember the Great Leap Forward that was supposed to bring China into the modern world but instead killed twenty or thirty million from famine, and they remember the Great Proletarian Cultural Revolution . . . These people worry that things may start well here, under China, but that someday – maybe someday soon – the central Government will decide that Hong Kong needs a lesson in humility.'

'Could that happen?' Susan asked.

'There have already been too many signs that Beijing is uncomfortable with the idea of Hong Kong as the financial center of China, and that they're troubled by Hong Kong's pride in its own economic power, and frightened by its political system.'

'Haven't they made promises?' David asked. 'That they won't interfere?'

'One country, two systems,' Sunny said. 'That's the phrase they use. We're supposed to think it means that our system of free-market capitalism and individual freedom in Hong Kong will co-exist with their system of corrupt, Communist-run capitalism and repression on the mainland. More likely, the *real* two systems will mean that foreigners and the richest Chinese capitalists in Hong Kong will enjoy

416

relative freedom and business as usual, and the vast mass of Chinese Hong Kong people will be treated to mainland-style repression. Especially those politicians and activists whose words might reach receptive ears on the mainland.'

'And where do *you* fit?' Susan asked.

'That's what's scary. We'd be in the middle somewhere. If it happened gradually we might not know where we really fit until it was too late . . . It's so hard to know what will last and what won't. Except the Hong Kong Bank and the RA – they're here to stay.'

'David and I were just talking about the Racecourse Association,' Susan said, 'I have this vague memory that it's a major factor in the life of the Colony.'

'Oh yes,' Sunny said. 'There used to be a saying: "Hong Kong is run by the RA, the Hong Kong Bank and the Government, in that order." '

'The *Racecourse* Association?' David asked.

'Truly. We Chinese gamble a lot, and horse racing is number one here. The RA dominates that part of life, and it gets very rich doing it. And from the beginning they decided they ought to give some of it back to the community, so they're involved in all kinds of charity. And they're good at organizing things, so they're called on to run big, complex projects.'

'Do you know about anything they do that involves computers – besides calculate odds?'

'You'd probably learn more about that from them. Or from anyone but me.'

She reached into her shoulder bag and took out a gray box that looked midway between a computerized address book and one of the handheld computers called personal data assistants.

'One thing they do is this.' She handed it to David. 'It's for betting. It gives up-to-the-second odds on every race and every kind of bet, including the crazy multiple ones. Plus you can actually place your bets with it, and move money in and out of your bank account to cover them. It hooks up straight to the RA's main computers.'

David turned it over in his hands, examined the membrane control keys and the multi-line screen.

'This is an old one,' Sunny told him. 'You have to plug it into a phone jack when you're ready to transmit. The new ones are like cellular phones.'

He handed it back to her.

'They have automated betting machines all over, too, just like bank teller machines. And they funded and built the technical university, and help run it. I'm sure they must use lots of computers there.'

A warbling noise came from the vicinity of Sunny's shoulder bag. 'Speaking of cellular phones . . .' She reached in and came up with one.

*'Wei?'* she said into it, and listened. Then, *'Hai?'* and *'Hai,'* and, sharply, *'Hai.'* She said a few sentences in Cantonese and hung up.

'I'm sorry,' she said, gathering herself. 'My son isn't feeling well so I have to go now and pick him up.'

'Nothing serious?' Susan asked.

'No, no. He'll be fine. Listen, I want to see you some more, and Bunny wants to see you. We'll have dinner before you leave.'

'I hope we'll have time.'

'We'll keep in touch. Our schedule is easy this week.'


'Sunny and Bunny?' David asked.

'I know. It's too precious, but that's how they are. It's weird, calling him Bunny, because he's a major banker, and kind of predatory, I think. But he can be the sweetest man with Sunny and their kids.'

'You know him?'

'They stop to see me when they're in New York, and once I went to Canada to spend some time with them.'


Susan suggested that in the time before dinner they take the tram up the face of the mountains. As the cable car purred smoothly up the mountain David marveled at the apartment blocks they were passing – built on a hillside too steep for anything but a cable car. The cable car's angle of climb was so extreme the slender towers along the tramway looked tilted. 'Are these all new, do you think?'

'Most of them.'

'They look so weathered.' Except for the ones still under construction, the buildings – white and gray and a variety of pastels – were streaked with grime and rust. 'Some of them look like they're crumbling already.'

'I think the climate has something to do with it,' she said. 'And I have the feeling they don't always build for longevity.'

Haze filtered the view from Victoria Peak. They started along the paved footpath that circled the summit.

'Sunny doesn't make Hong Kong's future sound too good,' David said.

'I think she exaggerates for effect. She's always been very dramatic.'

'Dynamic, for sure. I don't think I know anybody who talks that fast.'

'Pointless enthusiasm,' Susan said. 'That's what we call it at work. It's an occupational hazard of people in our business. After a while it infects your personal life, too.'

'Is she in your business?'

'Oh, yes, didn't I say? Pure coincidence.'

They paused at a break in the trees to look at the view. 'Okay,' she said. 'I've had enough. It's too hot for this. Too humid.'

To cool off, they stopped for a soft drink in the air-conditioned restaurant overlooking the harbor, tiny in the distance below, then took the tram back down.

Susan was in the hotel lobby at ten to eight, intent on being prompt for dinner. By the time David joined her she was edgy with impatience: she had made it clear to him that punctuality was a Chinese imperative.

Precisely at eight, a car pulled into the taxi queue at the hotel entrance with June Eng at the wheel. In the passenger seat next to her was a heavyset man with thinning black hair slicked back over his head. Oversize tortoise-shell eyeglasses accentuated the roundness of his face.

'This is my brother Peter,' June Eng said. 'Susan Chan and David Clark.'

'I hope you don't mind,' June Eng said when they had been seated at the restaurant, cavernous and elaborately decorated in the style of a Chinese empire Susan could not identify. 'We've asked someone to join us. He's a good friend of the family. He'll arrive shortly.'

While they waited June and Peter Eng asked polite questions about how Susan and David were enjoying Hong Kong. They made polite answers.

Susan did not find Peter as engaging as she had June, and there was an air of incompleteness hovering over the table that made the conversation seem particularly stilted. She wondered who the friend was and if he had anything to do with David's suspicion that there was more going on here than met the eye.

As their waiter was asking if they'd like another round of drinks a captain came to the table escorting a thickly-built man of medium height. He had dense, coarse black hair and a square face, deeply lined. Susan thought he might be in his late fifties. The waiter withdrew and Peter Eng rose to introduce the newcomer.

'This is Chan Kwok-Wing,' he said, 'an old friend of our family. David Clark and Susan Chan.'

'Ah,' Chan said to Susan, 'it appears we share our family name. Welcome to Hong Kong. I am pleased that you both have consented to let me join you.'

'We were about to hear how Mother and Father are doing, Uncle Wing,' Peter Eng said. Susan heard deference in his tone. 'Mr Clark and Ms Chan were among the people who judged the evidence against our parents.' He switched to Cantonese.

'He is explaining about what a grand jury is,' June Eng told them.

'Ah. I see,' Chan Kwok-Wing said. 'I do not think we have such a process in China.'

'Are you from China?' Susan asked.

Chan seemed surprised by the question. 'We are *all* from China, is that not so? Wherever we reside.' He bowed slightly in David's direction. 'My apology to Mr Clark.'

Susan decided not to press it. 'Is there anything you particularly want to hear about?'

'If you could tell us about the grand jury, that would be most appreciated,' June Eng said.

Susan had already left grand jury secrecy behind where the Engs were concerned. She had talked to David about it; they had decided that what she did was her own business and that being here with her put him under no obligation to keep her from violating the secrecy law.

She did her best to review the witnesses and the basics of their testimony. She aimed her narration at Peter and June Eng, including Chan Kwok-Wing occasionally. She quickly got the feeling that the Engs were listening only politely, but that Chan was vitally interested.

Her story was punctuated by the waiters bringing food and by Chan's descriptions of each dish. When she was finished detailing the evidence Mahoney had presented, she said, 'I think that's about all, except for your parents' testimony.'

The Engs and Chan conferred briefly in Cantonese and then June Eng asked, 'Did you say that the man who testified about the ledger books was an accountant?'

'That's what they told us.'

'And he was quite certain that they were the records of drug purchases and sales?' This was Chan's question, so intense that Susan instinctively turned it aside.

'David understood all that better than I did.' She looked at him guiltily after the words were out. She hadn't meant to put him on the spot that way.

'I don't know that I did understand it better,' he said. 'But, speaking generally, I do know that if you're trying to figure out a simple substitution code like that, based on internal evidence, you often have to look for hints in the context. And once you do that, the strength of your conclusions rests on how accurately you can read the context.'

'For instance,' Susan said: 'The prosecutors based their conclusions on some heroin they found. If that heroin didn't belong there, then their conclusions would be all wrong.'

Peter Eng said something in Cantonese to Chan, whose voice rumbled back.

'What did *you* think was in the books?' Peter Eng asked David.

'I thought it could be almost anything.'

Susan said, 'So did some of the others on the grand jury, including an accountant.'

'Accountant on the jury, not to give evidence?' Chan asked.

'Both. One to give evidence, one on the jury.'

Chan nodded, said something else in Cantonese. Peter Eng said, 'We're sorry to have interrupted. If Mr Clark would be willing to continue with our parents' testimony, Ms Chan will have more chance to eat.'

David looked at Susan with an expression she couldn't read, then shrugged. 'Okay,' he said and summarized the testimony quickly.

Susan joined in to describe how convincing and moving she had found the family's history in China. 'Your mother and father reminded me so much of my own parents.'

'We're flattered that you should think so,' June Eng said.

'Did Chu-Ming tell what was in the books?' Chan asked.

Susan was confused.

'That's our father,' June Eng explained. 'His Chinese name.'

'Yes, he did.'

'What did Chu-Ming tell?'

Susan and David had discussed how she should handle this. She was afraid Martin Eng's description of his last wishes, which included doling out huge amounts of money to people outside the family, might be seen as insulting to his children. David hadn't seen why she cared.

'There's the whole question of face,' she had told him. 'I know they're not exactly being disinherited, but I still don't think it's the kind of thing they'd want to have their parents announce in front of twenty-three strangers.'

In the end she had decided to tell the Eng children about that aspect of the testimony only if it seemed unavoidable and then only in private. Now here they were with a third party present, and he was the one pressing the question.

David seemed to sense her distress. He put his hand briefly on hers and began to answer Chan's question.

Susan was happy to let David do this part of it. While he spoke, she watched the Engs and Chan Kwok-Wing. Again, the younger Engs seemed to be maintaining an attitude of paying attention without actually becoming engaged – even though the subject concerned them intimately. Chan listened with a deep alertness in his eyes.

When David stopped talking, Chan was ready with a question. 'Mr Eng made list of people to receive money?'

'Yes, that's what he said. For when he died.'

'What kind of names?'

David didn't seem to get it.

'Chinese names,' Susan said. 'Is that what you're asking?'

'Yes. Chinese names. Do you remember them?'

'No,' Susan said. 'Only that he said some of them were friends and some were poor people. David, do you remember any specifics?'

'Not really.'

'Did he say why poor people?'

'For charity, I assumed,' David said, and Susan thought: what an odd question.

'Where is money now?' Chan asked abruptly.

'The police have it.'

'Police keep, after now?'

'It depends on what happens next,' Susan said. 'But it's hard to predict. There are times when you're not found guilty and they keep the money anyway.'

'How can that be?' June Eng asked.

'Because to prove criminal guilt, they have to convince all twelve trial jurors beyond a reasonable doubt. But they can also bring what's called a civil forfeiture action, to keep the money.' Susan was drawing now on David's research about asset forfeiture. 'That's like an ordinary lawsuit – the standard of proof is much lower, and they don't need a unanimous verdict.'

'Police keep money now?' Chan insisted.

'Yes.'

'How much money?'

'A million and one hundred thousand dollars, cash, give or take,' David said. 'Plus about three hundred thousand in bearer bonds, and there's some gold jewelry.'

'All with police?'

'Yes, as far as I know.'

'Police do not give back the money?'

'I don't think they do until at least after the trial,' David said.

'Trial? Again?'

The question produced a moment of confused silence.

'Oh, no,' Susan said. 'The grand jury is different. It's only for accusing people. The grand jury decides if there will be a trial. Then the trial decides if they are guilty or not. The grand jury is what I was just describing to June and Peter.'

423

'Ah.' The syllable was meant to indicate that Chan understood, but the furrow between his eyebrows belied it. 'This trial is soon?'

'I don't know. I think it has to be soon.'

'Next month?'

'I don't know. I don't think so.'

'Mr Eng and his wife are not in jail,' Chan said.

'No. I saw them at their apartment,' Susan said. 'Their flat.'

'Go to jail after trial?' Chan asked David.

'Only if they're convicted.'

'Before trial, must stay in country?'

'It's a crime not to appear in court when you're supposed to,' David answered. 'And they would lose all their bail money.'

'Oh, yes,' Chan said. 'Bail money.' This time he seemed to understand. 'Money paid so to be out of jail.'

'Yes.'

'Police keep bail money if people leave before trial?'

'Yes.'

'Thank you. Can you say what will happen at this trial? Guilty? Or no?'

'I don't know,' David said.

'Ms Chan?'

'It's so hard to know. There was a lot of doubt on the grand jury. We only indicted them by a small margin. If they have a good defense, I think it would be hard to convict them.'

'Unless the prosecutor has more evidence than he showed us,' David countered. 'In that case, again, it's hard to say.'

After dessert, Chan said to Susan, 'I have heard from Cheung Meiling the sad story of your parents. I hope you will permit me to hear it from you directly.'

She told him all she had told Meiling, trying not to leave out any detail – that with China opening to the West again her parents had come to visit old friends and war buddies and relatives. That after a short time they had stopped communicating with their children in America. 'I didn't expect to hear much from them,' she understated. 'They were keeping in closer touch with my brother.

'When weeks passed without a word, he contacted the American

424

State Department and the Chinese Government travel agency to see if our parents could be located. Nothing happened. He came to Hong Kong in the hope that being here would help get a response, and when he had to go back to America, I came. Finally they told us that my parents had been in the vicinity of Beijing and Tianjin during the big earthquake in July that year, that they had probably been killed there and their bodies were in one of the mass graves. They said they were sorry.'

'You do not believe this story?'

'I did, for a long time. My brother didn't. He hadn't really heard from them for two months *before* the earthquake. He said that didn't make sense, and he's right. And they didn't really have any reason to visit the north.'

Chan nodded. He was carefully maintaining an expression of serious thought, an expression in which it would be easy to read any emotion a person wanted to see. Susan tried not to fool herself into thinking it was concern or sympathy.

He asked her many questions about her parents, their history in China, their affiliations in China and Hong Kong and the U.S. Then he resumed his thoughtful expression.

'I will try to help,' he said. 'Peter or June will tell you.'

'That was odd,' David said when they were back at the hotel.

'What do you mean?'

'All that about the money.'

'And did you notice how Peter and June didn't seem to be listening that carefully?'

'I didn't get it right away, but eventually I did.' He and Susan were standing in the hotel lobby. 'Do you want to talk about this over a nightcap or a cup of coffee?'

'Not in a bar,' she said. 'I don't feel like being in public. How about room service?'

'Fine.' He did not say, 'My room or yours?' He did his best not to think about the possibilities.

They took their drinks out on her balcony. The night was humid and warm. David could see city lights on either side of the dark building

425

across the street. Traffic hummed by below.

'I think you may be right,' Susan said. 'There *is* something odd here. Mr Chan gave me the chills.'

'He seemed very interested in your parents.'

'Don't change your opinion on me just when I'm starting to agree with you.'

'I'm not. I still think there's something odd going on, and I agree with you about Chan.'

'I had the feeling he thought we were more a part of the legal system than we are,' Susan said.

'That much I can understand. I think that in a lot of places all the judging is done by judges, sometimes panels of judges, not by ordinary citizens off the street. He might have had trouble getting past that.'

'Who do you suppose he is?'

'They said he's a friend of the family.'

'But really, who do you suppose he is?'

'Not a clue,' David said. 'There was all that about bail, and going to jail or not. A friend would want to know about that, I suppose.'

'He was very interested in who Mr Eng said he was leaving his money to. I was hoping we could get past that, but he kept coming back to it.'

'Maybe he expected them to leave it to him.' The idea made David smile. 'But it *was* the money that he seemed to care about most. The way he went after it, you'd think it was his.'

'How could that be?'

'Maybe he's the guy who supplies the heroin.'

'David!'

'Sorry.'

She turned to him. 'You've been so great about this. It made a big difference having you there tonight. I'm sorry about putting you in a place where you had to talk about the grand jury.'

'I didn't *have* to, I chose to. I decided it was their parents' testimony, and their parents have a right to reveal it, and I took it for granted they'd approve. Besides, I was glad to give you a chance to eat.' He tried a small smile. 'And now I should give you a chance to get some sleep.'

'I'm ready for that. Let's talk some more in the morning.'

426

In his room down the hall, he was too restless for sleep. He turned on the television and flipped to the list of pay movies. There were several categories. At the bottom of the screen he saw ADULT MOVIES and, separately listed, JAPANESE ADULT MOVIES. Why not? he thought. Satisfy your curiosity if nothing else.

He pressed the appropriate numbers on the remote and was rewarded with another list, this one of specific selections. They had oddly straightforward names like *Woman Pleases Many Men* and *Schoolteacher in Short Skirt*. He pressed more buttons on the remote to get a five-minute sample.

He saw at once that he'd made a mistake. This wasn't what he wanted. He turned the set off.

For a while he stood on his balcony looking out into the night, then he took a warm shower and went to bed. He lay in the dark thinking about Susan Linwood until sleep took mercy on him.

# 3

Mahoney sat pondering the pages of phone calls made from the office of Mr M.C. Wu, who had shown up so often on the Engs's phone listings.

Most of the calls on Wu's Local Usage Details were to the Engs's home number. Another large group of local calls went to numbers at the China Society. Mahoney had tried those. The most frequent two were to the offices of a Mr Feller and a Mr Fox. Mr Feller, he'd found when he called the Society's main information number, was their executive director, and Mr Fox was director of information programs.

Wu's long-distance toll calls were almost all to Washington, D.C. That was the most interesting part. The feds were after the Engs for something that was not heroin and that was being handled by their Public Corruption Unit, and here were the Engs in almost daily contact with a person who spent a lot of time on the phone to the nation's capital. It was hard not to think there might be a connection. And Ned King had told him to keep his eyes open for anything that looked like what the feds were after.

The only problem with that, Mahoney had to remind himself, was that he had recently received new evidence that the Engs had been laundering money, so he ought really to be sticking to that part of the case. Horgan's big trial was going to the jury after the weekend, and Horgan would surely be on Mahoney's ass about the Engs as soon as the jury came in.

Besides, these phone calls could perfectly well be meaningless. So what if Eng talked to someone who talked to people in Washington? Looked at closely – from a defense attorney's point of view, say – that meant exactly nothing. The truth was, he would have paid zero extra attention to Mr M.C. Wu among the people on the Engs's LUDs if not for the fact that Wu and Eng were the same name.

He pondered the notion that the same written character with the same meaning could be pronounced completely differently in two different parts of the same country. It brought to mind the time he'd tried to use his college French in Quebec. Two different languages, really, though they were both called French and looked identical on the page. And Chinese was even worse.

*Wait a minute*. What dialect did those two waiters speak? Not Cantonese, because the interpreter he'd wanted, who had translated Mrs Eng's Cantonese just fine, didn't speak the right dialect for the waiters, so he hadn't been able to use her.

How had he missed that? He picked up the phone to call the interpreter who'd translated for the two waiters. He had to find out if he was right.

June Eng called Susan first thing in the morning.

'I hope I didn't wake you, but I wanted to give you this news right away. Mr Chan knows someone who may be able to tell you more about your parents. He plans to talk to the person later today to see if his guess is right and if the person is willing to see you.'

'Thank you,' Susan said. 'I'm very grateful.'

'We're grateful to you. I'm happy to be able to help. You should know that this person Mr Chan is speaking to is in China. You must go to the hotel concierge at once and ask them to arrange a visa for you, on a rush basis. It costs extra but you will have it for tomorrow.'

They needed pictures. The concierge directed them to the rapid transit station adjacent to the hotel. There, in the bright and spacious underground corridor, just past a shop selling fresh flowers, a silver picture-taking booth stood against the red-tile wall. They took turns sitting for their visa pictures.

Waiting for them to develop, Susan said, 'Let's take some together. Souvenirs.'

'Sure.'

They crowded into the booth together. Susan giggled as the light flashed. She made the kind of face Lara might have, and before she was ready the light flashed again. They sat pressed together for another moment, but the light didn't flash.

'I think that's it,' David said. 'Four pictures, two poses.' He backed out of the booth and made room for her to get out.

Her pictures were ready. 'Oh, they're awful,' she said.

'Mine aren't hot good either,' David said when they emerged.

'Let me see.' She snatched them from his hand.

'Hey.' He reached for hers but she danced away.

'Oh, no,' she said. She handed his back. 'Yours aren't so bad.'

David feinted another grab for her pictures and when she pulled back again he reversed ground and took up a position by the slot that dispensed the finished photos. Too late, she saw what he'd done.

He grabbed the pictures of the two of them together and cupped them in his hands so she couldn't see them. He burst out laughing.

'What?' she said.

He turned them so she could see: in the second pose her funny face was captured in all its juvenile glory. In the first she had apparently begun giggling before the flash went off. Her eyes were narrowed with laughter and her head was bent toward his, her hair draped over his shoulder. She snatched for the pictures, but he held them away from her.

'They're terrible,' she said. 'We have to destroy them.'

'Oh, no. You can have your half to destroy if you want, but I'm keeping mine. Souvenir.'

Susan didn't know how to account for her high spirits, but she was in no mood to question them. She suggested that they take the day for sightseeing. It was hot, but not quite as hot as it had been. 'It's probably our last chance. If I learn what I came for in China, we'll be going home.'

'I have to talk to the guy at the Racecourse Association,' David said. 'In fact, I should call him now.'

Susan, still giddy, made a disappointed face. She browsed in the hotel bookstore while he made his call. She was feeling the same kind of pang she had when he first told her about his contact at the RA. It made no sense. Why should she be the only focus of his trip? He wasn't, of hers.

430

'Okay,' he said when he came back. 'I've got an appointment with him at ten-thirty in the morning. That means I won't have time to go running, but I'll survive.'

'You run?'

'Most days, if I can. I especially like to get some miles in when I travel. It's a great way to see parts of town you might miss otherwise. And there's a jogging map in my room, looks interesting.'

'Speaking of rooms,' she said, 'I called the hotel people before I came down to meet you in the lobby just now. They'll move us out of our rooms and hold our things for us while we're in China. And they'll move us back in if we give them a few hours' notice. They're going to try to put us in the front of the building, so we can see the harbor. It'd be nice, even if it's only for one night.'

'Remind me to travel with you next time I go somewhere,' David said.

She felt herself flush. 'Service with a smile.'

The Royal Hong Kong Racecourse Association came as a revelation to David. The operations building was modern and technologically up-to-date, fully wired for computer networks and fiber-optic tele-communications. His host, a genial Scotsman named Macleod, gave him a general tour of the facilities, from the betting operations center to the control room for the twelve-hundred-square-foot television screens that showed live race action to the grandstand crowds at whichever of the Association's two alternately-used tracks was idle.

'We look to be fully built,' Macleod said. 'In truth, we're always planning for what our need will be tomorrow. Now we've got our university to think about as well. Hong Kong Institute of Technology – HKIT. We built it and we run it, and it's our special jewel. We fancy we can make it the MIT of Asia.'

They sat in an empty operations room overlooking the racetrack, and Macleod asked David about his background. Ordinarily, David wasn't inclined to tell people his whole story. But Macleod – an odd combination of taciturn, jolly and open – prompted him to tell more of it than usual.

'Bad luck,' Macleod said when David was done.

'I've been kind of laying low since then. Contract work, nothing

431

very stimulating, though, and I find it tends to narrow me. The headhunter I was working with liked to get me new jobs just like the old ones.'

'You can see his point of view, I imagine.'

'And the people who hire me, too. That doesn't make it good for me.'

'No, I fear you're right. And if you sink into a rut, you're doomed.'

'The sad truth. You need to stay in the technical mainstream . . . competing with kids out of school who get entry-level money.'

'All that energy, and the sense they can do anything,' Mcleod observed. 'We all had it once.'

'Now we have experience. And I don't notice that I've lost the passion to create.' Wishful thinking, right now, but a man could hope.

'Passion's what we run on, here.' Macleod stood. He was well over six feet tall, with a barrel chest and long legs. 'Passion and sweat.'

David watched Macleod put his computer systems through their paces with all the proprietary glee of a precocious teenager, until well past the start of the professional staff's lunch-hour. Macleod invited him to stay for lunch and took him to the clubhouse dining room, a vast space with two-story ceilings and a curving sweep of glass overlooking the track. They traded stories about the ways the world of computers had changed around them as they worked in it. Macleod was enough older than David to remember earlier days, when university science departments had proudly used computers with less power and less memory than might be found today in a good pocket calculator.

'We're not all technology here,' Macleod said as they shook hands in parting. 'You ought to come by and see the building on race nights. A different sort of place, entirely.'

The taxi taking David back to the hotel sat snarled in post-lunch-hour traffic. He got back just in time to meet Susan and climb into another taxi.

They had tea in a restaurant built into the shell of an elegant old hotel lobby on a green hillside overlooking a beach and a yachting harbor on Hong Kong island's south shore – lush and inviting as any tropical resort isle.

432

A taxi brought them back over the mountain to Hong Kong Central, where Susan decided she'd been in enough taxis. 'We have to try the subway, too. Or Metro, or Underground, or whatever they call it.'

'MTR,' David said. 'Mass Transit Railway.'

'Very good.'

'We were in the station this morning. I read the signs.'

They disembarked at the first stop after they'd gone under the harbor to Kowloon. Susan led them on a browsing and shopping tour of the open-fronted shops crowding Tsim Sha Tsui's narrow, twisting, teeming streets, then to a huge mall that turned out to feature mostly Western shops, and then – with frequent looks at a map as they wound through another maze of streets – to a store that sold goods imported from China. David bought a silk scarf and a cashmere sweater for his sister and a bagful of handicraft souvenirs for the twins.

'Nothing for your girlfriend?' Susan asked.

He didn't answer.

They took the MTR back to Hong Kong island and got off at a stop called Wan Chai. Here, as in Kowloon and Central, the station was spacious and airy and had maps showing where the exits were. Susan picked one that kept them walking underground for blocks.

They emerged in the three-story-high lobby of a new skyscraper faced in reflective glass and metal. The entire towering lobby space was floodlit, and it was fully open on the street side. Across the narrow street, in a gloom untouched by the bright white light, was a row of dilapidated, grayish apartment blocks, not more than six stories high, streaked black with rain and the soot of a million passing cars. Laundry hung disconsolately on the balconies, the washed-out colors of the clothes further muted by the night. Tendrils of humid air penetrated the curtain of air conditioning in the open skyscraper lobby, carrying with them the odors of decay and sewage that had accosted David's nose unexpectedly everywhere he'd been in Hong Kong.

'Quite a contrast,' he said.

'Hong Kong progress,' Susan said. 'In case you're homesick, this building is called Times Square.'

They took an escalator the full three-story height of the lobby and then an exterior, glass-walled elevator that looked down on the gray buildings across the street.

'Starting here, five stories of restaurants,' Susan informed him when they got off the elevator at the base of a bank of escalators.

'Sunny told me about this place,' Susan said as they waited to be seated, a few floors further up.

The décor was *faux* jungle, with a lot of rattan, and palm trees all over. There was a big oval bar, complete with a noisy bar scene, in a room to itself. In an adjacent room a pop-music band was playing to a restaurant full of diners.

A young man, tall and blond, with an Australian accent, led them to a table and took their drink order. Susan glanced around, confirming for herself what Sunny had told her.

'Take a look,' she said to David. 'At the people.'

He took a while at it. 'Isn't that something,' he said finally. 'Is this the night for it, or is it always like this?'

'Always, Sunny told me. Fifty percent or more of the couples here are white men with Chinese women. But I don't know if they're girlfriends, wives or mistresses.'

'A little of each, I'd guess,' David said. 'And a few who are only traveling companions.'

Mahoney went out to the reception desk to meet the interpreter. She was wearing the same too-tight blue suit she had the other times he'd seen her.

Back in his office he offered her tea or coffee; she took the coffee, black.

'Thanks for coming in,' he said. 'Here's what I need your help with. You've worked for me twice on this case, once in the grand jury and once here in the office. I'm confused about whether you were translating a different language each time.'

She smiled broadly. 'Same language, Chinese. Different dialect. Toishanese, Cantonese.' Her English in conversation had the same

434

abbreviated quality it did when she was interpreting, but there was nothing halting about the way she spoke. It was as if she was just leaving out the words she thought didn't matter. 'Also, sometimes translate Mandarin.' She seemed quite proud of the accomplishment.

'Let me be sure I understand. You're talking about different dialects of the same language.'

She nodded happily: he was being a good student. 'Toishanese not same, Cantonese. Some people say, subdialect. People speak in Toishan, county in south part of Canton province, now call Guangdong province. Toishan, part of Sze Yap. Sze Yap, mean Four District.'

That rang a bell. 'Give me a minute,' Mahoney said. He swiveled around to face his computer and called up the directory with the Eng grand jury minutes. Found Martin Eng's testimony and keyed in a search for the word 'district.' On the screen he saw I am president of Guangdong Three Districts Association. He turned back to the interpreter.

'Did you just say *Four* Districts?'

'Yes.'

'And this Toishan is part of that Four Districts?'

'Yes.'

'Is that the same as Three Districts?'

The interpreter looked amused. 'Not same. Three District, Four District. Different.'

'Do they speak the Toishan dialect in Three Districts, too?'

'Speak Cantonese, Three District. Toishanese, Four District.'

'So when you translated for these men, that was Toishanese, and when you translated for Ms Cheung, that was Cantonese.'

'Cheung Meiling speak very well. Educated, upper-class. Waiters you interrogate speak Toishanese, peasant-class, no education.'

'Could they speak to her, or her husband?'

The interpreter shrugged. 'Educated people, Guangdong province, speak Cantonese, Mandarin . . . also can understand some words Toishanese. Guangdong people, no reason to speak Toishanese, except maybe some people learn to boss factory worker in Sze Yap. These waiters not speak Cantonese, only Toishanese, maybe understand Cantonese a little, for work.'

435

'So they might be able to communicate with the Engs?'

She hesitated. 'Yes. Enough for making deposits in bank.'

'But they'd have some difficulty?'

'Depend, how much Mr, Mrs Eng speak Toishanese.'

So it wasn't as cut and dried as he'd thought. Still, he had to follow it up.

# 4

The food was good, but it arrived slowly. Susan nursed her glass of wine while David was imbibing two oversize bottles of beer.

'Thirsty work, all that walking around,' he said.

'I have to keep reminding myself we're in the tropics,' she said. 'So I shouldn't be surprised it's hot and humid.'

David looked around the room again, at the mixed couples. 'Does it make you homesick?'

'What an odd thing to say.'

'I'm feeling surly tonight.'

'Didn't you have a good morning?'

'Good enough.' Unsure how to feel about the ferry rides, talking about the audio tape.

'And you said you had a good time at the RA.'

'I did. But the sightseeing and shopping was a lot for me. I don't do much of either in my normal life.'

'Oh, yes, your normal life . . . we've never gotten around to talking about that . . . Unless you're feeling too surly.'

'What can I tell you about my normal life?'

'You could start with what you do.'

'The short version is that right now I get work through a headhunter who hears about computing jobs and matches them up with people who have the right skills.'

'How did you get into that kind of work?'

'By mistake.'

'If you don't want to talk about it, that's fine,' she said.

'Sorry. I'm kind of bitter about how things are at the moment. Sometimes I forget not to take it out on everyone in sight.'

437

'I really don't mean to pry.'

'You're not prying. And maybe it would be good for me to talk about it. But I'll have to give you some background.'

'Whatever you want.'

'Let me get a refill first.' He waved for the waiter and asked for another beer.

'All right. From the beginning. What makes me grumpy about where I am now is how different it is from where I was when I started. There was a sense of excitement then, a sense you could do something no one had ever done before. You never really knew how hard it was going to be – because everything always turned out harder than you thought. So you worked as hard as it took and you were happy to be doing it. Because every day, every minute of every day, there was this thought in the back of your mind – this is what I want to be doing. And it was a great time to be doing it. A revolutionary time.

'Everything was changing – the huge mainframe computers that everyone relied on were dinosaurs, but nobody really knew it yet. The hot technology then was called a minicomputer – only about the size of a refrigerator but powerful enough to handle a small business, or certain kinds of engineering work or laboratory analyses. And then there were these guys, mostly on the West Coast, who were fiddling with something really new, taking the first steps toward a kind of computer you could have in your own home.

'I had a friend in college, he was kind of a pothead and tended to be vague and spacey, but he was brilliant when it came to computers. He said: "I have one word for you, my boy." You know, like in that movie, *The Graduate*. Only his word wasn't plastics, it was "*microprocessors*."

'These days, there's a microprocessor everywhere you turn – cars, appliances, at the heart of every personal computer – and some of them are more powerful than mainframes were when I was in high school. But fifteen years ago, when Jon said that, microprocessors couldn't do much at all. Even so, I decided he was right – microprocessors were the future.

'I went off to get a Masters degree and then he coaxed me to come work for this company with him. By that time, personal computers

438

were starting to be a regular feature of the landscape, and we were in a position to be in on the early stages of developing them.'

He paused, looking toward the bandstand. Not seeing the band, Susan thought.

'Not quite the ground floor, not like the guys who founded Apple, or Microsoft. But close enough. Except there weren't a lot of steady jobs in that end of the business, not yet. So what we did instead was to get off into a very specialized little area that was paid for by Government contracts, nothing to do with what the public was ever going to see in a computer store.

'It could be very high-pressure work, if you let it. Some of us stayed until ten, twelve almost every night, no real time off, working so hard we were making our families unhappy or losing our girlfriends and not even noticing it, because we were doing the real thing. We were actually designing this new kind of machine that used lots of micro-processors to break big problems into little chunks and solve them faster that way – and we were doing it from the ground up. And that was what we seriously wanted to be doing.'

'And did the job make you lose your girlfriend?' Susan couldn't resist asking.

'It would have if I'd had one then, but not having time to meet anyone I just stopped thinking about it. All I did was work and sleep. Now and then I did my laundry or bought groceries. And wouldn't you know it, there was a woman I kept seeing at the laundry and at the grocery store – a very pretty woman, tall, with long blonde hair and big blue eyes, and a nice smile – and one night she was right behind me in the grocery line and the cash register broke and we were just standing there, waiting. And she said to me, "What is it you're always thinking about? Every time I see you, you've got this expression like you're looking at what's happening on the other side of the moon. All I can think of is either you're crazy or else you're playing chess like they do, without a board and an invisible opponent."

'So we got talking, because I thought that was kind of clever, what she said, and it turned out she was a singer, and she worked as a waitress and she was very smart and intuitive. She had an uncle she liked who was an engineer, so she sort of got off on what I was doing and how deep I got into it. And we started to go out. We had a good time, and it was a help that she had plenty on her mind and things to occupy herself with, including working late a lot of the time, so it didn't matter that much that I was working late, too. In fact, she liked it. It was part of the mystique.' He smiled. 'It made the other guys at work crazy once they found out about it. This one guy said to me, "You're the only guy in the history of the world who ever got laid for being a workaholic computer geek." But after a while it got to be too much for her, too, and we kind of drifted apart.'

He stopped, looking off in what Susan thought of as a version of what that woman in the laundry must have seen, but sadder.

'Well, anyway, you don't want to hear about my love life.'

*Yes, I do,* she knew not to say.

'The point I was trying to make,' he resumed, 'is we were working hard, sure, harder than some people could believe anybody would ever want to. But nobody told us we had to. We were doing it because it felt good. And you could sense it, just walking into the room.' As Susan could sense it, now, in his voice.

'And the thing was, you knew that once you signed on for a job like that there was no way you could leave in the middle. You're part of a team, people are breaking their hearts and their butts to get *their* parts done, relying on you for whatever part you're supposed to play. You can't let them down. And then there's the voice inside of you that tells you: you start something, you damn well finish it. You beat it, you don't let it beat you. No matter what it takes. And then, if you're lucky, you come out with something you can be really proud of.' He was smiling broadly, shaking his head. 'People are so crazy, sometimes.'

'It doesn't sound crazy to me,' she said. 'Were you lucky?'

'Yes and no. Jon, my friend that I told you about, came up with a new word. Two, actually – *innovation* and *independence*. So the two of us and a third guy left the company we were with and set up on our own.

'Because of what we'd been doing we thought we had a headstart on how to make a lot of incompatible machines and programs work together. And doing that was a huge unsolved problem out there in the world of microcomputers.

'It turned out to be a lot easier to see the solution than to make it work. In retrospect maybe that's one of the reasons why no one had done it.'

He paused. 'I'm kind of oversimplifying, but I don't want to get too technical.'

'This is just fine. And it's fascinating. What happened?'

'After about three years of really hard work, we thought we'd succeeded – not a hundred percent but close enough to have something to work with. And then we realized that three clever systems engineers had zero chance to launch a brand new product all on their own. So we found ourselves a huge company that bought the rights in what we'd done and hired us for five years to make it part of a bigger program they were designing.'

'That sounds wonderful.'

'That's what we thought. After all those years of work we were genuinely in on the real ground floor of something with the potential to be very big. And then, after two more years of our working even harder, they pulled the plug on us. Canceled the project.'

'How could they do that?'

'They didn't seem to have any trouble. Called us into the office and said, "You remember this clause in the contract where it says we are under no obligation to release any commercial product based on your work? Well, we're not going to." '

'Couldn't you take it somewhere else?'

'No, because our deal said they could make a lump-sum payment to buy out our rights.'

'That's awful.'

'Yes.'

'But what about your five-year contract?'

'We had three years to go on it. They could have put us to work in some other division, they had plenty of use for good systems engineers. But they made it clear we would not be happy staying and offered to release us from our obligation to them for some extra money on our buyout. Jon said the hell with them, he was going to stick it out and be in their faces and get some on-the-job training at their expense, until they got so sick of him they'd *really* make it worth his while to leave. I saw that he was right, but my situation was different. I took

441

their offer on the spot and they said I should be out of my office by the end of the day.'

'Can I ask why you had to leave that way?'

He looked at her. For a moment she could see regret in his eyes, then it was gone – replaced by something harder and colder.

'Sure – why not? Here we are, halfway around the world from home and hearth, watching a second-rate cover band in an overpriced watering hole for expatriates and their local girlfriends. What better subject to talk about?'

'I'm sorry,' she said. 'If this part's too unpleasant . . .'

He looked at her. She had the sense he was appraising her, coming to a decision about how much to trust her.

'I was just being surly again,' he said. 'Mad at the world.'

'I know how that feels.'

'I guess you do. It's odd, though. Sometimes, looking at you, I still think, there's somebody with a perfect life.'

'Not quite.'

'Anyway,' he resumed after a moment, 'what happened to me is simple enough. I made the mistake of going out with a woman who worked in the company we'd sold out to. It was a big stretch for me, in the first place. I'd never really known a woman like her, much less thought of going out with one. Born with a silver spoon, the best schools, smart and beautiful from day one—'

He stopped abruptly. 'Never mind that. The important thing was, she ran the division we were part of. Which indirectly made her my boss. And she played a big part in the decision to close the division down and abandon the project. *And* the decision to keep the rights they'd bought from us, even though they weren't going to use them for anything.'

'So you felt betrayed.'

'Betrayed right down the line. By the company, by the people there I trusted, and especially by the woman I loved, who I was dumb enough to think loved me.'

'She might not have had any control over what happened.'

'Maybe not, but it was sure funny how she dealt with it. No warning, no talk about how I might like to see it handled, or maybe how my partners and I could salvage the situation for her bosses. Or

442

disengage in a way that saved our ability to keep our creation alive.'

'But if she didn't have control over those things . . .'

'Whatever. Let's listen to the band.' He rubbed his forehead. 'Better yet, I'm thinking it's time for me to head back to the hotel. You're welcome to join me.' He signaled for the waiter.

'David.' She put her hand on his arm. 'I'm sorry. I didn't mean that the way it must have sounded. I wasn't defending her. I just thought, she could have loved you as much as she knew how and still not have known how to handle a situation like that. That's not to say she was right, only that loving someone doesn't always save us from our own shortcomings.'

He sat without speaking. She became acutely aware of her hand on his arm, uncomfortable leaving it there but feeling that removing it would somehow send a wrong message.

He smiled ruefully and put his hand on hers. 'You're right about loving someone not saving us from our shortcomings. A frequent blindness about women being one of mine.'

He squeezed her hand and took his away. It was a natural time for her to take hers back, too. She did, but she was sorry to.

'So you quit?' It was all she could think of to cover the awkwardness.

'So I quit. I assumed I was going to find another job right away. But my buyout contract said that for three years I had to stay out of the field I'd been in for the past five. And a lot of companies saw my other skills as being out of date, or they were worried because I had no experience with these dumbed-down computer languages they all had started working in while I was off doing my thing.'

He paused for a moment, then said, 'It's as if you were a surgeon and they told you the only job available was giving massages. You'd know right away that you'd be good at it – maybe better at it than most, because you knew so much anatomy and physiology. But first you'd have to convince people you could learn Shiatsu and Swedish and whatever other kinds there are.

'And assuming you did convince them, then you'd actually have to go and learn it all. And then spend every day doing it – perfectly good techniques for doing massage, but a long way from surgery. They're clumsy and limited and they stay on the surface of things. Not very

443

satisfying when you're used to getting in there and building new structures out of sinew and bone and blood vessels.'

'You make it very vivid. It must be very frustrating for you.'

'What bothers me most is the feeling that I'll never get to do real surgery again. I mean, don't get me wrong, for those two years when we thought we were going to be millionaires, that was a genuine rush. But the part that really mattered was the *doing* of it – that, and being way out on the leading edge of things. Making something that you knew was smart and well-designed and that people were going to be amazed by and happy to have.'

Hearing David talk that way brought Susan back to her earliest, almost forgotten, days with Richard – the kind of fire he'd had before he'd gotten swept up in the externals. Before his patients had become stepping stones to greater reputation, more power, more money.

Even if he were still intoxicated by the sheer virtuosity of it – a passion that seemed to move David – that would have been all right. But nothing Richard had done in many years had been done for itself, and all his goals seemed cold and ultimately without value.

'Do you not get any pleasure out of what you're doing now?' she asked David.

'Not much. It's mostly just massage of one kind or another. And the more I do, the more I wonder if I'll ever do anything else.' He looked at her. 'It makes me feel strange, talking about my frustrations – I mean, considering the kinds of problems *you're* dealing with, or the Engs. I had it good for a long time. I had satisfactions some people never have. I came close to having it all, and I came away with a decent consolation prize. I don't have anything to complain about.'

She knew not to contradict him. 'How about some dessert?' she said.

He smiled wanly. 'Go ahead. I couldn't, myself. Beer and self-pity are a lousy combination.'

At the hotel, they stopped by his door.

'Thanks for being a good listener,' he said. 'I needed that more than I knew. It put things in focus.'

444

'I'm glad we got to talk. I feel as if I know you so much better. And it's probably silly for me to say it, but I believe you'll find what you want. You have too much desire not to.' She put out her hand. 'I'm glad to know you, David Clark.'

Her hand in his, she felt suddenly, unaccountably panicky. She said a quick good night and tried not to run to her own door.

# 5

David woke early, his head and stomach feeling better than he had any right to expect. He took advantage of the early-morning cool to follow the hotel's jogging map.

He returned from his run sweaty but refreshed, and breakfasted on the bowl of fresh fruit that the hotel provided every day, plus coffee from room service. He squeezed in a late-morning visit with Macleod, and then it was time to leave for China.

They sat in the pointed bow cabin of the jetfoil to Macao, watching the harbor boats and the construction. David marveled at the graceful arc of cable slung between the slender suspension towers of the bridge to the new airport, rising six hundred and more feet over the water. Susan, who had seemed jumpy and distant since he'd met her and June Eng in the hotel lobby, responded without much enthusiasm when he pointed out how much it looked like the Golden Gate. Once they were out in clear water the jetfoil rose up for an hour's skimming flight over the choppy gray mouth of the Pearl River.

Arriving in Macao they could see a seemingly interminable green-and-red dragon with a flashing golden spine, borne by hundreds of dancing Macanese, twisting its way over a bridge connecting the outlying islands with the mainland.

'A greeting for the Prime Minister of Portugal,' June Eng explained after she'd inquired for them. 'It's not often such a high official comes here.'

'I thought it might be for us,' David said.

'Oh no,' June Eng began seriously, then saw her mistake and smiled.

446

They went to meet Chan Kwok-Wing at the Macao sister of their hotel in Hong Kong but here, instead of rich black marble and lavish chandeliers, the dominant note was wood and the obvious influence, Iberian. There was nothing like the crush of people David had experienced everywhere in Hong Kong, and the whole tempo of the place felt significantly slower. Even the Macanese air seemed more languid: no less hot and humid, but less oppressive.

Chan arrived in a van driven by a young man with thick, coarse black hair that stood up in tufts. Chan introduced him. 'He will be our driver until the hotel in China.'

The van was neither new nor old, its accommodation utilitarian. The bench seats were hard and covered in plastic, the ride firm and bumpy.

As they drove, David found his initial impression of Macao confirmed. Everything was more spread out, less populated and slower-paced here than in Hong Kong. There were many old buildings, clearly European in design, painted in fading shades of yellow and green and pink. They detoured to the top of a steep hill, where a park surrounding an old Portuguese church gave a commanding view of all Macao.

'China,' June Eng said, pointing. David looked, saw only a continuation of the coastline, green hills, stretches of dun earth.

At the border they got out; the driver and van went through Customs separately. Once in the Customs shed David and Susan and June Eng followed the signs for people with foreign passports. Chan went off toward the lines for Hong Kong people and returning citizens of China.

The austerity of the building and the severe demeanor of the uniformed men and women behind the passport-control desks made David uneasy. They were, after all, about to enter a country where, to judge by what he'd read, people were still routinely and swiftly executed for minor crimes and detained for years without trial. And much had been made in the early summer of the harsh penalties meted out in the latest anti-corruption campaigns, part of a larger struggle for power inside China.

He fumbled his entry-card form as he handed it to the officer with his passport. The man gave him a hard look and keyed his name and passport number into a computer terminal, examined his documents closely while he waited for the computer to respond. With a grunt he stamped the passport, detached the top copy of the entry card and thrust the carbon and David's passport across the desk.

Susan and June Eng were waiting for him beyond the exit doors. They walked out together into the bright sun, crossing a gated parking lot to the street.

'The van isn't here yet,' Susan said. 'Mr Chan has gone to see what's keeping it.'

Across a wide street David saw a large building with a colorful neon sign – two Chinese characters followed by the Roman letters O and K – 'kara-OK,' he had learned in Hong Kong. Beyond the karaoke bar was a kind of shopping square; a line of red taxis and a small white bus waited in front of it for people coming through passport control. Down a tree-lined alley he could see a flock of parked bicycles, colorful awnings, and a milling crowd of people.

'Street market,' June Eng said. 'For local people.'

A big new Mercedes – the most expensive model, in metallic gold with right-hand drive – pulled up to the gate of the parking lot. The driver leaned out and shouted something to the armed, uniformed guard – Army or Customs police, David guessed. The guard didn't move. The driver shouted again and waved a leather folder containing some kind of official pass. The guard jumped to open the gate.

The sedan pulled into the parking lot, having gained perhaps fifty feet for all the fuss, and two immaculately dressed Chinese business-men got out, took expensive-looking leather attaché cases from the trunk of the car and walked toward Customs.

'Hong Kong people?' David asked June Eng.

'Chinese,' she said. 'License plate is from here, Zhuhai –' the place name came out *Jeehoy* – 'and you can tell by their hair, very coarse and stiff, that they are likely to be from the mainland. But the car is from Hong Kong. Stolen, probably.'

'How can you tell?'

'Because it has right-hand drive, for driving on the left. Cars for sale in China are left-hand drive, like in the U.S.'

448

★ ★ ★

Chan Kwok-Wing walked up. 'Van coming. Sorry. Some wrong papers.'

The van drove up and they climbed aboard. The driver put their bags in back, behind the seats, except for June Eng's briefcase, which she clung to possessively.

Chan said, 'Take shortcut, here to factory, then Zhongshan –' *Chungsan* – 'for stay in hotel.'

'Factory?' David asked.

'Yes,' June Eng said. 'Part of our business here is investing in factories. Mostly garment factories. There's one here in the Zhuhai Special Economic Zone, and since we'll be going right by I wanted to talk to the manager and look around. And I thought you might find it interesting.'

On the way out of town, the road was crowded with bicyclists pedaling four and more abreast along the side of the road. Next to them were people on motorbikes and motor scooters and small motorcycles. All these open vehicles proceeded in a cloud of tan dust raised from the road and its unpaved shoulder by their own passage. The riders were all covered head to foot by a thick layer of the dust.

The van hurtled along past them, often perilously close. In the center lanes on the other side of the van, heavy trucks lumbered at lower speeds than the vans and cars.

'Isn't it dangerous having the fast traffic next to the bicycles and motorbikes?' Susan asked.

'It used to be worse,' June Eng told her. 'Slowest on the outside, fastest in the middle. But there are no lines to separate the lanes, and when the traffic got heavy it pushed the people in the center over too far, so you had cars going top speed straight at each other down the middle of the road. It still works that way some places. Here people started driving the slow trucks in the center lanes. Not so many head-on collisions, but you're right, a lot of people get sideswiped instead.'

At an intersection, unmarked and without a traffic signal, their driver squeezed to the right through the traffic of two-wheelers and turned onto a bumpy dirt road. Now the van was raising its own impressive cloud of dust.

449

'Shortcut,' Chan said.

The land they were crossing was mostly the same tan as the dust that seemed to be everywhere. They passed several buildings under construction.

'All this, reclaimed land,' Chan said.

'Reclaimed from what?' David asked.

'All rice farm, before.'

'And what's being built here?'

'Condominium housing,' June Eng said.

'Who's it for?' Susan asked.

'Whoever buys it.'

'They must have a market in mind,' Susan persisted.

'Retirees from Hong Kong.'

'You can't be serious.'

'Why not? Hong Kong is expensive. Living is cheap here. Once Hong Kong becomes part of China, what's the difference if you live here or there?'

'You're saying this is being built on speculation?' Susan ventured.

'Yes, that's what a lot of this activity is – people scrambling to make a dollar on all kinds of speculative projects.'

'And they're *reclaiming* rice farms to do it.'

'Of course they are. How much corn do you see growing in New York City?'

The van pulled onto a paved road and slowed down.

David looked around. He saw a broad open field, this one more green than tan, some paved roads, and several buildings, long and wide but only a few stories high. They were uniformly faced in large square tiles of gray and deep burgundy.

'What's this?'

'Have identification papers ready please,' Chan said. 'Army check-point. Shortcut across Army base.'

The atmosphere in the van, relaxed a moment before, went suddenly tense as the van rolled to a stop at a sentry booth. Soldiers, automatic rifles at the ready, stalked up and down alongside the van. David took his American passport from its case and held it up where its distinctive blue-and-gold cover could readily be seen. Chan and the driver handed their papers to a soldier through the driver's-side window.

More tense minutes passed before the soldier handed their papers back with what David thought might have been a fast salute. The soldiers withdrew, and the driver started along a road crossing the Army base.

'Army here, protect Special Economic Zone,' Chan said. 'Also, engage in industry.'

'We're partners with them,' June Eng said.

'Partners?' David asked.

'With the Army.'

'How can you be partners with the Army?' Susan asked.

'The People's Liberation Army isn't like other armies that way. They invest in businesses. They also provide workers – to help do construction, to run and maintain our factory buildings. The Army gives us soldiers, we pay their salary and house them. They're hard workers with great discipline, and the pay scale is very reasonable.'

'And the Army *invests*?' David found it hard to believe.

'It's one of the biggest capitalist organizations in China. The PLA owns factories, construction companies, transportation, hotels, casinos, night clubs. It operates them, as well. Every kind of enterprise there is.'

'And they're your partners?' David asked.

'Good partners,' Chan said.

The visit to the garment factory went quickly. Susan had an impression of broad, open floors brightly lit by overhead fluorescents and large windows. On each floor were row upon row of sewing machines or steam irons, more comfortably spaced than the tables in many an overpriced restaurant she'd been to. The women intently sewing and ironing did not, at a glance, look oppressed – a thought that made Susan wonder how quickly she would recognize any but the most blatant oppression, even staring straight at it.

On the ground floor were computer systems for optimizing the way the cloth was cut, to get more shirts and less waste; others were used for the computer-driven embroidery machines. David lingered in the computer room, asking questions that, translated, seemed to surprise the computer operators. He stopped, too, at a huge cutting machine that monitored the flatness of the multi-layered stack of cloth waiting

451

to be cut by scanning it with a laser beam.

Susan had not expected machinery this sophisticated, and she said so.

'China is part of the modern world.' June Eng spoke sharply. 'Not stuck in the middle ages the way some people want you to believe.'

Susan noticed something else that interested her: the deference that greeted Chan Kwok-Wing. On the main factory floors the workers who looked up at his approach all immediately resumed work with particular energy, and none of them looked up again until after Chan was well past her row. The people who had to speak with him all but kowtowed. None turned his back on Chan and they all appeared tongue-tied with eagerness for his approval.

None of this appeared to please him. He barked so loud at one poor floor manager, who actually did bow as he shook Chan's hand, that the man snapped to immediate attention and, when Chan waved him away, fled as if pursued by demons.

It made her think of the story of the Emperor going out into the countryside and pouring tea for his retainers. Chan should have had someone warn the factory people to tap their fingers on the table, instead.

Their destination for the night was a spa and golf resort outside Zhongshan. A billboard beside the monumental, pagoda-topped gate-way advertised HOT SPRING VILLAS BEVERLY HILL GARDEN, with a rendering of Chinese-style golf-course condos.

The hotel's lobby was enormous and coldly empty, staffed by pretty young women with eyes as chilly and vacant as the lobby. Even after Customs and the Army base, it was here that the words *Communist* and *totalitarian* came most strongly to Susan's mind.

They checked in quickly and left for dinner. Susan had a brief impression of her small room – austere in a way that matched the lobby in spirit. The air conditioning worked only feebly, and there were no screens in the windows. And this part of China was famous for its mosquitoes.

Dinner was in town at the International Hotel in Zhongshan, a recent building at least twenty stories high. Walking up the front drive under strings of colored lights Susan counted five Mercedes sedans and five BMWs, all top of the line. They were left-hand drive, so presumably they had been purchased through normal channels. Or stolen somewhere other than Hong Kong.

The spacious restaurant took up most of the top floor, but heavy draperies covered the windows. The food was superb. The fish steamed with ginger and scallions and the wine-cooked shrimp had been alive until virtually the moment they were cooked; the pigeon, smoked and roasted in the local manner, was meltingly tender; the pea sprouts tangy, slippery with just the right amount of oil. Even the soup of black-skinned chicken – 'good luck to eat, good for health,' Chan said – was just right, rich but not fatty.

Here, too, Chan was treated with exaggerated respect, and seemed annoyed by it. He called the manager over and spoke to him in stern tones. Listening, the manager was increasingly deferential, a reaction that only increased Chan's annoyance. The exercise complete, the staff served the table with eyes downcast, approaching by any route that did not bring them near Chan Kwok-Wing.


Mahoney thought the two Chinese waiters looked nervous to be back in his office. Interviewing the first one, he smiled a lot and lobbed easy questions at him, going back over the ground they had already covered, watching to see if he would drop his guard.

The language barrier and the man's general fidgetiness made it hard to pick the moment, but when Mahoney thought it was time he asked, almost casually, 'Did you get your instructions from Mr Eng or from Mrs Eng?'

'Mr Eng,' the interpreter reported.

'Did you ever get instructions from Mrs Eng?'

The waiter was slow answering. Mahoney saw dawning suspicion in his face before he spoke.

'Sometimes,' the interpreter said.

'Do you know where in China Mr and Mrs Eng come from?'

The waiter stared at him.

'Repeat the question,' Mahoney told the interpreter.

'Don't know,' was the answer.

'Do you remember if Mr Eng spoke Cantonese or Toishanese?'

'Toishanese,' the waiter responded after a pause.

'And Mrs Eng? What dialect did she speak?'

'Toishanese.' Much more quickly this time.

'Did they have any accent, when they spoke to you?'

This time the silence was longer, and the waiter's stare more perplexed.

'No accent,' the interpreter reported finally. She had barely finished when the waiter spoke again.

'*Cantonese* accent,' the interpreter said this time. 'Mr and Mrs – both.'


'You could see he was sweating,' Mahoney reported to Max Straus and Laurie Jordan. 'And when I pushed him harder he froze up. The other one was about the same except he kept repeating that he didn't know about any accent. I'd say it was pretty clear they were both lying about working for the Engs, and they're afraid of being caught at it. Not because of what *I* can do to them. There's somebody out there who scares them a lot more than I do.'

'You think Pullone put them up to it?' Laurie Jordan wanted to know.

'I don't see who else. Pullone or his snitch. Unless it's somebody with a bad grudge against the Engs.'

'In any event,' Max Straus broke in, 'somebody close to the case thinks it's necessary to trump up evidence at this point, and to my mind that puts Detective Pullone back on the front burner.' The D.A.'s counsel made a sour face. 'I'd better let Ned King know about this before he says the wrong thing to the Southern District.

'While I'm at it,' Straus added, 'should I be telling Ned anything more about your grand jurors?'

'They're both out of town, and at least one of them is out of the country,' Mahoney reported. 'I'm betting they're together. I've had Customs red-flag their passports to alert me when they come back. For all I know it's just a lovers' tryst, but with this case I'm not taking anything for granted.'

'You shouldn't,' Straus said. 'I'm beginning to think there's nothing and nobody innocent associated with these Eng people.'

He handed a file folder across the desk to Jordan. 'About Detective

Pullone – before Dan's waiters muddied the waters I'd begun putting together some background intelligence. I've got some notes there you might want to have a look at. It seems Messrs Pullone and Horgan have an interesting record with each other. They were handling forfeiture cases together even before Mr Horgan convinced the Boss to set him up in business for himself.

'The cases I picked out all have this in common – lots of money forfeited, and drugs, too. In most of them the probable cause behind the warrant came from an unregistered informant. They all ended with pleas *before* indictment, and the pleas were for essentially meaningless charges. You'll see sentences there of one-to-three and two-to-six. A couple, three-to-life.

'These are situations where Pullone and Horgan were pulling down thousands and thousands of dollars, and anywhere from an ounce to over a kilo of white powder. A-2 and A-1 felonies, every one of them. If the cases were any good, they should have been putting this slime away for the rest of their natural born lives.'

Jordan glanced over the file. 'But if they all smell like cheap pleas to cover bad arrests, why did they make arrests at all? Why not just run a pickup operation and be done with it?'

The same question, Mahoney thought, that he and Estrada had been kicking around about the Eng case.

'They couldn't let *all* the perps just walk,' he said. 'Not if they wanted to avoid somebody taking a hard look.'

'So Pullone scared the perps enough to make doing short time seem safer than gambling a not-guilty plea against twenty-five-to-life,' Jordan filled in. 'And everybody went away happy.'

'No doubt Pullone and Horgan even felt proud of themselves,' Straus pointed out. 'Perverse as that is. Because if they knew these searches were totally bad – which they must have been – then they also knew the perps shouldn't have done any time at all. And putting a skell away for one-to-three is better than letting him walk.'

What Straus and Jordan were outlining, Mahoney thought, was a whole lot worse than just one manufactured case. He could almost see Jordan adding up a prosecutorial two plus two in her head.

'But if *these* cases are bad –' she tapped the file folder with a precisely manicured fingernail – 'then don't we have to worry about every single case Horgan and Pullone ever made, together or separately?' Eager for the kill as Jordan was, her voice carried a certain dread. 'And then there's the question of who they might have taught and who taught them.'

'And who hired them and who promoted them and how they got away with it for so long,' Straus added.

'Scary,' Mahoney said.

'Very scary,' the D.A.'s counsel affirmed. 'If it's as bad as it looks, it'll be enough to keep Laurie and her colleagues busy for a long, long time.'


Back at the spa hotel, Susan and David said good night to their hosts and went into a small building called AMERICAN CAFE. The 'café' proved to be a single, dim room open to the sour night air, with a dirt floor and a dozen rickety tables draped in grimy oilcloth. They stood at the bar to get bottles of mineral water and took them to the table farthest from the few other patrons.

'Enjoying the trip?' David asked.

'It's a lot to absorb,' she said.

He looked hard at her in the gloom. 'Are you okay?'

The question surprised her. 'Why?'

'You've seemed tense, withdrawn, upset . . . all day.'

'Is it that obvious?' She wondered if she'd offended June Eng, or Chan.

'Not a bit,' David reassured her. 'I don't think anyone who didn't know you would have noticed.'

'I talked to my brother this morning.' There was no point concealing any of this from David, she thought, or why had she been so intent on having him here with her? 'And I talked to Richard. They didn't offer much support. My brother thinks I'm crazy to actually go into China to do this. He says if our parents got killed trying to make contact with people in China, what makes me think I won't?'

'It's a good question.'

'And I don't know the answer – I don't know how safe this is. That's part of the reason I've been upset.'

'What about your husband? What did he have to say?'

'He wants me to come home. He's decided I should never have said

456

yes to any of this, and he shouldn't have humored me about it – not even the Hong Kong part.'

'A little late for that.' As soon as the words were out David made a face. 'Sorry – that was past the bounds of being direct.'

'It's okay. You have permission to speak the truth even when you're accusing my husband of being an ass.'

'How's your son?' David asked, clearly uncomfortable. 'Any word?'

'Not really. And I'm not expecting any for a while. That's the way they work it where he is – for the first six weeks the family is completely out of contact. It makes me frantic not to know what's going on or how he is, but I'm told it's best for him, and for all of us.'

A woman came to their table and said something in Cantonese. Susan didn't understand even her usual one word in ten. The woman pointed at her watch, at the bar, at her watch again, and then at the door.

'I think she's telling us it's last call,' Susan said.

'This is all the mineral water I need for now,' David said.

Susan shook her head; the waitress didn't move. Susan tried again. This time the waitress shrugged and moved away.

'How was your morning?' Susan asked. 'Didn't you have another meeting at the RA?'

'Macleod took me to the university they sponsor. They've got a great computer setup over there, and they're planning some fascinating work. When you said the RA was the big time – that's not the half of it. The way Macleod talks, it's not only what he does in Hong Kong, but the projects they invite him in on, here.'

'In China?'

'So it seems. As a consultant, usually.'

'Did you learn anything useful?' She was interested, but the question came out flat and perfunctory.

'Useful to us, now, you mean? Not that I know of.'

'I meant useful for you.' She was exhausted, overloaded.

He seemed to sense it. 'We should get some sleep,' he said. 'You sure you're going to be all right?'

'You want the truth? The truth is I'm not sure at all. The truth is, I'm

457

frightened. Not that something's going to happen to me. I'm frightened of what I'm going to hear tomorrow.'

*There's nothing and nobody innocent associated with these Eng people.* I ought to put it on my bulletin board, Mahoney thought, or make it into a bumper sticker.

Nobody innocent – certainly not the waiters, prompted by money or threats from . . . someone . . . to lie about the Engs. And not Martin Eng's violent rival, Tony Ching of the Sam Yap Association.

And then there was Mr M.C. Wu, the Engs's daily phone companion – M.C. stood for Ming Chu, Mahoney had learned – a contributor to scholarly journals about Chinese history, according to Mr Feller at the China Society. And a regular phone caller to law firms and publicists and think tanks in Washington, where the Justice Department was hot on the trail of something that involved Martin and Meiling Eng.

And most puzzling of all, there were the two grand jurors, off somewhere, doing something . . .

The bed in Susan's room had been turned down and there was a candy on the sheet. In one corner of the room a small device topped by a metal coil was plugged into the wall. Some kind of mosquito repellent or killer was all she could think it might be. She hoped it worked.

She undressed and washed up and put on a lightweight, oversize T-shirt, started to get into bed – and stood up in surprise. She pushed at the bed and felt around its edges: it was a wooden slab with a dense mattress no more than an inch thick.

Well, she thought as she lay down, traditional Chinese beds were made of wood; this is a piece of history. An engaging thought, but it did not make the bed any more comfortable. She lay there with her eyes closed, trying not to think about the morning.

# 6

Susan woke early, her stiff and aching body only a minor distraction from her fear. She couldn't bear staying in her stuffy room so she braved the mosquitoes and took a walk around the grounds. Everything she saw struck her as incongruous – the foot-high ceramic pandas perched on low stone pedestals, the mermaid with the faint outline of a bra scratched into the bronze to defeat her nakedness, the laundry hanging limply on the balconies of guest rooms, the nearly empty swimming pool lined with blue tile, brackish brown water stagnating at the bottom.

The others were waiting for her at the main restaurant. Like the restaurant at the International Hotel, this was a vast room, more suitable for banquets than a quiet breakfast. Only four of the spacious tables were occupied.

They were seated and given tea and small bowls of pickled vegetables. Susan tried not to notice that the tablecloth was stained and the dishes flecked with old food.

She was not in the mood for conversation, and the others seemed subdued, as well. In her few exchanges with David, Susan saw concern in his eyes and did her best to produce a smile, though she doubted it was very reassuring.

Five minutes before their mystery guest was due, a waitress brought him to the table. Yu Wenli was small and frail, smaller than Martin Eng. His hair was thin and gray and unruly; his brownish, blotchy skin, all wrinkles; his hands, knobby with arthritis. His lively brown eyes surveyed the world from behind round, steel-rimmed glasses.

Susan endured the introductory civilities and the ordering of food

459

and made herself chat about her impressions of China. When the food arrived she smiled and forced herself to eat, though the congee – watery, greasy rice gruel reeking of fatty smoked pork and pickled vegetables, served in a bowl crusted with the residue of many previous breakfasts – almost brought her stomach into her mouth.

Yu Wenli noticed her distress. 'I apologize for the inadequacies of this place. I chose to come here in spite of them.' His clear, formal English was accompanied by a thick accent and delivered in a stiff cadence. 'I knew that few people would be here. Other places, we could not have so much privacy.'

He offered her the steamer of buns, some filled with pork, others with chopped vegetables. 'The food is not always the best taste, but it is healthy.'

Susan took a pale, gummy bun. 'Thank you. I'm not very hungry, I'm afraid. Traveling is not kind to my stomach.' A small, polite lie.

'Ah.' He returned to his congee.

Finally, he looked at her over his congee bowl and said, 'Chan Kwok-Wing has told me about your parents' visit to China many years ago.'

'Yes, I hope to learn what happened to them here.' She was beyond finding the proper circumlocution. 'Mr Chan said you might help.'

'When he first spoke of them, I was not sure that I could be of help. I hoped I was correct in thinking that the name of your father was like the name of a man I once knew. Names can be confusing here. My middle name, *Wen*, is Mandarin; in Cantonese, the same character is *Mun*. Miss Eng's family name is Cantonese; in Mandarin it is *Wu*. Very different.

'In this case, I knew your father's name – and your mother's name, too, was familiar. Two people's names that match is not so likely to be a mistake. I decided they were the people I was thinking of.

'We know that your parents came to China from America in the spring months of the Western year 1976. At that time the Cultural Revolution was ended and Deng Xiaoping was restored to power. Perhaps because of these signs your parents thought it was a safe time to come. Unfortunately, such signs can be misleading.

'It was a difficult year among many difficult years. Nothing stayed the same. Because of the death of Zhou Enlai, there was a large demonstration in Tiananmen Square in the spring, at the time of Qing Ming – the festival of cleaning and renewing graves and paying special homage to the dead. This happened in the same way that the famous Tiananmen Square demonstration in 1989 followed after the death of Hu Yaobang and the demonstrations beginning with the Qing Ming celebration in that year.

'Some people say many hundreds were beaten to death at the demonstration in 1976. The officials say many were hurt but none was killed. That was two decades ago. Who will contradict the officials now?

'After the demonstration, Deng Xiaoping was forced to flee from Beijing. Mao Zedong, the Great Helmsman, was dying. His wife and her Gang of Four, leaders of the Cultural Revolution, had been criticized by Mao in his last days. As he died the Gang of Four were preparing to take over the country. All this was during the time your father and mother came to China.

'The man I think was your father was a military hero from before. When he was very young he followed Mao Zedong on the Long March. In the war against the Japanese, Mao sent him to be liaison with the Nationalist Army. This was during that brief time when Mao Zedong and Chiang Kai-shek were pretending to join each other in a united front against the Japanese.

'When the break between Mao and Chiang came, your father had become close with American Air Force officers who were helping Chiang, and he did not wish to be separated from them. Because of this, his connection with Mao and the Communists was broken. But he did not make any firm connection with Chiang Kai-shek and his Nationalists.

'Soon after the war with the Japanese ended, your father went to Hong Kong. When Chiang and his people were forced out of China and went to Taiwan in 1949, your father did not follow.

'I do not know as much about your mother. I believe that for many generations, back into the Qing Dynasty, members of your mother's family played a role in the administration of Guangdong province.'

'My parents never told me any of this. I wonder if they told my brother.' And hadn't Meiling's family been imperial officers, too? So perhaps the two families *had* known each other.

461

'Many Hong Kong people must have known who your father was when he first went there. And when your mother arrived, many would have known her family as well.'

'My mother came to Hong Kong in 1949, I think,' Susan said. 'She met my father when he came back from college in the United States, and they were married in 1950. I was too young when we left Hong Kong to remember who their friends were or anything like that. I do know they were popular, and I know we weren't poor, though I don't think we were rich, either.'

'I think your father left Hong Kong because he wished to put past days behind him. I would not say that he was afraid of Mao Zedong or of Chiang Kai-shek, though I believe both leaders considered – incorrectly, I think – that he had failed in his loyalty to them. But he was a prudent man, and many prudent men in those days wanted to be as far from harm as possible. When he could, he left and went permanently to the United States. I believe he was helped by what he had done in the war, because at that time the United States was still almost closed to people from China.'

Susan saw now what she hadn't before. 'Once we were in America there was nothing about the old days. We didn't live near other Chinese people. My father was an executive in an American company, and his favorite expressions were things like, 'look ahead, the past is behind you,' and 'all that matters is what you do tomorrow.' He believed children should respect their parents for the work they did in raising them and for the knowledge they'd gained in living their lives, but aside from that he said the only achievements that matter are ones you haven't yet realized.

'My mother was different. She tried to get us to appreciate our heritage and be more Chinese, but we weren't that interested. And even when she did that, she never talked about her personal history, or my father's. She would say things about her family being very proper and well-regarded, but she never really said why. Just that she wanted us to be a credit to them.' She stopped short of describing her mother's anger and disappointment when Susan married a man whose ancestors came from England and Scotland. 'And I was so busy being an ordinary American I didn't want to ask questions.' A sharp sense of opportunities lost made her eyes sting; she blinked it away. 'But how

462

does all that affect what happened when they were here?'

'At the moment your parents came back to China,' Yu replied, 'Mao was sick, the Gang of Four was out of power, and Deng Xiaoping held a strong position. Your parents had no reason to suppose they would be noticed or bothered. They visited their old friends and they sought out your mother's family. Many in her family were gone, and also in your father's family. Many did not survive the Cultural Revolution. Many others had been sent out into the countryside, to the western provinces, to work on pig farms. No one knew where they were.

'During the time your parents were here everything changed. There was the demonstration in Tiananmen Square. I do not know if they were in Beijing at that time. It is possible they were. After the demonstration Deng Xiaoping was forced to flee from Beijing, as I said. He came here to Guangzhou. He was hidden here by friends in the Army.' Yu smiled. 'We have always been good revolutionaries, here in the south. The northerners don't like us. They don't trust us. We return the favor.

'At the time the situation changed so drastically, those people your parents came to visit – people who had survived the Cultural Revolution and were made to feel secure by the brief return of Deng Xiaoping to power – suddenly no longer were secure. No one with experience in political life was safe. In Shanghai at that time there was a separate army a million strong, preparing for a civil war.

'Your parents had been in America many years. They did not remember how dangerous it was simply to speak. The China they lived in was often full of treachery, but it was safe and simple compared to how things became later.

'I cannot say what happened to them. I think it is likely that someone who remembered your father from the war days learned that on this trip he had visited some person who had suddenly fallen under suspicion. Your father's past history was very dangerous to him.'

'But he'd been out of the country almost thirty years,' Susan protested. 'If what you say is right – I'm sorry, I don't mean to suggest that I doubt you, only that these ideas are so new to me that it's hard for me to take in – if I understand what you're saying, all he did during the war was to fight China's enemies.'

'To fight China's enemies is not enough. It matters how, and when, and what allies you fought beside. I do not mean to offer disrespect to your parents, but I think it was not prudent of them to come here when they did. They did not understand how easily things could change, or how quickly.'

'Could they have been so imprudent that it got them killed?'

'If people killed your parents, it did not happen by design. By that I mean that your parents were not aware of the dangers, and the killers – if that is what happened – did not set out to kill them. People are detained, people are interrogated. Sometimes they are hurt. Or perhaps it was during the demonstration in Tiananmen Square.

'If there was a mistake, then to report that two foreigners had a fatal accident is easier than to explain why they were imprisoned or abused or badly damaged. If such a mistake happened, it was a very bad mistake and I am sure the person or people responsible suffered for it.'

'You think my parents were killed.'

'Possibly. If so, the earthquake was very convenient.'

'It was a little late,' she said, trying to contain her emotions. 'There are the missing weeks, after all.'

'But what can you do with missing weeks, in the end? What *did* you do? The authorities have travel documents to show you and you cannot know if they are authentic. They send you a letter from a witness. And for almost twenty years, you believe them.'

But her brother hadn't. He'd even made almost the same comment about the earthquake. She had been the gullible one.

'How can you tell us all this now? Isn't it dangerous to make accusations like that?'

'I am an old man. Times have changed. I do not think this place – I apologize again for bringing you here – is full of listening devices. I do not think you will denounce me.'

He held the bowl of congee to his mouth and slurped some up with help from his spoon.

'When a man is as old as I am, he understands that history must be honored. The truth must be honored. I regret I do not have more to tell you. I know it is painful. I hope and believe this kind of pain is good for the spirit.'

'You know so much about my parents. So much more than I do. How is that possible?'

464

'I knew your father. Not well, and only briefly, long years ago. Also, he came to see me in 1976.'

'He did? When?'

'In the spring. Before the demonstration in Tiananmen Square.'

'Then did you know . . . did you know what happened to him?'

'I was concerned.' For a moment, Yu did not speak. 'After a time, I heard there had been an incident, but I did not know precisely what happened.'

She was suddenly wary. 'Is that why you think he might have been killed? For coming to see you?'

'I will admit it was not helpful in those uncertain days if my name was on a list of the people one spoke with.' Yu took brief refuge in slurping up more congee. 'No one, I think, was killed for that reason alone.'

Susan felt a sudden knot of pain in her stomach. She could not make herself look at Yu.

'Why did he come to see you?'

'He said he wished to say hello to an old commanding officer. He spoke with me about how he might locate members of his family and your mother's. I offered some ideas to him.'

'When were you his commanding officer?' She made her voice level, though she wanted to throw her congee bowl at Yu's lined face.

'I was your father's superior during the war against Japan, before he was assigned to Chiang's camp. And I knew him from the Long March.'

She put her shaking hands in her lap. 'How do you remember this so well, after so many years?'

'Because I thought your father was a good soldier and a man who loved his country, who was treated unfairly. And I knew that after he came to see me in 1976 something happened to him and your mother. I considered myself responsible. Why responsible? For not warning him clearly enough about how dangerous the times were. For not protecting him in that way from coming to harm.'

'But you've never said anything about it.'

'I never had anyone I could tell about it. And in the years since then I was myself often in a difficult position. I was protected by being in

465

the south, and by being in the Army, but no protection of that kind is perfect.'

Susan turned to Chan Kwok-Wing. 'It was good fortune that you talked to Mr Yu about this.'

'It was good fortune, indeed,' Yu said. 'My friend Wing came to me because he knows I have studied certain practices of that period. I was *reformed* by the Great Proletarian Cultural Revolution – I spent many years in a re-education camp. When my rehabilitation was arranged, after that sad, misguided period ended and after the trial of the Gang of Four, I was happy to be responsible for cataloging some of the abuses that occurred, to locate intellectuals and experienced officials who had been dispersed into the countryside or imprisoned as I had been, and return them to useful work. Chan Kwok-Wing thought that for this reason I could find out what had happened to your father. He did not know I had briefly known a person with that same name, in the Army, or that I had seen him when he visited in 1976.'

'I have one more question,' Susan said as Yu was leaving. 'Do you remember if my father said anything about visiting Shuntak?'

'No. I do not remember that. Shuntak is not far from here. On the way to Guangzhou. If it is the same family I think, then some of your mother's and father's relatives lived near there.'

'Do you know if any of their relatives are still there?'

'I inquired about both families. I found no people I could say were your relatives. Even if they survived all that came before, in almost twenty years many people move.'

'But don't people need special permission to move any distance, and new residence permits?'

'Yes. But people move without them.' He scratched his nose and seemed to drift away for a moment. 'There is another reason. Your parents came here as returning Chinese, but they were also Americans. The American Government might have decided to make serious inquiry about them after they disappeared. If so, the people your parents visited, particularly their relatives, could tell stories the authorities would find embarrassing and inconvenient. Those people would not be allowed to remain at their previous address.'

'You think they were killed? For speaking to my parents? Or being related to them?' Susan was horrified. Killing whole families to punish the transgression of a single member was part of Chinese imperial tradition.

'Not killed,' Yu reasured her. 'Relocated. And by now, the ones that did not die from the passing of time . . .' He shrugged. 'Who can say where they are?'

After they said goodbye to Yu Wenli, Susan excused herself to go back to her room. David asked if there was anything he could do but she said, no, she wanted to be alone.

He wandered the grounds and considered what it might be like to get the kind of news Susan had just received. Her parents had died twenty years ago. Was there any solace in knowing now how it might have happened, the cruelty and needlessness of it? Was that better than visualizing their death in an earthquake?

He'd heard anger in her voice at the end. Did it help to know that you had a terrible grievance you couldn't redress against people you couldn't identify?

He wondered how much more Yu knew than he was telling. How directly visiting Yu had really been a catalyst in her parents' death. And why he hadn't warned them more clearly.

Warned them that China was dangerous in the midst of a succession of power at the top, David thought. But China was going through that very kind of transition right now. Paramount leader Deng Xiaoping would lead no more. His cronies and his long-time rivals were dead and dying, too. The new president was scrambling to make his job more secure – the anti-corruption purges were just the opening shot.

Was Yu indirectly warning them of that now?

467

# 7

From the spa hotel they drove north toward Sam Yap. June Eng had scheduled a stop in Shuntak, but Susan said she didn't feel up to it. 'And if I won't be able to find my relatives, there's no point.'

June Eng apologized for having made an appointment in Panyu to visit a factory while they were in the neighborhood. 'I did not expect you would have such upsetting news.'

The road to Panyu seemed dustier to David even than the road from Zhuhai to Zhongshan. Long stretches were lightly traveled, but each time they approached a town, traffic clogged the road. David got accustomed to seeing trucks forging up the wrong side of the road to get to a turnoff, cars and trucks frozen in an intersection with no traffic signals, drivers ignoring the few traffic signals there were.

Sitting on the other side of June Eng from Susan, David felt frustrated: he wanted to comfort her, though he had no particular solace to offer and she had asked for none. She made the trip in silence, closed off in her thoughts, as she had been since breakfast.

In the hour before they left the spa hotel, Susan had lain on the hard bed in her room, trying to absorb what Yu had told her. She had been beyond tears, beyond any immediate ability to visualize what had happened to her parents – clubbed by police in a demonstration in Beijing, tortured by overzealous interrogators . . .

By the time they were on the road she had entered a merciful state of blankness. She spent the trip staring out the window. Along the road between towns she had an impression of virtually uninterrupted construction. Green hills had been bulldozed to flat, dusty plains. On some of the sites, buildings were going up, shrouded in a mesh of bamboo scaffolding. Many of the lots stood vacant, waiting.

Once, they hurried by a broad, wooded hillside high on whose flank she saw a grand house of many wings with a red pagoda roof. The entire hillside in front of and below the mansion had been bulldozed away, so that its front gate was at the edge of a sheer dirt cliff. Where the rolling, green lower slope of the hill had been, there was now only another empty, barren plain.

That's me, she thought, looking at the house – rich and imposing from a distance, but completely isolated. All access cut off and the foundations in danger of being eroded away if they don't collapse first.

Delayed by traffic jams, they stopped for lunch en route and arrived in Panyu later than June Eng had planned. It was a bustling city, the streets full of young people in Western dress. Nowhere did David notice the drab, high-button jackets and baggy pants that had once been a feature of every picture of China that he saw.

'A lot of soldiers,' he said. They strolled the street in twos and threes, automatic rifles slung from their shoulders.

'Yes,' Chan acknowledged without saying more.

Susan asked to stay in the factory manager's office while the others did their business, and David stayed with her, not wanting to leave her alone.

An elderly man who had been introduced to them as the factory's assistant manager came in with a pot of tea and asked in labored English if there was anything he could do for them.

'Is it possible to call the United States?' Susan asked.

He went off to see.

'I have to tell my brother,' Susan said to David. 'And my husband.'

The assistant manager came back and led Susan off to make her phone calls, then returned to the office, nodded to David, and sat down.

Making sure we don't steal the ashtrays? David wondered.

'Have you worked here long?' David asked him, not sure he would understand.

'Not work here long. This, new factory . . . Work for Eng family, Cheung family, almost whole life, from small boy.'

He reached for the teapot and poured some for David, and himself. David tapped the table with two fingers; the assistant manager grinned widely, showing an incomplete set of badly stained teeth.

'Many years, Mr Mao say – good for all people to work farm, not work factory for silk,' he went on. 'In here –' he grabbed his belly the way an American might press his hand to his heart – 'work for Eng family whole time.'

'Have they always had factories here?'

'Long, long time. My father work for Eng family – work for Eng grandfather of Eng Jung – Miss June, you call. Father of my father work for Cheung grandfather of mother of Eng Jung. Cheung Lung. Very famous.'

'They've been in the garment business here that long?'

'Many business. Cheung family own land all around, Panyu, Shuntak. Farm for animals, rice. Mulberry trees for silk. Many mulberry trees, many silk. Family very important. Father and grandfather of Cheung Lung, officials in Guangzhou for Qing Emperor. Cheung Lung and sons of Cheung Lung good friend, Sun Yatsen.' He repeated the name, turning it into a question. 'Sun Yatsen?'

'Yes, I think I know who that is.'

'Father of Republic. Cheung Lung important person, left wing of Sun Yatsen Nationalist Party. Communist cadre . . . Sun Yatsen Nationalist Party not like Chiang Kai-shek Nationalist Party.' The assistant manager made a sour face and hissed.

'But didn't the Communists and Nationalists fight a civil war against each other?' In which Susan's father, apparently, had been caught in the middle.

'Civil war come after. Mao Zedong Communists come after. First China Communist Government – Sun Yatsen Government, Guang-dong province.'

Susan came back into the office. 'I talked to my brother.' Her voice was stronger than it had been.

'What did he say?'

'Basically, "I told you so." But he's glad he doesn't have to wonder any more. Now he wants to find out exactly what kind of war hero our father was, and all about our mother's family.' Her lips compressed into a bitter smile. 'I told him he could come over here himself if he was so hot to know.'

She sank onto the lumpy vinyl-covered couch next to David. 'I'm exhausted. All I did was sit at breakfast and listen to a man tell a story, and I feel as if I've been carrying bricks uphill all day.'

She put her head back, but the couch did not support it well. She turned slightly and curled up; her forehead came to rest on his shoulder. 'Is this okay?' she asked.

'Sure it's okay.'

She was asleep immediately. The assistant factory manager grinned at David and left, closing the door behind him.

For almost an hour David sat without moving, not wanting to wake her. Her eyes opened and she sat up when Chan Kwok-Wing and June Eng came into the office.

'I must say goodbye,' Chan said. 'I have other business now.' He held out a hand to shake Susan's. 'Thank you. I am grateful to hear from you about my friends. Please bring good wishes to Eng Chu-Ming and Cheung Meiling.'

'I'm the one who should be doing the thanking,' Susan said in a dull voice. 'Thank you for finding Mr Yu. His answers were very helpful.'

Chan smiled broadly. 'One friend help another friend.'

The road out of Panyu was as dusty as the road in. Yet again, they sat in a traffic jam. Next to them was a truck full of hogs, its sides a wide-spaced lattice of metal pipes and wooden slats. The hogs were jammed in on two levels, but there seemed to be four layers of them, sitting and lying and leaning on each other, many on the bottom layers clearly in pain, some of the ones on the outside deeply cut and bleeding where they were pressed against the thin bars that contained them.

The van passed through the city of Guangzhou as quickly as the

471

congestion of trucks and cars and buses would allow. David had the impression of streets as full of traffic and pedestrians as those of Hong Kong, but here there were wide boulevards that would not have fitted in the narrow confines of Hong Kong island. There were massive old buildings here, too, a kind he hadn't seen in Hong Kong, looking transplanted from nineteenth-century Paris or London. The avenues he saw were filled with bicycles and motorbikes as well as cars and trucks, but there were traffic signals and here in town people seemed to obey them.

From an elevated highway, June Eng pointed out the main railroad station, massive and gray, with a broad plaza in front of it, embraced by the building's two substantial wings. The plaza was packed with people.

'An unofficial job market,' June Eng said. 'All those people have come from the countryside. It's that way every day.'

'Do they find any work?'

'Some do.'

'What about the others?'

'They wait till the next day, they lower their asking price or agree to do more menial work. Some of them beg, some go home. Some of the women are tricked into prostitution, some choose it.'

They dropped June Eng off at a luxury hotel in Guangzhou. She slung a small bag over her shoulder and kept a tight grip on the briefcase she'd been carrying since they'd left Hong Kong.

'I don't mean to abandon you,' she said. 'But I have an important meeting here this evening and I don't want to ask you to sit around waiting for me. I'll see you back in Hong Kong. And you're in good hands with Mr Li.'

Mr Li – June Eng's replacement as their English-speaking guide – was short and plump, almost roly-poly, David thought. He was a troubleshooter and roving factory manager for the Engs, he explained in colloquial American. A native of Hong Kong, he had been educated in the U.S. and had lived there for almost sixteen years.

'I was an engineer first, then I got laid off and I was a schoolteacher for a while. Then I got this idea to come back over here, and I got a job managing a factory. I've been working for the Engs for four years now. My family came with me, but because of the transition in Hong Kong and the succession of power here on the mainland they decided to go back to the U.S. Now I'm here alone.'

The van retraced its route through part of Guangzhou to get back to the road out.

'I hope you don't mind,' Li said. 'I have an errand to run for June. It's only a little out of the way, and it's different from what you've seen.'

The factory was outside a town called Dongguan, several traffic jams to the east of Guangzhou. They drove along roads lined on both sides with tall, slender trees. Beyond them, David glimpsed his first rice paddies, and a factory pipe gushing bright blue effluent into what looked like an irrigation canal.

'From stonewashing jeans,' Li commented. 'Dye runoff.'

They pulled into the factory parking lot at sunset and while Li took care of his errand Susan and David got a tour. They saw a machine cutting stuffed-animal ears out of a roll of leathery material densely covered with brown fur, bales of white cotton-wool standing by to be stuffed into the inside-out cloth shells of teddy bears, and women punching holes in empty cloth heads and pressing plastic eyes into the holes – a job for only the most senior workers, their guide told them, because the exact position of the eyes made so much difference in the finished animal's personality. David doubted Susan was really seeing any of it.

'I apologize for taking so long,' Li said when he rejoined them. 'There are fine hotels in Guangzhou. I know Miss June would want me to get you dinner and a comfortable room there as an apology for this. No need to travel at night.'

'I appreciate your kindness,' Susan said, 'but I'd rather get back to Hong Kong as soon as possible.'

'If you wish. There's a fast highway to Shenzhen' – *Sumchun*. 'You could take the train from there to Hong Kong, but you would arrive very late. Or you could stay in a hotel in Shenzhen and go through to

473

Hong Kong first thing in the morning.'

'If it's not too much trouble,' Susan said.

'No trouble. And there's no need to choose now. First we go to the main highway. We can decide which way to go, then.'

It was dark when they got underway, with a thin crescent moon peeking occasionally through the clouds. There were no lights on the road from the factory and not much traffic. Susan curled up in a corner of the van's rear seat. David, next to her, looked out into the night, watching the black-on-black silhouettes of the roadside trees flash by. For a few minutes at a time, he dozed.

He awoke to the realization that they seemed still to be on the same dark road.

'How are we doing?' he asked Li.

'That's a good question. It appears we're slightly lost.'

'Lost?' That did not sound good. China between Guangzhou and the toy factory had left David with the impression of a place where getting lost might mean really being *lost*.

'The driver thought he had a good, new way to get to the highway,' Li explained. 'Faster and simpler. He must have made a wrong turn somewhere. The problem is, around here the roads get built more quickly than the maps can be revised.'

At one intersection two old men were laying a concrete sidewalk by the light of kerosene lanterns. The driver asked them directions, but they could not help.

David sat back while they hunted through the night. He thought Susan must be asleep; she'd shown no reaction to his exchange with Li about being lost.

Gradually, David and Li fell into conversation. Li was interested to learn that David worked with computers; he had many questions about the future course of popular hardware and software.

He complained about the difficulty of getting some kinds of computer equipment in China. 'But there's always a way,' he said. 'You know about *guanxi*, I suppose – using connections and influence where it counts, one hand washes the other. That's very important here. Cash helps, too.'

'I wondered about that,' David said. 'There's been so much about anti-corruption campaigns.'

'People find ways . . .'

Li was telling a story. The driver said something over his shoulder.

'Excuse me,' Li said, and had a short talk with the driver. 'He says he knows where we are now. Ten or fifteen more minutes to the toll road. From there it should only be an hour or so to Shenzhen, if you still want to go that way.'

Their conversation shifted to Yu Wenli's comment about mistrust between northerners and southerners in China.

'It made me think about how many places that happens, around the world,' David said.

'Yes,' Li said. 'The United States itself is an example of that. You had a civil war between the north and the south in your country.'

'And in Asia there's Korea,' David said. 'And Vietnam.'

'British India, too, in a way,' Li added. 'In China it goes back centuries. The south, especially, has always had a broad independent streak. They have a saying down here – *"the mountains are high and the Emperor is far away."*

'I wonder about it, sometimes. Look at China, as it is now – more than a billion people, thousands of miles between borders. Why do we assume it's best for it to be all one country?

'The Tibetans would be happy to rule themselves. The people in Xinjiang, in the far west, look more like you than like me, and they're Muslims like their Western neighbors. In the north-east, Manchuria was a separate country until the Manchu Emperors invaded China. Between, in the interior provinces, people strike and riot against the central authority. And even within the boundaries of the old Han Chinese states near the coast – as we were saying, southerners and northerners don't mix. They don't look alike, don't use the same spoken language . . .'

He paused a moment, then said, 'For me, this is an interesting philosophical question. But there are some who see it as a matter of geopolitical realism and economic self-interest. Many people in business and in local and provincial Government resent having to pay taxes to a central government that demands much and provides little. For many years the regional governments have failed to pay part of the taxes Beijing levies. And some would like still more independence.' He took a long breath and shook his head. 'This is a dangerous time we live in.'

Abruptly, he looked up. 'What now?'

# 8

They were slowing down. David could make out an area of brightness ahead of the van, cold light on an obstruction in the road.

Li and the driver exchanged rapid Chinese.

'Something's wrong,' Susan said softly in the dark beside him.

The van slowed again, sharply.

Li twisted around in his seat to face them. 'It's a roadblock. We have to stop, maybe get out. No problem.'

'Is that usual?' Susan asked. 'Out here in the middle of nowhere?'

'To these people this is the middle of a main road.'

The van stopped. David could see now that the roadblock was a two-foot high bundle of the bamboo poles used for construction scaffolding, each pole long enough to span the road.

In front of the roadblock were three men in olive-drab army uniforms pointing their automatic rifles at the van. A fourth soldier was moving toward the driver. David sensed motion in the dark beyond the bamboo blockade – others, not fully seen.

The soldier poked the barrel of his automatic rifle through the driver's window and barked a few harsh words.

*'Mei you,'* the driver said, his voice hoarse with fright. *'Mei you.'*

'He's asking if we have any weapons or money,' Li whispered. 'The driver said we don't have any.'

The soldier banged his rifle barrel fiercely against the window frame and shouted. Immediately, Li faced the windshield and sat in rigid silence.

After a few more curt questions, all answered by the same denial, the soldier issued what was unmistakably an order.

'We have to get out now,' Li translated. 'The soldiers are going to search the van. No problem.' The last words were tacked on woodenly, with no apparent hope they would be believed.

The night air was close and muggy. Getting awkwardly out of the van, David could feel himself begin to sweat. He turned to help Susan.

The soldier jammed the muzzle of his rifle into David's kidney and shouted at him, shoved him forward.

David limped toward the front of the van, trying to ignore the pain in his back. Behind him he heard Susan getting out of the van, the soldier hurrying her along. She said a few words of Chinese that David took to be a protest against being pushed along or manhandled.

The soldier lined the four of them up with their backs to the van's front bumper. The three soldiers David had seen earlier had not moved except to point their rifles directly at their prisoners.

*Prisoners.* As the word came into his mind David felt a sudden rage. He wanted to take their guns and wrap them around their necks. For a moment, the pure heat of it drove away the chill of fear.

The soldier who had gotten them out of the van looked at David with sudden interest. He moved closer and poked the muzzle of his gun under David's chin, pushing up painfully. David stood his tallest, then raised up on his toes. Without a word, the soldier released the pressure, his eyes locked on David's until David looked away.

The soldier asked a question. Li responded with an affirmative grunt and half a step forward. The soldier shouted at him and he stepped back into place.

Having identified Li as the group's leader, the soldier engaged him in what sounded like an interrogation. As he shouted questions, he indicated first Susan, then David. Something seemed to be annoying him about the situation.

David, anger and frustration warring in him with prudence and fear, felt preternaturally alert despite the soporific tropical night. He wanted to communicate with Susan, who was close enough for him to feel the heat of her body next to his, but he sensed that even to glance at her now was to risk upsetting a precarious equilibrium.

The soldier broke off his interrogation of Li to shout orders to the three waiting by the bamboo roadblock. One detached himself from the group and went around to the side doors of the van; the other two spread out slightly, the better to cover the four prisoners.

478

With the bright lights in his eyes, everything beyond the roadblock was impenetrable blackness. David couldn't tell how many more men with rifles were out there, or where they were, but with every minute he was more convinced this was not the way an Army roadblock would be run.

He felt something brush his hand, looked down. It was Susan's fingers, reaching for his. He took them, trying not to let the slight movement of his arm draw the soldiers' attention.

Her hand was cool, and slick with perspiration. Her fingers pressed his; he returned the pressure.

The lead soldier was apparently finished with Li. They all stood in silence until his comrade-in-arms came out of the van carrying David's backpack and Susan's small bag. He emptied them onto the bamboo roadblock, with a running commentary on what he found, then stuffed everything back. The lead soldier, who had seemed increasingly displeased by what he was hearing, pointed his rifle at Li and issued a long order.

Li turned to them. 'We have to go with them now. It's best to do what they say.'

'What *is* this?' Susan asked, her voice tight but controlled. 'Who are they, why are they doing this?'

'It's an Army roadblock,' Li said, unconvincingly.

David said, 'I thought you were partners—'

The soldier yelled at them, took two long strides that put him within inches of David, and yelled threateningly in his face, the rifle muzzle again pressed painfully under his chin. With the threatening words came a blast of rancid, garlicky breath.

Li said something – an explanation – and the soldier turned and slapped him with the rifle butt. The factory manager staggered, blood welling from his mouth.

'No!' Susan cried, and immediately clapped a hand over her mouth.

The soldier now looked beside himself with fury but before he could act on it something else caught his attention. He gave a startled look over their shoulders at the same time David sensed a change in the light and heard a growling sound that resolved into the racing motor of a fast-approaching car. The soldier barked orders to the others, who raised their rifles.

479

David turned to look and saw the car rushing toward them, its headlights extinguished even as David caught sight of it. He wondered if it would plow into the van, hurtling it forward, crushing them. As his muscles tensed, the car slewed to a halt, its doors flying open.

He launched himself toward Susan just as she turned to him and the first bursts of automatic-weapons fire exploded in the night. He knocked her off her feet and bore her to the ground under him. He heard the breath go out of her with a sharp cry.

'Okay?' he whispered under the roar of the guns.

She nodded, gasping breath back into her lungs.

She started to crawl under the van. He held her back. It was shelter, but if a bullet caught the gas tank it could explode. He tried to tell her; he couldn't be sure if she'd heard, but she stopped resisting him.

His head was by the front wheel on the driver's side of the van. Looking up, he could see the verge of the road, where the roadblock lights cast only a faint glow. He thought there might be a ditch there, just past the line of newly planted young trees.

The gunfire was sporadic now, bursts punctuated by silences. Most of the firing, he thought, was coming from the direction of the roadblock, but he couldn't be sure what that meant. He wondered whether he and Susan could crawl to the side of the road unseen, to the shelter of the ditch. If they stayed where they were, they were bound to be hit by a stray bullet even if no one was firing at them directly. But by moving they might make themselves targets.

The van rocked under the impact of bullets. A line of hot pain seared the back of David's neck. 'We're not safe here,' he said. 'There's a ditch at the side of the road. If we crawl, slowly, we may be able to get there without drawing their fire.'

Susan rolled over so she could talk to him. Her face was streaked with dirt, and there was a bruise on her cheek. 'Why shoot at us?'

'Once they start . . .' None of this made any sense.

She nodded. 'You sure we shouldn't stay here?'

'No.'

There was brief silence, then another volley rocked the van.

Susan said, 'I guess—'

Bullets slammed into the ground just beyond their heads. David was stung by a spray of dirt and pebbles.

Susan clutched at him and buried her face in his chest. He held her close and tried to make them both small, invisible.

Gradually he became aware that the latest silence was not being interrupted. He looked up, saw only the road, trees, the shadow of the ditch. Another car screeched to a halt somewhere nearby. He held Susan tighter.

He heard the crunch of shoes approaching. Impossibly, they sounded louder and more ominous than the gunfire.

The footsteps stopped at his back.

'Mr Clark? Mrs Chan?'

David looked up, saw a thin Chinese man in a business suit.

'My name, Yee Kwok-Fung,' he said. 'Wing Chan, my cousin. All okay now.'

*Where did he come from?* David wondered, but nothing that happened this night was going to surprise him now. He stood up slowly, helped Susan up. Standing, she sank back against the van, her arms wrapped around herself, shaking.

David looked toward the roadblock, saw three burly men in business suits – business suits, in this heat – prodding at the bodies of the soldiers, apparently to see if they were dead. Each of the burly men held a machine pistol in one hand.

'We go now,' said Yee Kwok-Fung.

They left in the car that had brought Yee. Their rescuers stayed behind. None of the burly men, it seemed, had suffered more than superficial wounds. The van driver and Mr Li were dead, Yee told them, killed in the first hail of bullets from behind the roadblock.

There was no conversation in the car. Yee rode in the front. In the rear, Susan curled up and rested her head against the seatback and the window. David wanted to turn her around, rest her head on his shoulder, cradle her in his arms. He reached for her but she just curled up tighter.

He was drifting into exhausted sleep when he felt her stir beside him. She turned and curled up again, her head on his chest. He could feel the dampness of tears and sweat seep through his shirt. Her breathing settled into the regular pattern of sleep, and soon he was asleep, too.

★ ★ ★

They both came awake – the car was stopped in bright glare. David saw Army uniforms and automatic rifles.

'No worry,' Yee said quickly. 'All safe here. Migration control, Shenzhen special zone. Keep people out of Special Economic Zone without permit. Migration control very important.'

He smiled over the back of the seat at them. 'Very safe. No shooting for foreigners.'


They slept again until Yee woke them. They were in a coldly-lit basement garage whose concrete floor and concrete-block walls could have been anywhere in the world.

Yee helped them into an elevator. They got off in a carpeted hallway and he led them to a luxury hotel suite. Heavy drapes were drawn across the windows. A doctor and nurse were waiting for them.

The nurse took Susan off into one of the bedrooms. In the other, the doctor examined David and stitched up the wound in the back of his neck.

'Four stitches,' Yee told him. 'Doctor says no scar. Important you sleep now. Doctor give sedative.'

David held up a hand in protest. 'Susan?' It came out sounding ragged.

'Doctor say only mild shock.' Yee pressed his slender palms together and rested his cheek on the back of one hand. 'Sleep now. Tomorrow morning, both feel better.'

# 9

In the morning, Chan Kwok-Wing was there. He told them they had been the victims of road bandits. This kind of banditry was a recent phenomenon, he explained. Gangs of thieves bought or stole Army uniforms and weapons, sometimes even got actual Army roadblocks or checkpoint booths. They set up at a distance from population centers, where they could rob likely-looking travelers.

Fortunately, Chan told them, this gang was known to the authorities, and a group of investigators from the People's Armed Security Police had already been on their way to arrest them at the time they stopped the van. Also by good fortune Wing Chan's cousin Fung Yee was an officer in the security police. Chan had been visiting with his aunt and his aunt's family in Guangzhou when Cousin Fung heard a police call saying that bandits had ambushed a van carrying two Chinese, along with a white-ghost man and an overseas-Chinese woman. Chan had recognized the descriptions and told his cousin he knew the victims. Yee Kwok-Fung had then called Headquarters and insisted on going to the scene.

'Very persistent. Nobody say no to Chan Kwok-Wing or Cousin Fung.'

'Were the bandits all killed?' Susan asked.

'Yes. Eight.'

'Lucky number,' she said acidly. She looked distracted, David thought, as if she wasn't focusing on what was going on around her. 'What would they have done to us?'

'They take money, possessions. Everything.'

'But what would they have done to *us*?'

Chan shrugged, shook his head. David thought he knew and was holding back.

'They would have killed us,' Susan said. 'That's what they would have done, isn't it?'

Chan shrugged again. 'Some bandits kill victims, yes. Police say these do not. Rob, only, and kidnap. Kidnapping is Chinese way, solve many disputes. Also for money.'

'They killed Mr Li and our driver.'

'Accident.' Chan's mouth turned down in exaggerated sorrow. 'Too many bullets. Very sad.'

'He seemed like such a good, kind man.'

'Very sad,' Chan repeated. 'Good man, good worker, very valuable.'

'What will happen to his family?' Susan asked.

'Please, not worry,' Chan said. 'June and Peter, very upset. They help Li family.'

'You told June and Peter?'

'Yes. They send good wishes. Happy you are well. Sorry for bad experience.'

'Thank you,' Susan said without emotion.

'I apologize for China,' Chan said. 'No good to allow foreign people places where bandits practice trade. Road must be patrolled, catch bandits first.'


Susan and David had a room-service breakfast while they waited for the security police to interview them. The hotel was the Shenzhen branch of a South-Asian chain, amply stocked with the ingredients necessary for a Western breakfast, if the kitchen had only known how to prepare them.

'Amazing what just being alive can do for your appetite,' David said. He'd meant it lightly, but it made her put her fork down.

'They were going to kill us,' she said. 'I know it.'

'I don't know. That head guy seemed awfully confused, as if he wasn't finding something he expected.'

Susan looked at him oddly. 'He didn't seem confused about telling us what to do.'

'He was shouting a lot, but it looked more like a tantrum to me than like he was in control . . . But I guess we'll never know.'

'My parents came here, and they died here,' she said. 'My brother told me I was crazy to come, but I never imagined . . .' She pushed her plate away. 'I don't know whether to shake with fear or scream with anger.' She looked at him. 'You saved my life, didn't you?'

'I don't know about that.'

She reached over to touch the bandage on the back of his neck. 'I'd say you came close enough to get the credit.' She offered her hand. 'Thank you.'

He pressed her hand, held it a moment. He remembered standing next to her in the roadblock glare, her fingers searching for his . . .

The rest of the day they were at the beck and call of the security police. The officers who spoke to them offered a mixture of effusive apology and totalitarian rigidity. They interviewed Susan and David separately and repeatedly. It seemed odd to David, since there was so little to tell.

In the afternoon, at a time when they were together, Susan demanded that they be allowed to return to Hong Kong.

'If you're holding us here, it's against our will and I want to see the American consul.'

'Consul in Guangzhou,' the security-police captain told her.

'I want to call him.'

He left the room. Yee Kwok-Fung came in.

'Trouble?'

'I said I wanted to leave. Or talk to the American consul at once.' It was something they did, when they were serious – hold you *incommunicado*.

'No problem. Police only wish to learn what happened.'

'We've told them.'

'Three times, each,' David said.

'You must be tired, sitting in hotel,' Yee said. 'Beautiful day. You go for walk, I talk again to police.'

They went for their walk with two security policemen in business suits walking behind them. The boulevards in Shenzhen were as wide as the ones David had seen in Guangzhou, although the traffic was not as heavy. They passed tall, pale buildings with large windows – commercial buildings and hotels.

485

A small boy darted out of the parking area in front of a hotel and walked alongside David, chattering in Cantonese and holding out his hand. David smiled at him but kept walking.

The boy started to sing, or to recite a poem, David couldn't tell which.

'I suppose we shouldn't encourage him,' Susan said.

'That's the conventional wisdom. There are probably a million of them.'

The little boy tugged at David's sleeve, hung on. Their security-police escorts ran up, shouting. The boy fled.

Susan turned to the guards, indignant. David squeezed her arm in warning and she let it pass.

'He wasn't hurting anybody,' she said as they continued walking. 'But you were right to stop me.'

They paused to wait for the traffic light so they could cross a boulevard that looked as wide as a six-lane highway. On the other side, Susan said, 'Did you notice he didn't approach me, only you?'

'Because I look more like a sucker.'

'No, because I'm Chinese and you're not.'

'They wouldn't get far here, if they didn't beg from Chinese people.'

'I think it's the mix. You're a non-Asian male, I'm a Chinese woman. Here, I think that makes me your mistress.'

David kept walking, eyes ahead.

'Or a prostitute,' she said.

They were still on the same street, but they had reached a less prosperous part of town. Here, restaurants and shops were open-walled spaces in low buildings, like shops they had seen in Kowloon. In front of a restaurant, they saw a row of round, red plastic basins. In each was a different kind of fish or shellfish, swimming in water kept replenished with a garden hose lying nearby. On the other side of the restaurant's entrance was a stack of small cages that held three different kinds of chicken, including one of the kind with black skin – 'good taste, good for health' – its dense, puffy white feathers made it look like it came from the toy factory. Other cages held two rabbits and an animal that looked to David like a badger. He turned to point it out to Susan, but she had stopped by one of the red basins. He went back to see what had caught her attention. It was a thick brown snake, its coils filling the large plastic bowl.

'Nothing like knowing your food is fresh,' David said.

Everyone was all smiles and gratitude when Susan and David got back to the hotel. The security-police captain thanked them lavishly for their help and cooperation.

While they'd been walking, someone had returned their bags. Susan discovered a bullet hole through hers when she brought it into her bedroom. She poked a finger into the hole and then started laughing. The laughter took hold of her and would not let go until she fell gasping on the bed.

How was she going to explain *that* to Richard? She'd just have to leave the bag in Hong Kong and buy another one to travel home with. She emptied the bag to see if anything had survived unpunctured.

Most of her clothes had been in the path of the bullet. Finding a white silk T-shirt and a pair of jeans that were intact and only slightly smudged with road dust, she showered and put them on. She thought of her downtown dinner with Lara and of wearing a similar outfit at Jimmy Kelly's grand jury party. Too much had happened since then – too much had changed.

'You sure picked a lousy time to go to Mexico,' Mahoney told Joe Estrada on their way to a farewell party for a friend who was leaving the D.A.'s office.

'Life busy while I was gone?'

'Complicated.' Mahoney told him about the waiters and their made-up story about smurfing drug money for the Engs.

'Sounds like you handled it right.'

'Hindsight is wonderful, but there were times I could seriously have used a reality check.'

'Builds character, twisting in the wind all on your own,' Estrada said.

'Yeah, thanks.'

The farewell racket was at a midtown bar whose clientele alternated between prosecutors and wiseguys. They'd taken a private room in the back that had been declared immune for the night from the city's no-smoking ordinance.

Estrada started coughing on the way in.

'Hey,' Mahoney said. 'At least you won't have to waste money on a cigar. You can just breathe.'

'*You* breathe. I'm stopping till we're out of here.'

They elbowed toward the bar, getting caught up in conversations along the way.

'I didn't know Nick was this popular,' Estrada shouted to Mahoney over the din.

'I don't know if it's Nick or the entertainment.' There had been rumors that table dancers had been hired for the amusement of the guest of honor and other interested parties. 'Maybe that's why there aren't any women here.'

'Don't be so sure, Mahoney,' said a voice in his ear. He felt a warm presence at his side; mingled with the blue miasma of cigar smoke he could smell flowers and musk.

'Hello, Laurie,' he said, turning to face her. 'I didn't know you and Nick were friends.'

'We worked on something together a long time ago.' She smiled. 'Besides, I wanted to see how a roomful of you boys reacted to the entertainment.'

'You think that's more than a rumor?'

'I have it on good authority. I've even seen the ladies work before.' He looked at her.

'What's the matter, Mahoney? Something wrong with appreciating beautiful women?'

'I never thought so.'

'That's the spirit. You'd better get yourself a drink, though. This isn't a place to have empty hands.'

'You want one?'

'If you don't mind. I can't get near the bar without being groped.' She smiled again. 'And I'm very particular about who I let grope me.'

When he made it back to her with the drink she said, 'On a more serious note, I worked late yesterday, and I came across something I think might be interesting for us. I just stumbled onto it, going through the latest logs from Internal Affairs. I don't know if it's real – and if it is, I'm not sure it's our man – but if it's real and if it's him, then it's going to make a big difference.'

'What? Tell me.'

'Not here. How about tomorrow? You busy?'

'Nothing earth-shaking. It's Sunday, though. I kind of thought I'd take the day off.'

'I seem to remember that you play golf now and then.'

'Mostly I dig divots and curse.'

'I'll pick you up at nine. We can talk then.' She started to move off into the crowd.

'You want the address?'

'I'm in Official Corruption,' she said over her shoulder. 'I know everything.'

Susan and David had new rooms when they got back to Hong Kong, adjoining each other on the north side of the hotel, facing the harbor. The hotel staff had already moved their belongings into the closets and drawers.

'As I predicted,' Susan said.

'So you did. I'd forgotten.'

She laughed. 'I had, too, until they gave us our keys.'

'I want to take a shower and try for a little sleep,' David said. 'Dinner at eight?'

She put a hand on his arm. 'It's not that I don't love your company, but I think I need to be alone, tonight.'

'Sure . . . I understand.' He caught himself hoping his disappointment didn't show. But there was no reason to hide it. 'Though I'll admit I'm disappointed,' he said. 'More than a little.'

'I am, too. I really do enjoy being with you, and you really have been wonderful. I'm just kind of overloaded.' Her hand still on his arm, she kissed his cheek. 'Breakfast at eight tomorrow?'

'A deal,' he said.

He wanted to put his arms around her – to hold her for a moment, at least. He didn't like to think that after perhaps one more day and night they would be on their way back to their separate lives. Before he

489

could reach out for her she'd moved away.

'Isn't it a beautiful view?' she said, opening her balcony door and looking out across the harbor. 'I could almost forget all the ugliness we've been through.' She turned to him. 'See you tomorrow. Sleep well.'

He went to the Chinese restaurant at the top of the hotel and ate beautiful, expensive food he couldn't taste. Beyond the picture windows boats plied the harbor, glowing with light. He could see far to the east along the north coastline of the island – the same skyscrapers they'd first seen on the way in from the airport. He felt terribly alone.

He went downstairs to the informal grill and bar that featured scores of single-malt Scotch whiskies. He couldn't taste the rare, expensive spirits there any better than the food upstairs.

'I'm glad you were free,' Laurie Jordan said to Mahoney. 'It's too beautiful a morning to be inside.'

She was driving them north along a parkway through Westchester. Here and there the first hints of color were touching the leaves. The top was down on her red Jaguar – Estrada had been right about that – and she'd put a jazz CD on the changer.

'I didn't know you played golf,' he said.

'I have a lot of talents you don't know about.'

He started out playing ahead of his game. Jordan was better than he'd expected, fiercely concentrated when she was making a shot. Her drives weren't long but they were straight, and she had a sure eye on the green. By the end of the front nine, they were each eight strokes over par – not exactly tournament golf, but not bad, either.

On the tenth hole, Mahoney was feeling good. His swing felt perfect, as if all his joints were oiled. His eyes found the ball against the clear blue sky, high and already well down the fairway. As he watched the ball it curved gracefully to the right, the radius of the curve tightening as the ball lofted over the trees beside the fairway. It went out of sight as it came down deep into the rough, probably taking with it his chance to break ninety.

'Too bad,' Jordan said and hit her ball a hundred and sixty yards straight down the fairway.

Mahoney shouldered his bag. 'What was it the man called this damn game – a good walk ruined?'

# 10

When David got back to his room, the message light was flashing on his phone. He called the desk: the message was from Susan. Alarmed, he dialed her room number.

'Are you okay?'

'I'm fine . . . I just thought – I don't know how tired you are, but I've decided I wasn't right about needing to be alone. What I really need is to talk to someone. If you're not too tired.'

'I'm okay,' he said.

'I know you've been very tolerant of me, and I appreciate it. I hate to impose on you again.'

'No imposition. You're why I'm here.'

'Thanks,' she said. 'If you want, you can just come over.'

He hung up and checked himself in the dressing mirror. Went into the bathroom to splash water on his face and brush his hair and beard. *Talk*, he told himself: She said she needs to *talk*. To *somebody*. And we've both just been through hell. Don't get yourself all worked up for nothing.

'Do you want something to drink?' she asked him.

'Mineral water, maybe.'

She took a bottle from the mini-bar's refrigerator and poured for both of them. He sat in the easy chair and she sat on the edge of the bed.

'I'm still trying to assimilate the story Mr Yu told me about my parents,' she said, 'and all that's happened since. And I thought maybe it would help to talk. I told you what my brother said about Mr Yu's story. And my husband doesn't see what difference it makes in the end

492

whether it was an earthquake or a crazed Communist. But he's a pragmatist, he only cares what works. *Why* isn't really part of his repertoire. I used to think it was, but it isn't.'

'Some people are like that,' David said. 'Some people aren't. It's like what we were saying that first time we had lunch together, about needing to *know*. And knowing *why* is definitely part of that. For me, anyway. I think if you've got that impulse, it's hard to shake it off.'

'I'm just learning that,' she said. 'It's something new for me. Or if it was there all along, I didn't know it.

'There's so much I left unresolved about my parents,' she said quietly. 'Their death took me completely by surprise, left so much not done. It's as if all of that has been closed off inside me since then. And seeing the Engs, and getting involved in their story, brought it out in the light again.'

She got up and poured more water for them, then went back to sit on the edge of the bed.

'Family is so important for Chinese people. The duty of children to their parents. The desire of parents for their children to be rich and powerful and happy and carry on the line. It gets into your bones. It used to be only the boys. Girls, they left out to die. Now, modern Chinese people don't think that way – overseas Chinese, at least. They educate their daughters, and they don't feel quite as bad if there are no sons.

'But when I was growing up my brother was the one who counted. I got up early to help with the housework; he never did. I was in high school before I figured out that wasn't some kind of natural law. My parents were always saying how smart he was and how beautiful I was. How he was going to do great things in the world and I was going to marry well.

'So I gave them what they wanted, and I took it away at the same time. I married a man every woman wanted, a man who seemed destined for great things. Only he was white. Not just white – old-fashioned Establishment Anglo-Saxon white. And even though my parents had always made a lot of noise about how we Chans were all Americans now, that wasn't what they meant.'

'What happened to your brother?'

'He fulfilled their prophecy, too, in a way. He works on Wall Street doing mathematical analysis of something called financial products, whatever that means. Great things? I don't think so. But he makes plenty of money, and he has a nice Chinese wife who treats him the way a nice Chinese wife is supposed to, and he has two sons who are both at important universities studying science and math.

'Of course, most of that happened after my parents went to China. All my parents knew when they died was that Sandy was in graduate school and that he had a proper Chinese wife and one tiny son. And that I had a trophy-class white husband and a son who embarrassed them because he was so obviously half-white. I hated them so much for that, for being ashamed, even though in some ways I did it to them because they'd treated Sandy so much better than they treated me.

'I was barely talking to them when they died. It hit me so much harder than I expected. I'd always hoped that we could find each other and make up for some of what we had done wrong. That they would learn tolerance and love, and that I would be able to forgive them. But when they didn't come back from China that could never happen.'

'My sister left home at sixteen,' David said. 'She used to say she felt like an alien spaceship had dropped her in our parents' house by mistake, or out of malice.'

'Does she get along with them now?'

'They're gone, too. They married late and they were older than most when they had us. My mother went first, then my father, not that many months after I left my job.'

'That must have been hard.'

'I loved them. They were simple, unsophisticated people, not too educated, but they were honest and hard-working. How they had a daughter who ran away to be an actress was always beyond them. I think Alice wasn't the only one in the family who suspected an evil-minded alien of dropping her off at their house. I guess you can't always predict what kids will do, however careful you are bringing them up.'

The last thing he expected, talking about his own family, was to see Susan's eyes fill with tears.

'Sometimes you can.' She began to cry. 'Sometimes you can predict.'

She slumped forward, her hands over her face, her shoulders

shaking. She said something, muffled by her hands. He thought it might have been, 'I'm sorry.'

He looked around for tissues, but there was nothing in sight except the bare surfaces of the built-in desk-dresser and the night table. 'I'm going to look for some tissues,' he told her, not wanting to leave the room without explanation.

He came back quickly with a wad of them from the bathroom dispenser. She looked so forlorn sitting on the edge of the bed, sobbing more softly now, still slumped forward, that his impulse was to sit next to her – if only, he told himself, to give her something to lean on.

As he sat, pressing the tissues into her hand, she turned to him and buried her head in his shoulder. He put his arm around her. They sat that way until she had cried herself out.

'Sorry,' she said, then blew her nose. 'This is very attractive, I know.'

'It's okay. You've been through a lot. This is hard stuff you're doing.'

'I was thinking about my son, about what you said about being careful bringing kids up. The hard part is when you're not careful . . . and you know it.'

He had the sense not to say anything.

'God, how I screwed up,' she said. 'You do things and you think you have a good reason and you think you're being careful and you screw up your life anyway, and everybody else's around you.'

She put her head on his shoulder. 'Thank you for being here to lean on.'

He stroked her hair.

'Could you just hold me for a little while?' she said in a small voice. 'If it's not . . . I don't know, maybe it's not a good idea.'

'No, it's okay.' He put his arms around her, awkwardly, as they sat side by side.

She made a small noise and shook her head. He felt her weight shift in his arms and let go.

'Could we lie down?' she asked. 'Just for a minute?'

After a moment's hesitation he stretched out next to her. She nestled her head between his shoulder and neck, her chest resting partly on his, the rest of her body held chastely away.

He felt the warmth of her, the dampness of her face. He tried to think of her the way he might think of Jessie in a similar situation, a distressed little girl, but he was too aware of her grownup heft, the smell of her hair, the rise and fall of her breathing.

'You're shaking,' she said.

'Am I?' He could feel it now, a faint tremor running the length of his body. 'It must be this position,' he improvised.

He shifted, pulling her slightly closer. 'That should be better.' He concentrated on slowing his breathing and letting his muscles relax. The tremor subsided.

He turned his head to bring his nose closer to her hair, his lips dangerously close to her forehead. He ached to taste the salt in the tiny beads of sweat at her hairline.

They stayed that way, her breath warming his neck, for how many minutes he didn't know.

'I did an awful thing,' she said so softly he could barely hear it. 'Long ago, I did an awful thing.'

He realized he was holding his breath, let it out, concentrated again on keeping its rhythm steady.

'I can't believe I could have been so stupid.' She started to weep, much more quietly than before. Again, he stroked her hair.

'I'm sorry,' she said into his neck. 'I think I have to talk about this.'

'It's all right. Whatever you want.'

She lifted her head to look at him, her deep brown eyes searching his and then running over his face, returning to his eyes. His lips tingled with an anticipation he knew would not be fulfilled.

She let her head settle back onto his shoulder, looking up toward the line where wall joined ceiling above the bed.

'I've never talked about this,' she said in the same soft voice. 'Not to anyone. Not even to Richard. Especially not to Richard.'

She paused again. When she resumed it was in the tone of telling a story about someone else.

'It was when Charles was nine. Lara was six then. Richard was already the *enfant terrible* of neurosurgery, challenging the accepted ways, coming up with new procedures. I hadn't really worked since

Charles was born, except for some volunteer projects I did for the hospital and benefits for medical charities. My parents had been dead about eight years by then.

'I was miserable. My days were full – social events for Richard and for the children, parents' activities at their schools, my volunteer work, maintaining the house in New York and the one we had just bought at the beach. But I was miserable and restless and convinced that this life I had arranged for myself was missing something important. And Richard was so preoccupied with becoming the greatest neurosurgeon ever, and his doing that seemed important in a way my unjustified misery could never be . . . so I was afraid to tell him how I felt.

'I began to feel like I had no existence of my own. All I ever did was for other people – my husband, my children, the charities board at the hospital. I wanted something for myself.'

She turned onto her back, her head still on his arm.

'Charles was at a day school in those days, and his school had a drama department they wanted to expand. They had just hired a new teacher. He was trying to organize a regular season of school plays with paying audiences and even some professional actors to work with the older kids. The school knew I did volunteer public relations work, so they asked me if I would help them develop a concept they could use to present this new program to the world.

'It was exactly what I needed. I'd been thinking of going back to work in a serious way, and I wanted to have some more variety in my portfolio and some more recent work. They were offering me a chance to create a whole identity for the program – name, logo, theme, everything from the ground up. Even though it was just for a high-school drama program it was the broadest assignment I'd ever had. So I said yes immediately.'

She stopped. David sensed that the easy part of the story was over.

'The first meeting with the teacher, I saw I'd made a mistake. His name was David, oddly enough, and he was handsome and easygoing. He had a twinkle in his eye and he smiled a lot and he had a quality that made people want to be his friend and do things to make him like them. I had the feeling a lot of women were drawn to him. And he was Chinese. David Hsu.'

She rolled to face across the room, her back to him, her legs drawn up slightly.

'I couldn't have been more vulnerable right at that moment, and I don't know how, but I sensed that David Hsu was precisely what I was vulnerable to. I could have stopped right then, before it went any further. I could have discovered I was busy. I could have found a way to do the job without any personal contact with him. That would have been hard, but eventually I did end up having to do it, anyway, when it was too late.'

She paused. When she resumed her voice was so low and flat he had to work to hear her.

'I went ahead. I think I told myself it was safe, Chinese men didn't appeal to me, I'd never been with a Chinese man, I'd hardly ever even dated them. The truth was I had been running away from that all my life, and a part of me needed to stop running.

'I guess you can see where this is going now. Except it didn't, not exactly, not quite. We had that first meeting and then I had a lot of other meetings with him. Once a week, for two hours, sometimes three, we sat in his office, which seemed to me more like a living room than a teacher's office.

'We talked about the drama program and about how to present it, and we batted ideas back and forth with never a word about anything else, and all the while there was this other, unmentioned thing in the room with us. Until finally I couldn't stand it any more.'

She was silent for a moment, then resumed in a stronger voice, the words coming faster as if now she needed to get whatever it was over with.

'We were side by side, leaning over the table he used as a desk, looking at a poster I'd had the school's art department work up for me, and I . . . I put my hand on the back of his neck. I don't really know what I wanted at that moment, or what I thought would happen. I just had this tremendous desire to touch him.

'He knew exactly what was happening. As soon as he felt my fingers on his neck, he turned his head to kiss me. It was a nice kiss, not too long, almost chaste in a way. When it was over he had me in his arms and I said something like, "I don't know why I did that." He smiled and said, "I'm glad you did."

498

'Then he was kissing me again, and this time it wasn't chaste. It was much more intense. At first I let myself get swept up in it – in the thrill of this man wanting me so much, being so intent and focused. Then I was thinking, no, wait, this is going too far, this isn't what I wanted. My heart was racing and so was my mind, I was so scared.

'I was squirming to get away, trying to talk with his mouth smothering mine. I don't know, maybe he misunderstood, feeling me move like that. Suddenly he scooped me up and dumped me onto the table, on my back. The way he did it, so sudden – lifting me with his hands under my thighs and toppling me backward – there was nothing I could do.

'He was leaning over me and my legs were on either side of him. I could feel him pushing my skirt up and his hands on my legs. It was as if the shock of it all paralyzed me. I didn't have the strength or the will to scream, or even to protest. I was so terrified and confused. How had I let this happen to me? What had I done to make him think I wanted this?

'I don't know how far it would have gone. I don't think he would have kept on if I could have got my voice back and told him to stop. He wasn't the raping type, I don't think. But I don't know. He was very passionate and there was a kind of glazed look in his eyes . . . More than ten years ago, and I remember every instant of it.'

She paused, took a breath.

'I don't know what would have happened next because right then the door opened. It was a saggy door and the bottom of it scraped on the floor when it opened. The sound of it was so loud he stopped right away. I didn't know whether to be horrified to be caught that way or relieved.

'He turned to see who it was and I heard him make an odd noise in his throat. I sat up, my skirt up around my hips—'

She stopped again. For a time she said nothing. He waited.

'It was Charles. I pushed myself off the table and yanked my skirt down and there he was, standing by the door staring at me. My precious, trusting little boy.'

He felt her back begin to shake and then she turned toward him – quickly, almost violently – and clung to him.

'I can see it as if it happened this morning,' she said in a thin,

499

haunted voice when the tears had passed. 'And I see us both – me and this man – as if I were standing in the doorway the way Charles was when he saw whatever he saw. I never quite worked out how it happened. The way they did things at the school, the teachers were on call for the kids, unless they pulled down the shade over the window in the top part of the door. They only did that when they wanted to be left alone, grading papers or preparing for a class. The rule was, if the shade was up and you could see in through that window, it was okay to come in. Otherwise, no, you had to respect the teacher's privacy. And after David Hsu and I were interrupted a dozen times during our first meeting, he'd made kind of a joke of pulling the shade down as soon as I arrived.'

She took a long, ragged breath before she continued. 'I think Charles must have been on some errand – it was the middle of a class period so the halls were empty – and he knew I was going to be there and stopped to tell me some news he had that he was excited about. I don't know why he didn't knock, and I don't know how much he saw as he was coming in, before David Hsu stopped what he was doing.

'I went right to Charles and knelt down next to him and hugged him. I was shaking, my face was flushed, I couldn't really control my voice. I said something, his name or "How's my Charles?" I don't know what. Mr Hsu found an excuse to leave the room so we could be alone.

'So there we were. I was still shaking – if anything, worse now that we were alone. I could barely speak. I asked Charles then if there was anything he wanted to ask me about. He just stood there. I pulled him close to me, clung to him, as if somehow that would return me to the reality I'd known before, where none of this had happened. Finally, he said, so I could barely hear him, "Mommy, you're hurting me."

'I let him go, but I held onto his hand. I needed that contact. I said I was sorry if I hurt him, that I was just very glad to see him, and I *was* glad – so very relieved – for all that I was terribly afraid about what he'd seen. He still was looking at me with this blank expression, as if he was stunned.

'I knew I had to do my best to act normally. I asked him if he had any news, and that seemed to wake him up. He said he'd been picked to carry the school flag at lower-school assemblies. It was a big honor, but he said it so quickly, almost mumbled under his breath. I hugged him again, carefully this time, and told him how happy I was for him. He didn't hug me back and when I finally let go of him he said he had to get back to his class. By that time, I was completely numb. Charles ran off without saying another word and I just watched him go and I realized he'd never once looked me in the eye.

'I never knew what he saw, and I never knew what, if anything, he said about it to his father. He was nine, going on ten. I didn't know how much he knew about sex, and as for fidelity and adultery . . . I certainly didn't know.

'My husband never said a word about it. I told him that Charles and I had run into each other at school, but all he said was, "Oh, really?" Nothing more.

'At first I tried being extra nice to both of them, but that seemed like an admission of guilt so I did my best to get back to normal. I was sure Richard had become more distant, but he was already distant, so for every piece of evidence that convinced me Charles had told him some wild story, there was another I could use to prove to myself that nothing had changed.

'Charles changed, though. He went through a period of being erratic and absolutely awful – withdrawing into himself for weeks, and then throwing tantrums, beating up his sister, lying, then withdrawing again. And I was always ready to take his side and try to smooth things over for him. What else could I do? It was all my fault in the first place, and I was a Chinese mother and he was my husband's only son. I owed them both the duty of making Charles the Emperor of my world.

'So that was how I lived, in an agony of not knowing, afraid to bring it up myself for fear that I'd be opening a door that had been unlocked only in my imagination. And I couldn't think of how to talk about it without giving it so much more importance than it deserved.

'So I said nothing, and after a while the very fact that I had said nothing became a barrier against saying anything. The longer I said nothing, the more impossible it became to break my silence.

'And the more I tried to get Charles to respond to me, and the more he didn't, the harder I tried. And then I would get angry and resentful – why was he putting me through this? And that would make me feel guilty again until finally the constant up and down of it wore me out. Maybe that's acceptance. Whatever it is, I just couldn't do any more.

'I tried to make it up to Charles and Richard, and I tried to make it up to Lara, who was suffering, too – not getting support from me when she truly needed and deserved every bit of support I could give. There were so many times when I should have laid down the law for Charles but I didn't, because I was afraid to, or I felt guilty.

'Meanwhile Richard and I grew apart, and kept growing apart, so that now we're like polite roommates. He and Charles became great buddies. Ninety percent of the little time Richard allotted for family activities, he spent with Charles, playing squash or fishing.

'And I gradually froze over. I started a business and I made peace with my daughter and did my best to be a friend to her, and tried to tell myself that maybe everything was all right – Charles had a close relationship with his father and he was doing brilliantly in school, and Lara was doing well, too, and turning into a charming, funny and very beautiful young woman.

'So what if I didn't quite have a husband, or much of anything beyond occasional moments with Lara that gave me real happiness? Aside from that, everything seemed to be going just fine. But it wasn't, was it? Because Richard's perfect son was busy dealing dope and turning himself into a heroin addict, so estranged from me and so afraid of losing his father's approval that he came within an inch of killing himself.'

She sighed and turned so she could look at him and said in a clear calm voice, 'And all I could think, standing there in the hospital looking at Charles all hooked up to tubes and pumps and monitors was – I did this. It's my fault.'

'But you can't go through life beating yourself up like that,' David said. 'You can't make everything your fault.' He rolled toward her to pull her close. Her body stiffened.

'No, David,' she said with an edge of panic in her voice.

He let her go at once.

502

She put her hand to her head. 'I'm sorry, I'm just so jumpy.' She smiled ruefully. 'And I'm the one who asked you to hold me.' She moved closer to him, rested the whole length of her body against his. 'It just shows what a mess I am.'

She brushed the hair back from his forehead. 'I said once before that you were unusual. It's true. Unusual and very precious. Thank you.'

# 11

Laurie Jordan turned back Mahoney's attempts to talk about work. 'Not until we're off the course,' she said. 'It destroys my concentration.'

On the back nine Mahoney would have liked nothing better, when she birdied the tenth and then the short, dog-leg fourteenth.

He finished with a ninety-eight, better than he deserved but not better than her ninety-two. She was exhilarated by victory, throwing her arms around him, kissing him with abandon.

'That was fun,' she said. 'We have to do it again.'

'I'm ready when you are.' He was trying for her kind of innuendo, was surprised to hear how eager he sounded.

'Why, Dan,' she said, smiling, 'how sweet.' She leaned against him, kissing him lingeringly on the corner of his mouth. She'd caught his hand between them so his knuckles were pressed to the warmth at the top of her thighs. He didn't think it was an accident.

She pulled back, still smiling at him, pushed her sunglasses to the top of her head so he could feel the full force of her eyes – clear, bottomless green. 'Let's go get a drink and we can have that talk.'

'It was an Internal Affairs Bureau log,' she said as they sat on the clubhouse terrace overlooking the first tee. 'From a murder case – a low-level Chinese heroin distributor. And the log said he'd been bragging he got his heroin from a crooked cop who got it from a dealer to use for evidence.'

'That's a switch.' That kind of story usually went the other way – cops stole drugs from evidence and arranged to have them sold on the street. 'Did the log say how much heroin?'

504

She shook her head. 'Just what I told you.'

'Tantalizing,' Mahoney said, trying to hold back his excitement. 'If we knew more about the amount and the date . . .'

Instead of responding she leaned back in her chair and put her feet up on the terrace rail. She'd showered and changed when they came off the course: she was wearing a sheer skirt that draped softly over her long, smooth-muscled thighs. She fiddled with the paper umbrella in her drink and sipped through the tiny red straw.

'Actually, we do know more.' She was playing nonchalant. 'I tracked the story back through the log number to the detective who filed it. I got lucky and caught one of his bosses on Friday night, and he was obliging enough to read me the DD-5' – the detective's original report of his conversation with the street source.

'You going to make me pull this out of you one word at a time?' Mahoney asked her.

She swung her legs off the rail. 'Maybe if you handcuff me and threaten a little prosecutorial brutality . . .' She said it with a mock-wicked smile, but he heard the challenge and felt an echo of her body's heat against the back of his hand. He did his best to ignore it – for now, at least, he told himself.

'Okay,' she said. 'This time I'll tell you anyway. From what the detective put in his DD-5 – and we have to figure he was playing the whole thing down – the story on the street put the quantity at half a unit or a unit, and the time-frame in early July. The distributor who supplied the heroin is fairly high-level, does maybe five, ten units a month. That makes his monthly wholesale cost something like a million dollars.'

'The DD-5 didn't happen to name the detective who took the heroin from him?'

'I'm surprised the detective wrote it up at all,' Jordan said. 'What cop likes to memorialize a street rumor calling another cop dirty? And without the name, we don't have to worry it's a phony story planted to jam somebody up.'

'The time-frame is right for us, and the amount is right, too,' Mahoney said.

'Seems like.'

'So we'd better talk to Max about it in the morning.'

Her eyes were on his, her head cocked, her expression expectant.

'Am I missing something?'

'Aren't you going to congratulate me, or tell me I'm wonderful or something like that?'

'Better than that. I'm going to buy you a fancy dinner.'

She stood up so she was leaning over him, one hand on each arm of his chair. He could feel her breath on his neck. Her hair was a dark, fragrant tent over his face. 'I'd prefer handcuffs,' she said in his ear.

'Next time,' he said, sweating.


June Eng met Susan and David for breakfast in the hotel coffee shop, as she had on their first morning in Hong Kong. She bustled over to their table, pale and agitated.

'I was so upset to hear what happened. Uncle Wing told me.'

Even after she sat down she was in constant motion, shifting in her chair, her hands picking at the silverware. 'I can't apologize enough. I keep thinking that I told Li he should go to that factory.'

'You couldn't have known,' Susan said.

'If I'd been with you, maybe it wouldn't have happened that way.'

Susan wondered briefly what she meant, but June seemed so distraught Susan didn't want to press it. She was distracted by a waiter, bringing them coffee and a plate of fresh fruit.

June Eng was still playing with her silverware, but more subdued now. 'What if it was me?' The words were barely audible.

'I don't understand,' Susan said.

'What?' June looked up as if surprised to find other people at the table with her. 'Oh. Nothing. My imagination plays tricks on me.' Her eyes went to the plate of sliced papaya and pineapple and melon.

'Please, take some,' Susan said.

'Thank you.'

Susan traded glances with David. He seemed as perplexed as she was.

'It is not an accurate impression of China, to be subjected to such a horror,' June Eng said, eating a piece of melon. 'There is so much turmoil now. No one knows who will be in power next – capitalist-roaders or old-line Communists. Fear and greed make bad companions.' She pushed her plate away. 'I can't eat. How can you be so calm?'

'Right now, it feels more like a nightmare I woke up from than something real,' Susan said.

'We've decided to talk to someone from the American consulate,' David said.

'But what good would that do?' June sounded alarmed. 'Uncle Wing said the men were all killed.'

'But surely they aren't the only ones who do that kind of thing,' Susan said.

'Yes, I suppose that's right. Especially since the Triads have started to do business on the mainland.'

'Triads?'

'Criminal gangs.'

'People should know these things happen, don't you think?' David said.

'But everything will change once the succession in Beijing is determined. The atmosphere will be calmer.'

'Doesn't that depend on the outcome?'

'I'm sure whatever happens it will be better for foreign visitors.'

'Even so, in the meantime, people might be in danger.'

June Eng offered no response to that.

'Do you have time for more sightseeing before you leave?' she asked them.

'We have reservations to go back tomorrow,' Susan said. 'We've both planned a full day.'

'That's good. You should end with a better memory of your trip.'

As they parted she gave them both small packages. 'A token of our gratitude for how much you have helped our family. Peter was sorry not to be here; he sends his thanks as well.' She reached into her shoulder bag again. 'This is for our parents, if I can impose one last time. A recorded letter in return for the one they sent us.'

Susan took it, knowing David would object. She wasn't sure how she felt about it herself, but her affection for June Eng remained, and the woman had clearly been badly upset by Mr Li's death. There was nothing to be gained by making a scene here. If necessary she could have the hotel's messenger service return the tape after she and David had left.

507

The man at the consulate, John Gerard, had suggested they tell their story as well to an officer of the Royal Hong Kong Police. They all met in a small conference room in the hotel.

Gerard was tall and ruddy and bald – in his thirties, David guessed. Detective Chief Inspector Roger Hall was a British expatriate a good ten or fifteen years older, youthfully athletic-looking.

As Susan had requested, David assumed the burden of telling them the story of the roadblock. He kept it short and simple: easy enough, since there wasn't much available in the way of embellishment. Both men listened carefully. Occasionally the American took notes.

'Did you get the names of the men who interrogated you afterward?' Detective Chief Inspector Hall wanted to know.

'They may have told us. I don't remember.'

'I don't either,' Susan said. 'We weren't in the best of shape.'

'I'm sure you weren't,' the policeman said. 'Don't feel under pressure about this. The important thing now is that you're all right. But while we're on the subject, do you happen to remember if you heard anyone addressed by rank?'

'They called one man "Captain," I think,' Susan ventured.

'That's what I heard,' David said.

'And you believe that the bandits were all killed?'

'That's what we were told,' David said. 'Eight of them, I think he said.'

'And can you tell me again who this was, the man who told you?'

'His name is Chan Kwok-Wing.'

'And you say he's a businessman?'

'That's what he told us.'

'A cousin of the security policeman called Yee.'

'Again, that's what he told us.'

'But this Chan Kwok-Wing is from Hong Kong.'

'Yes,' Susan said. 'We met him here.'

'And how was it that you met him?'

'Through some business associates of his. June and Peter Eng.'

'And they're friends of yours, are they?'

'We know their parents in New York.'

'I see.' He turned to the man from the consulate. 'John, I don't mean to put myself front and center, here. I'm sure there are things you want to know.'

John Gerard's questions weren't very different from Detective Chief Inspector Hall's. He took David back over the incident briefly and ended with the Engs. 'I don't remember if you said how you know them. The parents.'

David was stymied. They hadn't expected the questioning to go this way. Susan came to the rescue.

'My family comes from the same part of China they do. I have an old aunt who knows them from a same-birthplace society in New York.'

'And you're married, is that right?' the policeman asked her unexpectedly.

'Yes.' Susan's face flushed with the answer.

'Mr Clark?'

'No.'

'And you're both friends from New York?'

'Yes . . .' David's answer was tentative – he wondered where Hall was headed.

'What's the point of these questions?' Susan challenged him. 'We're the *victims*.'

'Quite so. Sorry.' The policeman turned again to his companion from the American consulate. 'Well, John, that's it for me.'

'Yes, I think I know everything I need to, as well.' To David and Susan, Gerard said, 'I want to thank you for coming forward. It's a terrible thing that happened to you. We'll be getting a report eventually from the security police over there, but they can be very sluggish. This way we can keep after them about it.'

The two men stood up to leave.

'I wonder if you'd had any thought of going to the press about this,' Inspector Hall said.

David traded surprised glances with Susan.

'No, nothing like that,' she answered. 'I don't see anything to be gained. I'm sure you'll know best how to deal with it. We certainly don't want to be involved personally, ourselves.'

As they parted Hall reached into his jacket pocket for his wallet. 'Did I give you a business card?'

'When we met,' David said. 'We all exchanged them.'

'So we did. I must be getting old. Or else it's so automatic I don't notice I've done it.' He put his wallet away. 'Perhaps a bit of both.' As an apparent afterthought he added, 'You know, it does make me think – you don't by chance have one of Mr Chan's cards, do you?'

'No,' David lied quickly. 'I don't think he gave us one.'

'Why did you say that about not having Chan Kwok-Wing's card?' Susan asked when they were alone.

'It just seemed right. The truth is, I thought that whole thing was strange.'

'It was. I don't know what the Engs have to do with it,' she said. 'Or Mr Chan. I'm just glad he was there to help us.'

'Amen. I mean, it was the security police riding up at the right moment that really counted, but I'd still have hated to be there without someone who spoke better English than Mr Yee, or that captain or whatever he was.'

'Why do you think Inspector Hall was so interested in us?' Susan asked. 'Personally, I mean.'

'The only thing I can think of is that he was sniffing around to see if we were involved in something that could have made us targets. Or maybe he just has a nose for gossip.'

She looked for a smile behind his beard. 'Sometimes I can't tell when you're kidding.'

'That's okay – I can't always tell, myself.'

'Well, I thought he was just this side of rude, asking those questions.' Susan could feel her face flushing again, which made no sense: it wasn't as if she had anything to be embarrassed about.

'Not that I'm eager to change the subject,' David said, 'but did you hear June Eng say something at breakfast that sounded as if she thought it was her fault? *What if it was me?* or something like that?'

'You know, I wasn't sure. And it seemed so odd.'

'And what about the tape recording she gave you?' he probed. 'I suppose you're going to insist on bringing it back.'

'I don't know.' The prospect of conflict with David, even minor conflict, made her jumpy. 'Let's talk about it tomorrow, before we leave.'

★ ★ ★

For Susan, lunch alone with Sunny was like a year's worth of letters. They gossiped about all the things they'd held back, talking in front of David, although Susan still said nothing about Charles's run-in with heroin.

The restaurant Sunny had chosen was full of lunching ladies. Some of them had brought their children. In the Chinese manner the children had the run of the restaurant, and run they did. No one seemed to notice, or care.

Sunny told her about a job she'd had, working for a Hong Kong construction contractor that had been hired by a Government-owned company in Guangdong.

'At the last minute, the contractor got fired. I'd done a lot of work for them and spent a lot of money. But my deal was dependent on their contract, so I wasn't going to get paid.'

In the end, Sunny had exploited her connections to an important official in a neighboring Chinese province; he had put pressure on his opposite number in the Guangdong provincial government, and in due course money had trickled out of China and into Sunny's bank account.

'I got seventy-five cents on the dollar,' she said. 'Nobody else got a penny.'

'That's very impressive,' Susan said. 'You must have been relieved.'

'Relieved isn't the half of it. And the trouble with *guanxi* these days is you have to be sure you're making your connections in the right places. I was lucky because I could deal with people who were family friends. A lot of others have no choice but to *buy* influence. And it's hard for them to know if they're getting value.

'Remember we were talking about people wanting to emigrate?' Sunny continued. 'Well, there's a whole industry here of people who claim they can pave the way to get Hong Kong people citizenship, or at least permanent residence, someplace outside. Almost all these consultants are running scams, but people believe so strongly in having that kind of edge they don't look close enough. They're losing their life savings, or big chunks of it, because they think paying the money will put them at the head of the line out of here. It's sad.'

'But you don't have to worry.'

'So far it doesn't seem so. But sometimes I worry anyway.'

The waiter brought back Sunny's credit card. 'Let's go out and walk along the promenade by the harbor. Get a bit of sea spray in our faces.'

'That doesn't sound like you,' Susan remarked.

'Which part?'

'Getting spray in your face.'

'My new, nature-child incarnation. I'm practicing for my future life in scenic Canada.'

The promenade gave a clear view across the harbor to Kowloon. They stood and watched the boats go by.

'That's kind of a sexy fellow,' Sunny said.

Susan looked around to see who she meant.

'Not here – the fellow you're traveling with. David. He looks like he'd be great in bed.'

'Sunny!'

'Well, you're traveling with him.'

'Only traveling. He's smart and he's a good listener.'

'Why is he here?'

'I asked him to come. For some reason, I didn't want to come here alone.'

'You asked him to come so you wouldn't be alone.'

'Right.'

'And he said yes.'

'Obviously.'

'And you're not sleeping together. Come on, Susan – there has to be more to it than that.'

'I'm married.'

Sunny made a skeptical face.

'I think I intimidate him,' Susan blurted out. Then: 'Listen to me! I don't have a clue where that came from.'

'And *I* think he's in love with you.'

'That's silly,' Susan said, but she wondered if it really was.


The neighborhood where Susan had spent the first six years of her life, was – as she expected – unrecognizable. She had only a few memories of Hong Kong, as much a compound of her parents' stories and old photographs as of her own retained perceptions, but she knew that this complex of tall white apartment buildings had not been here when she was growing up.

At the side of one of the buildings was a small park. She found a bench and sat looking at the view – slivers of hillside and business-district skyscrapers and tinier slivers of harbor, visible between the new and decaying apartment houses that seemed to march in lock step toward the water.

She tried to recapture a sense of what it had been like growing up here, before they had packed up and flown to America. She remembered having a feeling of specialness and – leaving – a sense of her parents' long-time wish coming true. Yu Wenli was probably right: her parents had had some kind of influence, and when their efforts had paid off they were able to go to the Golden Mountain, taking their precious son and their daughter, a daughter who had been only too eager to find a place to live where little girls might be more valued than in Hong Kong or China.

She thought of what she had said to David about her parents – her view of herself as a rebellious daughter spitefully marrying a white-ghost man to get back at them for treating her badly. The fact was that they *had* treated her badly. And Richard, when she met him, could not have been more desirable. Intelligent and ambitious, rich, handsome, funny, sought after. Even – or so it had seemed then – sympathetic and understanding. How ridiculous to think she should have turned her back on him simply because he wasn't Chinese.

No wonder she felt that her parents had thought of her as Susan the symbolic daughter and not Susan the real person. No wonder she still felt the frustration of never having been reconciled with the parents who had rejected her. No wonder she had been so ready to embrace the illusion of having substitute parents that she had built around Martin Eng and his wife.

And yet, perhaps it was unfair to her parents to think of their behavior toward her as a matter of rational choice, unfettered by tradition. Susan's father had not been a young man when she was born. He himself had been born into the very beginnings of Republican China; his parents had lived almost all their lives under the Qing Dynasty. He was a sophisticated city man – and a war hero, it now seemed – but the old ways were not far in his past.

From her mother she could have expected better. Her mother had been younger, less tied to the old ways. Or so it should have been. But her mother had been the one who tried to teach them the old traditions and who selected for her daughter a private school with a sizeable Chinese student population. Her father had been the one who said the past was the past and all that mattered was the future.

Her parents' behavior had been confusing for her then and it was confusing, still. So when it came to her connection with the Engs, had she been too intent on seeing things as being simple and straight-forward? Without ever thinking it in so many words, had she been too eager to believe that Meiling's apparent responsiveness to her was real affection, that she could stand in for Meiling's long-dead daughter in some small fraction of the way she wished Meiling could be a substitute for her own dead mother?

Her thoughts of parents and children and the old traditions brought into focus something that had been bothering her since she'd heard Martin Eng – Chu-Ming, Chan had called him – testify in the grand jury. He had been very specific about the meaning of the entries in the ledger that corresponded to the markings on the money in his safe deposit boxes: it was a list of people he wanted the money to go to when he died. Friends and supporters and poor people – strangers, some of them, or relative strangers – were to get this money that, he had testified, included all he and Meiling had been able to salvage from the cumulative result of generations of effort.

That there was something inherently *off* about this had nagged at her from the beginning, coming to the front of her mind occasionally but never with so much clarity as now.

There was nothing more important in the Chinese view of the world than providing for the succession of generations. Even a *jook sing* knew that. It was one of the few bits of ancient wisdom she remem-bered from her Chinese education: marriage was a union between two people of different families with the double object of serving the ancestors in the temple and of perpetuating the coming generation.

The basic attitudes might be left over from the days when people had children as a way to be sure there would always be a living generation to venerate them when they were dead, but it didn't take

514

old-time religion to inculcate the Chinese love for children – male children, at least. She thought of the little ones running around the restaurant where she and Sunny had eaten lunch – being *kids*, because that's what kids did. Even if Chinese parents didn't always appreciate that, they understood it and tolerated it.

And though much face could be gained by having admirable off-spring, in the scheme of things that made children paramount it didn't ultimately matter whether yours happened to be smart or strong or successful in their own right. They still came before *any* outsider. Strengthening the family line was first priority.

And to the extent that wealth was and would continue to be the highest measure of success and strength, it made no sense to be doling out the family's money the way Martin Eng had claimed to be doing.

She remembered what she had said to David about it when they were discussing how to present it to June and Peter Eng. They had to be careful not to give offense; it wasn't something people would want the neighbors to know. All along, her instinct had been that Martin Eng's story of an encoded will ran counter to the ancient traditions she was sure he honored.

She no longer saw any convincing alternative to the conclusion that Martin Eng had been lying. Lying either about what the money was for, or that it was all the money they had.

*To become rich is glorious*, he had quoted. To give away money in those quantities – almost *all* your money – was hardly the path to glory. And as David had pointed out, Deng Xiaoping's economic rallying cry was about ends, not means.

The more Susan went over it all in her mind, the more certain she was Martin Eng had lied. But it was a long way from that certainty to knowing what the truth might be, and farther still to knowing what to do about it.

She had to focus on the first steps: what was the money's true source and what was its destination? And what was there about either or both of those things that had made Martin Eng lie?

There had to be some way to get closer to the truth. And she had to find it – not just for her own peace of mind, but because she had drawn David into this with her.

Had drawn him in because in her guilt-ridden and emotionally bereft state she had been unable to face, without support and alone, the emotional unknowns that lurked here in Hong Kong and in China. Reluctant at first, he had followed . . . Why? For the adventure of it? Because he was, after all, drawn to her – as Sunny had so overstated? She found it hard to imagine anyone could be drawn to the sorry shell she had become. *Hollow bamboo*, indeed. Not just in her ignorance of things Chinese – in her whole life.

David called her at the hotel at five-thirty: he was back from the Racecourse Association, did she want to have dinner alone or would she join him? In her turmoil, she hesitated, asked to call him back.

*Fool!* she said to herself as soon as she had hung up. She called him right back. 'I don't know what I was thinking of. Of course we should have dinner together, if that's what you want.'

'I sure do. It's our last night, after all.'

'Would it be all right with you if we didn't eat Chinese food? I know we're flying back to Western cuisine tomorrow, but—'

'How about the grill here in the hotel?'

'Great. I want to pack and shower first. Eight o'clock?'

'I'll make a reservation.'

# 12

Susan fussed over what to wear. The clothes she had left behind had at least escaped bullet-holes, but the selection that remained was limited and nothing seemed right. She settled on a pair of loose, unlined linen pants and a silk T-shirt. She started to do her hair up, then let it down and combed it out so it hung free. She put on a single gold bracelet and two gold rings on her right hand to balance the wedding and engagement rings.

That's way too much, she thought, looking at her diamond. It was the first time she'd had that thought in ages.

Brushing her hair one last time and checking herself in the mirror, she asked herself why she was acting like a kid going out on a date. But that was the wrong question, she told herself: she couldn't spend every minute crying over the way she'd screwed up her life, or horrified at having narrowly escaped the clutches of Guangdong bandits.

She'd embarked on an adventure and this was the conclusion of a major chapter. She might even have figured out what much of it was really all about. And this was going to be her last dinner in Hong Kong. Why not be in a party mood?

David was waiting for her in the lobby. He made a small production of admiring her.

'Even more beautiful than usual,' he said.

She noticed that he, too, seemed to have taken care dressing for dinner. His hair was still damp from his shower and his beard looked freshly trimmed. And he was wearing a suit she'd never seen – summer-weight wool, an elegant weave of dark gray and black.

'That's quite a suit,' she said.

517

He beamed. 'Do you like it?'

'It's beautiful.' She reached for the sleeve. 'May I?' It was buttery soft and smooth. 'Cashmere?'

'They told me merino.' He held out his arm for her. 'Shall we dine?'

They each had a glass of champagne. As he raised his glass she raised hers and said, 'Confusion to our enemies.' She wasn't up to dealing with a sentimental toast.

When they'd ordered she made conversation about the room and the other diners. David followed her lead, but she sensed he was somewhat bemused by her uncharacteristic bright chatter.

She wanted to try out her ideas about the Engs on him, but she wasn't ready. 'Tell me about the suit,' she said.

'Courtesy of a suggestion from Mr Macleod at the RA. He told me about a tailor on Nathan Road. Not like these big fancy ones in the hotel. This is a little hole-in-the-wall place in the back of an arcade across the road from the park in Tsim Sha Tsui. You go in and there's barely room to stand, and the guy I talked to wasn't even Chinese, I think he's from India. And all over the walls and under the glass counters are these testimonial letters. From British nobility, a couple of chairmen of the U.S. Joint Chiefs of Staff, cabinet secretaries, you name it . . .'

'Hong Kong is a surprising place that way.'

'The surprise is that I bought a suit. I thought, this is the only time in my life I'm ever going to have a suit custom-made. It's a crazy thing to do when you're unemployed—'

'But you're not unemployed. You're *self*-employed.'

'I suppose, but in the cold light of morning it looks a lot like unemployed. Anyway, the prices at this place aren't bad—'

'The only prices in Hong Kong that aren't.'

'—so it was too good to pass up.'

'You look great. You may never feel the same about that cotton suit of yours.'

'Kind of a sack, isn't it? You should see my winter suit.'

'I'll look forward to it.'

They were well into their main course before Susan had the courage to tell him her theory about Martin Eng. She gave it the full historical and cultural preamble, partly so she could be sure she was right, at least in her decision that the story of massive cash bequests to strangers didn't ring true. By the time she was done she had convinced herself again.

'He must have been lying. If the money is truly earmarked for others – when Martin dies or any other time – then it can't be his money, or if it *is* his money he's got to have a lot more of it somewhere.'

'Interesting,' David said. 'It could explain some things I didn't understand, like why Mr Chan was so much more interested in the ledgers and the money than he was in the health and safety of his friends. I think I said it at the time – he was asking about it as if it was *his* money.'

'Maybe it is.'

'But if it's Chan's,' David reasoned, 'then it's not going to be labeled for distribution to friends of Mr Eng's. So that part isn't likely to be true, either.'

'That's what I think – we don't know what the labeling really means.' Although she had an idea.

'It could just be heroin money, after all, the way the police say,' David ventured. 'The bills *did* have heroin dust on them.'

'Yes, but . . .' Her new theory aside, Susan did not want to think of the Engs as heroin dealers. It was too ugly, too tied up with her feelings about Charles, her memories of him in the hospital, struggling with death. 'Do you really think that's what it is?'

'Importing heroin is still the least complicated theory,' David said. 'It accounts for everything simply.'

'What about the fingerprints?'

'Right – no fingerprints on the heroin.'

'I have a different theory,' she said. 'A new one.' This was the part that took courage. What if it didn't hold up? What if he laughed at her?

'Let's hear.'

'We've been talking to people about how the British are giving up Hong Kong, and China is taking over?'

'Right.'

'And how a lot of people are getting ready to leave?'

'Chinese people.'

519

'Yes, because they're afraid. Especially the ones who left the mainland because they were fleeing oppression or had been in conflict with the mainland Communists.'

'After hearing Mr Yu, about how changeable and dangerous politics can be in China, I can't blame them for being frightened,' David said.

'And we talked about how some of those people might want to leave but they don't have enough money to buy themselves residency in Canada or Australia or the U.S.?'

'Yes . . .'

'Well, I heard some more about that, this afternoon.' She told him what Sunny had said about emigration-consulting scams.

'So some of these people really are getting desperate,' he said.

'It seems they are.' She took a breath – this was the last piece of her puzzle. 'Remember when we were at Kelly's, when I'd just heard the story from Uncle Eight about Tony Ching, the man who stole the presidency of the Sam Yap Association from Martin Eng? And you were telling the others about how men in Chinatown – any Chinatown – would deposit their money with a merchant they trusted or with the benevolent association?'

'Sure.'

'And you said that the account books for that kind of deposits might look a lot like Martin Eng's ledgers?'

'As they would.'

'And that was the theory that interested you the most – that the Engs were holding the money for other people.'

'I liked it better than the family-fortune story, I suppose.'

'Then, if you think about it, you already sort of know what my new theory is.' She hoped it would seem more plausible to him if he added up the pieces himself.

It took him a moment to say, 'Your theory is that people here in Hong Kong, the ones who are afraid they'll have to leave when China takes over, are sending money out, and Martin Eng – as head of the Three Districts Association – is collecting it and holding it for them.'

'Yes, right. And that's why there are coded names on the money in the Engs's safe deposit boxes. To show who the money belongs to.'

'There was about a million and a half dollars, altogether, in their house and in the safe deposit boxes,' David recalled.

'Yes. And if we're talking about people who don't have enough money to buy citizenship, that still might not be more than ten families, or even fewer. Because to invest, say, a few hundred thousand in your new country of choice, you have to *have* a lot more. So, the Engs could easily be handling a hundred thousand, a hundred fifty thousand per person, or per family. Or more.'

'The police accountant said twenty-five million over three years.'

'Yes, but who knows if that's right.'

'If it is, twenty-five million puts it in the range of a couple of hundred people at a hundred-plus thousand a person,' David said. 'That's a lot of people.'

'Hong Kong has almost six million.'

'You're saying two hundred is only one out of thirty thousand.'

She grinned. 'You're the numbers expert.'

'And, from what I read, if you're a Hong Kong person expecting to pay passage to one of those people-smugglers, a hundred and twenty thousand might just about cover a family of four, just to get from here to there.' He spent some time chewing a piece of his grilled lamb chop. 'But it's a hell of a logistical problem moving all that cash.'

'Drug smugglers have to do it all the time.'

'I think they try to use the banking system and international wire transfers as much as they can. And they're sending the money in the other direction.'

'They send out suitcases of money, too. Isn't that what those experts testified?'

'I suppose they did. But it's still going in the other direction.' He chewed some more, thinking. 'And where does Chan fit in? I really do think he was in a bad state about that money.'

'You said just now that it was a logistical problem. They'd need somebody here, Kowloon-side, to collect the money and to deal with getting it to the U.S.'

'What about June and Peter?' he proposed. 'Why couldn't they do it?'

'I don't know. Maybe they could.' It was her turn to ruminate over her food.

'They're not local,' she said. 'Chan is. He'd know more people, and

521

he'd inspire the right kind of confidence. June and Peter might not. And he's older, too. That helps.'

'I'm impressed,' David said. 'You seem to have this all figured out.'

'Some of it. Some is just saying whatever comes into my head.'

'However you do it, you're beginning to convince me.'

'Another thing,' she said. 'If Chan is vouching for them, then he's put himself on the line here. When you said he acted as if the money was his, well – it *is* as if the money is his. For him to lose money he was entrusted with, or let it be taken away, would mean an enormous loss of face – even if he could claim it wasn't his fault.'

'But if it's people getting their own money out of the country, why not use the banking system?' David asked. 'Drug smugglers have to be careful because the money calls attention to them, and they have something to hide. But these people would just be depositing their own money.'

Before she could respond David said, 'No, I can answer that one myself. Because you have to declare money to the Government if you bring in large amounts, which means the U.S. authorities would know about it. And if these people are coming in illegally they wouldn't want to pay for the trip with money that's officially part of the system. Besides, you need a social security number for a bank account, and there are tax problems—'

'And they don't necessarily trust banks.'

'Okay, then how do they move the money?'

'There's a way.' She watched him carve the last piece of his lamb away from the bone while she got the story straight in her head.

'It's something Sunny told me. One of our friends – call her Kerry – is having trouble in her marriage, so she's going to try to get away from her husband. Her problem is she likes money and doesn't want to take a chance she'll be cut off if she leaves. And she can't let her husband know she's setting up a bank account outside Hong Kong, because he'd figure out she was planning to leave and maybe make it hard for her to take the children. Or else find out where the money had gone and use it as a way to trace her, later.'

'Quite a dilemma,' David said. She thought there was sarcasm in his voice, but she ignored it.

'According to Sunny, here's what Kerry's doing. She gets money from her husband to buy gold jewelry. She wears it once, to some special occasion with him, then she takes it back to the gold store and gets cash for it. Her husband doesn't really notice what she's wearing so he mostly doesn't know if she has any given piece or not.'

'What happens to the cash?'

'She leaves it at the gold store. Then she has a friend in, say, Paris go to a gold shop there, and the owner of that gold shop in Paris gives her friend the money and keeps a small percentage as a fee.'

'How did the money get to Paris? What do they do, send it in a package with some jewelry?'

'No, that's the clever part. The actual cash never leaves Hong Kong. Because there's also bound to be somebody in Paris who wants to send money to Hong Kong. So he gives *his* money to the gold-shop owner in Paris, and Kerry's gold-shop owner gives *her* money to the Parisian's friend here.'

'You're saying Kerry's friend in Paris gets the Parisian's money there and the Parisian's friend gets Kerry's money here,' David recapped.

'Exactly. And no money ever crosses a border.'

'And if the amounts don't match, there's a constant flow of this kind of money, so it all evens out in the long run, or else the gold-shop owners settle up among themselves.'

'That must be how it works.'

David laughed. 'It's exactly like a bank – or a banking system, anyway.'

'For people who don't believe in banks.'

'And, most important, it's off the record,' he said. 'It would certainly work in this case, assuming a volume of money that large could be covered.'

'If it's true,' Susan said, 'then the New York Police took money from the Engs that actually belongs to innocent people here in Hong Kong. People who are counting on it so they can escape from what they're afraid will happen to them when the Chinese take over.'

'And the Engs couldn't use that as a defense, could they? Because they've probably broken the law by not declaring the money. And maybe they're guilty of some kind of conspiracy, violating the immigration laws.' He drummed his fingers on the table in frustration. 'I wish I knew more about the legal part of it.'

'They must have a good reason to risk fighting the heroin charge instead of telling the truth. And now these Hong Kong people may have lost their life savings.'

'It's a tragedy,' David said, 'if that's what it is. And I don't see what we can do about it.'

'There has to be something,' she said.

Neither of them had much appetite for dessert.

'If we believe the money the police took from the Engs came from Hong Kong,' Susan said, 'then that has to mean the heroin was planted. By the detective or the informant.'

'Okay, I can accept that. But will anybody else?'

'I know we'll think of something to do.' There had to be *something*, she thought. 'But we can't let this ruin our last night here.'

'You're right . . . And in that case, how about a nightcap?'

She started to say yes but shook her head instead. 'It seems a shame to have those beautiful rooms with a view of the harbor and Kowloon and almost no chance to enjoy them. If we're having a nightcap, we should go upstairs.'

Sensing his hesitation, she added, 'If I *promise* not to cry?'

He laughed. 'Okay. Upstairs it is. But only if you promise.'

'I had a talk first thing this morning with the detective who filed that DD-5,' Laurie Jordan said. 'I told him it was just routine, we had a new system of following up on reports like that as a matter of course.'

She and Mahoney were sitting in Max Straus's office. Knowing Straus's mid-morning preferences from their Appeals-Bureau days, Mahoney had suggested bringing coffee and Danish pastry from the wagon downstairs.

'I don't suppose he gave up the cop's name,' Straus said.

'No, but I got the rest of the story. The murder victim – his name was Ying – was a stranger to the neighborhood. He was offering to supply heroin to street dealers at cut rates, shooting his mouth off that he could sell so cheap because he got the drugs for free. That a cop gave him the drugs to plant on somebody, but it was more powder than he needed to plant so he got the extra for himself. Like a bonus. And the cop got the drugs from a distributor in Washington Heights he was tight with.'

Straus said nothing, but he'd stopped in the middle of sugaring his coffee.

'According to the detective,' Jordan went on, 'the story going around is that the late Mr Ying was peddling his heroin to street dealers whose regular supply came from the very same distributor Ying was naming as the cop's drug source.'

'Which I take it we think is what got him killed,' Straus said. The coffee stood neglected on his desk – a small testament, Mahoney thought, to how seriously he was taking this.

'Right. The theory is that the low-level supplier whose territory Ying was invading didn't like this Chinese guy underselling him, so he popped a cap on him. As to whether the distributor himself knew about it – they don't have a theory one way or the other.'

'But they don't think the shooting was to shut Ying up about the cop.'

'So the detective says. He wants the whole cop part of it to be a fairytale. And the supplier has a motive whether the story Ying was telling about the cop being the source of the heroin was true or not. Ying was underselling him if the heroin came from Mars.'

'But if it's *not* a fairytale about the cop, you can bet the distributor Ying put in his story would want Ying's mouth closed permanently,' Straus commented.

'So would the cop,' Mahoney heard himself say.

'But Ying never named the cop,' Jordan pointed out.

'No, but if he thought someone might connect the dots . . .' In for a nickel, in for a dime. Mahoney wondered if Pullone would really kill to cover up planting the heroin.

'We're getting carried away, here,' Straus said. 'Let's take it one step at a time. Do you have enough to identify the distributor?'

'I have a street name and a couple of addresses and a name that may or may not be the one his mother gave him,' Jordan said.

'Run a DECS check on him. If we're lucky, somebody's got a case working we can use against him. If not, we can talk about running a sting on him. If the dirty cop is real, we have to know who he is.'

525

# 13

There was a small bottle of cognac in the top section of the mini-bar.
'Is this okay?' Susan asked.

'You know, I think I've had enough alcohol tonight,' David said.
'I'd be happy just to sit and look at the view.'

'Shall we go out on the balcony, then?'

'Sure.' He turned that way.

'No, wait a minute,' she said.

He stopped. There was the hint of a smile at the corners of her
mouth.

'Would you . . .' She stopped, started again. 'I'd like you to kiss me.
If you want to.'

It took a moment for the words to register. When they did his
response was a long exhalation of breath he hadn't known he was
holding. He felt suddenly, unaccountably, shy.

'Okay,' he said. 'Sure.'

He looked at her. She was breathing so deeply he could see her chest
move, her breasts challenging the loose white silk.

She took half a step toward him.

He suddenly wanted everything and he wanted it all at once. He
made himself slow down.

Gently, he took her shoulders. He tilted his head toward her and let
his lips settle on hers. He wanted to feel their softness, their fullness.
They were not like any lips he had ever kissed. He was focused
completely on the sensation.

He did not want to rush. This was too special to hurry any of it. In
some part of himself he did not believe it could be happening. From
the beginning Susan Linwood had represented the kind of woman he

526

could barely hold a conversation with, the kind who – with a single painful exception – stood completely outside his romantic range.

Now, he held her in his arms, feeling her body against his – the firmness, the softness, the heat – and his lips pressed, felt, tasted, delighted in hers.

He did not know which of them ended the kiss. They stood clasped together, arms tight around each other. His hands explored her back – silk over soft, warm flesh – his palms as alive with sensation as his lips had been.

He leaned back so he could see her, kissed her brow, touched his lips to each of her eyes, to the tip of her sculpted nose, to the corners of her mouth. His breath came quickly. He wanted to kiss her neck, her shoulders—

'Wait,' she said softly.

He pulled away, releasing her.

'Oh, no,' she said, reaching for him. 'I don't mean we should stop. Not stop this, not stop anything. I just know if we get started . . . I just want to go slowly.'

He reached out to touch her face. 'Any speed you want.' The words came out cracked, from a suddenly dry mouth. He wet his lips, smiled. 'Not that I'm not eager, you understand.'

Her smile matched his. 'I understand.'

She took his hand. 'I think I want a drink, after all.'

She opened two mini-bottles of Scotch and poured them into brandy snifters from the shelf over the wet bar. She raised her glass to him but didn't speak.

'To your beautiful lips,' he said. 'To your beautiful brown eyes. To every beautiful part of you.'

'To my eyes?' she said after she'd sipped her drink. 'You think my eyes are beautiful?'

'Very beautiful.'

She nestled her head against his shoulder. 'I don't think I expect Europeans to think of my eyes as beautiful. Exotic, maybe. Fascinating, I suppose. Weird, definitely. But never beautiful . . .' She kissed the angle of his jaw. 'Sometime remind me to tell you a story about eyes.'

He put his drink down so he could cup her head in his hand. He kissed her eyes again, softly. Then he kissed her mouth.

This time was different – hotter, more intense. His fingers dug into her hair, pulling her head to him, her mouth against his, as if he could fuse them together.

He pulled his head back and then kissed her softly again. 'That was about to be not so very slow,' he said.

'Me, too,' she acknowledged. She stepped away from him. 'Can we sit on the balcony a while?'

They sat side by side in the dark, holding hands, looking at the lights of Kowloon, watching the sparkling boats skim across the harbor.

'Tell me a story,' he said.

'About eyes?' There was a wistful smile in her voice. 'Okay . . . It was when Lara, my daughter, was five . . . we had a birthday party for her, friends and family. Richard's parents came, and Richard's mother always brings a camera to family occasions and makes endless photo albums, all carefully labeled. And she wanted to take a picture of the birthday girl. She had Lara posed the way she wanted her, with the presents and the decorations, and before she clicked the shutter she looked out from behind the camera and said, "Lara dear, don't squint." So Lara smiled at her and posed some more. This happened three or four times – Lara would pose and smile and Grandma would look out from behind the camera and say, "Lara dear, don't squint." Until Lara finally said, completely exasperated, "I'm not squinting, I'm *half Chinese*." '

He laughed. 'Well done, Lara,' he said.

'Her brother still calls her "squinty." ' She sighed.

They sat a while in silence.

'I'm married,' she said.

'I know you're married. And I know you're a grownup.'

'I don't want this just for fun. I'm not asking for anything, not even anything beyond tonight. Just so it's not some meaningless roll in the hay.'

He lifted her hand to his mouth and kissed her palm.

'Not meaningless. Not for a minute.'

'I'm being silly. It's . . . I'm frightened, suddenly.'

'We don't have to, you know.' It was as hard a thing to say as any he could remember.

'No, no. That's not what I mean. But . . . This is what I want to say. I've wanted to kiss you before. I think I've wanted . . . everything. I just didn't know that was what I was feeling. Because I didn't think I worked that way.

'I know there are married women having affairs all over. But I never . . .' She looked at him, touched his face. 'I told you that story about the drama teacher. I used to torture myself that I must have really wanted him and that was why I didn't scream. But in my more rational moments I know better. I take things like commitment very seriously.

'So these feelings I've been having are . . . not the Susan Linwood I thought I knew. And I realized something just now as I was about to ask you to kiss me.'

She stopped. She did not speak for so long he was sure she had reconsidered whatever she had been about to say.

'I realized,' she said quietly into the night, 'that my marriage was over. It's probably been over for me for a long time, but I haven't recognized it. There are still words to be said between me and Richard, of course. Formalities. But in my heart I'm not married.'

Again, she fell silent, but only for a moment.

'I needed to hear myself say that out loud. And I wanted you to know it. And maybe that's why these feeings I'm having don't fit Susan Linwood. There is no more Susan Linwood. It's Susan Chan who feels this way.'

He sat, watching the harbor, feeling her presence beside him on the balcony. She lifted his hand to the arm of her chair and traced the lines on his palm with her forefinger. The sensation was so intense it was hard for him not to close his hand around hers.

She turned in her chair to face him.

'David, now that I've said all that, I don't know how ready I really am. I still want to go slowly. Very slowly. Can we do that?'

He nodded. He couldn't speak.

He undressed her, marveling. Her skin so smooth, her breasts so gracefully curved, the nipples tiny cylinders in the center of precise brown circles, all her body taut and sleek.

529

★ ★ ★

'I love the way you look at me,' she said. 'So full of lust.'

He led her to the bed and she lay down to watch while he undressed.

'You're good at looking, too,' he said.

She was smiling. 'That's because you're good to look at. I didn't realize you were so muscular.'

'I'm a computer guy with a beard,' he said with a grin. 'Kind of misleading.'

Lying next to her he ran his hand slowly over her body. Now and then she shuddered. The first time, he stopped.

'Don't stop,' she said. 'That's pleasure.'

He paused at the plump, soft flesh high on the inside of her thigh.

'Oh.' She sounded dismayed.

'No,' he said. 'I love it. So tender and sweet.'

He bent to kiss her there. She stiffened.

'Something wrong?'

'No. I didn't know what you were going to do.'

'This?' he said, and probed gently with his tongue.

'Oh, God!' she said. She put her hand on his head. 'Wait,' she said. 'I guess I'm not ready yet, after all.' And then, 'I'm sorry to stop you.' And, laughing, 'Believe me, I'm sorry.'

Impossible as it felt to hold himself back, he straightened out so they were side by side and took her in his arms 'We can just sleep if you'd like. We're both tired, we've had a lot to eat and drink. We don't have to do this all at once.'

He amazed himself with this ability to be patient. By the morning she was likely to change her mind entirely. And yet he knew that pushing now could ruin it all, and that was something he would not risk. If being patient meant this never went further than it had already, so be it.

Mahoney smelled Horgan's dead cigar even before the Organized Crime Narcotics chief came through the door.

'Got a minute?' Horgan parked his butt on Mahoney's desk and stared down at him. He took the cigar from his mouth and picked a flake of tobacco from the tip of his tongue. 'Just what do you suppose you're up to?'

It was the knowing rebuke of an omniscient father, offering redemption in confession – technique good enough that Mahoney was caught up in it for a dangerous moment. *How much does he know?*

In self-defense he pushed his chair away from his desk so that Horgan was no longer looming over him.

'What am I *up to*?' he faked. 'What does that mean?'

'You think you're getting away with this bullshit?'

Mahoney ground his teeth to keep himself from answering.

'I expect you to be here making a case. I expect it to be all ready for me. But no, you're out of the office doing shit behind my back. You interview a couple of Chinese waiters, but you don't say a word, there's nothing about it in the file, nothing at the unit meeting.'

'I found out they were lying.'

'What's so interesting on the eighth floor?' The new subject meant to catch him off-guard.

'I've been going to see Max Straus.' The truth will set you free. Up to a point. 'There are some cases from when he was my unit chief – I had them in the Appellate Division, and now they're going up to the Court of Appeals. Max asked me to give a hand.'

'That's bullshit.'

Again, Mahoney stifled the admission Horgan was trying to evoke.

'You have a job to do right here,' Horgan thundered. 'No, that's wrong – you *had* a job. I told you once. I should have done something then.'

'You're right.' Mahoney saw daylight and ran for it. 'I've been thinking it was time to say something myself. This was a mistake – I should never have left Appeals. I've already talked to Max about going back.'

'You're supposed to talk to *me*.'

'I knew you didn't like the way I work. I figured you'd be relieved to see me go.'

'That's one thing you got right.' Horgan got off the desk. 'I want a full review of the Eng case. Then start wrapping up everything else you've touched here. I'm going to do us both the favor of asking the front office to get you the fuck out of my sight.'

David awoke with the sun and lay in bed admiring Susan.

The night before he had sometimes found himself unprepared, looking at her. Being in bed with a woman of a different race wasn't something he'd ever given much thought, one way or the other. Life had presented him with blondes and brunettes and one magnificent redhead. The idea of actively seeking out otherness for its own sake – in the way perhaps of the expatriates here in Hong Kong – had always seemed forced and artificial to him. Condescending, at best, and possibly something nastier.

Now here he was in bed with Susan Linwood. Susan Chan. A woman very different from the unapproachable spoiled rich lady he'd initially thought she was. He knew her better now, knew something about her fears and her needs. They had been constant companions for little more than a week, but they had been through so much together that time was not a useful measure. He felt a surprisingly deep kinship with her – and, somehow, that very sense of being close made the physical newness of her all the more striking.

He sat up in bed and wrapped his arms around his knees and appreciated her.

Her eyes opened slowly. She closed them again. Wrinkled her face and stretched. She looked at him.

'Hi. I was awful last night, wasn't I?'

'No such thing.' He kissed her lightly. 'Good morning.'

She turned away from the kiss. 'Dragon breath. Me, not you. Do you remember when we leave?'

'We have until one.'

'Good.' She wrapped the sheet modestly around herself and dragged it behind her to the bathroom.

*Told you so*, he taunted himself.

'How do you want to spend the morning?' she asked when she came out of the shower, wrapped in a towel.

He looked at her.

'I know. But what's your second choice?'

'Take a walk? I know a place.'

'Someplace I don't know?'

'Wait and see.'

'Okay,' she said. 'Breakfast first.'


He led her to the Peak tram.

'I thought you were going to surprise me.' Not that she objected to Victoria Peak. She'd just been hoping for something less ordinary.

The tickets he bought were for the first stop on the way up the mountain, not the whole journey.

'Okay, I'm surprised.'

They got off and walked up a steep flight of steps to a mid-levels roadway.

'Where are we?'

'Just follow me.'

After a few blocks of apartment houses they were on a paved cliffside path bordered by tropical woods. The foliage broke from time to time to give views of the skyscrapers in Central and Wan Chai and then the Happy Valley racecourse. Only occasionally was the illusion of being insulated by natural beauty broken by a current of foul air, reeking of sewage or garbage or both. They were passed by joggers running singly and in pairs, and multi-generation Chinese families walking briskly together.

'Is this the trail where you went running?'

'Right the first time.'

'It *is* a surprise.'

'The best is yet to come.'

They kept walking, pausing to enjoy the views. As they turned a corner in the path, skirting a thick-trunked tree, David pointed.

Among the rocks at the tree's base was a niche bordered in strips of red paper bearing gold Chinese characters. In the niche, sticks of incense burned in front of a color picture of a Chinese god.

'A shrine!' Susan exclaimed. She looked along the path. 'There's another one.'

Not much farther along, on the hillside wall of the path, he pointed out a series of increasingly larger shrines, all honoring the same god.

Next came a narrow, winding stone stair, twisting up the steepest part of the hill. On either side of it was a profusion of red-bordered shrines. The bottom steps were painted red, the paint scarcely worn away, and there was a short handrail, only as far as the first small plateau reached by the stairs. On the handrail was a plaque with Chinese characters and the English legend LOVERS' ROCK GARDEN.

'How wonderful.' She threw her arms around him and kissed him and then quickly headed up the stairs.

She stopped by the first large shrine. It was on a sheer boulder far enough from the stairs to make David wonder how the red paper and the ceramic statue of the god and the incense had been perched there.

Susan pointed at the statue. 'You think he's related to the one sitting on Martin's heroin?'

'I don't know,' David said. 'They all look alike to me.'

She hit him. 'Typical white-ghost humor.'

They climbed further, past white incense braziers that looked to him like suburban charcoal grills, some of them holding burning incense.

It was a hard climb to the top, but Susan made it eagerly, and he stayed close behind. Even in the early morning they were both sweating.

At the top, the steps and path and some of the stones were painted red. Huge coils of incense hung from the branches of trees, swinging in the breeze, impossibly high.

'The higher you can hang it, the quicker your prayers get to heaven,' Susan said.

She went to stand on the farthest point of the round boulder at the very top of the garden of shrines. David joined her. The cliff fell away dramatically below them; the view of the harbor and Kowloon was as panoramic and unobstructed as any he'd seen. They were buffeted by a stiff wind that cooled the sweat on his back.

He put his arms around her and they stood there together. She lifted her face for a kiss. This time she was not holding back.

'I don't know how safe this is,' David said.

'I'm not worried.'

A gust of wind almost toppled them. 'Oh!' she exclaimed. 'I see what you mean. I thought it was the kiss that was making me feel unsteady.'

'I know a nice hotel.' He looked at his watch. 'But we'll have to hurry.'

'That's okay,' she said. 'We've already done slow.'

When they got back to the hotel all the stifled passion erupted at once, for both of them. For a moment as they explored each other's bodies, David was so beset with simultaneous desires he could not move to satisfy any one of them first.

Susan's hunger matched his own – they shared the same drive to touch to see to taste every part of each other. Every sensation heightened their need and sharpened the next sensation. Consummation itself was merely a continuation, an extension of a single protracted act of merging.

They lay in each other's arms, warm with pleasure.

'Well,' she said. 'That was something.'

'Oh, yes. Worth waiting for.'

'Can we do it again?' She blushed. 'I don't know how I got so brazen. Is it all right?'

'It's wonderful.'

'Good.' She kissed him. 'Can we?'

He laughed. 'Well, yes. But not immediately.'

She reached down and touched him. 'Such a friendly fellow.'

'Actually,' he said, 'some things we *can* do again immediately.'

'Oh, good,' she said. 'Let's.'

# 14

On the flight home they nuzzled and held hands. Susan was grateful when the eastward-bound plane met the westering sun, the cabin lights went out and their cabinmates went to sleep. She and David spread blankets over themselves to conceal their busy hands.

This is ridiculous, she told herself – you're acting like a teenager. She said as much to David.

'What's wrong with that?'

'I'm supposed to be a grownup.' She couldn't bring herself to say her age, though he already knew she had children in college, though they'd had sex more exciting than she had remembered was possible. I must be ten years older than he is, she thought. 'I'm past forty,' she made herself say.

'If I have the story right, you took a long vacation from having any pleasure in your life. I'd say you're entitled to act any way you want.'

She wasn't convinced but she didn't argue the point.

'I can't believe how much I want you,' she said a little later. 'How could I have waited so long, left us so little time?'

'We have all the time in the world,' he said, but she could tell she had hurt him by mentioning the ending they were speeding toward at six hundred miles an hour.

'I want you all the time,' she said. 'It doesn't stop.'

'The feeling's more than mutual.' He kissed her neck; under the blanket, his hand moved up her thigh.

'Oh, God! That just makes it worse.'

'We could try going in the back.'

'In the back?'

'Where we can lock ourselves in and have some privacy.'

'The washroom?' She looked at him in disbelief. 'Do people really do that?'

'I've never tried it, but they say people do.'

'I'm definitely too old for *that*.'

'Okay, Grandma.' He kissed her again.

Sitting there in the dark she couldn't get rid of the idea. 'Okay, let's try it,' she said finally.

'Try . . .?' He grinned. 'You sure?'

'We can try.'

In the dark of the airplane's night, they strolled back separately to the toilets and locked themselves in together.

'I can't believe we're doing this,' Susan whispered, giggling. 'I never really believed it was possible.'

'I'm not sure it is.'

'There's no room to undress.'

'I think you're mostly meant to keep your clothes on,' he said.

'All right. But you have to undo my bra.'

He reached around behind her and undid the clasp. She lifted her shirt and the bra so he could kiss her.

'That feels so good.' She reached down for him. 'So does that.'

It seemed to her she was discovering a whole new world – of sensation and of freedom. She had always thought of Richard as having awakened her, but it was only in contrast to the shy and relatively sheltered girl she had been when they married. And whatever abandon she had managed with Richard had dwindled after the children were born, then died totally when Richard seemed to lose interest in having sex with her, and Charles saw her with Mr Hsu.

'Isn't there a way to do it standing up?' she asked.

'No other way, in here.' He showed her.

'Oh, yes,' she said, her back pressed against the door. 'That works.' After that, they didn't need words.

Back in their seats, they napped, her head nestled in the curve of his

537

neck and shoulder, his head pillowed on her hair.

Dawn arrived as quickly as had night. The cabin attendant woke them for breakfast.

'I'd better go back and wash up,' Susan said.

'You know the way?'

She tugged his beard. 'I do now.'

He watched her go, not wanting to think how much closer they were to the United States, to New York, to reality. He had no idea how she was going to play it, didn't even want to bring it up.

'I think there's a hotel right in the airport,' he told her when she came back. They'd been talking about it before their nap – their last chance to be alone together on the trip. 'If not, there's one just outside the airport entrance, and they send courtesy buses every five minutes. We have a couple of hours, so as long as Customs isn't too bad . . .' Getting no response, he just let it trail off.

After their breakfast trays had been cleared she turned to him and put a hand on his. The expression on her face went with the tender gesture: all that was missing was the words, some form of *I'm sorry* . . . He swallowed hard to keep his breakfast down.

'David, I'm sorry,' she said, 'but I don't think the hotel would be such a good idea.'

*The hotel.* He felt immediate relief, guessed it was premature.

'It's just that I'm beginning to feel very confused. The closer we get to New York, the more I know I have to face reality. I thought – as long as we're in the air, as long as we're still traveling, I can just be with David and not worry about the world. But it's not as easy as that.'

Lord, how he did not want to hear this. 'It's okay, I understand.' He was trying to sound supportive, but there was a kind of defensive impatience in his voice.

'Let's not fight,' she said.

'I'm not—' he began sharply but stopped himself before he made things worse.

She tangled her fingers in his beard, turned his face toward her so she could kiss him. Her other hand tightened on the top of his thigh. 'I don't want to lose this,' she said. 'Not any of it. It means too much to me.'

538

He pulled her to him, held her as tight as he could in the awkward space. 'I don't want to lose it, either.' He could not make himself let go.

Walking into Max Straus's office, Dan Mahoney did his best to conceal his apprehension at seeing Ned King sitting in a chair next to Straus's desk.

'I've been keeping Ned up-to-date on our doings,' Straus explained as Mahoney sat on the couch with Laurie Jordan. 'He and I both thought this had reached the point where he should be a regular part of the team.'

Mahoney had assumed that Straus would be keeping the Chief of Investigation apprised of what they were up to – because it included the possibility of a bad A.D.A., and even more so because of the competition with the Southern District and the interest from the Boss prompted by the op-ed piece on asset forfeiture. But facing King this way raised questions Mahoney had hoped to avoid, such as how pissed-off King might be at Daniel J. Mahoney because he had gone to Max Straus with his tales of Pullone and Horgan, instead of going straight to Ned King – Horgan's boss – as he should have, doing it by the numbers.

'I've just been hearing nasty stories about you,' King said to Mahoney, boosting his apprehension. 'I hope you don't have a lot of friends like Kevin Horgan.'

'Before this is over, Mr Horgan's likely to wish he didn't have a lot of friends like Dan,' Max Straus said.

'He certainly is eager to have you out of his unit,' King said. 'I told him, "You know, I don't understand. When Mahoney requested his transfer out of Appeals, everybody there was full of good things to say about him – extra smart, hard worker, good instincts." I was stretching it some, for effect.

'Then I said, "I hear he's been doing some work with Max Straus lately, and Max thinks he's the best thing since sliced bread. So, tell me, Kevin – what's *your* problem?" ' The investigation chief was definitely enjoying himself, telling the story. 'I thought he was going to have a stroke.' He looked at Mahoney again. 'He can get really colorful about you when he gets going.'

539

Mahoney didn't even want to imagine it.

'The question I have,' said Straus, 'is how did he react when you mentioned my name?'

'That's why I brought you into it, to see what he'd do.' He turned to Mahoney. 'Max told me how you handled it when Horgan raised the eighth floor as an issue, so I knew you'd mentioned Max. But it's still a real question, whether he knows or suspects what you've all been up to.' To Max: 'I didn't see him flinch when I brought you up, and he didn't ask what you and Dan were working on. That worried me a little – you'd think he'd be curious, after the way I baited him with it.'

'What do you think?' Straus asked Mahoney. 'You're the one with the most first-hand experience.'

'When he confronted me, I was sure he knew something was up,' Mahoney answered. 'But at this point I think he was only fishing. He's uneasy, maybe he smells something wrong, but he might not know what it is yet. I think there's a chance he bought what I told him.'

'All right,' King said. 'We'll have to be careful, and most important we have to wrap this up before it explodes in our faces. Meantime, Max, maybe you can talk to Kathy Cody at Appeals about finding this man someplace to sit and a special assignment she can tell the world he's doing. She's going to scream about how overcrowded they are, but it can't be helped.'

'She owes me a couple,' Max said. 'I'll twist her arm a little.'

'Good,' King said. 'Now, about the main event—'

Max turned to Laurie Jordan. 'Progress?'

'I ran a DECS check on our heroin distributor,' she said. 'I got some hits. Our man, if this is our man, is listed by our friends right here in Special Narcotics.' She handed a sheet of paper to Straus, who skimmed it and passed it to King.

The Investigation Division chief glanced over it quickly. 'Good.' He reached for Straus's phone. 'Let me see if we can cut through the bullshit here.' He identified himself to the secretary who answered and when he was put through said, 'Billy, I need your help on something. You're going to get a call from Official Corruption about a drug distributor, street name El Coyote –' he read off the information

Jordan had on him – 'you've got him listed with DECS. I wanted you to know I have a strong interest in this, so I'd appreciate your stretching a little to help them out.'

King listened, said, 'First of all they're going to want to know where he falls in the hierarchy, what his activity is. If he's what they need, then if you can find a way to break free your case against him for them to use, I'd appreciate it. I know you won't want to compromise an informant or any wiretap information. If that can be avoided, all the better – if not, we may have to find a way to live with it . . . Yeah, it's that important. That's why I wanted to prepare the ground—'

He listened again. 'No, I can assure you pretty definitely they're not targeting anybody on your team. This is something outside what you're doing. And I appreciate the help, really appreciate it. You'll be hearing from the Copperhead, and the assistant on the case is called Laurie Jordan. Don't be distracted by how beautiful she is –' he winked at her – 'she's got one of the best minds in the office.'

He hung up. 'Okay. That ought to smoooth the way.' He looked intently at Jordan and Mahoney. 'I know you've gone over with Max how serious this could be for the office. Now that we're moving beyond this small group, we're making a real statement that we believe this is real and not a figment of our anxieties. I don't want to increase the pressure of an already difficult situation, but I do want you to know that when I leave here I'll be going straight in to brief the Boss.'

David and Susan disembarked blearily in lunch-time Los Angeles. Local clock and calendar registered a time before their departure from Hong Kong.

The Customs hall was spacious and airy, with high ceilings and plenty of light. David checked his declaration as he waited to be cleared. With his new suit and the gifts for Alice and the kids, he was over the allowance, but he had listed everything in detail, even the farewell gift from June Eng, a soapstone seal with the figure of an astrological animal on top and his name in English and Chinese carved into the bottom.

The passport-control officer swiped his passport over some kind of reader and waited while information came up on the computer. He looked closer at his monitor for a moment, then at David, tapped something into his keyboard, then computer-scanned David's Customs declaration. He stamped the passport, marked something on the declaration, handed back David's papers. 'Welcome back,' he said.

David went through the rest of the process without a hitch. The Customs inspector read his declaration and waved him through to the cashier to pay duty on his over-limit purchases.

As he wheeled his airport luggage cart from the Customs hall into the terminal, he heard himself being paged. 'David Clark, please pick up your message on any courtesy phone.' A few seconds later there was a similar announcement, this time for Susan.

She was waiting for him just inside the terminal.

'What do you think that's about?' she asked.

He shook his head – no idea. They found a courtesy phone and made their calls.

'Detective Chief Inspector Hall of the Royal Hong Kong Police,' he told her. 'Please call. Urgent. And he left a bunch of numbers.'

'The same,' she said. 'I don't understand.'

'I don't see how it can be good.'

'But how can it be bad? Maybe he learned something about the bandits.'

'Urgent?' David asked.

'No, I guess not. Maybe we should call and find out.'

'It's the middle of the night there.'

'I forgot. I suppose it can wait.'

'We've got too many other things to worry about, anyway.'

Paramount among them was June Eng's audio tape. He brought it up as soon as they were airborne on the way to New York.

'I'm going to call the Engs first thing tomorrow and arrange to bring it over,' Susan said. 'Then we can stop thinking about it.'

'It bothers me,' David countered. 'I'm more convinced than ever there's more to these tapes than some kind of greeting card.'

'But if they're helping people escape oppression then whatever's on the tapes is part of that, and I'm happy to help.'

542

'But we don't *know* that's what they're doing.'

'You were satisfied with it when we were discussing it.' Susan's tone was sharper.

David wondered if he was being unreasonable. But he couldn't let it go. 'Remember I told you about the guy I was partners with, on my shot at the big time? Jon knows all about encoding information and putting it where you wouldn't expect it to be. And he has some equipment that might help read whatever's on that tape.'

'Why? Why do you want to tamper with it?'

'I don't want to tamper with anything. But I think they're using us, and I want to know how.' He hastened to say, 'I do feel bad for them. And I feel worse for the people whose money they were holding.' Accepting that theory for argument's sake, and because he had to admit it seemed right. 'But I don't think it was necessary for them to manipulate us, and I'm uncomfortable being made a courier without my consent.'

'*I'm* the courier,' Susan countered. 'And it doesn't bother me. They came through for me exactly the way they said they would. I don't blame them for not telling us. How could they?'

'We got shot at in China, remember.'

'That didn't have anything to do with them.'

'I hope you're right.' He sat in silence. For the moment there didn't seem to be anything more to say.

'We've got to go see them,' she said. 'We can't just walk away from this. And it *is* a letter from their children. Whatever else it might be.'

'I'm not saying we shouldn't see them.' He was glad she'd decided to give him an opening. 'And I'm certainly not saying we should hold back the tape. All I want to do is take it to Jon for a day or so. Then I'll bring it back. If I go straight to Boston as soon as we get into New York, I can be back before you even talk to them.'

'But you'll have been traveling for a whole day. How can you just get on another plane?'

'I'll take the train. I can sleep on the way.'

'Do they run that late?'

'If not I'll take the first one in the morning. I can still be back before you can possibly arrange to see them.'

'All right.' She said it grudgingly. 'But only if you promise he's not going to tamper with it.'

'He's just going to put it on his equipment and play it. Maybe make a copy.'

She kissed him. 'See, I can't say no to you.'

David felt the thud of the landing gear dropping into place like a death knell.

'What next?' he said to Susan. They still hadn't really discussed it. She was married, she had a family; it had to be her call.

'I already said I don't want to lose this.' She leaned across to kiss him. 'I meant it. I can't bear the thought of being without you completely. But it may be difficult for us to see each other.'

'I expected that.'

'There's Charles. I can't do anything dramatic about my life until I know Charles is going to be all right. And there's going to be a lot waiting for me to do at work—'

'It's okay, I know you have a lot on your mind. I'm not saying it won't be hell for me not to see you, but I understand it's necessary.'

She turned away from him. 'You know, sometimes I just wish you weren't so accommodating.'

'What should I do? Forbid you to see your husband or worry about your son? Kidnap you and take you away somewhere?'

She turned back to him. 'I'm sorry, David. I hate this so much. I'm so on edge I don't really know what I'm saying.'

She was even more on edge when she got home. Richard was waiting for her. He gave her a quick hug and a kiss on the cheek.

'Welcome home.'

'It's good to be back.' Could he hear how false the words were?

He carried her bags into the bedroom. She followed him.

'Will you be staying around a while now, or do you have some more exotic trips in mind?'

'No more trips, not at the moment.' She lay down on the bed. 'But I don't know how long I'll be staying around.'

He turned from the closet where he was hanging her garment bag. 'And what does that mean?'

544

'I don't know, Richard, I don't know why I said that. I'm just tired. I've been in the air for almost twenty-four hours, and I didn't get much sleep.'

'Of course. We can talk in the morning.'

'How can we talk in the morning? You'll be at the hospital in the morning, or at your office.'

'I don't see what we have to talk about, in any case. You had a long, tiring trip, and you should get some sleep.'

She sat up. 'I meant what I said. I don't know how long I can keep living here.' She was surprised to find herself persisting: it was like asking David to kiss her – it felt natural and true, though it was dramatically unlike anything she could ever have imagined doing before.

'I suppose I can guess what prompted this,' Richard said. 'All I can say is, this conversation is unnecessary. There's no reason we can't go on as we have been. We have before.'

'What do you mean, *we have before*?'

'You know perfectly well what I mean.'

'No, I don't. What *do* you mean?'

'I'm not going to open all that up, not after so many years.'

So there it was – he *had* thought, all this time, that she'd had an affair with David Hsu. And never said a word about it.

'I think you should open it up. I think it's about time we stopped keeping silent about what's important.'

'You think I don't know why you take your so-called business trips to conventions in Las Vegas and Miami?' he said abruptly. 'Or why you have your late-night conferences?'

'Richard, for heaven's sake! You can't think—' But he could. And it had nothing to do with Charles.

He said, 'I'm not interested in a divorce. And I'm certainly not interested in a scandal.'

'Nobody said anything about a divorce.' She lay back again and covered her eyes with her hand. 'Not yet.'

'Not yet, and not in any future I can possibly foresee.'

'Richard, I can't even *think* about the future until I know how Charles is. But for now, at least, I don't see how I can keep living here.'

'You can't live with someone else, either. I won't have it.'

'Why would you care? You don't want to sleep with me. And do you think I don't hear rumors? The great neurosurgeon and his med-student groupies.'

'I know about those rumors. You can't think I'm that stupid.'

She sat up to face him. 'The truth is, Richard, I've tried not to think about it one way or the other. I always assumed it was mostly the rumor-mongers' jealousy talking. But now that we're talking about it – no, I don't think you're that stupid. I think you're that arrogant and that hungry for power and that oblivious to other people, for all your concern about appearances. I bet you have chamber-music groupies, too.'

'This is nonsense. Whatever this is, this fling of yours, get it out of your system. You have my blessing.'

She stared at him.

He left the room and returned quickly with his briefcase. 'Here,' he said. He took out a pad and a pen and wrote, handed her the result. In his neurosurgeon's scrawl he had written:

I hereby forgive my wife Susan for any sexual activity in which she may have engaged during her recent trip to Hong Kong and within two months of her return.

'Is that enough time?' he asked.

'Richard, why are you carrying on like this?'

'I like my life as it is. I won't sit by in silence and see it destroyed because of some pre-menopausal fling—'

'Richard, I'm forty-two.' Focusing on the detail because anything else would release too much anger.

'Empty-nest blues, then. Whatever it is. I'm trying to be rational about it. It doesn't have to change our lives. I know you'll think this is maudlin, but with everything that's happened, I do love you.'

'No, you don't. You love Richard Linwood. If you have any feeling for me it's affection for a prized possession.'

'I can see there's no point continuing this. Charles comes up for his evaluation in less than three weeks. Let's try to stay calm until then. If you want to move out to the beach—'

546

'Richard, I have a business.'

'A hotel, then, if that's what you want. I'd prefer something large and impersonal, if that's all right. I don't want them noticing your boyfriend's comings and goings.'

'I don't have a boyfriend.'

'Whatever you say.' He went to his closet for his pajamas. 'I'm going to sleep in the guest room. You've had a hard trip, I don't want to disturb you when I get up.'

In the morning Mahoney had a call from Max Straus. 'I got your notification from Customs.'

Mahoney had made the request to Customs in Straus's name. He didn't want information about David Clark and Susan Linwood coming in on Horgan's fax machine.

'They're back?'

'L.A., yesterday afternoon,' Straus told him. 'New York late last night.'

'Where were they?'

'China. Hong Kong and China.'

Mahoney whistled. 'That's a long way to go to get laid. At least in the Poconos you get a heart-shaped bed.'

'Didn't you say one of them was Chinese?'

'The woman.'

'Maybe she was visiting family.'

'And who was *he* visiting? What did they declare?'

'Custom-made suit, cashmere sweaters, silk scarves,' Straus said. 'Very touristy.'

'I suppose I didn't really expect them to declare a half-dozen units of Double UoGlobe.'

'Why don't you have a chat with them – see what they have to say about all this.'

Susan slept late. She awoke feeling nervous about the conversation with Richard. She wanted to move out immediately, if only to avoid another encounter like the one the previous night, but she knew that even if she did they had a lot more to get through before they were done.

She checked the clock – too early to call David. He was probably still en route to his friend Jon's in the suburbs north-west of Boston. But it might not be too late to call Hong Kong. If Detective Chief Inspector Hall was the early-to-bed type, she'd probably wake him, but too bad if she did: he'd said the message was urgent.

He was at the second number she called, very much awake. He thanked her for calling. She thought he sounded strained.

'Mrs Linwood, could you tell me if you had a chance to see June Eng before you left?'

'We had breakfast with her when we got back to Hong Kong. The day before we left.'

'The day before yesterday, then.'

'I think so. The time change is so disorienting.'

'Quite. And how did she seem, at breakfast?'

'Seem? She seemed fine. Well, no, actually, she seemed upset. But I assumed it was because of what happened in China, and Mr Li's death. That's what she was talking about. Why? Is there some kind of trouble?'

'If you could just answer a few more questions. Do you know her parents at all well?'

'Not well, no.'

'And do you know what sort of business they're in?'

'I believe they're retired.' Why was he asking all these questions? Something had to be wrong.

'What about the younger Engs? Their business – did they talk much about that?'

'I know they're in the garment business, because we visited some of the factories. And real estate, and construction, I think. Their mother said something about infrastructure development.'

'I see.'

'And the Army,' Susan said.

'Beg pardon?'

'They're in some kind of business with the People's Liberation Army. June told us that.'

'Did she tell you what sort of business with the PLA?'

'I assumed it was the garment business.'

'But she didn't say?'

'No.'

'What about Mr Chan? Was he involved in this Army business with them?'

'Yes, I think they said he was. Inspector, what's wrong? I'm trying to cooperate, but I have to know what this is about, before I can say another word.'

He was silent. She listened to the hum and crackle of interference on the international line.

'Yes, well, Mrs Linwood, I'm afraid I have to tell you that your friend June Eng is dead.'

'She's— Oh, no!' It took Susan a long time to get her breath. 'How?'

'Very unpleasantly, I'm afraid. There's an ancient Chinese method of execution, sometimes called death by slicing. Her murderer – or murderers, more probably – apparently had a certain reverence for tradition, that way.'

Susan's legs felt weak. Hall should have asked if she was sitting before he told her the news. She sat on the floor. 'When? When was she . . .'

'Last evening. Six hours or so after you left.'

The policeman had more questions. She answered without really listening to what either of them was saying.

'Why?' she asked him suddenly. 'Why was she killed like that?'

'I believe you're asking two distinct questions,' he responded. 'Why? and Why like that? I regret to say I can't answer either of them. That's why I wanted to talk with you. I hoped you might help me understand. My next question for you was going to be, have you any reason to think the Engs have made any particularly vindictive enemies?'

'I don't know what this has to do with Hong Kong,' Susan said. 'But I do know one story.' She told him about Tony Ching and the dispute over the election at the Sam Yap Association.

'Yes, that's interesting. As you say, though, perhaps a bit remote.'

'Do you think June's death has anything to do with what happened to David and me in China?'

He hesitated. 'Why do you ask?'

'June said something at breakfast, something like . . . it might not have happened if she'd been there. I thought she meant we'd have taken a different route, or we wouldn't have gotten lost. Now I'm not sure.'

'You suppose she might have had something else in mind that ties her more closely to the incident in China? And ties the incident to her death.'

'I'm just asking – I don't know enough to *suppose* anything. That's your job.'

# 15

As soon as she was off the phone with Hong Kong, Susan called the Massachusetts number David had given her.

'Please tell him it's urgent,' she told Jon Levi. 'I need him to call me the minute he gets there.'

She sat by the phone, waiting for David to call, until anxiety impelled her to get up and begin packing. She had no idea what or how much to take with her, and no ability to make a decision. She pulled clothes from her closet without aim or plan.

The phone startled her. Her first thought was that she could not handle more bad news, then she thought of David and raced to answer it.

'Are you okay?' he asked immediately.

'No.' That was all she could say, at first.

'What is it? What's wrong?'

The concern in his voice helped. 'It's okay – I'm all right. Did you call Hong Kong?'

'No. What was it?'

'David . . . June Eng is dead.'

'Oh, Lord. How?'

'Murdered. Chief Inspector Hall called it death by slicing,' she made herself say.

'I've read about that, it's—' He stopped short. 'How horrible. Do they know who did it, or why?'

'No. That's why he called. He wanted to know who she did business with and who her enemies might be.'

'Did you tell him about the grand jury?'

'Just about Tony Ching.'

'Are you sure you're okay?'

'I'm a mess, but it's nothing that won't pass. Richard was awful last night. I'm moving into a hotel.'

'What happened?'

'We can talk about it when I see you.'

'And what's this about a hotel?'

'It's just for now, I just can't face Richard every day. I'll call you when I check in. In the meantime, you have to bring the tape back right away.'

'I can have it back tomorrow.'

'We shouldn't keep it from them.'

'I came all the way up here. The least I can do is take the time to accomplish something.'

'Everything is different now. This is the last chance the Engs will ever have to hear from their daughter.' The words bore in on her. 'It's so awful. They've already lost two children, and now June.' She thought of Charles in the hospital, at the edge of life, barely holding on. To lose *any* child was inconceivable. To lose three?

'Do you think they'll even be able to listen to it? I mean, knowing she's dead?'

'That's not for us to decide. All that matters is to give them the tape, and say how sorry we are.'

'All right. Give me a while to catch my breath. I'll take a train back later. Where will I find you?'

'I'll leave you a message.'

'What was that?' Jon Levi wanted to know when David got off the phone.

'Trouble,' David said. He took the tape from his briefcase, described what he thought might be on it. 'I need to have it back in New York by tonight.'

'That doesn't give me much time. I don't have everything here I need to do the job right.'

'Can't you make a copy and analyze that?'

'It's not the same.'

'It's the best we can do.' He checked his watch and the train schedule. 'You've got about five hours.'

'Hey, guy, when you ask a favor, you really ask a favor.'

'I wish it could be easier. And I don't know how much help I can give you with it – my brain is still on Hong Kong time. We'll be lucky if I can stay awake.'

Jon turned the tape over in his hands, musing. 'Tell you what – why don't you take a nap? If I need you, I'll wake you up. That way maybe you'll be some use.'

'Good idea.' David put a hand on his old partner's arm. 'Be careful with it, okay? The woman who recorded it is dead.'

'Dead! When?'

'The day after she gave it to us.'

'How did she die?'

'Very slowly, very unpleasantly.'

'Oh, shit, Davey, what are you getting us into?' Jon glared at him. 'I don't need this, you know. I really don't need this.'

'The hell – you eat it up. You always loved the intrigue best.'

Jon took a poke at him. 'Get outta here. Go get some sleep, before I send you *and* your tape back where you came from.'


Susan finished packing and realized she had no idea where to go. Much as she despised Richard's obsession with appearances, no one would profit by her flaunting their separation or her connection with David.

That meant avoiding the prominent hotels clustered along Fifth and Park Avenues toward the south end of Central Park, and the ones near the Metropolitan Museum. She finally settled on a new luxury hotel in midtown. It was expensive but big enough to be anonymous, and she was not about to cower in some dive.

Her doorman wished her a good trip as he lifted her bags into the cab he'd hailed for her. She told the cabby to take her to the airport and let him get out of sight of the building before giving him the hotel's address, in the other direction. She arrived feeling like a secret agent.


Mahoney sat staring at his phone list. He had already tried David Clark and gotten an answering machine. A woman in Susan Linwood's office said she hadn't been in and wasn't expected for the rest of the week.

Finding her at home presented more of a challenge. His subpoena to the phone company for all the unlisted Manhattan Linwoods had been answered: there was no residence phone for a Susan Linwood. Among the Linwoods with telephones were a Charles and a Lara – both listed, both at the same Park Avenue address. Husband and wife, he'd thought at first. But among the unlisted Linwoods he found a Dr Richard, also of that same Park Avenue address. Coincidence? Or was it one big happy family? And if it was, would they have a phone line each for their kids but only one for Dr and Mrs to share? Possible.

He called a medical referral service, asked about Dr Richard Linwood and got an earful. Board-certified neurosurgeon, Fellow of prestigious colleges of surgery. Clinical Professor of Neurosurgery and member of the board of directors at a major teaching hospital. Author of, and so on . . .

Mahoney called the public library and asked them to check WHO'S WHO. There he was, in even more detail. Wife, Susan, née Chan; children, Charles and Lara. Bingo!

Mahoney called the doctor's Park Avenue residence and got a machine. The voice on the outgoing message was a woman's, her tones rich and warm. He didn't remember grand juror Number Nineteen's voice well enough to recognize it on an answering machine, but rich and warm seemed about right.


It took Susan most of the afternoon to work herself up to calling Meiling Cheung. The prospect of talking about June was not pleasant.

'We were so anxious to hear from you,' Meiling said when she heard Susan's voice. 'Have you brought any news of our children?'

She sounded so eager it broke Susan's heart. 'Oh, Meiling, I'm so sorry—'

'You know?'

Susan was derailed by the abruptness of the question. 'Yes.'

'Who told you?'

'A policeman from Hong Kong.'

'How do you know a policeman from Hong Kong?'

'We were held up by bandits in China. I don't know if . . . if June told you.'

'Yes.'

554

'The policeman questioned us about it in Hong Kong.'

'Why did he call you now?'

Again, the question was sharper than Susan was prepared for. She was suddenly wary.

'I don't really know why he called. He asked when David and I last saw June, and how she seemed.' Leaving out Hall's other questions.

'What did you say?'

'That she seemed upset, but we thought it was about the shooting in China – two of her employees were killed, a driver and a factory manager.'

'China is like a place at war, now. People always die in war.'

'And that wasn't why June was upset, was it?' Susan challenged, and then said quickly, 'Forgive me, please. I think this hit me harder than I realized. I liked June very much, even in the short time I knew her. I felt as if she could be the sister I never had.' Stretching the truth, in the interest of kindness. 'And it gives me great pain to think how this must hurt you.'

'You are very kind to say so. We are old people, and we have seen much tragedy in our lives. We learn to live with what the world inflicts on us.'

Susan didn't know what more to say.

Meiling said, 'Did June give you something for us?'

'Yes, a tape like the one you sent to her.'

'It would be a comfort to us, to have it. I am sure you are tired from your trip, but my husband's grief is very great and I know it would soothe him to hear her voice. If you could please bring it to us today, it would mean so much. I would be happy to send a car for you, so you are comfortable on your way.'

'Thank you, that's very kind. But I don't have it. I'm sorry.'

'I don't understand.' There was a new iciness in Meiling Cheung's voice. 'What does that mean, you *don't have it*?'

'David . . . my friend who made the trip with me . . . David's gone –' her wariness stopped her before she said where – 'gone away on a short business trip. And I forgot to ask him for it before he left. So he still has it – either with him or at home. But he'll be back . . . tomorrow, I'm sure.'

'I don't understand,' Meiling said again. 'You gave it to him?'

'Just to carry back from Hong Kong.'

A cold silence. 'I see. And he went away.'

'For a day, at most.'

'How is your son?' Meiling asked in a tone that could have been a parody of her former warmth.

'My son?'

'Yes. We spoke of your son. You said he was . . . having a problem.'

'He's fine. Thank you.' All Susan wanted now was to get out of this conversation – politely, if she could, but soon.

'I have read that a Western thinker once spoke of children as hostages to fortune,' Meiling said. 'An interesting idea. Don't you think so?'

'I never . . . Yes, very interesting.'

'My two children drowned long ago, and now June is gone. All I have left is Peter. It is as if he is all four children in one. And yet I do not think he is more precious to me than your Charles is to you.'

Susan was too stunned to speak. Talking to the Engs, had she ever spoken of Charles by name?

'Heroin is such a difficult problem,' Meiling said. 'Once you have been its victim you are always in danger. No one truly recovers. The temptation is always waiting. And there are always people who have reason to exploit that temptation. Isn't it so?'

'Yes.' Susan didn't recognize her own voice. 'I suppose.'

'There are so many evil people in the world, and they all have ways of finding the vulnerable ones. There is no way to hide from them. They are like vampires who smell blood.' Meiling gave a short laugh, like a snort. 'I have become so morbid in my old age. Forgive me. It must be my grief that is speaking now. We will be so relieved when we have June's message and we can hear her voice, this one last time.'

Susan was shaking when she got off the phone. She couldn't catch her breath. She sat on the edge of the hotel bed, her arms clasped about her body.

As soon as she could, she picked up the phone again and called David's friend Jon.

'Did David leave?'

'No, he fell asleep.'

556

'Oh, no! Get him up, please! Right away!'

'Okay, okay.'

It was agonizing minutes before David came to the phone. 'Susan? What's wrong?'

She tried to talk but at first all she could do was moan.

'Susan, what is it?'

'Charles. Meiling.' She took a long breath. 'I'm so scared. Meiling threatened Charles.'

'What! How?'

'Heroin. She threatened . . . It doesn't matter. Just come back. Please come back. Bring the tape. She threatened Charles if I don't give them the tape.'

'I think there's a train in half an hour or so. Call them and say I'm on my way. I'll let you know I'm on the train, or Jon will. You can meet me at Penn Station, or they can, or you all can. And if I miss the train I'll try for the late shuttle to La Guardia.'

She gave him the hotel's phone number and her room. 'David, be careful. I'm so frightened.'


Mahoney tried David Clark and Susan Linwood often enough to know their answering-machine messages by heart. He left no messages, himself.

Between phone calls he worked on the files for the Eng case, separating out what Horgan would need if he ever prosecuted the case from the material that was ammunition for Ned King to use in the battle with the feds. Like Mr Ming Chu Wu's phone records – all those calls to Washington. He had a paralegal checking out the people on the list; he called to tell her to get as much done as she could before the day was over. Her report would go with him to his new desk in Appeals, along with a copy of the whole case file for Ned King.

As the day wore on with no human response at either David Clark or Susan Linwood's home phone, Mahoney toyed with the idea of calling Dr Richard to ask where his wife might be – but that, he decided, would only raise them up unnecessarily. This is only one afternoon of one day, he told himself.

★ ★ ★

Susan was at the train station half an hour early. Ten minutes later the Engs arrived, Martin in a white suit and Meiling in a white cheongsam – the color of mourning. Susan watched them approach, thinking of how eager she had been to see them, to thank them for helping her transform her life. Of how shocked she had been to hear of their daughter's death. Now it was all she could do to suppress a shudder in the face of their greeting.

The three of them stood neither together nor apart, waiting in awkward silence amid the bustle of the train station. Susan didn't know how she was going to greet David – the first time they'd been away from each other since . . . since Hong Kong. The first time they'd be in public together this way.

As soon as they caught sight of each other, her questions vanished. They rushed together and clung tight.

'Oh, David, I'm so glad to see you,' she breathed in his ear.

'I should never have left.'

'They're here,' she said.

'I see them. Let's get this over with.'

'Be civil.'

'Why?' he snapped, and then, 'All right, if that's what you want.'

'Please.' She took his hand and they walked to where the Engs were waiting for them.

'You remember David Clark,' she said.

'Yes,' Martin Eng said. 'It is pleasant to see you again.'

'I'm sorry about your loss,' David said.

'Thank you.'

'Your daughter was very kind to us in China. We'll remember her with great fondness.'

'You are generous to say so.'

David opened his backpack. 'She gave us something for you. I apologize for having carried it away. I hope the delay in getting it didn't cause you too much discomfort.' He handed Martin the tape.

'We are happy to have it now,' Martin said. 'We regret any inconvenience it caused you in bringing it to us.'

Some of the tension went out of the air. Meiling smiled.

'I am so pleased to see you,' she said to Susan. 'I already thought of

558

you as another daughter. Now, in a way, you are my only one.'

The thought made Susan shiver, remembering their last phone conversation.

'I must apologize for being so unpleasant on the telephone,' Meiling said. 'I am quite distraught. It expresses itself in morbid thoughts, as I said. I hope I did not upset you by talking about your son that way. I am sure he will be fine. Always.'

'Thank you.' Susan felt a moment's relief – had she been imagining the threat in what Meiling had said? 'I'll admit you scared me.'

'I grew up on old Chinese ghost stories. There are still demons everywhere, in my mind. They come out when I am unhappy.'

People hurrying from a newly arrived train pushed by them.

'This is not a good place for conversation,' Martin said. 'Would you join us for a late supper?'

'No,' David said quickly. 'No, thanks. I'm exhausted, and I'm sure Susan is, too. We should go. Another time.'

Martin smiled coolly. 'Another time, then. We have a car waiting. Please let us take you where you are going.'

'It's not very far,' David said. 'And I'd like to get a breath of fresh air.'

'Perhaps you'll walk with us to our car,' Meiling persisted. 'If you're tired you may change your mind.'

'Of course,' Susan said, squeezing David's hand.


'Did you meet our friend Chan Kwok-Wing?' Meiling asked as they left the station.

'Yes, we spent a lot of time with him,' Susan said. 'We had dinner and then he accompanied us to China. He arranged my conversation with Mr Yu, who told me about my parents. And he was most helpful after the incident with the bandits.'

'Were you very frightened?'

'I've never been shot at before. It's still hard to believe it really happened.' She felt awkward talking about this: their daughter had suffered far worse than bullets whizzing past. 'For me, the important thing was talking with Mr Yu.'

'And that was helpful?'

'Very.'

559

'What was your impression of Chan Kwok-Wing?' Meiling asked.

'He was very gracious, and he seemed very interested in your well-being.'

'Tell us about that, please,' Martin Eng requested. 'What questions did he ask?'

Susan turned to David. 'Do you remember?'

'He was interested in how you were, as Susan said. He was also very interested in the legal system here, and especially in what would happen to the money the police took from you.'

'Oh? Did he ask about that specifically?'

'Yes, he asked several questions about it. The money was very interesting to him.'

'Was he satisfied with your answers?'

'Yes, I'd say so.'

'Did you have any other impressions of him?'

'He seemed to be an important person. Wherever we went, people were very respectful. I had the feeling it embarrassed him.'

'Did you find the factories interesting?' Martin asked blandly.

'It was a surprise to have a chance to see them,' David said. 'And a bigger surprise to hear that you are partners with the Army.'

To this the Engs said nothing. Martin looked up the block for their car.

'We saw a lot of people who'd come to town looking for work,' David said. 'It didn't look as if they were getting any.'

'This is a dangerous time for China,' Martin said. 'As you know from your encounter with the bandits. As we were reminded in a more permanent way.'

The car pulled up in front of them before the silence became too painful. It was a stretch limousine. The driver was Chinese, in full livery.

'Our Association is kind enough to provide this, for now,' Martin explained. 'To make our life easier in this difficult time. Are you sure we cannot take you where you are going?'

'No, thank you very much,' Susan said.

'That was something,' David said. They watched the limousine drive away, then he stepped into the street and flagged a cab.

'I'm glad you said no, about the car,' Susan said on the way to her hotel. 'I might have been too polite.'

'I couldn't see being in close quarters with them like that, and I didn't want them to know where either of us lived. I don't know why I bothered, though – I'm in the phone book.'

'I've been having the same kind of impulses. Like not telling Chief Inspector Hall about the indictment. It's like being part of a conspiracy but you don't know what it's about.'

'Or even who the good guys and the bad guys are.'

At the hotel she took his arm and led him to the elevator. 'You really kept after them.'

'I was looking for a reaction . . . I'm sure you noticed how eager they were to talk about the way people deferred to Mr Chan. Or about their business with the Army.'

'Chief Inspector Hall was interested in that,' she said. 'Their connection with the Army. But, you know, the fact that Chan was interested in the money, and the fact that Martin and Meiling were so interested in how Chan behaved and what he wanted to know . . . it all fits with our theory that they're holding money for Hong Kong people, and that Chan is the organizer over there – collecting the money and vouching for their reliability.'

They were alone together in the elevator. David wrapped his arms around her.

'To tell the truth,' he said, 'I don't like those people. I don't care how altruistic they are.'

'And what was all that about your being like her daughter?' he asked in the hotel room. 'I wanted to tear her throat out. To say something like that on the same day she threatened you – threatened your *son* – and scared you out of your wits.'

'I don't know, David, I'm so confused. She seemed to be taking the threats back. Saying it was all a misunderstanding, or apologizing.'

'Sure she was. Now that she has the tape.'

She kissed him. 'One thing I do know – the way you handled it at the beginning, you could almost be Chinese. I was very impressed.'

He grinned. 'A little more practice and I'll be up there being indirect with the best of them.'

'I don't think I want to encourage that.'

She sank onto the bed. 'All of a sudden I'm totally wiped out. Would you please come over here and hold me?'

'At your service.'

They both dozed. When they woke up, she showed him Richard's note. He looked at it and handed it back.

'That's what I meant when I told you he was awful,' she said.

'I don't want to screw up your life.'

'Thank you, I can do that just fine by myself. You get none of the credit.'

He reached out to touch her face. 'Every time I see you next to me like this, I'm surprised.'

'Because I look funny.'

He pulled her close. 'Because you're so beautiful.'

'People tell me that,' she said. 'But when I was little, and I first went to school, I was the only Chinese kid there. The other kids would come up to me and just stare. You can't imagine what that feels like to a six-or seven-year-old girl in a strange new place where she can't speak the language all that well.'

'It doesn't sound like fun. But you must have had them falling at your feet, starting not much after that.'

'I'm glad you think so.'

'Well, you sure have me falling at your feet. And at some other parts of you, too.'

'Demonstrations are always welcome,' she said.

'It's over, with the Engs, isn't it?' she said later. 'There was a moment, talking to them, when I was somewhere between angry and hopeful about them, but now it's all just making me sad, and confused.'

'I think it's time to put it behind us. We seem to have done what they wanted us to. I don't know what more there is.'

'You're right – I should just let it go,' she said. 'I know that, but it's so hard. I can't make it add up. The way Meiling threatened me – if that's really what it was. The horrible way June died. The possibility

562

that what happened to us in China was related to them somehow. And yet they seem to be doing something good and worthwhile. Even if they are helping people come here illegally.' She sat pondering it. 'I just wish I understood.'

# IV

*OFFICIAL CORRUPTION*

# 1

In the morning they made love, without the sadness David had sensed in Susan the night before. Afterward, she lay in silence, her head propped on her hand, studying him.

'How could I have thought I wasn't going to see you?' She kissed his shoulder, ran a finger along the ridges of muscle over his stomach. 'It's so wonderful to feel this way.'

Their breakfast arrived on a table draped in a starched white cloth and adorned with napkin pyramids and a kaleidoscope of cut flowers. The room-service waiter rolled it to the patch of sunshine by the window.

'You may get more of me than you bargained for,' David joked as they moved chairs over to the table.

'Only if I'm very lucky.'

He pulled back the curtains to reveal blue sky and skyscrapers sheathed in gray metal and black glass and muted colors of stone, and bits of Long Island.

'You just like the surroundings,' she teased.

'The best view I can see is right across the table.'

'My apartment has been invaded,' he told her as they ate.

'Invaded?'

'It seems Alice takes this movie job as a sign she can be an actress, after all. L.A. is better than New York for the movies but she doesn't want to move Zack and Jessie in the middle of a school term, so they'll stay till January or maybe through the spring.'

'Is there enough room for all of you?'

It was not a tempting image. 'The way it looks right now, I get to

567

sleep with my computer, Alice gets the room I've been using as a bedroom, and the twins have to fight over the second bedroom. Either they share it or one of them gets the bedroom and the other sleeps in the dining room.'

'If I were twelve years old, I wouldn't want to live in the dining room. And at that age I'd've slept on the fire escape before I'd share a room with my brother.'

'Now *there's* something to picture.' That she almost certainly had never endured a shortage of bedrooms, or of anything else, was no longer a source of resentment for him or a reason to see her as beyond reach. 'I'm sure Jessie feels exactly that way. I'm betting on her to get the bedroom.'

'Have you thought about getting another place?'

'I've thought about leaving the country.' He made it into a joke, true though it was – nothing about the future seemed clear. For now, the important thing was being with Susan.

'I've decided to go to work today,' she announced. 'I was going to wait until Monday, but I can't really afford to stay out any longer.'

He watched her pick her day's outfit from the closet, captivated by the texture and tone of her skin, the proportions of her body, familiar and still surprising.

'I'm usually so shy about my body,' she said. 'And here I am parading around in my underwear.'

'And very businesslike underwear it is.'

She turned from the closet holding her dress in front of her. 'No fair making fun of me.'

He hugged her tight.

She pulled away. 'Hey! You're crushing my dress.' She was grinning. 'This is all so silly. And wonderful.'

Mahoney felt increasingly unreal as he compiled and reviewed the material for *People v. Eng* and made notes for a cover memo to Horgan. He remembered how he had sweated, preparing the case for the grand jury. Now he was making witness lists and lists of evidence as a combination of busy work and camouflage.

The paralegal's report on the Washington phone connections of

Martin Eng's friend Mr Wu went into the not-for-Horgan file. A weak reed on which to build anything, even if the names turned out to be interesting, but they were still almost the only hint Mahoney had found of something that might be related to what the feds were after. Wu's phone records, and whatever David Clark and Susan Linwood might have to say.

He saw a name on the list that surprised him – a law firm he recognized. One of the lawyers Wu talked to in Washington was a partner in Ellen Hyams's law firm. That answered the question of where the Engs had come up with their high-powered Washington-based defense lawyer. Apparently she, or her firm, had been recommended by Mr Wu. Mahoney wasn't sure what to make of that, but there'd be time to think about it after he was done here and settled in at Appeals. He made himself a note to follow it up and went back to his cataloging.

He was happy to be interrupted by a phone call from Laurie Jordan. 'I have a present for you,' she said.

'Oh?'

'Ms Linwood is in her office this afternoon.'

'And how do you come by that information?'

'I was feeling restless, so I called and asked.'


Susan wasn't having much luck paying attention to the Consolidated campaign. Her mind kept turning to thoughts of David. She didn't know what to make of her feelings. Was she simply intoxicated by the sex, after years of near-celibacy? Or was it some kind of mid-life rebellion, as Richard had accused? Or was she genuinely changed—

The intercom buzzed. Mona said, 'There's a man here to see you—'

*David?* she thought. Not Richard. Richard was 'Dr Linwood,' and he would never come unannounced – even in the unlikely event the reality of losing her had penetrated the armor of his narcissism. And while she was sure David would respect her privacy he was not beyond a romantic gesture.

She was suddenly aflutter, her misgivings gone. Just like a teenager in love. She smoothed her hair.

'—a Mr Mahoney from the New York County District Attorney's office.'

She had been getting up to greet David with a hug; Mahoney's name stopped her. What could he want? Why was he here?

'All right.'

The tall, imposing prosecutor came in and closed the door behind him.

'I'm Dan Mahoney,' he said. 'Maybe you remember me from the grand jury.'

'Yes, I do. Can I ask what brings you here?' Doing her best to conceal her fear in a cloak of efficiency. 'I have a busy day.'

'I wouldn't disturb you if it wasn't important.' He indicated a chair opposite her desk. 'May I?'

'If you won't be too long.'

He sat down; somehow he managed still to be imposing. 'I'll get right to the point. I'm here because I'm worried about you. I have every reason to believe you're a smart woman, but what you've been doing lately isn't smart – it's dangerous.'

*Oh my God*, she thought with a new flash of apprehension. How much has he found out?

He said, 'I know you've been in touch with the Engs. And I know you've been to Hong Kong and China. You and David Clark.'

She closed her eyes. Why had she thought they could do whatever they wanted and no one would know?

Another part of her mind barked at her to pull herself together: Mahoney would be studying her reactions – she had to reveal as little as possible.

'Why would you be interested in where I take my vacation?'

'Don't get me wrong, Ms Linwood – I'm not here to accuse you of anything. I want to help.' He was leaning toward her earnestly. 'This isn't just a question of whether the Engs are heroin dealers, or whether they're laundering money. It's bigger than that, a lot bigger and a lot more complicated. I'm afraid you're getting into it so deep that you're going to end up in very bad trouble. Trouble that's not easy to get out of. I want to help you avoid that.'

'I don't know what you're talking about.' She could hear how wooden and unconvincing she sounded.

Mahoney's eyes hadn't left hers. 'I'm not sure how to make this clear enough to you,' he said. 'Before you go another step, you have to stop and think twice about what you're doing. What you're doing, and who your real friends are.

'And when you're thinking about who your real friends are, bear this in mind – defense attorneys are paid to win their cases at all costs, guilty or not, but my job isn't like that. I'm not in business to convict people who aren't guilty.

'I know from your questions in the grand jury that you were skeptical of this case. If you have new reasons to believe the Engs are not guilty of the heroin charges, I need to know about it. If there's any information that could help them, I've got a responsibility to find out what it is. More than a responsibility, I *want* to know.'

It was all coming at her so fast, and he seemed so sincere. But that would be his job. He had to fool people into talking to him, didn't he? Get people to do what he wanted them to.

'The one point I can't stress strongly enough,' he said, 'is that this is far bigger than you know. Bigger than a simple question of why they had heroin in their house. I'm talking about crimes with far more serious implications than just another unit of heroin on the streets . . . implications that go beyond the borders of Chinatown, and even of the United States.' He relaxed a bit, almost smiled. 'But you must know that already, considering where you've just been.'

He could be bluffing, she thought, he sounds a bit like he is. But he did know where she and David had been, and that they'd been in touch with the Engs. And David had warned her about the tape.

'The problem is,' Mahoney continued, ominously now: 'You've already made things more difficult for everyone by your travels and your contacts. At this point, I'm not sure how much longer I can protect you.'

'Protect us!' she said before she could censor it. 'Protect us from what? From whom?'

He shook his head. She thought he looked genuinely worried. 'All I can tell you is that I'm very concerned about what you've been doing. And I'm even more concerned about what you might do next.

'As it stands, you're further complicating an already complicated situation. You're putting yourself in real danger. Legal danger, and danger from the people who are involved in all this.'

'And how do you propose to save us?' She tried to make it sound

571

sarcastic, as if she knew she wasn't in danger at all.

'First of all, we have to talk. I want you to tell me everything that's happened, so I can match it with what I already know and be sure I'm finding the best way to get you out of this undamaged. That's the most important thing. We've got to cooperate with each other. It's the only safe way out.'

'I don't know,' she said. 'I don't know what to say.' It was the truth – he had frightened her badly, especially in light of yesterday's drama with the Engs. But she needed to catch her breath, figure out what to do next. Talk to David. She looked at her watch, trying to seem like a busy executive. 'I don't know about talking more, but I do know this isn't the time or the place.' She made the words sound more definite than she felt.

'I have to urge you to make it as soon as possible,' Mahoney said. 'Later today, tomorrow—'

'I've been out of town a long time, as you seem already to know,' she countered. 'I have work to catch up on, and family obligations.' She turned the pages of her desk calendar, hoping he couldn't see her hand shake.

'We can't afford delay,' he said sternly. 'I really want your coopera-tion – it's in your interest as well as mine. I don't want to be talking to you as an adversary.'

'Don't strongarm me, Mr Mahoney. Next week is the best I can do.'

His eyes narrowed as if he was about to snap back at her but all he did was to take a pen and his wallet from his jacket pocket.

'Please try to understand that I do have your best interests at heart,' he said. 'I know you think of me as someone who puts people in jail. But I also try to keep people *out* of jail if they don't belong there. And above all I want to keep well-intentioned people like you and your friend David from getting themselves into bad trouble they have no way of forseeing. The only way I can do that is if you'll tell me what's going on.'

He scribbled something on the back of a business card. 'I'm going to give you my beeper number and my home phone number, so you can contact me any time. Any time you think something's going on, whatever it is, if you have any concerns at all, let me know right away – any time of the day or night.'

When he stood to leave he seemed toweringly tall to her, bigger than when he had come into the room. 'I'm making myself available to you this way because you're really in this over your head. You're smart people, but you're way out of your depth.'

From the door he said, 'Please think about this. Do yourself a favor and call me – sooner rather than later.'

As Mahoney left, he was analyzing Susan Linwood's reactions. He'd bit her hard because he knew she'd be well defended, and it had been the right approach. He was sure now that she and David Clark were involved with the Engs somehow. Behind the innocent-citizen bluster, she had been scared.

He stopped at a pay phone and called David Clark. He got a busy signal – chances were it was Susan Linwood, already on the phone with him.

Mahoney hopped in a cab and gave the driver Clark's address on the off-chance he could catch him.

David listened to Susan's report of the visit from Mahoney and tried to reassure her.

'We're out of that, now,' he told her. 'The Engs have their tape—'

'But Mahoney says he doesn't want to prosecute them if they're not guilty. Maybe we should talk to him. I mean, if they could get the money back . . .'

'He doesn't want to prosecute them for *heroin* – that doesn't mean he wouldn't be happy to get them for something else. Those crimes with far-reaching implications . . . Anyway, it's not up to us to save them.'

'What about the people in Hong Kong whose money it is?'

'I still don't think it's up to us.' He wanted to make the world go away, so all they had to think about was each other.

'He said we're in legal trouble. We can't just ignore him.'

'You're right – I suppose we can't.' Reluctant as he was.

'He's going to want to talk to you, too.'

Reality intruding further. 'I'll bet he's on his way here right now. I'd better get out of the house.'

'How about meeting a friend at Jimmy Kelly's?'

★ ★ ★

The twins were just home from school. He told them he had to go out.

'Right away?' Zack asked.

'Why? Something I can do for you?'

'I need to talk about school. I need some help.'

'Okay, grab a jacket and let's take a walk in the park. I have a few minutes.'

It was a bleak day, cool for early autumn. Kids and grownups were tossing footballs on the grassy median of the riverside promenade, their dogs running free, chasing squirrels.

'What's up?' David asked his nephew.

'It's about China. I have to do a report for school.'

'I don't know much about reports for school, but China could be an exciting subject.'

Zack shrugged. 'I guess.'

'What's the report about?'

'Something about Ancient Rome and modern China.'

'You don't sound very enthusiastic.'

'I don't like this school much, and I don't like the teacher, either.'

'I don't think I can be much help with that.'

'Mom doesn't care, she just moves us anywhere she wants to go.'

'But you like Colorado okay, don't you?'

'Yeah but we're not in Colorado now.'

'What she's doing matters a lot to her,' David said. 'But she's thinking of you guys all the time. You're the most important thing in her life.'

'Yeah, great.'

'What about that report?' Back to a subject David thought he might be able to handle. 'What's it actually supposed to be?'

'About how, you know, the Roman Empire kind of fell apart because it was so big and they, like, couldn't govern it over such large distances. And China's big, too, and it has a lot of different parts . . .' His voice trailed off in uncertainty.

'Well, that's something I can talk about. I had a conversation about that with a man in China. About how it has a lot of parts that don't necessarily go together so well.'

'Yeah? Cool. Can you tell me about it?'

574

David thought about Mr Li, ruminating on China's future in the dark van as, all unknowing, he rode toward his death.

'Sure I can.'

'You just missed him,' the elevator man told Mahoney. 'Went out about five minutes ago.'

Mahoney thanked him and headed over to Broadway for the subway trip downtown. He could call when he got back to the office.

Though it meant violating his prohibition against the twins going into the computer room while he wasn't there, David told Zack where on the bookshelves to find his China research.

'There's plenty – books and pamphlets. That ought to keep you busy for a while. Then, when you're ready, we can sit down and you can ask me questions and I'll try to answer them.'

Walking into the Shamrock, he spotted Susan at the bar, talking to Jimmy Kelly. The redhead gave David a big hello and a hearty handclasp. Susan just smiled at him, but he could feel the warmth in it, and he knew he must be shining with his own pleasure at seeing her. Kelly would not be missing a moment of it.

'Susan was telling me about China. Sounds like you two had a great time.' There was a broad wink in his voice.

'It's a fascinating place,' David said.

'And you'll never guess who was in here the other night,' Kelly said. 'Our old friend Mr Mahoney from the grand jury. The one who presented the heroin case you were both so interested in.'

David was frozen, and he could see that Susan was too. Kelly didn't seem to notice.

'He was asking after the old grand jury crowd, too.' He cocked his head. 'The two of you in particular, if I remember it right.'

'Do you remember what he wanted to know about?'

'Can't say I do. Just if I was in touch with anybody. I mentioned how you helped me with the computer, and he said he could use somebody like that. I told him you were out of town, and then I finally shut my great flapping mouth and that was all.' Kelly looked from one of them to the other. 'And I'm not asking any questions, now, either.

Susan said you two want to talk. My office is yours as long as you need it.'

In the privacy of Kelly's office Susan clung to David, pressing herself against him as if she could draw from the contact some greater strength for herself.

'He was looking for us,' she said into his chest. 'Looking for us here!'

'I wonder how he knew we were in touch with the Engs.'

She pulled back to look at him. 'They must have cameras. And he saw our pictures and recognized us.'

'I guess I was wrong to think we could ignore this.' He took her hand and led her to the couch.

'We have to talk to him,' she said.

'But we'd be crazy to go in there unprepared and alone.'

'I know. I was thinking that same thing.'

'Do you know any criminal defense lawyers?'

'I know some lawyers socially, but they're Wall Street corporate types. Do you?'

'I don't know *any* lawyers. But it suddenly occurs to me that we both know somebody we can ask.'

At first, she didn't see what he was driving at. Then she remembered: 'Jimmy!'

'Right. And here we are in his office.'

Kelly's friend was named Michael Ryan. He was a former federal prosecutor who had been in private practice for years, Kelly said, trying major commercial lawsuits. He'd begun his criminal-defense career a few years before with a famous murder case.

'Which is to say, a famous murder case the way we once thought of such things,' Kelly observed. 'In those innocent days before life became a constant parade of murder trials.

'And Michael's wife, Kassia – they're partners – she's had some big cases herself. A real big one not long ago . . . *People v. Morales* it was called. They're good lawyers, both of them. Good people, too.'

Kelly called them and after a brief conversation with Michael Ryan handed the phone to Susan.

'And now if you'll excuse me, I'll go back to tending my bar,' he said to David. 'And give you folks a bit of privacy.'

David listened while Susan gave Ryan a sketchy version of the background and told him about her visit from Mahoney.

'He says he can call Mahoney and find out what this is about,' she told David when she got off the phone. 'But he wants to talk to us first.'

# 2

The law offices were spacious, modern in a low-key way. Michael Ryan came out to greet them. He was craggily handsome, with wavy salt-and-pepper hair and intensely blue eyes, businesslike without being brusque.

'I've put us in a small conference room. I wanted to have a colleague sit in on this.'

The colleague was a petite, dark-haired woman in a red dress. Seeing them together, Susan remembered having met them briefly at Jimmy Kelly's.

'This is Kassia Miller,' Ryan said.

'The first thing we have to tell you is that there are some potential problems in having us represent you both,' Ryan said. 'We have to worry about what happens if your interests conflict.'

'Why should they?' Susan challenged. 'There's nothing that either of us did alone. Everything we did, we did together.'

'It's true,' David said.

'Even so . . . Suppose what you did was a crime – I'm not making a judgment here, I don't know yet what either of you did – but suppose one or both of you committed a crime, and suppose one of you wants to make a deal and admit guilt of a lesser offense, but the other wants to plead innocent and stand trial.'

'The prisoner's dilemma,' David said.

'Sorry?' Ryan was perplexed.

'It's a standard teaching problem in mathematics, part of what's called the theory of games and decisions. The idea is you have two prisoners, isolated from each other, with a choice of whether to talk to

578

the prosecutor or not. The way the problem is set up, if they both refuse to talk they'll both end up in jail for four years each. If they both confess and implicate each other, they'll each do ten years. So far so good . . . it's easy to see they're better off keeping their mouths shut.

'But the prosecutor offers a deal – if one confesses and the other doesn't, the snitch gets out in a year and the one who kept his mouth shut gets put away for fifteen. The problem is to find a strategy for one prisoner that maximizes his chances to get the best outcome he can.

'The way it works out, each prisoner figures – whatever the other guy does, I'm better off if I talk. I get ten years instead of fifteen if he talks, and one year instead of four if he doesn't talk. And I'm especially a sucker if I don't talk in the hope that he won't, and then it turns out he does.

'Not only that, but each prisoner has to assume the other one is thinking the same way – that no matter what *I* do *he's* better off talking . . . So the way it's set up, they're both going to talk and they're going away for ten years.'

'Even though they could both get out in four if they both kept their mouths shut,' Kassia Miller said. 'That's the kind of dilemma that makes a prosecutor happy.'

'Right. But the only reason it's such a dilemma for the prisoners is because they're being kept apart, so one of them can't know what the other is doing and they can't agree to cooperate.'

'I'm glad they don't teach that in law school. Prosecutors don't need any help making our lives miserable.'

'But Susan and I aren't prisoners, and so far nobody's keeping us apart. So why should we do it to ourselves?'

'A good question,' Ryan said. 'But I have to warn you of something – if we go ahead now and you both tell us your story, you're protected by the fact that everything you say to us is privileged. We can't repeat it, we can't use it in a way that will harm you. But if your interests do turn out to diverge, then the very protection given by that privilege is sure to put some information we need to defend one of you out of bounds because we learned it in a way that makes it privileged. It might even mean you'd both have to find new lawyers.'

'Wait,' Susan said, 'why are we talking as if we're going to be *accused* of something. He said he wanted cooperation.'

'But didn't he also say he didn't want to be an adversary,' David asked, 'as if he might be?'

Miller said, 'If they're extending the possibility of cooperation, we want to keep them thinking that way. But a lawyer's job is to protect against the bad things that can happen if everything doesn't go just right. This is a criminal matter and Mahoney seems to think you've gotten yourselves tied up in it. We have to assume the possibility of criminal exposure even if right now everybody's saying we all want to cooperate with each other.'

'All right, but we're still in this together.' Susan looked to David for confirmation.

'Absolutely.'

'Okay,' Ryan said. 'Let's assume for the moment we're going ahead together. The first thing we need is a better understanding of what's been happening. And that's something I'd prefer to do separately, the first time around, even if you're cooperating with each other.'

Kassia Miller said, 'It's the best way for us to get a three-dimensional view of the story – each of you is going to remember what happened from a slightly different angle and put emphasis on different things. Later on, when we put the two versions together, we can see it all much more clearly.'

The two lawyers left Susan and David alone in the conference room to discuss what they wanted to do.

'That was impressive,' Susan said. 'What you said about not isolating us from each other.'

'It's too soon for us to be separated any way at all, if we can help it.'

She took his hand, pressed it tight.

'I like them,' she said. 'They seem honest and smart.'

'And careful. I don't see any reason not to go ahead with them.'

Susan told the lawyers a summary version of her story, from her conversation with Mrs Liu to her theory that the Engs were involved in a kind of underground banking system for people preparing to flee from Hong Kong.

'If it really is their money the police took, that's very sad,' Michael

Ryan said. 'Unfortunately, I don't know how sympathetic the D.A.'s office will be. The bigger question for us is, what are the prosecutors after? Mahoney said it was more than just heroin.'

'More than heroin, or else that it was about something else. He may have said both things.'

'And he said it was international?'

'Yes. I think he said "implications that go beyond the borders of the United States." And he didn't mean heroin smuggling.'

'That goes with your theory. And it tends to rule out jury tampering or violating grand jury secrecy as their major concerns. That doesn't mean that they won't try to use those crimes as some kind of leverage against you.'

'I see.' That didn't sound good to her.

Ryan said, 'What strikes me most is the fact that Mahoney is talking about international matters at all. That's not exactly the province of a state prosecutor. If he were an Assistant U.S. Attorney it would make more sense.'

'But remember, Michael,' Kassia Miller said, 'this is the same state prosecutor's office that made cases against a major international bank for what were basically international crimes.'

'That's a point. Of all the D.A.'s offices they've always had the longest reach. And it's also possible that the international talk is misdirection, that he's aiming somewhere else and doesn't want to spook you about it. We'll just have to talk to Mr Mahoney and see what he has to say.' He stood up to usher Susan out of the conference room. 'After we have our session with Mr Clark.'

'There's one thing I left out,' Susan said, thinking of David's story of the two prisoners. 'As a favor to the Engs, I carried an audio-cassette letter to their children, and I brought one back from June Eng to her mother.'

'Did you really.' A cloud of what Susan supposed was Celtic anger darkened Ryan's face.

'I'm glad you remembered,' Kassia Miller said evenly. 'It's probably important. June Eng is the one who was killed?'

'Yes.'

'Do you know what was on the tape?'

'No. David wanted to try to find out, but there was no time. The

Engs were very anxious to have it – it was their last contact with June.'
She left out the threat to Charles. They'd never actually *threatened*
her, it could just have been conversation that she'd exaggerated in her
own mind.

'This is bound to be important,' Ryan said.

'But how could the District Attorney's office know about it?' Susan
asked. It genuinely seemed impossible to her, unless the Engs themselves were talking about it.

'Off-hand I don't know,' Ryan said. 'But if they do know about it, I
don't want them sandbagging me with it. And that holds true in
general. You have to tell us about anything Mahoney could be after,
whether you think he knows about it or not.'

'There's nothing else. If I think of anything I left out, I'll tell you
right away.'

Ryan checked his watch. 'I have a quick phone call to make. I'll let
you and Kassia talk to each other for a minute.'

At first they sat in silence. Susan tried to collect herself, to convince
herself she hadn't done anything wrong getting involved with the
Engs.

'Have you and David been together long?' Kassia Miller asked. Her
tone was warm and sympathetic.

Susan looked at her in surprise.

'I'm sorry to make life more difficult,' Miller said quietly. 'But if
the two of you are having a romance we have to be prepared for
questioning along those lines.'

Susan was suddenly overwhelmed by the weight of everything. 'It's
no crime if we are.'

'No, but it could be something for them to use against you.'

'Only if I let them.' Defiant, despite herself.

'Does your husband know?'

'He thinks he does.' She told Miller about the piece of paper he'd
given her.

'At this point,' Miller said, 'I don't know if that helps or hurts.'

After the lawyers interviewed David, they assembled everyone in the
conference room again.

'We wanted to get the two of you together and talk some more about

582

the things that happened to you in China and Hong Kong,' Ryan explained. 'First of all, the bandits who ambushed you on the road. Was there anything to indicate it wasn't a random attack?'

David said, 'I had the feeling at one point that they were looking for something specific.'

'Any idea what?'

'No.' He tried to visualize it. 'Just that their leader seemed very intent on something, and angry and confused when it wasn't there.'

'But it could just have been . . . valuables,' Susan said. 'Money. Maybe they thought we were rich tourists.'

'In that van?' David said.

'Or they could have known we were coming from the toy factory and thought we had some money from there.'

'Why would they think that?' Miller asked.

'That's why Mr Li went there, to straighten out some problems about a payroll delivery.'

'Anything else?' Ryan prodded.

'Didn't June Eng say it wouldn't have happened if she'd been there?' David asked Susan.

'Something like that. I didn't understand why, and she said it was just because she was feeling guilty.'

'Do you know anything at all about why she was killed?'

'No,' David said. Susan shook her head.

'Or if the robbery and the killing were connected?'

'I don't see how,' Susan said.

'Let's say they were,' David said. 'What then? We still have no reason to think it had anything to do with *us*. Or whatever Mahoney is after.'

'You spent a lot of time in her company when these things were happening,' Miller said. 'You went to see her on behalf of her parents. Mahoney is very interested in her parents and some sort of international implications. We have to consider the possibility all that is connected.'

'In any case, we're out of it now,' David said.

'What about the tapes you carried?' Ryan wanted to know. 'Do you have any idea what was on them?'

'I said, they were just letters,' Susan responded.

'But her parents were very anxious to get the one you brought from their daughter.'

'She was dead!'

'All right,' Miller said quickly. 'Maybe that's enough for one day. Let's see what we can learn from Mahoney about what he wants, then we'll talk again.'

In the cab uptown Susan and David reassured each other they'd picked the right lawyers. The conversation felt awkward to David, but he didn't know what to do about it, or how to draw Susan out of the silence that followed.

'Is everything okay?' he asked her finally.

'It's so awful. Miller said they might make an issue of you and me.'

'Ryan implied as much to me. I didn't know what to say to him.'

'There's nothing to say.' She fell silent again.

At her hotel she asked him to wait in the lobby while she went up to her room. She came back down with a bulging garment bag.

'Going somewhere?' He said it lightly, but the idea of Susan carrying luggage out of the hotel scared him. Was she moving back home?

'It's my clothes,' she explained. 'When I left the house I just threw things together. I want to bring back the ones I can't use and get some I can.'

Susan dropped David off and took the cab across town. The doorman on duty at her apartment building was not the one who'd seen her leave initially, but going in with a full garment bag and then coming out again minutes later with that much and more was certain to get tongues wagging among the building staff. There was nothing she could do about it, and despite the scare she'd had at the lawyers – or maybe because of it – she was no longer sure she cared.

The man on the door was relatively new, someone she hadn't gotten to know yet. He greeted her with a hearty and unaccustomed, 'Hello, Mrs Linwood,' and welcomed her back.

'No welcome necessary – I'm just in transit,' she said. 'I'll be down in a minute.'

Walking through the lobby to the elevator she had the impression of someone on the couch in the lobby sitting area, but she paid no attention.

Mahoney told Ned King and Max Straus and Laurie Jordan about his conversation with Susan Linwood and his feeling that she was frightened – and that she had something to be frightened about.

'I still haven't talked to David Clark. I'm sure by now she's warned him about me.'

With the Chief of Investigation a regular part of their action group, the meetings had been moved to his office. 'Keep trying,' he said. 'If your grand jurors started poking around in this Eng mess based on their suspicions about the evidence, we really have to find out what they've learned. Bear in mind – if the late Mr Ying *was* tied up with Detective Pullone, these people could be making themselves targets if they keep poking around in that end of it.'

'If they haven't already,' Straus added.

'Another thing to remember,' King said. 'The heroin case may be bad, but these Eng people are still *our* defendants, and when we get to the day of reckoning with the Southern District I want to be holding the good cards. And that means at the very least finding out what took your grand jurors to Hong Kong and China.'

'You think they'll lawyer up?' Straus asked.

'I'd say yes just on the basis of class and education,' Mahoney replied. 'But if they're this far into it on their own – talking to the defendants and running off to Hong Kong and China – and no lawyers in sight . . . maybe not.'

'The visit from you is likely to be a wake-up call in that regard,' King said. 'Let's get back to Mr Ying for a minute. Laurie, anything on that?'

'My unit chief and I sat down with Special Narcotics. This El Coyote we're looking at is an upper-middle-level distributor. Mostly he deals in units and fractions of a unit, but he puts together some bigger deals than that, and he's got contacts all the way to the top in the organization Special Narcotics is going after. In one way, we're lucky, because they were planning to flip him anyway, so the case they've been building against him separates out of the bigger case without involving any of the informants or compromising any wiretaps or surveillance.'

'Sounds good,' King said. 'Nice and clean.'

'Unfortunately, they weren't ready to flip him yet so we had to haggle over the terms, but I think we're okay. We'll give him to them when we're done, and we'll let them know what we've learned, once that's safe from our point of view.'

'I'll have another talk with Billy just to be sure they give you enough room,' King said. 'Do you have a plan for picking him up?'

'From what they told us, Thursday's a big night for him. He works late and then he goes to an after-hours club. He usually leaves alone, and he takes a gypsy cab home. My people tell me they can have a cab in place. If he catches some other cab we'll pull him over and make sure the driver keeps his mouth shut, but obviously it's best if the driver's ours, too.'

'Tonight, then?' Straus said.

Mahoney's beeper went off. It was a paralegal from Official Corruption: the only reason she'd beep him instead of Jordan was if Susan Linwood called. 'Excuse me, I need to get this. It may be our grand juror.'

'You can use the phone in my office,' Straus said.

Mahoney went down the hall and called Offical Corruption.

'You had a call from a Michael Ryan,' the paralegal said. 'Representing Susan Linwood.' That Mahoney had reason to expect it didn't make it welcome.

The lawyer's name rang a bell for him. He tried to place it as he dialed, figured it out just as Ryan came on the line.

'Mr Mahoney, I understand you're interested in talking to my client, and I thought we ought to sit down and have a chat about that.'

'I'm available any time starting right now.'

'Well, Ms Linwood just informed me of this, and I've got a full calendar, so why don't we say Tuesday? I might be able to make late Monday, but I can't promise.'

'I ought to make something clear,' Mahoney said, King's words fresh in his mind. 'It's a mistake to treat this casually. You don't know me, but let me assure you that I'm not talking for effect here. Your client is involved in something she doesn't understand, and this can't wait until Tuesday or even late Monday.'

'Due respect, Mr Mahoney – as you say, I don't know you, but I was a prosecutor myself for a lot of years and I do know this – when a prosecutor says "This is important," sometimes it actually is important. And sometimes – a lot of the time, in my experience – it's just that the prosecutor is awfully impressed with the matter as *he* sees it, in his own universe. And the sad truth is, what's important to you is not necessarily important to me, or to my client.'

'I hear what you're saying,' Mahoney conceded, 'and you're not completely wrong, in theory. But this isn't theory, this is real. And that's no bullshit.' Mahoney had to find a way to cut through Ryan's notion that he was doing what was right for his client. 'Let me ask you a question. Are you the Michael Ryan who's Kassia Miller's partner?'

'Yes, I am . . .' Warily.

'We were just saying you don't know me. But there's an easy way for you to fix that. I'm good friends with Joe Estrada, have been for years. I did some of the law work for him on *People v. Morales*, and he came to me for reality checks, beginning to end. So I know some things about how your colleague works. I know Joe thinks very highly of her, and I have to assume she knows by now that she can trust Joe. What I'm suggesting is, I can have Joe call her, or she can call him, and he'll tell her anything she wants to know about me. Maybe that'll increase your comfort level.'

'Could be.'

'I still want to move this along. So let's figure on tomorrow morning.'

'Suppose I call you about that after Kassia talks to Joe.'


On Susan's way out of her apartment building, half an hour after she'd arrived, the doorman offered to hail her a cab. As he stepped out into the avenue to find one, she became aware of someone approaching her from behind. Suddenly afraid, she turned and found herself face to face with a burly Chinese man in a business suit.

'Susan Linwood?'

'What?' Her mind was crowded with images of the Chinese night, the glare of the roadblock, burly men in business suits carrying machine pistols.

'Are you Susan Linwood?'

'Yes.' Not here, she thought, not in broad daylight on Park Avenue with the doorman steps away.

The man reached under his suit jacket. Susan stood petrified.

He handed her a piece of paper. 'This is a subpoena to appear before a grand jury in United States District Court.'

He left her standing there holding it, shaking with relief.

'Mrs Linwood?'

She jumped at the voice. 'What?'

'I have a cab waiting,' the doorman said.


David checked his e-mail. Nothing from Jon. He'd been wondering if the copy of the Engs's tape was yielding anything interesting but knew Jon well enough not to nag him about it. He started to compose a note to Angus Macleod at the Racecourse Association, a follow-up to their last conversation.

Zack knocked on the door and came in. 'Uncle David?'

'What's up?'

Zack handed him a brochure: it was from the China Society. 'Can we go to this?'

It was an announcement for a symposium, no doubt one of a bunch of papers and pamphlets he'd picked up on his first visit there. The program title was *Whither China? An Ancient Empire Enters the Twenty-First Century*.

He skimmed over it, looking for registration information. In his business, conferences like this one could easily cost most of a thousand dollars if you attended all the special instructional sessions, but there was sometimes a general-admission category that was cheaper, or free.

It took him two passes through to find the small print: *Admission by invitation only. Please request space on your letterhead, stating relevant affiliations and reason for attendance.*

The conference, he noted, had started Wednesday – yesterday – and the formal presentations would end late Saturday afternoon followed by a cocktail party and dinner in honor of the speakers. On Sunday there would be small discussion meetings and a closing brunch.

He checked his watch. It was after five, but he called the China

Society anyway and got a woman who told him she was sorry but registration was closed and there was no provision for non-participants to get the program materials. 'But we will be publishing a summary pamphlet in a few months.'

'I had something more immediate in mind.'

'What did you say your affiliation was?'

He hadn't. 'The Royal Hong Kong Racecourse Association,' he said because it was on the computer screen in front of him.

In that case, she said, he was welcome to send a fax or e-mail to the conference director, but she didn't see the point.

Instead, he added a few lines to his e-mail note to Angus Macleod. To Zack, he said, 'I don't think there's much chance to get in, but we'll try to get something for you. Anyway it's really for grownups.'

'Okay. Thanks for trying.'

'Some of these topics might be just what you need,' David said, looking over the schedule again. A lot of them fascinated him, too, especially yesterday's opening address, *The Past as Prediction: Modern China in Historical Perspective*, a topic reprised with the conference-closing summary panel featuring the symposium's principal speakers. The opening speaker and summary moderator was called Wu Chu-Ming.

'I just had a chat with Kassia Miller,' Estrada told Mahoney. 'She wanted to know if you were prone to exaggeration, or other similar defects of character.'

'And?'

'It was a tough call, what with the obligations of truth on the one side and friendship on the other.'

'The question is, did she buy it?'

'Yeah, I think so. I wish she'd been as willing to believe me during the Morales trial.'

'You sound more sincere now that you're a boss. You know anything about Michael Ryan?'

'The usual stories about his battle-royal with the unlamented Franky Griglia' – a thoroughly disliked one-time Acting District Attorney. 'Aside from that, all I can say is he's the husband and law partner of a defense lawyer who's smart and tough and tenacious and

589

honest. That's on the plus side. On the minus side, he used to be a star prosecutor for the Southern District.'

The phone rang while David was in the shower. He shaved and dressed and got ready to leave; neither of the twins gave him a message.

'Anything I should know?' he asked when he came out into the living room.

'There was someone here to see you,' Jessica told him. 'We said you were busy and had to go out. He wanted to come in and wait, but we said we weren't supposed to let anybody in. I hope that's right.'

'Exactly right. Never let anybody in. Where's Maria, by the way?'

'She should be here any time,' Jessica said, very grownup. 'Sometimes she gets out of work late. And I think sometimes she has, like, auditions?'

An old acting-class buddy of Alice's had jumped at the chance to house-sit while David was in China and Alice was off on location. In return for the space, she had promised to stay in, evenings, so Zack and Jessica wouldn't be alone. The twins also had the cook-housekeeper David was paying for, but she only worked afternoons, and she left promptly at five.

For the time being, while Alice was still away, Maria had agreed to stay on. It suited her to be out of the Greenwich Village railroad apartment she shared with three other women and six cats, and David was happy to have the freedom to be with Susan. But the freedom was only an illusion if Maria wasn't reliable.

'Did the man leave his name or a business card or anything like that?'

'No.'

'What did he look like?'

'He was wearing a suit, and we think he was Chinese. Zack was mad at me for not letting him in. He wanted to ask him questions.'

'It's okay, you did the right thing.'

Maria arrived, full of apologies, just as David was losing patience. As he was hurrying out, Zack called after him. 'Uncle David? I forgot to tell you – you had a phone call.'

He waited.

'It was a woman.'

'That's all?'

Zack shrugged: what more could there be?

'You have a visitor,' the elevator operator told him on the way down.

*'Have?'*

'Guy's in the lobby, waiting for you. You're having a lot of visitors don't quite catch you these days. Only, the last one didn't wait.'

'The last one? What did he look like?'

'Ah, you know, like anybody else.'

'Tall, short, white, black?'

'Oh, yeah, well – tall. Plenty tall. Good-looking, athletic. White guy, maybe your age, something like that.'

*Mahoney.* 'Thanks. And the guy in the lobby?'

'Some kind of slope, you know? No offense, but I can't tell 'em apart. Looks tough, though.'

'You know, maybe you ought to take me to the basement,' David told him. 'I think this is somebody I don't want to deal with tonight.'

The elevator operator stopped the car between two and three and cast a skeptical eye at David. 'We're not supposed to let people go out that way, you know. If the gate gets left open down there, I'm the one who takes shit for it.'

David folded a ten-dollar bill and tucked it into the breast pocket of the operator's uniform. 'I promise I'll close the gate.'

'Well, okay, this once.' He started the car moving again and took David straight down to the basement.

'Don't say anything to the guy in the lobby about seeing me leave, okay?' David said. 'And don't take him upstairs again. I don't want him bothering the kids.'

# 3

David bought an armload of flowers at the local fruit-and-vegetable market. The hotel concierge gave him a vase big enough to hold them.

'What am I going to do with you?' Susan said, taking the flowers from him. She clung to him for a moment, then let him go and went to the wet bar to run water into the vase.

She put the flowers on the nightstand, spent a moment arranging them. 'They're beautiful,' she said. 'But . . . no roses?'

He started to explain, saw she was teasing.

She kissed him lightly and sat on the bed facing out the window. The curtains were pulled back and the window was crowded with lights, skyscrapers transformed into grids of glowing yellow and blue-white.

'I was waiting and waiting for you to call,' she said.

'Zack isn't the most reliable message-taker. By the time he told me a woman called I was on my way out the door.'

'It's okay, I'm just upset.'

He went to her. 'What's wrong?'

'It's on the desk.'

He found a formal-looking notice – two pages, the first with an Old-English heading: United States District Court, Southern District of New York.

'To Susan Linwood,' it said, and gave her address on Park Avenue. 'GREETING.'

'*Greeting*. That's a nice touch.'

'Don't stop there. It gets better.'

'We *command* you,' he read aloud. 'And in capital letters, too. Another nice personal touch.'

592

He read further, to himself –

WE COMMAND YOU that all and singular business and excuses being laid aside, you and each of you appear and attend before the GRAND INQUEST of the body of the people of the United States of America for the Southern District of New York—

'We ought to call the lawyers. It says next Wednesday – that's not much time.'

'I called them right after I called you, but they weren't in, so I left a message.' She rested her head in her hands. She looked exhausted. 'What do they *want* from us, David?'

'I don't know,' he said, stroking her hair. 'I don't know.'

They lay down together the way they had that first night in bed together in Hong Kong. She curled up in his arms and fell asleep. After a time, he drifted off into a state that was neither sleep nor waking – he was aware only of her weight against him and the gentle rise and fall of her body with her breathing and his own.

When she woke up he suggested that they go out for some dinner.

'I'm not hungry,' she said. 'And I'm not up to facing the world.'

'We ought to eat something.' He called room service. 'Just like Hong Kong.' He smiled but she didn't respond.

When the food came Susan sat at the table with him and picked at the grilled-chicken salad he'd ordered for her, drank some of the minibar wine. Gradually she seemed to perk up.

'We ought to talk about this,' he said.

'I suppose.'

There was no mistaking that for enthusiasm, but he went on. 'I don't understand why this is for the United States District Court. That's not Mahoney. Our grand jury was in the New York State Supreme Court. That's completely different.'

'That's what upset me so much. Mahoney was enough. How do these other people even know about us?'

'Our friends the Engs seem to have a wide and attentive following.'

'And now they're all following us.'

593

'So it seems' He was glad she was up to attempting humor. 'How did you get this thing?'

'A Chinese man. He accosted me in front of my house when I went to get my clothes. He'd been waiting in the lobby. He looked just like those armed security police at the roadblock, the ones with the guns.'

'He came looking for me, too.' He told her about the man Zack had wanted to interview for his homework, and how the elevator operator had reluctantly helped David avoid him. He related it as broadly as he could and succeeded in making her laugh.

When Michael Ryan called they both got on the phone. The news of the federal subpoena startled him.

'Do you have any idea what it could be about?'

'No,' they both said.

'Read me the statute they're citing – that's where it says some numbers on either side of the initials U.S.C.'

' "To testify and give evidence in regard to a violation of Section," ' Susan read. 'That's printed, and then it says, typed in, "18 U.S.C. section 371." Is that what you mean?'

'Yes . . . and that's the criminal conspiracy statute. Conspiracy is very broad, it could include almost anything. Is there a second page, for documents?'

'Yes. It says, "All documents relating in any way" and then there's a number one, "to any travel to Hong Kong and/or China, including departure and return, and/or" number two, "to any communication with Martin Eng and/or Meiling Cheung." '

'And read me the name of the assistant at the bottom.'

He had her spell the name out, then said, 'I should have a copy – if you could fax it to my office that would help.' He gave them the number. 'It's too late to do anything about it today. I've got a meeting with Dan Mahoney at the D.A.'s office first thing in the morning. After I talk to him I'll call some people over at the Southern District and see what I can find out about this. You're sure you don't know what it could be?'

'We told you everything,' David said from the extension in the bathroom. 'All we can think of is they're watching the Engs and they saw us with them.'

594

'How do they know who you are?'

'They could have followed us.'

'Unlikely. Have you talked to the Engs on the phone?'

'Not me,' David said.

'I have,' Susan said.

'From a phone listed in your name?'

'There is no phone listed in my name, exactly.'

'Then that's not it – though even if it were I can't imagine they'd subpoena everyone who's on the phone lists. Well, we'll figure it out. Meantime, try to get a good night's sleep.'

'Easy for him to say,' Susan said when they got off. 'I'm so furious with all of these people. Every one of them, starting with the Engs. And the trouble is I can't even wish I'd never heard of them, because if not for them I wouldn't have you.'

They got ready for bed slowly. With the lights out, the room was illuminated by the glow of the unsleeping city.

Lying next to Susan, David was not surprised he wanted her. Just thinking about her was enough for that.

He'd anticipated she would be too distracted; instead, her desire for him seemed heightened, though it had an undertone of melancholy that made their lovemaking slower and softer. There were tears on her cheeks when they finished. He kissed them away and asked no questions.

The phone call from Laurie Jordan got Mahoney out of bed at six.

'We've got him!'

'Huh?' Mahoney managed.

'El Coyote. Our gypsy cab picked him up smooth as butter.' There was no mistaking the excitement in her voice. 'They're taking him to a safe house for debriefing.'

'That's great,' Mahoney told her. 'Congratulations.'

'Let's see what he says first.'

There was no way Mahoney was getting back to sleep, so he put in an unaccustomed morning half-hour at the gym, in the hope it would wake him up. As insurance he had extra coffee with breakfast.

As planned, he called in sick and went straight to Official Corruption. Laurie Jordan was looking her usual spectacular self, despite what must have been a sleepless night. She set him up at the conference table in the Copperhead's office, one of the few in the open loft that was fully enclosed, and told the receptionist he was expecting Michael Ryan.

The defense lawyer arrived promptly at nine-thirty. Mahoney had looked Ryan up after he talked to Estrada about him, knew the highlights of his career as federal prosecutor, civil litigator and criminal defense lawyer, knew he had to be at least fifty, though in person he didn't have the air of seen-everything weariness Mahoney associated with veteran defenders.

They exchanged pleasantries, like boxers feeling each other out with light jabs. Talked about how they had both worked on the Morales trial without ever meeting – Mahoney as behind-the-scenes adviser for the prosecution, Ryan in a similar role for the defense. Then Ryan got down to business.

'When we spoke it was in terms of Susan Linwood, but I want you to know that my office is also representing David Clark, and we have the impression that you have some interest in him as well.'

'I assume you've considered the real possibility for conflict that presents.'

'Do you have something specific in mind?' Ryan asked.

Mahoney ignored the question. 'If you're telling me they're acting together, that's their privilege.' Though he didn't like the idea. 'You're right about my interest in David Clark. I need to talk to both of them.'

'And *I* need to know what kind of interest it is. Do you see them as targets? Witnesses? I need to know what their exposure is. And I can't help but notice that you've invited me to the Official Corruption Unit. Unless I have stale information you're not assigned to Official Corruption.'

Mahoney took a breath. 'I want to be as forthcoming with you as I can on this,' he said. 'I need your clients to come in and talk to me, and I need them to trust me. And that means I need *you* to trust me. So I'm going to tell you everything I can without compromising my case.

'To begin with, I don't know where your clients are sitting right now. I can't tell you they're not targets, not yet – I do have some concerns about what they've done.'

'It would help if you could give me an idea what the arena is,' Ryan said. 'I hear heroin and money, and I hear about international implications, and I see Official Corruption. I don't want to get the wrong answer, adding it up myself.'

'It's the right question. I can tell you that if my main concern were the case I presented to them in the grand jury – disclosure of that material – they would certainly be targets, because I have no doubt they were engaged in that kind of behavior. But the truth is, this thing is so much bigger than Susan Linwood and David Clark that I'm way past that.'

'They're not targets, then,' Ryan prodded.

'At the moment. At the moment my focus is on the fact that your clients appear to have been conducting their own investigation. I'm going to tell you, for the purposes of this conversation only, that I have some of the same concerns about the case as they expressed when I was presenting it in the grand jury. But that doesn't mean we're ready to give anybody a clean bill of health – the Engs or anyone else.

'What I need is information. I need to know what your clients have been doing, and why – and what they found out. Then I can have a sense of where they fit. But I told Susan Linwood, and I'll tell you – what they're getting into is way over their heads.'

Ryan sat with that a moment. Mahoney watched him, but the defense lawyer was not giving anything away.

Ryan said, 'When you say over their heads – how much does that have to do with what the Southern District is looking for?'

Mahoney did his best to cover his surprise that Ryan was asking about the feds. 'Just how do you mean that?'

'For one thing, as soon as I hear the word international, I think of the Southern District. I know how they operate – I used to work there. If it's major and international, they're not likely to be letting it go by unnoticed.'

'I'd like to be able to talk to you about that, but I really can't.' The regret in Mahoney's voice was real enough – regret not that he couldn't talk about it but that there was anything to talk about.

'Well, if you can't talk about it then I'll just have to go down the street and talk to them myself.'

Where was this coming from? 'I don't see where that's a choice that helps your clients.'

'It's no *choice*. My clients may have some problems there. We already have one grand jury subpoena from them, and we're expecting another one.'

It was a bolt out of the blue. His protective reflexes jumbled by fatigue and coffee, Mahoney just looked at Ryan, a fraction of a second too long.

'You don't know about that,' the defense lawyer ventured.

'I wasn't aware of any subpoenas.' Mahoney was furious – working to keep it out of his voice, though he knew he wasn't being completely successful. And trying to think of a way to salvage the situation. 'I'm glad you told me. There's a chance I may be able to solve your problem with them.'

Mahoney could see he'd piqued Ryan's interest with that.

'It would uncomplicate things if you could,' the defense lawyer said.

'If I can take care of that, I'll want to talk to your clients as soon as possible.'

'I'm still not comfortable doing anything that's going to increase their exposure.'

'Mr Ryan,' Mahoney said, redirecting at Ryan his anger with the feds. 'Let me put it simply – we can work together on this and both come out ahead, or we can make it into a tug of war and that way we all lose, especially your clients. I'm promising nothing, but I'll say again that right now your clients are not the main event here. I want their help, and if I get it, I'll be grateful.'

'Well and good,' Ryan said. 'But if you're not going to assure me they're not subjects or targets, I need to know what the conditions are going to be if we do decide to come in.'

'That's not a problem. I can give them our standard Queen for a Day.' Basically, a guarantee not to use anything in the interview against them, preserving the right to use it as a source of leads and a benchmark for later testimony.

'If I remember the details, the standard terms aren't going to do it,' Ryan was quick to say, 'but that's something we can talk about. Meanwhile, my clients are still under federal subpoena, so I'd suggest you call me when you've done what you can down the street. And before we come in – if we do – I need to spend some time with my clients—'

'If I haven't made myself clear,' Mahoney interrupted, 'time is of the essence here.' With El Coyote already being questioned, Mahoney was feeling crowded. He needed to know what Ryan's clients had learned about Pullone and the Engs.

'I was about to say, I should be able to accomplish that over the weekend,' Ryan told him. 'So, assuming you and I can get the conditions straightened out, any time Monday should be fine.'

'If we can make it in the morning. I really do need to talk to them sooner rather than later.'

As soon as Ryan was gone Laurie Jordan came into the office.

'How'd it go?' She looked closer at Mahoney. 'Is that *smoke* I see coming out of your ears?'

'We've got a problem.' He headed for the door. 'Let's go see Max and Ned.'

She held back. 'I don't think we should be marching over there together – especially since you already banged in sick. Why don't I give Ned a call?'

David and Susan left the hotel together. She went to her office and David went home.

He'd decided it was time to get some paying work. He had legal bills to look forward to – substantial ones, probably – and that wasn't going to help his dwindling nest egg.

He checked his e-mail. There was a message from his old head-hunter wanting to know if he was back in the market. How timely, he thought, but he didn't answer it. A typical message from Jon Levi: THINKING OF YOU.

And one from Angus Macleod, who had arranged for David to attend the symposium at the China Society –

You are on the list for the afternoon session Saturday and the cocktail party, with a guest if you prefer. Sorry, no dinner. Also regret, no one under 18 yrs.

Macleod closed with a request—

If you do choose to go, please try to hear Wu
Chuming. Mr Wu is something of an enigma. He
almost never appears in public, though he
publishes interesting papers, frequently
with an historical foundation. He is quite
free of academic or diplomatic credentials or
institutional support and has made his way
entirely on the quality of his mind. I will be
most interested in your opinion of him.

Ned King and Max Straus came over to Official Corruption. 'We can
sit out on the roof deck,' King had said to Jordan. 'Nice and private
and out of everybody's way.'

Mahoney was too full of fire to sit. 'These are the people we want to
cooperate, and the fucking Southern District is serving subpoenas on
them!' His fury felt as boundless as the open sky on this cloudless day.
'We have a standstill agreement, and they're subpoenaing my grand
jurors! Just when I'm getting them to cooperate.'

'Maybe we shouldn't jump to too many conclusions,' Max Straus
said when Mahoney paused for breath. 'Do we have any reason to
believe the Southern District *knows* that these two people were grand
jurors?'

Mahoney took his cue from Straus's measured delivery. He made
himself sit down and consider his answer before he spoke.

'I don't think we know, either way. And Ryan doesn't seem to know
what the feds are after. So I have to assume he doesn't know how they
got onto his clients, either. That's the main question, I suppose.'

'Remind me how *you* got onto them,' Ned King said.

'I found them in the FBI's surveillance photos.'

'Maybe the feds did, too,' Laurie Jordan suggested. 'Though a
picture wouldn't tell who they were, would it?'

'There's no point in our playing guessing games,' King said. 'I'll
get on the phone and set up a meeting, and we can see what the feds
have to say for themselves.'

'Anything more on El Coyote?' Max Straus asked Laurie Jordan as
they all parted.

'So far he's being fairly stubborn, but they did get a waiver of speedy arraignment out of him, and they're keeping the pressure on. He doesn't like it that they keep talking to him as if they think he did the murder.'

'Is he a suspect?'

'He could be,' she said, 'but it's more likely to be someone lower down the ladder. This is to soften him up.'

David called Susan and told her about the China Society symposium. 'It started out as something I was doing for my nephew, but it sounds fascinating, especially with what Macleod said.'

'I don't know,' she said. 'We already have a meeting scheduled with the lawyers tomorrow, and Sunday is my daughter's birthday. I don't know if I'll have time.'

It wasn't the response he'd expected. He realized it was the first time since Hong Kong that she'd said no to something they could do together. He got off the phone feeling at a distance from her. It was not a good way to feel.

Mahoney and King went over to the Southern District at six. They met in the same combination conference room and library that had been the scene of the first confrontation over the Engs.

The Chief of the Criminal Division greeted them pleasantly enough and made a show of remembering Mahoney's name, though Mahoney was sure King had specified in advance who would be accompanying him.

'Tell me exactly what the problem is,' the Southern District Chief said.

King said, 'Dan informs me you've subpoenaed at least one and possibly two people who were on the grand jury that indicted Martin Eng and his wife. Susan Linwood and David Clark.'

'Yes, as you said on the phone. I have to tell you we definitely had no knowledge they were grand jurors.' He got a confirming nod from the fourth man in the room, the Assistant U.S. Attorney in charge of the federal case. 'If we had known that they were your grand jurors, and that you were looking at them, we wouldn't have gone near them without consulting you first.

601

'But it does raise a question,' he continued. 'Why are your grand jurors hanging out with the people they indicted? And, more to the point, why do you care if we subpoena them or not?'

'I really want to resolve this,' King said. 'So I'm going to skip fencing with you about it and give you our bottom line. We're pretty sure the heroin case against the Engs is bullshit. It looks very much like there's police corruption involved. We're moving on that, as we speak. In fact, we're fully operational. That's the heart of our problem – your subpoena is going to put a complete monkey wrench in what we're doing.'

'Ned, I promise you, if we caused you any trouble, it really was inadvertent.' The federal boss took off his round eyeglasses and polished them on his tie as he spoke. 'There was no intention to do anything like that.'

Mahoney thought: Maybe if he could meet somebody's eye while he was being so sincere, there would be a chance of believing him.

'But let me get clear on one thing,' the federal prosecutor said, putting his glasses back on. 'If it's police corruption you're worried about, what do *grand jurors* have to do with it?'

'These grand jurors are right smack in the middle of it,' King told him. 'We have strong reason to believe they've been conducting their own parallel investigation. And as part of that we think they may have found out some things we might want to know more about. Plus, they may be able to corroborate what we *do* know. We were all set to debrief them when your subpoena dropped, and spooked them.'

'You can rest assured that our interest in them is completely different from yours,' the federal boss responded. 'It stems from their trip to China. We take it you're aware they were in China.'

'Yeah, we know about that,' Mahoney interjected, with the disdain it deserved.

'As it happens we're paying a lot of attention at the moment to the Asian end of our investigation,' the fed went on. 'Your grand jurors were in Hong Kong and China, and they showed up on our radar there.'

King waited for more. This time, Mahoney waited with him.

The Chief of the Criminal Division obliged them: 'You're talking about police corruption in a local case about heroin possession and

602

conspiracy to sell. I'm not going to denigrate the importance to you of *any* police corruption case, however large or small. But I'm looking at an international conspiracy that Washington thinks may impact national security.'

'It seems to me you've got it exactly backwards.' King sounded to Mahoney like a man working hard to stay reasonable. 'I've got a significant case that I'm right in the middle of – ongoing, substantial and serious. You've got a bunch of second-hand theories and a fishing expedition that may go somewhere and may not. These two people you subpoenaed are vital to me and peripheral to you, if they're even that.'

'They are *not* peripheral to me.'

'Then how come they just popped onto your radar a week ago?'

The federal prosecutor had no response.

'I'll tell you why,' King supplied. 'These are grand jurors who had a problem with a case they heard in *my* grand jury and decided to go out snooping on their own. In the process they got tangled up with the defendants, which is the only reason they showed up on your screen at all. I need what they learned to help make my case, and I need it right now.'

'Okay – I hear you. There's no need for us to go to war over this. You're right about one thing – when we subpoenaed these people we had them down as conspirators. Our whole thrust here is finding out who the players are. If you're telling me they're grand jurors doing their own investigation – that's news and it puts it in a different light. As I said, if we screwed you up any, we did it inadvertently, and I'm happy to back off for now.'

'That's appreciated.'

'But only for now.' The federal boss wasn't about to roll over and play dead. 'These grand jurors of yours are still my best way to link our targets with their principals in China. And I think we have to assume that once your people got *tangled up* in this, as you say, it's not unlikely that they became part of the conspiracy.'

'These aren't conspirators, they're a couple of amateur detectives on a sightseeing trip,' King overstated.

'If they are, they had an unusual trip. In China they were the subjects of police activity that involved several shooting deaths, and they were also in the vicinity of June Eng in Hong Kong immediately before she got killed. And, frankly, I can't afford to have you poking around in any of that and getting them all lit up about it.'

Mahoney listened in unruffled silence to this remarkable news. I must be getting better at not registering shock or surprise, he thought.

The fed wasn't done. 'Nasty business, that murder, wasn't it?' He was raising the stakes, probing to see what they knew.

'Come on, get serious,' King bluffed. 'Look at who these people are. Do you honestly believe they were involved in that kind of murder? Or *any* kind, for that matter.'

King's incredulity was modulated just right to tempt the fed into setting him straight. It was a good recovery, and for a moment Mahoney thought it would work, but the federal boss sidestepped it.

'I'll be frank with you,' he said. 'I don't know what they got involved in over there. Amateurs out conducting an investigation are a well-known pain in everybody's ass, and God only knows what they're capable of.' He gave King and Mahoney an us-against-them smile. 'Look, I'm sure you don't want to screw me up on this any more than we wanted to screw you up. So go ahead – take your shot at them. But I want to know what they have to say. And when you're done with them, they're ours.'

'Do you know anything about police shootings in China?' King asked Mahoney when they got outside. 'Or June Eng – is that the daughter? *Nasty business.* I wonder what that means.'

'You sounded in there like you did the investigation yourself,' Mahoney said.

'I doubt I fooled him. You think your grand jurors could have had anything to do with it?'

Mahoney hoped they hadn't. He wanted to think of them as honest, well-meaning people who would be glad to cooperate with law enforcement once the situation was explained to them. 'I don't see how they could have,' he said. 'But you never know, do you? I'll see if I can get something on it from Hong Kong.'

'Let me know.'

'And it ought to give me a good line of questioning when I see them on Monday. Assuming it's not off limits.'

'I don't remember agreeing to put it off limits. Especially if the grand jurors are the ones who open the door.'

Easier to say than do, Mahoney thought. 'And if they don't?'

'Let's say I'd prefer to be able to say with a straight face that they did. But under any circumstances it would be a shame to let that whole line of inquiry get by.'

Mahoney went to pick up his briefcase at Official Corruption. Laurie Jordan was waiting for him. She pulled him into her office and wrapped herself around him.

'He did it! El Coyote gave up Pullone! I'm so excited.' She kissed him, then broke away. 'Okay, I'll behave now.'

She sat down at her desk. 'You were right,' she told him. 'A hundred percent right. Pullone extorted the heroin from El Coyote.'

'Tell me.' Relieved – more relieved than he'd have expected.

'They'd worked together before. El Coyote was one of the unregistered snitches that Pullone got disciplined for. He never gave up much – mostly stuff about his competitors.

'He says Pullone came to him and said he needed the heroin, he knew it was worth a lot of money but he expected to return it next time he scored big on an arrest, and if El Coyote said no, Pullone would make sure he had more trouble in his life than he could handle. Or words to that effect. Pullone told him it was for evidence against someone he needed to jam up.

'So when this guy Ying – the deceased – starts selling at cut rates right in the territory of one of El Coyote's best customers, and bragging how he got the heroin for free, from a cop, and how the cop got it from a distributor to use as evidence . . . Well, you can imagine El Coyote was not pleased.'

'What about the murder?' Not knowing what answer he wanted.

'No surprise, really – he gave us the guy whose territory Ying was working. El Coyote figures the guy had one of his bodyguards do the actual shooting.'

'Not Pullone?'

'No, thank God.'

'You're right – this is bad enough.'

'And then some. But they were right to go for the murder first. Once

El Coyote gave up what he knew about the murder, Pullone was that much easier.'

'Does he know how Ying got the heroin?'

'He claims he doesn't. But Pullone couldn't have planted the heroin himself, so we have to assume he gave it to his snitch to plant and the snitch held out a little and sold it to Ying.'

'But didn't Ying say he got it for free?'

'Maybe he was lying.'

'Or maybe Ying was the snitch.'

'Only if he was unregistered.'

'Why not? That's Pullone's style.'

'Ying had no record. Not the greatest snitch material.'

'Well, the important thing is, El Coyote gave us Pullone,' Mahoney said.

'Except so far it's only conversation. Uncorroborated accomplice testimony, at best.' Insufficient for a conviction in New York. 'We still need to get El Coyote fully on board, so he's willing to get what we need from Pullone. And then he's got to be prepped. I don't think we'll be able to turn him loose on Pullone until Sunday or Monday, the earliest.'

'Congratulations, anyway.'

'For what?' Jordan asked.

'Didn't you say, when he gives up Pullone, then we can congratulate each other?'

'I'm superstitious. I don't want any congratulations until it's over.'

# 4

Friday night Alice came home and David went out to dinner with her and the twins at one of the tourist-and-pre-teen traps on West Fifty-seventh Street. Her acting job had gone wonderfully, Alice informed them all, and now she'd been hired as a production assistant, a chance to meet more people and to learn about that side of the business. At evening's end she announced that as a treat for the twins she was taking them on a weekend trip to the beach before she returned to the movie location. They made no attempt to pretend enthusiasm.

'It's too cold to swim in the ocean,' she acknowledged. 'But it's totally beautiful out there this time of year and the house is great and there's a heated swimming pool.'

News of the pool perked them up, and they immediately tackled the question of which of their new school friends they could invite along.

'This was supposed to be for *us*,' Alice protested, but it was *pro forma* – she clearly knew when she was outnumbered and outgunned.

The whole household was up and running Saturday at dawn, David not excepted. There was much fuss about what to pack and who was coming and setting up the new two-mailbox answering machine Alice's new status demanded. After she and the twins left David read the morning paper and sat down at his computer to check his e-mail.

There were a few responses to his job queries, but none of them excited him. He typed out a message to Angus Macleod asking for more details on one of the research programs at the Hong Kong Institute of Technology. It was already Saturday night in Hong Kong, so Macleod probably wouldn't get the message until Monday morning – Sunday night in New York – but there was no rush.

607

There was a message from Jon Levi. It said INCONCLUSIVE SO FAR. KEEP TRYING, he replied. RAPID ENCRYPTED RESPONSE APPRECIATED, IF POSSIBLE.

He closed down the computer and got dressed for the meeting with Michael Ryan and Kassia Miller. And Susan.


'There's good news,' Ryan said. 'Dan Mahoney persuaded the U.S. Attorney's office to withdraw their grand jury subpoenas. For the time being, at least, you don't have to worry about that.'

'Did he say why they wanted to see us?' Susan asked.

'I don't think he knows – he was surprised to hear they'd served you with subpoenas.'

'How about Mahoney?' David wanted to know. 'Do we know what he has in mind, or are we in the dark about that, too?'

'We have some clues. For one thing, Mahoney is pretty sure you violated grand jury secrecy—' Ryan held up a hand to keep them from jumping in. 'Just hear me out. Mahoney said he's not interested in prosecuting you for that, he's after bigger fish.'

'One fascinating thing,' Kassia Miller said: 'We checked out the Assistant U.S. Attorney who issued the federal subpoena, and he's in their Public Corruption Unit. And when Mahoney met with Michael yesterday, it was at the Official Corruption Unit of the D.A.'s office, even though Mahoney isn't assigned to that unit.'

'That's a lot of corruption,' David noted. 'What does it have to do with us?'

'It might have to do with that theory you both sketched out for us,' Ryan speculated. 'That the Engs are holding money for people who intend to leave Hong Kong. That kind of scheme lends itself to bribing public officials – immigration officials or consular officials to get people into the country, or Customs to get the money in.'

David realized that they hadn't told the lawyers Sunny's story about the gold shops and how they transferred money from one place to another without ever moving it physically. He supposed that didn't invalidate Ryan's point that the Engs might be engaged in bribery. And China seemed to be a place where people believed that the world was best dealt with by spreading money around.

'Of course, bribing federal officials is a federal crime, not a state

608

crime, so that doesn't explain Mahoney's interest,' Miller said. 'But you mentioned the possibility that the heroin case you heard in the grand jury involved planted evidence.'

'That's what we thought,' Susan said.

'Well, the D.A.'s Official Corruption Unit prosecutes cops who go wrong. The Public Corruption Unit at the U.S. Attorney's office is more likely to deal with federal officials, but they're always delighted to expose and punish bad apples in local law enforcement.' She gave her partner a mocking look. 'It nourishes their superiority complex.'

'We tried to ask about planted evidence in the grand jury, but Mahoney wouldn't listen,' Susan said. 'Why does he care what we think, now?'

'That *is* the question, isn't it?' Ryan said. 'What do you know that makes you so interesting to both the federal and the local prosecutors?'

'I don't see what it could be,' Susan said. 'We didn't commit any crimes and we don't have any evidence of crimes. All we have are some theories.'

'That's one reason why – before we talk about how you should answer Mahoney's questions – we have to go over carefully what you did and what you saw. It's a fair bet you're full of information you don't know you have.'

David saw Susan's distress when the lawyers' questions turned to the audio tapes.

'You don't have any idea what was on them?' Ryan asked.

'No,' David said quickly. 'As Susan said last time, I wanted to find out but I never had a chance.' Hurrying by it, for her sake.

'This is another area that's more likely to be federal than state,' Ryan said. 'And frankly it's also one area where you're vulnerable. The fact that you claim ignorance isn't enough, especially when it comes to conspiracy.'

'What do you mean?' Despite her naturally glowing complexion, Susan looked decidedly pale.

'First of all, you should know that – unlike the state grand jury, which I know you're familiar with – going into the federal grand jury can be a perilous thing,' Ryan said. 'Witnesses in the federal grand jury don't get automatic immunity the way state grand jury witnesses do. Anything you say in federal grand jury can be used against you – directly, or as a source of leads for an investigation which turns up further evidence.'

'Then why would anybody testify?' David wanted to know.

'If they subpoena you, you don't have much choice. They'll generally tell you if you're the subject of their investigation, or a target for indictment. But even when you think you know why you're there it's full of pitfalls.

'In practice,' Ryan continued, 'if we're afraid there's anything at all that might come back and bite us later, we notify them that you're going to assert your Fifth Amendment right not to incriminate yourself. Across the board. That's how it's done, not one question at a time.

'And because it's not proper to call somebody into the grand jury purely for the purpose of making them take the Fifth Amendment, they then have two choices – either they cancel your appearance or they get a court order compelling you to come in and testify and granting you immunity for all of that testimony.'

'That doesn't sound so bad,' Susan said. 'Can we do that?'

'The problem is, it's only *limited* immunity,' Miller said. 'Not like in the state grand jury, where the immunity covers any transaction involving anything mentioned in the testimony. Transactional immunity is New York State's special craziness. Unfortunately, the federal system doesn't work that way.

'With federal grand jury immunity, the prosecutors are prohibited from using your specific testimony against you, and they can't go out and drum up evidence based on what they learn from that testimony. But if they get the evidence anywhere else, they can convict you of anything they want to. Which is not something that could happen after you testify in the state grand jury.

'And there's another problem,' Ryan added. 'If they were only thinking of you as a witness, not a subject of the investigation – or, worse, a target – then if you take the Fifth they may wonder what you're hiding and look at you a lot more closely.'

'Do you really think we'll have to testify for them?' Susan asked.

'Federal prosecutors use the grand jury for investigation much more aggressively than the state does,' Ryan said. 'A lot depends on how badly the Southern District wants the information they think you have, and whether they have somewhere else to get it. And it may make a difference how Mahoney convinced them to let him have the first shot at you.'

'The first shot!'

'I know that sounds ominous, but unless the Southern District has only a minimal interest in you, chances are Mahoney just got them to back off until he's done with you.'

'Then what's the point?'

'Don't underestimate it – it's going to be hard enough to deal with one set of prosecutors at a time. And we can hope to learn from the questions Mahoney asks you. But in the end, we're going to have to deal with both.'

'You'd think they'd have better ways to spend their time than going after us,' David said.

'They obviously don't think so,' Ryan said. 'Which brings me back to the question of your exposure. If the U.S. Attorney is going to consider prosecuting you, a lot will depend on how she frames the charges.

'As an example, let's assume they know about the tapes and they're looking at you as members of a conspiracy to export and import them. The question then becomes how much you knew about the criminal nature of the conspiracy.'

'How can anyone think we're part of a conspiracy?' Susan demanded.

'Because you are,' Ryan said. 'To be convicted of participating in a conspiracy in federal court, you have to knowingly participate in the scheme that's being charged. So if that scheme involved exporting an audio tape, or importing one, then you clearly participated in it knowingly – they asked you to carry it for them, and you did, and you knew you were carrying it. The question then is, was it a criminal conspiracy? Was the scheme unlawful and if so, did you have any knowledge of its unlawful aims?'

'Of course we didn't.'

'That would be the line we'd follow. But it may not be that simple, because the prosecution can ask if the reason you didn't know was that you consciously avoided knowing.

'Basically, they'd be saying you *should* have known, or easily *could* have known that what you were doing was illegal – either illegal in and of itself, or part of an illegal scheme – and that you wilfully turned away from that knowledge. Using the tapes as an example – the fact that you didn't listen to them before you transported them on behalf of accused heroin distributors demonstrates a desire *not* to know what you were doing was illegal.'

'You mean we had some *obligation* to listen to the tapes before we carried them?'

Susan asked the question looking intently at Ryan. Watching her, David had the feeling she was avoiding his glance.

'Yes, you might have had an obligation,' Ryan said. 'In fact, I'm beginning to think about this seriously.'

'What do you mean?' David asked.

'You have this theory about the Engs helping people get their money here from Hong Kong. Arguably that involves at least *some* illegal activity on the part of the Engs, and some sort of conspiracy along with it. And that gives you plenty of reason to be suspicious about the tapes, besides the heroin charges.'

David took another quick look at Susan. She was staring at the floor.

'You told us you had one of the tapes with you when you went to Boston.' Ryan was studying David. 'And you wanted to find out what was on it but you didn't have a chance. Is there something more about that, that you might have left out because you didn't think it mattered?'

Be happy you have a sharp lawyer, David told himself. He said, 'I have a friend in the Boston area who knows some things about encoding computer data. I took the tape up there for him to look at.'

'Did he find anything?'

'Not yet. He's got a copy he's looking at.'

'A copy.' Ryan looked at Miller.

'Does he still have it?' she asked.

'Is that a problem?'

'This is a tricky area of the law,' Ryan said. 'We have to assume that if the Government knew a copy of the tape existed, they'd say the document subpoena covers it. But bear in mind, it's the Government's job to prove the tape existed in the first place and that you had it in your

612

possession. And we can't be placed in the position of doing any of that for them.

'But if you gave them a copy of the tape, by that very act you would be *admitting* that the tape itself existed and also that you'd had possession of it. Because how else could you have made a copy? So the only way to avoid incriminating yourself is not giving it to them at all. And not telling them that's what you're doing, because by telling them you'd admit that the *copy* exists . . .'

'I don't see how they could know there's a copy,' David said, 'even if they know about the tape.'

'If they don't know there's a copy,' Miller said, 'we can leave it with your friend, and they might never know to look there, and as long as it's under his power and control and not yours, the subpoenas they served on you don't even cover it. Unfortunately, though, if they *do* know it's there, they can subpoena it from him, and he has no right against self-incrimination to protect it with, because he didn't do anything criminal.'

'I don't think we can afford to rely on the Government's failing to find out about anything,' Ryan said. 'We had some trouble seeing how they could know about you, too. And they do.

'Here's what I think you should do. Get the tape back. Give it to me as custodian. I'll hire an audio lab – or your friend, if he's willing and you think he's the man for the job – so that I retain legal custody of the tape even when it's being analyzed, and all the results will be subject to lawyer-client privilege.'

David glanced at Susan again, wondered if he was as pale as she was. It made his head buzz to think they had gone so quickly from being grand jurors themselves to being the potential targets of a grand jury. A federal grand jury.

'I have a question,' Miller said to them. 'I can understand your delivering the first tape, in Hong Kong. But by the second one you must have had plenty of reason to think there was something on the tape besides "Hello, Mother, hello, Father." So why did you deliver it to them at all?'

'They threatened Susan,' David said and saw, too late, that Susan didn't want him to open that door.

Miller jumped on it right away. 'How did they threaten you?'

'They never actually threatened me,' Susan said. 'Meiling was so desperate to hear her daughter's voice she spoke a little harshly. I might have imagined it was a threat.'

'If it *was* a threat, what was the nature of it?'

'It was about my son, Charles,' she said so softly it was hard to hear.

'What were they going to do?'

'To get him hooked on heroin.' Barely audible.

'Why that?'

Susan sat frozen. David thought she looked worse than pale.

'You don't think they deal in heroin,' Miller prodded.

'No.'

'But they threatened your son with heroin, not some other kind of violence—'

'Can't you see she's upset?' David broke in.

'That's nothing to how she's going to feel in the grand jury if we're not prepared,' Miller said evenly. 'I don't know how to make it clearer to you – you have to tell us everything.'

'Her son had some trouble with heroin,' David said. 'I think he's in rehab.'

They spent a half-hour on it – what Charles's problem had been and how Meiling had couched the threat, which Susan only reluctantly agreed had been more than a colorful form of expression prompted by Meiling's agitation. David thought Susan was angry with him, but she seemed to calm down as they got further into it.

'It's another sign that the tape is important to the Engs,' Ryan said. 'And we'll be careful how we handle it. But we also have to be careful not to confuse ourselves. What's important to the Engs and what's important to the federal prosecutors may not be the same. Didn't you say there was a consular official at your meeting with the Hong Kong policeman?'

'Yes,' Susan said.

'And it was the connections among the Engs and all the people you saw in China that they seemed most interested in?'

'Yes.'

'And one or the other of them must have taken some identification from you,' Ryan said.

'Yes. Both of them did.'

'Okay. If the Southern District is looking at some kind of international conspiracy, whether it includes the tapes or not, chances are they also have their eye on the Hong Kong and China end of it.

'From Mahoney's unhappy reaction to the federal subpoenas, I doubt the U.S. Attorney learned about you from the D.A.'s office. But they may well have learned about you, and your contact with the Eng family, from the man you spoke to at the Hong Kong consulate. And if that's their source, they're likely to be focusing on what you did over there. They'll want to know everything about what you saw, who you spoke to, what was said . . . Because if they're onto this rescue scheme for Hong Kong residents that you've described to us, they're probably trying to put all the pieces together, just the way you were.

'It seems likely to me that they're fishing around to find out what role you played, probably ready to believe the worst. There's no real reason to think they know about the tapes, yet. But once they do, they're going to be very interested in everything to do with them. Our problem will be convincing them you were innocent dupes.' Ryan smiled. 'If you'll excuse the characterization.'

They took a break and then Ryan and Miller put them through another grilling, starting with everything and everyone they'd had contact with in Hong Kong and China, then back over the tapes and the bandits and what Detective Chief Inspector Hall had told Susan about June Eng.

Susan and David rode uptown together. She was silent, staring out the window. Her dismay was almost palpable.

'They didn't kid around,' he said, trying for a tone of normalcy. 'But they do really seem to be on top of it.'

She didn't turn away from the window.

Neither of them spoke as the cab slalomed northward through the Saturday shopping traffic. As they neared midtown David said, 'The China Society's not far from your hotel. I still want to go to that symposium . . . I could come by and get you on my way.'

'I don't think so, David.' Her voice was flat; she barely glanced at him. 'But you go. I just don't think I'm up to it.'

This was something more than just the strain of talking to the lawyers. 'Are you okay?'

At first she was silent and he wasn't sure he'd asked the right question, but then some of the stiffness went out of her body.

'It's not just all this,' she said in a weary voice. 'It's Richard. We had another scene. He's been a different person since Charles . . . since he went away. It's as if all Richard's anger and suspicion of the past ten years has come out at once. God knows what he thought I was doing all those years, or where he thought I found the energy or the time to run around while I was managing his house and his social life, raising Charles and Lara, and building a business . . .' She sighed. 'Even though I don't want to be married to him, and I know I don't, I still don't want this. And it's so like him to make things as difficult as possible just when we're supposed to be celebrating Lara's birthday.'

'Does she know what's happening? I mean, between you and Richard?'

'I told her I'd learned some things in China that I needed to figure out so I was staying in a hotel for a while to give myself a chance to think about it. I didn't even want to say that much . . . She took it very hard about Charles, and college is still new and strange for her. That's plenty for her to deal with.'

'I wish there was something I could do,' he said.

'You do just fine.'

David called her at the hotel an hour later. 'I'm on my way to the conference but I've got something to tell you first. Can I come by?'

'Any time you want. I may not be up to going to a symposium or a cocktail party, but that doesn't mean I stop wanting to see you.' The right words, but he heard no energy in them.

The first thing he did when she let him in was to hug her. Once he had her in his arms, he didn't want to let go.

'It feels as if you're not sure I'm real,' she said.

'It's good to be reminded.'

'Is that why you came by? I'm flattered.'

'That's the most important reason. And I had something to tell you, about the Engs. I know your mind's on other things—'

616

'To tell the truth, right now I don't think I care. No matter how concerned I am about the Hong Kong people they're helping – and I *am* concerned about them – if I never see Martin or Meiling again, that's fine with me.'

'Okay, I understand that, but just hear me out. I think you'll see this is important.'

'All right.' She sank into the easy chair by the window.

'Something's been bothering me,' he said, 'and I finally figured out what. All that talk about Hong Kong and China has got June and Peter Eng's friend Chan Kwok-Wing stuck in my mind. I just keep thinking how I always felt there was more to him than met the eye.'

'I suppose we don't really know much about him,' Susan acknowledged. 'He's a friend of the Eng family, he's in business with them, and people in the factories treated him with a lot of respect.'

'Not just in the factories – in that restaurant, too. In Zhongshan. In *China*, not Hong Kong.'

'That's true.' Displaying her first real sign of interest.

'So I had him in the back of my mind, wondering about him, and then just a little while ago something came to me.'

'Yes?'

'You know how sometimes you see something and it doesn't register and then later the memory comes back to you and you can't believe you missed it the first time around? Coming out of the shower just now, getting ready for the symposium, I had that exact kind of memory about Chan Kwok-Wing.

'Remember when we were going through Customs from Macao into China? We had to use the passport-control line for foreigners, and so did June Eng. And Chan went off toward where it said Hong Kong travel permits and returning residents.'

'I wasn't paying attention. Customs always makes me nervous. Especially going into China, because my parents never came out again.'

'I wasn't paying much attention either, but I realize now that I saw something that didn't fully register at the time. Chan didn't get onto the line for people with Hong Kong travel permits. He got on the line for *returning citizens of China*.'

'Are you sure?'

'What I remember is – the returning-citizens line was shorter than the Hong Kong line. I guess I put it down to that, when I first noticed it – that he was going to the shorter of the two lines the way anybody would. But the thing is, it was *much* shorter. So why didn't other people move over from the longer one? The only answer is, because they didn't qualify. They were Hong Kong residents, so they had to stay in the longer line.'

'You think he's Chinese? China Chinese?'

'It would help explain why he's so well-known and so well-connected in Zhongshan.'

'And how he knows Yu Wenli, who used to be an Army officer in China, and who was chosen to write an official report on abuses of the Cultural Revolution.' The energy was returning to her voice. 'And Chan's cousin is an officer in the People's Armed Police. And there was that odd thing he said when we first met, when I thought he said he was from China – about how we're all children of the Yellow Emperor . . .'

'It looks pretty convincing when you put it all together, doesn't it?'

'So it could be he's Chinese and important,' she said.

'I think so.'

'Some kind of official?'

'Possibly . . . And the trouble with all that is –' he began and she broke in to finish the thought – 'that a mainland-Chinese official is hardly the right man to earn the trust of Hong Kong people who are afraid of the Chinese Government.'

'Right. They're certainly not going to give him their money to send ahead for them so they'll have it waiting in America when they flee.'

Susan sat forward. 'If that's true – if Chan is from China, and he's not transferring money for potential emigrants – then what's this all about?'

# 5

By the time Susan and David arrived, the auditorium on the main floor of the China Society was almost full. To sit together they had to climb to the top of the steeply-raked rows of red-plush seats and ask a distinguished-looking, white-haired man if he would mind moving over one seat.

'I'm glad you got me out of that hotel room,' Susan said, 'but do you really think this is going to help us?'

'It can't hurt. And if Mr Chan is from China and our whole Hong Kong theory is out the window . . . this is as good a place as any to get up-to-date on what the issues in China are.'

'Why do I think there's something else?'

'There *is* something else, but I'm not sure about it.' He seemed reluctant to say more. 'If I'm wrong we can always leave.'

Susan looked at the program they had been given on their way in. The morning speeches had been Beijing – 'How Many Successions?'; 'Regionalism vs. Central Government'; and 'The Army as Entrepreneur.' Earlier in the afternoon, there had been a speaker on 'Corruption as a Moderating Force' and a panel on 'U.S. Policy – Dragon of Influence or Paper Tiger?' The program was closing with a summary panel moderated by a speaker named Wu Chuming who had opened the conference three days before with a talk on 'The Past as Prediction: Modern China in Historical Perspective.'

The conference chairman, rotund and florid, with graying blond hair, sat alone at a table on the moderate-size stage. Four empty chairs, each with a microphone in front of it, awaited the panel discussion. The chairman rose and went to the lectern.

'We've had a very stimulating few days, I know you'll all agree,' he said, 'and to put it all in perspective we're closing with a panel of our speakers.' He introduced the panelists one by one and when they were all seated at the table he said, 'To set the stage for our summary panel and to lead it we are privileged to have a scholar who has often helped us see the present through the clarifying lens of the past – through his insightful writings, and on rare and special occasions in public talks. Ladies and gentlemen it is my honor to present to you Mr Wu Chuming.'

For no reason Susan could name her hand felt for David's, found it, held it tight.

A short, slight man in a beautifully cut dark-blue suit came up the aisle and mounted the stage. From where they were sitting Susan could see the back of his large head and a hint of skin as smooth as Martin Eng's.

You're being ridiculous, she chided herself. Now you're going to start seeing them everywhere you turn.

The conference chairman moved to greet Wu Chuming, to shake his hand, obscuring Susan's view. It was only when the chairman moved away and left the stage, when the speaker approached the lectern, tugging his notes from his inside jacket pocket, that Susan could see clearly and without a doubt that the man introduced as Wu Chuming was Martin Eng.

'Ouch,' David said.

Her nails were digging into his palm. She let go.

'You knew!' she breathed, breaking her fascination with Martin Eng – Wu Chuming – long enough to look sharply at David.

'I suspected. I was nowhere near sure.'


Martin Eng placed his notes on the lectern and poured himself a glass of water. Looked at his audience.

'In the great historical epic *San Guo Zhi Yen-yi*,' he began, '*The Romance of the Three Kingdoms* – we read at the beginning of the story these words.' He spoke a flowing, almost melodic Chinese sentence. 'This means, "They say that the movement of history has always been this way: the empire, long divided, must unite; long united, it must divide." ' He paused, then repeated: ' *"The empire, long divided, must unite; long united, it must divide." '*

He paused again, sipped some water.

'In this hall, we have the privilege to hear many thoughtful and intelligent speakers. Their words add up to a picture of China today, where much is possible, for good and for ill.

'My perspective on this picture is the perspective of the past. I think that for us here today there is one central question – where in the great rise and fall of Chinese history do we stand at this moment? Is this a time for the empire, long divided, to be united again, or is it a time like so many in China's long story, when the united empire must draw new strength from a period of division?'

The rest of his talk was a blur to Susan, trying to think of Martin Eng in this new light, to adjust to the idea of his second identity. Meiling had said her husband was a scholar, and Mrs Liu had also said that was his reputation. It was typical for a scholar or poet to assume a name for that role that was different from his childhood name or the name he used at home – a pen name, really. And yet given this and what she and David had decided about Chan Kwok-Wing . . .

She heard snatches of the panel discussion, a mixture of today's China and the distant past. There was a lot about warrior states as a continuing historical force, and the Army's modern economic and political role, about Hong Kong and Guangdong . . . Special Economic Zones . . . court eunuchs and palace intrigues . . . conflict between north and south in imperial China and the twentieth century . . . the effect of American policy on Chinese politics . . . the universality of corruption in the waning days of powerful dynasties . . .

And then Martin Eng was reading his closing remarks, before she was ready, before she had digested what was happening.

'It is said that China is weakest and most subject to foreign domination when it is most fragmented. This is a narrow view. In times of great change – when technologies are changing, philosophies are changing, political systems are changing, China has been well served by having strong and independent regions – even when this has meant that they are at war with each other.

'Things cannot move everywhere at the same rate, and to pretend that they can destroys progress and brings stagnation and hardship.

Ancient China's greatest teachers and sages flourished in a period when an old empire broke into many pieces that we now call the Warring States.

'All Han Chinese people know the story of the Yellow Emperor. He is the ancestor of us all and the great symbol of the unity of China.

'The sages tell us the Yellow Emperor had four faces, so he could look in all directions. The greatest sage of all, Master Kung, whom Westerners call Confucius – and who lived at the dawn of the Warring States period – explained this mythical image in simple words. Master Kung said, "The Yellow Emperor gathered around him four men and had them rule the four quarters. They were his four faces."

'In modern times, empires rise and fall in the lifetime of a single person, and we must keep careful watch against the rise of false Emperors. We must understand that China is a country of great size and complicated problems, and so the true modern heir to the Yellow Emperor must also have separate faces.

'One face cannot see in all directions. And the quarter where each face rules is different from the others. The people, the languages, the resources are different, and so the needs are different. The most important task of this age is to honor the need for separate ruling faces and at the same time to keep them together – distinct and independent aspects of a single will.'

The cocktail party was in a ballroom up a sweeping flight of marble stairs. There were three bar tables; waiters circulated with champagne and hors d'oeuvres.

David and Susan drifted through the room, trying to look as if they were chatting with each other while they picked up pieces of other conversations. At one large group, David stopped.

'You can't seriously think the country is going to come apart,' said a woman with frosted silver hair and a suit to match.

'It's all going to depend on the Army,' countered a man who looked to David as if he'd spent most of his life in uniform. 'Just as Wu was saying. The old leaders are too corrupt to make anything work.'

'I think he had the wrong emphasis, on corruption,' a plump, bankerish fellow said. 'If the children of the ruling élite are getting to be billionaires, corrupt or not, they're going to want a system that

622

protects the rights of owners and capitalists. It has to foster the growth of a stable middle class.'

'That's nonsense,' said a Japanese man with an intense, brooding look. 'China has been a garden of corruption from the beginning of time, and the blossoms always stink.'

As David and Susan stood listening, the group widened slightly to accommodate them. The conversation went on.

'That's what Wu was saying,' the old soldier offered. 'That every dynasty, including the mythical ones, ended after corruption overwhelmed everything else.'

'It's what Sun Yatsen was talking about at the end of the Qing Dynasty,' said the woman with the silver suit. 'It's why his revolution succeeded.'

'I think the country is going to come apart,' said a newcomer to the group, a tall, reed-thin woman with her dark hair twisted high on her head around jeweled chopsticks. 'It has to, for its own sake. Wu is right about that.'

'He never said that.'

'Didn't he?' She raised one penciled eyebrow. 'Then I will. People talk about Greater China, but the only Greater China that makes sense is Greater South China. Guangdong and Fujian and Hainan, plus Hong Kong and Singapore and Taiwan. When you come down to it, Hong Kong and Singapore and Taiwan are a lot more Chinese than Tibet or Mongolia or Xinjiang.'

'It's all well and good to talk about Greater South China, but the Army won't let the country come apart,' the old soldier countered.

'I'd say there's going to be a façade of unity, lip service but no more,' said an African-American man in a red-and-white bow-tie, his thumbs hooked into matching suspenders. 'The regions are already paying taxes to the central government at their own whim. The restrictions on internal travel are going to have to increase still more, to the point of introducing internal passports.'

'I don't see that,' said the woman in silver.

'Then take another look,' bow-tie retorted. 'You have a country with one of the smallest amounts of agricultural land, per person, in the entire world – and in the coastal regions they're building condos on what little they have. Peasants are leaving the countryside by the millions with nowhere to go and nothing to do, there are already food riots and work riots in the internal provinces. A big fraction of the state enterprises are bankrupt.'

'China's a country of regional strongmen, always has been,' said a man with gnarled hands, leaning on a walking stick. 'You need that kind of thing to keep a big country like China from stumbling over itself, especially when big changes are happening. Call it "federalism with Chinese characteristics." The Yellow Emperor's four faces might be enough, or it might take more. And nothing any of us can do or say is going to change that.'

'Besides, now that the south is on the rise why should they sit still for the north to dominate them?' the tall woman challenged. 'They've had enough of that over the centuries, and I can't say as I blame them for being fed up with it.'

That was a conversation-stopper. The bankerish man who thought corruption could be a good idea turned to David and Susan.

'Hello, I don't think I've had the pleasure. Harold Pinkson, Hong Kong Bank.' He introduced the others: the silver-suited woman was also a banker, the military type was an Army officer, as David had guessed – a member of the National Security Council; the man with the walking stick, an expert in Asian securities markets; bow-tie, a college professor; and the intense Japanese man, a journalist.

'I'm Susan Chan, and this is David Clark.'

'Pleasure,' said Pinkson. 'And what brings you here?'

'The Royal Hong Kong Racecourse Association,' David said, sensing Susan's hesitation.

'Really? How is it I don't know you?'

'It's a recent connection. I've been consulting with Angus Macleod.'

'Ah, yes, the computer whiz. Natural resource, that man is. How is old Angus?'

'Working hard on the new telecommunications links with China.'

'That's what we want to hear. Keep everything running. Through train to the new era, no stops along the way. And Ms Chan?'

'I'm a friend of Wu Chuming and his wife.'

'Are you? Quite a fellow. Amazing how he can make three thousand years ago seem like yesterday. And on top of that his wife is an expert

624

on early- and mid-twentieth-century Chinese politics.'

'Really?'

'Didn't you know?'

'I don't know her that way. We eat dim sum and talk girltalk,' Susan said with a sweet smile.

Pinkson glanced over her shoulder. 'I think that's them now.'

She turned to look. 'So it is.'

'Well, you'll want to say hello, no doubt.'

'Nice to meet you all,' Susan said and took David's arm, leading him in the direction of the Engs.

'Don't they look splendid,' she said in his ear. 'Martin ought to wear a suit more often, it gives him stature. And don't you love that discreet ton of gold around her neck? I guess they didn't sell quite every bit of it, after all.'

David looked at her. She squeezed his arm.

'A side of me you haven't seen? Catty cocktail-party lady. I must be angrier with them than I realized.'

'Are we really going to say hello to them?' David asked.

'We have to make a show of it or old Pinkson's going to call in the Horse Guards. I don't think he was completely convinced.'

'Why should he care?'

'People get territorial at these things. Don't want to have the feeling that while they had their back turned, someone let in the riffraff.'


The Engs were all but invisible in the center of a circle of admirers. Standing outside the ring with David, Susan could hear the conversation of two nearby men waiting to have their minute with Wu Chuming.

'You know, you want to talk about the value of public relations,' one said, 'I was talking to Jake the other day and he was saying how there was this family, made all its money in heroin and now the kids are investing in legitimate enterprises. They just broke ground on this powerplant-cum-industrial park development in Zhuhai, and, don't ask me how, but Jake got them congratulatory videos from two actual ex-presidents.'

'Of the U.S.?'

'Of the U.S.'

'You think they knew?'

'I'd say they didn't, but you know Jake – he might have sold it to them anyway.'

Abruptly, a gap opened in the crowd around the Engs and Susan saw Meiling register their presence. For an instant she was as immobile as the ancient terra-cotta armies of Xian, then her smile returned and she continued to chat with the man closest to her. Susan wondered if the man even noticed the momentary stillness or the vacant expression in her eyes that had replaced her earlier social warmth.

At a break in the conversation around them, she whispered in her husband's ear. Susan couldn't see his face as he listened, but soon enough, nodding and smiling to the congratulators and well-wishers, they made themselves a path to where she and David were standing.

'How nice to see you,' Meiling said. 'I wasn't aware you were on the invitation list.'

'A friend arranged it,' David said.

'Your scholarship is very impressive,' Susan said to Martin.

'You are kind to say so. I did not know you were so interested in China's future, or its past.'

'Only since I met you and your friend Mr Chan.'

David wanted to squeeze her hand, to signal her to be careful, but he knew it would not go unnoticed. Instead he tried for a diversion. 'From what we heard today, you're very fortunate to be in business with the Army.'

'We are not in business with anyone,' Meiling said. 'Our children are in business—' Her voice broke in mid-sentence. She pulled a handkerchief from her purse and dabbed at her eyes. 'Forgive an old lady's emotions.'

'No, I have to ask you to forgive me,' David said. This wasn't the kind of diversion he'd had in mind.

'Thank you for coming,' Martin said. 'Now there are others we must speak to.'

'How did you know?' Susan said as they walked out between the stone lions.

'Well . . . Martin's name is Chu-Ming, Chan told us that. I'd forgotten it until Macleod sent me a message about Wu Chuming. And I remembered that Mr Yu was talking about how Chinese names can be misleading, and one of the examples he gave was about June. I thought he'd said Eng and Wu were the same but I wasn't sure so I called the China Society, and sure enough.'

'So you thought – same name, same person.'

'For all I knew, Wu Chuming could be the John Smith of China, but I figured it was worth a chance.'

They walked in silence down Park Avenue. Late rush-hour traffic streamed by; the sidewalks were full of hurrying people.

'Did you see who was there?' Susan asked after a few blocks. 'I don't mean just Colonel James from the National Security Council.'

'I saw a lot of men in fancy business suits and a lot of women in expensive clothes – none as beautiful or well-dressed as you.'

'You know just what to say. But . . . you really didn't recognize anybody?'

'I'm not much good at that. One guy I know I've seen on TV. Gray suit with a red tie. He was talking to Meiling just as we left. Sort of looked like one of our former vice-presidents.'

'Right. Him. That's who it was. And the one built like a fireplug with the *basso profundo* voice? He used to be a national security adviser.'

'I kind of thought it might be, only I couldn't see how it was possible.'

'It was him. Plus two members of what some people still think of as the richest family in the country. And one genuine incumbent U.S. Senator. Martin seemed to know them all, but if you ask me, it was Meiling they were paying attention to.'

'How do you know all this?'

'I do this a lot. Or, I used to. Benefits for the hospital. Benefits organized by the wives of Richard's fellow board members. Affairs I go to for my clients. There was actually one man there from the hospital's board, but I don't think he recognized me. I'm missing my most identifiable feature.' In answer to David's unspoken question she said: 'Richard. That's how people think of me -- that Asian woman who came in with Richard Linwood.'

627

'We ought to figure out what we've just seen,' she said when they got back to her hotel. 'As soon as I get out of these tight shoes and into something more comfortable.'

'Good idea.' He scooped her up in his arms 'How about a nice warm shower?'

'Hey. Put me down. I only get in the shower with my clothes off.'

'That sounds like a *really* good idea.'

'Maybe we should have dried off first,' he said later.

'Maybe we should have gotten out of the shower first.'

He ran his finger down her body, stopped at dense black hair. 'Do you trim this?'

'A little. I have to strike a balance between too long and too short. Otherwise sometimes it pokes out through sheer cloth. Why?'

'I like it.'

'Not so curly as you're used to. Or as soft as your beard, say.'

'How's that, for you?'

She cupped his chin in her hands. 'I love it. Any extra sensation is always welcome.' She stretched. 'It's nice feeling so decadent. Too bad there's a real world out there we have to pay attention to.'

'We've got to decide what to do about Mahoney,' David said. 'How much are we going to tell him?'

'I don't know. Until a few hours ago I was sure I didn't want to tell him anything. I've already told Ryan that. That I wouldn't answer any questions, not in Mahoney's office and not in the grand jury, and if it meant going to jail for contempt of court I'd face that when I had to.'

'You told him that?'

'I did. Because, whatever else, I still believed the Engs were doing something worthwhile. Humanitarian. And I have tremendous sympathy for the Hong Kong people I thought they were helping.'

'What did Ryan say?'

'That I should think it over and whatever I decided he wanted to see me on Monday morning.'

'When did you decide this?'

'After you and I last talked. I thought I'd never be able to live with

628

myself if I did it any other way. And I knew right away that I didn't want to put any pressure on you. I'm glad we have a joint defense, but under normal circumstances you wouldn't know what I was doing, so you shouldn't base your decision on that.'

'If you feel so strongly about it, how could I undermine it?'

'But if you disagree with me—' She stopped herself. 'This is silly. After our conversation about Chan, and especially after what we just saw and heard, none of that makes sense any more. If Chan Kwok-Wing is from China, and Martin Eng is actually an expert on the history and future of China called Wu Chuming who's preaching the gospel of Greater South China and Hong Kong-Guangdong solidarity to a select group of American politicians and decision-makers, then everything I thought I knew is out the window. And so is my decision about what to do on Monday. I just wish we knew more.'

'Suppose we could know more? Suppose we can get some more information?'

'How?'

'From Hong Kong.'

'But it's Sunday there.'

'Yes, but tomorrow night when it's Sunday here it will be Monday there, and we have all of our Sunday night – the whole working day, Hong Kong time – before we have to go see the lawyers on Monday.'

# 6

At home Sunday morning, David turned on the computer to see if Jon Levi had replied to his message asking for the copy of the Engs's tape. He had, twice. His first message said: GOT YOURS. IN THE MIDDLE OF WORKING ON IT - CAN'T STOP NOW. The second said: DATA ON BOARD! DEFINITELY CAN'T STOP NOW.

MUST HAVE IT NOW. WILL RETURN IT TO YOU AS DESCRIBED FOR FURTHER WORK, David replied. He couldn't help being excited that Jon had found a concealed message on the tape, though he knew it would complicate things with the federal prosecutors, even if the Engs's data was encrypted and there was almost no chance of finding out what it said.

He sent an e-mail query to Angus Macleod asking if he could check on one Chan Kwok-Wing, possibly of China, Guangdong province, possibly of the city of Zhongshan or Guangzhou, possibly a significant personage. *I know this is vague, but it could be of considerable importance to me,* he typed.

He sat in front of the screen debating whether he should send a similar message to Detective Chief Inspector Hall. The Royal Hong Kong Police surely had resources that Macleod didn't. On the other hand, Hall – or more likely his friend from the consulate – had probably been the source of the federal prosecutors' interest in David Clark and Susan Linwood, so anything David sent him now was likely to end up coming back to haunt them.

Thinking about Hall reminded David of the Hong Kong policeman's request for Chan Kwok-Wing's business card. David hunted it down. It gave a Hong Kong address. Discouraging, but Chan had been

630

posing as a person from Hong Kong, so the card was consistent with that. The more important question was – if the address was phony, what about the name?

He had to gamble that the name was real; otherwise he had nothing to go on. It was a choice between searching for someone who might not exist and not searching at all.

Mahoney was on the golf course fighting a stiff October wind and rueing his decision to rise with the sun on a morning he could just as well have stayed in bed. It only compounded the day's folly to have his beeper go off as they got to the tenth tee. He recognized Laurie Jordan's office phone number: too important to wait until he got back to the clubhouse after the back nine.

Inevitably, one of his foursome had a cell phone. 'We're on an open line,' Mahoney warned Jordan when she answered.

'Our canine friend really delivered,' she said. 'I've got something for you to hear.'

That had to mean El Coyote had come through. He told her where he was.

'It's too nasty out for golf, anyway,' she said. 'Besides, just sneaking off for eighteen holes on the odd Sunday won't make you good enough to beat me.'

'I'll be there in an hour,' he said.

The tape was unusually clear and easy to understand. Jordan had it cued up to a place where El Coyote was saying, 'I gave you five hundred grams of powder, it wasn't to have some Chink selling it in my people's territory. Bragging how he got it for free. What kind of shit is that? You hear what I'm sayin'? That's one dead Chink, man. Bang, bang.'

'Hey, listen, he deserved it.' Pullone sounded unconcerned. 'His dickbrain brother Leon, too. The dickbrain Ying brothers. The cock-suckers stole that powder, and they could have fucked me up royally, doing it.'

It was a shock for Mahoney, hearing the detective's voice. A bigger shock hearing him talk about the heroin so off-handedly. Jordan was right – this really was what they wanted.

'What's this shit, they *stole* it?' El Coyote wanted to know. 'You told me you're *giving* it to him, you need it for evidence or some shit.'

'I gave it to fucking Leon and that's the last I saw of it,' Pullone said. 'He was supposed to plant it all, but the asshole had to get greedy.'

'He leave over *any* to fuck up those people, or he just steal it all?'

'Listen, my friend, you worry about what you need to worry about, and I'll worry about what I need to worry about.'

Pullone sounded wary, maybe even suspicious. Mahoney glanced at Jordan. She was listening expectantly, as if the best was still coming.

'What? You think I give a fuck?' El Coyote was playing indignant. Convincingly. 'You're the one fuckin' brought me into this. And I'm the one fuckin' got burned.'

'Yeah, they left enough,' Pullone said, humoring him. 'Then some butthole A.D.A. decided the evidence didn't smell right. Has his head up his ass, is what he was smelling. Almost blew the fucking indictment and then the pussy starts crying about how he needs more evidence.'

Mahoney glanced at Jordan again: this time she was watching for his reaction, grinning.

'They're *all* pussies,' El Coyote sneered. 'What I want to know – when you gettin' me my fuckin' junk back?'

'I told you you'd get it back.' Pullone sounded impatient. 'Nothing's come up.'

'That's fuckin' bullshit, you know what I'm sayin'? I don' need to hear that shit. I waited long enough. I got a business to run.'

'Listen, asshole. You just be happy I don't fuck you up for twenty-five to life. You want it sooner, give me one of your competitors. I'll make the bust and you've got your powder back with interest.'

'Fuckin' cops.' El Coyote sounded genuinely exasperated. 'Next time lift the fuckin' heroin from some fuckin' *evidence* room, okay? Leave me the fuck out of it.'

'Hey! Stealing from the evidence room is a crime,' Pullone said. 'What do you think I am?'

El Coyote wasn't amused: 'I think you're a fuckin' lyin' scumbag, is what I think, and I want my fuckin' heroin back.'

Jordan clicked the tape off. 'I'll bet if Detective Pullone knew he

632

gave such a hot performance he'd want a dozen copies of this.'

'Copies, hell. He'd want the original. I know that's what I want. Plus your sacred oath you haven't played it for anybody.'

She laughed. 'I'll bet you do.'

Susan looked across the table at Lara, hoping to see again the radiance that had so powerfully struck her barely over a month before. She saw the same strong, beautiful young woman, but tonight there was a muted quality about her.

Susan handed her a package, wrapped in handmade paper of red and gold-leaf. A jade dragon pendant, Susan's one truly extravagant purchase in Hong Kong. Real Burmese jadeite, the jeweler had assured her – though only a small piece, the dragon carved around its impurities, not the quality that went into million-dollar bangles and necklaces.

Lara put the unopened package on the table next to her wine glass. 'Daddy says Charles has to stay at the clinic at least another two months.'

'I didn't know we'd heard anything from the clinic.' Susan was distressed. 'Did your father say who told him that?'

'I think he talked to the director of the clinic.'

'I understood we weren't supposed to have any contact with them for another two weeks. Did he say anything about Charles? How is he?'

'Daddy told me he was sure that if Charles wasn't all right the man would have said something. Except Daddy's worried about the two more months.'

Susan was speechless. How much of this was true, and how much was Richard being Richard? What did it mean to say Charles would have to be there so much longer? Why hadn't Richard told her?

Lara looked at her. 'I have to say – this is a hell of a birthday present you've arranged, Mother.'

'I don't know what you mean.' But she was afraid she did.

'You and Daddy living apart. I thought it was just something about China you were thinking about for a few days.'

Oh, Richard, she thought: How like you. On your daughter's birthday.

'It's true,' she acknowledged in as calm a voice as she could manage. 'Your father and I are having some difficulties. It does have to do with some things I learned about myself in China, but . . . I didn't want to burden you with it. You have enough on your mind.'

'Mother! What could be more important?'

'I'm not saying it's not important. But it's between me and your father, and we'll work it out, one way or the other. And until we do there's nothing to be gained by involving you in it.' She was momentarily stymied. 'You're nineteen now, a college woman. Old enough to understand that people's relationships change—'

'So it *is* a birthday present. Now that I'm old enough you're free to mess up each other's lives—' Lara pushed herself away from the table and ran toward the rest room.

When Lara came back, Susan tried to find words that would make some connection between them. So many of the feelings that were driving her now were brand new for her – she'd barely learned to think about them: speaking of them seemed impossible. And she knew that right now even hinting that Richard might be at fault would be the worst thing she could do.

Whether it was her own clumsiness or Lara's being stubborn, Susan didn't know, but her efforts to explain had no visible effect. The rest of the dinner was a study in awkwardness. Lara gave perfunctory answers to questions about college. Susan told stories about Hong Kong and China – vaguely aware she was probably repeating the few she'd already told Lara on the phone.

'Aren't you going to open your present?' Susan asked as they sat in silence waiting for the waiter to bring back her credit card.

Lara tucked the package into her purse. 'Maybe later.'

*Maybe later.* Susan told herself not to be surprised by her daughter's ability to wound her. Sharper than a serpent's tooth, indeed, she thought in a moment of anger.

Susan returned to the hotel unsure whether she should call David, feeling the way she did. Her uncertainty was resolved by the message slips the front desk gave her. David had left three messages asking her to call back as soon as she could. *Call at once*, the last one said. *Any hour.* It was only a few minutes old.

'I've got something,' David told her on the phone. 'Can you come over here? It's best if I tell you about it where I have access to my computer.'

'Can it wait till the morning? I'm in the middle of a family crisis.'

'What's wrong?'

'It's just something I have to get through ... there's not really anything you can do.' But she knew that was wrong as soon as the words were out. 'I'd love just to have you hold me. Could you come here instead?'

'I can, but it would be better if you came here. We're going to have questions we want answered before our appointment with the lawyers in the morning, and the answers have to come from Hong Kong tonight.'

Susan could not help responding to the urgency in his voice. 'All right, I'll be right there.'

He held her, not asking any questions. After a time, the warmth of his body and the strength of his arms revitalized her.

'Okay, I'm better now. Now tell me what's got you so excited.'

He showed her a printout of an e-mail message from Angus Macleod.

```
As you rightly surmised, finding a particu-
lar person of importance named Chan in the
Pearl River delta is not a task lightly to be
undertaken. We start with the problem that
there are twelve different characters that
can be used to represent the Romanized
(Cantonese) CHAN surname. In the absence of
the character your Chan uses, any attempt to
identify him would be fruitless. With
regret, A.M.
```

'That can't be all,' she said. 'Otherwise why are you so excited?'

'Luckily enough, I kept Mr Chan's business card – that's a great custom, exchanging business cards with everybody. The characters on the card are so small the fax blurs them, so it took some back and forth with Macleod for him to pick the right ones.'

'It's great you made friends with him the way you did.'

'I think he just likes a good puzzle. He seems to have gotten right to work on this one. We picked the name characters live on line with each other, and it only took him a few hours after that to follow up. I made that last call to you as soon as I got this.' He handed her some pages from his printer. The top one read:

```
Having  the  Chinese  name  characters  was  a
considerable  aid.  Unfortunately,  we  could
not  find  mention  of  a  person  named  Chan  with
the  offered  given  names.  This  does  not  mean
your  man  is  unknown  here,  since  it  is  common
for  traditional  Chinese  men  to  have  several
given  names  which  they  use  according  to  the
circumstance.  In  particular  there  may  be  a
courtesy  name  and  the  equivalent  of  one  or
more  nicknames,  as  well  as  the  person's
original  given  name.  I  have  made  some
inquiries  of  people  in  Guangdong  on  the
subject  of  prominent  men  named  Chan  of
approximately  the  correct  age,  and  with
their  help  I  have  secured  press  photographs
of  several  candidates.  I  have  had  my  people
enhance  them  slightly  for  transmission.  If
the  images  you  receive  are  inadequate,  do
please  let  me  know  and  we  shall  try  again.
Please  advise  further  if  you  locate  your
Chan  Kwok-Wing.  Cheers.  A.M.
```

'I couldn't resist looking at them,' he confessed. 'See what you think.'

The pictures were contrasty and lacking in fine detail, with areas that were too muddy to decipher.

'Is this him?' Susan pointed at a figure on a reviewing stand.

'Could be. Let's put that one aside.'

Two pictures later she said, 'There.' A man at a lectern making a speech. 'I think that's him.'

'Okay. If that's what he looks like in a not-so-hot newspaper photo, let's look at that other one again.'

'It's him,' Susan said. 'It is. Standing right there among the dignitaries looking very important.'

'I wasn't sure at first, myself, but I think you're right. I picked the same two pictures.'

They sat contemplating the pictures. It made her feel dislocated and apprehensive seeing Chan looking so . . . official.

'Hey!' David said. 'Who's this over here? The one in the military uniform next to the tall guy in the middle?'

Susan looked. 'It can't be. Can it? Yu Wenli?'

'Why not? He's the one Chan went to for answers about your parents. They must know each other.'

'He's in uniform. And this is recent. So he must still be an Army officer.'

'All of the above,' David said.

'Is there anything that tells what the pictures are?'

'There's a list. The one of Chan at the podium is "provincial vice-chairman in charge of industrial development addresses businessmen's meeting." '

'Provincial vice-chairman.'

'In charge of industrial development. That's what it says.'

'What's the other one?'

'Provincial government officials and regional commanders of the People's Liberation Army view October tenth parade celebrating founding of People's Republic.'

'I don't believe it,' Susan said. 'Are we sure it's him?'

'It's not a great picture. I'll e-mail Macleod right away to see if he has more caption material and maybe some other pictures. I think he purposely didn't send us the names so we'd have to go strictly by appearance. And I didn't ask him about Yu. I will this time.'

# 7

'No point sitting here waiting,' David said after he'd sent the message to Hong Kong. 'He'll get it and turn it around and I'll check in with my e-mail every half-hour.'

'Fifteen minutes?'

'If you want.'

She looked around. 'So this is where you live . . .'

'Home sweet home.'

'Give me a tour?'

'Not much to see. Feel free to take a look.'

He walked with her while she explored.

'Is this is your room? With the computer?'

'For now. And Alice is at the end of the hall in what's usually my bedroom. Jessica is in the bedroom in between, and Zack got the dining room. He's sort of camping out there.'

'Where are they all?'

'Away for the weekend.'

'It's a nice apartment, I like the way it rambles.'

'It's great when it's just me. At the moment we could use another bathroom and a couple of extra bedrooms. And a separate phone line or two, with their own answering machines.'

He made them some coffee and they went into the living room to talk about what they'd learned.

'Before we start,' she said, 'you have to tell me where your friend at the Royal *Hong Kong* Racecourse Association gets such good information about officials in Guangdong.'

'I think he's well-connected all up and down the coast. The RA does consulting work for the provincial governments. They're major experts on large-project design and project management. Computers and telecommunications, too. They're right close to home for people in eastern China, and as a bonus for Guangdong, almost everybody at the RA speaks at least some Cantonese.'

'Good thing for us.' Susan kicked off her shoes and stretched her legs out on the couch. 'All right, I'm ready.'

'Let's start with Mr Chan. He's a major provincial official in Guangdong province – a fact he did not want us to know. He's connected in some way with Yu Wenli, who we now think may be a regional commander of the Army.'

'Chan said he and the Engs are in business with the Army, remember?'

'Right.'

'Chan was very concerned about what happened to all that money Martin Eng had around, and Martin was worried about what Chan wanted to know and his reaction to what we said about the money.' Susan picked at a loose thread on the couch. 'It looks as if our conversation with Chan was a lot more important than we thought.'

'It looks that way. The tape, too.'

'What about the tape?'

'I heard from Jon. There's data on it.'

She wasn't surprised, and yet it was a blow. 'It all makes me feel so dumb.'

'They fooled me as much as you, and they did help you learn about your parents.'

'Yes, but—'

'Whatever we did is done. The question is, what do we do next?'

She couldn't help thinking how much that sounded like her father – the past is over, only the future matters. But for her father and mother the past *had* mattered – it had reached out and taken away their future . . .

She shook her head to banish the thought. 'We have to assume that Chan is a big player in whatever Martin and Meiling are up to . . . at least that he has some kind of serious interest in the money.'

'Right,' David agreed. 'But what?'

'That's the frustrating part. At least our old theory gave us a starting point.'

'Let's take it from a different angle,' he suggested. 'Start with the Eng and Cheung families. They were friends and supporters of Sun Yatsen's, but they were close to the left wing of his party – the earliest serious Communists in China. They knew Chiang Kai-shek, too, but whatever connection they had with him and the right wing of the Nationalist Party wasn't enough to protect them from being brutalized when his troops took over south China after the Second World War. So both families had to flee to Hong Kong.'

'But then Martin and Meiling went back to China after the Communists were in power,' Susan said. 'And they kept running their factory, not only up to the time it was nationalized but right on after that.'

'So they must have had family connections in the Communist Party at least as high as the regional government,' David deduced. 'They were major capitalists, after all, and the worst that happened to them in almost fifteen years living under the Communists – through all kinds of purges and anti-this-and-that campaigns – was that Martin spent a couple of years in jail. And came right back to his family and his factory.

'Then,' he continued, 'at the beginning of the Cultural Revolution, when good Party officials were starting to be deposed wholesale by mad bands of students, and killed or jailed or sent to the inner provinces to work on farms, the Engs finally decided they had to flee again. Which means that their family's Communist past wasn't pure enough to get by that kind of crazed scrutiny.'

'The old connection to Chiang Kai-shek can't have helped,' Susan said. 'And all their protectors were probably being deposed, too.'

'You're right, that's probably the biggest part of it. Didn't Yu say something about having suffered during the Cultural Revolution?'

'I think he said he was reformed. That probably means a long time in jail or at hard labor, maybe torture to make him confess his crimes, plus endless indoctrination sessions.'

'So Martin and Meiling saw there was no one to protect them and they fled to Hong Kong in a panic, probably just in time, and from Hong Kong they came here.'

'It's amazing to think that with all they've been through in China and Hong Kong they can have been in the U.S. thirty years,' Susan reflected. 'I have to keep reminding myself they're almost eighty, and they were in their forties when they got here.'

'And since then Martin has been an entrepreneur and community association head, and at the same time a scholar of Chinese history under the Mandarin form of his name.'

'And now that people like Chan and Yu are back in power,' Susan observed, 'they're all in business together.'

'Speaking of Yu, we're overdue to check the computer.'

YOU HAVE MAIL David read off the computer screen. 'Let's see.' Susan watched him play the keyboard, making text jump on the screen. 'There it is,' he said.

'Where? All I see is strange abbreviations.'

'That's the addresses and the routing information. Look under that, where it says, Chan Ka Kim, former Colonel of the People's Liberation Army, Guangdong provincial official since 1982, currently vice-chairman in charge of industrial development. Okay, we knew that last part.'

'But not about the Army.'

'No.' He hit another key and the text scrolled up the screen. 'And look at that. Yu Wenli, senior officer of the People's Liberation Army since World War Two, stripped of rank and re-educated, 1967-1976. Currently regional vice-commander.'

And there were more photos too – from the Politics Department at HKIT. You see - we're not only a technical university, Macleod had written.

The new pictures left no doubt: Vice-chairman Chan and Regional Vice-commander Yu were the men they had met.

'So now we know,' David said. 'We were in some impressive company.'

'But what does it add up to?'

A noise from the direction of the living room made Susan jump. 'What was that?'

'The front door.' David was getting up from the computer.

'You think they're coming after us?' Susan was joking but there was a tremor in her voice.

It was a boy and a girl – the niece and nephew David had talked about. Perfect twelve-year-olds, Susan thought: thin and full of energy, both of them vibrant with health. They were darker than David but Susan saw a family resemblance in the clean lines of cheekbone and brow, the strong, straight nose.

'Where's your mom?' David asked them.

'Parking the rent-a-car,' the girl said. 'Hi, who're you?'

'I'm Susan.'

'I'm Jessica.'

'I thought you might be. And you must be Zack.'

'How come you know our names? What'd he tell you about us?' Zack demanded.

'Wouldn't you like to know.'

'You're teasing, right?' Jessica said.

'Right.'

'Are you his girlfriend?' Zack asked.

'I guess directness runs in the family,' Susan said.

'Did you meet him in China?'

Susan looked at David before she answered. 'I met him in court.'

'Were you on the grand jury? Cool,' Jessica said, and to David, 'You didn't tell us you had a girlfriend there.'

'In case you hadn't noticed, it's the middle of the night,' David said. 'Time for you two to get into bed and stop doing your best to embarrass all of us.'

'I'm not embarrassed,' Jessica said, deadpan. 'Are you, Zack?'

'Nope.'

'See,' David said. 'That's what happens when you tease them.'

While David was making more coffee, his sister came in, dripping wet.

'It's pouring out there. Hi, I'm Alice. You must be the one from the grand jury.'

'Yes.' As opposed to the one from . . . where? 'Susan . . . Chan.'

'Well, it's nice to meet you finally. Sorry things are so cramped around here.' Alice yawned. 'I don't guess you'll mind if I get dry and shuffle off to bed.'

★　★　★

David poured them both coffee and they went into his cramped bedroom-office. Susan sat on the convertible couch and David took the computer chair.

'Okay,' he began, 'we have a couple of people here who seem to have much better connections with the power structure than they want to let on.'

'Locally, at least.'

'Right – the governing hierarchy, civilian and military, in Guangdong province, where the Eng and Cheung families came from.'

'At a time when the governmental future of the whole country is in question.'

'And one of the principal questions is the balance of power between the regions and the central government.'

'Or even whether the country is going to hold together at all,' Susan said. 'If we can believe what we heard yesterday.'

'And with everything in flux a person might want to cement his connections with the people he thought would come out on top after it all shakes out.'

'True.'

'And we're talking about a country where people as a matter of course engage in behavior idealistic Americans like you and me tend to lump under the heading "corruption," a word that was on everyone's lips at that cocktail party,' David said.

'Even though they execute people for that sort of thing . . . I don't know about you, but the death penalty would make me think twice about taking a few dollars under the table.'

'Me, too. But they find ways to get around it. Mr Li told me a story about that while you were sleeping in the van.'

'Poor Mr Li.' Not a memory Susan wanted to dwell on. 'What kind of story?'

'About installing a fancy new high-capacity boiler in a factory he was managing, and how the city inspector came and told him it didn't pass because the welds were bad. But it was a state-of-the-art boiler from West Germany and the welds had all been X-rayed or radiographed so Mr Li knew they were fine. He asked what he could do to get approval and the inspector gave him the name of a repair company.

'So along comes the repair-company guy and walks around the

boiler, tapping it here and there and peering at it with a flashlight, just the way the inspector did. Then he opens the door to the oil burner and swings it back and forth and clucks his tongue. He takes an ordinary ballpeen hammer and gives the hinge of the oil-burner door a whack, then he smiles and says "okay now" and hands Mr Li a bill for ten thousand dollars, U.S., which Mr Li pays on the spot. Next day, the inspector comes by and gives him the okay to run his boiler.'

'And the repairman was the inspector's brother.'

'Close – the repair company was owned by the inspector's cousin.'

'Not very imaginative,' Susan said.

'But apparently it did the trick. And maybe that's the moral of the story – death penalty or no, they don't even bother to be all that imaginative about it.'

'You think Martin Eng's money was to bribe somebody in China . . . Chan maybe, since he was so nervous about the money?'

'I think we ought to follow the idea out – that Martin was either going to bribe Chan or send money to him so he could bribe someone else.'

'Maybe that's why there were those labels on the money,' Susan suggested. 'To identify who was getting the bribes.'

'And that's why Martin kept the ledger, to keep track of who was getting bribed.'

'And the whole thing was a record of bribes? Because Martin had been sending bribe money over to China for years? And it added up to twenty-five million dollars?'

'I don't know . . . I like it about the labels and the ledger, but I have the feeling something doesn't fit. Let's leave it there and come back.'

'I still want to know why their money had heroin on it,' Susan said. 'That always slips by somehow.'

'Could Chan be shipping heroin on the side?'

'Not to Martin and Meiling. The more I know about them the less I can imagine them involved with heroin. Look at how they were at that reception. Would they jeopardize all that?' She had an image of the cocktail party – the powerful and the would-be powerful . . . 'Those people aren't about to hang out with dope peddlers, and they certainly aren't going to take money from them.' And that answered another question. 'That's got to be why the Engs were so intent on avoiding publicity about the heroin charges. The more publicity there is, the more likely it is somebody might connect Martin Eng and Wu Chuming.'

'Don't you think those people would put two and two together anyway, just from what's already out there?'

'The police and prosecutors seem to know him only as Martin Eng. And how many people know Eng is the same as Wu?'

'And I suppose even if you do know, Martin Wu and Wu Chuming isn't exactly two and two.'

'Would you have thought twice about it, yourself, if Chan hadn't let Martin's Chinese name slip out like that?'

'Not a chance. So . . . we conclude that Chan wasn't shipping heroin to them on the side. That means you still think the heroin in their apartment was planted by Tony Ching and/or the police.'

'I'm not so sure about Tony Ching any more,' Susan said. 'I mean, it could be Tony Ching, but if Martin and Meiling are dabbling in power politics in Guangdong, who knows what kind of enemies they have? Or what those enemies might do to stop that money from getting over there to be put to whatever use Mr Chan and Mr Yu have for it.'

She stopped. 'What those enemies might do . . .' she repeated. 'Like kill June Eng.'

David nodded bleakly. 'It's a real possibility, isn't it?'

'I'm glad we gave them their tape,' she said. Wondering how close they had come to something truly dangerous.

David sipped at his coffee, apparently lost in thought. 'Ah!' he said.

'Yes? What?'

'Well, look. Who are they going to bribe over there?'

'I don't know. I haven't thought about it until just now.'

'And I don't know either. But you saw what it's like in Guangdong – all that construction, all those huge projects, hundred-thousand-dollar cars all over the place.'

'*Stolen* hundred-thousand-dollar cars.'

'Not all of them. Not even most of the ones we saw. The amount of money people are making has to be staggering.'

Susan nodded. 'They were talking about billionaires at that cocktail party.'

'Right. China has become a country where people with power can become U.S.-dollar billionaires in a few years. But how do you bribe someone who has a real shot at becoming a billionaire? Or even a hundred-millionaire? You'd have to be offering millions at least, don't you think?'

'There must be other people to bribe. People lower in the hierarchy who'd be happy with an extra hundred thousand. I know some people like that, myself,' she told him. 'And not what you'd call insignificant people, either.'

'Right, sure you do. Here.'

'Um.' He was right – it might not work to judge Chinese greed by American standards.

'And the people in China who'd be interested in smaller amounts of money are by definition people who can't get more,' he said. 'So how powerful can they be, over there? And what good does it do to bribe them? Remember, we're talking about a country where it takes ten thousand U.S. dollars just to buy a one-shot approval from a local boiler inspector.'

Susan thought about it. 'That's true, I suppose. It's not a bottom-up kind of culture, it's more top-down. You deal with the biggest shot possible, and everybody else scurries into line. She told him about Sunny and the fee she wasn't going to get from her canceled contract. She went to the top of the provincial government just for that. She used personal connections, so it wasn't a question of bribing anybody, and all she wanted was to have them honor a just debt . . . but she went all the way to the top. And the people who couldn't do that didn't get their invoices paid.'

'And we have to assume that a million and a half dollars – or even twenty-five million over a bunch of years – won't buy much at the top levels, especially if you're seriously bribing a lot of people.'

'What if it's just courtesy payments? Not bribes the way you're thinking, but money to remind people you're their friend. I think a lot of that goes on, too.'

'Okay. But why send money for that all the way to China from here? Or even swap it via gold shops?'

She rubbed her temples. 'That's a good question.'

'And where did Martin Eng get twenty-five million dollars to send from here to China, anyway? Unless you want to go back to his selling heroin.'

'No.' She was definite about that.

'And one big reason you say that is because if he did sell heroin it would jeopardize all those fancy American connections. Politicians and philanthropists, and investment bankers and national security advisers.'

'Right.'

'And why does he have all those connections?'

'Because he's legitimately a scholar and they legitimately like to hear him give speeches and talk to him at parties. I thought it was interesting yesterday – about the Three Kingdoms and the Warring States and the Yellow Emperor.'

'I suppose. And I suppose it's gratifying for him to have powerful people think he's smart. But it occurs to me that there might be other reasons to have friends like that, and something besides his grasp of history that buys him those connections.'

'What do you mean?'

'That he might be using better currency than clever speeches.'

She didn't say anything at first, just looked at him. 'It couldn't be.' The Engs bribing the people at that party, and others like them?

'Why not?'

'I just . . . it couldn't be.'

'Why not?' he persisted. 'It makes perfect sense. And I'll tell you what else – it explains why your federal subpoenas came from the Public Corruption Unit. Ryan was speculating how the immigration scheme might involve bribes to public officials who hand out visas, but I'll bet that for your average federal prosecutor, paying off visa clerks isn't nearly as sexy as bribing national security advisers and high-level government consultants.'

'God, how awful. It makes my skin crawl. All those fancy folks, fawning over Martin and Meiling – for *money*?'

'Sure,' he said. 'After all, not so long ago one of our beloved ex-presidents jumped to take a few million dollars from a foreign government that's arguably our economic enemy.'

'And two ex-presidents, knowingly or not, made a promotional video for the heirs of a Chinese heroin-importing family,' she added.

'If we can believe the cocktail party chatter.'

'Right. So it's not a stretch for all those big shots to be fawning over the Engs – excuse me, the Wus – in return for their every-so-often donation of sixty or eighty or a hundred thousand dollars.'

'But *why*?' she asked.

'There have to be a million reasons to buy influence with that kind of people. I doubt the Engs are doing it for themselves.'

'No, you're right. It would be for Chan and Yu . . .' She let it all sort itself out in her mind. It didn't make her happy. 'I have to admit it fits the facts a lot better than my romantic story of rescuing poor endangered Hong Kong people. That was a nice notion, all about solidarity and mutual assistance. This is different – this is the real world. They have so much money over there that they can buy influential Americans with what amounts to pocket change for them.'

'So what we're saying now is that the money came here from China,' David said, 'not the other way around.'

'It makes sense.' Though she hated to think about it.

'Via gold shops?'

'Let's say.'

'Then we're back to why did the money have heroin on it?'

'Detective Pullone could have put some white powder into the evidence bags when they seized it,' she said.

'That's fine for the money from the house – assuming he could sneak it in, or else that the whole squad of police was in on it. But what about the safe deposit boxes?'

For a moment they were both stumped.

'Wait a minute,' Susan said. 'We're forgetting something. If they got the money through the gold shops, then the actual physical money was here in this country all along.'

'It must have been,' David agreed. 'That's how it works, right?'

'That's how I think it works. Somebody brought money to the gold shop here and said I want to make this much money available in China. So the gold-shop owner made contact with another gold-shop owner in China – or Hong Kong – who was holding money to be matched up with money here. In this case, Chan's money.'

'Right.'

'Okay,' Susan said, 'then tell me this – who in New York wants to send twenty-five million dollars to China?'

David took a minute to see it. 'Heroin dealers?'

She leaned over to give him a kiss. 'It's perfect. It answers all the questions.'

'So it *is* heroin money, in a way,' David said. 'But the Engs didn't need to come anywhere near the heroin trade – or heroin traders – to get it.'

'And Detective Pullone planted the package of heroin in their house so he could make the arrests and take the money, the way I've been saying all along. And he just lucked out that the money had heroin on it.'

'We're still missing one thing,' David said. 'Exactly what are they trying to accomplish with the bribes?'

'You said yourself there are a million reasons to buy influence.'

'Yes . . .'

'Didn't somebody on the panel yesterday say that the American Government could tip the balance in Beijing by changing its policies in ways less obvious than the ones we usually hear about. He was talking about trade policy, but I'll bet it could be all kinds of things . . . military policy, international monetary policy, policy toward other countries on the Pacific Rim – South-east Asia and the Philippines in particular. Any of those things could have an effect on China.'

'We're really talking about this seriously, aren't we?' He was struck by the passion the idea had aroused in her. 'Trying to influence U.S. policy. It's so much bigger than anything we imagined.'

'But it makes sense. Look what happened just this summer when Congress decided it was okay to let the president of Taiwan come here for his college reunion. Just a small personal gesture, not an official visit, but small gestures about Taiwan have big meaning in China. And you can bet some people in Beijing lost a lot of face over it. That's why they did so much shouting and stamping their feet – withdrawing their ambassador from Washington and the rest of it – presumably to show the world the U.S. couldn't treat them badly and get away with it. But I'm sure a lot of that was really for internal consumption – damage control so somebody at the top would keep from seeming weak to the others in power.'

'And the idea would be that if every so often you can make a rival look bad or make yourself look good, then in the long run you come out way ahead of the game.'

'Yes, and the more often you can do it, the better. One incident wouldn't be enough to bring a powerful person down, but a lot could make a difference over time, even small things . . . Face is so important.'

The death of a thousand cuts, he thought.

'And I'll bet this isn't only about trying to influence U.S. policy,' Susan was saying. 'They'd want to buy information, too. That might be the most important. Policy information of all kinds. So their allies in China would know what was happening here, and they'd be in a better position to make accurate predictions about what the U.S. was about to do and to judge how it would respond to something they might do. And that way they'd also know who on this side would be receptive to a well-timed word in his ear. With darling Martin and Meiling right here in the States to do the whispering for them.'

'But policy-making is such a diffuse process,' David said, only partly playing devil's advocate. 'A lot of people get their oar in.'

'It's true that some kinds of policy take hundreds of people to make, but how many of those people have a real voice? If you can get to the right advisers – top advisers to significant people in the executive branch or to the congressional leadership, say – then you're more than halfway home. And even if it doesn't always work you'd want to be trying all the time, because the effects are probably cumulative, and you'd want the mechanisms in place as insurance in case anything truly major came up.'

'You're enjoying this,' David said and watched the words bring a smile to her face.

'What I'm saying horrifies me, but yes, I'm enjoying figuring it out, putting myself in the shoes of people with big ideas to sell. It's a lot like what I enjoy most about my work.

'And this is so clearly what's got to be happening. So deliciously devious, and in a genuinely Chinese kind of way. I can't tell you how many Chinese folk stories there are where the villain fools his victim with false advice. And the advice convinces the victim to help the villain get what he wants – at the victim's expense.'

650

# 8

'I guess we're going to give Mr Mahoney an earful tomorrow morning,' David said.

Susan looked at her watch. '*This* morning. It's almost two a.m., and all of a sudden I'm exhausted.'

The rain and their fatigue made David's crowded computer room seem more attractive than a trip to Susan's hotel. In the bathroom, Susan marveled that she was sharing David's toothbrush, an act that in her former fastidiousness she would have found impossible. That she could not only do it but even delight in the quiet intimacy of it told her how much she had changed. It was a revelation strong enough to push the night's conversation temporarily from her mind.

She got back to find the couch made into a bed, taking up almost all the floor space. David went to wash up. She undressed slowly, relishing each separate movement, feeling the texture of the cloth and the pleasantly cool air of the room on her bare skin. She lay down and let her hands roam over her body, feeling the intensity of the double touch: her fingers responding to the silky textures while her skin tingled with the warmth and pressure of her hands.

When David returned, he stood a moment admiring her and then, his eyes never leaving her, slipped off his shorts and lowered himself to the bed. They made urgent love and she plunged into sleep still wrapped around him.

They were jolted into bleary consciousness when the rest of the household erupted for Monday morning.

'What are they doing out there?' Susan asked. 'Rebuilding the place or demolishing it?'

'Weren't your kids like this?'

'I don't think so.' She kissed him good morning and slid the sheet down so she could admire his body. 'Do you think they'd hear us if we made love?'

'Depends on if we can be really quiet.'

They could, but it wasn't easy.


'We should go someplace and have some coffee,' David suggested.

'The hotel. Coffee and a shower and everything. I have to stop at home before we go to the lawyers, but there's time for both.'


Over room-service coffee they talked about what they were going to say to Mahoney.

'I don't think we should mention the tapes,' David said. 'Not without some assurance we won't be accused of conspiracy.'

'I thought what we say today can't be used against us, and that Ryan got them to agree they wouldn't use it for finding other evidence against us, either.'

'That's with Mahoney. But maybe the U.S. Attorney's office can use it, if what we say to Mahoney isn't secret.'

'We'll have to ask.' She was dismayed that the tapes continued to be a threat. 'I keep thinking how naive I was, not to realize there might be more on the tapes than they were telling me.'

'You couldn't know.'

'But *you* did – at least you suspected . . . And after last night I'm sure they have to be a major part of all this. Instructions from Chan and Yu to the Engs, reports from the Engs about what they've learned and what progress they've made. Maybe even lists of who got how much money . . . And I don't see how we can tell our story and hold that back.'

'If it will make you feel better, even if they had the tapes in their hands there's next to no chance Mahoney or anybody else in law enforcement would be able to find out what they say.'

'What do you mean? Why not?'

'Because there are too many ways to make codes unbreakable.

652

Unless you have the key to the code, or at least some part of it.'

'But the Government has whole agencies to do that.'

'And they're very good at it. I know, because some of that work I did with multiple-processor computers was for that very purpose.'

'And there are really codes they can't break?'

'There's an old motto – "the difficult we do immediately, the impossible takes a little longer." When it comes to decryption these days, the impossible sometimes takes longer than anybody could ever afford to spend.'

'Unless you have the key.'

'Right. Then you just feed everything to your computer and out comes the decrypted message. More or less.'

'Is there a different key for every message?'

'There could be, but it's not very efficient, because each time you'd have to find a secure way to get the new key to whoever you're communicating with. Usually, once you have a key established you stick with it for a while.'

'And if somebody else gets it, they can read all your messages.'

'No reason why not.'

They went over their theory again, trying to poke holes in it. The more they talked, the more convinced they both were that it fit the evidence too well for it to be anything but the truth.

'And the beautiful part about it from Martin's point of view,' Susan said, 'is that he's found a way to come right out in public and argue his case, and be applauded for it. Dine out on it.'

'You think that's what he's doing?'

'Well . . . he's a scholar of the earliest Chinese dynasties and the Warring States period and the Three Kingdoms. He writes his articles and goes to these meetings on rare occasions, and I'm sure he has a lot of private, intimate conversations with these people, and what he says, basically, is that we all ought to make ourselves comfortable with the idea of a relatively fragmented, decentralized China. That important growth in ancient Chinese history came in the periods of fragmentation, and that's what led to the strongest empires.

'And meanwhile his patrons in China are in the provincial government and the regional Army command group of Guangdong and south-east China. And his family's businesses link Guangdong and Hong Kong.'

'Greater South China is the only Greater China that makes sense,' David said, imitating the woman at the cocktail party.

'And you remember what Yu Wenli said – "*We have always been good revolutionaries in the South.*" '

'I was thinking about something you told me last night,' David said later. 'About Chinese folk tales that feature a villain who tricks the victim into acting against his own best interest.'

'By pretending to be a friend who's giving the victim helpful advice.'

'It occurred to me that Martin and Meiling are playing a sort of variation on that theme. Bribing some of these people to do what they already think good for this country. It seems to me there have always been people who believe it's best for the U.S. if China isn't a single, strong, unified entity. And if you're going to corrupt people it's got to be easiest to corrupt them in a direction they're already inclined to take. Some of these folks may be accepting the bribes and listening to the Engs and then just doing a pumped-up version of what comes naturally.'

'But they're not doing it naturally,' Susan argued. 'They're doing it because somebody paid them to. And there must be people who think the other way, too – that the U.S. can benefit from good relations with a strong central government in Beijing.

'The point is,' she said with real heat, 'decisions like that shouldn't be made because American policy-makers are secretly on the payroll of one side or the other in China's internal power struggle.'

'It's getting late,' Susan realized. 'I want to get over to the apartment and say goodbye to Lara before she heads back to college. I just have time to do that and meet you at the lawyers' office.'

'Okay.' He kissed her.

'Don't start without me.'

Mahoney kept his eyes on Ned King's golf trophies while Laurie Jordan played the tape of El Coyote's conversation with Mick Pullone.

He was aware of Ned King and Max Straus and the Copperhead listening intently. In the easy chair in the other corner of the room, beyond Mahoney's peripheral vision, the District Attorney was a silent presence.

Mahoney hadn't been able to figure out an appropriate attitude for listening to the tape, had bounced the question off Joe Estrada: they'd decided on emotionless and efficient, not a trace of gloating or I-told-you-so. It was good in theory, but listening again to Pullone bad-mouthing him it was hard to stay calm.

The room was silent when Jordan clicked off the tape.

The Chief of Investigation spoke first. 'Nice work. Very nice,' he said. 'It's a great first step. Let's see if we can keep the rest just as neat. Pullone is the key – he's been at this a long time, and there's no reason to assume he just got dirty. We're going to nail him and we're going to nail everybody who's had any piece of it with him. Especially Kevin Horgan.'

'Ned's right.' The District Attorney's voice was as strong and dignified as the man; it would have drawn everybody's attention even if he hadn't been the Boss. 'Horgan has got to be first and foremost. I want whatever dirty cops we can get, too, but no one case is going to wash out those stables. An A.D.A. who's wrong is another matter, entirely. I will not tolerate that for one minute.

'I want Kevin Horgan, and I don't want him slipping out through a hole in the evidence or a crack in the procedure. This is a personal priority for me.'

He stood up – tall and gaunt, dressed like a diplomat – nodded at them, and left the office.

'I don't have to tell you the Boss doesn't talk like that every day,' Ned King said. 'From now on, Kevin Horgan is job one.'

Straus said, 'That means when we go for Pullone we have to be all set up and ready for Horgan, too. It's got to be absolutely smooth and seamless.'

'You have enough manpower?' King asked the Official Corruption Unit Chief.

'As long as you're paying for the overtime.'

'Whatever you need,' King assured him.

The Copperhead, sleepy-looking as ever, nodded. 'Good.'

655

Mahoney watched his hooded eyes fasten on Jordan. 'We'll be ready.' It was both a promise to King and a warning to Jordan.

'What's the plan?' King asked.

Jordan said, 'We'll want to follow Pullone right after he signs out for his RDOs –' regular days off – 'to give ourselves the biggest window before anybody misses him. We need to check how that fits with where Horgan will be, to make sure we can get to him when we need to.'

'Let me know your schedule as soon as you have it,' King told her. 'I'm going to keep the Boss a hundred percent up to date, but I don't want to bring Internal Affairs on board any sooner than I absolutely have to.'

'I've got the grand jurors coming in this morning,' Mahoney said. 'They may have some information we can use.'

'Good,' Straus said. 'Whatever they have, we need it.'


On the way into the apartment Susan saw Lara's backpack and garment bag by the door. She called out, got no answer. A quick look around confirmed that Lara wasn't home.

Susan waited, fretting about where Lara might be, checking the clock. She thought of calling Ryan to see if he could postpone their meeting at the D.A.'s office, but that seemed wrong. Mahoney had been so full of urgency, and knowing what she did now his concern didn't seem overdone.

She got out her stationery and wrote a note—

Darling Lara,

We have so much to talk about and I wish we could have started this morning but I have to run off to my lawyers' office. After the grand jury and Hong Kong and China it's finally time for me to strike a few serious blows for truth and justice.

If you get this before eleven or so, please call me at the lawyers' to say goodbye.

She signed it 'with much love' and added Ryan and Miller's phone number. She sealed the note in an envelope and left it on top of Lara's backpack.

★ ★ ★

The doorman offered to get Susan a cab, but she saw there were none in sight on Park Avenue so she headed for the corner, where she might be able to intercept one headed crosstown.

'Excuse me.' A man's voice, heavily accented. Asian.

She turned. He was no taller than she, stocky in a muscular sort of way, with a moon face and narrow eyes.

'Yes?' Ready to pretend she was someone else. She didn't think they could serve a subpoena if you didn't admit who you were.

'Excuse me.' He seemed to be having trouble finding the next word. He said something in rapid Cantonese.

She shook her head – *don't understand* – and looked closer. South China, she thought, and his unruly shock of coarse black hair made her think he was from the mainland. He was younger than he looked at first glance, a lot younger than the man who had served the federal subpoena.

'Lost,' he finally squeezed out. 'Rock' fell' Cent'.'

Not a subpoena, then. She pointed. 'That way.'

He looked, nodded. He was not menacing in any way, yet she was uneasy. All that talk last night of the Engs . . .

'Fifth Avenue.' She held up her hand with the fingers spread.

'Say, driver?'

At first she didn't get it, then she looked toward the curb and saw a black sedan with another stocky Chinese man in a business suit standing by the open driver's door. Even younger than the moon-faced one.

Maybe they'd seen her come out of the building, stopped because she was Chinese. She wanted to be done with this. 'Fifth Avenue,' she said to the driver, pointing west. 'Downtown,' pointing south.

He smiled at her and opened the rear door. She moved to let the other man get in but found that he was close beside her.

His hand gripped her elbow. 'Get in car, please.'

She started to pull away but he moved his free hand and she saw a large black pistol, concealed from the world by their bodies and the car. The driver was still smiling at her, almost bowing, as if she were an honored guest.

She tried to stifle her panic. 'No. You're making a mistake,' she said, knowing they weren't.

'In car, Chan Huiling.' He squeezed her elbow sharply and pain cut away her thoughts of resistance. She stumbled on the curb as she moved toward the car. The driver caught her arm and between them the men pushed her into the rear seat with enough force to topple her onto her side. In the confusion that preceded terror, *he knows my name* was the only coherent thought she could manage.

David felt odd in the hotel room without Susan. He was apprehensive about the upcoming meeting with Mahoney. How much of what they had figured out about the Engs did the prosecutor already know? Was this what he'd meant when he told Susan they were in over their heads, and that it had international implications?

He went over their reasoning, reviewing the pictures and text he'd gotten from Macleod. It made even more sense this time.

He put the printouts in his backpack and left the hotel. It was a clear day, the sky washed a brilliant blue where he could see it at the ends of the streets and in the rare gaps between midtown skyscrapers.

By the time Susan had recovered enough to get herself sitting upright, the car was on its way down Park Avenue. She felt a sting in her side, looked to see that Moonface had replaced his gun with a long, thin-bladed knife.

'No move, no speak,' he said.

She couldn't completely stifle the protests that arose in her: there must be a misunderstanding, this would accomplish nothing . . . When she opened her mouth to speak, the knife bit into her side. She choked back the words.

Fear warred in her with fury, leaving her in a state of false calm: This had to be about the Engs. But what? And how? She told herself there must be a simple explanation. But she had nothing anyone wanted, posed a threat to no one . . . No, of course that wasn't true – she had been on her way to expose the Engs's true crimes to the man who was already prosecuting them as heroin dealers. Except how could anyone have known that? Even her own lawyers still thought she was going to refuse to cooperate . . .

The car entered the Queens-Midtown Tunnel. In the sudden dimness Moonface growled, 'Lift sleeve.'

She looked at him, uncomprehending.

He said it again, and again she did nothing. He grabbed her wrist and with a deft flick of the knife slit the sleeve of her jacket to the elbow. The tip of the knife left a thin trail of blood on her arm.

Swiftly, he wrapped her upper arm with a length of rubber surgical tubing. She didn't see where it had come from. As swiftly, the knife was back in his hand, the tip pricking gently at the side of her neck. She sat immobile, in terror again at the thought of what might be coming next. Someone had killed June Eng with a knife, horribly.

With his free hand, Moonface opened a leather case and extracted a syringe and hypodermic needle. The knife momentarily laid aside, he again clamped her wrist painfully in one hand and with the other he injected something into the swollen vein at her elbow. Immediately, he whipped the tourniquet from her arm.

She had a moment of stark fear – had he given her something fatal? – and then pleasure washed over her, warm and frighteningly welcome, suffusing her limbs and making her whole body tingle, almost too intense. Her stomach roiled with it, heaved. There was a white bucket held ready, a hand directing her face toward it and even with her stomach clenching she could think only of the pleasure.

As the light of Queens rose ahead of them in the tunnel, she sensed that she was being laid down on her side, a blanket wrapped around her shoulders.


David got to the lawyers' office five minutes late. The reception area was empty: he assumed Susan was already in with the lawyers. Kassia Miller came out and brought him to the same conference room where they'd had their original conversation.

'Susan isn't here yet,' she told him.

There was coffee on the sideboard, and the morning's papers. At Miller's suggestion he helped himself to both. Twenty minutes later he had drunk too much coffee and absorbed none of the news he'd read.

There was a phone next to the coffee maker. He picked it up, uncertain how to get an outside line. The conference-room door opened. It was Miller, alone.

'Susan still hasn't arrived,' she said, 'and it's getting close to the time we have to leave. Do you have any idea where she could be?'

'I was just going to make some calls.'

Susan didn't answer the phone at the hotel. At her office, neither Mona nor Annette had heard from her.

'She said she had an appointment outside the office,' Annette told him. 'We don't expect her until this afternoon.'

He called his own number. The machine informed him – in Zack's voice – that he could leave a message for Alice or for the twins. Nothing about David Clark. And it didn't respond to his call-in code.

'When Susan left me she was going home to see her daughter,' he told Miller. 'They'd been having some family trouble and I know Susan was upset about it. It's possible she got so involved talking to her daughter she lost track of the time.'

'Did you try her there?' Miller asked.

'I don't think her husband would respond too well to hearing from me. I assume he's at the hospital, but if he isn't, if he's at home . . .'

'I'll call, then,' Miller said.

'I don't think she's told him about any of this – Mahoney, or the subpoena.'

'I can be a new friend as easily as a lawyer.'

David checked Susan's home number in his electronic agenda, dialed it and handed Miller the phone. She got an answering machine, left her name and number. 'Please call right away,' she said to the machine, and to David, 'What about a cell phone? Or a car phone?'

'She doesn't believe in cell phones, but I think her car service has phones in the cars.'

'Do you know which one she uses?'

'No, sorry.'

'But if that was how she was coming, she'd have a phone.'

'She might. But she takes cabs, too. Even the subway, sometimes.'

'All right, let's give it another little while. She could just be caught in traffic. I'll go tell Michael.'

Miller returned quickly. 'Michael is calling Mahoney to say we've been delayed and we'll be at least a half-hour late. Meanwhile, he wants to know if you got the tape back.'

The tape! 'No, damn it, we've been so busy . . . I did send an e-mail

660

message to hurry my friend along, but I haven't checked for a response since last night.'

'You can log in from here.'

'The message'll be encrypted. It won't mean anything if I get it from here.'

'How about calling?'

He tried, got Jon's machine, left a message. He wondered if Susan had left a message on his machine. It made him furious not to be able to get through.

'You know,' he said, 'if we've got a few minutes, as long as Susan isn't here yet, I could be home and back fairly soon . . . check the e-mail, fix my answering machine . . .'

'What's wrong with your machine?'

'I think my niece and nephew were playing with it before they went away for the weekend, so they could get messages from their friends.'

'I don't think you should worry about it. And I definitely don't think you should leave. Susan could turn up any minute.'

'But she could be trying to get me, too, and so could my friend with the tape.' David was more worried about Susan than he wanted to let on. He felt like he was imprisoned here, his hands tied.


Susan was in the dark. She was sitting on the floor, propped in a corner. Her hands were bound behind her and her arms were bound above the elbows. Her legs were stretched out in front of her, tied at the ankles and above the knees.

There was a thin strip of light coming under the door, not enough for her to see anything. But she knew where she was. She was in a closet. Not a very big closet.

She hadn't been gagged and her nose wasn't covered so breathing was okay, though the heavy, stagnant air was pungent with frightened sweat and there was a sour taste of stomach juices in her mouth.

Her whole body was still filled with pleasure, like an intense and lingering sexual afterglow. The details of the world seemed distant and blurred – the closet, the way she was tied, the foul air. Tendrils of panic plucked at her mind but could not take hold. What had they given her? Heroin? Or something else?

She wriggled a little, trying to find a more comfortable position. Not to get out, she just wanted to be less burdened . . . Her bonds wouldn't budge, but that was all right. She thought of calling out, but if she was quiet maybe the men who brought her here would leave her alone, and that was better. All she wanted was to have the world leave her alone.

# 9

Kassia Miller brought David into Michael Ryan's office. There was still no word from Susan. They'd called the hotel again, and Susan's home and office.

'The only other thing I can think of is her son,' David said. 'If there was a crisis . . .'

'Do you know where he is?' Miller asked.

'A clinic in the Midwest. That's all I know.'

'We'll have to call the husband about that,' Ryan said.

Miller picked up the phone. David listened, fascinated, as she bluffed her way past telephone operators, medical secretaries and nurses.

'I'm sorry to bother you, Dr Linwood,' she said when she reached him. 'I'm a friend of Susan's and we were supposed to meet about something important. She's over an hour late, and no one seems know—'

Cut off by whatever Linwood said, she fought her way back into the conversation. 'But it's not like her—' Cut off again, she kept trying. 'I was afraid it might be something about Charles—' . . . 'I know he's been in detox, so I was afraid—' . . . 'Only because Susan is so reliable—'

She hung up. 'Charming fellow. I'd say he doesn't know where his wife is, and I doubt there's any emergency with the son. Even when he asked why I thought there might be trouble, it was just a way to dismiss me. Either the boy's all right, or Dr Richard Linwood has icewater in his veins.'

'It's a good bet he does,' David said. 'But not where his son is concerned.'

663

'She's almost an hour late, now,' Ryan said to him. 'She didn't strike me as a person who'd stay out of touch that long.'

'Not if she could help it.' It was just a standard expression, the sort of thing people said, but once said the words called up more than David had intended.

Ryan apparently heard it the same way. 'It may be time for us to consider that,' he said. 'That she's out of touch because she *can't* help it. That she's been in an accident, for instance.'

'Unless she left a message on my answering machine. If she did, she may think it's all taken care of.'

'Even so,' Ryan said, 'wouldn't she have called here? She knows this is where you'd be.'

'If what she's doing is important enough to make her this late, maybe she doesn't want to interrupt it any more than she has to.' But David could see that Ryan had made up his mind how to handle this.

'We need to call Mahoney,' Ryan said. 'He's expecting us. We'll have to tell him we don't know where Susan is or why she isn't here—'

'Why?' As far as David could see, Mahoney was no friend of theirs. 'Can't we just postpone this, say Susan is sick or something like that, until we know more?'

'No, we can't, and if we tried we wouldn't fool him. But whatever we say about Susan, Mahoney is going to want to see *you* right away.'

'Not a chance. Not without Susan.'

That didn't make Ryan happy. 'I have to tell you that trying to avoid Mahoney isn't a good idea. He'll know something's going on, and he'll know he's not getting the cooperation he needs. So instead of a potential ally, we'll have an enemy. And we need him as an ally.'

'Why?'

'To keep the federal grand jury off your backs, for one. Not to mention Mahoney himself.'

'The most important thing right now,' Miller said, 'is that Dan Mahoney is a lot better equipped to find out about Susan than we are. If there is some reason she can't be in touch with us . . . if there's been an accident . . . the D.A.'s office has lists of hospitals and police stations to call, and they're in a much better position than we are to get answers.'

That was the heart of it, David thought, never mind alliances with Mahoney. Finding Susan was what mattered. 'All right. If he can help find out where Susan is . . . but I won't talk to him about anything except that.'

Mahoney, waiting in an office at the Official Corruption Unit for Susan Linwood and David Clark and their lawyers, was running out of patience by the time Kassia Miller called. When he got off the phone, he called Joe Estrada.

'I just heard from your friend Miller. She says Linwood's still not there. They want me to check the hospitals and police stations and all the rest of it.'

'You're looking for more reassurance that they're being straight with you?'

'Something like that.'

'She's too good a lawyer not to be straight about something like that,' Estrada said. 'Anyway, what are you thinking of besides an accident?'

'Murder, kidnapping, and flight due to a consciousness of guilt all come to mind.'

'If you've got that kind of mind,' Estrada said. 'I don't know about murder and kidnapping, but I'd say people like your grand jurors don't run. They hire tough lawyers like Michael Ryan and Kassia Miller, and they stand and fight.'

'I suppose you're right – they're too well-established and tied-down to run. Linwood, anyway. That must have been wishful thinking. Settling disputes by murder and kidnapping are altogether too common in Chinatown, and I don't like the picture either one of them makes.'

In the dark closet Susan had slid herself into a position that took some of the strain off her neck and shoulders. Her head was resting against the wall, comfortable enough so she was less distracted by the awkward way she was bound.

There was no sound from beyond the closet door. Maybe there was no one out there. Or maybe they were just sitting very still. Could anyone sit that still? She could, feeling this way.

But maybe it wasn't good to sit so still, all tied up like this. She had a dreamy sense that she should avoid whatever it was that happened when your circulation was cut off for too long. She had no idea how long that was. But what did it matter if she was going to die here anyway?

Alone in the lawyers' conference room, David felt imprisoned more than ever.

Mahoney had started the search, but in the meantime he was insisting that David come in and answer questions: if Mahoney knew the whole story, Ryan and Miller had said, it would help him find Susan. David didn't believe that was the real reason. A list of hospitals was a list of hospitals.

He was worried about all the things that had so far gone unspoken. There had been so much violence – the deadly roadblock in China, the murder of June Eng . . . Knowing now the real stakes for the Engs and for Chan and Yu, David knew too that the lives of two nosy grand jurors were insignificant in comparison.

But the Engs couldn't know that he and Susan had planned to talk to Mahoney, any more than they could know that he and Susan had figured out what they were up to.

Or maybe they could, depending on what they had made of Susan and David's presence at the China Society. At the least they would want to know why he and Susan had been there. He doubted the Engs would do anything extreme, not until they knew more. Might they waylay Susan and hold her somewhere – in effect, kidnap her – to get answers to their questions? They might. Would they hurt her? The threat to hook Charles on heroin seemed more their style. Wu Chu-ming would exert pressure through the mind, indirectly.

As for the Engs's enemies, that was a different story. Presumably, they had already killed June Eng. Possibly they had arranged the roadblock. But why would they target Susan? For the tape? The Engs had the tape, not Susan . . . though their enemies might not know that.

He had to do something – at least find out if Susan had tried to reach him . . . or if someone else had. If he left here now he'd be out of touch for a half-hour on his way home, but when he got there he'd know.

How much of a problem was that half-hour? If Susan was okay but delayed for some reason, it didn't matter if he was in touch or not. If she *wasn't* okay – hit by a car, say, or something worse – then there was nothing he could do to help, and it didn't matter where he was, either.

The only way he could make a difference to Susan was if she was trying to get him, or if someone who knew what had happened to her was trying to get him. And then it *did* matter where he was.

Because anyone who tried to reach him here would at least get Miller or Ryan. But if there was someone who was trying him only at home – Susan, if she had a reason not to call here, or someone else who didn't know anything about their connection with Ryan and Miller or didn't want to call a lawyers' office – then he needed to be at home, or at least to fix his answering machine or forward his calls. Otherwise he would miss the information he most needed and Susan most needed him to have.

Even as that thought formed in his mind, he was walking to the reception area and through, with a pleasant nod to the woman at the desk. The elevator came quickly, before anyone noticed he wasn't where they wanted him to be.

He was ignoring his lawyers' advice, David thought as he waited on the subway platform, and maybe that wasn't smart. On the other hand, he barely knew them and had no way to tell what their priorities were. They'd promised Mahoney he'd have a witness – maybe something rode on that for them. Maybe if they didn't deliver they'd lose credibility that was a vital part of their professional capital. Lose face.

Still, they were the only defense he had against Mahoney and the rest of them. Just walking out on them without a word was not a good idea. He found their card in his wallet and called from the pay phone on the platform.

'Where are you?' Ryan demanded. 'We just heard from Susan's daughter. She says Susan was on her way here more than two hours ago. She left a note that she was running to see her lawyers. Something's definitely wrong. You could be in serious danger out there. We've got to get you protected.'

'I have to go home, first.' If Susan had left some kind of message . . .

The express train roared around the corner and into the station, pushing a blast of air ahead of it, erasing Ryan's words.

'This is my tràin.'

The brakes squealed as the train pulled to a halt.

'—investigator. Craig Lawrence. He'll meet you at your place. Don't go anywhere or do anything without him.'

'Got it.' He dove for the door as the chime sounded, just slipped in between the closing doors.

As the express raced uptown, David's thoughts raced faster. Could the Engs's enemies have been at that symposium, too? And could they have recognized him and Susan? Surprising if they *didn't*, he thought: we've been front and center with the Eng family on both sides of the globe by now.

So if anybody had kidnapped Susan, it suddenly seemed all too likely to be not the Engs but their enemies. The people who had sliced June Eng to death.

Susan still tingled with pleasure. But she could feel the panic rising in the back of her mind. At some point her jailers – whoever they were – were going to come back and kill her. Or they would just leave her here. Get killed themselves or be chased away or get stoned and forget her . . . and she would be left tied up in a closet with no food and no water and no way to get any. And she would die here. Eventually. And there was nothing she could do about it.

She was getting tired. She wanted to go to sleep, but she didn't want to. Everything was so dreamy and so frightening. It was hot and stuffy in the closet like the inside of a coffin. But it would be good to sleep.

There was a gray 4 x 4 double-parked in front of David's apartment building. Ryan's investigator?

As David got closer he saw a Chinese youth lounging against the 4 x 4's front fender. Before David could react, the youth spotted him. He pushed himself upright and beckoned.

'Hey, Klok!'

He was smiling, working hard to look friendly, David thought. As good a way as any to begin an abduction in the bright light of day. The youth headed toward the sidewalk, on an interception course. The engine of the utility vehicle turned over and caught.

David picked up his pace. The elevator operator wasn't in sight: there would be no safety in the empty lobby. And running wouldn't accomplish much. The young man approaching him looked fit and quick, and in any case David wasn't about to outrun the vehicle.

He scanned the street for Ryan's investigator. Nothing but parked cars. A woman pushing a stroller.

He stopped. If he couldn't run, he'd just have to stand his ground. The young man stopped, too, about ten feet away.

'You come with us, no danger,' he said. 'Talk about girlfriend.'

He rode in back. The young man sat in front with the driver. They paid no attention to him. Maybe this really wasn't a kidnapping. They'd known that once they mentioned Susan he would want to come with them. He wished he could be sure they weren't just lulling him so he'd come along quietly to his death.

The driver surprised him by turning north, away from Chinatown. They went up the West Side Highway.

One thing he was sure of: his only interest was protecting Susan. He would tell these people whatever they wanted to know about Martin and Meiling Eng. If they asked for it, he would get them Jon's copy of the tape. The hard part would be to make sure everything he did went to ensuring Susan's safety.

He was fairly certain now he knew what they had wanted from June Eng – the Engs's encryption key. And if they had gotten it from her, they would be able to decrypt the tape, so it would be worth killing for, too.

The driver got off the highway at the George Washington Bridge. Instead of taking the ramp to the bridge they stayed on city streets, through neighborhoods he'd never seen.

They parked on a residential street that looked more like the outer boroughs than Manhattan. 'You wait,' the driver told him and walked off. The other one stood on the sidewalk next to the car.

The driver came back. 'Okay, you come.'

They led David to an alley and through the back door of a restaurant. The driver took his backpack. 'Give back later,' he said.

The restaurant was deserted, apparently closed. At one large, round table sat Martin Eng and his wife. There was nothing on the table but a teapot and three cups.

★ ★ ★

David sat down, stunned. Cheung Meiling poured tea for him. He did not tap his fingers on the table or pick up the cup to drink.

'We were surprised to see you at the China Society,' she said.

He changed his mind about the tea: his mouth and throat were too dry for speech. He took a sip of tea and said, 'It was a surprise for Susan and me, too. I saw the announcement for the symposium and it seemed interesting. I didn't connect the name Wu Chuming with anyone I knew, though I knew Martin's name was Chu-Ming.'

'Yes, it is confusing, that two family names seemingly so different are actually the same. There are many. Guo and Kwok. Wen and Mun. Xu and Tsui. All names with different sounds in Mandarin and Cantonese.'

'Not so different as Wu and Eng.'

Martin Eng smiled thinly. 'No, not so different as Wu and Eng.' He sipped some tea. 'It was a closed session, if I am not mistaken.'

'Yes. A friend in Hong Kong arranged for us to be invited.'

'A friend in Hong Kong,' Meiling said as brightly as if they were in her living room. 'Would that be someone we know?'

'I doubt it,' David said. He wished the occasion for this sparring match were not so serious, was amazed that they could continue to avoid the main event: *Talk about girlfriend.*

Could it be that they were the victims in this, along with him and Susan? That they wanted to make some sort of alliance? But then why the elaborate effort to keep this conversation secret?

He said, 'I enjoyed listening to Martin. So did Susan.' Stressing her name, to make an opening.

'How is she?' Meiling asked, picking up on it. 'Have you heard from her?'

'She's missing.'

'Really? How distressing. How long since you saw her?'

'We had an appointment this morning. She wasn't there. I hoped you might have some idea where she might be.'

They gazed at him blankly, offering neither encouragement nor denial.

'Did I tell you about the tape you and Susan brought from Hong Kong?' Martin asked.

'No. What about it?'

'Some bad thing happened to it.'

'I don't understand.' Putting it mildly. 'What could have happened to it?' Jon. What the hell did he do?

'I hope you know the answer to that,' Martin said. 'The same as you hope we know the answer about Susan.'

There it was. The tape, and Susan: If you have an answer for me, I have one for you. Not an alliance, then. For a moment David couldn't breathe.

'I just carried it,' he forced out in an almost normal voice. 'I don't know anything more about it than that.'

'Perhaps the tape you carried was not the original.'

'How could it be anything else?' How, indeed? Knowing Jon's unwillingness to take no for an answer, David had checked the tape when Jon gave it back to him: It had June Eng's label on it, undisturbed – Chinese characters in her handwriting, no way could Jon have duplicated that. And no way that David could see, either, for the tape to have been damaged by Jon's making a copy to analyze. 'Why do you think it's not the original?'

'The tape has a greater legacy from our poor daughter than only her voice,' Martin replied. 'Sadly, some parts are . . . missing.'

'Maybe something happened when June and Peter recorded it. A bad connection with the microphone or a dirty recording head.' David was letting words come out of his mouth while he tried to figure out what to do. 'I wish I could be more help.'

'I wish the same. You see, my problem is simple. Right now I take so much time to worry – where is original tape? If I have original tape, I can take more time, think more about where is Susan.'

David almost choked on his fury. He could not keep up his part of the game. 'You know where she is. You kidnapped her.'

Martin Eng looked at him reproachfully. 'I am sorry to hear you say that.'

'She is like a daughter to us,' his wife said. 'Like our poor June. We wish your Susan only long life and prosperity.'

*Like our poor June.* David did not need an interpreter for that.

'I don't have your tape. I gave you your tape. I'm sorry for your loss, but at least you have your daughter's voice.' His anger talking.

671

'It is cruel to mock grieving parents,' Meiling told him. 'If I say to you – you can have Susan's voice, only, never Susan, does that make you happy?'

Right to the heart. *Watch your tongue*, David told himself.

'In the grand jury, you remember, there was much talk of gambling,' Martin said. 'I do not gamble now. All cards on the table, no bluff.'

'I want to put my cards on the table, too,' David said. 'I'm very worried about Susan. Nothing is more important to me than her safety.'

'You are right to value Susan so highly,' Meiling said.

'Last night in my dream,' said Martin, 'my spirit left my body and traveled to a distant place. My enemies were all gathered in a great banquet hall listening to the voice of my daughter while they crunched her bones for their dinner. My spirit cried out to Guan Di, god of war, and his two brethren of the peach orchard – the heroes of the story of the Three Kingdoms that you heard me speak of – and they came to earth and hacked to pieces everyone in the great banquet hall and put their heads on stakes for an example.'

'I don't see how that dream could ever come true.' David was as chilled as he knew Martin Eng meant him to be. 'Believe me, if I can think of any way to help you, I will. I wish I could do more right now, I truly do.' But until he spoke to Jon all he could do was play for time.

'I am sorry to hear you say that.' Martin Eng looked genuinely sad. 'Very sorry. Sorry, too, to say police will not help you find Susan. Best is to rely only on yourself. We have a saying in China – "Ask help from officials, open door of house to grief." '

'Please don't get me wrong,' David said quickly. 'I only want to help. I'm sure there's something I haven't thought of. I have a friend who's an expert in these things. He may know what to do. As soon as I can come up with anything, I'll let you know.' From somewhere he remembered to say, 'But I can only think clearly about this if I know that Susan is safe and well.'

'I am sure she will be fine,' Meiling said blandly.

'How do I get in touch with you?' David asked as he stood to leave.

Martin gave him a beeper number. 'You call any time, we call right back.'

'If only you will think hard,' Meiling added. 'For Susan's sake.'

672

# 10

David's escorts dropped him off at an uptown subway station. He spent the short ride there convincing himself he had said the right things, the only things he could have.

He had to keep the Engs hoping for something: he was afraid of what they might do to Susan if they decided he couldn't help them. The horror of it was that he didn't see how he could. The copy Jon had made – David's only hope for ransoming Susan – wouldn't be any better than the original it was made from. If anything, it would be worse. Enhancement was sometimes possible, but not in the time he had given Jon with the tape.

There was no point speculating. He needed to get in touch with Jon and get hold of the copy, however inadequate it might be. He tried not to think of what Susan might be going through.

He searched the station platform for a pay telephone. The one he found didn't work. He went upstairs and searched on Broadway. It was three blocks before he found a phone that worked and that wasn't being used.

Jon wasn't in, or he wasn't answering. 'You can't reach me,' he told the answering machine. 'I need the tape *immediately*. Life or death, and I mean life or death. Don't do anything that would harm it in any way.' Hoping that at least the copy might convince the Engs there was no missing 'original.'

The next thing he had to do was send an e-mail message to Jon, who often ignored the telephone completely, and the place to do that from was his own computer. But going home meant Ryan's investigator, and David wasn't ready to deal with Ryan because Ryan would push him toward Mahoney and the Engs had clearly warned him against that.

The hot, stuffy closet was getting worse, Susan thought, waking up, stiffer and more uncomfortable. She was afraid to move too much or make too much noise. But then she thought – if she had been left here to die, attracting attention was the only way to save herself. But who would hear . . . and if the wrong people heard what might they do to her? As if it made any difference.

It was her fault for getting involved in all this . . . nobody to blame but herself. She felt so sad and alone and defeated. No one knew where she was, no one could help . . . and she had thrown away her life, led herself to this place, on a foolish whim . . .

David went to Susan's hotel and used the room key she'd given him. The bed had been changed and the room made up, yet she pervaded it. He turned on the light of the walk-in closet and stood for a moment inhaling the faint scent of her, his memory filling out the empty folds of her clothes with her substance and warmth.

He called home thinking he might catch Alice. He got the answering machine and while he was at it tried some possible access codes. No luck. Those twins, he thought, but he didn't blame them . . . nobody could have known this was going to be a life-or-death kind of day—

*Alice and the twins.* Could they be in danger, too?

It wasn't out of the question. If the Engs had taken Susan as a way to put pressure on him, Alice and the twins could be next.

Getting Jon's copy of the tape was the best he could do. There was a remote possibility it would not be as useless as he thought: that Jon had made a good copy of a clear original and somehow damaged the original while the copy was being made. Or that he had made more than one copy and the original got screwed up on the second pass . . .

David called the hotel's business center to see if they could send Internet e-mail. They could but he had to make an appointment.

'It's an emergency,' he said.

'Everybody has an emergency. All we have time for is emergencies.'

David wasn't about to argue the relative merits of his emergency and the emergencies of investment bankers and traveling salesfolk. He called Michael Ryan.

'Where have you been?' the lawyer wanted to know.

Not a question he was ready to answer. 'Have you heard anything?' On the off-chance that the Engs were bluffing, despite Martin Eng's disclaimer.

'Nothing good. Mahoney hasn't found a sign of her anywhere. He wants to talk to you more than ever. He thinks you have information that will help more than you realize.'

'I'm not ready for that.' The Engs's warning still loud and frightening.

'Susan's life may be at stake.'

'I know that.' Better than you do.

'You've got to come in and talk to us.'

He hesitated. He knew the lawyers would insist on his handling this their way.

'Are you okay, where you are?' Ryan asked. 'Not under any pressure?'

'No, no, it's not that.' Nobody's holding a gun to my head at the moment – not literally, anyway.

'Where were you all this time?'

The question was, could he trade Jon's copy of the tape for Susan, without help? Afraid as he was of doing anything that might hurt Susan, he was no longer sure bringing in help was more dangerous than going it alone. And Ryan wasn't the police . . . though for the Engs that might be a distinction without a difference.

'I got taken for an unexpected ride.'

'We can't talk on the phone.' Alarm in Ryan's voice.

Especially not on this hotel telephone, the ultimate open line. 'I'm on my way.'


Mahoney was getting more and more worried. Susan Linwood had been missing for almost six hours – not long as those things went, very long for a person with a solid history of reliability and a known itinerary. And David Clark was not making himself available.

Mahoney called Michael Ryan. 'I still don't have anything. Where's your client?'

'I finally heard from him, not ten minutes ago.'

'Is he coming in?'

'I'm working on it.'

'Working on it isn't enough. Whatever these Eng people are into, it got their daughter murdered.' He was still waiting to hear from the Royal Hong Kong Police exactly how. 'Within hours of your clients' last contact with her.

'Right now the only thing any of us can afford to think about is Susan Linwood. Locating her and making sure she's safe, and nothing else. So get your client in here. You know as well as I do that on his own he's only going to make things worse.'

This is my fault, David thought on his way to the lawyers' office. If I hadn't had to know more about the tape, if I'd left well enough alone, none of this would have happened.

It was a thought he'd been avoiding, holding it back because it was too much to deal with. But there it was and no getting away from it. If Jon had damaged the tape, it was only because somebody had been stupid enough to give it to him in the first place.

And even if the tape had been bad to begin with, the Engs – with no way to know that – would still be blaming him because he had taken the tape to Boston in the first place and brought it back to them only under pressure. And because he'd had to follow up his curiosity about Wu Chuming . . . and drag Susan to the China Society.

Mahoney called Ned King. 'There's still no sign of Susan Linwood, and David Clark is playing hard to get. My guess is she's been kidnapped and he's afraid to get close to law enforcement. Or he may have already been told to avoid us.'

'Their lawyers any help?'

'They're trying to get him in here.'

'These people have information on Pullone?'

'I think they do.'

'Keep me posted.' King made sure Mahoney had his beeper number. 'If it is a kidnapping, my worry is the Southern District will stumble over it and get somebody killed. I'm going to call right now and tell them something may be breaking.'

★ ★ ★

David found Ryan and Miller waiting for him in the law firm's reception area. They hustled him back to Ryan's office.

'I think Susan's been kidnapped,' David said. He'd decided there was no point trying to keep them out of this.

'You *think*?'

'Nobody came right out and said so.'

'You think the kidnappers took you for a ride?'

'Yes.'

'Where?'

'A Chinese restaurant near the George Washington Bridge.'

'And they let you go.'

'Right.'

'Did they know you were coming here?'

'I wasn't, when I left them. I went to Susan's hotel.'

'Were you followed?'

'I don't know.' *Genius!*

Ryan shook his head. 'Who was it?'

'The Engs.'

'Why?' Amazed.

'There's something wrong with the tape they have. They claim it's not the original. They think I have it.'

'Is that possible?'

'No.'

'What about the copy your friend made? Can you give them that?'

'It's all I can do. I need to get on the Internet . . .'

'Kassia's the one who knows about computers,' Ryan said.

On the computer in Miller's office, David connected up with his service provider and checked his mailbox. There was a message from Jon but it was encrypted, and he needed the decryption software on his own computer to read it.

He sent a reply: Must have PLAINTEXT messages only. URGENT I have best possible copy of tape IMMEDIATELY. DROP EVERYTHING ELSE and bring it to New York. Advise of ETA, etc. For safety's sake he appended the law firm's e-mail address, though it would appear in the routing header of the message.

'How good do you think the copy is?' Ryan asked him.

'Not good enough. Jon was bitching and moaning about how hard it was to be sure he could get a copy of everything on the original. He hated the fact that he didn't have more time.'

'Are you sure there's no way the original and the copy could have been switched somehow?' Miller asked.

'I don't see how.'

'Why not?'

David, unprepared to be cross-examined by his own lawyers, stifled an impatient response. 'I had it in my hands. I saw what I gave him and what he gave back. It was definitely the same cassette. It had all June Eng's handwritten labels—'

He stopped talking. 'Do you have an audio cassette?'

Ryan looked at him, held back the questions that were clearly on his mind. 'Sure.' He went and got one.

David turned it over in his hands. He'd known what he was going to see but the concrete object made his conclusion seem stronger. 'That bastard!'

'Who?' Kassia Miller asked.

'Jon. He might have switched it, after all. That bastard! He must have.'

'You're sure?' Ryan asked.

'Oh yeah. It's just his kind of thing.'

Miller said, 'But a minute ago you were so sure—'

'And I was so wrong. You see these –' the tiny screws that held the plastic cassette shell together – 'All he had to do was make a copy on a tape of the same type as the original, then unscrew both cassette shells and switch the tapes so that the original tape was in the new shell and the copy was in the shell that used to hold the original, the one with all the handwritten labels. A person looking at the original cassette shell would have no way to tell the switch had been made, except maybe some tiny scratches on the screws.

'And that way Jon could keep the original recording and have all the time he wanted to analyze it, and at the same time return the original shell to me, to pass on to the Engs.'

'That's pretty devious,' Miller observed.

'Not from Jon's point of view. He wanted to satisfy his curiosity and he went straight for it. And what makes me doubly sure, now that I've

678

thought of it, is that since I left Boston with the so-called original Jon hasn't complained once about how it's my fault he has to work with a lousy copy.'

'That's good news, then, isn't it?' Miller said.

'It gives me something to trade for Susan.' But it also magnified his certainty that he had caused all this. If he'd never gone to Jon with the tape, the Engs would have had the pristine original – and no reason to be upset, nothing to force him to give back. 'But I've got to send another message right away.'

I KNOW WHAT YOU DID the new message said. Bring ORIGINAL only. I MUST have ORIGINAL. Nothing else will do. LIFE OR DEATH.

You can't give up, Susan told herself through her fear: you have to fight.

She labored to get her feet under her. Though her ankles and thighs were bound together, she could bend her knees, and with effort she could get her feet on the floor. She was making a noise now but she told herself not to care – she had to do something.

She pushed herself back into the corner in the hope that she could lever herself upward against the wall, but all that did was put strain on her shoulders. She pushed and pulled at her bonds. More pain in her shoulders. She tried to guess from how the bonds felt what she was tied with, got a mental picture of Moonface and his tourniquet of surgical tubing. That was what she was tied with, wrapped enough times around so that it didn't stretch in any way that would allow her to escape.

Her efforts to stand had made her sweat again, with the ugly odor of fear. Resting, trying to keep from plunging back into despair, she thought she heard noises from outside. She froze, straining to hear.

A metallic sound that might be a lock opening. Then a whole series of noises, rapid and overlapping – heavy footfalls, a door slamming, the lock again, voices in coarse Chinese. The scrape of chairs on the floor. Other noises, not so loud – the crackle of paper, softer sounds she could not identify. Faintly, she caught the odor of food – cheap, greasy Cantonese food. It made her stomach turn.

She tried to hear the voices, to tell them apart, to guess how many

679

there were. Two. Or three. Possibly four. She couldn't tell. The fear, the strain of not knowing, the mixture of odors were making her dizzy and weak. They were out there having lunch or dinner and chatting and laughing. For now, at least, they seemed to be giving no thought to her.

'All right,' Ryan said. 'What we've got to do now is talk to Mahoney.'

As David had expected. 'They told me that Susan would suffer if I went to the police. They made that very clear.' As clear as they ever made anything.

'That's what kidnappers always say.'

'It's also the truth. Kidnappers kill their victims to avoid being identified.'

'And they kill them whether or not law enforcement is involved, and often whether or not the ransom is paid. The only time they don't is if they're stopped first.'

'These are serious people. They're playing for high stakes.'

'Yes, though it does seem hard to reconcile kidnapping with helping the poor oppressed people of Hong Kong flee to a better, safer life.'

David grimaced. 'With all this, I never told you – Susan and I figured out we were wrong about all that.' He told the lawyers about the symposium at the China Society and the cocktail party and what he and Susan had made of it all.

'So when Mahoney told Susan you were in over your heads, it was no exaggeration,' Ryan said.

David had nothing to say to that.

'I'm a defense lawyer these days,' Ryan said, 'but I used to be a prosecutor, and I'm going to tell you what I'd say in Mahoney's place . . . You're at a decision point. You can't have it all ways. The stakes here are simple, you're gambling with Susan's life.

'Trying to deal with this on your own would be a huge mistake, a *fatal* mistake. You've gotten yourselves – both of you – in the middle of something very dangerous. People have died. Now Susan's been kidnapped.

'I asked you if you were followed when you left the Engs,' Ryan reminded him. 'You said you don't know.'

'No, I don't.'

'Because you didn't even think of it.'

'And I admit it was stupid of me not to. If you're about to say I'll make other mistakes, I can't say you're wrong.'

'For a complete amateur you've handled yourself fairly well, but – yes – that's just a sample of the kind of mistake you're sure to make. These are serious people, you said it yourself. Susan's only hope is to have equally serious people on her side.

'There's no time for playing games with this. You have to decide right now who your friends are and who you can trust.

'Mahoney and his people are professionals at this. It's what they're trained to do, and they have a lot of experience at it. You don't. You're David Clark, not James Bond. And this is not something one person can do alone.'

'If we go to Mahoney, what happens next?'

'We'll meet with him and you'll tell him your story and you'll answer all his questions. Kassia and I will do our best to make sure you and Susan are protected. All you have to worry about is giving him the information he needs to do his job.'

'You trust this guy?'

Ryan didn't answer at once. He turned to Miller, who said, 'As much as you can trust somebody you don't know. And he's good friends over there with Joe Estrada, whom I *do* know and trust, and who tells me Mahoney is a straight-shooter. If it'll make you feel more comfortable I'll see if we can get Joe to the first meeting, too.'

David closed his eyes. He saw Susan, standing atop the red-painted rock that surmounted the Lovers' Garden, her face in the wind, full of joy, her black hair whipping behind her. And then an image of Detective Chief Inspector Hall, saying the words Susan had reported: *an ancient method of judicial execution called death by slicing.*

'All right,' David said. 'Let's do it.'

Mahoney beeped Ned King as soon as he got off the phone with Ryan.

'There's definitely been a kidnapping. David Clark is on his way over here with his lawyers. They want protection for both families, full immunity for Clark and for Linwood if we get her back, a non-prosecution letter for both of them from the Southern District. Ryan says they'll cooperate fully and reminds us there are lives at stake.'

'Yeah – thank him very much for that. All right, we can deal with our part of it, no problem. I don't know how far I can push the Southern District.'

'Ryan says if we prefer Miller will call her friend the U.S. Attorney directly. They're buddies from one of the women-lawyers' breakfast clubs.'

'I'll bet she'll call direct. Just what we need. You told them we'd take care of it for them?'

'I did.'

'Good . . . The Boss just took off for some damn D.A.'s conference in Colorado. I'll try to reach him in the air so he can have a telephone chat with *his* friend the U.S. Attorney. You just go ahead as if it's all settled.'

'Understood.'

'I'll need to talk to this Clark, too, before I go over to the Southern District. As soon as I get the Boss I'll come straight to Official Corruption – we can do all our debriefing and preparation there. I don't want to be dragging the man all over law-enforcement heaven, a block from Chinatown.'

# 11

Mahoney unlocked the door for David Clark and his lawyers.

Mahoney had watched Kassia Miller work during the Roberto Morales retrial, facing Joe Estrada as prosecutor. He'd seen Michael Ryan in that courtroom once or twice as well, there as a spectator or to offer Miller support. Now, as then, the two lawyers made an oddly comfortable pair – the tiny, intense Miller and her cooler, black-Irish-looking husband, almost a foot taller.

David Clark was more or less as Mahoney remembered him from the grand jury – on the tall side of medium height, and fit; alert blue eyes under thick, wavy brown hair; the reddish beard neatly trimmed. Watching him come into Offical Corruption Mahoney saw a man working to hold himself together.

Mahoney introduced Laurie Jordan. To start, she was the only D.A.'s-office person in evidence besides himself. Clark was clearly wary, looking around, getting his bearings, assessing everything and everyone.

'Before we start,' Ryan said, 'let's be sure we've settled David and Susan's status when we come out the other side of this.'

'Right this way.' Mahoney led Ryan into Jordan's office, motioning for her to join them.

David was doing his best to keep up. The surroundings were far from what he'd expected. Hard to reconcile the double-height ceilings and wall of windows and modern fixtures with the aged, shabbily institutional building where he'd been a grand juror.

Mahoney seemed nervous, he thought – a host throwing a party where he knew the guests might not get along. By contrast, the striking woman with dark hair and penetrating green eyes – Jordan? – had been a model of cool self-possession. This was her office, Mahoney had said, making the introductions, and her investigators would be the ones providing support.

Ryan came out from behind the modular room divider where he had gone with Mahoney and Jordan.

'We've got a signed agreement for today,' Ryan reported. 'When this part is over Mahoney is going to want you and Susan to testify about the investigation you did, and for that he'll put you in the grand jury so you'll have full transactional immunity from prosecution for state crimes.'

David assumed this mutual dance was necessary, but for now he could not bring himself to care about it. All he could think of was Susan.

'As far as the no-prosecution letter from the U.S. Attorney goes,' Ryan continued, 'it's not fully up to him, but in principle there's no problem and the District Attorney will be working on that with us. But it won't come for free. Knowing how the federal government works, they're going to insist on full cooperation as well.'

'I understand that.' Something else to worry about later.

'For now, here, we have the improved Queen-for-a-Day agreement we already talked about.' Ryan showed him the agreement. He signed it without looking.

'From here on, we're putting all those questions of testimony and immunity aside,' Ryan said. 'All we're going to talk about is Susan.'

Mahoney led them all into an office up a step on the platform that ran along the wall of floor-to-ceiling windows. He started by reintroducing A.D.A. Jordan. 'As I said, she's a prosecutor here in the Official Corruption Unit. This is her case now as much as mine. But I want to be very clear that making a case is not important to us here. Not now. Our only purpose is to get Susan back safely. And we're going to do anything and everything we can to accomplish that. *Anything and everything.*

'But we need your help to do it, and I'm going to ask you to bear with us because you may not understand why we need to ask some

684

things, and you may not see why we do things the way we do. The thing to remember is we all have the same goal. I'm not going to risk human life for *any* case. I've seen too much to make that mistake.'

He paused, his eyes on David, as they had been throughout. 'To begin with we need to get as much information from you as we can in a very short period of time. We don't have the luxury of having you repeat it for seven different people, so I'm going to get everybody together right here. Once we start, things are going to go very fast. There won't be much time for explanation, so I'll try to anticipate some of your questions.

'The first thing I want to tell you about is the people who are going to be working directly with you on this. We have two main investigators to run the surveillance on you and the Engs. One is Richie Eilewitz, he was a police detective – a veteran of the special squad that works out of the D.A.'s office. And Frank Perez, he's also an ex-police detective and he's got a degree in electronics. He's our chief investigator. They're the ones who are going to be out in the street and they're going to have to react at a moment's notice so they have to hear your story.

'Frank and Richie are both full-time investigators with the Offical Corruption Unit, and that means they spend their time investigating corrupt cops and other law-enforcement people. Their bread and butter is making recordings of people saying incriminating things, and maintaining surveillance on the subjects of their investigations.

'If you think about it, there's nobody who's harder to run surveillance on than a dirty cop, especially a detective. They do surveillance themselves, so if they're also committing crimes they're very aware of how careful they have to be and what techniques are going to be used against them. That means the investigators who do surveillance on them have to be the best in the business, and that's what Frank and Richie are.

'And their skills are exactly the ones we need now. We need to find out what the Engs are up to and we need to follow them very carefully and discreetly to find Susan. You couldn't be in better hands.'

Mahoney paused again. David looked to Ryan and Miller; they seemed satisfied with what the prosecutor was saying, and it made sense to David. 'Okay,' he said.

'There'll also be a third investigator at the meeting – Bob Marion, from the Asian Gang Unit. He'll be there to give us an opinion on the Chinatown aspects.

'And the other person who's going to join us is my boss. His name is Ned King, and he's the Chief of Investigation for the D.A.'s office. He's my boss and Laurie Jordan's boss, and he works closely with the District Attorney. He's got to be here because starting right now I need blanket authority to spend money and to deploy troops, and in order for me to do that Ned King has to be involved. He can smooth the way within the office for the money and the manpower and the equipment, and again, we don't have the luxury of time, and we can't waste it bucking the bureaucracy. So he makes sure there are no snags of that kind. And he maintains contact with the head of the Criminal Division at the U.S. Attorney's office, so down the line when you're worried about your relationship there, Ned King is the one who's going to do the most to be sure you get your non-prosecution letter.'

This time Mahoney seemed to be pitching to Ryan and Miller as much as to David. Again David looked to the lawyers for their reaction. Ryan nodded: this was as agreed.

'Okay,' Mahoney said. 'If you have any questions about any of that I'll be happy to answer them. Otherwise, as I said, we have a lot to cover and not a lot of time.'

'I just want to know how it's going to work,' David said. 'I understand that you've got good people here. But I want *you* to understand that I've been warned against bringing anybody like this into it. So just by being here I may be endangering Susan's life, and the last thing I want to do is make the situation any worse.'

'I respect that,' Mahoney said. 'But to respond to that concern I need to understand what the situation really is. All of us do. So we need to start with you telling your story, and then we'll see where we go from there.'

In the dark, in the closet, breathing the foul air, feeling the growing numbness in her bound hands and feet, smelling the sweat of her own terror, glad in some corner of her mind that she had not wet herself – yet – Susan's despair was sharpened by rage.

She raged at herself and at the Engs and at the men who had taken her and tied her and locked her in here and injected her with heroin, and let it wear off and not given her any more to dull the pain and take away for another little while the deadening bleakness and the knowledge she was going to die here.

She raged, too, at Richard, who if he even knew she was missing would do nothing except make publicly proper statements of dismay, because that was all he was capable of, because he had never known how to rescue anyone but himself. And she raged at David Clark.

She knew she was here because of the Engs. She blamed herself for getting involved with them, blamed herself for agreeing to take the tapes. It was her fault, she should have known better. But in the end it would all still have been all right if David had left it alone.

Whoever had put her in here must want that tape and whatever was on it. What else could it be? But she didn't have it any more. And if she did have it, why would they want to stuff her in a closet to die? Who could they get anything from, by keeping her here? Not Richard. The Engs? Once she would have thought so. Meiling needed a daughter. But the Engs didn't really care. Did David? Could they make David do things for them by stuffing her in a closet?

Could they make him give them the tape? Did he have it? Did someone think so? Why did David have to take it to Boston for his friend to copy or analyze or whatever he had done? Why? To satisfy his curiosity? He said himself it was nothing anybody could even read.

And if he *could* read it, what difference would it make? Could it possibly be worth dying for, hogtied and deserted in a dark, stinking closet, far from the sun and the sweet fall air and the sight of her children's faces?

They moved into a a bigger office along the double-height wall of windows – one with a conference table in it – and Mahoney brought in the others. David was at the head of the table. On his left were his own two lawyers and the investigator from the Asian Gang Unit. On his right were Mahoney and A.D.A. Jordan and the two Official Corruption investigators. At the far end of the table was Ned King, the D.A.'s Chief of Investigation.

Five lawyers and three top cops, all here to listen to David Clark. An honor he would happily have forgone.

687

'Right,' Mahoney said to him. 'If it's okay with you I'm going to turn this over to Laurie Jordan, because this is her area of expertise.'

'Mr Clark, I know you're under a lot of strain,' she said, 'but we need to have you start at the beginning and tell us the whole story. And it's very important not to leave anything out. If there's anything you or Susan did that you're worried about, just remember we're not here to think about anything like that. All we care about is Susan.'

'What do you mean by start at the beginning?' David asked.

Mahoney said, 'We know that you and Susan were on the grand jury that indicted the Engs, and we know that you weren't happy with the case I presented. We need to know what happened starting right there – what led you and Susan to get involved in this after the grand jury, and everything from then on.'

'What's the point?' For the first time, David let his impatience show. 'God knows where Susan is or what she's going through. Why waste time with all that history? Let's get to what we're here for.'

'We understand how you feel,' Jordan said. 'But in a situation like this it can be fatal to react out of haste or ignorance. That's why we need you to tell us everything you can possibly think of, and to be patient with us when we have questions for you. Mr Ryan has been a prosecutor, himself, and I'm sure he'll bear me out on this.'

'Ms Jordan's right,' Ryan said. 'You've got to tell them everything, and that means *everything*. You're in no position to decide which details are important and which aren't. That's *their* job. And their expertise.'

'And when it's over,' Kassia Miller added, 'you don't want to be thinking – "if only I had told them more it might have turned out better." '

Not an option, he thought. He already had enough to blame himself for.

Once he got underway, it went surprisingly quickly. There were frequent interruptions for clarification or to follow along a path he might not have taken himself.

The questions came mostly from Jordan and the investigators, with some from Mahoney and very few from their boss. They were sharp questions, David thought, quick and to the point, and he found himself surrendering more and more to the process.

They were particularly interested in the Engs, in anything he could remember about their habits, their surroundings, their conversation. He did his best to repeat what Susan had told him about the Engs's apartment, though he supposed they must have access to some information about that from the original arrest.

They paid close attention to his description of the conference at the China Society and the cocktail party that had followed, and they were frustrated by David's inability to identify people whom, he was sure, Susan would have been able to name in an instant. They were interested, too, in his impressions of who the Engs's enemies might be, in China as well as in Chinatown.

The audio cassette Susan had brought back from Hong Kong got their attention most completely. They took him repeatedly through everything he could say about it, and Jordan called a break so David could access his e-mail to see whether Jon Levi had sent a response to his messages.

He had. It said AMTRAK 159 ; - )

Just like Jon – making life complicated. They checked with the railroad: the train was en route, running on time and due at Penn Station at 9:26. Why Jon had appended a winking-face emoticon was anybody's guess.

Thinking of Lara and Charles had made Susan ache, had reduced her to sobbing. She so missed her children. She had done so much wrong. It was her fault that Charles was where he was and that Lara mistrusted her. And now before she had any chance to make it better, to tell them how she really felt . . . she was going to die. Die here in this closet and leave them alone in the world with no one but a father who knew how to care only for himself.

And David . . . where was he? She had entrusted herself to him, had let him reawaken her, had thought he cared. He cared, all right – about the same thing all men did . . . David Clark and David Hsu, and both times she had suffered, suffered so much. *She* had, not the men, never the men . . . Even Richard, cold as he was, was no different – uninterested in his wife but he'd always had his adoring residents and post-residency fellows. That she had turned a blind eye didn't mean it hadn't happened. Men were all the same.

Men were all the same . . . and she was locked in a closet at the mercy of who knew how many men. What would they do to her, what violation, what indignity – rape her for fun, rape her to make her submissive, to make her do . . . what? The images pressed in her the way she feared the men themselves would.

She could scarcely breathe. The sweat turned cold on her body. Now for the first time her fear was palpable, it had a name and a shape she could see and a taste and a smell. Murder she could not keep in her mind, not even after the horrible death of June Eng. She had imagined suffering as June had and the image did not stick, it was too abstract, too terrifying to be real. But rape was concrete and believable, every kind of brutal rape, one after another after another . . .

While the investigators briefed David Clark on the hardware he'd be wearing – a digital recorder they called an F-bird, plus a beeper-transmitter – Mahoney and Jordan had a quick meeting with Ned King.

'Laurie and I were thinking that with the evidence from El Coyote there's a chance to go after Pullone for extorting the heroin from him, and for distributing it,' Mahoney told King. 'But when this all first came up, we talked to Max about how far Pullone's immunity would reach, and we're still worried about it. I had him testify in the grand jury about finding heroin at the apartment. It's possible that any crime he committed that has *anything* to do with that heroin – not just as evidence in the Eng case, but *any* contact Pullone had with it – is going to be covered by his grand jury immunity.'

'That's been in the background all along. We may just have to litigate it.'

'Unless we let the feds prosecute him.'

'I hate to give it to them,' King said. 'But with all this . . . And it's a good bargaining chip – they're always ready to take down a cop.' He came to a decision. 'Horgan's the one we really want to keep for us – that's what counts. And to get Horgan we need Pullone, so we can't let him think for a minute he can squeak out of this.'

'That's why I thought we should talk before you went over to the Southern District.'

'Absolutely right. I'll have to do a deal with them that covers this whole business. It's all one thing – Horgan, Pullone, the Engs, your two grand jurors – everything. And I'm going to make damn sure they stay out of the action until we're ready for them.'

The Investigation Division Chief spent a moment in thought. 'What do you make of this theory of Clark's that the Engs are bribing people in Washington?' he asked them.

'It fits what we know,' Mahoney said.

'And it sure explains why our Southern District friends are so damn interested,' King reflected. 'Something for me to use over there. He seems smart, this guy Clark.'

'When he's not being dumb,' Jordan said.

# 12

The twins were home when David called from the Official Corruption office.

'Where's your mom?'

'She went out. She said you'd get us dinner.'

He didn't remember anything about that.

'It's kind of late for dinner,' Zack said, on the extension.

'We raided the fridge,' Jessica added.

'Good thing you did. We're going on an adventure.' He told them to pack enough clothes for a week.

'Does Mom know about this?' Jessica was wary.

'It's a surprise.'

When he got home, David went upstairs with one of Mahoney's investigators. She waited in the hall.

David said hi to the kids and went to check on their progress. They'd been doing everything but packing. He hurried them along, trying not to snap at them despite his sense of urgency. He had to meet Jon Levi at Penn Station in less than two hours, and the plan was to beep the Engs and talk to them before that. If everything went smoothly there might still be a chance to save Susan from spending the night in danger and fear.

While they finished packing he checked the answering machine. There was a message giving only a phone number and the words "please call" in what sounded like a Chinese accent – likely to have been left as backup in case he missed Martin Eng's errand boys. A message from Alice about her plans for the evening with a request to feed the kids dinner, and several impatient messages from Michael

Ryan, left while David was on his ride to northern Manhattan. And the twins had definitely been playing with the access codes.

Finally the twins had their duffle bags packed. On the way out he remembered to ask them about schoolbooks.

'I thought this was an adventure,' Jessica protested. She saw the investigator waiting in the hall and stopped short. 'Who are you?'

'I'm Annie Ross. I'm part of the adventure.'

'We're playing cops and robbers,' David said. 'Ms Ross is going downstairs with you and there's a car that'll take you all to the airport. Then another car will pick you up and take you to a hotel. There'll be somebody to stay with you, and your mom will be there as soon as she comes back from wherever she is.'

'Uncle David, are you kidnapping us?' Jessica asked with a straight face.

'Do I look like a kidnapper?' Ross said.

'No, really,' Jessica insisted. 'This is what they always tell kids to watch out for – your nice uncle promises you a trip to the country, and then he takes you someplace nasty and locks you up and does bad things to you.'

'In those stories do the nice uncles have women accomplices with badges?' David asked her.

'I don't think so.'

'Hey, do you really have a badge?' Zack wanted to know.

Deadpan, Ross flashed her badge.

'Cool,' Zack said. 'Do you have a gun, too?'

'What is this really?' Jessica demanded.

'Something to do with when I was in the grand jury,' David said. 'There are some people who might come looking for me here and it's better if you're not around for a while.' There was an investigator on the way to get Lara Linwood at her college dorm, too.

'Oh.' Jessica was suddenly subdued. 'What about you? Are you coming with us?'

'No, I can't, not right away. But I won't be staying here, either.'

After Ross left with the twins David forwarded his calls to Official Corruption and left a note for Alice, enough to keep her from worrying and to get her to call Kassia Miller, but not so much that it would tell anyone else what was going on.

Susan thought she must have fainted, because she was aware of coming back to consciousness. There was an acrid smell in the closet with her. It took her a moment to realize that she had finally wet herself. Her instinctive humiliation was washed away by a kind of relief. This was a good thing. Her body's fluids were her friends. Let the men outside find her filthy and disgusting. If only she were having her period, the blood might scare them off . . .

She could hear them out there – a cough, the scrape of a chair, a few words. There were at least two, but it could have been any number of men with harsh voices, speaking Chinese in an accent that sounded coarse and uneducated even to her ears.

She had to do something to keep her sanity. She had to plan what she would do, how she would appeal to them, to their human side, but that made no sense because she couldn't speak their language and they had no human side, they were serving some master whoever it was and they would do what their master wanted and she was no more a human being to them than June Eng had been to whoever had sliced her to death.

But she couldn't sit here shivering in the dark, her mind dominated by the growing fear that her hands would go gangrenous or her body would be torn by unspeakable assaults. There had to be something that hostages did to stay in control of themselves, to rise above hopeless despair. Some way not to be completely at the mercy of these people. To be alert enough to take advantage of an opportunity if there should ever be one.

After some evasive maneuvers – being last through a traffic signal as it turned red, using buses or trucks as screens for unexpected turns – the driver dropped David at Grand Central Station.

As instructed, he went straight through and out the other side and took a cab – also driven by one of Mahoney's investigators – downtown to the Public Theater. He mingled with the last-minute lobby crowd and stood in the box-office line for people picking up tickets. Just before it was his turn he left, feeling awkward and conspicuous.

Resisting the temptation to look around, he walked the few blocks to the restaurant across the street from the Official Corruption Unit, pausing on the way at a pay phone to let them know where he was. He ordered some takeout dinner; when it was ready he called again and got an all-clear. No one had been seen following him to the restaurant, and there was no one lurking obviously in the vicinity.

Upstairs, he got a last-minute briefing while he ate barbecued chicken and greens, not a big meal but enough to give him some sustenance. He hadn't eaten since breakfast with Susan.

Could that be right – breakfast with Susan? Could he have touched her, kissed her, talked to her not even twelve hours ago?

Mahoney was saying, 'We all know this is a dangerous thing we're asking you to do. If there was another way to do it, we would. But the Engs have already told you not to bring anyone else into it. And you *know* them. You know the background and the context, you know how to talk to them and how to hear what they're really saying.'

'I understand that.' And more: he had put Susan in danger, he had to do whatever it took to get her out. 'I know I'm the only one who can do this.'

'Good. But I want to remind you of something else – there's no need for you to do things you're not trained for. Wherever you and the Engs agree to meet, you won't be going in alone. You'll have the best people in the business in there with you from the very first minute. You won't see our people, you won't recognize them, but they'll be there – covering you, watching what's happening, ready to step in and protect you. And Susan, if necessary.'

'Just so long as the Engs don't see them, either. I don't want to do anything that would endanger her.'

'They won't reveal themselves unless it's absolutely necessary. The important thing is that they'll be there. And there are going to be people outside, too, monitoring your conversation so we can know exactly how things stand all the time.'

Mahoney stopped talking for a moment, as if he might be afraid he was selling too hard.

'The message I want you to get is how much backup you'll have, for your protection – and for Susan's if you can get them to deliver her. All you have to think about is having your conversation with the Engs and getting them to produce Susan for you if you can.'

★ ★ ★

695

Susan was awakened by a banging and shouting at the outside door.

Her heart jumped. *The police!* There was shouting inside the apartment, too. Her captors were defying whoever was outside.

The shouting match continued until it was drowned out by the roar of automatic weapons fire. Even in the closet the noise was deafening. Susan cradled her head on her raised knees. The screams coming from the room outside were so near, so horrible, so insistent, they filled her with a terror so deep, that she felt her only release would be to scream as well. She clamped her lower lip between her teeth to keep herself mute. The intruders might not know she was there and she was not so sure now they were the police.

She didn't recognize the silence immediately. Even after she realized the shooting and the screams had ended, she sat huddled against the closet wall, head on her knees, eyes clamped shut so tight her head hurt.

She heard footsteps, pressed herself into the corner, tried to breathe so shallowly no one would hear her. The footsteps drew closer, stopped. There was a conversation out there in Chinese – a dialect she didn't recognize.

The door burst open and light flooded in. She squeezed her eyes shut against the pain of the brightness. She heard a coarse laugh, a guttural comment in Chinese followed by another laugh. Even in the impenetrable dialect she recognized the tone of sexual innuendo. The man standing in the closet doorway said a few words she did not understand. When she did not respond he reached in and grabbed her by the hair and pulled.

Now she screamed. He barked an angry word and yanked again, as if to pull her up onto her feet. She struggled to get them under her as she toppled forward into the room. The third time he pulled she had enough balance to use the momentum to help herself stand.

The room stank of gunpowder and other things she did not want to identify. There was nowhere to look without seeing blood, but she kept her eyes high, off the red-streaked bundles on the floor that could only be human corpses. Her legs shook under her, pierced by the sharp needles of too much time in one position.

The man who had pulled her from the closet was shorter than she was but thick in the torso and limbs. He let go of her hair and kept her upright by her arm, fingers digging into her flesh. He smiled at her and flicked open a long-bladed knife. 'Okay now,' he said, his accent so heavy the words were barely intelligible.

The hand with the knife darted behind her. She screamed again.

'Okay now,' the man said, louder.

She felt a tugging sensation in her arms and shoulders and the surgical tubing holding her arms behind her parted, whipping around and lashing her chest. The man knelt quickly to cut the tubing around her legs.

He traded a few more words with one of the others – there were four – and then marched her out into the hallway. The others followed quickly.

They hurried her down the stairs and out into the street. Two dark-colored sedans pulled up at the curb and they all piled in, shoving her into the back of the first car.

Frank Perez taped the digital recorder solidly to the hollow at the top of David's buttocks and gave him the microphone wire to loop under his groin and back up the front. The microphone went into his navel.

'If they pat you down seriously they might find it, but meeting in a public place – like a restaurant or something – that's not too likely.'

When David had his shirt tucked in and his belt buckled, Perez gave him the separate transmitter he was going to be wearing, concealed with its own microphone inside an ordinary pager.

'These beeper-transmitters don't work a hundred percent. There may be times we can't hear you. We'll be in the surveillance van listening, and if we decide you're in trouble we'll move in.'

'How can you talk about moving in before Susan is safe? It could get her killed.'

'We can't let them hurt you either.'

'They're not going to hurt me.' Easier to say than to believe. 'Not as long as they think I'm following their instructions.'

'Let's hope not.' Perez checked that the pager was secure on David's belt. 'Remember, the microphone's pretty sensitive, which means it'll pick up what they say even if they don't talk all that loud, but it also picks up all the noises around, which can make it hard for us to hear. And also if your jacket rubs against it too much or you play with it or anything like that, it picks up those noises, too. So you don't want to be fiddling with it or anything like that. It's best if you try to forget it's there.'

'Right. Sure. And don't think of elephants.'

'It's getting late,' Mahoney said. 'If you're going to call, now's the time.'

Susan's new captors made no attempt to hide where they were going. She was too disoriented to know where they were – Queens, perhaps, maybe somewhere near the new Chinatown in Flushing – and her attention was diverted by the fresh night air and the welcome pain of circulation returning to her arms and legs.

They pulled her out of the car on a block of three-story attached houses and hurried her up the stairs and inside. The room they shoved her into was empty except for an iron-frame bed with a small table next to it.

Two men pulled her, struggling, toward the bed. When they saw she would not go easily they stopped pulling. One left the room and returned with the man who had freed her from the closet.

'Okay now,' he said, smiling. 'No fuck.' Meaning, apparently, to be reassuring.

And she believed him – long enough to let them lead her to the bed and make her lie down and shackle her to the corners of its frame with handcuffs on her wrists and ankles. Then they all left the room, turning off the lights as they went out.

In the darkness she tried to focus on what had happened. Someone had kidnapped her. Someone had rescued her, only to imprison her again. Different factions. How to tell which was which? It got her mind running in circles, but it helped ward off the sexual images her position brought to mind, and the renewed possibility that she would be left and forgotten. She wished they had let her use the bathroom, then remembered that soiling herself had its advantages.

Five minutes after David called the Engs's pager number the phone rang in Official Corruption – the line taking calls forwarded from David's home number. David steadied himself and answered it. The prosecutors and investigators put on headphones to listen in, while the tape-recorder reels turned.

'Mr Clark?' asked a male voice David couldn't quite place. Not Martin Eng.

'Yes. Who's this?'

'Peter Eng. We met in Hong Kong.'

'Oh, yes. I didn't know you were in New York.'

'I've only just arrived. I'm calling on behalf of my parents.'

Jordan shook her head, no.

'I was hoping to talk to *them*,' David said.

'They're really quite exhausted, tonight. They did want me to tell you, though, that they hope and believe you're wrong about Susan Chan having been kidnapped.'

'It's kind of them to say so.' Waiting for the other shoe to drop.

'Because if you did happen to be right they would be very concerned. In Chinatown, kidnapping is often by proxy, and the people hired to do the kidnapping sometimes treat the victims far worse than the ones who initiated the kidnapping intended. You even hear stories of kidnappers cutting off parts of the victim's body as proof they have them, and to encourage the friends and relatives to pay the ransom money.'

*Fucking bastard.* 'So far no one's asked for ransom money.'

'Really? Perhaps that's a good sign. I didn't mean to add to your burden of worry.'

Not much you didn't.

Peter Eng went on: 'I'm being rude. You called. Do you have news?'

'I don't know if I'd call it news.' After the flash of fear and anger, David felt oddly calm. 'I beeped your parents because I have some new thoughts about their problem. They may be right to think I gave them a copy of that tape, not the original.'

'You're talking about the tape from me and June – the one Susan Chan was supposed to deliver to them.'

'Yes, that one. I was certain that I'd delivered the original to them. But I see now it's possible I gave them a copy.'

'You didn't tell my parents about a copy.' Peter Eng's tone was cool, almost matter-of-fact. 'How interesting that you made one.'

'Susan and I knew the tape would be precious to your parents, even before we learned that June had been killed. We were afraid we might

699

lose it, so I made a copy as a precaution.' The lie he had come up with and rehearsed. 'I didn't tell your mother and father when we talked recently because I didn't think a copy would help them. I was sure they had the original, and if the original was bad, why should the copy be better?' A lie close enough to the truth to be easy to tell.

'And do you know where the original is now?' Peter asked, only partly concealing his eagerness.

'I don't have it at the moment. I believe I can get it soon, maybe in as little as an hour. But I need some assurance that Susan is alive and well.'

'I don't know anything about that. But Chinatown can be a small place. I may be able to learn something. And if you can return the original tape, my family will owe you a large favor.'

This time it was Frank Perez who shook his head, holding his fingers to eyes like eyeglasses.

'I want to see her.' Risking a direct request.

'I know what you want, Mr Clark,' Peter Eng said with quick impatience. 'We can't always get what we want.'

'That goes two ways.' Fear made David's voice come out in a croak he hoped sounded tough. He covered the mouthpiece so he could catch his breath.

'No need to fight,' Peter Eng said. 'I suggest we pick a public place to meet, at a time when you'll have the tape.'

Perez scribbled on a pad and held it up for David to see.

'Ten-thirty,' David said. 'And there's a restaurant in Tribeca—'

'I'm sure. There's also a nice quiet Chinese restaurant uptown, in Inwood. They'll be closed soon, but I believe I can persuade them to stay open for us.'

The one where David had talked to Martin and Meiling. Perez shook his head and turned a thumb down.

'An empty restaurant where you know the owner isn't my idea of public,' David said.

They settled on a restaurant on the edge of Chinatown, one that would be neither full nor empty that late.

'You did good,' Perez told him when he was off the phone.

'Time to get over to the train station,' Mahoney said.

700

The gang kid who came in with a plate of food for Susan looked different from her other captors: sloppier, dirtier. He leered at her, studying her body, and when he set her plate on the bedside table he put his hand on her, pressing and probing.

He pinched her nipple. He was grinning at her when he did it, and somehow she knew it was important not to react. When he released the handcuffs on her wrists so she could sit up and eat she was amazed to find herself trying to pummel him, keening with anger and frustration.

He caught one of her hands and bent it sharply back at the wrist, his thumb in her palm, his fingers pressing into the back of her hand. The pain was so intense it narrowed her world to that and nothing else. He pushed on her hand and she fell back onto the bed. Even after he let go, her hand throbbed so badly she barely noticed when he squeezed her disdainfully between the legs.

Without a word, he locked her wrists to the bedframe again and pulled the rings from her fingers. He took away the food he had brought.

Amtrak train number 159 was on time. Jon Levi came bounding up the stairs from the platform looking around for David, who was standing alone under the annunciator board.

'I had plans tonight,' Jon said almost before he got within range. 'I just hope you appreciate that I dropped everything the way you said and made this ridiculous trip. The least you can do is buy me a beer and tell me a good story about why I had to do it.'

'I'll buy you all the beer you want, but I can't stay to watch you drink it. And the story will have to wait, too. I have to deal with this, first.' He held out his hand.

Jon looked at the outstretched hand a moment as if he didn't understand, then brightened. 'Oh, right.' He took an envelope from his jacket and handed it to David.

The weight and shape of the cassette in his hand brought David a surge of relief. He opened the envelope and saw a standard plastic audio-cassette box with a cassette in it.

'Happy?'

'It was an asshole stunt, switching it on me in the first place.' With the tape in his hand, David's anxiety was transformed into anger.

'Yeah, well, you got even, pulling all this life-and-death bullshit to get me down here with it.'

'No bullshit.'

'This is Jon you're talking to. What's life and death about anything you'd get tied up in, even a Chinese audio tape with data hidden on it?'

David grabbed him by the front of the shirt as a way to keep from hitting him.

'Listen, dickbrain, these people kidnapped the woman I –' he caught himself, let go of Jon's shirt – 'went to Hong Kong with.' He brandished the cassette. 'This is the ransom.'

Jon stared. 'You're shitting me, right?'

'No, I'm not shitting you. You said if there were separate data tracks you couldn't get it all onto a quick copy. Well, how in hell could you expect that kind of copy to fool the very people who were looking for the data?'

'They really kidnapped her?'

'Listen, I wasn't supposed to say that. I'm not supposed to talk about it at all, because that could get her killed, too. But yeah they really did. And they just threatened to cut pieces off her to prove they're serious.'

'Oh, shit, David, how could I know they'd want it that bad?'

'And they don't want it getting into other hands, either. This is dangerous stuff.'

Jon's eyes filled with eager curiosity. 'Do you know what it is?'

'You asshole.'

'Okay, you're right, now's not the time. You'll let me know, though – and how it comes out with your friend. I'm really sorry. Honestly. I had no idea. And listen, uh, about that tape . . .'

David grabbed him again. 'Don't fuck with me, Jon. If this isn't the original, they're going to kill her. And if they do—'

'Hey, hey, okay. Listen, that cassette you have in your hand has better audio than the original. But I have to tell you, if you give me a chance – the data isn't on the tape.'

'*What?* What are you talking about?'

'It's so beautiful. The recording tape – it's just audio. They put the data on the *leader* . . . head and tail. Optical, not magnetic. It's a miracle I thought to look. If I wasn't so brilliant . . . if I didn't pull my *asshole stunt* . . . we'd never have found it.'

'And this one –' David pushed the cassette at him – 'with *better* audio . . . what kind of data is on this one?'

'It's all there—' He saw David's face and immediately reversed ground. 'But if you want the original instead, sure. I was just trying to help out.'

He took another cassette from his jacket pocket. 'Here, I'll swap you.'

David, livid with anger and fear, snatched the cassette from Jon's hand.

'Okay, okay,' Jon said.

David pocketed both cassettes, knowing Jon was sure to have left another copy behind in case David demanded both of the ones he was carrying.

'If I were you, I'd keep real quiet about this,' David said. 'There's more than one party after it, and they have friends in surprising places. People have already died. You don't want to make yourself a target.'

Mahoney and Jordan were going over the plans for covering David Clark and rescuing Susan Linwood, if the opportunity was there.

'I'm worried about anything that's going to raise up the cops,' Mahoney said. 'Pullone's got to have buddies everywhere. If it gets back to him, or to Horgan, that there were Official Corruption investigators all over the Engs . . . I think we stand a real chance of losing them.'

Jordan thought about it. 'I wish I could say you were wrong. But this has to be our priority.'

'I'm not saying no. I just hope we can keep it contained.'

The phone that was getting David Clark's forwarded calls jangled Mahoney out of his other worries. He looked at Jordan.

'Are we expecting anything?'

'The man must get some ordinary phone calls.'

The answering machine picked up. They listened to the message Clark had recorded and waited for the signal tone.

'Mr Clark,' a male voice said. 'My name is Tony. I have newly acquired something you want. And I believe you have something I want. We must talk about an exchange. This is very important.' He ended with a phone number he repeated twice. 'Call at once, please.'

'That was a Chinese accent, right?' Mahoney offered.

'Sounded like.'

'Tony. Not a very Chinese name.'

'Why not? Isn't Eng's name Martin?'

'Come to think of it,' Mahoney acknowledged. 'And there's a Tony in this someplace, if I could remember where.'

'You think the message is real? You think this Tony has Susan?'

'That's what he seemed to be saying.'

'Then what about Peter Eng?'

'Somebody's lying,' Mahoney said. 'We'd better call the car, have him bring Clark in right away.'

# 13

'Change of plans,' David's driver said.

'Why? What?'

'They don't tell me these things. They want you back at Official Corruption.'

'I can't do that. I'm due to meet Peter Eng at the restaurant in twenty minutes.'

'It's on the way.'

The lights came on abruptly. Susan squeezed her eyes shut to hold out the glare, opened them slowly. Two men were converging on the bed. One was the man who had pulled her from the closet. He smiled at her: the same emotionless grimace as before.

'Feel good,' he said.

The other man was carrying a narrow leather belt and a hypodermic needle and syringe. She thought about resisting but knew it would be futile.

The tingling, warm pleasure swept through her again, again too much for her stomach. When the first rush was past they brought her a tape recorder and a piece of paper with words to read. They hurt her once while she was reading. She wished they would leave her alone.

'What's going on?' David demanded as he burst into the loft office.

'You had a phone call.' Mahoney played him the answering-machine tape.

'What's it mean?'

'It looks as if we have two teams both claiming they captured the flag. Do you know who Tony is?'

705

'There was a Tony Ching who was a rival of Martin Eng's. They had a dispute over an election at the association Martin used to belong to, and I think Tony had him beat up.'

'Right . . . that's what I remember – thinking maybe Tony put Mick Pullone's snitch in motion. So Tony and the Engs could be rivals over this tape, too.' Mahoney held out his hand. 'I assume you got it.'

'I got two.' He gave them to Mahoney. 'The one in the envelope is a copy. There's computer data stored on the leader, not the tape.'

'We can worry about that later. You'd better call Tony. You don't want to be late for Peter Eng.'

'If Tony's got Susan, what difference does Peter Eng make?'

'If.' Mahoney handed him the phone and put on earphones.

David sat down and caught his breath.

The phone was answered on the first ring. 'Wei?'

'I returning a call from Tony. This is David Clark.'

'This is Tony.'

'You said you have something I want.'

'Yes, something that was taken from you by Martin Eng.'

Stunned by the openness of it, David looked at Mahoney, who made a keep-him-talking motion with his hand.

'How do I know that?'

'Martin Eng *did* take something from you.'

'Suppose he did. I still don't know you have it.'

'Unfortunately I am not in the proper location to provide immediate proof. We can arrange something. If you have what I want in exchange.'

'And what would that be?'

'A recording tape. The same one Martin Eng wants.'

'I might have it.'

'Can you bring it to me at eleven o'clock?'

Jordan shook her head vigorously, flashed ten quick fingers and then two more.

'Twelve,' David said.

'All right. There is a late-night vegetable market under the Manhattan Bridge overpass. If you are there at midnight, someone will pick you up in a black Volvo and bring you to where you can see that I have what you want.' He hung up without giving David time to reply.

'Shit,' Mahoney said.

'This one doesn't beat around the bush.' Jordan.

'But do we believe him?' Mahoney asked.

'I've been worried about the Engs's enemies from the beginning,' David told them. 'Somebody killed June Eng. There's no reason to suppose they don't operate here. Or hire people here to do their work for them.'

'And somebody wound up Mick Pullone's snitch and set that whole thing in motion,' Mahoney said. 'Could be the same people. Let's listen to Tony again.'

They played the recording of David's phone conversation with him.

'Is he saying that he took Susan away from the Engs?' Jordan asked.

'That's what it sounds like.' Mahoney turned to the investigator from the Asian Gang Unit. 'Bob, does that make sense?'

'If you figure the Engs hired a youth gang to do the abduction and to hold onto her for them, then – yeah. I mean, these gang kids don't maintain military discipline or security. They talk and brag among themselves and among their peers. If Tony had his ear to the ground he could hear about it. Then all he'd have to do is hire a rival gang to snatch her away. He might even be able to buy off the gang that took her in the first place, or pull some kind of influence on them.'

'Okay. So we have to figure he's for real. And we need to work out a way to deal with this I'll-pick-you-up-and-take-you-somewhere business.' He looked at the clock. 'But first we have to get David over to his ten-thirty date.'

'What about the tape?' David asked.

'We do everything the way we planned. It can't hurt to have the tape in reserve, and the fewer last-minute changes we make, the better. If you need the tape, you call the number we gave you and somebody'll bring it into the restaurant.'

The men came back and unshackled Susan and walked her into a bathroom. Moving made her queasy. They put her in the tub, wearing her reeking dress, and turned on the water.

One of them took out a knife. She thought she ought to be frightened, but she wasn't, it was all too much like a dream. He cut the dress off her. Soon she was naked. What difference did it make? He shoved

something at her. Soap. Barked some command she did not understand. Why didn't they just let her be? When she did nothing, he put
his hand over hers and forced her to make harsh rubbing motions with
the soap on her body.

'Okay, let me,' she mumbled, making pushing-away gestures. She
soaped herself languidly, enjoying the sensation of the lather on her
body, just feeling good. The times she stopped, they pushed her hand
around to remind her what she was doing.

They took the soap away and made her rinse off and dry herself.
Then they gave her some clothes.


David was five minutes late for Peter Eng. By the time he got to the
restaurant, the remains of his pumped-up confidence had drained
away. The room was vast, at least twice as big as the Official Corruption loft, though the ceiling was not as high. Banks of fluorescent
lights exaggerated the garishness of the pale walls and red-and-gold
trim. There was Chinese music, loud enough to be distracting.

In the entrance area a Chinese woman in a blue dress was sitting on
a red banquette, waiting for a takeout order or perhaps a late date.
Huge goldfish swam in a long fish tank that divided the entrance area
from the rest of the restaurant.

A hostess smiled David in. 'One?' she asked, her voice barely
carrying over the music.

'I'm meeting someone.'

She nodded, still smiling, with no sign she'd understood, and led
him into the restaurant, past large, partly-occupied tables.

The room was divided into quadrants of which only one was in use
at this hour. Twenty or thirty patrons were spread among a dozen of the
large round tables that seemed the only kind the restaurant had. In
the three closed-off areas, the empty tables were all perfectly set,
ice-white tablecloths glaring under the bright overhead lights. Not
surprisingly given the phone call from Tony Ching, there was no sign
of Susan.

David spotted a heavyset Chinese man with thinning black hair
slicked back over his head and oversize tortoiseshell eyeglasses. At
the same time, the man saw him and waved.

'Miss,' David called to the hostess, and headed that way.

Peter Eng stood as David reached the table. He held out his heavy arms in greeting.

'David, my good friend.'

It was odd behavior, completely artificial, but Peter Eng's expression told David he was expected to cooperate. He allowed Peter Eng a quick, comradely hug and felt hands pat quickly over his back and sides.

'Look at you,' Peter Eng said, keeping up the charade. He opened David's jacket. 'You've taken off weight.' He patted David's stomach as if in confirmation. 'Wearing a beeper, too.'

'Doesn't everybody?' David said, sitting down. He was badly rattled. Peter Eng's pat-down had only narrowly missed the recorder and the microphone.

The hostess asked David if he wanted a drink.

'One of those,' David told her, pointing at the beer in front of Peter Eng.

'Were you able to get what I asked for?' Peter Eng asked when the hostess had left.

'The audio tape your parents wanted? Yes, I got it.' Naming things – as he had been instructed to – for the benefit of the recorder taped to his back and the one that was presumably picking up the conversation in the surveillance van, transmitted by his pager. Assuming they could hear him over the music.

'Do you have it with you?'

A touch too eager, David thought, recovering his equilibrium. 'It's where I can get at it.'

'I don't understand.'

'And I don't see Susan.'

'Not having Susan here is a precaution. We don't want to expose her. But once I know you have the tape, we can see about getting her to you.'

At least he had stopped being cagey, David thought. But that didn't change the fact that he didn't have her and was pretending to.

'I don't think you understood me,' David said. Knowing that nothing real was at stake, he was beginning to enjoy the sparring. 'I'm not doing anything, and I'm certainly not putting you within range of the tape, until I know Susan is unharmed.'

'Then I think we have a problem,' Peter Eng said.

709

The phone rang in Official Corruption. Perez.

'I can't hear a fucking thing,' he told Mahoney. 'Since he sat down in there, I'm getting a huge amount of static. It's still transmitting, but between the static and the music they're playing I only get stray words and syllables.'

'Have you checked the receiver?' Mahoney asked him.

'First thing we did. As far as we can tell it should be okay. It was fine when we went out. And the receiving antenna, too.'

'Isn't there anything you can do?'

'We're going to try moving the van. Maybe the interference is local or directional and if we're listening from somewhere else it won't be as bad.'

'Okay, let me know.'

Mahoney relayed the bad news to Jordan. 'We'd better make sure the equipment works in time for the meeting with Tony.'

When Susan was dressed they took her outside to a big black car. They had to help her off the curb or she would have stumbled and fallen. They got her into the back of the car and pushed and pulled her so she was in the middle of the seat. Then one of them sat on either side of her. The car pulled away. Once they stopped moving her, she drifted into a reverie in which none of them was real.

The hostess returned with David's beer and stayed to pour it for him.

When she left David said, 'I thought the whole point of meeting in a place like this was – you have your thugs bring her here and I get to see she's okay without being able to do anything about it until we figure out a way to make the exchange.'

'I don't have any thugs.'

'But the point remains.'

'Yes.'

'And . . .'

Peter Eng shook his head and drank some beer.

'Tell me something,' David said. 'Why did your parents think they had to kidnap Susan in the first place? If they'd told us about the problem, we would have figured out why and gotten the original for them.'

'They were very upset to see you at the China Society. When they added that to the bad tape, they felt sure you were in league with their enemies. And they also felt they had to act quickly.'

'Enemies? You mean the people who killed June?'

'Possibly.'

David looked at him.

'Probably.'

'And did these same enemies arrange the ambush near Dongguan?'

'Yes, probably.'

'Why?'

'They wanted something June had. She was in the vehicle with you from Zhuhai until Guangzhou. They may not have known she got out.'

'And is that why they killed her, to get what she had?'

'Possibly.'

'Did they get what they were looking for?'

'I have to assume they did. Personally, I think they killed her the way they did in part as a warning to my parents.'

'That's some serious warning. How do you follow up a warning like that?'

A waitress wheeled a dim-sum cart to their table. Peter Eng waved her away.

'They follow up by killing *me*,' he said. 'Sons are more valuable than daughters. So if they kill June as a demonstration, my parents may change their behavior, to protect me. But instead they called me back from Hong Kong.'

'Can't those people kill you here?'

'It's possible.'

'Why don't you all stop?'

'You have to think of us as soldiers in a civil war. We are concerned with the future of our ancestral country. And the future of the United States, too.'

'That sounds very noble, but Susan and I don't want any part of it.' Though it is consistent with our theory.

'You took sides when you took away that tape.'

'We didn't mean to. And I promise we'll never have anything to do with either you *or* your enemies ever again. We're out of this as soon

711

as you prove you can give me Susan back in return for your tape.' As if he could.

'I can't.'

Now we get to the nitty-gritty. 'Then forget your tape. I'm keeping it for someone who can.'

'You misunderstand. The reason I can't show Susan to you here is to protect her from our enemies. Did you get a phone call this evening?'

'What do you mean?'

'A phone call. About Susan.'

Something was wrong here, something unexpected. *Is anybody listening?*

Another dim-sum cart came by. This time Peter Eng selected two miniature steamers – one holding tiny shrimp dumplings; the other, stuffed mushroom caps. The waitress marked their check with her chop and wheeled the cart away.

'Suppose I did get a phone call,' David said.

'All right, suppose,' Peter Eng played along. 'If you did, what would this phone call have said?'

'That someone had taken Susan from you.'

'And what would his name have been, the man who made this supposed phone call?'

'Tony.' No point holding it back.

'Just Tony?'

'That's all he said.'

'And you believed that he had Susan.' The supposing dropped, now.

'Pending further proof.'

'There won't be any further proof. Tony is wrong. He only thinks his – thugs, did you call them? – his thugs took Susan from the people who were holding her.'

'What are you talking about?' Something *was* wrong.

'There was a raid. It was very bloody. Susan could have been killed – many others were. But the people Tony hired did not succeed. Only one of them survived, and he was persuaded to call Tony to say the mission had gone as planned.'

David downed the beer in his glass and poured himself the rest.

'The problem is,' Peter Eng continued, 'Tony will not stay fooled for long. So you and I have to conclude our business and you have to get Susan well out of harm's way immediately, at least until Mr Tony and his masters in China calm down. And that's why I can't display her to you. Not in Chinatown.'

'That's a good story,' David said, trying to recover. 'Tell me one reason why I should believe it.'

'You fool!' Peter Eng blanched at his own fury. 'Sorry. I didn't mean—'

'That doesn't answer the question.' David was intent on keeping focused, not get carried away by emotion and conjecture. If this was a bluff, it was a clever one. But if it was the truth . . .

'I can show you this,' Peter Eng said. He pulled a small cloth bag from his pocket and passed it across the table.

David guessed from the heft of it what it would contain: Susan's engagement and wedding rings. He put them back in the bag and put the bag in his pocket. 'That proves you had her at some point,' he said. 'No, not even that. You could have bought them or stolen them.'

'What's the point of this obstinacy?' Peter demanded. 'Don't you see that we have common interests?'

'And don't you see that you and your family have forfeited any claim to my belief or trust? That by your actions and your parents' you've made it impossible for me to believe a word you say.'

'All right.' Exasperated. 'We can't afford to go on like this. I can show you Susan, for just a moment. It's risky. But then we have to move our negotiations elsewhere immediately. Out of Chinatown.'

'Let's get to it.'

'Can you have the tape here in five minutes?'

'Less.' David hoped.

'How?'

'Leave that to me.'

Peter Eng studied him a moment, then stood up. 'I'll be right back.' He headed for the rest rooms – and presumably the pay phones.

'Did you guys get that?' David said for the benefit of his beeper-transmitter. 'Peter Eng says he has Susan, and Tony doesn't. And I may need the tape right away.'

'It's hopeless,' Perez reported from the van. 'I get maybe one word in three. I think he said he needs the tape, but I don't know. You want us to go in there?'

'Laurie?' Mahoney said. She was the one with experience in this kind of thing.

Jordan, on the line with them, said, 'I don't think so, not as long as you're not hearing anything like a threat, or any panic in Clark's voice.'

'I'm telling you, all I'm getting is static and weird music and stray syllables. Tone of voice, forget it.'

'Just sit tight. Remember we've got Benny and the others in there for emergencies. If anything breaks we'll hear from them.'

Inside the black car, Susan thought she heard a phone ring. She opened her eyes but the motion of the scenery going by the windows made her feel sick. She closed her eyes again.

'Okay,' Peter Eng said to David, returning from the pay phone. 'She'll be here in a few minutes.' From his jacket pocket he took a thin, flat cassette player. 'I can tell you that this won't distinguish the original from a copy. All it will tell me is that you aren't trying to ransom Susan with the Rolling Stones. We'll have to work out a better test later.'

Indeed they would – an audio playback would let him hear his own voice and his dead sister's, but it would reveal nothing about the optical data track.

'We don't need any test,' David said. 'Your parents have demonstrated their ability to reach out for both me and Susan. I'm sure they could do it again, enemies or not. I don't think for a moment it would be remotely healthy for me to try to fool you.'

'What about copies?' Peter Eng asked. 'Do you have any others?'

'No,' David lied. 'What good would they do me?'

'They might do you harm, if Tony and his friends knew about them.'

Or they might be insurance, David thought. He said: 'It looks to me as if we're at a kind of stalemate. Like the end of a game of Go – I think it's called Wei Kai, in Chinese –' the ancient Asian board game had been an enthusiasm of David's college days – 'when the board is

714

almost full and neither player can make any advantageous move.'

'Perhaps,' Peter Eng said. 'Or perhaps it's more like that stage of the game when a position can change back and forth between the same points again and again, alternating for ever unless one player can distract the other with a threat in another part of the board and end the stalemate to his own advantage.'

'See it that way if you want,' David told him. 'But trying to come out ahead is only going to make this harder.' There seemed to be no more to say.

In Official Corruption the second action line rang – the one for the team inside the restaurant. Mahoney grabbed the phone before the bell stopped vibrating.

'What's up, Benny?'

'Peter Eng just made a phone call. And he put some kind of radio or cassette player on the table.'

'Interesting. How do they look?'

'Calm and businesslike. Eng patted our guy down at the beginning but he didn't find anything.'

'No trouble?'

'I don't think so.'

'The transmitter's screwed up some way. Frank isn't getting anything useful. He said something about music.'

'Chinese opera. Can't you hear it?'

'Yeah. Kind of sour.'

'A specialized taste.'

'Keep on your toes – if Frank can't hear, you're all we have.'

'There's something I want you to hear,' Peter Eng said. He gave David a pair of earphones and plugged them into the cassette player.

David put the earphones on and heard hissing and some harsh words of Chinese and then a woman's voice – Susan's, he realized, but dull and listless in a way he had never heard it.

'Hello, David,' she said. 'This is Susan. Please do what they tell you. Don't go to the police.' There was a brief silence, more Chinese, and then a cry from Susan. 'Please David. They'll hurt me.'

'You bastard.' He pulled off the earphones. He had never before

715

been able even to imagine wanting to kill someone. Now he didn't need his imagination.

'No one's hurt her,' Peter Eng said quietly. 'As far as I know, no one's hurt her at all. What you heard was more surprise than pain. But you have to understand that we're serious. It would be unfortunate for Susan if you tried to play some trick to resolve our stalemate in your own favor.'

'I never doubted you were serious,' David said. 'But I swear, if you hurt her I'll kill you. I don't know how, but I'll find a way.'

'I'm sure you mean what you say, but none of these threats is really necessary now. Just give me the original tape and it will all be over.' He waved for a waiter. 'Bring us two more beers, please.' To David he said, 'Take a minute to calm down. I apologize for having to upset you.'

As the waiter was pouring their beer, David's peripheral vision caught motion near the restaurant entrance. He looked and saw three Chinese youths coming in. They reminded him of the three gang kids at the Chinatown game arcade Zack had wanted to try. These three were all in black jeans, too, with black leather jackets that looked capable of concealing an arsenal. One wore sunglasses and a baseball cap turned backward on his head. He moved more slowly than the others, feet dragging and head down, as if he was stoned.

'Don't stare,' Peter Eng said, and it was only then that David realized that the third young man was Susan.

# 14

'You have a tape for me,' Peter Eng said abruptly.

Disoriented, David at first didn't know what to say. 'I need to make a phone call,' he managed.

'I don't think so. Not while she's here.'

'Come and listen, if you want. I won't be saying anything.'

'Who are you calling? You were told not to bring anyone in on this.'

'I needed somebody to hold the tape while we talked and to bring it to me when the time came. I wasn't about to carry it around with me.'

'Where is he?'

'Close.'

'How do you get him here?'

'I beep him. He knows to come in and find me.'

'Can you talk to him?'

'No.'

'All right. Let's beep him and then you stand by the fish tank. When he comes in, hold out your hand for the tape and do not speak. Susan will be in the men's room with one of her friends until he's gone. If you say a word, if there's any trouble, Susan will suffer for it.'

It worried David but he couldn't think of a reason to object. He wondered if Mahoney's people, whoever they were, had spotted Susan.

'It's clever to dress Susan up like a boy,' he said for Perez's benefit. 'But I want to see her up close. I want to talk to her.'

'No. Not before I have the tape.'

David sat in silence, intending to seem obstinate. Peter Eng was unimpressed.

'Okay,' David conceded. They both got up and walked to the pay

717

phone in the corridor by the rest rooms. David made the call and keyed in the beeper number that would signal Richie Eilewitz to bring the tape.

As he hung up, the woman in the blue dress came into the corridor. Peter Eng stiffened and put a hand under his jacket.

*Reaching for a gun*, David thought.

The woman glanced at them in passing and went into the ladies' room.

Peter took his hand from under his jacket, empty.

'Well,' he said. 'It seems we're all touchy tonight.'

The number-two phone rang again. This time it was Grace Tsui.

'Clark made a phone call.'

The other phone rang.

'Hang on, here's Frank.'

Jordan answered the phone, listened, hung up. 'Clark beeped Richie. He wants the tape.'

Mahoney relayed the news to Grace Tsui. 'You see any sign of Susan Linwood?'

'Not so far.'

'Something's weird.'

Standing by the hostess desk, David watched the woman in blue go back to her table and Susan and one of her guards get up and go to the men's room. He tried to smile at Susan as she passed, but she didn't seem to notice him. Seen closer up, she looked even more stoned.

Having drawn a blank on a good way to signal Eilewitz, David had decided it was too risky even to try, especially since everybody out there would be keeping up, based on what came over the transmitter. He watched the fish glide to and fro over the ceramic pagoda at the bottom of their prison.

The outside door opened and Eilewitz came in. He moved lightly, with the look of a man expecting surprise and ready for whatever might come at him, from whatever direction.

He saw David and stopped.

David held his hand out.

'What's up?' the investigator asked.

718

David pushed his hand farther forward. He didn't want to shake his head or nod.

'You want the tape?'

David stayed silent.

Eilewitz took the tape out and extended it toward David.

'She here?' he said without moving his mouth, but before David could even grunt Eilewitz looked past him and said, 'Hi,' in a conversational voice.

David turned. Saw, standing next to him, Peter Eng.

'Everything all right?'

'Fine,' David said.

'Who are you?'

'Name's Richie, friend of Dave's.' The investigator held his hand out.

'Peter.' He shook Eilewitz's hand. 'Thanks for your trouble. Sorry we can't ask you to join us. Good night.'

'Who was that?' Peter Eng asked, back at the table.

'A friend.'

'I didn't know you had friends on the police.'

David stared at him, heart hammering. 'He's a computer programmer.'

'He looks like a policeman.'

'Definitely something weird,' Eilewitz reported. 'He met me at the entrance, stuck his hand out for the tape, wouldn't talk, wouldn't even nod his head. The Eng guy came up before Clark could say if Linwood was there.'

'What do you think?'

'Something's got him spooked. Some new threat, maybe.'

'Could be whatever Eng played him on the tape recorder,' Mahoney speculated. 'I could kill whoever made that fucking transmitter.' Not to mention every one of the opera musicians, and the composer.

David put the cassette on the table, his hand over it. 'Okay. This is what you want.' His mouth was dry again. It was hard to form the words.

Peter Eng slid the tape player across the table to him. David put the cassette in it while Peter put on the earphones. David pressed PLAY.

After a minute, David turned the player off and took the tape out. He put the tape in its case and put it in his pocket.

'I'm ready to make the exchange now,' he said. 'Have your friends bring Susan over here and then go to the men's room.' The rehearsed instructions coming out on their own. 'You can walk with Susan and me to the door and I'll give you the tape as we leave.' There was something more, but it was eluding him. Then he remembered: 'Just to avoid dangerous misunderstandings – I'm not alone here. And I won't be alone when I leave. Not just Richie, out there. I have friends in here, too. I know better than to try to take Susan from you. And you should know better than to try to take the tape from me.'

'We can all go out together,' Peter Eng said. 'Right now. I don't want to make myself an easy target. And I'm not walking around with the tape, unprotected, any more than you would.'

'All right,' David said. He didn't know how Frank Perez and the others would react to the change, but he was too frozen with the need to get Susan free of danger to think of clever alternatives, and he was afraid to lose the moment.

They paid the cashier. One of Susan's guards waited behind them to pay while she and the other guard stood near the table. David still wasn't sure if she had seen him or recognized him.

'Vehicle,' Perez reported. 'Large black sedan, European. Stopped by the fireplug in front of the restaurant. I see two, no, three males. Asian, I think. Heading for the restaurant. Motor running on the car.'

'Motor running?' Mahoney didn't like the sound of that.

'Yeah.'

'What kind of car?'

'Not a Mercedes. It's getting kind of pea-soupy out there, hard to see details through the mist. Could be, I don't know, an old BMW. Or one of those Swedish cars.'

David and Peter walked past the fish tank toward the door. Susan and her two guards were behind them. David turned to wait for Susan.

'I'll take the tape now,' Peter Eng said to David.

'I want Susan over here.'

Peter said something in Cantonese to the two gang youths.

'A Volvo?' Mahoney asked Perez.

'Yeah, a Volvo.'

'That's trouble. Get moving.'

The taller and thinner of the leather-jacketed youths took Susan by the elbow and turned her in David's direction. Behind them a couple were paying their check – the woman in blue and her date.

The outside door opened and three burly Chinese men in business suits came in. For an instant, everyone stopped. One of the newcomers pointed at Peter Eng and barked something in Chinese, then pointed at David.

Before anyone else could move, another of the business-suited men grabbed Peter Eng and held a knife to his throat. The third was pulling something dark and angular from under his coat. David didn't wait to see what it was. He threw himself at Susan, grabbing her waist and trying to knock her down and out of the way as sound erupted all around him: shouts of *'Police!'* and Chinese words and screams and strange chuffing sounds he didn't recognize.

David and Susan bounced off the skinny gang member and hit the fish tank. As Susan fell David snatched off her hat, releasing a cascade of black hair.

He turned, shielding her with his body, glimpsed the bloody forms of her two guards slumped on the floor. Peter Eng, sweating with fear, was held immobile by the man with the knife. The other two men were holding ugly, efficient-looking guns like the machine pistols in action movies. With his free hand the closer of the men yanked David away from Susan – hurling him into the arms of the man who had barked the orders – then bent to lift Susan.

*'Police! Freeze!'* a woman's voice called and the man reaching for Susan turned, raising his gun toward . . . the woman in the blue dress, her pistol extended in both hands.

Shots exploded from her gun and the man was hurled backward, his finger clamped tight on the trigger of his machine pistol, firing it as he fell, the gun's silencer making the chuffing noises David had heard before, suddenly obliterated by a cataract of glass and water as bullets shattered the fish tank.

The man holding David with a single, choking arm around his neck began backing toward the door, using him as a shield. His companion – still holding a knife at Peter Eng's throat – was already there, on his way out. Susan lay slumped on the floor, drenched with water from the fish tank. A goldfish struggled for breath in the hollow above her hip, another at her feet. Blood streaked the water between her and the fallen gunman.

The woman in blue and her partner were following, their guns extended. Another man with a gun was following behind them. The restaurant was a bedlam of yelling and confused motion.

David struggled, but the arm holding him did not yield. He could barely breathe and his vision was going blurry. His captor's other hand held one of the silenced machine pistols. He fired it at the pursuing investigators and they hit the floor. David pushed at the gun arm. The hold on his throat tightened.

David felt the cool, damp night air as they backed through the restaurant's front door. Behind him he heard a thud and a high scream. Sounds of scuffling.

The man holding him stopped moving. His grip tightened. As David blacked out, he felt himself spun around. He thought he heard shouting but he wasn't sure.


'Dave?' he heard through ringing ears. 'You okay?'

He was lying on his back in some kind of van. It took a corner fast enough to slide him along the floor.

Somebody held him steady. Frank Perez.

'Susan!' he tried to say, but his voice wasn't working right. 'Where's Susan?'

'She's okay. What about you?'

'Don't know,' he croaked. 'I think I'm okay.' He tried to sit up and was instantly dizzy.

'Take it easy,' Perez said. 'We'll get you someplace safe.'


Mahoney got off the phone with Perez. 'Frank has them,' he told Jordan. 'He thinks they got clear in time.'

'We'd better get over there and start doing some damage control,' she said, but he was already on the line with Ned King, who was following the action from the Southern District with the chief of the federal criminal division.

'There was a shootout at the restaurant—'

'Baby Jesus! What—'

'—we have Linwood and Clark, they're on their way to a safe house, and I've got a police surgeon headed there to look them over—'

'Good.'

'—I don't have the details on the shootout yet, but Grace Tsui and Benny Yeung and Richie Eilewitz were all involved. Three people down, probably dead. I don't know who – Chinese gang members. None of our people got hurt. And we've got Peter Eng, too. Laurie wants to go over and do some damage control—'

'Okay, but she won't carry enough weight by herself. The police bosses are going to be out in force. I'll reach out for the Chief of Patrol and the First Deputy Commissioner so they know we have this under control and they should just go through the motions for now, and then I'll get over there myself. Tell Laurie to keep as low a profile as she can . . . there are too many Official Corruption people visible in this already. And you stay put. I don't want you showing your face anywhere near there.'


Frank Perez brought David into a sparsely furnished apartment with small, boxy rooms and low ceilings. David's throat hurt from the pressure that had been put on it, he was still disoriented, and his whole body felt cold.

'Where's Susan?'

'She's here,' Perez told him.

*'Where?'*

'In one of the bedrooms, but she's kind of out of it and I don't want you in there until the doctor's had a look at her.'

David didn't like being kept away from her, but he didn't see what he could do.

'They were dead, weren't they?' he asked.

'Who?'

'Those two gang kids in the restaurant. And the other one, too – the one the woman shot.'

'I don't know. I wasn't in there.'

The doorbell rang. Perez took out a gun and went to answer it.

He came back with the gun out of sight again. With him was a tall, dark-haired man in khakis and a white shirt carrying a medical bag. Perez took him in to look at Susan.

---

Ned King called Mahoney. 'I got them to put the brakes on at the police department, but something's still bound to get out. You've got a Wild West shootout at a Chinese restaurant, a million press people, reports of missing witnesses . . . I'm hoping nobody gets as far as a major operation by Official Corruption around someone called Peter Eng, but one or two are already sniffing at the possibility that the cops are under pressure to keep the investigation contained.

'Once word gets out, we run a real risk it'll spook Pullone or Horgan,' King said. 'It means moving all that up. We can't afford to wait for Pullone's RDOs.'

'We can catch him when his tour ends tomorrow,' Mahoney proposed.

'You'd better pick him up on the way in, in the morning. Have him bang in sick, to keep from lighting anybody up. I know it's going to take time with Pullone, but get to Horgan as soon as you can. This makes it all a lot trickier, but it's the only way.'

---

Susan knew she was in another bed, with no handcuffs this time. Something was binding her right thigh, which throbbed with pain, but she wasn't tied down.

There had been another shooting, more people killed, she thought, all of it strange as a dream. And someone who looked like David. He'd knocked her down when the shooting started, just the way David had in China. Maybe it *was* a dream. Even though her head hurt where she remembered hitting it.

The door opened and a man came in. She hoped he would leave her alone. Everybody had been pushing and pulling her . . . she just wanted to lie here.

The man had stopped by the bed. He was looking at her very intently.

'Ms Linwood?' the man said tentatively. 'Susan Linwood?'

'Who are you?'

'Alan Tanzer. I was Dr Linwood's student . . . it must be ten or twelve years ago, now. We met at the hospital. You were doing public relations for them, I think.'

'Did Richard send you?' Could that be? Could this man be from the safe, solid world beyond the dream? But he didn't answer.

'If it's all right, I'd like to give you a quick examination and have a look at that cut on your leg,' he said. 'I understand you've been through quite an ordeal.'

The Official Corruption team was gathered in the office. Ned King and the feds' criminal-division chief were on the sidelines, paying close attention.

'You up to talking about what happened out there?' Mahoney asked Grace Tsui.

'I'm a little in shock, but I'll tell you what I remember. Benny and I were on our way to the lobby of the restaurant, keeping an eye on Clark and Eng and what we thought were three gang kids in leather jackets.

'At that point we were flying kind of blind, because after our last update we had no reason to believe Peter Eng had access to Susan Linwood. But we saw Clark get the tape from Richie and he did some kind of demonstration with it, so we figured something was up. Benny and I were keeping close, just in case, while Ahn and Eric hung back a little.'

'We're going to have to ask Clark about that part of it,' Mahoney said. 'I don't know where Linwood came from, either.'

'Wherever she came from, it's a damn good thing she lost that hat,' Benny Yeung said. 'Those three Hong Kong crazies would have shot her, sure as day, if they hadn't seen her hair.'

'It was kind of tense,' Grace Tsui said. 'A lot going down all at once and hard to tell the good guys from the bad guys.'

'You get the medal,' Benny Yeung said. 'If you hadn't shot that guy we'd both probably be dead.'

'Okay,' Mahoney said. 'Let's slow down a bit here. Grace was saying—'

'In hindsight it looks they were there to snatch Eng and Clark, and probably Linwood, too, if they found her. They grabbed Eng first, one of them holding a knife to his throat. And as soon as that happened, before Benny and I had our guns out or a chance to identify ourselves, Clark tackled one of the gang kids – who it turned out wasn't a gang kid at all, it was Linwood. That took her out of the action, and not a moment too soon, because the crazies had their artillery working and the two actual gang kids were dead meat.'

'By that time,' Benny Yeung said, 'Grace and I were shouting *'Police!'* in every dialect we knew, but these guys didn't flinch. One of them grabs Clark and kind of tosses him to the other and I don't know what he was going to do then. Something with Linwood.'

'I shouted again,' Grace Tsui said. 'I was scared enough so it came out real loud. One good thing was, there was a good clean field of fire, with Linwood and Clark out of the way. And this guy finally hears me and I can see he's like – "okay, now I have to swat this fly," and he's turning his gun on me, and the next thing I know for sure I have an empty gun and a sore hand from the recoil and this crazy is flat on the floor in a big pool of water with fish flopping all around.'

'Saved both our lives, for sure,' Benny Yeung put in. 'Ahn's, too, because by then he was right there backing us up.'

'While Eric tried to hold back the screaming hordes in the restaurant,' added Ahn Ling.

'What a zoo,' Eric Leo said. 'I thought they were going to trample each other trying to get out through the kitchen, and then the chef or whoever was chasing them back out of there with a cleaver.'

'Not to mention Richie and his tire iron,' Perez said.

'Yeah, Richie, what about that?' Jordan said.

'It was just – I had it in the car and when this all started to come down I thought, hell, there's plenty of us with guns, maybe a little silent persuasion is going to be in order. It was just luck I was over by the door when this bozo comes backing out with the point of his pig-sticker under Peter Eng's chin. If he'd had the blade up against Eng's throat, I'd have let him walk right by. But the way it was I thought I could wallop him good and he wasn't going to slit Eng's throat by accident.

'So I let him get a fair distance out the door, to where he was getting confident nobody was going to bother him, and I gave him a good overhand shot on the elbow. He yelled like a stuck pig and the knife went flying and he just crumpled.'

'I think his pitching days are over,' Jeff Cavanaugh said.

'Well, by the way he screamed he can sing opera. The guy with Clark heard it and turned around, and there's his buddy on the deck. He threw Clark at Frankie, maybe figuring he was going to shoot his way to the car, but by then he had a gun in each ear and one up his nose and nobody in front of him to shoot. So he folded.'

'By this time Frank decided we were a little too public,' Benny Yeung said. 'On account of we had these serious security questions to worry about. So he got Eng and Clark and Linwood and the van and a half-dozen investigators out of there before patrol started to arrive. He only beat them by about a minute, but when they got there there was nobody in sight except us and the dead and wounded, and pieces of fish tank.'

'What a mob scene that turned into,' Grace Tsui said. 'I haven't seen that much police brass in one place since the St. Patrick's parade.'


After he examined Susan, the doctor looked at David.

'This one's going to be okay,' he told Perez as David put his pants and shirt back on. 'I think you should get the woman to a hospital.'

'You're sure?' Perez prodded. 'We really want to keep this quiet.'

'I'm a doctor, not a tactician.' He sounded angry. 'The cut on her leg didn't hit any major vessels, but it's deep and there's a piece of glass in it that's got to be dealt with – and God knows what it carried in with it. And there's a chance she might have a concussion.'

'Okay. I'd better call to ask where to take her.'

'Do you know who she is?' the doctor asked.

David thought he knew what was coming, and it didn't make him happy. You're being ridiculous, he told himself – this is no time for jealousy.

'Her husband's a prominent neurosurgeon,' the doctor was saying. 'World famous. He's the one who should be deciding on her care.'


'Here's how it looks,' Jordan said to the team at Official Corruption. 'We're getting decent cooperation from the police bosses on not pushing too hard investigating our little shooting party. But even so, the eleven o'clock news was already full of "conflicting eyewitness reports" and "missing witnesses." Molly O'Hara was interviewing somebody about a "mystery woman." We have to assume our targets have their antennae up for something like this. And once they get wind of it, they'll find ways to learn more, so we have to get moving on them right away.

'We're going to need some of you as early as six tomorrow morning,' she said. 'This morning, that is. Frank and Richie, definitely. Not Grace and Benny – being under fire gets you a by on this one.' She stood up. 'Okay, everybody get some sleep. Dan and I'll close up.'

David stood in the doorway of the bedroom, looking at Susan. She was curled up on her side like a kid, the fear and turmoil of the past day erased from her features by sleep.

When the ambulance arrived for her, he asked to ride along, but even before the ambulance driver said no, the investigator who had relieved Perez did.

'You're here till further notice,' he told David. 'We don't know how safe it is for either of you out in the world.'

'You can't hold me prisoner. Suppose I say I need to go to the hospital myself?'

'Tell you what – you want to call your lawyer, you can do that. That's what they told me you're supposed to do as soon as you feel strong enough. That and sit down with me and tell me everything you remember about what just happened.'

'The important thing is, you're both safe, and you're both okay,' Ryan said. 'For now, I'd say the best place you can be is right where you are. Talk to the investigator, if you're up to it. Then get some sleep and you can give us the details in the morning.'

'Some damn reporter is bound to wonder about so many Official Corruption investigators just happening to be in that restaurant right then,' Mahoney said to Jordan as they locked up the office. 'Even picking up Pullone first thing in the morning, I'm still afraid too much

728

of this is going to get around too soon and by the time we can flip Pullone, Horgan will know something's rotten.'

She smiled at him. 'You always worry this much?'

'I don't always have this much to worry about.'

# 15

'It's the waiting that's getting to me,' Mahoney said at just past seven in the morning; he and Laurie Jordan were at a motel not far from Mick Pullone's home, expecting to hear from Richie Eilewitz. 'Do you ever get used to it?'

'Not if it's something that matters.'

When the phone rang the only question was, good news or bad. Jordan picked up the receiver and listened. 'We're ready,' she said, and hung up.

'They got him,' she told Mahoney. 'They're on their way.'

'Great.' Mahoney swung his legs off the bed, stood up and stretched. His fingertips grazed the acoustical tiles of the ceiling.

Minutes later he heard tires on gravel. Three cars, pulling in quickly. He went to the window and eased the curtain away from the wall far enough to expose a sliver of view. He saw the two investigators' cars and Pullone's ride – a 4 x 4 on steroids – pull to a halt. Richie Eilewitz jumped from the driver's seat of the 4 x 4. Mahoney waited to see Frank Perez climb out of one of the cars with Pullone, then let the curtain fall back into place.

'It's them.'

He heard the door of the next room open and close.

'Now we wait some more,' Jordan said.


Sunlight on the wall of the room woke Susan up. She was groggy and disoriented. And afraid. The last thing she remembered was being in a closet. No, handcuffed to a bed. And then a ride in a car. And then . . . there was more but increasingly she didn't want to know what was dream and what was real. Something about Richard, too . . .

This was someplace new, but it smelled familiar. She was bound again, one hand strapped to the bed. Her leg still throbbed. She let her eyes close, afraid to give any sign of being awake, and listened for the sound of someone in the room with her. She heard the ticking of a clock. It mesmerized her back to sleep.

The motel walls were thin but not thin enough to follow what was happening next door. Now and then, Mahoney could hear raised voices.

'You might try getting some air,' Jordan suggested. 'You look kind of strung out.'

'I'd be afraid I'd miss something.'

'If you stay here pacing and fidgeting you're going to drive me nuts.'

'Sorry.'

'It happens to everybody.'

He took as long a walk as he could. She was right, there was no reason not to. His part in this wouldn't come until after hers, and they weren't ready for her yet. The problem was, there wasn't anywhere to go. He walked along the highway, but even on the verge beyond the shoulder the wind from the eighteen-wheelers blasting by threatened to knock him flat.

'Anything?' he asked when he got back.

'Not yet.'

The light was brighter when Susan woke up. She glanced at the arm strapped to the bed. There was a tube going into her vein. Were they keeping her drugged that way?

She heard footsteps approaching the door and quickly shut her eyes. The door opened, closed. Footsteps again, coming toward the bed.

The footsteps stopped. Someone was standing beside her. Susan could feel the heat of his body.

'You awake, hon?' A warm voice with a Caribbean accent.

Susan opened her eyes and saw a smiling ebony-skinned woman in white – a nurse – and burst into tears of relief.

731

It was another hour before Eilewitz knocked on the motel-room door.

'He's hungry. He didn't have his breakfast.'

'How's it going?' Mahoney asked.

'Could be worse. He thinks he's a tough guy. He started with the usual routine – "I don't know what you're talking about but I'll be happy to talk to you." Looking to get an idea of what our case looks like.

'So we obliged him. We played him the El Coyote tape and showed him the surveillance pictures of the two of them, nice and cosy. I had the feeling he maybe wondered if we were going after him for murdering Ying.'

'Should we be?' Jordan asked.

'Nah. Frank let him worry about it a little while, is all. You could see his mind work. He knew he didn't do it, but he didn't know we wouldn't try to hang it on him as a conspirator. Probably figured *he* would have, in our place.'

'Has he seen the light yet?' Mahoney asked.

'He's getting there, but slow. Playing it cagey – *"Can I get a walk out of this?"* I tell him, "Hey, the way it looks to me, you're going away for a long time, one of those nice prisons upstate with all the guys you ever put away, and all their buddies." '

'You give him a Christian Burial speech?' Jordan wanted to know.

'Cop to cop. Like . . . I know you've given this speech yourself a thousand times, but it's God's own truth. You're at the crossroads of your life, and the decision you make now is the most important decision you've ever made, budabing budaboom.'

'And?'

'Like I said, he needs to think he's a tough guy. But underneath he's like a lot of them – he knew something like this was coming, he just didn't know when. So now he's kind of relieved. He knows he's been a bad boy and he's ready for his spanking.'

'My turn, then.'

But for the ferocity of Jordan's smile it might have seemed like one of her jokes. Watching her, Mahoney thought – I wouldn't want to be the reason for that smile.

She said, 'He can wait for his food until he's talked to me.'

732

Having slept soundly and long, David awoke in a strange bed in a strange room. He dressed quickly, full of worry about Susan.

The investigator was sitting in the kitchen drinking takeout coffee. He pulled another container from a big white bag and put it in the microwave for David.

'There's donuts, too.'

'Do you know how Susan is?' David asked him.

'She's okay. They got the glass out of her leg.'

'I'd like to see her.'

'I don't think so. Not now.'

'Suppose we call Mr Mahoney and see what he has to say.'

'He's busy.'

'It's worth a try.'

'No, he's really busy. In the middle of something important.'

Important! Compared to what? David thought. He said: 'I need to call my lawyer.'


Mahoney tried watching television but couldn't concentrate on it. All he could think was that in the next room Mick Pullone was or wasn't agreeing to cooperate with them. And Pullone was the key to Kevin Horgan.

Jordan had said she was convinced Pullone would flip, that the only real questions were how much he'd give up and how useful it would be. And whether he would put his heart into it when they sent him out after Horgan. Mahoney hoped she was right. The further into this he got, the more important it seemed.

It wasn't only what Horgan had done, himself, that so infuriated Mahoney, although that was more than bad enough – cutting corners and bending the rules, ultimately breaking the law. What compounded it was the kind of example he'd been setting. Mahoney had seen how the other A.D.A.s in the unit looked up to Horgan. If he wasn't stopped they might not all go bad the way he had, but their judgment would be distorted, their susceptibility to the dangers of wielding prosecutorial power would be increased. And real people's real lives would be ruined as a result. Mahoney didn't believe that was how the office ought to work, and he was only now coming to understand how passionate he was about it.

On the phone, David gave Ryan and Miller a quick rundown on the adventure of the night before.

'It's in all the papers,' Miller said. 'Though nothing like the way you described it. More a Chinatown gang war – Hong Kong Triad versus local boys. And one paper is making a fuss about a mysterious missing bearded man and a dragon-lady gang leader who disappeared before the police arrived.'

'Dragon lady?'

'That's what it says,' Miller affirmed. 'Except for that, there's no hint that you or Susan were ever there.'

'What about Peter Eng?'

'Not a word,' Ryan said.

'Have you talked to Susan?' Miller asked.

'I was just saying I wanted to go see her, but the guy they have babysitting me says no. They claim they're protecting me, but I feel more like a prisoner.'

'We need to be sure this has blown over before you go back to normal. We called Mahoney to see what he thinks; we're waiting to hear back.'

'They tell me he's busy.'

'From what he's told us, and the way they're keeping the story out of the press, I'm sure he has something to finish before full word of all this gets out.'

'I don't know about that. All I know is I want to see Susan.'


There was a knock on the motel-room door. Eilewitz.

'You're up next, Counselor,' he told Mahoney.

'What happened?'

'Laurie did it. That's one tough lady. Too bad you couldn't see her in action.'

'He's on board, then?'

'About ninety percent. He's given it all up, and he's smart enough to know what's coming next. But we're letting you have the pleasure of telling him.'

'Let's go.'

'First he gets to eat and think about his choices.'

'That's generous of everybody.'

'All part of the game,' Eilewitz said.

Jordan brought Pullone his lunch, then joined the others in the next room.

'I was telling Dan how it's too bad he couldn't see you operate,' Eilewitz said.

'It was pretty standard,' she said. 'Though I have to admit, that man is one serious scumbag.'

'She laid it all out for him, beginning to end,' Eilewitz said. 'Sounded like everything he ever did wrong in his life. And the best Christian Burial speech I ever heard.'

Jordan smiled, still fierce. 'He doesn't have anywhere else to turn at this point. He's thoroughly dirty and he's looking at a lot of time in a state prison. And you know what that means for a cop.

'So I let him think about that and then I dropped the Southern District into the conversation. Told him he'd better not count on getting any mileage from his grand jury immunity because the feds were going to have his ass for violating the Engs's civil rights, anyway. And he saw a lifeline – maybe if he plays his cards right, he can make a deal to do federal time.'

'Almost as good as a pardon,' Eilewitz said.

'At least he might live through the first month,' Frank Perez put in.

Jordan said, 'In the end I just told him, "Look, *I* know you have to push for some assurances from me, and *you* know I can't give them to you. So do yourself a favor, stop screwing around and make up your mind. Because the truth is we both know you've made it up already. You made it up a long time ago." And he didn't say no.

'Then I said, "You want some time to compose your thoughts? I can understand that. Take a half-hour, take an hour. We'll get you some lunch. When you're ready, you can make the phone call. Because it's either that or you're under arrest and we call a press conference this afternoon to tell the world all about the adventures of Mick Pullone, and your life is over." '

Jordan went in to see how Pullone was doing, came back and gave Mahoney a thumbs-up.

'Let's go get him.'

Mahoney was the third one in the door, after Eilewitz and Jordan. Pullone did a take when he saw him.

The detective was sprawled in the easy chair in the corner of the room. He had a cigar in one hand, was balancing a cardboard coffee cup on the chair arm with the other.

Mahoney stood close to Pullone, arms crossed over his chest. It was a calculated use of his size: he loomed even more intimidatingly than Horgan.

'We need to talk about Martin Eng and his wife.' Mahoney said it simply, no great weight.

Pullone closed his eyes for a moment. When he opened them he took a pull at his coffee.

'What do you want to know?'

'Might as well start at the beginning. And you don't need to leave anything out, we have plenty of tape.'

The story Pullone told, haltingly at first, bore out what Mahoney already knew or had guessed. When Pullone faltered or strayed, Mahoney had a question to put him back on track.

Pullone's snitch, name of Leon Ying, a Chinese plumber and sometime gang member Pullone had used only a couple of times before, had come to him with a tip: there were some people who handled dirty money, and if Pullone raided them soon he could catch them with a lot of cash, maybe millions. Leon thought it might be drug money, but the problem was these people never actually handled drugs. If Pullone could provide some drugs, Leon could get access to the house to plant it.

Pullone had asked him where he got the information. 'From someone who doesn't like these people,' Leon had said. A very reliable source – men with a lot of face.

Pullone hadn't loved it, but he needed money and he was expecting a piece of the finder's fee.

'I'm the one with my ass on the line,' he offered defensively. 'Why should the snitch get all the fucking money?'

'What happened then?' Mahoney asked, neutral.

Pullone had thought of El Coyote as a source of the heroin. But before he went to El Coyote he had to know the case would have a home with someone he could trust.

'That means Kevin Horgan,' Mahoney said.

'Who else? He's the one who assigned you the case, isn't he?'

There it was. Mahoney struggled to keep the eagerness out of his voice. 'How much did he know?' Sounding almost bored – as if he already knew the answer.

Mahoney could see the decision take hold: the tension went out of Pullone's face.

Pullone polished off his coffee. 'You kidding?' He snorted. 'You think I'm going to pull a stunt like that – put myself on the line with some scumbag heroin dealer – without being a hundred percent sure of the follow-up? Kevin Horgan knew every fucking thing I did.'

Mahoney was going to ask a question when he caught something in Pullone's face that told him to shut up and wait. Use silence as a tool.

For an agonizingly long moment there was nothing. Then Pullone said, 'Not just the Eng thing – from the first day we started to work together.'

'Was he taking money, with you?'

'You know, Kevin never gave a shit about money for himself. He wanted the forfeiture numbers. He wanted the money for the office so he could be a big hero and have his own unit with a big budget. He even wanted to put bad guys away. Ambitious motherfucker, but nothing like greedy.'

Pullone was talking to Mahoney like a bar-room buddy now. Mahoney grabbed a chair and sat, straddling it, back to front, his arms folded on top of the chair back.

'How did you and Horgan get started together?'

'We had a couple of cases, maybe five, six years ago, and one of them, the search wasn't exactly kosher and we were sitting in this bar and he said, "You know, these fucking skells you collared ought to go away for twenty-five to life." And I said "Yeah," and he said, "I don't want to put anybody I work with in the position of committing perjury, and we both know that fucking warrant won't stand up on its own feet." And I said, "Yeah," and he said, "I don't want to see these scumbags walk, either – them or their money."

'That was it,' Pullone said. 'That was how we got started.'

'You get this going with some other A.D.A. s, too?'

'Just Horgan. I mean, taking money from snitches, putting in warrants with bullshit probable cause – that was me and a lot of other guys I worked with. Cops, not D.A.s. But we didn't go around talking about it, if you know what I mean. Horgan was the only D.A. who as much as said, "I don't care if you cut corners, I don't care what you do, I just want to make cases." '

Susan's hospital room was large and airy, almost like a room in an expensive apartment. An investigator from the D.A.'s office sat outside the door.

David sat next to Susan's bed watching her sleep.

Her eyes opened. 'David?'

'Yes.'

She just looked at him. He couldn't tell what she was thinking.

'How long have you been here?' she asked.

'I don't know. A while.'

He thought she smiled, he couldn't tell. Her eyes closed and she was asleep again.

'All right,' Mahoney said when it looked as if Pullone was about dry. 'Let's make that phone call. You understand the deal?'

'Yeah. I talk to Kevin and I get him to say the right things, and then I cop a plea that puts me in the federal system.'

'One step at a time,' Mahoney warned. 'Anything's possible, but you've got to do what's right, first. And I'm talking about what's right for you. Because that's what everybody else is going to do – what's right for them. Kevin Horgan is going to save Kevin Horgan's ass if he can, and if it's at Mick Pullone's expense, too bad. You bring us Kevin Horgan the way we need him, we'll do what we can for you. And you know that's the only deal we can make. No guarantee.'

Pullone took a minute with it. 'Okay, where's the phone?'

'Hang on,' Jordan said. 'We need to know where you're going to meet him. Is there someplace the two of you hang out?'

'A couple of bars. An Italian place where we have lunch, but it's all cops and prosecutors.' He puffed on his cigar, shook his head. 'Outside. This has got to be outside. Someplace where's there's nobody at the next table.'

'Let me check,' Jordan said. She went to the other end of the room and had a quick, whispered conference with Eilewitz. 'Okay, we can deal with that.'

She took the phone off the nightstand, checked that it was wired up to the tape recorder, and handed it to him.

Mahoney put his earphones on.

'Where've you been?' Horgan demanded, clearly annoyed. 'I've been looking for you all morning. You called in sick, but you're not at home, and you don't call back when I beep you—'

Mahoney didn't like the sound of this. Horgan had something on his mind. Not responding to the beeper had been a calculated risk: they couldn't let Pullone make any calls until they knew he'd signed on for real.

'—There's something going on here,' Horgan was saying. 'You hear anything about this Chinatown shootout last night?'

Oh shit, Mahoney thought.

'Listen, I got no time for bullshit here,' Pullone told Horgan. 'I've got to see you – right now.'

'I can't—'

'You fucking can, and you fucking will. You don't want to think about the alternative.'

'What's—'

'In person.'

They settled on a place to meet and Pullone hung up.

'Good job,' Jordan told him.


Susan was still sleeping. David had not tired of watching her.

A man strode into the room. He was tall and trim, with a straight nose between penetrating, close-set gray eyes. His wavy brown hair was lightly streaked with gray and his suit fit better than the one David had had made for him in Hong Kong.

'Who are *you*?' he snapped at David, and David knew at once who was asking.

'David Clark.'

'From the grand jury.' Not a question.

'Yes.'

'How did you get in here?'

739

Through the door, David was tempted to say. Richard Linwood was one of those men who made him feel instantly combative. Or maybe it was the situation. He said nothing.

'I'd like you out of here,' Linwood told him. 'This minute.'

David almost complied – the man had that much presence. He looked at Susan. Her eyes were still closed.

'If she asks me to leave.'

'She doesn't look in much condition to ask for anything. If you'll excuse me, I'd like to examine her.'

David stood to face him. 'I thought it was against medical ethics to treat your own relatives.' He couldn't take the thought of this man touching Susan, husband or not.

'I didn't think she'd take up with someone so dense,' Linwood said with distaste.

'Richard?' Susan said in a thin voice. 'Is that you?'

They both turned to look at her.

'Are you two fighting?'

'I've asked him politely to leave so I can examine you.'

'He *is* a doctor,' Susan said. 'I suppose we should let him do some doctoring.'

David was shaken to be dismissed like that, virtually the first time he had seen Susan awake since she'd been kidnapped. He wanted to talk to her, to see how she was. He was afraid she blamed him for what had happened to her, the way he blamed himself.

If they couldn't talk, if he had to go, he wanted at least to kiss her, however chastely, or even just touch hands – make some kind of contact. But anything like that seemed too much, too pointed a challenge. Reluctantly, he turned and walked out the door.

# 16

Pullone and Horgan met in an empty parking lot at the base of the Brooklyn Bridge. The heavy span of the bridge and its spidery cables loomed overhead against a low silver sky. Across the East River, the downtown skyline of Manhattan challenged the harbor, stolid as a banker. Only the banners of the South Street Seaport provided an element of frivolity.

Mahoney and Jordan were with Frank Perez in the Official Corruption van, parked behind the stone wall of a restaurant next door to the parking lot. The investigator was preparing a brace of shotgun microphones.

'There'll be two of us out there,' he said. 'One on the barge, and one in the building on the far side of the lot. These things are real sensitive, so we should each be able to get every word they say. With two we can be a lot surer we'll get what we need. And if there are any doubtful places on one recording, we can clear them up with the other.'

In the van, Mahoney concentrated on what he was hearing. Closed his eyes and tried to visualize the scene.

'What the fuck is this about?' Horgan led off.

'We've got to talk.'

'I figured that out.'

'First pat me down.'

'What are you talking about? Out here in the open?'

'Over by the wall. Nobody's there.'

'I still don't . . . why am I patting you down?'

'I'll tell you why – we're going to have a frank conversation here, but first I'm going to make sure you're not wired. I'm going to satisfy

741

*my*self, and you'd better satisfy *your*self.'

'Jesus, you *are* spooked.'

'Fucking A.'

'Okay, here, go ahead.'

Silence. Faint noises. The shuffle of feet.

'Okay.' Pullone. 'Your turn.'

'This is too fucking dumb.'

Another shuffle of feet, a perfunctory series of slapping noises.

'All right, satisfied?' Horgan. 'Now are you going to tell me what the fuck this is about?'

'They're onto us.'

'Who? What are you talking about?'

'I'm talking about every fucking thing we did, the last eight years. Every bad case, every phony warrant, every scumbag we sweated a plea out of based on no evidence, every snitch we paid to lie.' Pullone named a string of cases.

'Where do you get this *we* shit?'

'Are you listening, or what? They have us on the whole Eng thing. Beginning to end.'

'What *they*?'

'IAB – who the fuck else?'

'And how do you come by this?' Horgan, sounding more skeptical than scared.

'Two ways. First, you don't live my kind of life and not get yourself an early-warning system in Internal Affairs. And then I got it from Ventimiglia's office, too. Fucking lucky thing for us, this new system where IAB brings the local commanders in on what they're doing.'

'And just what are they doing, that you or I should be worried about?'

'You hard of hearing all of a sudden? They're onto us. And you've got to know there's no way I'm going down for this myself. You're in this with me up to your fucking eyeballs.'

'So what are you proposing? That we go in there hand in hand and cop a plea? A plea to what?'

Listening to Horgan play dumb, Mahoney seethed with frustration, and concern: had Horgan been warned somehow? Was he toying with

742

Pullone? Mahoney wanted to go out there himself and wring an admission from Horgan.

'I'm *proposing* that the only way to save both our asses is if I get the fuck out of town,' Pullone said. 'And you're going to help me. I'm *proposing* that you find me enough money to live on until the heat dies down.'

Silence. Then: 'How much are you talking about?'

'Twenty, minimum. I need I.D., I need a driver's license, maybe a passport. That doesn't come free. Plus I need to live.'

'Where the fuck am I going to put my hands on twenty thousand dollars?' Now Horgan was angry. 'Where's all the money you've been pulling down all these years?'

'Do you know what happens to you if they take me down?' Pullone shot back. 'Do you think they can't figure out it took two of us? And you're being so helpful and generous right now, why the fuck should I stand up for you when they have me by the balls? Fuck you, asshole – I'll take my chances if I have to. See what I can buy with your hide.'

Mahoney was stunned by Pullone's audacity: goading Horgan with the image of what he was already doing.

'You bastard. You fucking bastard,' Horgan erupted. 'Threatening me! Threatening me like this was my fault. Like I *owe* you something. We were doing fine until you got greedy and sloppy. If you hadn't pushed me into this Eng business, none of this would be happening. I told you, you didn't know enough about them. I told you, make sure there's nothing that's going to bite us on the ass. The next thing I know, the feds are all over me and I'm going to meetings at the Southern District with Ned King, all about these Eng people. *Nice quiet case nobody's ever going to think twice about*. You fuckhead.'

'Listen, I told you what I told you.' Pullone was unmoved. 'You could have said no. You could have put the fucking thing in the grand jury yourself instead of giving it to that asshole Mahoney.'

'What are you talking about? That's the one good thing that happened. It takes me out of it. Nobody can say I put you in the grand jury and asked you questions to get you immunity.'

'Takes you out of it? *Nothing* fucking takes you out of it. Except if they don't have me to squeeze for evidence against you.'

Silence.

'Keep pushing,' Mahoney exhorted the empty air in the van. 'You've got him going.'

The next voice was Horgan's: 'All right. I can get you ten. Maybe. That's all there is. And don't even think about coming back for more. Get your ass out of the country and stay there, wherever. I don't want to know where.'

'Yeah, like I'm going to keep in touch.'

Another silence.

'All right, I'm going back to work.' Horgan. 'I don't know what I'm going to tell my wife about the money.'

'I need it today.'

'Today! How the fuck am I—'

'Listen, the sooner you give it to me, the sooner I'm out of your life.'

'*There's* a bonus. Where you going to be?' Horgan, sounding resigned.

'You'll get a call from a snitch named Hector, and you'll need to go meet him, on zero notice. Got that?'

'Yeah, I got it – Hector.'

'Be there.'

They all listened to the tape in the van.

'It's enough,' Jordan said. 'From the minute Horgan starts talking about the money.'

'I thought he was going to hold out for ever,' Mahoney said.

'Pullone got him going, though.'

'Finally.' Mahoney could hardly believe it. 'When do we go get him?'

'Let's see what Ned and Max have to say.'

When David could no longer bear sitting and pacing in the waiting room he went back down the hall to Susan's room. The investigator was still there, his chair moved in front of the door. On the door was a red sign: NO VISITORS.

'What's this?' David asked.

'Doctor's orders.'

'But I'm her . . .' What? Boyfriend? Lover? Partner in crime? He didn't have any words.

*'Be there.'*

Pullone's words sounded less resonant in the bright, open office than they had in the crowded van. Jordan turned off the tape recorder.

Mahoney waited for Ned King's reaction.

'Okay. I've already let the Boss know what we've got, and he's heading back early from Colorado. Basically the question now is do we have what we need, and it sounds like we do.' There was no emotion in King's voice, as if the Chief of Investigation was keeping himself at a distance from the enormity of arresting one of his own people. 'Is somebody keeping an eye on Horgan?'

'He's in the office,' Jordan said. 'He went to the bank on the way back from the meeting. It's just a question of getting Pullone to call him.'

'Let's finish it, then.'

Jordan called to tell Eilewitz, in the safe house with Pullone, that it was time for 'Hector' to get in touch with Kevin Horgan.

'Good,' King said. 'And as soon as you get him in, I want to bring the Engs in, and get all that underway. That means your grand jurors, too.'

This time neither Pullone nor Horgan bothered to pat the other down. And the beeper-transmitter Pullone was wearing worked fine.

'You have it?' Pullone said, his transmitted voice clear in the stuffy van.

'Yeah, I have it,' Horgan replied. 'You ready to leave town?'

'I already called in sick for tomorrow. And Thursday and Friday are my RDOs. By the time anybody misses me I'll be on another planet.'

'Just so I never see you again.'

There was a brief silence.

'I don't suppose I have to count this,' Pullone said.

In the van, Jordan whispered *go* into her microphone.

Mahoney burst from the back of the van and ran across the street toward the vacant lot where Perez and Cavanaugh and Eilewitz were already converging on Horgan.

Watching them, Mahoney slowed to a walk, then stopped, just past the unit's cars. They'd have to come this way.

745

★ ★ ★

As Eilewitz walked his prisoner past Mahoney, Horgan turned. They were face to face.

Not a word. Mahoney held the stare. He could see the color rise in Horgan's face and his eyes widen. His fists clenched. Eilewitz tightened his hold.

Horgan kept staring, as if he could sear Mahoney with his hatred and anger.

Mahoney stood there, absorbing it, letting the intensity of Horgan's emotion nourish him, knowing that beneath the heat was the icy certainty of utter defeat.

That's right, he thought: Feel it. Take a good long look, so you won't forget this moment.

Horgan turned his head away. 'Get me out of here,' he said to Eilewitz.

Ryan and Miller had succeeded in getting themselves and David past the NO VISITORS sign on Susan's door. They were sitting around Susan's bed. She was propped into a sitting-up position, looking more alert than she had the last time David had been in the room.

'Where do we stand?' she asked.

'To be honest,' Ryan said, 'nobody loves the idea that the two of you mixed in the way you did . . . but they have to be grateful to you for giving them a handle on these people that they never would have gotten on their own. I had a quick conversation with Mahoney, and he thinks the Southern District is trying hard to get the Engs to cooperate – give evidence about what they've been doing.'

'How?' David was surprised they even thought it was possible.

'I'm guessing here,' Ryan said. 'They're old people and they've been through a lot. Chinese patriots though they are, they're tired. Most important, Peter is all they have left. Their son, the only surviving child of four, the only way to carry on the name. Except if he goes to jail. Or if their enemies kill him.

'And your grand jury testimony is going to put all the more pressure on them to cooperate, because once you've revealed some of what they're doing they have much less to protect.'

'Isn't that dangerous for us?' David asked.

'It could be,' Ryan acknowledged. 'We need to find a way to hide you both until it's time to testify. I think the biggest danger is in advance, when they might think they can stop you. Once you're done, it shouldn't be as urgent.'

'One other thing,' Miller said. 'Testifying about China aside, the State will want to put David in the grand jury about the shooting in the restaurant. There has to be a grand jury investigation when the police shoot somebody.'

'Well, I wanted to see what a grand jury looked like from the front of the room,' David said. 'Now I'll have plenty of chances.'

'And a federal grand jury is a whole different thing,' Ryan said. 'You'll have great stories to tell your grandchildren.'

Susan was blushing. David thought he must be, too.

'Well,' Ryan said. 'You know what I mean.'


David stayed when Ryan and Miller left. Susan was sitting in the raised hospital bed with her eyes closed.

'They tell me you saved my life,' she said.

'Who told you that? Not your doctor, I'll bet.'

His tone opened her eyes. 'The people from Mahoney's office.'

'They're the ones who really saved you. All I did was knock you down and give you some bruises and a minor concussion.'

'Richard can be terrible,' she said. 'I'm sure he must have been terrible to you.'

David let it go.

'You mustn't let him bother you,' she said. 'If he's nasty to you it's because you have something he wants.'

That made a difference. 'I was beginning to think it looked the other way.'

She took his hand. 'You can be very silly, sometimes.'

'I suppose. After all, I'm in love with you. They say that makes people silly.'

'There's nothing silly about it. Nothing at all.'


In the morning, David came to the hospital to take Susan home. He stopped at the threshold of her room. There was someone next to the bed, a young woman taller and slimmer than Susan and – seen in profile – almost as beautiful.

'Come in,' Susan said, and the young woman turned to see who was there. She was unmistakably Susan's daughter.

'This is Lara,' Susan said. 'Lara, this is David Clark.'

'Hi. You're from the grand jury, aren't you?'

'Yes . . .'

'I saw you there once.' Her eyes stayed on him – memorizing him? Judging him? 'Well, I'd better be going. I have to get back to school.'

David stayed by the door while mother and daughter said their goodbyes.

'Nice meeting you,' Lara said on her way out, still appraising him, he thought.

'She's something,' he said to Susan.

'Isn't she? I'm very proud of her.'

'Come on,' he said after they kissed hello. 'Let's get you ready to go.'

'Isn't it early?'

'I promised Kassia Miller I'd have you home by noon.'


Home, for now, was her hotel room. David had a limousine waiting at the hospital door to take them the two miles.

'This is crazy,' she said, kissing him, but she was glad to have the space and the comfort.

He made a production of ushering her into the room. It was full of roses, a vase on every surface – red roses, yellow roses, pink, white, peach – dozens of them.

'This time, I got roses,' he said.

She laughed and fell into his arms. 'You're so wonderful.' The laughter turned briefly to tears. 'This is happiness,' she said. 'My emotional wiring is a little screwed up.'

He kissed her and sat her down facing the television. 'It's past noon,' he said and turned it on.

'What is this?'

'I'm not sure myself.'

It was a press conference. The District Attorney sat at a long, microphone-covered oak table flanked by several serious-looking men, one with odd orange hair, and one woman. The only one Susan recognized was A.D.A. Mahoney. David pointed out people at the

748

table, names she knew from the story of what had happened to her – Laurie Jordan and Ned King, Frank Perez and Richie Eilewitz.

'—a superb job by the members of the Official Corruption Unit,' the District Attorney was saying. 'The investigation continues in the police department, but we are confident that within the District Attorney's office no other individuals are involved. As part of his plea arrangement, Detective Pullone continues to cooperate with this office and with the U.S. Attorney's office for the Southern District of New York. Charges against Kevin Horgan will be pursued exclusively by this office, with Ms Lauren Jordan as lead prosecutor . . .'

There was more, and they watched it all, including the commentary by the station's veteran police and court reporter, Molly O'Hara.

'It's a major event for the D.A.'s office to arrest one of its own,' she said in answer to a question from the noon-news anchor. 'I'm sure today must be a hard day for the District Attorney – proud as he must be to have cleaned his own house, it's got to hurt that one of his people went that far wrong.'

'What about the people who were falsely charged?'

'We don't have much word about that. The charges related to the evidence planted by Detective Pullone and his informant are going to be dropped, of course, but there are rumors that other charges against the same people may be forthcoming.'

'Well, we'll have more about that at six.'

David turned it off. 'We did it!'

'*They* did it,' Susan corrected.

'*Somebody* did it. That's what counts.' He took her in his arms and danced her around the room.

'Hey! I'm supposed to take it easy.'

'Oh. Sorry.' He laid her gently on the bed.


Ryan found them a cabin in the Massachusetts woods. They had a week there together. It would have been more, but Ryan was pressing to get their testimony done and over as soon as possible.

Mostly, they managed to make the rest of the world go away. They hiked in the woods, among the last of the autumn leaves. They swam in the chill waters of a nearby lake, emerged shivering and wrapped each other in huge towels to hug themselves warm. In the easy mornings and at sunset and sometimes deep in the night they made love. Those times especially, in the silent darkness, Susan felt closer to David than she ever remembered feeling to anyone.

'I'm considering going to Hong Kong,' David said as they walked in the woods one afternoon.

'To work for Angus Macleod?' Susan didn't seem as surprised as he'd expected.

'He's doing interesting things, some of them in my old line of work, and I don't think my buyout agreement prohibits teaching and research halfway around the world.'

'Is there such a thing as halfway around the world any more?' He didn't think she was talking about geography.

'Maybe I should use a pseudonym, if I go.'

'Considering how many friends we have in that part of the world.'

He was silent. It was one of the questions he'd been wrestling with for days.

'I suppose if they want us, that way, they'll find us wherever we are,' he said.

'And we can't spend our lives looking over our shoulders.'

'Except for each other.'

She kissed him. 'How long do you think you'll be gone?'

He put his arms around her. 'In one way, I don't want to be gone at all. It just seemed like I ought to get out of your way for a while. I hate the idea of not seeing you, but every time I think of being here while you . . .' He couldn't think of how to put it, just left it hanging.

They walked together in silence, the gold and brown leaves softening their steps.

'You mean so much to me,' she said. 'There's no one I can talk to like you. I spent a long time thinking while I was in that closet, when my mind wasn't all twisted with heroin or with coming down from being high, and when I wasn't being flat-out terrified. I was so sure I was going to die.'

He moved to comfort her, saw it wasn't what she wanted.

'There's so very much I want to do now. I can't stay with Richard, but I'm determined to work that out without its being any messier than

750

it has to be and that means taking time. And there's so much I have to say to my children, to build a new bond based on what life is like for us now, with as little of the old baggage as possible. With Charles, of course, but Lara, too . . .

'When I've thought about all that these past days, it's been so clear that having you to talk to, having your support, would make a tremendous difference. But then that started to scare me. So much of this I need to do alone, and I need to know it's me who's doing it. So you're probably right that the best way is for us to be apart for a while, as much as that hurts. The last thing I want, years from now, is not to be clear in my mind how and why I made these changes in my life.' She held out her arms for a hug. 'Which doesn't for a minute mean I don't love you.'

There was a knock on the door of the Appeals Bureau cubicle that was Mahoney's temporary office. Laurie Jordan.

'I was just down the hall talking to Ned and Max, so I thought I'd drop by and say hi.'

'Hi.' He was inordinately glad to see her, supposed it was written all over his face. What the hell, he thought, she probably sees that a hundred times a day.

'Anything new on our friends?' she asked, perching on the corner of his desk.

'They went for it.' Mahoney was the D.A.'s liaison with the Southern District on the Eng case. He wasn't supposed to talk about it now that the cases against the Engs and Horgan were on separate tracks, but she'd done too much to shut her out completely. 'They even gave up the key to their code.'

'The one their daughter died for?'

'That was the sticking point. But in the end they didn't really have a choice. They're too old to go back to jail, and they know prison will destroy their son.'

They feds were still drafting the Engs's plea agreement, and it would be sealed once it was finished, pending whatever indictments grew out of the evidence they were giving. But Mahoney knew the agreement contained a summary of the tape's secret contents: names, dates, amounts of cash payments to be made – the kind of information that was in the ledgers, too, but fresher and in greater detail – plus instructions about what activities were expected as *quid pro quo* for the money. Clark and Linwood had hit it right on the button.

'What about your case?' he asked Jordan.

She touched the tip of his nose with a fingernail. 'Wouldn't you like to know.'

'You bet I would.'

'What do I get in return?'

'Whatever you'd like.' Maybe two *could* play this game.

'Deal. And since I trust you to pay on demand, I'll tell you that Kevin Horgan has decided to plead.'

That was major news. 'I thought he was going to fight it.'

'Rumor is, his wife laid down the law – the kids couldn't take the publicity of a long trial.'

'That's great! That's just great. Congratulations.'

'I don't know. I was kind of looking forward to the trial.'

'There'll be others.' But he knew that was no consolation, because it would be a long time before there was another one like *People v. Horgan*. 'And this way, you don't have to worry about losing.'

'*Losing?* You must mean some other prosecutor.'

'I must.'

'Anyway,' she said, 'I was thinking we ought to celebrate.'

'Absolutely. We earned it. How about a fancy dinner, with plenty of champagne?'

'I was thinking of a weekend in the country. I can get us into a great golf club in Pennsylvania.'

That stopped him. Dream come true, he thought. Or was it? 'Sure,' he said.


Ryan interrupted Susan and David's idyll with a call on Friday afternoon.

'I wanted you to know the schedule. You have Monday to get back to the city and begin preparing. David will do the state grand jury on Tuesday about the police shooting. Wednesday is the grand jury about Susan's kidnapping for both of you. Thursday off and preparing for the federal grand jury about the Engs's China activities. Testimony in the federal grand jury for both of you on Friday.'

'That's a full week,' David said.

'The good news,' Ryan continued, 'is that the Engs are cooperating with the federal government. That means your testimony is mostly a way to make sure they're being honest and complete. And the federal no-prosecution letter is all drafted and ready for you to sign when you get back.'

'What's going to happen to the Engs?' Susan asked.

'They'll probably go into some form of witness protection . . . but we'll never know what actually happens, not unless somebody screws up very badly.

'On the subject of screw-ups, the Engs were apparently happy to help Mahoney make a case against the man who tried to kidnap Susan from her kidnappers. Tony Ching, I believe is his name. He's also the one who planted the rumor about the Engs being heroin dealers. It seems the Engs and Mr Ching are allied with opposing factions in China.'

'Nice of them to pick New York for their little civil war,' David said.

As Mahoney and Jordan blasted westward in her red Jaguar, top down despite the autumn chill, she said, 'Listen, there's something I thought might matter to you.'

'Oh?'

'I broke up with the banker.'

'Does that mean you have to give the car back?'

'Not on your life. I put up with enough from that s.o.b. to earn three of these.'

'Then congratulations.'

'What I mean to say is, in case that was a problem for you . . .'

He didn't answer at once. Then he said, 'I have some news, too.'

'Oh?'

'I'm putting in for a transfer to Official Corruption.'

'Really?'

'Yeah.'

A long silence. 'Hmmm.'

'I gather that means something.'

'Yeah, it does.' She was uncharacteristically hesitant. 'I don't . . . I mean, I'm glad you told me now. Before we, um . . . before. Most guys wouldn't.'

'I'm not looking for a good-conduct medal. And it's not that I'm not interested.'

She laughed, a little shyly. 'That's been evident, now and then.'

'I think we make a good team.'

'I do, too. It was great. All of it. You're good, Mahoney.'

'And so are you. The best. It's an education watching you work.'

She laughed. 'Mutual admiration society.'

'It'd be a shame to complicate it, in ways that might make it awkward down the line,' he said.

She glanced at him quickly, then kept her eyes on the road.

A while later she said, 'It's going to be fun, having you in the unit. And while we're out here we might as well keep going and play ourselves some golf.'

Sunday night, David and Susan's last night before going back to be grand jury witnesses, they sat on the cabin porch. The sun was behind the mountains, the sky a pale blue overhead, darkening toward the silhouettes of the mountains. Across the small lawn, night was already taking hold among the evergreens.

They sat next to each other, their fingers intertwined. David thought of the first time they had held hands, sitting together on the balcony of Susan's hotel room in Hong Kong.

'I won't be gone that long,' he said. 'The initial contract's six months, and I want to give the takeover a wide berth.'

'It might be interesting to stick around for it.'

'From what I've seen, I don't think it's for me. Unless you want to see it.'

'I'm not sure I ever want to go back there. My heritage matters to me, but the future matters more.'

'There's not much we can do about the past.'

'Understand it and try not to repeat it, they say, but even that takes too much looking backward. I think my father was right, after all . . . the past is over. Only what we do next matters.'

They kissed again.

She said, 'One thing I *am* going to do is get myself a personal e-mail address so I can correspond with my friends in foreign lands. Maybe even coax them to come home for a visit if they get tempted to stay away too long.'

'Sounds good to me.'

Three weeks later, David came back from his morning run along Bowen Road and sat down at the computer. Pulled up Susan's e-mail address and began to type—

```
I stood on our red rock today, at the summit
of the Lovers' Rock Garden. The wind tried to
push me off, but I was too strong for it. I
was rooted by my thoughts of you and by the
conviction that what we share in the future
will be even better than our memories. For
both of us.
```

At the end, he added a rose: @}—>—.

Poised to start the message on its electronic voyage, he stopped and went back. An ordinary rose wasn't enough. What he really wanted to send her was a *long-stemmed* rose: @}—>———.

# AUTHOR'S NOTE

Writing this book was a voyage of discovery. It started at a museum in Chinatown, now called the Museum of Chinese in the Americas, which truly is located in a former school building only a few blocks from the criminal courts and the District Attorney's office, and which has just built a wonderful new main exhibit space. There is also a real organization in the East Village that monitors violence against Asians and helps the victims: it's called the Council Against Anti-Asian Violence.

In general, the world portrayed in these pages is as I found it, from the Manhattan D.A.'s office to the back roads of China. Of course, none of the people in *Grand Jury* represent anyone real, and I've substituted, renamed and somewhat altered versions of a few real-life organizations, to emphasize the distance between fact and fiction.

As for the physical realities, Hong Kong changes too fast to be sure that anything will endure, but the Lovers' Rock Garden off Bowen Road is likely to be there a while, and the Star Ferry will no doubt keep running even after the new cross-harbor links to Kowloon and the airport at Chek Lap Kok are finished.

While I was in Hong Kong I stayed at the Mandarin Oriental Hotel, overlooking the harbor in the Central district of Hong Kong island. I got to Hong Kong on Cathay Pacific Airways. Though it has never been my practice to name the real hotels, restaurants, etc., which my characters visit in the course of their adventures, in this case I am happy to acknowledge the value of my experience with those two excellent organizations. Most important, my sanity during a long and consistently hectic stay in Hong Kong was preserved by the graciousness of virtually everyone on the staff at the Mandarin.

I rely for much of my material on people who work in law enforcement, and I'm always impressed by the professionalism of the ones I talk to, and by the real concern and thought they put into what they do.

Among the prosecutors and policefolk in New York and Hong Kong who gave me invaluable assistance were:

James Clemente, David Hodson, William Hoyt, Richard LaMagna, Jim McGuire, Gilda Mariani, Bruce Moskowitz, Chauncey Parker, Luke Rettler, Anne Rudman and Tommy Ullo.

I also had many helpers in the civilian world. The people who shared their knowledge with me include:

Kathryn Cordes. Patty Hassler. David Wachsmann and Karen Romer. Jessica Parsons. Floyd Sikes. Richard Konigsberg. Pamela Morton.

Peter Van Den Beemt and Joseph Pane.

Also Jeanne Larsen, whose delightful novels of ancient China I heartily recommend, Cheryl Imes, Herbert Huncke and Steven Watson.

Phoebe Eng, Amy Jedlicka and David Chan. Peter Kwong. Jennifer Lee, Donald Leo, Eileen Lim, Robert Lin and Lichia Yiu.

Sandy Hom, Ann Hsiung and M.B. Lee.

The directors and staff of the China Institute and the Museum of Chinese in the Americas, and the volunteers at CAAAV.

At the Hong Kong government information office, Thomas Rosenthal in New York, and Mark Pinkstone and Betty Chan in Hong Kong.

Also in Hong Kong: Serena Cheung and Maria Kwok. Frank Ching and Anna Wu. David Vong, Manu Melwani. Julie Amann at the Mandarin. James Tang, lecturer, and Professor Byron Weng. Gordon Wu. And most especially Robert Neeley.

In China, Eric Mak and Peter Yeung and many others at YGM.

Valuable introductions were made by many of the people already mentioned and by: Ellen Yaroshefsky, Cyrana Longest, Michael Tanzer, Sybil Wong, Philip Olivetti, Mike Parish, John Briggs and Harry Elish. For past favours, thanks to Hillel Hoffman.

★ ★ ★

Special thanks to my literary friends and advisers Jeanne Larsen, Katherine Finkelstein, Peter Stern and Tina Bennett.

Much of this book was written at the Virginia Center for the Creative Arts, whose staff seems more like family each time I have the privilege of going there. I thank them all.

And my continuing heartfelt gratitude goes to Lawrence Block, Lynne Bundesen, E.W. Count and Francisco Drohojowski.

As always, all these good people (and the ones mentioned earlier) are responsible only for what is true and just in these pages. The errors of omission, commission and misinterpretation are all my own.

## A selection of bestsellers from Headline

| | | | |
|---|---|---|---|
| BODY OF A CRIME | Michael C. Eberhardt | £5.99 | ☐ |
| TESTIMONY | Craig A. Lewis | £5.99 | ☐ |
| LIFE PENALTY | Joy Fielding | £5.99 | ☐ |
| SLAYGROUND | Philip Caveney | £5.99 | ☐ |
| BURN OUT | Alan Scholefield | £4.99 | ☐ |
| SPECIAL VICTIMS | Nick Gaitano | £4.99 | ☐ |
| DESPERATE MEASURES | David Morrell | £5.99 | ☐ |
| JUDGMENT HOUR | Stephen Smoke | £5.99 | ☐ |
| DEEP PURSUIT | Geoffrey Norman | £4.99 | ☐ |
| THE CHIMNEY SWEEPER | John Peyton Cooke | £4.99 | ☐ |
| TRAP DOOR | Deanie Francis Mills | £5.99 | ☐ |
| VANISHING ACT | Thomas Perry | £4.99 | ☐ |

*All Headline books are available at your local bookshop or newsagent, or can be ordered direct from the publisher. Just tick the titles you want and fill in the form below. Prices and availability subject to change without notice.*

Headline Book Publishing, Cash Sales Department, Bookpoint, 39 Milton Park, Abingdon, OXON, OX14 4TD, UK. If you have a credit card you may order by telephone – 01235 400400.

Please enclose a cheque or postal order made payable to Bookpoint Ltd to the value of the cover price and allow the following for postage and packing:

UK & BFPO: £1.00 for the first book, 50p for the second book and 30p for each additional book ordered up to a maximum charge of £3.00.

OVERSEAS & EIRE: £2.00 for the first book, £1.00 for the second book and 50p for each additional book.

Name ................................................................................................

Address ............................................................................................

............................................................................................................

............................................................................................................

If you would prefer to pay by credit card, please complete:
Please debit my Visa/Access/Diner's Card/American Express (delete as applicable) card no:

| | | | | | | | | | | | | | | | | | |
|---|---|---|---|---|---|---|---|---|---|---|---|---|---|---|---|---|---|
| | | | | | | | | | | | | | | | | | |

Signature ................................................... Expiry Date ..............